THE AUTHOR

Edward Frederic Benson was born at Wellington College, Berkshire in 1867. He was one of an extraordinary family. His father Edward White Benson – first headmaster of Wellington – later became Chancellor of Lincoln Cathedral, Bishop of Truro, and Archbishop of Canterbury. His mother, Mary Sidgwick, was described by Gladstone as 'the cleverest woman in Europe'. Two children died young but the other four, bachelors all, achieved distinction: Arthur Christopher as Master of Magdalene College, Cambridge and a prolific author; Maggie as an amateur egyptologist; Robert Hugh as a Catholic priest and propagandist novelist; and Fred.

Like his brothers and sisters, Fred was a precocious scribbler. He was still a student at Cambridge when he published his first book, *Sketches from Marlborough*. While he was working as an archaeologist in Athens, his first novel *Dodo* (1893) was published to great success. Thereafter Benson devoted himself to writing, playing sports, watching birds, and gadding about. He mixed with the best and brightest of his day: Margot Asquith, Marie Corelli, his mother's friend Ethel Smyth and many other notables found their eccentricities exposed in the shrewd, hilarious world of his fiction.

Around 1918, E. F. Benson moved to Rye, Sussex. He was inaugurated mayor of the town in 1934. There in his garden room, the collie Taffy beside him, Benson wrote many of his comical novels, his sentimental fiction, ghost stories, informal biographies, and reminiscences like *As We Were* (1930) – almost one hundred books in all. Ten days before his death on 29 February 1940, E. F. Benson delivered to his publisher a last autobiography, *Final Edition*.

The Hogarth Press also publishes *Mrs Ames, Paying Guests, Secret Lives, As We Were* and *As We Are*.

DODO
AN OMNIBUS
E. F. Benson

New Introduction by
Prunella Scales

THE HOGARTH PRESS
LONDON

Published in 1986 by
The Hogarth Press
Chatto & Windus Ltd
40 William IV Street, London WC2N 4DF

Dodo first published in Great Britain by Methuen 1893
Dodo the Second first published in Great Britain by
Hodder and Stoughton 1914
Dodo Wonders first published in Great Britain by Hutchinson 1921
The collected edition, *Dodo, An Omnibus*, first published in Great Britain by
The Hogarth Press 1986
Copyright the Executors of the Estate of the Revd K. S. P. McDowall
Introduction copyright © Prunella Scales 1986

British Library Cataloguing in Publication Data

Benson, E.F.
The dodo omnibus
I. Title
823'8[F]   PR6003.E66
ISBN 0 7012 0696 9

Printed in Finland by
Werner Söderström Oy

INTRODUCTION

The first thing to be said is that I am not what is called 'a
Benson addict'. I had read very few of his books before 1984,
when I swallowed all the *Lucia* novels at once while preparing
to attempt Miss Mapp in a television serial. Throughout
rehearsals and shooting, the whole cast had constant recourse
to the books, and we learned to be truly thankful for Benson's
meticulous details of character and behaviour, particularly
in the dialogue. But I never became *addicted*, and indeed
approached the *Dodo* trilogy (with some trepidation) only at
the kind invitation of The Hogarth Press.

Dodo, A Detail of the Day, was first published in 1893, one year
after the first production of Oscar Wilde's *Lady Windermere's
Fan*, eight years before the death of Queen Victoria, eleven
years before Saki's first volume of short stories, eighteen years
before Max Beerbohm's *Zuleika Dobson*, and twenty-seven
years before the first of Benson's own *Lucia* novels. In the
Concise Oxford Dictionary of English Literature it is the only one
of his novels mentioned, and in the *New Oxford Companion* the
only one named apart from *Queen Lucia*.

Dodo was a runaway success on publication. The *Athenaeum*
hailed Benson as 'a writer of quite exceptional ability', the
Spectator called it 'a delightfully witty sketch of society', the
Guardian 'unusually clever and interesting' and the *Bookman*
'the most modern and up-to-date book that has yet appeared'. It
remained constantly in print until Benson's death in 1940. Even
assuming its contemporary *succès de scandale* sprang from
imagined references to well-known society figures (and perhaps
from its author's kinship with the Archbishop of Canterbury),
Dodo is clearly something of a literary curiosity, and re-publica-
tion long overdue, not least to reveal what all the fuss was about.

It is a pretty astonishing work – three separate archives of the vanished world of Saturdays-to-Mondays, dressing-bells and cotillion toys: *Dodo*, a late Victorian gadfly caught in the amber glow of the Nineties; *Dodo the Second*, a unique chronicle of the pre-1914 Bright Young Things; and *Dodo Wonders*, a first-hand social history of the Great War in Mayfair and the Shires. Yet the people moving in this ancient world are astoundingly modern: it is almost impossible to think of Dodo herself, for instance, wearing whalebone stays and wielding Lady Windermere's fan; though that is how she must have appeared when she took London by storm in 1893.

There were some dissenting voices. The celebrated hostess Margot Asquith later wrote:

Dodo was a novel that made a sensation at the time of publication as the heroine – a pretentious donkey with the heart and brains of a linnet – was supposed to be myself . . . I told everyone I could not have been the heroine, as I was not beautiful, and did not hunt in summer; nevertheless, there was an exact description of my sitting-room and other details, which proved that the author had me in his mind . . . The Prince of Wales . . . addressed me as 'Miss Dodo' when we met at a ball, which gave great pleasure to bystanders.

And we can certainly hear a creak of stays in the strictures of the *Spectator* on Dodo:

We are chiefly sorry for the forlorn female intellect, unballasted by love, drifting hither and thither . . . unstayed by any unseen power even of passion . . . It were breaking a butterfly upon a wheel to say much of what these female portraits mean. As long as an inheritance of good custom and secure police [sic] remains, they need only amuse the lookers-on. But we are sorry for Adam if he has no better Eve by his side.

Some ninety years later, we are sorry for this Eve. We may not be as amused as were her contemporaries – indeed, a good deal of Dodo's 'brilliant chatter' (the *Athenaeum* again) strikes us today as insufferably arch – but her plight is poignant, and we see her less as a villainess than a sensual, energetic, highly intelligent woman, undereducated and underemployed, made for love and terrified of sex, victim rather than queen of the society around her. Her energy, her erratic musical and literary talents, her vocabulary peppered with quotations from the Authorised Version and the Book of Common Prayer, she shares with Lucia. But the tenderness, the passionate yearning and incapacity for love are her own, and very surprising they are to readers only familiar with the Tilling novels. The young Benson was evidently much preoccupied with such yearnings, repeating and intensifying them in Dodo the Second, her daughter Nadine. With archaeological fervour he digs around in the female psyche and comes up with some remarkable artefacts: some of the monologues suggest the improvisations of a 1960s' Method actor. Never mind Queen Victoria or Saki: it is quite hard enough to believe that *Dodo* appeared seven years before the first English translations of Sigmund Freud.

And despite some splendid jokes, it is all leagues away from Tilling-on-Sea.

From time to time there are the flashes we expect from the author of *Miss Mapp*. 'Mrs Vane's smile always suggested a reformed vampire who had permanently renounced her blood-thirsty habits, but had not quite got out of the way of gloating on what would have been her victims in the unregenerate days.' There is Edith Staines, a portrait of Ethel Smyth (gleefully acknowledged by the subject): 'When I'm composing a Symphony I want something more exciting than two poached eggs . . . A brandy-and-soda and a grilled bone is what one really wants for a scherzo.' And in *Dodo the Second* there is the wonderful Seymour Sturgis, not so much a sketch for Georgie Pilson of Tilling, as a distillation of Pilsonism, the scent itself rather than the *eau de cologne*:

Seymour Sturgis (who, Berts thought, ought to have been drowned when he was a girl) . . . lived in a small flat just off Langham Place, with a large capable middle-aged Frenchwoman . . . He always alluded to her as 'my maid', and used to take her with him, as valet, to country houses . . . he did this largely to annoy, and he largely succeeded. He had a ruby ring, a sapphire ring, and an emerald ring; they were worn singly and matched his clothes . . . All these depressing traits naturally enraged such men as came in contact with him, but . . . they could not openly laugh at him, for he had a tongue, when he chose, of quite unparalleled acidity, and was markedly capable of using it when required and taking care of himself afterwards . . . somewhere in his nature there was a certain grit which quite refused to be ground into the pulp of a spoiled young man . . . He was fond of food, and drank a good many glasses of port rather petulantly, after dinner, as if they were medicine.

Benson himself seems to have underestimated his own gift for this sort of portrait: 'the difficulty I have is with the minor characters, which I have consciously to whip up. Unless they, too, are developed in the course of the story, they become mere lay figures which do not help the drama in any way. The neglect of this is I think, one of the chief faults of "*Dodo*".'

For us today, the minor characters are among the chief delights of *Dodo*. What we find far harder to take are the passages of shameless sentimentality and barefaced melodrama occurring in all three novels. They are quite separate from the genuine anguish and passion in much of the writing, and nothing we know of his ideals and method prepares us for them beforehand or explains them afterwards.

Among the many contemporary articles and reviews zealously researched and generously supplied to me both by the E. F. Benson Society and the Tilling Society of Rye, there is an enchanting interview between Benson and Raymond Blathwayt of the *Bookman*. It took place in November 1893 in the somewhat incongruous surroundings of the old Library at Lambeth Palace.

For some time past he has been engaged in digging up Megalopolis, the ancient capital of Arcadia . . . Literature he told me, comes naturally to him . . . Mr Benson is a hard worker; indeed he takes his holiday chiefly in the alternation of work.

'It is the best way of working,' he said to me in his quiet manner, 'to have two occupations, and then one is a holiday from the other' . . . He is, as I have said, a quite young man, who takes a rather thoughtful and philosophical view of life . . . 'I had for long been interested in the Modern Time, and in its curious development . . . I thought therefore, that I would write a book which should be strictly modern . . . Dodo, by-the-bye, is not the portrait of any one person . . . Dodo is – to put it briefly – a compound of many characters blended in one type. She is the incarnation of the contrast that exists between this and the previous generations . . . And for the type you can't take a model, you must take several models.'

'Do you consider the book an exact photograph of Society as it is?'

'No, certainly not,' replied Mr Benson, 'I simply do not agree with people who try to describe society *as it is* . . . Photography is not only inartistic, it is nowadays unnatural. The tendency among cultivated people is towards Impressionism . . . the so-called 'smart' people, with which class my book chiefly deals . . . and many others of today draw their conclusions from their impressions, and so the impressionist school in literature as in art specially appeals to them . . .'

'Who do you best like to treat in your books, men or women?'

'Women, I think; they are more complex and inconsistent, and I love the inconsistent character, it is so interesting to work out . . . At the same time, whilst very fond of depicting character, I don't admire the analytical tendency carried to extremes as it is by W. D. Howells and Henry James. Character ought to tell its own story. It is a confession of weakness if a novelist has to tell you why . . .'

Benson is speaking as a connoisseur, and thinking and working like a good character actor. We know that his models were Jane Austen, Mrs Gaskell, George Eliot and Emily Brontë. We know that he aimed to 'convey character by means of conversation rather than analysis' and believed 'there must be no patches, even purple ones, in the perfect narrative'. So why does he give us passages like these, reminding us of the worst excesses of Mills and Boon?

'Stay,' she said. 'Not yet, not yet . . .'

'Oh, my husband, my husband, live to forgive me!'

. . . She clung to him, she sheltered under his shoulder unconsciously, instinctively, as an animal trusts his master without knowing it is trusting. And that to his aching hunger for her was something.

And finally:

'My dear, are you content?' she asked.

His eyes answered her . . .

Even in Benson's own time such passages misled the critics. A long and exceptionally unfavourable notice in the *Saturday Review*, 17 June, 1893, attributes *Dodo* to a woman writer, and castigates 'her' for sending her heroine hunting in September. (September is indeed a surprising howler for Benson, who was reputedly a keen sportsman.) And a later commentator, Bonamy Dobrée, in *The Victorians and After* (London, 1938), says of *Dodo*: 'Its psychological level is about that of Ouida's, but though the representation of 'high society' is more accurate than hers, it lacks her gusto.'

With shame I realise that I have never read Ouida, and race to look her up in the *Oxford Companion to English Literature*. Goodness, her entry is four times as long as Benson's. The note says: 'Ouida (1856–1939) suffered frequent ridicule for her extravagantly portrayed heroines . . . and for her inaccuracies in matters of men's sports and occupations.' Great heavens. Have I unearthed a massive literary hoax? This could become the Bacon/Shakespeare controversy *de nos jours*. Were Benson and Ouida collaborators, or even *one and the same person*? Intoxicating fantasies ensue, where I give up the acting, become bookish bloodhound and get into the *Oxford Companion to English Literature*. Or perhaps Benson was engaging in deliberate Ouida pastiche? Or did he include the uncharacteristic purple passages with one eye on the circulating libraries? Either way, he had grown out of them by the time he arrived in Tilling.

I dismiss the unworthy, though intoxicating fantasies. *Dodo* remains a wonderful read. And one must not be too frivolous about this dear, gentle, funny writer, with his romantic cynicism and demure extravagance, his faultless ear and wicked tongue, who, years after his death, has inspired a worldwide minor cult.

And all right, so I've joined the E. F. Benson Society. But I'm still not an addict. Not a *real* addict. I can kick it any time, I tell you.

Prunella Scales, London 1985

CONTENTS

BOOK 1

DODO
A Detail of the Day

1

Poets of all ages and of all denominations are unanimous in assuring us that there was once a period on this grey earth known as the Golden Age. These irresponsible bards describe it in terms of the vaguest, most poetic splendour, and, apart from the fact, upon which they are all agreed, that the weather was always perfectly charming, we have to reconstruct its characteristics in the main for ourselves. Perhaps if the weather was uniformly delightful, even in this nineteenth century, the golden age might return again. We all know how perceptibly our physical, mental and spiritual level is raised by a few days of really charming weather; but until the weather determines to be always golden, we can hardly expect it of the age. Yet even now, even in England, and even in London, we have every year a few days which must surely be waifs and strays from the golden age, days which have fluttered down from under the hands of the recording angel, as he tied up his reports, and, after floating about for years in dim, interplanetary space, sometimes drop down upon us. They may last a week, they have been known to last a fortnight; again, they may curtail themselves into a few hours, but they are never wholly absent.

At the time at which this story opens, London was having its annual golden days; days to be associated with cool, early rides in the crumbly Row, with sitting on small, green chairs beneath the trees at the corner of the Park; with a general disinclination to exert oneself, or to stop smoking cigarettes; with a temper distinctly above its normal level, and a corresponding absence of moods. The crudeness of spring had disappeared, but not its freshness; the warmth of the summer had come, but not its sultriness; the winter was definitely over and past, and even in Hyde Park the voice of the singing bird was heard, and an old gentleman, who shall be nameless, had committed his annual perjury by asserting in the *Morning Post* that he had heard a nightingale in the elm-trees by the Ladies' Mile, which was manifestly impossible.

The sky was blue; the trees, strange to say, were green, for the leaves were out, and even the powers of soot which hover round London had not yet had time to shed their blackening dew upon them. The season was in full swing, but nobody was tired of it yet, and "all London" evinced a tendency to modified rural habits, which ex-

3

pressed themselves in the way of driving down to Hurlingham, and giving water parties at Richmond.

To state this more shortly, it was a balmy, breezy day towards the middle of June. The shady walks that line the side of the Row were full of the usual crowds of leisurely, well-dressed people who constitute what is known as London. Anyone acquainted with that august and splendid body would have seen at once that something had happened; not a famine in China, nor a railway accident, nor a revolution, nor a war, but emphatically "something." Conversation was a thing that made time pass, not a way of passing the time. Obviously the larger half of London was asking questions, and the smaller half was enjoying its superiority, in being able to give answers. These indications are as clear to the practised eye as the signs of the weather appear to be to the prophet Zadkiel. To the amateur one cloud looks much like another cloud: the prophet, on the other hand, lays a professional finger on one and says "Thunder," while the lurid bastion, which seems fraught with fire and tempest to the amateur, is dismissed with the wave of a contemptuous hand.

A tall, young man was slowly making his way across the road from the arch. He was a fair specimen of "the exhausted seedlings of our effete aristocracy"—long-limbed, clean-shaven, about six feet two high, and altogether very pleasant to look upon. He wore an air of extreme leisure and freedom from the smallest touch of care or anxiety, and it was quite clear that such was his normal atmosphere. He waited with serene patience for a large number of well-appointed carriages to go past, and then found himself blocked by another stream going in the opposite direction. However, all things come to an end, even the impossibility of crossing from the arch at the entrance of the Park to the trees on a fine morning in June, and on this particular morning I have to record no exception to the rule. A horse bolting on to the Row narrowly missed knocking him down, and he looked up with mild reproach at its rider, as he disappeared in a shower of dust and soft earth.

This young gentleman, who has been making his slow and somewhat graceful entrance on to our stage, was emphatically "London," and he too saw at once that something had happened. He looked about for an acquaintance, and then dropped in a leisurely manner into a chair by his side.

"Morning, Bertie," he remarked; "what's up?"

Bertie was not going to be hurried. He finished lighting a cigarette, and adjusted the tip neatly with his fingers.

"She's going to be married," he remarked.

Jack Broxton turned half round to him with a quicker movement than he had hitherto shown.

"Not Dodo?" he said.

"Yes."

Jack gave a low whistle.

"It isn't to you, I suppose?"

Bertie Arbuthnot leaned back in his chair with extreme languor. His enemies, who, to do him justice, were very few, said that if he hadn't been the tallest man in London, he would never have been there at all.

"No, it isn't to me."

"Is she here?" said Jack, looking round.

"No I think not; at least I haven't seen her."

"Well, I'm——" Jack did not finish the sentence. Then as an after-thought he inquired: "Whom to?"

"Chesterford," returned the other.

Jack made a neat little hole with the ferrule of his stick in the gravel in front of him, and performed a small burial service for the end of his cigarette. The action was slightly allegorical.

"He's my first cousin," he said. "However, I may be excused for not feeling distinctly sympathetic with my first cousin. Must I congratulate him?"

"That's as you like," said the other. "I really don't see why you shouldn't. But it is rather overwhelming, isn't it? You know Dodo is awfully charming, but she hasn't got any of the domestic virtues. Besides, she ought to be an empress," he added loyally.

"I suppose a marchioness is something," said Jack. "But I didn't expect it one little bit. Of course he is hopelessly in love. And so Dodo has decided to make him happy."

"It seems so," said Bertie, with a fine determination not to draw inferences.

"Ah, but don't you see——" said Jack.

"Oh, it's all right," said Bertie. "He is devoted to her, and she is clever and stimulating. Personally I shouldn't like a stimulating wife. I don't like stimulating people, I don't think they wear well. It would be like sipping brandy all day. Fancy having brandy at five o'clock tea. What a prospect, you know! Dodo's too smart for my taste."

"She never bores one," said Jack.

"No, but she makes me feel as if I was sitting under a flaming gas-burner, which was beating on to what Nature designed to be my brain-cover."

"Nonsense," said Jack. "You don't know her. There she is. Ah!"

A dog-cart had stopped close by them, and a girl got out, leaving a particularly diminutive groom at the pony's head. If anything she was a shade more perfectly dressed than the rest of the crowd, and she seemed to know it. Behind her walked another girl, who was obviously intended to walk behind, while Dodo was equally obviously made to walk in front.

Just then Dodo turned round and said over her shoulder to her,—

"Maud, tell the boy he needn't wait. You needn't either unless you like."

Maud turned round and went dutifully back to the dog-cart, where she stood irresolutely a few moments after giving her message.

Dodo caught sight of the two young men on the chairs, and advanced to them. The radiant vision was evidently not gifted with that dubious quality, shyness.

"Why, Jack," she exclaimed in a loudish voice, "here I am, you see, and I have come to be congratulated! What are you and Bertie sitting here for like two Patiences on monuments? Really, Jack, you would make a good Patience on a monument. Was Patience a man? I never saw him yet. I would come and sketch you if you stood still enough. What are you so glum about? You look as if you were going to be executed. I ought to look like that much more than you. Jack, I'm going to be a married woman, and stop at home, and mend the socks, and look after the baby, and warm Chesterford's slippers for him. Where's Chesterford? Have you seen him? Oh, I told Maud to go away. Maud," she called, "come back and take Bertie for a stroll: I want to talk to Jack. Go on, Bertie; you can come back in half an hour, and if I haven't finished talking then, you can go away again— or go for a drive, if you like, with Maud round the Park. Take care of that pony, though; he's got the devil of a temper."

"I suppose I may congratulate you first?" asked Bertie.

"That's so dear of you," said Dodo graciously, as if she was used to saying it. "Good-bye; Maud's waiting, and the pony will kick himself to bits if he stands much longer. Thanks for your congratulations. Good-bye."

Bertie moved off, and Dodo sat down next to Jack.

"Now, Jack, we're going to have a talk. In the first place you haven't congratulated me. Never mind, we'll take that as done. Now tell me what you think of it. I don't quite know why I ask you, but we are old friends."

"I'm surprised," said he candidly; "I think it's very odd."

Dodo frowned.

"John Broxton," she said solemnly, "don't be nasty. Don't you think I'm a very charming girl, and don't you think he's a very charming boy?"

Jack was silent for a minute or two, then he said,——

"What is the use of this, Dodo? What do you want me to say?"

"I want you to say what you think. Jack, old boy, I'm very fond of you, though I couldn't marry you. Oh, you must see that. We shouldn't have suited. We neither of us will consent to play second fiddle, you know. Then, of course, there's the question of money. I must have lots of money. Yes, a big must *and* a big lot. It's not your fault that you haven't got any, and it wouldn't have been your fault if you'd been born with no nose; but I couldn't marry a man who was without either."

"After all, Dodo," said he, "you only say what every one else thinks about that. I don't blame you for it. About the other, you're wrong. I am sure I should not have been an exacting husband. You could have had your own way pretty well."

"Oh, Jack, indeed no," said she;—"we are wandering from the point, but I'll come back to it presently. My husband must be so devoted to me that anything I do will seem good and charming. You don't answer that requirement, as I've told you before. If I can't get that— I have got it, by the way—I must have a man who doesn't care what I do. You would have cared, you know it. You told me once I was in dreadfully bad form. Of course that clinched the matter. To my husband I must never be in bad form. If others did what I do, it might be bad form, but with me, no. Bad form is one of those qualities which my husband must think impossible for me, simply because I am I. Oh, Jack, you must see that—don't be stupid! And then you aren't rich enough. It's all very well to call it a worldly view, but it is a perfectly true one for me. Don't you see I must have everything I want. It is what I live on, all this," she said, spreading her hands out. "All these people must know who I am, and that they should do that, I must have everything at my command. Oh, it's all very well to talk of love in a cottage, but just wait till the chimney begins to smoke."

Dodo nodded her head with an air of profound wisdom.

"It isn't for you that I'm anxious," said Jack, "it's for Chesterford. He's an awfully good fellow. It is a trifle original to sing the husband's praise to the wife, but I do want you to know that. And he isn't one of those people who don't feel things because they don't show it—it is just the other way. The feeling is so deep that he can't. You know you like to turn yourself inside out for your friend's benefit, but he doesn't do that. And he is in love with you."

"Yes, I know," she said, "but you do me an injustice. I shall be very good to him. I can't pretend that I am what is known as being in love with him—in fact I don't think I know what that means, except that people get in a very ridiculous state, and write sonnets to their mistress's front teeth, which reminds me that I am going to the dentist to-morrow. Come and hold my hand—yes, and keep withered flowers and that sort of thing. Ah, Jack, I wish that I really knew what it did mean. It can't be all nonsense, because Chesterford's like that, and he is an honest man if you like. And I do respect and admire him very much, and I hope I shall make him happy, and I hear he's got a delightful new yacht; and, oh! do look at that Arbuthnot girl opposite with a magenta hat. It seems to me inconceivably stupid to have a magenta hat. Really she is a fool. She wants to attract attention, but she attracts the wrong sort. Now *she* is in bad form. Bertie doesn't look after his relations enough."

"Oh, bother the Arbuthnot girl," said Jack angrily. "I want to have this out with you. Don't you see that that sort of thing won't do with Chesterford? He is not a fool by any means, and he knows the difference between the two things."

"Indeed he doesn't," said Dodo. "The other day he was talking to me, and I simply kept on smiling when I was thinking of something quite different, and he thought I was adorably sympathetic. And, besides, I am not a fool either. He is far too happy for me to believe that he is not satisfied."

"Well, but you'll have to keep it up," said Jack. "Don't you see I'm not objecting to your theory of marriage in itself—though I think it's disgusting—but it strikes me that you have got the wrong sort of man to experiment upon. It might do very well if he was like you."

"Jack, you sha'n't lecture me," said Dodo; "I shall do precisely as I like. Have you ever known me make a fool of myself? Of course you haven't. Well, if I was going to make a mess of this, it would be contrary to all you or anyone else knows of me. I'm sorry I asked your opinion at all. I didn't think you would be so stupid."

"You told me to tell you what I thought," said Jack in self-defence. "I offered to say what you wanted, or to congratulate or condole or anything else; it's your own fault, and I wish I'd said it was charming and delightful, and just what I had always hoped."

Dodo laughed.

"I like to see you cross, Jack," she remarked, "and now we'll be friends again. Remember what you have said to-day—we shall see in time who is right, you or I. If you like to bet about it you may— only you would lose. I promise to tell you if you turn out to be right, even if you don't see it, which you must if it happens, which it won't, so you won't," she added with a fine disregard of grammar.

Jack was silent.

"Jack, you are horrible," said Dodo impatiently, "you don't believe in me one bit. I believe you are jealous of Chesterford; you needn't be."

Then he interrupted her quickly.

"Ah, Dodo, take care what you say. When you say I needn't be, it implies that you are not going to do your share. I want to be jealous of Chesterford, and I am sorry I am not. If I thought you loved him, or would ever get to love him, I should be jealous. I wish to goodness I was. Really, if you come to think of it, I am very generous. I want this to be entirely a success. If there is one man in the world who deserves to be happy it is Chesterford. He is not brilliant, he does not even think he is, which is the best substitute. It doesn't much matter how hard you are hit if you are well protected. Try to make him conceited—it is the best you can do for him."

He said these words in a low tone, as if he hardly wished Dodo to hear. But Dodo did hear.

"You don't believe in me a bit," she said. "Never mind, I will force you to. That's always the way—as long as I amuse you, you like me well enough, but you distrust me at bottom. A woman's a bore when she is serious. Isn't it so? Because I talk nonsense you think I am entirely untrustworthy about things that matter."

Dodo struck the ground angrily with the point of her parasol.

"I have thought about it. I know I am right," she went on. "I shall be immensely happy as his wife, and he will be immensely happy as my husband."

"I don't think it's much use discussing it," said he. "But don't be vexed with me, Dodo. You reminded me that we were old friends at the beginning of this extremely candid conversation. I have told you that I think it is a mistake. If he didn't love you it wouldn't matter. Unfortunately he does."

"Well, Jack," she said, "I can't prove it, but you ought to know me well enough by this time not to misjudge me so badly. It is not only unjust but stupid, and you are not usually stupid. However, I am not angry with you, which is the result of my beautiful nature. Come, Jack, shake hands and wish me happiness."

She stood up, holding out both her hands to him. Jack was rather moved.

"Dodo, of course I do. I wish all the best wishes that my nature can desire and my brain conceive, both to you and him, him too; and I hope I shall be outrageously jealous before many months are over."

He shook her hands, and then dropped them. She stood for a moment with her eyes on the ground, looking still grave. Then she retreated a step or two, leaned against the rail, and broke into a laugh.

"That's right, Jack, begone, dull care. I suppose you'll be Chesterford's best man. I shall tell him you must be. Really he is an excellent lover; he doesn't say too much or too little, and he lets me do exactly as I like. Jack, come and see us this evening; we're having a sort of

9

Barnum's Show, and I'm to be the white elephant. Come and be a white elephant too. Oh, no, you can't; Chesterford's the other. The elephant is an amiable beast, and I am going to be remarkably amiable. Come to dinner first, the Show begins afterwards. No, on the whole, don't come to dinner, because I want to talk to Chesterford all the time, and do my duty in that state of life in which it has pleased Chesterford to ask me to play my part. That's profane, but it's only out of the Catechism. Who wrote the Catechism? I always regard the Catechism as only a half-sacred work, and so profanity doesn't count, at least you may make two profane remarks out of the Catechism, which will only count as one. I shall sing, too. Evelyn has taught me two little nigger minstrel songs. Shall I black my face? I'm not at all sure that I shouldn't look rather well with my face blacked, though I suppose it would frighten Chesterford. Here are Maud and Bertie back again. I must go. I'm lunching somewhere, I can't remember where, only Maud will know. Maud, where are we lunching, and have you had a nice drive, and has Bertie been making love to you? Good-bye, Jack. Remember to come this evening. You can come, too, Bertie, if you like. I have had a very nice talk with Jack, and he has been remarkably rude, but I forgive him."

Jack went with her to her dog-cart, and helped her in.

"This pony's name is Beelzebub," she remarked, as she took the reins, "because he is the prince of the other things. Good-bye."

Then he went back and rejoined Bertie.

"There was a scene last night," said Bertie. "Maud told me about it. She came home with Dodo and Chesterford, and stopped to open a letter in the hall, and when she went upstairs into the drawing-room, she found Dodo sobbing among the sofa cushions, and Chesterford standing by, not quite knowing what to do. It appeared that he had just given her the engagement ring. She was awfully pleased with it, and said it was charming, then suddenly she threw it down on the floor, and buried her face in the cushions. After that she rushed out of the room, and didn't appear again for a quarter of an hour, and then went to the Foreign Office party, and to two balls."

Jack laughed hopelessly for a few minutes. Then he said,—

"It is too ridiculous. I don't believe it can be all real. That was drama, pure spontaneous drama. But it's drama for all that. I'm sure I don't know why I laughed, now I come to think of it. It really is no laughing matter. All the same I wonder why she didn't tell me that. But her sister has got no business to repeat those kind of things. Don't tell anyone else, Bertie."

Then after a minute he repeated to himself, "I wonder why she didn't tell me that."

"Jack," said Bertie after another pause, "I don't wish you to think that I want to meddle in your concerns, and so don't tell me unless you like, but was anything ever up between you and Dodo? Lie freely if you would rather not tell me, please."

"Yes," he said simply. "I asked her to marry me last April, and she said 'No.' I haven't told anyone till this minute, because I don't like it to be known when I fail. I am like Dodo in that. You know how she detests not being able to do anything she wants. It doesn't often happen, but when it does, Dodo becomes damnable. She has more perseverance than I have, though. When she can't get anything, she makes such a fuss that she usually does succeed eventually. But I do just the other thing. I go away, and don't say anything about it. That was a bad failure. I remember being very much vexed at the time."

Jack spoke dreamily, as if he was thinking of something else. It was his way not to blaze abroad anything that affected him deeply. Like Dodo he would often dissect himself in a superficial manner, and act as a kind of showman to his emotions; but he did not care to turn himself inside out with her thoroughness. And above all, as he had just said, he hated the knowledge of a failure; he tried to conceal it even from himself. He loved to show his brighter side to the world. When he was in society he always put on his best mental and moral clothes, those that were newest and fitted him most becomingly; the rags and tatters were thrown deep into the darkest cupboard, and the key sternly turned on them. Now and then, however, as on this occasion, a friend brought him the key with somewhat embarrassing openness, and manners prevented him from putting his back to the door. But when it was unlocked he adopted the tone of, "Yes, there are some old things in there, I believe. May you see? Oh, certainly; but please shut it after you, and don't let anyone else in. I quite forget what is in there myself, it's so long since I looked."

Bertie was silent. He was on those terms of intimacy with the other that do not need ordinary words of condolence or congratulation. Besides, from his own point of view, he inwardly congratulated Jack, and this was not the sort of occasion on which to tell him that congratulation rather than sympathy was what the event demanded. Then Jack went on, still with the air of a spectator than of a principal character,—

"Dodo talked to me a good deal about her marriage. I am sorry about it, for I think that Chesterford will be terribly disillusioned. You know he doesn't take things lightly, and he is much too hopelessly fond of Dodo ever to be content with what she will grant him as a wife. But we cannot do anything. I told her what I thought, not because

I hoped to make any change in the matter, but because I wished her to know that for once in her life she has made a failure—a bad, hopeless mistake. That has been my revenge. Come, it's after one, I must go home. I shall go there this evening; shall I see you?"

2

Jack went home meditating rather bitterly on things in general. He had a sense that Fate was not behaving very prettily to him. She had dealt him rather a severe blow in April last, which had knocked him down, and, having knocked him down, she now proceeded in a most unsportsmanlike way to kick him. Jack had a great idea of fair play, and Fate certainly was not playing fair. He would have liked to have a few words with her on the subject. The world had been very kind on the whole to him. He had always been popular, and his life, though perhaps rather aimless, was at least enjoyable. And since the world had been kind to him he was generous to the world in general, and to his friends in particular. It had always held a high opinion of him, as a thoroughly healthy-minded and pleasant companion, and he was disposed to hold a similar opinion of it. Consequently, when Dodo had refused him that spring, he had not thought badly of her. He did not blame her, or get bitter about it; but though he had flattered himself that he was used to Dodo's ways, and had always recognised her capabilities in the way of surprising her friends, he had not been quite prepared for the news of her engagement. In fact, he was surprised, and also rather resentful, chiefly against the general management of mundane affairs, but partly also against Dodo herself. Dodo had not told him of her engagement; he had been left to find it out for himself. Then, again, she was engaged to a man who was hopelessly and entirely in love with her, and for whom, apart from a quiet, unemotional liking, she did not care two straws, except in so far as he was immensely rich and had a title, two golden keys which unlocked the most secret doors of that well-furnished apartment known as Society, which constituted Dodo's world. Hitherto her position had been precarious: she had felt that she was on trial. Her personality, her great attractiveness and talents, had secured for herself a certain footing on the very daïs of that room; but she had always known that unless she married brilliantly she would not be sure of her position. If she married a man who would not be always certain of commanding whatever money and position—for she would never have married a wealthy brewer—could command, or, worst of all, if in her unwillingness to accept anything but the best she could get, she did not marry at all, Dodo knew that she never would have that unquestioned position that she felt was indispensable to her. Jack knew all this perfectly well—in fact Dodo had referred to it that morning—and he accepted it philosophically as being inevitable. But what he did not like was being told that he would not have done on general grounds, that he was too fond of his own way, that he would not have given Dodo rein enough. He had known Dodo too long and too well, when he proposed to her, to have any of a lover's traditional blindness to the faults of his love. He knew that she was, above all things, strongly dramatic, that she moved with a view to effect, that she was unscrupulous in what she did, that her behaviour was sometimes in questionable taste; but this he swallowed whole, so to speak. He was genuinely attached to her, and felt that she possessed the qualities that he would most like to have in his wife. Bertie had said to him that morning that she was stimulating, and would not wear well. Stimulating she certainly was—what lovable woman is not?—and personally he had known her long, and she did wear well. The hidden depths and unsuspected shallows were exactly what he loved her for; no one ever fell in love with a canal; and though the shallows were commoner than the depths, and their presence was sometimes indicated by a rather harsh jarring of the keel, yet he believed, fully and sincerely, in the dark, mysterious depths for love to lose itself in. Besides, a wife, whose actions and thoughts were as perfectly calculable and as accurately calculated as the trains in a Bradshaw, was possessed of sterling qualities which, however estimable, were more suited to a housekeeper than a mistress.

These reflections were the outcome of an intimate knowledge of Dodo in the mind of a man who was in the habit of being honest with himself and the object of his love, a quality rare enough whether the lover is rejected or accepted.

He had had time to think over the matter quietly to himself. He knew, and had known for many weeks, that Dodo was out of his reach, and he sat down and thought about the inaccessible fruit, not with the keen feelings of one who still hoped to get it, but with a resignation which recognised that the fruit was desirable, but that it must be regarded from a purely speculative point of view.

And to do him justice, though he was very sorry for himself, he was much more sorry for Chesterford. Chesterford was his cousin, they had been brought up together at Eton and Oxford, and he knew him with that intimacy which is the result of years alone. Chesterford's old friends had all a great respect and liking for him. As Dodo had said, "He was an honest man if you like." Slight acquaintances called him slow and rather stupid, which was true on purely intellectual grounds. He was very loyal, and very much devoted to what he considered his duty, which consisted in being an excellent landlord and J.P. of his county, in voting steadily for the Conservative party in the House of Lords, in giving largely and anonymously to good objects, in going to Church on Sunday morning, where he sang hymns with fervour, and read lessons with respect, in managing a hunt in a liberal and satisfactory manner, and in avoiding any introspection or speculation about problems of life and being. He walked through the world with an upright gait, without turning his eyes or his steps to the right hand or the left, without ever concerning himself with what was not his business, but directing all his undoubtedly sterling qualities to that. He had a perfect genius for doing his duty. Nobody had ever called him shallow or foolish, but nobody on the other hand had ever called him either deep or clever. He had probably only made one real mistake in his life, and that was when he asked Dodo to marry him; and we have seen that Jack, who knew Dodo well, and whose opinion might be considered to be based on good grounds, thought that Dodo had committed her first grand error in accepting him. The worst of the business certainly was that he was in love with Dodo. If he had been a different sort of man, if he had proposed to Dodo with the same idea that Dodo had, when she accepted him, if he had wanted a brilliant and fascinating woman to walk through life with, who could not fail to be popular, and who would do the duties of a mistress of a great house in a regal fashion, he could not have chosen better. But what he wanted in a wife was someone to love. He loved Dodo, and apparently it had not entered his calculations that she, in accepting him, might be doing it from a different standpoint from his own in proposing to her. Dodo had smiled on him with the air of a benignant goddess who marries a mortal, when he offered her his hand and heart, and he had taken that smile as a fulfilment of his own thought. Decidedly Jack might have justification for feeling apprehensive.

Jack's only hope lay in that vein which did exist in Dodo, and which she had manifested in that outburst of tears the night before. He put it down to her dramatic instincts to a large extent, but he knew there was something besides, for Dodo did not care to play to an empty house, and the presence of her future husband alone constituted anything but a satisfactory audience. Jack had always had a considerable belief in Dodo: her attractiveness and cleverness were, of course, beyond dispute, and required proof no more than the fact that the sun rose in the morning; but he believed in something deeper than this, which prompted such actions as these. He felt that there was some emotion that she experienced at that moment, of which her tears were the legitimate outcome, and, as he thought of this, there occurred to him the remark that Dodo had made that morning, when she expressed her regret at never having felt the sort of love that she knew Chesterford felt for her.

Mrs. Vane was perhaps perfectly happy that night. Was not her daughter engaged to a marquis and a millionaire? Was not her house going to be filled with the brightest and best of our land? She had often felt rather resentful against Dodo, who alternately liked and despised people whom Mrs. Vane would have given her right hand to be in a position to like, and both hands to be in a position to despise. Dodo was excellent friends with "London," only "London" did not come and seek her at her own house, but preferred asking her to theirs. Consequently, on Mrs. Vane and Maud devolved the comparatively menial duty of leaving their cards and those of Dodo, and attending her in the capacity of the necessary adjunct. They would be asked to the same houses as Dodo, but that was all; when they got there they had the privilege of seeing Dodo performing her brilliant evolutions, but somehow none of Dodo's glory got reflected on to them. To be the mirror of Dodo was one of Mrs. Vane's most cherished ideas, and she did not recollect that there are many substances whose nature forbids their acting as such to the most brilliant of illuminations. Mr. Vane was kept still more in the background. It was generally supposed that he was looking after his affairs in the country, whilst the rest of the family were amusing themselves in London. It was well known that he was the proprietor of a flourishing iron foundry somewhere in Lancashire, and apparently the iron needed special care during the months of May, June and July. In any case he was a shadow in the background, rather than a skeleton at the banquet, whom it was not necessary to ignore, because he never appeared in a position in which he could be ignored. Mrs. Vane had two principal objects in life, the first of which was to live up to Dodo, and the second to obtain, in course of time, a suitable brilliant son-in-law. The latter of these objects had been practically obtained by Dodo herself, and the first of them was in a measure realised by the large and brilliant company who assembled in her rooms that night.

Mrs. Vane was a large, high-coloured woman of about middle age, whose dress seemed to indicate that she would rather not, but that, of course, may only have been the fault of the dressmaker. She had an effusive manner, which sometimes made her guests wonder what they could have done to have made her so particularly glad to see them. She constantly lamented Mr. Vane's absence from London, and remarked, with a brilliant smile, that she felt quite deserted. Mrs. Vane's smile always suggested a reformed vampire, who had permanently renounced her bloodthirsty habits, but had not quite got out of the way of gloating on what would have been her victims in the unregenerate days. It is only fair to say that this impression was due to the immensity of her smile, which could hardly be honestly accounted for by this uncharitable world. She was busily employed in receiving her guests when Jack came, and was, perhaps, more stupendously cordial than ever.

"So kind of you to come," she was just saying to a previous arrival when Jack came in. "I know Dodo was dying to see you and be congratulated. Darling," she said, turning to Maud, "run and tell Dodo that Lord Burwell has arrived. So good of you to come. And how do you do, dear Mr. Broxton? Of course Dodo has told you of our happiness. Thanks, yes—we are all charmed with her engagement. And the Marquis is your cousin, is he not? How nice! May I tell Maud she may call you Cousin Jack? *Such* pleasure to have you. Dodo is simply expiring to see you. Did she see you this morning? Really! she never told me of it, and my sweet child usually tells me everything."

Dodo was playing the amiable white elephant to some purpose. She was standing under a large chandelier in the centre of the room, with Chesterford beside her, receiving congratulations with the utmost grace, and talking nonsense at the highest possible speed. Jack thought to himself that he had never seen anyone so thoroughly charming and brilliant, and almost wondered whether he had not been doing her an injustice all day. He saw it was impossible to get near her for the present, so he wandered off among other groups, exchanging greetings and salutations. He had made the circuit of the room, and was standing about near the door, feeling a little lonely, when Dodo came quickly towards him. She was looking rather white and impatient.

"Come away out of this, Jack," she said; "this is horrible. We've done our duty, and now I want to talk. I've been smiling and grinning till my cheeks are nearly cracked, and everyone says exactly the same thing. Come to my room—come." She turned round, beckoning to him, and found herself face to face with Chesterford. "Dear old boy," she said to him, "I'm not going to bore you any more to-night. I shall bore you enough after we are married. Jack and I are going away to talk, and he's going to tell me to be a good girl, and do as his cousin bids me. Good-night; come again to-morrow morning."

"I came here on purpose to congratulate you," said Jack, grasping Chesterford's hand, "and I wish you all joy and prosperity."

"Come, Jack," said Dodo. "Oh, by the way, Chesterford, ask Jack to be your best man. You couldn't have a better, and you haven't got any brother, you know."

"I was just going to," said Chesterford. "Jack, you will be, won't you? You must."

"Of course I will," said Jack. "All the same we're all awfully jealous of you, you know, for carrying Dodo off."

"So you ought to be," said he, enthusiastically. "Why, I'm almost jealous of myself. But now go and talk to Dodo, if she wants you."

The sight of Chesterford with Dodo made Jack groan in spirit. He had accepted Dodo's rejection of him as quite final, and he never intended to open that closed book again. But this was too horrible. He felt a genuine impulse of pure compassion for Chesterford, and an irritated disgust for Dodo. Dodo was an admirable comrade, and, for some, he thought, an admirable wife. But the idea of her in comradeship with Chesterford was too absurd, and if she could never be his comrade, by what perversity of fate was it that she was going to become his wife? Jack's serenity was quite gone, and he wondered what had become of it. All he was conscious of was a chafing refusal to acquiesce just yet, and the anticipation of a somewhat intimate talk with Dodo. He felt half inclined to run away from the house, and not see her again, and as he followed her up to her room, he began to think that his wisdom had followed his serenity. After all, if he asked her again about her resolution to marry Chesterford, what was he doing but continuing the conversation they had in the Park that morning, in which Dodo herself had taken the initiative. "These things are on the knees of the gods," thought Jack to himself piously, as the door of Dodo's room closed behind him. Dodo threw herself down in a low arm-chair with an air of weariness.

"Go on talking to me, Jack," she said. "Interest me, soothe me, make me angry if you like. Chesterford's very nice. Don't you like him immensely? I do."

Jack fidgeted, lit a match and blew it out again. Really it was not his fault that the conversation was going to be on this subject. He again laid the responsibility on the knees of the gods. Then he said,—

"Dodo, is this irrevocable? Are you determined to marry this man? I swear I don't ask you for any selfish reasons, but only because I am sincerely anxious for your happiness and his. It is a confounded liberty I am taking, but I sha'n't apologise for it. I know that it isn't any business of mine, but I risk your displeasure."

Dodo was looking at him steadily. Her breath came rather quickly, and the look of weariness had left her face.

"Jack," she said, "don't say this sort of thing to me again. You are quite right, it is a confounded liberty, as you say. I shall do as I please in this matter. Ah, Jack, don't be angry with me," she went on as he shrugged his shoulders, and half turned away. "I know you are sincere, but I must do it. I want to be safe. Jack, old boy, don't make me quarrel with you. You are the best friend I have, but I'm sure you're wrong about this."

She rose and stood by him, and laid one hand on his as it lay on the mantelpiece. He did not answer her. He was disappointed and baffled. Then she turned away from him, and suddenly threw up her arms.

"Oh, my God," she said, "I don't know what to do. It isn't my fault that I am made like this. I want to know what love is, but I can't—I can't. You say I shall make him unhappy, and I don't want to do that. I don't believe I shall. Jack, why did you come here suggesting these horrible things?"

There was a great anger in her voice, and she stood trembling before him.

Just then the door opened, and a middle-aged lady walked in. She did not seem at all surprised. Nobody who had known Dodo long was often surprised.

She walked up to Dodo and kissed her.

"I came late," she said, "and your mother said you were in your room, so I came up to congratulate you with all my heart."

"Thank you very much," said Dodo, returning the kiss. "Jack, do you know Mrs. Vivian?—Mr. Broxton."

Mrs. Vivian bowed, and Jack bowed, and then nobody seemed quite to know what to say next. Mrs. Vivian recovered herself first.

"I wish you would show me the necklace Lord Chesterford has given you," she said to Dodo. "Mrs. Vane said the diamonds were magnificent."

"Certainly, I will fetch it," said Dodo, with unusual docility. "Don't go away, Jack."

Dodo left the room, and Mrs. Vivian turned to Jack.

"My dear young man," she said, "I am old enough to be your mother, and you mustn't mind what I am going to say. This sort of thing won't do at all. I know who you are perfectly well, and I warn you that you are playing with fire. You were at liberty to do so before Dodo was engaged, and I daresay you have burned your fingers already. Several young men have—but now it won't do. Besides that, it isn't fair on either Chesterford or Dodo herself."

Jack wanted to think "what an impertinent old woman," but there was something in her manner that forbade it.

"I believe you are right," he said simply; "but it wasn't wholly my fault."

Then he felt angry with himself for having shifted any of the blame on to Dodo.

"Honi soit," said the other ambiguously. "I don't mean that—Ah, here is Dodo."

The diamonds were duly shown and admired, and the three went downstairs again.

Mrs. Vivian took her leave shortly. She was very gracious to Jack, and as they parted she said,—

"Come and see me at any time; I should like to talk to you. Here is my address."

Jack sought Mrs. Vane to inquire who Mrs. Vivian was. Mrs. Vane was even more effusive than usual.

"Oh, she is quite one of our leading people," she said. "She has not been in London, or, in fact, in England for two years. She was unhappily married. Her husband was a scamp, and after his death she suddenly left London, and has only just returned. She is quite an extraordinary woman—everyone used to rave about her. She never gave herself airs, but somehow she was more looked up to than anyone else. Quite royal in fact. I feel immensely honoured by her presence here. I hardly dared to ask her—so fascinating, and so clever."

Dodo came up to Jack before he left.

"Jack," she said, "I was angry with you, and I am sorry. Don't bear me malice. If Mrs. Vivian had not come in, I should have said something abominable. I am afraid of her. I don't quite know why. She always seems to be taking stock of one, and noticing how very small one is. Don't forget to-morrow. We're all going on a water-party at Richmond. Mind you come."

"I think I had better not," said Jack bluntly.

Dodo lifted her eyebrows in surprise that may have been genuine. "Why not?" she asked.

Jack had no reasonable answer to give her.

"What did Mrs. Vivian say to you?" asked Dodo suddenly.

Jack paused.

"A few polite nothings," he said; "and half the royal motto. Mrs. Vane said she was quite royal, which, of course, explains it."

"I can't conceive what you're talking about," remarked Dodo. "It seems to me to be sheer nonsense."

Jack smiled.

"On the whole, I think it is sheer nonsense," he said. "Yes, I'll come."

Dodo swept him the prettiest little curtsey.

"How good of you," she said. "Good-night, Jack. Don't be cross, it really isn't worth while, and you can behave so prettily if you like. Oh, such a nice gentleman!"

"No, I expect it isn't worth while," said Jack.

3

There is a particular beauty about the Thames valley for which you may search for years elsewhere, and not find; a splendid lavishness in the way that the woods are cast down broadcast along the river, and a princely extravagance of thick lush hayfields, that seem determined not to leave a spare inch of land between them and the water. The whole scene has been constructed with a noble disregard of expense, in the way of water, land, and warm woodland air. The tall, clean-limbed beech-trees have room to stretch their great, lazy arms without being prosecuted for their clumsy trespasses, and the squirrels that chatter at you from their green houses seem to have a quite unusual sleekness about them, and their insolent criticisms to each other about your walk, and general personal unattractiveness, are inspired by a larger share of animal spirits than those of other squirrels. As you row gently up in the middle of the stream, you may see a heron standing in the shallows, too lazy to fish, too supremely confident to mind the approach of anything so inferior as yourself, and from the cool shadow of the woods you may hear an old cock pheasant talking to himself, and not troubling to practise a new and original method of rocketing in June, for he knows that his time is not yet.

At this time of year, too, you need not trouble to look round, to see if there are large boats full of noisy people bearing down on you; like the pheasant, their time is not yet. But now and then the long strings of creamy bubbles appearing on the deep, quiet water, and a sound rich in associations of cool plunges into frothy streams, warns you that a lock is near. And above you may see some small village clustering down to the river's edge, to drink of its sweet coolness, or a couple of shaggy-footed cart-horses, looking with mild wonder at this unexpected method of locomotion, lifting their dripping noses from the bright gravelly shallows to stare at you, before they proceed to finish their evening watering.

Dodo was very fond of the Thames valley, and she really enjoyed giving up a day of June in London to the woods and waters. They were to start quite early in the morning, Dodo explained, and everyone was to wear their very oldest clothes, for they were going to play ducks and drakes, and drink milk in dairies, and pick buttercups, and get entirely covered with freckles. Dodo herself never freckled, and she was conscious of looking rather better for a slight touch of the sun, and it would be very dear of Mrs. Vivian if she would come too, if she didn't mind being silly all day; and, if so, would she call for them, as they were on her way? Chesterford, of course, was going, and Jack, and Maud and her mother; it was quite a small party; and wasn't Jack a dear?

Mrs. Vane had got hold of a certain idea about Mrs. Vivian, distinctly founded on fact. She was one of those women who cannot help making an impression. How it is done, or exactly what it is, one would be puzzled to define, but everyone noticed when she came into a room, and was aware when she went out. It was not her personal appearance, for she was short rather than tall, stout rather than graceful, and certainly middle-aged rather than young. Dodo has mentioned the effect she produced on her, and many people felt in the same way that Mrs. Vivian was somehow on a higher plane than they, that her mind was cast in a larger mould. Happily for our peace of mind such people are not very common; most of our fellow-men are luckily much on the same level, and they are not more than units among units. But Mrs. Vivian was much more than a unit. Dodo had said of her that she was two or three at least. And evidently nothing was further from Mrs. Vivian's wishes than trying to make an impression, in fact, the very impressive element was rather due to her extreme naturalness. We are most of us so accustomed to see people behave, and to behave ourselves, in a manner not quite natural, that to see anyone who never does so, is in itself calculated to make one rather nervous.

Mrs. Vivian evidently intended to take her life up again at the point where she had left off, so to speak—in other words, at the period before her marriage. Of her husband, perhaps, the less said the better. He died, owing to an accident, after ten years of married unhappiness, and left Mrs. Vivian poorer than she had been before. After his death she had travelled abroad for two years, and then returned to England to live with her sister, who had married a rich judge and kept house rather magnificently in Prince's Gate. Lady Fuller had always disapproved of her sister's marriage, and she was heartily glad to see her well quit of her husband, and, on her return to England, received her with open arms, and begged her, on behalf of her husband and herself, to make their home hers. Mrs. Vivian accordingly settled down in the "extremely commodious" house in Prince's Gate, and, as I said, took up her life where it had left off. A standing grievance that her husband had had with her was, that she interested herself in the poor, and in the East End slums, that she went to cabmen's shelters, and espoused the cause of overdriven factory girls. He had told her that it was meddling with other people's business; that nothing was so objectionable as an assumption of charitable airs; that a woman who went to balls and dinner-parties was a hypocrite if she pretended to care about the state of the poor, and that she only did it because she wished to appear unlike other people. But he altogether failed to perceive that her actions were entirely uninfluenced by the impression they were to make, and mistook her extreme naturalness for the subtlest affectation. However, Mrs. Vivian resolutely banished from her mind the remembrance of those ten years, and, being unable to think of her husband with tenderness or affection, she preferred to forget her married life altogether. The Vanes had been their neighbours in the country for many years, and she had known Dodo since she was a child. Dodo had once asked to accompany her in her visits to the East End, and had been immensely struck by what she saw, and determined to be charitable too. This sort of thing seemed extremely chic to Dodo's observant mind. So she took up a factory of miserable match-girls, and asked them all to tea, and got Mrs. Vivian to promise her help; but when the afternoon came, Dodo particularly wished to go to a morning concert, and on Mrs. Vivian's arrival she found, indeed, plenty of match-girls, but no Dodo. Dodo came back later and made herself extremely fascinating. She kissed the cleanest of the girls, and patted the rest on the shoulder, and sang several delightful little French songs to them to her own accompaniment on the banjo, and thanked Mrs. Vivian for being "such a dear about the slums." But on the next occasion when she had nothing to do, and called on Mrs. Vivian to ask to be taken to another of those "darling little slums," Mrs. Vivian hinted that, though she would be charmed to take her, she thought that Dodo had perhaps forgotten that the Four-in-hand Club met that day in Hyde Park. Dodo had forgotten it, and, as she had bespoken the box seat on one of her friends' coaches, she hurried home again, feeling it freshly borne in upon her that Mrs. Vivian thought she was very contemptible indeed.

Altogether Mrs. Vivian knew Dodo well, and when she went home that evening, she thought a good deal about the approaching marriage. She was glad to have had that occasion of speaking to Jack, he seemed to her to be worth doing it for. She knew that she ran the risk of being told, in chillingly polite English, that she was stepping outside her province, and that Jack did not belong to the East End class who welcomed any charitable hand; but she had a remarkably keen eye, and her intuitive perception told her at once that Jack's sense of the justice of her remark would stifle any feeling he might have that she was officious and meddlesome, and the event had justified her decision.

In the course of the next few days she met Jack several times. They both went to the water-party Dodo spoke of, and she took the opportunity to cultivate his acquaintance.

They were sitting on the bank of the river below the Clivedon woods, a little apart from the others, and she felt that as he had behaved so well, she owed him some apology.

"It was very nice of you, Mr. Broxton," she said, "to be so polite to me last night. To tell you the truth, I did know you, though you didn't know me. I was an old friend of your mother's, but I hadn't time to explain that, and you were good enough to take me without explanations. I always wonder what our attitude towards old friends of our mothers ought to be. I really don't see why they should have any claim upon one."

Jack laughed.

"The fact was that I knew you were right as soon as you spoke to me, though I wanted to resent it. I had been putting it differently to myself; that was why I spoke to Dodo."

"Tell me more," she said. "From the momentary glance I had of you and her, I thought you had been remonstrating with her, and she had been objecting. I don't blame you for remonstrating in the general way. Dodo's conduct used not to be always blameless. But it looked private, and that was what I did object to. I daresay you think me a tiresome, impertinent, old woman."

Jack felt more strongly than ever that this woman could not help being well-bred in whatever she did.

"It sounds disloyal to one's friends, I know," he said, "but it was because I really did care for both of them that I acted as I did. What will happen will be that he will continue to adore her, and by degrees she will begin to hate him. He will not commit suicide, and I don't think Dodo will make a scandal. Her regard for appearances alone would prevent that. It would be a confession of failure."

Mrs. Vivian looked grave.

"Did you tell Dodo this?"

"More or less," he replied. "Except about the scandal and the suicide."

Mrs. Vivian's large, grey, serious eyes twinkled with some slight amusement.

"I think while I was about it I should have told her that too," she said; "that's the sort of argument that appeals to Dodo. You have to scream if you want her to listen to what she doesn't want to hear. But I don't think it was quite well judged of you, you know."

"I think she ought to know it," said Jack, "though I realise I ought to have been the last person to tell her, for several reasons."

Mrs. Vivian looked at him inquiringly.

"You mean for fear of her putting a wrong construction on it? I see," she said.

Jack felt that it could not have been more delicately done.

"How did you know?"

"Oh," she said, "that is the kind of intuition which is the only consolation we women have for getting old. We are put on the shelf, no doubt, after a certain age, but we get a habit of squinting down into the room below. That is the second time I have shown myself a meddling old woman, and you have treated me very nicely both times. Let us join the others. I see tea is ready."

Dodo meanwhile had walked Chesterford off among the green cool woods that bordered the river. She had given Jack's remarks a good deal of consideration, and, whether or no she felt that he was justified in them on present data, she determined that she would make the event falsify his predictions. Dodo had an unlimited capacity for interfering in the course of destiny. She devoted herself to her aims, whatever they might be, with a wonderful singleness of purpose, and since it is a fact that one usually gets what one wants in this world, if one tries hard enough, it followed that up to this time she had, on the whole, usually got her way. But she was now dealing with an unknown quantity, which she could not gauge. She had confessed to Jack her inability to understand what love meant, and it was with a certain sense of misgiving that she felt that her answers for the future would be expressed in terms of that unknown quantity "x." To Dodo's concrete mind this was somewhat discouraging, but she determined to do her best to reduce things to an equation in which the value of "x" could be found in terms of some of those many symbols which she did know.

Dodo had an inexhaustible fund of vivacity, which was a very useful instrument to her; like a watch-key that fits all watches, she was able to apply it as required to very different pieces of mechanism. When she wished to do honour to a melancholy occasion, for instance, her vivacity turned any slight feeling of sorrow she had into hysterical weeping; when the occasion was joyful, it became a torrent of delightful nonsense. To-day the occasion was distinctly joyful. She had a large sense of success. Chesterford was really a very desirable lover; his immense wealth answered exactly the requirements of Dodo's wishes. Furthermore, he was safe and easily satisfied; the day was charming; Jack was there; she had had a very good lunch, and was shortly going to have a very good tea; and Chesterford had given orders for his yacht to be in readiness to take them off for a delightful honeymoon, directly after their marriage—in short, all her circumstances were wholly satisfactory. She had said to him after lunch, as they were sitting on the grass, "Come away into those delicious woods, and leave these stupid people here," and he was radiant in consequence, for, to tell the truth, she had been rather indulgent of his company than eager for it the last day or two. She was in the highest spirits as they strolled away.

"Oh do give me a cigarette," she said, as soon as they had got out of sight. "I didn't dare smoke with that Vivian woman there. Chesterford, I am frightened of her. She is as bad as the Inquisition, or that odious man in Browning who used to walk about, and tell the king if anything happened. I am sure she puts it down in a book whenever I say anything I shouldn't. You know that's so tantalising. It is a sort of challenge to be improper. Chesterford, if you put down in a book anything I do wrong, I swear I shall go to the bad altogether."

To Chesterford this seemed the most attractive nonsense that ever flowed from female lips.

"Why, you can't do anything wrong, Dodo," he said simply; "at least not what I think wrong. And what does it matter what other people think?"

Dodo patted his hand, and blew him a kiss approvingly.

"That's quite right," she said; "bear that in mind and we shall never have a quarrel. Chesterford, we won't quarrel at all, will we? Everybody else does, I suppose, now and then, and that proves it's vulgar. Mrs. Vivian used to quarrel with her husband, so she's vulgar. Oh, I'm so glad she's vulgar. I sha'n't care how much she looks at me now. Bother! I believe it was only her husband that used to swear at her. Never mind, he must have been vulgar to do that, and she must have vulgar tastes to have married a vulgar person. I don't think I'm vulgar, do you? Really it's a tremendous relief to have found out that she's vulgar. But I am afraid I shall forget it when I see her again. You must remind me. You must point at her and say V, if you can manage it. Or are you afraid of her too?"

"Oh, never mind Mrs. Vivian," said he, "she can wait."

"That's what she's always doing," said Dodo. "Waiting and watching with large serious eyes. I can't think why she does it, for she doesn't make use of it afterwards. Now when I know something discreditable of a person, if I dislike him, I tell everybody else, and if I like him, I tell him that I know all about it, and I am *so* sorry for him. Then he thinks you are charming and sympathetic, and you have a devoted admirer for life."

Chesterford laughed. He had no desire to interrupt this rapid mono-logue of Dodo's. He was quite content to play the part of the Greek chorus.

"I'm going to sit down here," continued Dodo. "Do you mind my smoking cigarettes? I'm not sure that it is in good form, but I mean to make it so. I want to be the fashion. Would you like your wife to be the fashion?"

He bent over her as she sat with her head back, smiling up at him.

"My darling," he said, "do you know, I really don't care a straw whether you are the fashion or not, as long as you are satisfied. You might stand on your head in Piccadilly if you liked, and I would come and stand too. All I care about is that you are you, and that you have made me the happiest man on God's earth."

Dodo was conscious again of the presence of this unknown quantity. She would much prefer striking it out altogether; it seemed to have quite an unreasonable preponderance.

Chesterford did not usually make jokes, in fact she had never heard him make one before, and his remark about standing on his head seemed to be only accounted for by this perplexing factor. Dodo had read about love in poems and novels, and had seen something of it, too, but it remained a puzzle to her. She hoped her calculations might not prove distressingly incorrect owing to this inconvenient factor. But she laughed with her habitual sincerity, and replied,—

"What a good idea; let's do it to-morrow morning. Will ten suit you? We can let windows in all the houses round. I'm sure there would be a crowd to see us. It really would be interesting, though perhaps not a very practical thing to do. I wonder if Mrs. Vivian would come. She would put down a very large bad mark to me for that, but I shall tell her it was your suggestion."

Chesterford laughed with pure pleasure.

"Dodo," he said, "you are not fair on Mrs. Vivian. She is a very good woman."

"Oh, I don't doubt that," said Dodo, "but, you see, being good doesn't necessarily make one a pleasant companion. Now, I'm not a bit good, but you must confess you would rather talk to me than to the Vivian."

"Oh, you are different," said he rapturously. "You are Dodo."

Dodo smiled contentedly. This man was so easy to please. She had felt some slight dismay at Jack's ill-omened prophecies, but Jack was preposterously wrong about this.

They rejoined the others in course of time. Dodo made fearful ravages on the eatables, and after tea she suddenly announced,—

"Mrs. Vivian, I'm going to smoke a cigarette. Do you feel dreadfully shocked?"

Mrs. Vivian laughed.

"My dear Dodo, I should never venture to be shocked at anything you did. You are so complete that I should be afraid to spoil you utterly, if I tried to suggest corrections."

Dodo lit a cigarette with a slightly defiant air. Mrs. Vivian's manner had been entirely sincere, but she felt the same sort of resentment that a prisoner might feel if the executioner made sarcastic remarks to him. She looked on Mrs. Vivian as a sort of walking Inquisition.

"My darling Dodo," murmured Mrs. Vane, "I do so wish you would not smoke, it will ruin your teeth entirely."

Dodo turned to Mrs. Vivian.

"That means you think it would be very easy to spoil me, as you call it."

"Not at all," said that lady. "I don't understand you, that's all, and I might be pulling out the keystone of the arch unawares. Not that I suppose your character depends upon your smoking."

Dodo leaned back and laughed.

"Oh, this is too dreadfully subtle," she exclaimed. "I want to unbend my mind. Chesterford, come and talk to me, you are deliciously unbending."

4

Lord and Lady Chesterford were expected home on the 6th of December. The marriage took place late in August, and they had gone off on the yacht directly afterwards, in order to spend a few warm months in the Mediterranean. Dodo had written home occasionally to Mrs. Vane, and now and then to Jack. To Jack her letters had never been more than a word or two, simply saying that they were enjoying themselves enormously, and that Jack had been hopelessly wrong. Mrs. Vane also had much reason to be satisfied. She had spent her autumn in a variety of fashionable watering-places, where her dresses had always been the awe and wonder of the town; she had met many acquaintances, to whom she had poured out her rapture over Dodo's marriage; had declared that Chesterford was most charming, and that he and Dodo were quite another Adam and Eve in Paradise, and that she was really quite jealous of Dodo. When they left England, they had intended to spend the winter abroad and not come back till February, but early in December a telegram had arrived at Winston, Lord Chesterford's country house, saying that they would be back in ten days. About the same time Jack received a letter, saying that their change of plans was solely owing to the fact that Dodo was rather tired of the sea, and the weather was bad, and that she had never been so happy in her life. Dodo's eagerness to assure Jack of this struck him as being in rather bad taste. She ought to have entirely ignored his warnings. The happiness of a newly-married woman ought to be so absorbing, as to make her be unaware of the existence of other people; and this consciousness in Dodo of her triumphant superiority of knowledge, led him to suppose he was right rather than wrong. He was unfeignedly sorry not to be sure that she had

been right. When he told Dodo that he wished to be jealous of Chesterford, he was quite sincere. Since he could not have Dodo himself, at
any rate let her make someone happy. Dodo also informed him that
they were going to have a house-party that Christmas and that he
must come, and she had asked Mrs. Vivian, to show that she wasn't
afraid of her any longer, and that Maud was coming, and she wished
Jack would marry her. Then followed a dozen other names belonging
to Dodo's private and particular set, who had all been rather disgusted
at her marrying what they chose to call a Philistine. It had been quite
hoped that she would marry Jack. Jack was not a Philistine at all,
though the fact of his having proposed to her remained a secret. Maud,
on the other hand, was a Philistine; and it was one of Dodo's merits
that she did not drop those who originally had claims on her, when
she became the fashion. She was constantly trying to bring Maud
into notice, but Maud resisted the most well-meant shoves. She had
none of Dodo's vivacity and talents; in fact, her talents lay chiefly in
the direction of arranging the places at a dinner-party, and in doing
a great deal of unnecessary worsted work. What happened to her
worsted work nobody ever knew. It was chiefly remarkable for the
predominance of its irregularities, and a suggestion of damaged goods
about it, in consequence of much handling. To Dodo it seemed an
incredible stupidity that anyone should do worsted work, or, if they
did do it, not do it well. She used to tell Maud that it was done
much more cheaply in shops, and much better. Then Maud would
drop it for a time, and take to playing the piano, but that was even
more oppressively stupid to Dodo's mind than the worsted work. Maud
had a perfect genius for not letting her right hand know what her
left hand was doing, a principle which was abhorrent to Dodo in every
application. The consequence of all this was, that Dodo was apt to
regard her sister as a failure, though she still, as in the present instance,
liked giving Maud what she considered a helping hand. It must be
confessed that Dodo's efforts were not altogether unselfish. She liked
her environment to be as great a success as herself, as it thus added
to her own completeness, just as a picture looks better in a good frame
than in a shabby one. Maud, however, had no desire to be a success.
She was perfectly happy to sit in the background and do the worsted
work. She longed to be let alone. At times she would make her escape
to the iron works and try to cultivate the domestic virtues in attending
to her father. She thought with a kind of envy of the daughters of
country clergymen, whose mediocre piano-playing was invaluable to
penny readings and village concerts, and for whose worsted work there
was a constant demand, in view of old women and alms-houses. She
had hoped that Dodo's slumming experiences would bring her into

connection with this side of life, and had dispensed tea and buns with a kind of rapture on the occasion of Dodo's tea-party, but her sister had dropped her slums, as we have seen, at this point, and Maud was too shy and uninitiative to take them up alone. She had an excellent heart, but excellent hearts were out of place in Mrs. Vane's establishment. Dodo had confessed her inability to deal with them.

Dodo's general invitation to Jack was speedily followed by a special one from Winston, naming the first week in January as the time of the party. Jack was met on his arrival by Chesterford, and as they drove back the latter gave him particulars about the party in the house.

"They are chiefly Dodo's friends," he said. "Do you know, Jack, except for you, I think I am rather afraid of Dodo's friends, they are so dreadfully clever, you know. Of course they are all very charming, but they talk about character. Now I don't care to talk about character. I know a good man when I see him, and that's all that matters as far as I can judge. Dodo was saying last night that her potentiality for good was really much stronger than her potentiality for evil, and that her potentiality for evil was only skin deep, and they all laughed, and said they didn't believe it. And Dodo said, 'Ask Chesterford if it isn't,' and God only knows what I said."

Jack laughed.

"Poor old fellow," he said, "you and I will go to the smoking-room, and talk about nothing at all subtle. I don't like subtleties either."

"Ah, but they expect great things of you," said Chesterford ruefully. "Dodo was saying you were an apostle. Are you an apostle, Jack?"

"Oh, that's only a nickname of Dodo's," he said, smiling. "But who are these dreadfully clever people?"

"Oh, there's Ledgers—you know him, I suppose—and a Miss Edith Staines, and a girl whom I don't know, called Miss Grantham, whom Ledgers said, when she was out of the room last night, that he had 'discovered.' What he meant Heaven knows. Then there's Maud, who is a nice girl. She went round to the keeper's with me this afternoon, and played with the baby. Then there's Bertie Arbuthnot, and I think that's all."

Jack laughed.

"I don't think we need mind them," he said. "We'll form a square to resist cavalry."

"Bertie's the best of the lot," said Chesterford, "and they laughed at him rather, I think. But he is quite unconscious of it."

They drove on in silence a little way. Then Chesterford said,—

"Jack, Dodo makes me the happiest of men. I am afraid sometimes that she is too clever, and wishes I was more so, but it makes no difference. Last night, as I was in the smoking-room she sent to say she wanted to see me, and I went up. She said that she wanted to talk to me, now she had got rid of all those tiresome people, and said so many charming things that I got quite conceited, and had to stop her. I often wonder, Jack, what I have done to deserve her. And she went on talking about our yachting, and those months in London when we were first engaged, and she told me to go on smoking, and she would have a cigarette too. And we sat on talking, till I saw she was tired, and then I went away, though she would hardly let me."

This communication had only the effect of making Jack rather uncomfortable. Knowing what he did, he knew that this was not all genuine on Dodo's part. It was obviously an effort to keep it up, to use a vulgar term. And since it was not all genuine, the doubt occurred as to whether any of it was. Jack had a profound belief in Dodo's dramatic talents. That the need for keeping it up had appeared already was an alarming symptom, but the real tragedy would begin on that day when Dodo first failed to do so. And from that moment Jack regarded his prophecy as certain to be fulfilled. The overture had begun, and in course of time the curtain would rise on a grim performance.

They drove up to the door, and entered the large oak-panelled hall, hung all round with portraits of the family. The night was cold, and there was a fire sparkling in the wide, open grate. As they entered, an old collie, who was enjoying the fruits of a well-spent life on the hearthrug, stretched his great, tawny limbs, and shoved a welcoming nose into Chesterford's hand. This produced heartburnings of the keenest order in the mind of a small fox-terrier pup, who consisted mainly of head and legs, which latter he evidently considered at present more as a preventive towards walking than an aid. Being unable to reach his hand the puppy contented himself with sprawling over his boots, and making vague snaps at the collie. It was characteristic of Chesterford that all animals liked him. He had a tender regard for the feelings of anything that was dependent on him. Dodo thought this almost inexplicable. She disliked to see animals in pain, because they usually howled, but the dumb anguish of a dog who considers himself neglected conveyed nothing to her. From within a door to the right, came sounds of talking and laughter.

There was something pathetic in the sight of this beautiful home, and its owner standing with his back to the fire, as Jack divested himself of his coat. Chesterford was so completely happy, so terribly unconscious of what Jack felt sure was going on. He looked the model of the typical English gentleman, with his tall stature and well-bred face. Jack remembered passing on the road a labourer who was turning into his cottage. The firelight had thrown a bright ray across the snow-covered road, and inside he had caught a momentary glimpse of the wife with a baby in her arms, and a couple of girls laying the table-cloth. He remembered afresh Dodo's remark about waiting until the chimney smoked, and devoutly hoped that the chimney of this well-appointed house was in good order.

Chesterford led the way to the drawing-room door, and pushed it open for Jack to enter. Dodo was sitting at the tea-table, talking to some half-dozen people who were grouped round her.

As Jack entered, she rose and came towards him with a smile of welcome.

"Ah, Jack," she said, "this is delightful; I am tremendously glad to see you! Let's see, whom do you know? May I introduce you to Miss Grantham? Mr. Broxton. I think you know everybody else. Chesterford, come here and sit by me at once. You've been an age away. I expect you've been getting into mischief." She wheeled a chair up for him, and planted him down in it. He looked radiantly happy.

"Now, Jack," she went on, "tell us what you've been doing all these months. It's years since we saw you. I think you look all right. No signs of breaking down yet. I hoped you would have gone into a rapid consumption, because I was married, but it doesn't seem to have made any difference to anybody except Chesterford and me. Jack, don't you think I shall make an excellent matron? I shall get Maud to teach me some of her crochet-stitches. Have you ever been here before? Chesterford, you shut it up, didn't you, for several years, until you thought of bringing me here? Sugar, Jack? Two lumps? Chesterford, you mustn't eat sugar, you're getting quite fat already. You must obey me, you know. You promised to love, honour and obey. Oh, no; I did that. However, sugar is bad for you."

"Dodo keeps a tight hand on me, you see," said Chesterford, from the depths of his chair. "Dodo, give me the sugar, or we shall quarrel."

Dodo laughed charmingly.

"He would quarrel with his own wife for a lump of sugar," said Dodo dramatically; "but she won't quarrel with him. Take it then."

She glanced at Jack for a moment as she said this, but Jack was talking to Miss Grantham, and either did not see, or did not seem to. Jack had a pleasant impression of light hair, dark grey eyes, and a very fair complexion. But somehow it produced no more effect on him than do those classical profiles which are commoner on the lids of chocolate boxes than elsewhere. Her "discoverer" was sitting in a chair next her, talking to her with something of the air of a showman exhibiting the tricks of his performing bear. His manner seemed to say, "See what an intelligent animal." The full sublimity of Lord Ledgers' remark had not struck him till that moment.

Miss Grantham was delivering herself of a variety of opinions in a high, penetrating voice.

"Oh, did you never hear him sing last year?" she was saying to

Lord Ledgers. "Mr. Broxton, you must have heard him. He has the most lovely voice. He simply sings into your inside. You feel as if someone had got hold of your heart, and was stroking it. Don't you know how some sounds produce that effect? I went with Dodo once. She simply wept floods, but I was too far gone for that. He had put a little stopper on my tear bottle, and though I was dying to cry, I couldn't."

"I always wonder how sorry we are when we cry," said Lord Ledgers in a smooth, low voice. "It always strikes me that people who don't cry probably feel most."

"Oh, you are a horrid, unfeeling monster," remarked Miss Grantham; "that's what comes of being a man. Just because you are not in the habit of crying yourself, you think that you have all the emotions, but stoically repress them. Now I cultivate emotions. I would walk ten miles any day in order to have an emotion. Wouldn't you, Mr. Broxton?"

"It obviously depends on what sort of emotion I should find when I walked there," said Jack. "There are some emotions that I would walk further to avoid."

"Oh, of course, the common emotions, 'the litany things,' as Dodo calls them," said Miss Grantham, dismissing them lightly with a wave of her hand. "But what I like is a nice little sad emotion that makes you feel so melancholy you don't know what to do with yourself. I don't mean deaths and that sort of thing, but seeing someone you love being dreadfully unhappy and extremely prosperous at the same time."

"But it's rather expensive for the people you love," said Jack.

"Oh, we must all make sacrifices," said Miss Grantham. "It's quite worth while if you gratify your friends. I would not mind being acutely unhappy, if I could dissect my own emotions, and have them photographed and sent round to my friends."

"What a charming album we might all make," said Lord Ledgers. "Page 1. Miss Grantham's heart in the acute stage. Page 2. Mortification setting in. Page 3. The lachrymatory gland permanently closed by a tenor voice."

"Poor old Chesterford," thought Jack, "this is rather hard on him."

But Chesterford was not to be pitied just now, for Dodo was devoting her exclusive conversation to him in defiance of her duties as hostess. She was recounting to him how she had spent every moment of his absence at the station. Certainly she was keeping it up magnificently at present.

"And Mrs. Vivian comes to-morrow," she was saying. "You like her, don't you, Chesterford? You must be awfully good to her, and

take her to see all the drunken idlers in the village. That will be dear
of you. It's just what she likes. She has a sort of passion for drunken
cabmen, who stamp on their wives. If you stamped on me a little
every evening, she would cultivate you to any extent. Shall I lie down
on the floor for you to begin?"

Chesterford leant back in his chair in a kind of ecstasy.

"Ah, Dodo," he said, "you are wonderfully good to me. But I must
go and write two notes before dinner; and you must amuse your guests.
I am very glad Jack has come. He is a very good chap. But don't
make him an apostle."

Dodo laughed.

"I shall make a little golden hoop for him like the apostles in the
Arundels, and another for you, and when nobody else is there you
can take them off, and play hoops with them. I expect the apostles
did that when they went for a walk. You couldn't wear it round your
hat, could you?"

Miss Grantham instantly annexed Dodo.

"Dodo," she said, "come and take my part. These gentlemen say
you shouldn't cultivate emotions."

"No, not that quite," corrected Jack. "I said it was expensive for
your friends if they had to make themselves miserable, in order to
afford food for your emotions."

"Now, isn't that selfish?" said Miss Grantham, with the air of a
martyr at the stake. "Here am I ready to be drawn and quartered for
anyone's amusement, and you tell me you are sorry for your part,
but that it costs too much. Maud, come off that sofa, and take up
the daggers for a too unselfish woman."

"I expect I don't know much about these things," said Maud.

"No; Maud would not go further than wrapping herself in a winding-
sheet of blue worsted," remarked Dodo incisively.

Maud flushed a little.

"Oh, Dodo!" she exclaimed deprecatingly.

"It's no use hitting Maud," said Dodo pensively. "You might as
well hit a feather bed. Now, if you hit Jack, he will hit back."

"Well, I'd prefer you hit me," said Jack, "than that you should hit
anyone who can't hit back."

"Can't you see that I have determined not to hit feather beds,"
said Dodo in a low tone. "Really, Jack, you do me an injustice."

Jack looked up at her quickly.

"Do you say that already?" he asked.

"Oh, if you are going to whisper, I shall whisper too," remarked
Miss Grantham calmly. "Lord Ledgers, I want to tell you a secret."

"I was only telling Jack he was stupid," said Dodo. "I thought I would spare him before you all, but I see I have to explain. Have you seen Bertie yet, Jack? He's in the smoking-room, I think. Edith Staines is probably there too. She always smokes after tea, and Chesterford doesn't like it in the drawing-room. You know her, don't you? She's writing a symphony or something, and she's no use except at meal-times. I expect she will play it to us afterwards. We must make Bertie sing too. There's the dressing-bell. I'm going to be gorgeous to-night in honour of you, Jack."

Jack found himself making a quantity of reflections, when he retired to his room that night. He became aware that he had enjoyed himself more that evening than he had done for a very long time. He questioned himself as to when he had enjoyed himself so much, and he was distinctly perturbed to find that the answer was, when he had last spent an evening with Dodo. He had formed an excellent habit of being exactly honest with himself, and he concluded that Dodo's presence had been the cause of it. It was a very unpleasant blow to him. He had accepted her refusal with an honest determination to get over it. He had not moped, nor pined, nor striven, nor cried. He had no intentions of dying of a broken heart, but the stubborn fact remained that Dodo exercised an unpleasantly strong influence over him. He could have repeated without effort all she had said that night. She had not said anything particularly remarkable, but somehow he felt that the most striking utterances of other men and women would not have produced any such effect on him. It really was very inconvenient. Dodo had married a man who adored her, for whom she did not care two pins' heads, and this man was one of his oldest friends. Decidedly there was something left-handed about this particular disposition of destiny. And the worst of it was that Chesterford was being hopelessly duped. About that he felt no doubt. Dodo's acting was so remarkably life-like, that he mistook it at present for reality. But the play must end some time, and the sequel was too dark and involved to be lightly followed out. He could not conceive why this elaborate drama on Dodo's part did not disgust him more. He wished he had been deceived by it himself, but having been behind the scenes, he had seen Dodo, as it were, in the green-room, putting on the rouge and powder. But failing that, he wished that a wholesome impulse of disgust and contempt had superseded his previous feelings with regard to her. But he believed with her that under the circumstances it was the best thing to do. The marriage was a grand mistake, true, but given that, was not this simply so many weeks of unhappiness saved? Then he had an immense pity for Dodo's original mistake. She had told him once that she was no more responsible for her philosophy than for the fact that she happened to be five foot eight in height, and had black eyes and black hair. "It was Nature's doing," she had said; "go and quarrel with her, but don't blame me. If I had made myself, I should have given myself a high ideal; I should have had something to live up to. Now, I have no ideal. The whole system of things seems to me such an immense puzzle, that I have given up trying to find a solution. I know what I like, and what I dislike. Can you blame me for choosing the one, and avoiding the other? I like wealth and success, and society and admiration. In a degree I have secured them, and the more I secure them the more reason I have to be satisfied. To do otherwise would be like putting on boots that were too large for me— they are excellent for other people, but not for me. I cannot accept ideals that I don't feel. I can understand them, and I can sympathise with them, and I can and do wish they were mine; but, as Nature has denied me them, I must make the best of what I have."

Jack felt hopeless against this kind of reasoning, and angry with himself for letting this woman have such dominion over him. In a measure he felt himself capable of views bounded by a horizon not so selfishly fatalistic, and the idea of the smoking chimney in the cottage did not seem to matter, provided that Dodo was sitting on the other side of the hearthrug. He would willingly have sacrificed anything else, to allow himself to give full reins to his thought on this point. But the grand barrier which stood between him and Dodo, was not so much her refusal of him, but the existence of her husband. At this Jack pulled himself up sharp. There are certain feelings of loyalty that still rank above all other emotions. Miss Grantham would certainly have classed such among the litany things. There was nothing heroic about it. It simply consisted in a sturdy refusal to transgress, even in vaguest thought, a code which deals with the most ordinary and commonplace virtues and vices. There is nothing heroic in a street boy passing by the baker's cart without a grab at the loaves, and it sounds almost puritanical to forbid him to cast a glance at them, or inhale a sniff of their warm fragrance. "Certainly this side of morality is remarkably dull," thought Jack; and the worst of it is, that it is not only dull but difficult. With practice most of us could become a Simeon Stylites, provided we are gifted with a steady head, and a constitution that defies showers. It is these commonplace acts of loyalty, the ordinary and rational demands of friendship and society, that are so dreadfully taxing to most of us who have the misfortune not to be born saints. Then Jack began to feel ill-used. "Why the deuce should Chesterford be born a marquis and not I? What has he done to have a title and fortune and Dodo that I have been given the chance to do?" It struck him that his reflections were deplorably commonplace, and that his position ought to be made much more of. He wondered whether this sort of situation was always so flat. In novels there is always a touch of the heroic in the faithful friend who is loyal to his cousin, and steadily avoids his cousin's wife; but here he is in identically the same situation, feeling not at all heroic, but only discontented and quarrelsome with this ill-managed world. Decidedly he would go to bed.

Owing to a certain habit that he had formed early in life he slept soundly, and morning found him not only alive, but remarkably well and hearty, and with a certain eagerness to follow up what he had thought out on the previous night. He was in an excellently managed household, which imposed no rules on its inhabitants except that they should do what they felt most inclined to do; he was in congenial company, and his digestion was good. It is distressing how important those material matters are to us. The deeper emotions do but form a kind of background to our coarser needs. We come down in the morning feeling rather miserable, but we eat an excellent breakfast, and, in spite of ourselves, we are obliged to confess that we feel distinctly better.

As Jack crossed the hall, he met a footman carrying a breakfast tray into the drawing-room. The door was half open, and there came from within the sounds of vigorous piano-playing, and now and then a bar or two of music sung in a rich, alto voice. These tokens seemed to indicate that Miss Edith Staines was taking her breakfast at the piano. Jack found himself smiling at the thought; it was a great treat to find anyone so uniformly in character as Miss Staines evidently was. He turned into the dining-room, where he found Miss Grantham sitting at the table alone. Dodo was lolling in a great chair by the fire, and there were signs that Lord Chesterford had already breakfasted. Dodo was nursing a little Persian kitten with immense tenderness. Apparently she had been disagreeing with Miss Grantham on some point, and had made the kitten into a sort of arbitrator.

"Oh, you dear kitten," she was saying, "you must agree with me, if you think it over. Now, supposing you were very fond of a tom-cat that had only the woodshed to lie in, and another very presentable tom belonging to the Queen came—Ah, Jack, here you are. Chesterford's breakfasted, and there's going to be a shoot to-day over the home covers. Edith is composing and breakfasting. She says she has an idea. So Grantie and I are going to bring you lunch to the keeper's cottage at half-past one."

"And Bertie?" asked Jack.

"Oh, you must get Edith to tell you what Bertie's going to do. Perhaps she'll want him to turn over the pages for her, or give her spoonfuls of egg and bacon, while she does her music. He's in the drawing-room now. Edith's appropriated him. She usually does appropriate somebody. We told Chesterford to get Bertie to come if possible, but Edith's leave is necessary. Maud is going to meet Mrs. Vivian, who comes this afternoon, and, as she has some shopping to do, she will lunch in Harchester, and drive out afterwards; Ledgers has had a telegram, and has made a blasphemous departure for town. He comes back this evening."

"Well, Dodo," remarked Miss Grantham, "now let's go on with what we were discussing. Mr. Broxton will make a much better umpire than the kitten."

"Oh, shut up, Grantie," said Dodo, with fine candour, "Jack agrees with neither of us."

"Tell me what it is," said Jack, "and then I'll promise to agree with somebody."

"I don't care about your agreeing with me," said Miss Grantham. "I know I'm right, so it doesn't signify what anybody else thinks."

Miss Grantham, it may be noticed, showed some signs of being ruffled.

"Oh, now, Grantie's angry," said Dodo. "Grantie, do be amiable. Call her Grantie, Jack," she added with feeling.

"Dodo, darling," said Miss Grantham, "you're really foolish now and then. I'm perfectly amiable. But, you know, if you don't care for a man at all, and he does care for you a great deal, it's sure to be a failure. I can't think of any instance just now, but I know I'm right."

Dodo looked up and caught Jack's eye for a moment. Then she turned to Miss Grantham.

"Dear Grantie, please shut up. It's no use trying to convince me. I know a case in point just the other way, but I am not at liberty to mention it. Am I, Jack?"

"If you mean the same as the case I'm thinking of, certainly not," said Jack.

"Well, I'm sure this is very pleasant for me," said Miss Grantham, in high, cool tones.

At this moment a shrill voice called Dodo from the drawing-room.

"Dodo, Dodo," it cried, "the man brought me two tepid poached eggs! Do send me something else. Is there such a thing as a grilled bone?"

These remarks were speedily followed up by the appearance of Miss Staines at the dining-room door. In one hand she held the despised eggs, in the other a quire of music paper. Behind her followed a footman with her breakfast-tray, in excusable ignorance as to what was required of him.

"Dear Dodo," she went on, "you know when I'm composing a symphony I want something more exciting than two poached eggs. Mr. Broxton, I know, will take my side. You couldn't eat poached eggs at a ball—could you? They might do very well for a funeral march or a nocturne, but they won't do for a symphony, especially for the scherzo. A brandy-and-soda and a grilled bone is what one really wants for a scherzo, only that would be quite out of the question."

Edith Staines talked in a loud, determined voice, and emphasised her points with little dashes and flourishes of the dish of poached eggs. At this moment one of them flew on to the floor and exploded. But it is an ill wind that blows nobody any good, and at any rate this relieved the footman from his state of indecision. His immediate mission was clearly to remove it.

Dodo threw herself back in her chair with a peal of laughter.

"Go on, go on," she cried, "you are too splendid. Tell us what you write the presto on."

"I can't waste another moment," said Edith. "I'm in the middle of the most entrancing motif, which is working out beautifully. Do you mind my smoking in the drawing-room? I am awfully sorry, but it makes all the difference to my work. Burn a little incense there afterwards. Do send me a bone, Dodo. Come and hear me play the scherzo later on. It's the best thing I've ever done. Oh, by the way, I telegraphed to Herr Truffen to come to-morrow—he's my conductor, you know. You can put him up in the village or the coal-hole, if you like. He's quite happy if he gets enough beer. He's my German conductor, you know. I made him entirely. I took him to the Princess the other day when I was at Aix, and we all had beer together in the verandah of the Beau Site. You'll be amused with him."

"Oh, rather," said Dodo; "that will be all right. He can sleep in the house. Will he come early to-morrow? Let's see—to-morrow's Sunday. Edith, I've got an idea. We'll have a dear little service in the house—we can't go to church if it snows—and you shall play your Mass, and Herr What's-his-name shall conduct, and Bertie, and Grantie, and you and I will sing. Won't it be lovely? You and I will settle all that this afternoon. Telegraph to Truffler, or whatever his name is, to come by the eight-twenty. Then he'll be here by twelve, and we'll have the service at a quarter past."

"Dodo, that will be grand," said Edith. "I can't wait now. Goodbye. Hurry up my breakfast—I'm awfully sharp-set."

Edith went back to the drawing-room, whistling in a particularly shrill manner.

"Oh, did you ever!" said Dodo, who was laughing feebly in her chair. "Edith really is splendid. She is so dreadfully sure of herself, and she tells you so. And she does talk so loud—it goes right through your head like a chirping canary. Chesterford can't bear her."

Jack laughed.

"She was giving him advice about the management of his kennels at dinner last night," he said. "I heard her say to him impressively, as she left the room, 'Try brimstone.' It took Chesterford at least five minutes to recover. He was dreadfully depressed."

"He must take Mrs. Vivian in to-night," said Dodo. "You'll hear them talking about slums, and over-crowding, and marriage among minors, and the best cure for dipsomaniacs. The other night they were talking about someone called 'Charlie,' affectionately but gravely, and I supposed they meant your brother, Jack, but it was the second laundress's young man. Oh, they shook their heads over him."

"I don't think common people are at all interesting," said Miss Grantham. "They only think about things to eat, and heaven, and three aces, and funerals."

She had by this time finished her breakfast, and stood warming her back in a gentlemanly manner by the fire.

The door opened and Lord Chesterford came in.

"Morning, Jack," he said, "what a lazy chap you are. It's half-past ten, and you're still breakfasting. Dodo, what a beastly smell of smoke."

"Oh, it's Edith," remarked Dodo. "You mustn't mind her, dear. You know she's doing a symphony, and she has to smoke to keep the inspiration going. Dear old boy, you are so sweet about these things; you've never made a fuss since I knew you first. You look very nice this morning. I wish I could dress in a homespun Norfolk jacket and knickerbockers. Grantie and I are going to bring you lunch. What should you like? You'd better have some champagne. Don't step in that egg, dear; it will make your nice brown boots all beastly. It's awfully cold. You'd better have two bottles. Tell Raikes to send you two. Chesterford, I wish you'd tell Raikes to cut off the end of his nose. I'm always afraid he'll hit me with it when he hands things. He might have it grafted into his chin, you know; he hasn't got any chin. Jack, have you finished? Yes, you'd better start. We'll meet you at the bothy. I'll go and ask Edith if she can spare Bertie."

"What does she want Bertie for?" said Chesterford.

"Oh, I expect she'll let him come," remarked Dodo; "she's really busy this morning. She's been composing since a quarter past eight."

Dodo went across the hall and opened the drawing-room door. Edith was completely absorbed in her work. The grilled bone lay untouched on a small table by the piano. Bertie was sitting before the fire.

"Bertie," said Dodo, "are you coming shooting?"

This woke Edith up.

"Oh, it's splendid," she said. "Dodo, listen to this."

She ran her hands over the piano, and then broke out into a quick, rippling scherzo. The music flew on, as if all the winds of heaven were blowing it; then it slowed down, halted a moment, and repeated itself till Dodo burst out: "Oh, Edith, it's lovely! I want to dance." She wheeled a table out of the way, kicked a chair across the room, and began turning and twisting with breathless rapidity. Her graceful figure looked admirable in the quick movements of her impromptu dance. Bertie thought he had never seen anything so deliciously fresh. Dodo danced with peculiar abandon. Every inch of her moved in perfect time and harmony to the music.

She had caught up a thin, Indian shawl from one of the sofas, and passed it behind her back, round her head, this way and that, bending, till at one moment it swept the ground in front of her, at another flew in beautiful curves high above her head, till at last the music stopped, and she threw herself down exhausted in an arm-chair.

"Oh, that was glorious," she panted. "Edith, you are a genius. I never felt like that before. I didn't dance at all, it was the music that danced, and pulled me along with it."

"That was the best compliment my music has ever received," said Edith. "That scherzo was meant to make you want to dance. Now, Dodo, could I have done that after eating two poached eggs?"

"You may have grilled bones seven times a day," said Dodo, "if you'll compose another scherzo."

"I wanted a name for the symphony," said Edith, "and I shall call it the 'Dodo.' That's a great honour, Dodo. Now, if you only feel miserable during the 'Andante,' I shall be satisfied. But you came about something else, I forget what."

"Oh, about Bertie. Is he coming shooting?"

"I wish it was right for women to shoot," said Edith. "I do shoot when I'm at home, and there's no one there. Anyhow I couldn't to-day. I must finish this. Dodo, if you are going to take lunch with them, I'll come with you, if you don't go too early. You know this music makes me perfectly wild, but it can't be done on poached eggs. Now set me down at the Handel Festival, and I'll be content with high tea—cold meat and muffins, you know. Handel always reminds me of high tea, particularly the muffins. He must have written the 'Messiah' between tea and dinner on Sunday evening, after an after-noon service in summer. I've often thought of taking the Salvation Army hymn-book and working the tunes up into fugual choruses, and publishing them as a lost work of Handel's, Noah, or Zebedee's children, or the Five Foolish Virgins. I don't believe anyone would know the difference."

Dodo was turning over the leaves of Edith's score book.

"I give it up," she said at last; "you are such a jumble of opposites. You sit down and write a Sanctus, which makes one feel as if one wants to be a Roman Catholic archbishop, and all the time you are smoking cigarettes and eating grilled bone."

"Oh, everyone's a jumble of opposites," said Edith, "when you come to look at them. It's only because my opposites are superficial, that you notice them. A Sanctus is only a form of expression for thoughts which everyone has, even though their tastes appear to lie in the music-hall line; and music is an intelligible way of expressing these thoughts. Most people are born dumb with regard to their emotions, and you therefore conclude that they haven't got any, or that they are expressed by their ordinary actions."

"No, it's not that," said Dodo. "What I mean is that your Sanctus emphasises an emotion I should think you felt very little."

"I!" said Edith with surprise. "My dear Dodo, you surely know me better than that. Just because I don't believe that grilled bones are necessarily inconsistent with deep religious feeling, you assume that I haven't got the feeling."

Dodo laughed.

"I suppose one associates the champions of religion with proselytising," she said. "You don't proselytise, you know."

"No artist does," said Edith; "it's their business to produce—to give the world an opportunity of forming conclusions, not to preach their own conclusions to the world."

"Yes; but your music is the expression of your conclusions, isn't it?"

"Yes; but I don't argue about it, and try to convert the world to it. If someone says to me. 'I don't know what you mean! Handel seems to me infinitely more satisfactory, I can understand him,' I simply say, 'For Heaven's sake, then, why don't you go to hear Handel? Why leave a creed that satisfies you?' Music is a conviction, but Handel's music has nothing to do with my convictions, nor mine with Handel's."

Edith sat down sternly, and buried herself in her convictions.

5

It was a perfect winter's day, and when, two hours afterwards, Dodo and the others drove off to meet the shooting-party, the grass in the shadow was still crisp with the light, hoar frost, but where the sun had touched it, the fields were covered with a moist radiance. It had just begun to melt the little pieces of ice that hung from the bare, pendulous twigs of the birch-trees, and send them shivering to the ground. Through the brown bracken you could hear the startled scuttle of the rabbit, or the quick tapping of a pheasant, who had realised that schemes were on foot against him. A night of hard frost had turned the wheel-ruts into little waves and billows of frozen mud, which the carriage wheels levelled as they passed over them.

They caught up the shooting-party shortly before lunch, and, as it was cold, Edith and Dodo got out, leaving Miss Grantham, who preferred being cold to walking under any circumstances, to gather up the extra rugs round her.

"See that there's a good fire, Grantie," called Dodo after her, "and tell them to have the champagne opened."

The sight of abundant game was too much for Edith, and, as Lord Chesterford fell out of line to join Dodo, she asked him if she might have a couple of shots.

The keeper's face expressed some reasonable surprise when he observed Edith snapping the cartridges into her gun with a practised hand. His previous views with regard to women in connection with guns were based upon the idea that most women screamed, when they saw a gun, and considered it a purely unaccountable weapon, which might go off without the least encouragement or warning, and devastate the country for miles round. He was still more surprised when he saw her pick off a couple of pheasants with precision and deadliness of aim. She gave her gun back to Lord Chesterford as they neared the lodge, and volunteered to join them after lunch for an hour, if they didn't mind. Chesterford stole an appealing glance at Dodo, who, however, only gave him a half-amused, half-pitying look, and nodded assent.

"The worst of it is," said Edith, "I care for such lots of things. There's my music, and then there's any sort of game—have you ever seen me play tennis?—and there isn't time for everything. I am a musician, and a good shot, and an excellent rider, and a woman, and heaps of other things. It isn't conceit when I say so—I simply know it."

Dodo laughed.

"Well, you know, Edith, you're not modest. Your worst enemies don't accuse you of that. I don't mean to say that I am, for that matter. Did you ever play the game of marking people for beauty, and modesty, and cleverness, and so on? We played it here the night before you came, and you didn't get a single mark from anybody for modesty. I only got eleven, and five of those were from Chesterford, and six from myself. But I don't believe your husband will ever give you five. You see, Bertie didn't give you any, if you're thinking of marrying him."

"Oh, I'm not going to marry anybody," said Edith. "You know I get frightfully attached to someone about three times a week, and after that never think of any of them again. It isn't that I get tired of them, but somebody else turns up, and I want to know him too. There are usually several good points about everyone, and they show those to new acquaintances first; after that, you find something in them you don't like, so the best thing is to try somebody else."

"Oh, that depends on the people," said Dodo, meditatively. "Some people wear well, you know, and those improve on acquaintance. Now I don't. The first time a man sees me, he usually thinks I'm charming, and sympathetic, and lively. Well, so I am, to do myself justice. That remains all through. But it turns out that I've got a bad temper, that I smoke and swear, and only amuse myself. Then they begin to think they rated me too high at first, and if they happen to be people who wear well themselves, it is just then that you begin to like them, which is annoying. So one goes on, disgusting the people one wants to like, and pleasing people whom one doesn't like at all. It's fate, I suppose."

Dodo plucked a piece of dead bracken, and pulled it to bits with a somewhat serious air.

"You oughtn't to complain, Dodo," said Edith. "You're married to a man who, I am sure, wears well, as you call it, though it's a dreadfully coarse expression, and he doesn't seem to get tired of you. I always wonder if it's really worth while trotting oneself out or analysing one's nature in this way. I don't think it is. It makes one feel small and stupid."

"Ah, but it's better to do it yourself, than to feel that other people think you small and stupid," said Dodo. "That's disagreeable, if you like. Wait till Mrs. Vivian comes, and she'll do it for you. She's the only person who makes me feel really cheap—about three-halfpence a dozen, including the box."

"Oh, but she won't make me feel small," said Edith coolly, "because I'm not small really. It's only myself that makes me feel small."

"I don't think I should call you morbidly modest," said Dodo. "But here's the keeper's cottage. I'm awfully hungry. I hope they've brought some *pâté*. Don't you like *pâté*? Of course one's very sorry for the poor, diseased goose with a bad inside, but there are so many other things to think about besides diseased geese, that it doesn't signify much. Come on, Chesterford, they can count the dead things afterwards. Grantie's waiting. Jack, pick up that pheasant by you. Have you shot well? Look at the sun through those fir-trees—isn't it lovely? Edith, why aren't we two nice, little simple painters who could sit down, and be happy to paint that, instead of turning ourselves inside out?

But, after all, you know, one is much more interesting than anybody or anything else, at least I am. Aren't you? What a blessing it is one didn't happen to be born a fool!"

Dodo was sitting alone late in the afternoon. The shooting-party had come back, and dispersed to their rooms to wash and dress. "You all look remarkably dirty and funny," Dodo had said when they came in, "and you had better have tea sent up to you. Does shooting bring on the inspiration, Edith? Take a bath."

Edith had gone up to her room, after insisting on having two of Dodo's bottles of eau-de-cologne in her hot bath. "There is nothing so refreshing," she said, "and you come out feeling like a goddess." Certainly Edith looked anything but a goddess just now. Her hat was pushed rakishly on to the side of her head, there was a suggestion of missing hair-pins about her hair; she wafted with her about the room a fine odour of tobacco and gunpowder; she had burned her dress with a fusee head that had fallen off; her boots were large and unlaced, and curiously dirty, and her hands were black with smoke and oil, and had a sort of trimming in the way of small feathers and little patches of blood. Decidedly, if she came out feeling or looking like a goddess, the prescription ought to want no more convincing testimonial. But she insisted she had never enjoyed herself so much, she talked, and screamed, and laughed as if nothing serious had occurred since breakfast. As Dodo sat in the drawing-room, opening a few letters and skipping all except the shortest paragraphs in the *Times,* she heard the noise of wheels outside, and hurried into the hall to meet Mrs. Vivian. Somehow she looked forward to Mrs. Vivian's coming with a good deal of pleasure and interest. She was aware that another strain in the house might be advisable. Bertie and Jack, and Miss Grantham and Edith, were all somewhat on the same lines. Personally, she very much preferred those lines; and it was chiefly for her husband's sake that she wanted the new arrival. Lord Chesterford had done his duty nobly, but Dodo's observant eye saw how great an effort it was to him; at lunch he had been silent, at tea even more so. Dodo acknowledged that Edith had relieved the party from any sense of the necessity of supporting conversation, but it was obvious to her that Chesterford was hopelessly out of his element, and she felt a keen desire to please him. She had sat by him after lunch, as they smoked and talked, before resuming the shooting, and Dodo had patted his hand and called him a "dear old darling" when nobody happened to be listening, but she had a distinct sense of effort all day in attending to him, and enjoying the company of the others as much as she wished. There was certainly a want of balance in the party, and Mrs. Vivian's weight would tend to keep things even. Dodo had even aroused herself to a spasmodic interest in the new curate, but Lord Chesterford had exhibited such unmistakable surprise at this new departure, that she at once fell back on the easier and simpler expedient of blowing smoke rings at him, and drinking out of the same glass by mistake.

Mrs. Vivian was extremely gracious, and apparently very much pleased to see Dodo. She kissed her on both cheeks, and shook both her hands, and said what a pleasant drive she had had with dear Maud, and she hoped Lord Chesterford was as well and happy as Dodo appeared to be, and they both deserved to be.

"And you must have a great talk with me, Dodo," she said, "and tell me all about your honeymoon."

Dodo was pleased and rather flattered. Apparently Mrs. Vivian had left off thinking she was very small. Anyhow, it was a good thing to have her. Lord Chesterford would be pleased to see her, and he was building some charming almshouses for old women, who appeared to Dodo to be supremely uninteresting and very ugly. Dodo had a deep-rooted dislike for ugly things, unless they amused her very much. She could not bear babies. Babies had no profiles, which seemed to her a very lamentable deficiency, and they were not nearly so nice to play with as kittens, and they always howled, unless they were eating or sleeping. But Mrs. Vivian seemed to revel in ugly things. She was always talking to drunken cabmen, or workhouse people, or dirty little boys who played in the gutter. Dodo's cometic interest in the East End had been entirely due to her. That lady had a masterly and efficient way of managing, that won Dodo's immediate admiration, and had overcome for the moment her distaste for the necessary ugliness. Anything masterly always found a sympathetic audience in Dodo. Success was of such paramount importance in her eyes, that even a successful organiser of days in the country for match-girls was to be admired, and even copied, provided the other circumstances of success were not too expensive.

Mrs. Vivian was a complete and immediate success on this occasion. Dodo made a quantity of mental notes on the best way to behave, when you have the misfortune to become middle-aged and rather plain. Everyone who already knew her seemed to consider her arrival as the last drop in their cup of happiness. Lord Chesterford, on entering the room, had said, "My dear Mrs. Vivian, this is too delightful of you. We are all charmed to see you," and he had sat down by her, and quite seemed to forget that Dodo was sitting on the other side of the fire. Jack also had, so to speak, flown into her arms. Dodo immediately resolved to make a friend of her; a person who could be as popular among the aristocracy as she was among cabmen was distinctly a person to cultivate. She decidedly wanted the receipt.

"It is so good of you, Dodo, to ask me like this," said Mrs. Vivian, when Dodo went and sat by her. "It always seems to me a great compliment to ask people quietly to your house when only a few friends are there. If you have a great houseful of people, it does not matter much whom you ask, but I mean to take this as a sign that you consider me an old friend."

Dodo was always quick at seeing what was required of her.

"Of course I do," she answered. "Who are my old friends if you are not?"

"That is so nice of you," said Mrs. Vivian. "I want to have a long talk with you, and learn all about you. I am going to stay with your mother next week, and she will never forgive me unless I give a full and satisfactory account of you. Satisfactory it cannot help being." She looked across to Lord Chesterford, who was talking to Miss Grantham, and laughing politely at her apostolic jokes. "Oh, Dodo, you ought to be very happy!"

Dodo felt that this was rather like the ten minutes before dinner. She had a vague idea of telling Chesterford to sound the gong, but she was skilled at glances with meaning, and she resorted to this method.

"Lord Chesterford tells me you have Miss Staines with you," continued Mrs. Vivian. "I am so anxious to meet her. She has a wonderful gift for music, I hear."

At this moment the sound of hurrying feet was heard in the hall. The drawing-room door flew open and Edith entered. Dodo laughed inwardly and hopelessly. Edith began to talk at the top of her voice, before she was fairly inside the room.

"Dodo, Dodo," she screamed, "we must settle about the service at once. I have heard from Herr Truffen, and he will be here by twelve; and we must have everything ready, and we'd better do my Mass in G flat; on the whole it's the easiest. I suppose you couldn't hire four or five French horns in the village. If you could, we might do the one in A; but we must have them for the Gloria. We must have a practice to-night. Have you got any musical footmen or housemaids?"

"Mrs. Vivian, Miss Edith Staines," remarked Dodo sweetly.

There was a moment's silence, and then Dodo broke down.

"Oh, Edith, you are a good chap; isn't she, Mrs. Vivian? Mrs. Vivian was just talking about you, and you came in so opportunely that, until you began talking about Masses, I really thought you must be the other thing. Oh, Chesterford, I haven't told you. We're going to have a delicious little service in the drawing-room to-morrow morning, and we are going to sing a Mass. Grantie can't possibly go to church

in this weather, and Jack and Bertie are not as good about it as they
might be, so you see it would be really removing the temptation of
not going to church if we have church here, and can you sing, Mrs.
Vivian? Will you come, Chesterford? You might go to church first,
and then come in here afterwards; that will be two services. How
dreadfully unbearably conceited you will be all the afternoon. You
might read the second lesson for us; no, I think I shall read both.
Yes, Edith, I'll come in a few minutes. I don't know of any muscial
footmen. You might have them up one by one and make them sing
scales, and Jack can try the housemaids' voices. I'm awfully glad Herr
Truffen is coming. He's a tremendous German swell, Mrs. Vivian, and
conducts at the Crystal Palace, and St. James's, and St. Paul's and
everywhere."

"That will be charming," said Mrs. Vivian. "I shall certainly avail
myself of it, Dodo, if I may, only I think I shall go to church first
with Lord Chesterford. He has promised to show me all his schemes
for the village. I think Maud means to go too. But if you will let
me, I will go to my room, and write a few letters, and then you will
be free to practise. It will be a great pleasure to hear your Mass, Miss
Staines; I am very fortunate in coming just in time."

"Really, Dodo," said Edith, "you ought to cultivate the musical talents of your establishment. Last winter I was in the Pyrenees, and
there was only an old sexton, who was also a charcoal burner, and
my maid, and Charlie and his valet and his wife, but we had magnificent
music, and a midnight service on New Year's Eve. Charlie took tenor,
and Sybil treble, and I alto, and the sexton bass. You have no idea
of the trouble it was to get the sexton to learn his part. I had to
hunt him up in those little brutal sheds, and thrust the book into
his hand, and forbid him to eat chestnuts, and force him to drink
porter and Spanish liquorice. Come on; let's begin."

The practice went off satisfactorily, and Edith expressed herself as
pleased. She and Dodo then had a talk to arrange what Dodo called
the "Play-bill." Dodo had arranged to read the lessons, and wished
to make a small selection of prayers, but there Edith put her foot
down.

"No, Dodo," she said, "you're taking a wrong idea of it. I don't
believe you're serious. Now I am. I want to do this Mass because I
believe we can do it well, but I haven't the least confidence in your
reading prayers well, or caring at all about them. I am rather in doubt
about the lessons, but I suppose we can have those."

It was distinctly news to Dodo that Edith was serious. For herself
she had only wished to have a nice little amusement for Sunday morning, which, in Dodo's experience, was rather a tiresome time if you

stopped at home, but on the whole preferable there than at a country church. But Edith was really in earnest whatever she did, whether it was shooting, or music, or playing lawn-tennis. Frivolity was the one charge she could not brook for a moment. Her amusements might, indeed, be frivolous, but she did them with all her heart. So the service was arranged to consist of a lesson, a Mass, and another lesson. The choice of lessons was left to Dodo. Accordingly, next morning Lord Chesterford and Mrs. Vivian drove off with Maud to eleven o'clock church, leaving the others still at breakfast. After that meal was over Dodo announced she was going to get the drawing-room ready.

"We must move all the sofas out of the room, because they don't look religious," she said: "and I shall cover up the picture of Venus and Adonis. I have got the sweetest little praying-table upstairs, and a skull. Do you think we'd better have the skull, Edith? I think it makes one feel Sunday-like. I shall put the praying-table in the window, and shall read the lessons from there. Perhaps the skull might frighten old Truffler. I have found two dreadfully nice lessons. I quite forgot the Bible was such a good book. I think I shall go on with it. One of them is about the bones in Ezekiel, which were very dry— you know it—and the other is out of the Revelation. I think——"

"Dodo," broke in Edith, "I don't believe you're a bit serious. You think it will be rather amusing, and that's all. If you're not serious I sha'n't come."

"Dear Edith," said Dodo demurely, "I'm perfectly serious. I want it all to be just as nice as it can be. Do you think I should take all the trouble with the praying-table and so on, if I wasn't?"

"You want to make it dramatic," said Edith decidedly. "Now, I mean to be religious. You are rather too dramatic at times, you know, and this isn't an occasion for it. You can be dramatic afterwards, if you like. Herr Truffen is awfully religious. I used to go with him to Roman Catholic services, and once to confession. I nearly became a Roman Catholic."

"Oh, I should like to be a nice little nun," said Dodo; "those black and white dresses are awfully becoming, with a dear trotty rosary, you know, on one side, and a twisty cord round one's waist, and an alms-box. But I must go and arrange the drawing-room. Tell me when your conductor comes. I hope he isn't awfully German. Would he like some beer first? I think the piano is in tune. I suppose he'll play, won't he? Make him play a voluntary, when we come in. I'm afraid we can't have a procession though. That's a pity. Oh, I'm sorry, Edith. I'm really going to be quite serious. I think it will be charming."

Dodo completed her arrangements in good time, and forebore to make any more frivolous allusions to the service. She was sitting in the drawing-room, regarding her preparations with a satisfied air, when Herr Truffen was announced. Dodo greeted him in the hall as if it was the most natural thing in the world that he should be called upon to accompany Edith's Mass.

"We're going to have service directly, if you're ready. We want you to accompany Miss Staines's Mass in G flat, but you mustn't take the Kyrie too quick, if you don't mind. Bertie Arbuthnot's singing tenor, and he's not quick—are you, Bertie? Oh, by the way, this is Bertie. His other name is Mr. Arbuthnot."

Herr Truffen was most gratified by so charming an arrangement, and so great a musical treat. When Edith came down she greeted him effusively.

"My dear Professor, this is delightful," she said. "It's quite like old times, isn't it? We're going to do the Mass in G flat. I wanted the one in A, only there are no French horns in the village—isn't that benighted? And would you believe it, Lady Chesterford has positively got not one musical footman."

Herr Truffen was a large, spectacled German, who made everyone else look unnecessarily undersized.

He laughed and fitted his fingers together with great nicety.

"Are we to begin at once?" he asked. "The congregation—haf they arrived?"

"Oh, there's no congregation," explained Dodo; "we are all performers. It is only a substitute for going to church. I hope you aren't shocked; it was such a disgusting morning."

"Lady Chesterford is surely a congregation in herself," remarked Herr Truffen, with elephantine elegance.

"Lord Chesterford is coming by-and-by," continued Dodo. "He has gone to church. I don't know whether he will be in time for the Mass."

"Then you haf all the service in a little chapel here, no doubt," said the Professor.

"Oh, no," said Dodo; "we're going to have two lessons and the Mass, and there isn't a chapel, it's only in the drawing-room. I'm going to read the lessons."

Herr Truffen bowed with undiminished composure, and Dodo led the way back into the drawing-room.

Miss Grantham and Jack were introduced, and Dodo took her place at the praying-table, and Herr Truffen at the piano. Dodo gave out the lesson, and read the chapter through.

"Oh, it is nice!" she exclaimed. "Sha'n't I go on to the next chapter? No, I think I won't."

"It would spoil the delightful impression of the very dry bones?" interrogated Herr Truffen from the piano. "Ah, that is splendid; but you should hear it in the Fatherland tongue."

"Now, Dodo, come here," said Edith. "We must go on with this. You can discuss it afterwards. On the third beat. Will you give us the time, Professor?"

The Mass had scarcely begun when Lord Chesterford came in, followed by Mrs. Vivian and Maud. The Professor, who evidently did not quite understand that he was merely a sort of organist, got up and shook hands all round with laboured cordiality. Edith grew impatient.

"Come," she said, "you mustn't do that. Remember you are practically in church, Professor. Please begin again."

"Ah, I forgot for the moment," remarked the Professor; "this beautiful room made me not remember. Come—one, two. We must begin better than that. Now, please."

This time the start was made in real earnest. Edith's magnificent voice, and the Professor's playing, would alone have been sufficient to make it effective. The four performers knew their parts well, and when it was finished, there followed that silence which is so much more appreciative than applause. Then Herr Truffen turned to Edith.

"Ah, how you have improved," he said. "Who taught you this? It is beyond me. Perhaps you prayed and fasted, and then it came to you."

As Edith had chiefly written the Mass while smoking cigarettes after a hearty breakfast she merely said,—

"How does anything come to anyone? It is part of oneself, as much as one's arms and legs. But the service is not over yet."

Dodo meanwhile had gone back to the praying-table.

"I can't find it," she said, in a distracted whisper. "It's a chapter in the Revelation about a grey horse and a white horse."

"Dodo," said Edith, in an awful voice.

"Yes, dear," said Dodo. "Ah, here it is."

Dodo read the chapter with infinite feeling in her beautiful clear, full voice.

Chesterford was charmed. He had not seen this side of Dodo before. After she had finished, he came and sat by her side, while the others got up and began talking among themselves.

"Dodo," he said, "I never knew you cared about these things. What an unsympathetic brute I must seem to you. I never talked to you about such things, because I thought you did not care. Will you forgive me?"

"I don't think you need forgiveness much," said Dodo softly. "If you only knew——" She stopped and finished her sentence by a smile.

"Dodo," he said again, "I've often wanted to suggest something to you, but I didn't quite like to. Why don't we have family prayers here? I might build a little chapel."

Dodo felt a sudden inclination to laugh. Her aesthetic pleasure in the chapter of Revelation was gone. She felt annoyed and amused at this simple-minded man, who thought her so perfect, and ascribed such fatiguingly high interpretations to all her actions. He really was a little stupid and tiresome. He had broken up all her little pleasant thoughts.

"Oh, family prayers always strike me as rather ridiculous," she said, with a half yawn. "A row of gaping servants is not conducive to the emotions."

She got up and joined the other groups, and then suddenly became aware that, for the first time, she had failed in her part. Jack was watching her, and saw what had happened. Chesterford had remained seated at the window, pulling his long, brown moustache, with a very perceptible shade of annoyance on his face. Dodo felt a sudden impulse of anger with herself at her stupidity. She went back to Chesterford.

"Dear old boy," she said, "I don't know why I said that. I was thinking of something else. I don't know that I like family prayers very much. We used to have them at home, when my father was with us, and it really was a trial to hear him read the Litany. I suppose it is that which has made me rather tired of them. Come and talk to the Professor."

Then she went across to Jack.

"Jack," she said, in a low voice, "don't look as if you thought you were right."

6

The same afternoon Chesterford took Mrs. Vivian off to see "almshouses and drunkards," as Dodo expressed it to Jack. She also told him that Edith and her Herr were playing a sort of chopsticks together in the drawing-room. Maud had, as usual, effaced herself, and Bertie was consuming an alarming number of cigarettes in the smoking-room, and pretending to write letters.

It was natural, therefore, that when Jack strolled into the hall, to see what was going on, he should find Dodo there with her toes on the fender of the great fireplace, having banished the collie to find other quarters for himself. Dodo was making an effort to read, but she was not being very successful, and hailed Jack's entrance with evident pleasure.

"Come along," she said; "I sent the dog off, but I can find room for you. Sit here, Jack."

She moved her chair a little aside, and let him pass.

"I can't think why a merciful providence sends us a day like this," she said. "I want to know whom it benefits to have a thick snowfall. Listen at that, too," she added, as a great gust of wind swept round the corner of the house, and made a deep, roaring sound up in the heart of the chimney.

"It makes it all the more creditable in Chesterford and Mrs. Vivian to go to see the drunkards," remarked Jack.

"Oh, but that's no credit," said Dodo. "They like doing it, it gives them real pleasure. I don't see why that should be any better, morally speaking, than sitting here and talking. They are made that way, you and I are made this. We weren't consulted, and we both follow our inclinations. Besides, they will have their reward, for they will have immense appetites at tea."

"And will give us something to talk about now," remarked Jack lazily.

"Don't you like Grantie, Jack?" asked Dodo presently. "She and Ledgers are talking about life and being in my room. I went to get a book from here, and the fire was so nice that I stopped."

"I wish Ledgers wouldn't treat her like a menagerie, and put her through her tricks," said Jack. "I think she is very attractive, but she belongs too much to a class."

"What class?" demanded Dodo.

"Oh, the class that prides itself on not being of any class—the all things to all men class."

"Oh, I belong to that," said Dodo.

"No, you don't," said he. "You are all things to some men, I grant, but not to all."

"Oh, Jack, that's a bad joke," said Dodo, reprovingly.

"It's quite serious all the same," said he.

"I'm all things to the only man to whom it matters that I should be," said Dodo complacently.

Jack felt rather disgusted.

"I wish you would not state things in that cold-blooded way," he said. "Your very frankness to me about it shows you know that it is an effort."

"Yes," she said, "it is an effort sometimes, but I don't think I want to talk about it. You take things too ponderously. Don't be ponderous; it doesn't suit you in the least. Besides, there is nothing to be ponderous about."

DODO

Dodo turned in her chair and looked Jack full in the face. Her face had a kind of triumph about it.

"I want to say something more," said Jack.

"Well, I'm magnanimous to-day," said Dodo. "Go on."

"All you are doing," said he gravely, "is to keep up the original illusion he had about you. It is not any good keeping up an illusion, and thinking you're doing your whole duty."

"Jack, that's enough," said Dodo, with a certain finality in her tone. "If you go on, you may make me distrust myself. I do not mean that as a compliment to your powers, but as a confession to a stupid superstitious weakness in myself. I am afraid of omens."

They sat silent a minute or two, until a door at the far end of the hall opened and Miss Grantham came through, with her showman in tow.

"Lord Ledgers and I were boring each other so," said Miss Grantham, "that we came to bore someone else. When you are boring people you may as well do it wholesale. What a pity it is that one hasn't got a tail like a dog, that cannot help wagging if the owner is pleased, and which stops wagging when he isn't."

"I shall certainly buy a tail," said Dodo, with grave consideration. "One or two, in case the first gets out of order. Must you wag it whenever you are pleased, Grantie? Is it to be an honest tail? Suppose you only think you are pleased, when you are not really, what does the tail do then? Oh, it's very complicated."

"The tail shares the same illusions as the dog," said Miss Grantham.

"Jack and I were talking about illusions," said Dodo.

"I'm going to get a quantity of illusions," said Miss Grantham. "In any case, what did you find to say about them?"

"Jack said it was a bad thing to keep an illusion up," said Dodo, broadly.

Miss Grantham was staring pensively at the fire.

"I saw two boys sitting on a gate yesterday," she said, "and they pushed each other off, and each time they both roared with laughter. I'm sure it was an illusion that they were amused. I would go and sit on a gate with pleasure and get my maid to push me off, if I thought it would amuse either of us. Mr. Broxton, would you like me to push you off a gate?"

"Oh, I'm certain that the people with many illusions are the happiest," said Dodo. "Consequently, I wouldn't willingly destroy any illusion anyone held about anything."

"What a lot of anys," said Miss Grantham.

Lord Ledgers was leaning back in his chair with a sense of pleased proprietorship. It really was a very intelligent animal. Jack almost expected him to take a small whip from his pocket and crack it at her.

53

But his next remark, Jack felt, was a good substitute; at any rate, he demanded another performance.

"What about delusions, Miss Grantham?" he said.

"Oh, delusions are chiefly unpleasant illusions," she said. "Madmen have delusions that somebody wants to kill them, or they want to kill somebody, or that King Charles's head isn't really cut off, which would be very unsettling now."

"Grantie, I believe you're talking sheer, arrant nonsense," said Dodo. "It's all your fault, Tommy. When one is asked a question, one has to answer it somehow or other in self-defence. If you asked me about the habits of giraffes I should say something. Edith is the only really honest person I know. She would tell you she hadn't any idea what a giraffe was, so would Chesterford, and you would find him looking up giraffes in the *Encyclopoedia* afterwards."

Lord Ledgers laughed a low, unpleasant laugh.

"A very palpable hit," he murmured.

The remark was inaudible to all but Jack. He felt quite unreasonably angry with him, and got up from his chair.

Dodo saw something had happened, and looked at him inquiringly. Jack did not meet her eye, but whistled to the collie, who flopped down at his feet.

"I really don't know where I should begin if I was going to turn honest," said Miss Grantham. "I don't think I like honest people. They are like little cottages, which children draw, with a door in the middle, and a window at each side, and a chimney in the roof with smoke coming out. Long before you know them well, you are perfectly certain of all that you will find inside them. They haven't got any little surprises, or dark passages, or queer little cupboards under the stairs."

"Do you know the plant called honesty, Grantie?" asked Dodo. "It's a very bright purple, and you can see it a long way off, and it isn't at all nicer when you get close than it looks from a distance."

"Oh, if you speak of someone as an honest man," said Miss Grantham, "it implies that he's nothing particular besides. I don't mind a little mild honesty, but it should be kept in the background."

"I've got a large piece of honesty somewhere about me," said Jack. "I can't always lay my hand on it, but every now and then I feel it like a great lump inside me."

"Yes," said Dodo, "I believe you are fundamentally honest, Jack. I've always thought that."

"Does that mean that he is not honest in ordinary matters?" asked Miss Grantham. "I've noticed that people who are fundamentally truthful, seldom tell the truth."

"In a way it does," said Dodo. "But I'm sure Jack would be honest in any case where it really mattered."

"Oh, I sha'n't steal your spoons, you know," said Miss Grantham.
"That's only because you don't really want them," remarked Dodo.
"I can conceive you stealing anything you wanted."

"Trample on me," said Miss Grantham serenely. "Tell us what I should steal."

"Oh, you'd steal lots of things," said Dodo. "You'd steal anyone's self-respect if you could manage to, and you couldn't get what you wanted any other way. Oh, yes, you'd steal anything important. Jack wouldn't. He'd stop just short of that; he would never be really disloyal. He'd finger things to any extent, but I am pretty sure that he would drop them at the last minute."

"How dreadfully unpleasant I am really," said Miss Grantham meditatively. "A kind of Eugene Aram."

Jack was acutely uncomfortable, but he had the satisfaction of believing that what Dodo said about him was true. He had come to the same conclusion himself two nights ago. He believed that he would stop short of any act of disloyalty, but he did not care about hearing Dodo give him so gratuitous a testimonial before Miss Grantham and the gentleman whom he mentally referred to as "that ass of a showman."

The front door opened, and a blast of cold wind came blustering round into the inner hall where they were sitting, making the thick tapestry *portière* belly and fill like a ship's sail, when the wind first catches it. The collie pricked his ears, and thumped his tail on the floor with vague welcome.

Mrs. Vivian entered, followed by Lord Chesterford. He looked absurdly healthy and happy.

"It's a perfectly beastly day," he said cheerfully, advancing to the fireplace. "Mrs. Vivian, let Dodo send you some tea up to your room. You must be wet through. Surely it is tea-time, Dodo."

"I told you so," said Dodo to Jack.

"Has Jack been saying it isn't tea-time?" asked Chesterford.

"No," said Dodo. "I only said that your virtue in going to see almshouses would find its immediate reward in an appetite for tea."

Mrs. Vivian laughed.

"You mustn't reduce our virtues to the lowest terms, as if we were two vulgar fractions."

"Do you suppose a vulgar fraction knows how vulgar it is?" asked Miss Grantham.

"Vulgar without being funny," said Jack, with the air of helping her out of a difficulty.

"I never saw anything funny in vulgar fractions," remarked Lord Ledgers. "Chesterford and I used to look up the answers at the end of the book, and try to make them correspond with the questions."

Dodo groaned.

"Oh, Chesterford, don't tell me you're not honest either."

"What do you think about honesty, Mrs. Vivian?" asked Miss Grantham.

Mrs. Vivian considered.

"Honesty is much maligned by being called the best policy," she said; "it isn't purely commercial. Honesty is rather fine sometimes."

"Oh, I'm sure Mrs. Vivian's honest," murmured Miss Grantham. "She thinks before she tells you her opinion. I always give my opinion first, and think about it afterwards."

"I've been wanting to stick up for honesty all the afternoon," said Dodo to Mrs. Vivian, "only I haven't dared. Everyone has been saying that it is dull and obtrusive, and like labourers' cottages. I believe we are all a little honest, really. No one has got any right to call it the best policy. It makes you feel as if you were either a kind of life assurance, or else a thief."

Chesterford looked a trifle puzzled.

Dodo turned to him.

"Poor old man," she said, "did they call him names? Never mind. We'll go and be labelled 'Best policy. No others need apply.'"

She got up from her chair, and pulled Chesterford's moustache.

"You look so abominably healthy, Chesterford," she said. "How's Charlie getting on? Tell him if he beats his wife any more, I shall beat you. You wouldn't like that, you know. Will you ring for tea, dear? Mrs. Vivian, I command you to go to your room. I had your fire lit, and I'll send tea up. You're a dripping sop."

Mrs. Vivian pleaded guilty, and vanished. Sounds of music still came from the drawing-room. "It's no use telling Edith to come to tea," remarked Dodo. "She said the other day that if anyone ever proposed to her, whom she cared to marry, she will feel it only fair to tell him that the utmost she can offer him, is to play second fiddle to her music."

Edith's music was strongly exciting, and in the pause that followed, Dodo went to the door and opened it softly, and a great tangle of melody poured out and filled the hall. She was playing the last few pages of the overture to an opera that she had nearly completed. The music was gathering itself up for the finale. Note after note was caught up, as it were, to join an army of triumphant melody overhead, which grew fuller and more complete every moment, and seemed to hover, waiting for some fulfillment. Ah, that was it. Suddenly from below crashed out a great kingly motif, strong with the strength of a man who is pure and true, rising higher and higher, till it joined the triumph overhead, and moved away, strong to the end.

There was a dead silence; Dodo was standing by the door, with her lips slightly parted, feeling that there was something in this world better and bigger, perhaps, than her own little hair-splittings and small emotions. With this in her mind, she looked across to where Chesterford was standing. The movement was purely instinctive, and she could neither have accounted for it, nor was she conscious of it, but in her eyes there was the suggestion of unshed tears, and a look of questioning shame. Though a few bars of music cannot change the nature of the weakest of us, and Dodo was far from weak, she was intensely impressionable, and that moment had for her the germ of a possibility which might—who could say it could not?—have taken root in her and borne fruit. The parable of the mustard seed is as old and as true as time. But Chesterford was not musical; he had taken a magazine from the table, and was reading about grouse disease.

7

Dodo was sitting in a remarkably easy-chair in her own particular room at the house in Eaton Square. As might have been expected, her room was somewhat unlike other rooms. It had a pale orange-coloured paper, with a dado of rather more intense shade of the same colour, an orange-coloured carpet and orange-coloured curtains. Dodo had no reason to be afraid of orange colour just yet. It was a room well calculated to make complete idleness most easy. The tables were covered with a mass of albums, vases of flowers, and a quantity of entirely useless knick-knacks. The walls were hung with several rather clever sketches, French prints and caricatures of Dodo's friends. A small bookcase displayed a quantity of flaring novels and a large tune hymn-book, and in a conspicuous corner was Dodo's praying-table, on which the skull regarded its surroundings with a mirthless and possibly contemptuous grin. The mantelpiece was entirely covered with photographs, all signed by their prototypes. These had found their quarters gradually becoming too small for them, and had climbed half way up the two sides of a Louis Quinze mirror, that formed a sort of overmantel. The photographs were an interesting study, and included representatives from a very wide range of classes. No one ever accused Dodo of being exclusive. In the corner of the room were a heap of old cotillion toys, several hunting-whips, and a small black image of the Virgin, which Dodo had picked up abroad. Above her head a fox's mask grinned defiantly at another fox's brush opposite. On the writing table there was an inkstand made of the hoof of Dodo's favourite hunter, which had joined the majority shortly after Christmas, and the "Dodo" symphony, which had just come out with great *éclat* at the Albert Hall, leant against the wall. A banjo case and a pair of castanets, with a dainty silver monogram on them, perhaps inspired Dodo when she sat down to her writing-table.

Dodo's hands were folded on her lap, and she was lazily regarding a photograph of herself which stood on the mantelpiece. Though the afternoon was of a warm day in the end of May, there was a small fire on the hearth which crackled pleasantly. Dodo got up and looked at the photograph more closely. "I certainly look older," she thought to herself, "and yet that was only taken a year ago. I don't feel a bit older, at least I sha'n't when I get quite strong again. I wish Jack could have been able to come this afternoon. I am rather tired of seeing nobody except Chesterford and the baby. However, Mrs. Vivian will be here soon."

Dodo had made great friends with Mrs. Vivian during the last months. Her sister and brother-in-law had been obliged to leave England for a month at Easter, and Dodo had insisted that Mrs. Vivian should spend it with them, and to-day was the first day that the doctor had let her come down, and she had written to Jack and Mrs. Vivian to come and have tea with her.

A tap was heard at the door, and the nurse entered, bearing the three weeks' old baby. Dodo was a little disappointed; she had seen a good deal of the baby, and she particularly wanted Mrs. Vivian. She stood with her hands behind her back, without offering to take it. The baby regarded her with large wide eyes, and crowed at the sight of the fire. Really it was rather attractive, after all.

"Well, Lord Harchester," remarked Dodo, "how is your lordship to-day? Did it ever enter your very pink head that you were a most important personage? Really you have very little sense of your dignity. Oh, you *are* rather nice. Come here, baby."

She held out her arms to take it, but his lordship apparently did not approve of this change. He opened his mouth in preparation for a decent protest.

"Ah, do you know, I don't like you when you howl," said Dodo; "you might be an Irish member instead of a piece of landed interest. Oh, do stop. Take him please, nurse; I've got a headache, and I don't like that noise. There, you unfilial scoundrel, you're quiet enough now."

Dodo nodded at the baby with the air of a slight acquaintance.

"I wonder if you'll be like your father," she said; "you've got his big blue eyes. I rather wish your eyes were dark. Do a baby's eyes change when he gets older? Ah, here's your godmother. I am so glad to see you," she went on to Mrs. Vivian. "You see his lordship has come down to say how do you do."

"Dear Dodo," said Mrs. Vivian, "you are looking wonderfully better. Why don't they let you go out this lovely day?"

"Oh, I've got a cold," said Dodo, "at least I'm told so. There—good-bye, my lord. You'd better take him upstairs again, nurse. I am so delighted to see you," she continued, pouring out tea. "I've been rather dull all day. Don't you know how, when you particularly want to see people, they never come. Edith looked in this morning, but she did nothing but whistle and drop things. I asked Jack to come, but he couldn't."

"Ah," said Mrs. Vivian softly, "he has come back, has he?"

"Yes," said Dodo, "and I wanted to see him. Did you ever hear of anything so ridiculous as his going off in that way. You know he left England directly after his visit to us in January, and he's only just back. It's too absurd for Jack to pretend he was ill. He swore his doctor had told him to leave England for three months. Of course that's nonsense. It was very stupid of him."

Mrs. Vivian sipped her tea reflectively without answering.

"Chesterford is perfectly silly about the baby," Dodo went on. "He's always afraid it's going to be ill, and he goes up on tiptoe to the nursery, to see if it's all right. Last night he woke me up about half-past ten, to say that he heard it cough several times, and did I think it was the whooping cough."

Mrs. Vivian did not seem to be listening.

"I heard from Mr. Broxton once," she said; "he wrote from Moscow, and asked how you were, and three weeks ago he telegraphed, when he heard of the birth of the baby."

"I don't know what's the matter with Jack," said Dodo, rather petulantly. "He wrote to me once, the silliest letter you ever saw, describing the Kremlin, and Trèves Cathedral, and the falls of the Rhine. The sort of letter one writes to one's great-aunt. Now I'm not Jack's great-aunt at all."

There was another tap at the door.

"That's Chesterford," remarked Dodo, "he always raps now, and if I don't answer he thinks I'm asleep, and then he goes away. You just see."

The tap came again, and after a moment's interval the door opened.

"Jack!" exclaimed Dodo.

She got up from her chair and went quickly towards him. Jack was pale, and his breath came rather short, as if he had been running.

"Why, Dodo," he cried, "I thought I couldn't come, and then I thought I could, so I did."

He broke off rather lamely, and greeted Mrs. Vivian.

"Dear old Jack," said Dodo, "it does me good to see you. Your face is so nice and familiar, and I've wanted you awfully. Jack, what do you mean by writing me such a stupid letter? especially when I'd written to you so nicely. Really, I'm not your grandmother yet, though I am a mother. Have you seen the baby? It isn't particularly interesting at present, though of course it's rather nice to think that that wretched little morsel of flesh and bones is going to be one of our landed proprietors. He'll be much more important than you will ever be, Jack. Aren't you jealous?"

Dodo was conscious of quite a fresh tide of interest in her life. Her intellectual faculties, she felt, had been neglected. She could not conceive why, because she had a husband and baby, she should be supposed not to care for other interests as well. Chesterford was an excellent husband, with a magnificent heart; but Dodo had told herself so often that he was not very clever, that she had ceased trying to take an intellectual pleasure in his society, and the baby could not be called intellectual by the fondest parent at present. There were a quantity of women who were content to pore on their baby's face for hour after hour, with no further occupation than saying "Didums" occasionally. Dodo had given what she considered a fair trial to this treatment, and she found it bored her to say "Didums" for an indefinite period, and she did not believe it amused the baby. She had a certain pride in having given birth to the son and heir of one of the largest English properties, and she was extremely glad to have done so, and felt a certain pleased sort of proprietorship in the little pink morsel, but she certainly had experienced none of the absorbing pleasures of maternity. She had got used to not being in love with her husband, and she accepted as part of this same deficiency the absence of absorbing pleasure in the baby. Not that she considered it a deficiency, it was merely another type turned out of Nature's workshop. Dodo laid all the blame on Nature. She shrugged her shoulders and said: "You made me so without consulting me. It isn't my fault!" But Dodo was aware that Nature had given her a brain, and she found a very decided pleasure in the company of clever people. Perhaps it was the greatest pleasure of her life to be admired and amused by clever people. Of course Chesterford always admired her, but he was in love with her, and he was not clever. Dodo had felt some difficulty before her marriage in dealing with this perplexing unknown quantity, and she had to confess it puzzled her still. The result was, that when it occurred, she had to admit her inability to tackle it, and as soon as possible to turn to another page in this algebra of life.

But she still felt that her marriage had been a great success. Chesterford had entirely fulfilled what she expected of him: he was immensely rich, he let her do as she liked, he adored her. Dodo quite felt that it was better that he should adore her. As long as that lasted, he would be blind to any fault of hers, and she acknowledged that, to a man of Chesterford's character, she must seem far from faultless, if he contemplated her calmly. But he was quite unable to contemplate her calmly. For him she walked in a golden cloud that dazzled and entranced him. Dodo was duly grateful to the golden cloud.

But she felt that the element which Jack, and Mrs. Vivian, and other friends of hers brought, had been conspicuously absent, and she welcomed its return with eagerness.

"You know we haven't been leading a very intellectual life lately," Dodo continued. "Chesterford is divinely kind to me, but he is careful not to excite me. So he talks chiefly about the baby, and how he lost his umbrella at the club; it is very soothing, but I have got past that now. I want stimulating. Sometimes I go to sleep, and then he sits as still as a mouse till I wake again. Pity me, Jack, I have had a dull fortnight; and that is worse than anything else. I really never remember being bored before!"

Dodo let her arms drop beside her with a little hopeless gesture.

"I know one's got no business to be bored, and it's one's own fault as a rule if one is," she went on. "For instance, that woman in the moated Grange ought to have swept away the blue fly that buzzed in the pane, and set a mouse-trap for the mouse that shrieked, and got the carpenter to repair the mouldering wainscot, and written to the Psychical Research, how she had heard her own sad name in corners cried, and it couldn't have been the cat, or she would have caught the shrieking mouse. Oh, there were a hundred things she might have done, before she sat down and said, 'He cometh not.' But I have had a period of enforced idleness. If I had set a trap for the mouse, the doctor would have told me not to exert myself so much. I used to play Halma with Chesterford, only I always beat him; and then nobody ever cried my name in sad corners, that I remember; it would have been quite interesting."

Jack laughed.

"What a miserable story, Dodo," he said. "I always said you had none of the domestic virtues, and I am right, it seems."

"Oh, it isn't that," said Dodo, "but I happen to have a brain as well, and if I don't use it, it decays, and when it decays, it breeds maggots. I've got a big maggot in my head now, and that is, that the ineffable joys of maternity are much exaggerated. Don't look shocked, Geraldine. I know it's a maggot, and simply means that I haven't personally experienced them, but the maggot says, 'You are a woman, and if you don't experience them, either they don't exist, or you are abnormal.' Well, the maggot lies, I know it, I believe they do exist, and I am sure I am not abnormal. Ah, this is unprofitable, isn't it. You two have come to drive the maggot out."

Mrs. Vivian felt a sudden impulse of anger, which melted into pity.

"Poor Dodo," she said, "leave the maggot alone, and he will die of inanition. At present give me some more tea. This really is very good tea, and you drink it the proper way, without milk or sugar, and with a little slice of lemon."

"Tea is such a middle-aged thing any other way," said Dodo, pouring out another cup. "I feel like an old woman in a workhouse if I put milk and sugar in it. Besides, you should only drink tea at tea. It produces the same effect as tobacco, a slight soothing of the nerves. One doesn't want to be soothed at breakfast, otherwise the tedious things we all have to do in the morning are impossible. Chesterford has a passion for the morning. He quoted something the other day about the divine morning. It isn't divine, it is necessary; at least you can't get to the evening without a morning, in this imperfect world. Now if it had only been 'the evening and the evening were the first day,' what a difference it would have made."

Mrs. Vivian laughed.

"You always bring up the heavy artillery to defend a small position, Dodo," she said. "Keep your great guns for great occasions."

"Oh, I always use big guns," said Jack. "They do the work quicker. Besides, you never can tell that the small position is not the key to the large. The baby, for instance, that Dodo thinks very extremely insignificant now, may be horribly important in twenty years."

"Yes, I daresay Chesterford and I will quarrel about him," said Dodo. "Supposing he falls in love with a curate's daughter, Chesterford will say something about love in a cottage, and I shall want him to marry a duke's daughter, and I shall get my way, and everybody concerned will be extremely glad afterwards."

"Poor baby," said Mrs. Vivian, "you little think what a worldly mother you have."

"Oh, I know I am worldly," said Dodo. "I don't deny it for a moment. Jack and I had it out before my marriage. But I believe I am capable of an unworldly action now and then. Why, I should wish Maud to marry a curate very much. She would do her part admirably, and no one could say it was a worldly fate. But I like giving everybody their chance. That is why I have Maud to stay with me, and let her get a good look at idle worldly people like Jack. After a girl has seen every sort, I wish her to choose, and I am unworldly enough to applaud her choice, if it is unworldly; only I shouldn't do it myself. I have no ideal; it was left out."

Jack was conscious of a keen resentment at Dodo's words. He had accepted her decision, but he didn't like to have it flaunted before him in Dodo's light voice and careless words. He made an uneasy movement in his chair. Dodo saw it.

"Ah, Jack, I have offended you," she said; "it was stupid of me. But I have been so silent and lonely all these days, that it is such a relief to let my tongue wag at all, whatever it says. Ah, here's Chesterford. What an age you have been! Here am I consoling myself as best I can. Isn't it nice to have Jack again?"

Chesterford saw the fresh light in her eyes, and the fresh vivaciousness in her speech, and he was so unfeignedly glad to see her more herself again, that no thought of jealousy entered his heart. He thought without bitterness, "How glad she must be to have her friends about her again! She looks better already. Decidedly I am a stupid old fellow, but I think Dodo loves me a little."

He shook hands with Jack, and beamed delightedly on Dodo.

"Jack, it is good of you to come so soon," he said; "Dodo has missed you dreadfully. Have you seen the boy? Dodo, may I have him down?"

"Oh, he's been down," said she, "and has only just gone up again. He's rather fractious to-day. I daresay it's teeth. It's nothing to bother about; he's as well as possible."

Lord Chesterford looked disappointed, but acquiesced.

"I should like Jack to see him all the same," he remarked. "May he come up to the nursery?"

"Oh, Jack doesn't care about babies," said Dodo, "even when they belong to you and me. Do you, Jack? I assure you it won't amuse you a bit."

"I can't go away without seeing the baby," said Jack, "so I think I'll go with Chesterford, and then I must be off. Good-bye, Dodo. Get well quickly. May I come and see you to-morrow?"

"I wish Chesterford wouldn't take Jack off in that way," said Dodo rather querulously, as they left the room. "Jack came to see me, and I wanted to talk more to him—I'm very fond of Jack. If he wasn't so fearfully lazy, he'd make no end of a splash. But he prefers talking to his friends to talking to a lot of Irish members. I wonder why he came after he said he wouldn't. Jack usually has good reasons."

Dodo lay back in her chair and reflected.

"You really are the most unnatural mother," said Mrs. Vivian, with a laugh. "I am glad Mr. Broxton went with your husband, or he would have been disappointed, I think."

Dodo looked a little anxious.

"He wasn't vexed, was he?" she asked. "I hate vexing people, especially Chesterford. But he really is ridiculous about the baby. It is absurd to suppose it is interesting yet."

"I don't suppose he would call it interesting," said Mrs. Vivian. "But you know there are other things beside that."

Dodo grew a trifle impatient.

"Ah, that's a twice-told tale," she said. "I consider I have done my duty admirably, but just now I confess I am pining for a little amusement. I have been awfully dull. You know one can't exist on pure love."

Mrs. Vivian rose to go.

"Well, I must be off," she said. "Good-night, Dodo; and remember this, if ever anything occurs on which you want advice or counsel, come to me for it. You know I have been through all this; and—and remember Lord Chesterford loves you very deeply."

Dodo looked up inquiringly.

"Yes, of course, I know that," she said, "and we get on magnificently together. In any case I should always ask you for advice. You know I used to be rather afraid of you."

Mrs. Vivian stood looking out of the window. Her eyes suddenly filled with tears.

"Ah, my dear, don't be afraid of me," she said.

Dodo wondered, when she had gone, what made her so suddenly grave. Her own horizon was singularly free from clouds. She had been through an experience which she had looked forward to with something like dread. But that was over; she and the baby were both alive and well. Chesterford was more devoted than ever, and she?—well, she was thoroughly satisfied. And Jack had come back, and all was going delightfully.

"They all talk about love as if it were something very dreadful," she thought. "I'm sure it isn't dreadful at all. It is rather a bore sometimes; at least one can have enough of it, but that is a fault on the right side."

The door opened softly, and Chesterford came in.

"I am glad to find you alone, darling," he said. "I haven't seen you all day. You are looking much better. Get Jack to come and see you again as soon as he can."

Dodo smiled benignantly on him.

"The baby really is wonderful," he continued. "It was sitting up with its bottle just now, and I really believe it winked at me when it saw me. Do you think it knows me?"

"Oh, I daresay it does," said Dodo; "it sees enough of you anyhow."

"Isn't it all wonderful," he went on, not noticing her tone. "Just fancy. Sometimes I wonder whether it's all real."

"It's real enough when it cries," said Dodo. "But it is rather charming, I do think."

"It's got such queer little fists," said he, "with nice pink nails."

Dodo laughed rather wearily.

"Are you a little tired, darling?" he said. "Won't you go to bed? You know you've been up quite a long time. Perhaps you'd like to see the baby before you go."

"Oh, I said good-night to the baby," said Dodo. "I think I will go to bed. I wish you'd send Wilkins here."

He bent over her and kissed her forehead softly.

"Ah, my darling, my darling," he whispered.

Dodo lay with half-shut eyes.

"Good-night, dear," she said languidly.

8

The questions about which a man is apt to say that he alone can judge, are usually exactly those questions in which his judgment is most likely to be at fault, for they concern him very intimately—a truth which he expresses by saying that he alone can judge about them, and for that very reason his emotions are apt to colour what he considers his sober decision.

Jack was exactly in this position when he left the Chesterfords' door that afternoon. It was only six o'clock when he went away, and he wished to be alone, and to think about it. But the house seemed stuffy and unsuggestive, and he ordered a horse, and sat fuming and frowning till it came round. It fidgeted and edged away from the pavement when he tried to mount it, and he said, "Get out, you brute," with remarkable emphasis, and asked the groom whether he hadn't yet learned to hold a horse quiet. This was sufficient to show that he was in a perturbed frame of mind.

The Row was rather empty, for a great race meeting was going on, and Jack cantered quickly up to the end, and cursed his stupidity for not having gone to Sandown. Then he put his horse to a quiet pace, and determined to think the matter out.

He had left the Chesterfords in January with a full realisation of his position. He was in love with Dodo, perhaps more deeply than ever, and Dodo was hopelessly, irrevocably out of his reach. The only thing left to be done was to get over it; but his ordinary circle and its leisurely duties were quite impossible just at present, and he adopted the traditional English method of travelling, and shooting unoffending animals. Whether the absence of faith was responsible, is an open question; at any rate, the remedy did not result in a cure. He was intensely bored with foreign countries; they were quite as distasteful

as England, and, on the whole, had less to offer. And he came back
to London again as suddenly as he had left it. He only remembered
one incident in his four months abroad which gave him any pleasure;
that was when he received a letter from Dodo at Berlin, which said
nothing particular, and wound up with a little mild chaff on the absurdity of his going abroad at all. "I hope you are really better," wrote
Dodo, "though I didn't know that you were in any immediate danger
of breaking down when you left us. Anyhow, come back. London is
particularly wholesome, and, to tell you the truth, it's just a wee bit
dull. Don't be conceited."

Of course he came back; it was no good remaining abroad, and
yawning in front of the Sistine Madonna, who, in her impossible serene
mildness, had no message whatever for him. He wanted to see Dodo;
why on earth shouldn't he? She was the only thing he really cared
about, and she was quite out of his reach. Where was the harm?

For two days after his arrival in London he was still undecided,
and made no effort to see her, and on the third day her note came.
London was as bad as Dresden, and again, where was the harm? He
wrote a note saying he would come, then he tore that up and sent a
refusal, offering no excuse; and after all, he had gone, and parted from
her with the words that he would come again the next day. But ah,
how sweet it was to see her again! Such were the facts upon which
Jack wished to form a conclusion. All this indecision was really too
annoying. What was the use of a conscience that took the sugar out
of your tea, and yet could not prevent you from drinking it? It was
not strong enough to prevent him going to see Dodo, and it took
the malicious line of making the visit as little enjoyable as possible.
Well, it must be settled one way or the other.

The problem obviously depended on one question. Did his desire
for Dodo grow stronger with seeing her? He decided that it did not
make much difference to the quality or degree of his longing, but,
on the other hand, her society gave him an inestimable pleasure. When
she had refused him a year ago, he had gone on seeing her day after
day, without the horrible, unsatisifed emptiness he had felt abroad.
That absorbing craving for her, he remembered, began when she was
on her wedding tour. Then why not see her freely and frequently?
No harm could possibly come out of it. Dodo, he thought, cared for
him only as she cared for a dozen other friends, why should he, then,
who cared so deeply for her, cut himself off from her? Again his deep-
rooted affection and respect for her husband was an immense safeguard.
Quixotism was a doubtful virtue at the best, and decidedly out of
date, and besides, what would Dodo think if she suddenly found that
one of her best friends invariably declined to meet her under any

circumstances? She would certainly guess the reason, and if there was one possible solution of this stupid problem more undesirable than another, it was that. And Jack made up his mind.

Well, that was settled, and here was Bertie riding down upon him. He felt as if he wished to record a deliberate and sober conclusion. They joined forces and rode up together.

Then Jack said suddenly,—

"Bertie, I have been making a fool of myself, but I am better now."

"That's good," said Bertie placidly.

There was something indefinably soothing about Bertie's manner. Jack determined to be more explicit. It is often a relief to tell a friend one's own resolutions, especially if one does not expect unseasonable objections.

"It's about Dodo," he said. "You see I'm dreadfully in love with her. Awkward, isn't it?"

"Devilish," said Bertie, without a shade of emotion passing over his face.

"And the less I see of her," said Jack, "the worse I get, so I've determined that the more I see of her in the ordinary way, the better. It sounds an unusual treatment, I know, but you must acknowledge I gave the other method a fair chance. I went and killed pigs in Austria, and climbed the Matterhorn, but it wouldn't do."

They rode on a little time in silence. Then Bertie said,—

"Do you want my advice?"

"Well, yes," said Jack rather dubiously.

"Then I'm dashed if I like it, Jack," he said. "It's too dangerous. Just think——"

But Jack broke in,—

"Don't you see my friendship for Chesterford is an absolute safeguard. Dodo gives me more pleasure than anyone I know, and when I can't see her, life becomes unbearable. Chesterford is one of those men to whom one couldn't do a mean thing, and, furthermore, Dodo doesn't love me. If those two facts don't ensure safety, I don't know what would. Besides, Bertie, I'm not a rascal."

"I can't like it," said Bertie. "If one has a propensity for falling into the fire, it's as well to keep off the hearthrug. I know you're not a rascal, but this is a thing one can't argue about. It is a matter of feeling."

"I know," said Jack, "I've felt it too. But I think it's outweighed by other considerations. If I thought any mischief could come of it, I should deserve to be horse-whipped."

"I don't like it," repeated Bertie stolidly.

Jack went to see Dodo the next afternoon, and for many afternoons during the next fortnight he might have been seen on Chesterford's doorstep, either coming or going. Her husband seemed almost as glad as Dodo that Jack should come often. His visits were obviously very pleasant to her, and she had begun to talk nonsense again as fluently as ever. With Jack, however, she had some rather serious talks; his future appeared to be exercising her mind somewhat. Jack's life at this time was absolutely aimless. Before he had gone abroad he had been at the Bar, and had been called, but his chambers now knew him no more. He had no home duties, being, as Dodo expressed it, "a poor little orphan of six foot two," and he had enough money for an idle bachelor life. Dodo took a very real interest in the career of her friends. It was part of her completeness, as I have said before, to be the centre of a set of successful people. Jack could do very well, she felt, in the purely ornamental line, and she by no means wished to debar him from the ornamental profession, but yet she was vaguely dissatisfied. She induced him one day to state in full, exactly the ideas he had about his own future.

"You dangle very well indeed," she said to him, "and I'm far from wishing you not to dangle, but, if it's to be your profession, you must do it more systematically. Lady Wrayston was here yesterday, and she said no one ever saw you now. That's lazy; you're neglecting your work."

Jack was silent a few minutes. The truth of the matter was that he was becoming so preoccupied with Dodo, that he was acquiring a real distaste for other society. His days seemed to have dwindled down to an hour or two hours each, according to the time he passed with Dodo. The interval between his leaving the house one day and returning to it the next, had got to be merely a tedious period of waiting, which he would gladly have dispensed with. In such intervals society appeared to him not a distraction, but a laborious substitute for inaction, and labour at any time was not congenial to him. His life, in fact, was a series of conscious pulses with long-drawn pauses in between. He was dimly aware that this sort of thing could not go on for ever. The machine would stop, or get quicker or slower, and there were endless complications imminent in either case.

"I don't know that I really care for dangling," said Jack discontentedly. "At the same time it is the least objectionable form of amusement."

"Well, you can't dangle for ever in any case," said Dodo. "You ought to marry and settle down. Chesterford is a sort of apotheosis of a dangler. By performing, with scrupulous care, a quantity of little things that don't matter much, like being J.P., and handing the offertory plate, he is in a way quite a busy man, to himself at least, though nothing would happen if he ceased doing any or all of these things; and the dangler, who thinks himself busy, is the happiest of men, because he gets all the advantages of dangling, and none of the disadvantages, and his conscience—have you got a conscience, Jack?—so far from pricking him, tells him he's doing the whole duty of man. Then again he's married—to me, too. That's a profession in itself."

"Ah, but I can't be married to you too," remarked Jack.

"You're absurd," said Dodo; "but really, Jack, I wish you'd marry someone else. I sha'n't think you unfaithful."

"I don't flatter myself that you would," said Jack, with a touch of irritation.

Dodo looked up rather surprised at the hard ring in his voice. She thought it wiser to ignore this last remark.

"I never can quite make out whether you are ambitious or not," she said. "Now and then you make me feel as if you would rather like to go and live in a small cathedral town——"

"And shock the canons?" suggested Jack.

"Not necessarily; but cultivate sheer domesticity. You're very domestic in a way. Bertie would do admirably in a cathedral town. He'd be dreadfully happy among dull people. They would all think him so brilliant and charming, and the bishop would ask him over to dine at the palace whenever anyone came down from London."

"I'm not ambitious in the way of wanting to score small successes," said Jack. "Anyone can score them. I don't mind flying at high game and missing. If you miss of course you have to load again, but I'd sooner do that than make a bag of rabbits. Besides, you can get your rabbits sitting, as you go after your high game. But I don't want rabbits."

"What is your high game?" asked Dodo.

Jack considered.

"It's this," he said. "You may attain it, or at any rate strive after it, by doing nothing, or working like a horse. But, anyhow, it's being in the midst of things, it's seeing the wheels go round, and forming conclusions as to why they go round, it's hearing the world go rushing by like a river in flood, it's knowing what everyone thinks about, it's guessing why one woman falls in love with one man, and why another man falls in love with her. You don't get that in cathedral towns. The archdeacon's daughter falls in love with the dean's son, and nobody else is at all in love with either of them. The world doesn't rattle in cathedral towns, they take care to oil it; the world doesn't come down in flood in cathedral towns, there is nothing so badly regulated as that. I don't know why I should choose cathedral towns particularly to say these things about. I think you suggested that I should live in one. If you like you can plunge into the river in flood and go down with it—that's what they call having a profession—but it's just as instructive to stand on the bank and watch it; more instructive, perhaps, because you needn't swim, and can give your whole attention to it. On the whole, that is what I mean to do."

"That's good, Jack," said Dodo; "but you're not consistent. The fact that you haven't been going out lately, shows that you're standing with your back to it, with your hands in your pocket. After all, what you say only comes to this, that you are interested in the problem of human life. Well, there's just as much human life in your cathedral town."

"Ah, but there's no go about it," said he. "It's no more like life than a duck pond is to the river in flood."

"Oh, you're wrong there," said Dodo. "It goes on just the same, though it doesn't make such a fuss. But in any case you are standing with your back to it now, as I said."

"I'm going into details, just at present," said Jack.

"How do you mean?"

"I'm watching a little bit of it."

"I suppose you mean Chesterford and me. Do you find us very interesting?" demanded Dodo.

"Very."

Jack was rather uncomfortable. He wanted to say more, and wished he hadn't said so much. He wondered how Dodo would take it.

Dodo did not take it at all. She was, for the time at any rate, much more interested in Jack's prospects as they concerned him, than as they bore on herself.

"What is the upshot of all your observations?" she asked.

Jack hardly knew whether to feel relieved or slighted. Was Dodo's apparent unconsciousness of the tenor of what he had said genuine or affected? On that he felt a great deal depended. But whether it was genuine or not, the matter was closed for the present. Dodo repeated her question.

"My observations on you, or on the world in general?" he asked.

"Either will do," said Dodo; "we're very normal. Any conclusion you have formed about the rest of the world will apply to us."

"My conclusion is that you are not quite normal," said he.

Dodo laughed.

"Oh, I'm dreadfully normal," she said; "all my inconsistencies lie on the surface—I'm married, I've got a baby, I'm honest, I'm lazy. I'm all I should and shouldn't be. And Chesterford——"

"Oh, then Chesterford's normal too," said Jack.

9

June was drawing to a close in a week of magnificent weather. It was too hot to do much during the middle of the day, and the Park was full of riders every morning from eight till ten. Dodo was frequently to be seen there, usually riding a vicious black mare, that plunged and shied more than Lord Chesterford quite liked. But Dodo insisted on riding it.

"The risks one runs every moment of one's life," she told him, "are so many, that one or two more really don't matter. Besides, I can manage the brute."

On this particular morning Dodo descended the stairs feeling unusually happy. The period of enforced idleness was over, and she was making up for lost time with a vengeance. They had given a dance the night before, and Dodo had not gone to bed till after four; but for all that she was down again at half-past eight, and her mare was waiting for her. She turned into the dining-room to have a cup of tea before starting, and waited somewhat impatiently for Lord Chesterford to join her. He came in, in the course of a few minutes, looking rather worried.

"You look as if you had not gone to bed for a week," said Dodo, "and your hair is dreadfully untidy. Look at me now. Here I am a weak little woman, and I feel fit to move mountains, and you look as if you wanted quinine and iron. Don't come, if you'd rather not. Stop at home and play with the baby."

"I'm all right," said he, "but I'm rather worried about the boy. The nurse says he's not been sleeping much all night, but kept waking and crying, and he looks rather flushed. I think I'll send for the doctor."

Dodo felt a little impatient.

"He's as right as possible," she said. "You shouldn't worry so, Chesterford. You've wanted to send for the doctor a hundred times in the last month, either for him or me. But don't come if you'd rather not. Vivy is coming to breakfast at half-past nine; I quite forgot that. If you feel inclined to stop, you might give her breakfast, and I'll lengthen my ride. I shall be back at half-past ten. She's going to take me to see Wainwright's new Turner."

"Are you sure you don't mind, Dodo?" said he, still wavering. "If you don't, I really think I will stop, and perhaps see the doctor about him. The nurse says she would like to have the doctor here."

"Just as you like," said Dodo. "You'll have to pay a swinging bill anyhow. Good-bye, old boy. Don't worry your silly old head. I'm sure it's all right."

Dodo went off perfectly at ease in her mind. Chesterford was rather fussy, she thought, and she congratulated herself on not being nervous. "A pretty pair we should make if I encouraged him in his little ways," she said to herself. "We should one of us live in the nursery." She put her horse into a quick trot, and felt a keen enjoyment in managing the vicious animal. The streets were somewhat crowded even at this hour, and Dodo had her work cut out for her.

However, she reached the Park in safety, and went up the Row at a swinging gallop, with her horse tearing at the rein and tossing its head. After a time the brute grew quieter, and Dodo joined a well-known figure who was riding some way in front of her.

"Good old Jack," she cried, "isn't it splendid! I had no idea how I loved motion and exercise and dancing and all that till I began again. Didn't you think our ball went off rather well? Did you stop to the end? Oh, of course you did. That silly dowager What's-her-name was quite shocked at me, just because we had the looking-glass figure in the cotillion. It's the prettiest of the lot, I think. Old Major Ewart gave me a pair of ivory castanets with silver mountings last night, the sweetest things in the world. I really think he is seriously gone on me, and he must be sixty if he's an hour. I think I shall appeal to Chesterford for protection. What fun it would be to make Chesterford talk to him gravely like a grandson. He stopped at home this morning to look after the baby. I think I shall get jealous of the nurse, and pretend that he's sweet on her, and that's why he goes to the nursery so much."

Jack laughed.

"Between you, you hit the right average pretty well," he said. "If it wasn't for Chesterford, the baby would certainly have fallen downstairs half a dozen times. You don't half realise how important he is."

"Oh, you're entirely wrong, Jack," said Dodo calmly. "It's just that which I do recognise; what I don't recognise is that I should be supposed to find ineffable joys in watching it eat and sleep and howl. You know one baby is very much like another."

"In other words, supposing the boy had no expectations," said Jack, "and was not the heir-apparent of half Staffordshire, you would find him much less interesting."

"Would you think me very heartless if I said 'Yes'?" asked Dodo.

"Well, I never held a very high opinion of your heart, you know," said Jack, laughing, "and I don't know that I think much worse of it now."

"You judge so stupidly," said Dodo; "you elevate matrimony into a sacrament. Now I don't. It is a contract for mutual advantage. The husband gives wealth, position and all that, and the wife gives him a housekeeper, and heirs to his property. Don't frown, Jack. That's my eminently common-sense view of the question. It answers excellently, as I find by experience. But, of course, there are marriages for love. I suppose most of the lower middle-class marry for love, at least they haven't got any position or wealth to marry for. But we, the disillusioned and unromantic upper classes, see beyond that. I daresay our great grandfathers married for love, but the fact that so many of us don't, shows that ours is the more advanced and probably correct view. You know all wine-tasters agree on the superiority of one wine, and the inferiority of another. That's the result of education. The amateur thinks they are all more or less alike, and very probably prefers some sweet bad kind. That's the middle-class view of love-marriages. The more I think of it, the more I feel that love is an illusion. Think of all the people who marry for love, and get eternally tired of each other afterwards. They can't keep it up. The lovers grow into friends, and the friends into enemies. Those are the enviable ones who remain friends; but it is better to marry as a friend than as a lover, because in the latter case there is a reaction and a disappointment, which may perhaps ruin the friendship. Aren't I a wise woman, Jack? I think I shall set up a general advice office."

Jack was rather pale, and his fingers twitched nervously at his reins.

"Have you never felt that illusion?" he asked, in a low voice.

"Really, Jack," said Dodo, "you behave as if you were the inquisition. But I don't see why I shouldn't tell you. For Chesterford I never have. He is the most excellent husband, and I esteem and admire him immensely. Don't make your horse so fidgety, Jack. As I was saying, I don't see why I shouldn't tell you, considering you proposed to me once, and confessed to the same illusion yourself. Have you got over it, by the way? If I had married you, you certainly would have by this time."

There was a long pause. Then Jack said,——

"No, Dodo, I have never got over it."

The moment after he had said it, he would have given his right hand to have it unsaid. Dodo was silent for a moment, and Jack found himself noticing the tiny, trivial things about him. He observed a fly trying to alight on his horse's ear, but the animal flicked it off with a little jerk, before it got fairly settled. He wondered whether the fly had illusions about that ear, and whether it imagined that it would be happy for ever and ever, if it could once settle there.

"You know we are saying the most frightfully unconventional things to each other," said Dodo. "I am very sorry for you, Jack, and I will administer consolation. When I said 'No' to you, I did it with real

regret, with quite a different sort of feeling to that which I should
have had if I had said 'No' to Chesterford. It was quite an unreasonable feeling, I couldn't define it, but I think it must have been because——"

Then Jack recovered his self-respect in a moment, by one of those
strange contradictions in our nature, which urged him to stop his ears
to what, a week before, he had been almost tempting her to say.

"Ah, stop, stop," he said, "you don't know what you are saying.
Dodo, this won't do. Think of Chesterford."

"Chesterford and the baby," said Dodo softly. "I believe you are
right, Jack. This is unprofitable. But, Jack, since we renounce that,
let us still be friends. Don't let this have made any difference to us.
Try and realise that it is all an illusion."

Dodo half turned towards him, with a long glance in her brown
eyes, and a little smile playing about her mouth.

"Yes, yes," said Jack, laughing nervously. "I told Bertie so the other
day. I have been a madman for half an hour, but that is over. Shall
we turn?"

They wheeled their horses round, and cantered down the Row.

"Oh, this beautiful world," exclaimed Dodo. "You've no idea what
it is to me to come out of the house again, and ride, and dance and
sing. I really believe, Jack, that I enjoy things more than anyone else
I know. Everything that enjoys itself appeals to me. Jack, do enjoy
yourself, although we settled you mustn't appeal to me. Who is that
girl standing there with the poodle? I think I shall get Chesterford
to buy me a poodle. There's a woman next her awfully like Vivy,
do you see, shading her eyes with her hand. It is Vivy."

Dodo's face suddenly grew grave and frightened. She reined her
horse in opposite to where Mrs. Vivian was standing.

"Quick, quick," she said, "tell me what has happened!"

Mrs. Vivian looked up at Dodo with infinite compassion in her eyes.

"Dodo, darling," she said, "give your horse to the groom. Please
help her to dismount, Mr. Broxton."

Dodo got off, and Mrs. Vivian led her to a seat. Dodo had a sudden
flash of remembrance of how she had sat here with Jack a year ago.

"Tell me quickly," she said again.

"My poor Dodo," said Mrs. Vivian, softly stroking the back of Dodo's hand. "You will be brave, won't you? It is worth while being
brave. It is all over. The baby died this morning, half an hour after
you had gone."

Dodo's first feeling was one of passionate anger and resentment.
She felt she had been duped and tricked in a most unjustifiable manner.
Fate had led her to expect some happy days, and she had been cruelly

disappointed. It was not fair; she had been released from two tedious
months of inactivity, only to be caught again. It was like a cat playing
with a mouse. She wanted to revenge herself on something.

"Oh, it is too awful," she said. "Vivy, what can I do? It is cruel."
Then her better nature came to her aid. "Poor Chesterford, poor dear
old boy," she said simply.

Mrs. Vivian's face grew more tender.

"I am glad you thought of him," she said. "His first thought was
for you. He was there all the time. As soon as it was over he said to
himself, 'Please, God, help Dodo to bear it.' You bear it very well,
dear. Come, the carriage is waiting."

"Oh, I can't, I can't," said Dodo passionately; "let me sit here a
little while, and then go away somewhere else. I can bear it better
alone. I can't see Chesterford."

"No, Dodo," she said, "you must not be cowardly. I know it is
the worst part of it for you. But your duty lies with him. You must
comfort him. You must make him feel that he has got you left. He
is terribly broken, but he will be brave for your sake. Be brave for
his."

Dodo sighed wearily.

"I suppose you are right," she said; "I will come."

She turned and looked round on to the gay scene. The Row was
full of riders, and bright with the flooding sunlight.

"Oh, it is cruel," she said. "I only wanted to be happy, and I mayn't
even be that. What is the good of it all, if I mayn't enjoy it? Why
was the baby ever born? I wish it never had been. What good does
it do anyone that I should suffer?"

Mrs. Vivian felt horribly helpless and baffled. How could she appeal
to this woman, who looked at everything from only her own
standpoint?

"Come, Dodo," she said.

They drove back in silence. Chesterford was standing in the hall
as they entered, waiting for them. He came forward to meet Dodo.

"My poor, poor darling," he said, "it is very hard on you. But we
can bear it together, Dodo."

Dodo turned from him passionately, and left him standing there.

. . . .

Dodo was sitting in the window of her morning-room late on the
same afternoon. She and Lord Chesterford had been together to look
at the baby as it lay there, with the little features that had been racked
and distorted with pain, calm and set again, as if it only slept; and
Dodo had at that moment one real pang of grief. Her first impulse,
as we have seen, was one of anger and impatience at the stupidity

of destiny. She had been enjoying herself, in a purely animal way so intensely, at that moment when she saw Mrs. Vivian waiting for her under the trees. She was just released from a tedious period of inactivity, and inactivity was to Dodo worse than anything in the Inferno.

"I daresay I should get accustomed to being roasted," she had said once to Miss Grantham. "It really would be rather interesting seeing your fingers curling up like fried bacon, but imagine being put in a nicely-furnished room with nobody to talk to, and a view over Hyde Park one side and Melton Mowbray the other, and never being able to get out! The longer that lasted, the worse it would become." And so she had felt the sort of rapture with which "the prisoner leaps to loose his chains" when she had gone out that morning, and again knew the infinite delight of feeling a fine horse answer to her hand, under a sort of playful protest. Then this had come upon her, and Dodo felt that language failed her to express her profound contempt and dislike for the destiny that shapes our ends.

But her generosity and sense of fair play had come to her aid. She was not alone in this matter, and she quite realised that it was worse for Chesterford than herself.

Chesterford had evinced the most intense interest in the baby in itself. Dodo, on the other hand, had frankly declared that the baby's potentialities possessed a far greater attraction for her than its actualities. But she had voluntarily linked her life with his, and she must do her part—they had had a great loss, and he must not feel that he bore it alone. Dodo shook her head hopelessly over the unknown factor, that made her so much to him, and left him so little to her, but she accepted it as inevitable. Almost immediately after she had left him in the hall, she felt angry with herself for having done so, just as she had been vexed at her reception of his proposal of family prayers, and a few minutes afterwards she sent for him, and they had gone together to see the baby. And then, because she was a woman, because she was human, because she was genuinely sorry for this honest true man who knelt beside her and sobbed as if his heart was broken, but with a natural instinct turned to her, and sorrowed more for her than for himself, her intense self-centeredness for the time vanished, and with a true and womanly instinct she found her consolation in consoling him.

Dodo felt as if she had lived years since this morning, and longed to cut the next week out of her life, to lose it altogether. She wanted to get away out of the whole course of events, to begin again without any past. From a purely worldly point of view she was intensely vexed at the baby's death; she had felt an immense pride in having provided an heir, and it was all no use, it was over, it might as well never have been born. And, as the day wore on, she felt an overwhelming disgust of all the days that were to follow, the darkened house, the quieted movements, the enforced idleness. If only no one knew, Dodo felt that she would fling herself at once, this very minute, into the outside world again. What was the use of all this retirement? It only made a bad job worse. Surely, when misfortune comes on one, it is best to forget it as soon as possible, and Dodo's eminently practical way of forgetting anything was to absorb herself in something else. "What a sensible man David was," she thought. "He went and oiled himself, which, I suppose, is the equivalent of putting on one's very best evening dress." She felt an inward laughter, more than half hysterical, as to what would happen if she went and oiled Chesterford.

She got up and went languidly across to the window. Lord Chesterford's room was on the story below, and was built on a wing by itself, and a window looked out on her side of the house. Looking down she saw him kneeling at his table, with his face buried in his hands. Dodo was conscious of a lump rising in her throat, and she went back to her chair, and sat down again.

"He is such a good, honest old boy," she thought, "and somehow, in a dim-lit way, he finds consolation in that. It is a merciful arrangement."

She walked downstairs to his study, and went in. He had heard her step, and stood near the door waiting to receive her. Dodo felt infinitely sorry for him. Chesterford drew her into a chair, and knelt down beside her.

"You've no idea what a help you have been to me, darling," he said. "It makes me feel as if I was an awful coward, when I see you so brave."

Dodo stroked his hand.

"Yes, yes," she said, "we must both be brave, we must help one another."

"Ah, my own wife," he said, "what should I have done if it had been you? and I was dreadfully afraid at one time! You know you are both the baby and yourself to me now, and yet I thought before you were all you could be."

Dodo felt horribly uncomfortable. She had been aware before that there had been moments when, as Jack expressed it, she was "keeping it up," but never to this extent.

"Tell me about it, Chesterford," she said.

"It was only half an hour after you went," he said, "that he suddenly got worse. The doctor came a few minutes after that. It was all practically over by then. It was convulsions, you know. He was quite quiet, and seemed out of pain for a few minutes before the end, and he opened his eyes, and put out his little arms towards me. Do you think he knew me, Dodo?"

"Yes, dear, yes," said Dodo softly.

"I should be so happy to think he did," said Lord Chesterford. "Poor little chap, he always took to me from the first, do you remember? I hope he knew me then. Mrs. Vivian came very soon after, and she offered to go for you, and met you in the Park, didn't she?"

"Yes," said Dodo; "Jack and I were together. She is very good to us. Would you like to see her to-night?"

"Ah no, Dodo," he said, "I can't see anyone but your dear self. But make her come and see you if you feel inclined, only come and talk to me again afterwards."

"No, dear," said Dodo. "I won't have her, if you feel against it."

"Then we shall have an evening together again, Dodo," he said. "I seem to have seen you so little, since you began to go about again," he added wistfully.

"Oh, it must be so," said Dodo; "you have one thing to do, and I have another. I've seen so many different people this last week, that I feel as if I had seen no one person."

"You are so active," he said; "you do half a dozen things while I am doing one."

"Oh, but you do great important man things," said Dodo, "and I do silly little woman things."

She felt the conversation was becoming much more bearable.

Chesterford smiled. Dodo seized on it as a favourable omen.

"I like seeing you smile, old boy," she said; "you look more yourself than you did two hours ago."

He looked at her earnestly.

"Dodo, you will not think me preaching or being priggish, will you, darling? You know me too well for that. There is one way of turning this into a blessing. We must try and see why this was sent us, and if we cannot see why, we must take it in faith, and go on living our lives simply and straightforwardly, and then, perhaps, we shall know sometime. Ah, my darling, it has taught me one thing already, for I never knew before how much I loved you. I loved you all I could before this, but it has somehow given me fresh power to love. I think the love I had for the boy has been added to the love I had for you, and it is yours, darling, all of it, always."

10

That same evening Edith Staines and Miss Grantham were seated together in a box at the opera. The first act was just over, and Edith, who had mercilessly silenced every remark Miss Grantham had made during it, relaxed a little. Miss Grantham's method of looking at an opera was to sit with her back to the stage, so as to command a better view of the house, and talk continuously. But Edith would not stand that. She had before her a large quarto containing the full score, and she had a pencil in her hand with which she entered little corrections, and now and then she made comments to herself.

"I shall tell Mancinelli of that," she murmured. "The whole point of the motif is that rapid run with the minim at the end, and he actually allowed that beast to make a rallentando."

But the act was over now, and she shut the book with a bang.

"Come outside, Grantie," she said, "it's so fearfully hot. I had to hurry over dinner in order to get here in time. The overture is one of the best parts. It isn't like so many overtures that give you a sort of abstract of the opera, but it hints at it all, and leaves you to think it out."

"Oh, I didn't hear the overture," said Miss Grantham. "I only got here at Mephistopheles' appearance. I think Edouard is such a dear. He really looks a very attractive devil. I suppose it's not exactly the beauty of holiness, but extremes meet, you know."

"I must open the door," said Edith. "I want to sit in a draught."

"There's Mr. Broxton," remarked Miss Grantham. "I think he sees us. I hope he'll come up. I think it's simply charming, to see how devoted he still is to Dodo. I think he is what they call faithful."

"I think it's scandalous," said Edith hotly. "He's got no business to hang about like that. It's very weak of him—I despise weak people. It's no use being anything, unless you're strong as well; it's as bad as being second-rate. You may be of good quality, but if you're watered down, it's as bad as being inferior."

Jack meantime had made his way up to the box.

"We've just been saying all sorts of nice things about you," remarked Miss Grantham sweetly. "Have you seen Dodo to-day?"

"Haven't you heard?" asked Jack.

Edith frowned.

"No; what?" she asked.

"Their baby died this morning," he said.

Edith's score fell to the ground with a crash.

"Good heavens! is it true?" she asked. "Who told you?"

"I was riding with Dodo this morning," said he, "and Mrs. Vivian met Dodo and told her. I knew something had happened, so I went to inquire. No one has seen either of them again."

"Did you try and see her?" said Edith severely.

"Yes, I went this evening."

"Ah!" Edith frowned again. "How does he take it?" she asked.

"I don't know," he said; "no one has seen them since."

Edith picked up her score.

"Good-night, Grantie," she said. "Good-night, Mr. Broxton. I must go."

Miss Grantham looked up in astonishment. Edith was folding her opera cloak round her. Jack offered to help her.

"Thanks, I can do it," she said brusquely.

"What are you going for?" asked Miss Grantham, in surprise.

"It's all right," said Edith. "I've got to see someone. I shall come back, probably."

The door closed behind her.

"Of course it's awfully sad," remarked Miss Grantham, "but I don't see why Edith should go like that. I wonder where she's gone. Don't you adore the opera, Mr. Broxton? I think it's simply lovely. It's so awfully sad about Marguerite, isn't it? I wish life was really like this. It would be so nice to sing a song whenever anything important happened. It would smooth things so. Oh, yes, this is the second act, isn't it? It's where Mephisto sings that song to the village people. It always makes me feel creepy. Poor Dodo!"

"I am more sorry for him," said Jack; "you know he was simply wrapped up in the baby."

"Dodo certainly finds consolation quickly," said Miss Grantham. "I think she's sensible. It really is no use crying over spilt milk. I suppose she won't go out again this season. Dear me, it's Lady Bretton's ball the week after next, in honour of Lucas's coming of age. Dodo was to have led the cotillion with Lord Ledgers. That was a good note. Isn't the scene charming?"

"I don't know what Dodo will do," said Jack. "I believe they will leave London, only—only—"

Miss Grantham looked at him inquiringly.

"You see Dodo has to be amused," said Jack. "I don't know what she would do, if she was to have to shut herself up again. She was frightfully bored after the baby's birth."

Miss Grantham was casting a roving London eye over the occupants of the stalls.

"There's that little Mr. Spencer, the clergyman at Kensington," she said. "I wonder how his conscience lets him come to see anything so immoral. Isn't that Maud next him? Dear me, how interesting. Bring them up here after the act, Mr. Broxton. I suppose Maud hasn't heard?"

"I think she's been with her father somewhere in Lancashire," said Jack. "She can only have come back to-day. There is Mrs. Vane, too. Dodo can't have telegraphed to them."

"Oh, that's so like Dodo," murmured Miss Grantham; "it probably never occurred to her. Dear me, this act is over. I am afraid we must have missed the 'Virgo.' What a pity. Do go, and ask them all to come up here."

"So charmed," murmured Mrs. Vane, as she rustled into the box. "Isn't it a lovely night? Dear Prince Waldenech met me in the hall, and he asked so affectionately after Dodo. Charming, wasn't it? Yes. And do you know Mr. Spencer, dear Miss Grantham? Shall we tell Miss Grantham and Mr. Broxton our little secret, Maud? Cupid has been busy here," she whispered, with a rich elaborateness to Miss Grantham. "Isn't it charming? We are delighted. Yes, Mr. Spencer, Miss Grantham and Mr. Broxton, of course—Mr. Spencer."

Mr. Spencer bowed and smiled, and conducted himself as he should. He was a fashionable rector in a rich parish, who had long felt that the rich deserved as much looking after as the poor, and had been struck with Maud's zeal for the latter, and thought it would fit in very well with his zeal for the former, had won Maud's heart, and now appeared as the happy accepted lover.

Mrs. Vane was anxious to behave in the way it was expected that she should, and, finding that Miss Grantham sat with her back to the stage and talked, took up a corresponding attitude herself. Miss Grantham quickly decided that she did not know about the death of Dodo's baby, and determined not to tell her. In the first place, it was to be supposed that she did not know either, and in the second, she was amused by the present company, and knew that to mention it was to break up the party.

Mr. Spencer had a little copy of the words, with the English on one side and the Italian on the other. When he came to a passage that he thought indelicate, he turned his attention to the Italian. Maud sat between him and Miss Grantham.

"I am so delighted, Maud," Miss Grantham was saying, "and I am sure Dodo will be charmed. She doesn't know yet, I suppose? When is it to be?"

"Oh, I don't quite know," said Maud confusedly. "Algy, that is Mr. Spencer, is going to leave London, you know, and take a living at Gloucester. I shall like that. There is a good deal of poverty at Gloucester."

Miss Grantham smiled sympathetically.

"How sweet of you," she said; "and you will go and work among the poor, and give them soup and prayer-books, won't you? I should love to do that. Mrs. Vivian will tell you all about those things, I suppose?"

"Oh, she took me to an awful slum before we left London," said Maud, in a sort of rapture—"you know we have been away at Manches-

ter for a week with my father—and I gave them some things I had
worked. I am doing a pair of socks for Dodo's baby."

Miss Grantham turned her attention to the stage.

"The Jewel song is perfectly lovely," she remarked. "I wish Edith
was here. Don't you think that girl sings beautifully? I wonder who
she is."

At that moment the door of the box opened, and Edith entered.
She grasped the situation at once, and felt furiously angry with Miss
Grantham and Jack. She determined to put a stop to it.

"Dear Mrs. Vane, you can't have heard. I only knew this evening,
and I suppose Mrs. Vivian's note has missed you somehow. I have
just left her, and she told me she had written to you. You know Dodo's
baby has been very ill, quite suddenly, and this morning—yes, yes—"

Mrs. Vane started up distractedly.

"Oh, my poor Dodo," she cried, "I never knew! And here I am
enjoying myself, when she—Maud, did you hear? Dodo's baby—only
this morning. My poor Dodo!"

She began crying in a helpless sort of way.

Maud turned round with a face full of horror.

"How awful! Poor Dodo! Come, mother, we must go."

Mr. Spencer dropped his English and Italian version.

"Let me see you to your carriage," he said. "Let me give you an
arm, Mrs. Vane."

Maud turned to Jack, and for once showed some of Dodo's spirit.

"Mr. Broxton," she said, "I have an idea you knew. Perhaps I am
wrong. If I am, I beg your pardon; if not, I consider you have behaved
in a way I didn't expect of you, being a friend of Dodo's. I think—"
she broke off, and followed the others. Jack felt horribly uncomfortable.

He and Edith and Miss Grantham stood in silence for a moment.

"It was horrible of you, Grantie," said Edith, "to let them sit here,
and tell them nothing about it."

"My dear Edith, I could do nothing else," said Miss Grantham, in
an even, calm voice. "There would have been a scene, and I can't
bear scenes. There has been a scene as it is, but you are responsible
for that. You are rather jumpy to-night. Where have you been?"

"I have been to see Mrs. Vivian," said Edith. "I wanted to know
about this. I told her I was coming back here, and she gave me this
for you, Mr. Broxton."

She handed him a note. Then she picked up her big score, and sat
down again with her pencil.

The note contained only two lines, requesting Mr. Broxton to come
and see her in the morning. Jack read it and tore it up. He felt undecided

how to act. Edith was buried in her score, and gave no sign. Miss Grantham had resumed her place, and was gazing languidly at the box opposite. He picked up his hat, and turned to leave. Edith looked up from her score.

"I think I ought to tell you," she said, "that Mrs. Vivian and I talked about you, and that note is the result. I don't care a pin what you think."

Jack opened his eyes in astonishment. Edith had always struck him as being rather queer, and this statement seemed to him very queer indeed. Her manner was not conciliatory.

He bowed.

"I feel complimented by being the subject of your conversation," he replied with well-bred insolence, and closed the door behind him.

Miss Grantham laughed. A scene like this pleased her; it struck her as pure comedy.

"Really, Edith, you are very jumpy; I don't understand you a bit. You are unnecessarily rude. Why did you say you did not care a pin what he thought?"

"You won't understand, Grantie," said Edith. "Don't you see how dangerous it is all becoming? I don't care the least whether I am thought meddlesome. Jack Broxton is awfully in love with Dodo, anyone can see that, and Dodo evidently cares for him; and that poor, dear, honest fool Chesterford is completely blind to it all. It was bad enough before, but the baby's death makes it twice as bad. Dodo will want to be amused; she will hate this retirement, and she will expect Mr. Broxton to amuse her. Don't you see she is awfully bored with her husband, and she will decline to be entirely confined to his company. While she could let off steam by dancing and riding and so on, it was safe; she only met Mr. Broxton among fifty other people. But decency, even Dodo's, will forbid her to meet those fifty other people now. And each time she sees him, she will return to her husband more wearied than before. It is all too horrible. I don't suppose she is in love with Jack Broxton, but she finds him attractive, and he knows it, and he is acting disgracefully in letting himself see her so much. Everyone knows he went abroad to avoid her—everyone except Dodo, that is, and she must guess. I respected him for that, but now he is playing the traitor to Chesterford. And Mrs. Vivian quite agrees with me."

"Oh, it's awfully interesting if you're right," said Miss Grantham reflectively; "but I think you exaggerate. Jack is not a cad. He doesn't mean any harm. Besides, he is a great friend of Chesterford's."

"Well, he's got no business to play with fire," said Edith. "His sense of security only increases the real danger. If Chesterford knew exactly how matters stood it would be different, but he is so simple-hearted that he is only charmed to see Jack Broxton, and pleased that Dodo likes him."

"Oh, it's awfully interesting," murmured Miss Grantham.

"I could cry when I think of Chesterford," said Edith. "The whole thing is such a fearful tragedy. If only they can get over this time safely, it may all blow over. I wish Dodo could go out again to her balls and concerts. She finds such frantic interest in everything about her, that she doesn't think much of any particular person. But it is this period, when she is thrown entirely on two or three people, that is so dangerous. She really is a frightful problem. Chesterford was a bold or a blind man to marry her. Oh, I can't attend to this opera to-night. I shall go home. It's nearly over. Faust is singing hopelessly out of tune."

She shut her book, and picked up her fan and gloves.

"Dear Edith," said Miss Grantham languidly, "I think you mean very well, but you are rather overdrawing things. Are you really going? I think I shall come too."

Jack meantime was finding his way home in a rebellious and unchristian frame of mind. In the first place, he had just lost his temper, which always seemed to him to be a most misdirected effort of energy; in the second place, he resented Edith's interference with all his heart and soul; and in the third, he did not feel so certain that she was wrong. Of course he guessed what Mrs. Vivian's wish to see him meant, for it had occurred to him very vividly what consequences the death of the baby would have on him and Dodo: and he anticipated another period like that which had followed the birth. Jack could hardly dare to trust himself to think of that time. He knew it had been very pleasant to him, and that he had enjoyed Dodo's undisturbed company during many days in succession, but it was with a certain tingling of the ears that he thought of the events of the morning, and his mad confession to her. "I have a genius for spoiling things," thought Jack to himself. "Everything was going right; I was seeing Dodo enough to keep me happy, and free from that hateful feeling of last autumn, and then I spoilt it all by a stupid remark that could do no good, nor help me in any conceivable way. How will Dodo have taken it?"

But he was quite sure of one thing—he would not go and see Mrs. Vivian. He was, he felt, possessed of all the facts of the case, and he was competent to form a judgment on them—at any rate Mrs. Vivian was not competent to do it for him. No, he would give it another chance. He would again reason out the pros and cons of the case, he would be quite honest, and he would act accordingly.

That he should arrive at the same conclusion was inevitable. The one thing in the world that no man can account for, or allow for, is change in himself. If Jack had been able to foresee, when he went abroad, that he would be acting thus with regard to Dodo, he would have thought himself mad, and it would have been as impossible for him to act thus then, as it was inevitable for him to act thus now. If we judge by our own standards, and our own standards alter, we cannot expect our verdicts to remain invariable. Under a strong attachment a man drifts, and he cannot at any one moment allow for, or feel the force of the current, for he is moving in it, though he thinks himself at rest. The horrible necessities of cause and effect work in us, as well as around us. As Edith had said, his sense of security was his danger, for his standard of security was not the same as it had been.

He sat down and wrote a note to Mrs. Vivian, saying that he regretted being unable to call on her tomorrow, and purposely forebore to give any reason. He had considerable faith in her power of reading between the lines, and the fact, baldly stated, was an unnecessary affront to her intellect.

Mrs. Vivian read the note with very little surprise, but with a good deal of regret. She was genuinely sorry for him, but she had other means at her disposal, though they were not so pleasant to use. They involved a certain raking up of old dust-heaps, and a certain awakening of disagreeable memories. But it never occurred to her to draw back. Naturally enough she went to see Dodo next morning, and found her alone. Mrs. Vivian had her lesson by heart, and she was only waiting for Dodo to tell her to begin, so to speak. Dodo hailed her with warmth; she had evidently found matters a little tedious.

"Dear Vivy," she said, "I'm so glad you've come; and Chesterford told me to ask you to see him, before you went away, in case you called. So you will, won't you? But I must have you for a long time first."

"How is he?" asked Mrs. Vivian.

"Oh, he's quite well," said Dodo, "but he feels it frightfully. But he is fortunate, he has spiritual consolation as his aid. I haven't, not one atom. It's a great nuisance, I know, but I don't see how to help it. Can the Ethiopian change his skin?"

"Ah, Dodo," said she, with earnestness in her tone, "you have a great opportunity—I don't think you realise how great."

"Why, what do you mean?" said Dodo.

"Of course I know what you feel," said Mrs. Vivian, "and it is necessary that with your grief there must be mixed up a great deal of vexation and annoyance. Isn't it so?"

"Yes, yes," said Dodo. "You don't despise me for feeling that?"

"Despise you!" said Mrs. Vivian. "You know me better than that.

But you must not dwell on it. There is something more important than the cancelling of your smaller engagements. You have a big engagement, you know, which must not be cancelled."

Dodo rose from her chair with wide eyes.

"Ah, Vivy," she said, "you have guessed it, have you? It is quite true. Let me tell you all about it. It is just that which bothers me. These days when I only see Chesterford bore me more than I can say. I don't know why I tell you this; it isn't want of loyalty to him, but I want help. I don't know how to deal with him. Yes, he bores me. I always foresaw this, but I hoped I shouldn't mind. I was wrong and Jack was right. He warned me of it, but he must never know he was right. Of course you see why. I think I did not expect that Chesterford's love for me would last. I thought he would cease being my lover, and I am terribly wrong. It gets stronger and stronger. He told me so last night, and I felt a brute. But I comforted him and deceived him again. Ah, what could I do? I don't love him. I would give anything to do so. I think I felt once what love was, but only once, and not for him."

Mrs. Vivian looked up inquiringly.

"No, I shan't tell you about that," said Dodo, speaking rapidly and excitedly; "it would be a sort of desecration. There is something divine about Chesterford's feeling for me. I know it, but it doesn't really touch me. I am not capable of it, and what happens is that I continue to amuse myself on my own lines, and all that goes over my head. But I make him believe I understand. It makes him happy. And I know, I know, that when I am out of this, I shall go on just as usual, except that I shall feel like a prisoner escaped, and revel in my liberty. I know I shall. Sometimes I almost determine to make some sacrifice for him in a blind sort of way, like a heathen sacrificing to what he fears, yes, fears, but then that mood passes and I go on as usual. I long to get away from him. Sometimes I am afraid of hating him, if I see him too much or too exclusively."

"Yes, Dodo, I know, I know," said Mrs. Vivian. "I don't see how you are to learn it, unless it comes to you; but what you can do, is to act as if you felt it, not only in little tiny ways, like calling him an 'old darling,' but in living for him more."

"Ah, those are only words," said Dodo impatiently. "I realise it all, but I can't do it."

There was a long silence. Then Mrs. Vivian said,—

"Dodo, I am going to tell you what I have never told anyone before, and that is the story of my marriage. I know the current version very well, that I married a brute who neglected me. That he neglected me is true, but that is not all. Like you, I married without love, without even liking. There were reasons for it, which I need not trouble you with. I used to see a good deal of a man with whom I was in love, when I married Mr. Vivian. He interested me and made my life more bearable. My husband grew jealous of him, almost directly after my marriage. I saw it, and, God forgive me, it amused me, and I let it go on—in fact, I encouraged it. That was my mistake, and I paid dearly for it. I believe he loved me at first; it was my fault that he did not continue to do so. Then my baby was born, and, a month afterwards, somehow or other we quarrelled, and he said things to me which no woman ever forgets. He said it was not his child. I never forgot it, and it is a very short time ago that I forgave it. For two years after his death, as you know, I travelled abroad, and I fought against it, and I believe, before God, that I have forgiven him. Then I came back to London. But after that day when he said those things to me, we grew further and further apart. I interested myself in other things, in the poor, and so on, and he took to drinking. That killed him. He was run over in the street, as he came back from somewhere where he had been dining. But he was run over because he was dead drunk at the time. When I was abroad I came under the influence of a certain Roman Catholic priest. He did not convert me, nor did he try to, but he helped me very much; and one day, I remember the day very well, I was almost in despair, because I could not forgive the wrong my dead husband had done me, somehow a change began in me. I can tell you no more than that a change comes, and it is there. It is the grace of God. There, Dodo, that is my history, and there is this you may learn from it, that you must be on your guard against making a mistake. You must never let Chesterford know how wide the gulf is between you. It will be a constant effort, I know, but it is all you can do. Set a watch on yourself; let your indifference be your safeguard, your warning."

Mrs. Vivian stood up. Her eyes were full of tears, and she laid her hands on Dodo's shoulders. Dodo felt comfort in the presence of this strong woman, who had wrestled and conquered.

Dodo looked affectionately at her, and, with one of those pretty motions that came so naturally to her, she pressed her back into her chair, and knelt beside her.

"Dear Vivy," she said, "my little troubles have made you cry. I am so sorry, dear. You are very good to me. But I want to ask you one thing. About that man your husband was jealous of—"

"No, no," said Mrs. Vivian quickly; "that was only one of the incidents which I had to tell you to make the story intelligible."

Dodo hesitated.

"You are sure you aren't thinking of anyone in my case—of Jack, for instance?" she suddenly said.

Mrs. Vivian did not answer for a moment. Then she said,—

"Dodo, I am going to be very frank with you. He is an instance—in a way. I don't mean to suppose for a moment that Chesterford is jealous of him, in fact, I know he can't be—it isn't in him; but he is a good instance of the sort of thing that makes you tend to neglect your husband."

"But you don't think he is an instance in particular?" demanded Dodo. "I don't mean to bind myself in any way, but I simply want to know."

Mrs. Vivian went straight to the point.

"That is a question which you can only decide for yourself," she said. "I cannot pretend to judge."

Dodo smiled.

"Then I will decide for myself," she said. "You see, Jack is never dull. I daresay you may think him so, but I don't. He always manages to amuse me, and, on the whole, the more I am amused the less bored I get in the intervals. He tides me over the difficult places. I allow they are difficult."

"Ah, that is exactly what you mustn't allow," said Mrs. Vivian. "You don't seem to realise any possible deficiency in yourself."

"Oh, yes, I do," said Dodo, as if she was announcing the most commonplace fact in the world. "I know I am deficient. I don't appreciate devotion, I don't appreciate the quality that makes one gaze and gaze, as it says in the hymn. It is rather frog-like that gazing; what do you call it—batrachian. Now, Maud is batrachian. I daresay it is a very high quality, but I don't quite live up to it. There are, of course, heaps of excellent things one doesn't live up to, like the accounts of the Stock Exchange in the *Times*. I fully understand that the steadiness of stockings makes a difference to somebody, only it doesn't make any difference to me."

"Dodo, you are incorrigible," said Mrs. Vivian, laughing in spite of herself. "I give you up—only, do the best you can. I believe, in the main, you agree with me. And now I must be off. You said Lord Chesterford wished to see me. I suppose he is downstairs."

"I think I shall come too," said Dodo.

So they went down together. Lord Chesterford was in his study.

"Do you know what Mrs. Vivian has been saying to me?" remarked Dodo placidly, as she laid her hand on his shoulder. "She has been telling me I do not love you enough—isn't she ridiculous?"

Mrs. Vivian for the moment was nonplussed, but she recovered herself quickly.

"Dodo is very naughty to-day," she said. "She misconstrues everything I say."

"I don't think it's likely you said that," said he, capturing Dodo's hand, "because it isn't true."

"I am certainly *de trop,*" murmured Mrs. Vivian, turning to go.

Dodo's hand lay unresistingly in his.

"She has been so good and brave," said Lord Chesterford to Mrs. Vivian, "she makes me feel ashamed."

Mrs. Vivian felt an immense admiration for him.

"I said you deserved a very great deal," she said, putting out her hand to him. "I must go, my carriage has been waiting an hour."

He retained Dodo's hand, and they saw her to the door.

The footman met them in the hall.

"Mr. Broxton wants to know whether you can see him, my lady," he said to Dodo.

"Would you like to see Jack?" she asked Chesterford.

"I would rather you told him you can't," he said.

"Of course I will," she answered. She turned to the footman. "Say I am engaged, but he may come again to-morrow and I will see him. You don't mind my seeing him, do you, Chesterford?"

"No, no, dear," he said.

Dodo and Chesterford turned back to the drawing-room. Jack was on the steps.

"I thought you were engaged at this hour," Mrs. Vivian said to him.

"So I was," he answered. "Dodo asked me to come and see her."

11

It was just three weeks after the baby's death, and Dodo was sitting in her room about eleven o'clock in the morning, yawning dismally over a novel, but she was conscious of a certain relief, a sense of effort suspended. Late the evening before, Lord Chesterford had consulted her about some business down at Harchester, and Dodo, in a moment of inspiration, had said that it must be done by someone on the spot, that an agent was not to be trusted, and that if Chesterford liked she would go. This, of course, led to his offering to go himself, and would Dodo come with him? Dodo had replied that she was quite willing to go, but that there was no need of both of them making a tiresome journey on an infernally hot day. Chesterford had felt, rather wistfully, that he would not mind the journey if Dodo was with him, but he had learned lately not to say such things. Dodo was apt to treat them as nonsense. "My coming with you wouldn't make it any cooler, or less insufferably dusty," she would have said. The result was that Chesterford went, and Dodo was left alone in London, with a distinct sense of relief and relaxation.

Dodo's next move was to send a note to Jack, saying that he was going to come and lunch with her. She was not conscious of any sense of deception in this, but she had seen that Chesterford had not cared to see anybody since the baby's death, except Mrs. Vivian, whereas she longed to be in the midst of people again. So, whenever opportunities occurred, she had been in the habit of seeing what she could of her friends, but was very careful not to bore her husband with them. She was quite alive to the truth of Mrs. Vivian's remarks.

But though Dodo felt a great relief in her husband's absence, she was more than ever conscious of the unutterable stupidity of spending day after day doing nothing. It was something even to keep it up with Chesterford, but now there was nothing to do—nothing. Still, Jack was coming to lunch, and perhaps she might get through a few hours that way. Chesterford had said he would be back that night late or next morning.

The footman came in bearing a card. "Jack already," thought Dodo, with wonder. But it was not Jack. Dodo looked at it and pondered a moment. "Tell Lady Bretton I will see her," she said.

A few moments afterwards Lady Bretton rustled into the room. Dodo had always thought her rather like a barmaid, and she was sure that she would attract many customers at any public-house. She was charmingly pretty, and always said the right thing. Dodo felt she ought to know why she had come, but couldn't quite remember. But she was not left in doubt long.

"Dearest Dodo," said Lady Bretton, "I have wanted to come and see you dreadfully, only I haven't been able. You know Lucas has been at home all this week."

Then it flashed upon Dodo.

"He comes of age to-day, you know, and we are giving a ball. I was so dreadfully shocked to hear your bad news, and am delighted to see you looking so well considering. Is Lord Chesterford at home?"

"No," said Dodo, as if weighing something in her mind. "He may come to-night, but I don't really expect him till to-morrow morning."

"Has he gone on some visit?" asked she. "I didn't suppose—"

"No, he's only gone on business to Harchester. He hasn't, of course, been out at all. But—"

Dodo paused.

Then she got quickly up from her chair, and clapped her hands.

"Yes, I will come. I am dying to go out again. Who leads the cotillion with me? Tommy Ledgers, isn't it? Oh, I shall enjoy it. I'm nearly dead for want of something to do. And he can dance, too. Yes, I'll come, but I must be back by half-past two. Chesterford will perhaps come by the night train getting here at two. I daresay it will be late. Are you going to have the mirror figure? Do have it. There's no one like Ledgers for leading that. He led it here with me. It will be like escaping from penal servitude for life. Talk of treadmills! I'm at the point of death for want of a dance. Let it begin punctually. I'll be there by ten sharp if you like. Tell Prince Waldenech I'm coming. He wrote to say he wouldn't go unless I did. He's badly in love with me. That doesn't matter, but he can dance. All those Austrians can. I'm going to have a regular debauch."

"I'm delighted," said Lady Bretton. "I came here to ask you whether you couldn't possibly come, but I hardly dared. Dear Dodo, it's charming of you. It will make all the difference. I was in despair this morning. I had asked Milly Cornish to lead with Ledgers, but she refused, unless I asked you again first. We'll have a triumphal arch, if you like, with 'Welcome to Dodo' on it."

"Anything you like," said Dodo; "the madder the merrier. Let's see, how does the hoop figure go?"

Dodo snatched up an old cotillion hoop from where it stood in the corner with fifty other relics, and began practising it.

"We must have this right," she said; "it's quite new to most people. You must tell Tommy to come here for an hour this afternoon, and we'll rehearse. You start with it in the left hand, don't you? and then cross it over, and hold your partner's hoop in the right. Damn—I beg your pardon—but it doesn't go right. No, you must send Ledgers. Shall I want castanets? I think I'd better. We must have the new Spanish figure. Ah, that is right."

Dodo went through a series of mysterious revolutions with the hoop.

"I feel like a vampire who's got hold of blood again," said Dodo, pausing to get her breath. "I feel like a fish put back into the water, like a convict back in his own warm nest. No charge for mixed metaphors. Supplied free, gratis, *and* for nothing," she said, with emphasis.

Lady Bretton put her head a little on one side, and gushed at her. Her manners were always perfect.

"Now, I'm going to send you off," said Dodo. "Jack's coming to lunch, and I've got a lot to do. Jack who? Jack Broxton, of course. Will he be with you to-night? No? I shall tell him I'm coming. You see if he doesn't come too. You sent him a card, of course. After lunch

I shall want Tommy. Mind he comes. Good-bye."

Dodo felt herself again. There was the double relief of Chesterford's absence, and there was something to do. She hummed a little French song, snapped her castanets, and pitched her novel into the grate.

"Oh, this great big world," she said, "you've been dead, and I've been dead for a month. Won't we have a resurrection this evening! Come in, Jack," she went on, as the door opened. "Here's your hoop. Catch it! Do you know the hoop figure? That's right; no, in your left hand. That's all with the hoop. Now we waltz."

Jack had a very vague idea as to why he happened to be waltzing with Dodo. It seemed to him rather like "Alice in Wonderland." However, he supposed it was all right, and on they went. A collision with the table, and a slow Stygian stream of ink dropping in a fatal, relentless manner on to the carpet, caused a stoppage, and Dodo condescended to explain, which she did all in one sentence.

"Chesterford's gone to Harchester after some stuffy business, and I'm going to the Brettons' ball, you must come, Jack, I'm going to lead the cotillion with Tommy, I simply must go, I'm dying to go out again; and, oh, Jack, I'm awfully glad to see you, and why haven't you been here for the last twenty years, and I'm out of breath, never mind the ink."

Dodo stopped from sheer exhaustion, and dropped a blotting-pad on to the pool of ink, which had now assumed the importance of an inland lake.

"Blanche has been here this morning," she continued, "and I told her I'd come, and would bring you. You must come, Jack. You're an awfully early bird, and I haven't got any worms for you, because they've all turned, owing to the hot weather, I suppose, and I feel so happy I can't talk sense. Tommy's coming this afternoon to practise. What time is it? Let's go and have lunch. That will do instead of worms. If Chesterford goes to attend to bailiff's business, why shouldn't I go and dance? It really is a kindness to Blanche. Nothing ought to stand in the way of a kindness. She was in despair; she told me so herself. She might have committed suicide. It would have been pleasant to have a countess's corpse's blood on your head, wouldn't it?"

"I thought Chesterford was here," said Jack.

"Oh, I'm not good enough for you," remarked Dodo. "That's very kind of you. I suppose you wouldn't have come, if you had known I should have had no one to meet you. Well, there isn't a soul, so you can go away if you like, or join the footmen in the servants' hall. Oh, I am so glad to be doing something again."

"I'm awfully glad you're coming to-night," said Jack; "it'll do you good."

"Ain't it a lark?" remarked Dodo, in pure Lancashire dialect, helping herself largely to beefsteak. "Jack, what'll you drink? Do you want beer? I'll treat you to what you like. You may dissolve my pearls in vinegar, if it will give you any satisfaction. Fetch Mr. Broxton my pearls, I mean some beer," said Dodo, upsetting the salt. "Really, Jack, I believe I've gone clean cracked. I've upset a lot of salt over your coat. Pour some claret upon it. Oh, no, that's the other way round, but I don't see why it shouldn't do. Have some more steak, Jack. Where's the gravy spoon? Jack, have you been trying to steal the silver? Oh, there it is. Have some chopped carrots with it. Who's that ringing at our door-bell? I'm a little— Who is it, Walter? Just go out and see. Miss Staines? Tell her there's lunch going on and Jack's here. There's an inducement. Jack, do you like Edith? She's rather loud. Yes, I agree, but we all make a noise at times. Can't she stop? Oh, very well, she may go away again. I believe she wouldn't come because you were here, Jack. I don't think she likes you, but you're a very good sort in your way. Jack, will you say grace? Chesterford always says grace. Well, for a Christian gentleman not to know a grace! Bring some cigarettes, Walter, or would you rather have a cigar, Jack? And some black coffee. Well, I'm very grateful for *my* good dinner, and I don't mind saying so."

Dodo went on talking at the top of her voice, quite continuously. She asked Jack a dozen questions without waiting for the answer.

"Where shall we go now, Jack?" she continued, when they had finished coffee—Dodo took three cups and a cigarette with each. "We must go somewhere. I can leave word for Ledgers to wait. Let's go to the Zoo and see all the animals in cages. Ah, I sympathise with them. I have only just got out of my cage myself."

Dodo dragged Jack off to the Zoo, on the top of a bus, and bought buns for the animals and fruit for the birds, and poked a fierce lion with the end of her parasol, which the brute bit off, and nearly fell over into the polar bear's tank, and had all her money stolen by a pickpocket.

Then she went back home, and found Lord Ledgers, whom she put through his paces, and then she had tea, and dressed for the ball. She had ordered a very remarkable ball-dress from Worth's, just before the baby's death, which had never yet seen the light. It was a soft grey texture, which Dodo said looked like a sunlit mist, and it was strictly half mourning. She felt it was a badge of her freedom, and put it on with a fresh burst of exultation. She had a large bouquet of orchids, which Lord Bretton had caused to be sent her, and a fan painted by Watteau, and a French hairdresser came and "did" her hair. By this time dinner was ready; and after dinner she sat in her room smoking and singing French songs to Lord Ledgers, who had come to fetch her, and at half-past nine the carriage was announced. About the same moment another carriage drove up to the door, and as Dodo ran downstairs she found her husband in the hall.

She looked at him a moment with undisguised astonishment, and a frown gathered on her forehead.

"You here?" she said. "I thought you weren't coming till late."

"I caught the earlier train," he said; "and where are you off to?"

"I'm going to the Brettons' ball," said Dodo frankly; "I can't wait."

He turned round and faced her.

"Oh, Dodo, so soon?" he said.

"Yes, yes, I must," said Dodo. "You know this kills me, this sticking here with nothing to do from day to day, and nothing to see, and nobody to talk to. It's death; I can't bear it."

"Very well," he said gently, "you are quite right to go if you want to. But I am not coming, Dodo."

Dodo's face brightened.

"No, dear, they don't expect you. I thought you wouldn't be back."

"I shouldn't go in any case," said he.

Lord Ledgers was here heard to remark, "By Gad!"

Dodo laid her hand on his shoulder, conscious of restraining her impatience.

"No, that's just the difference between us," she said. "Go on, Tommy, get into the carriage. You don't want me not to go, dear, do you?"

"No, you are right to go, if you wish to," he said again.

Dodo grew impatient.

"Really, you might be more cordial about it," she said. "I needn't have consulted you at all."

Lord Chesterford was not as meek as Moses. He was capable of a sense of injustice.

"I don't know that you did consult me much," he said. "You mean to go in any case."

"Very well," said Dodo, "I do mean to go. Goodnight, old boy. I sha'n't be very late. But I don't mean to quarrel with you."

Lord Chesterford turned into his room. But he would not keep Dodo, as she wished to go, even if he could have done so.

Ledgers was waiting in the carriage.

"Oh, the devil," said Dodo, as she stepped in.

Lady Bretton's ball is still talked about, I believe, in certain circles, though it ought to have been consigned, with all other events of last year, to oblivion. It was very brilliant, and several princes shed the light of their presence on it. But, as Lord Ledgers was heard to remark afterwards, "There are many princes, but there is only one Dodo."

He felt as if he was adapting a quotation from the Koran, which was somehow suitable to the positive solemnity of the occasion. Dodo can only be described as having been indescribable. Lucas, Lady Bretton's eldest son, in honour of whose coming of age the ball was given, can hardly allude to it even now. His emotions expressed themselves feebly in his dressing with even more care than usual, in hanging round Eaton Square, and in leaving cards on the Chesterfords as often as was decent.

Dodo was conscious of a frenzied desire to make the most of it, and to drown remembrance, for in the background of her mind was another picture, that she did not care to look at. There was a man she knew, leaning over a small dead child. The door of the room was half open, and a woman, brilliantly dressed, was turning to go out, looking back over her shoulder with a smile, half of impatience, half of pity, at the kneeling figure in the room. Through the half-open door came sounds of music and rhythmical steps, and a blaze of light. This picture had started unbidden into Dodo's mind, as she and Ledgers drove up to Lady Bretton's door, with such sudden clearness that she half wondered whether she had ever actually seen it. It reminded her of one of Orchardson's silent, well-appointed tragedies. In any case it gave her a rather unpleasant twinge, and she determined to shut it out for the rest of the evening, and, to do her justice, no one would have guessed that Dodo's brilliance was due to anything but pure spontaneity, or that, even in the deepest shades of her inmost mind, there was any remembrance that it needed an effort to stifle.

Many women, though few men, were surprised to see her there, and there was no one who was not glad; but the question arose more than once in the minds of two or three people, "Would society stand it if she didn't happen to be herself?" Dodo had treated a select party of her friends to a private exhibition of skirt-dancing during supper-time. The music from the band was quite loud enough to be heard distinctly in a small, rather unfrequented sitting-out room, and there Dodo had displayed her incomparable grace of movement and limb to the highest advantage. Dodo danced that night with unusual perfection, and who has not felt the exquisite beauty of such motion? Her figure, clad in its long, clinging folds of diaphanous, almost luminous texture, stood out like a radiant statue of dawn against the dark panelling of the room; her graceful figure bending this way and that, her wonderful white arms now holding aside her long skirt, or clasped above her head; above all, the supreme distinction and conscious modesty of every posture seemed, to the little circle who saw her, to be almost a new revelation of the perfection of form, colour and grace.

Jack knew Dodo pretty well, but he stood and wondered. Was she a devil? Was she a tiger? or was she, after all, a woman? Dodo had told him what had happened that evening, and yet he did not condemn her utterly. He knew how prison-like her life must have been to her during the last month. It was a thousand pities that Dodo's meat was Chesterford's poison, but he no more blamed Dodo for eating her meat than he blamed Chesterford for avoiding his poison; and to advance the conventional argument against Dodo, that her behaviour was not usual, was equivalent to saying, "Why do you behave like yourself?" rather than, "Why don't you behave like other people?" Dodo's estimate of herself, as purely normal, was only another instance of her very abnormalness. No, on the whole, she was not a devil. The other question was harder to settle. Jack remembered a tigress he had seen that day with her at the Zoo. The brute had a small and perfectly fascinating tiger cub, in which she took a certain maternal pride; but when feeding-time came near, and the cub continued to be importunate, she gave it a cuff with her big velvety paw, and sent it staggering to the corner. Dodo's tiger cub was a mixture between Chesterford and the dead child, and Dodo's feeding-time had come round. Here she was feeding with an enviable appetite, and where was the cub? The tigress element was not wholly absent.

And yet, withal, she was a woman. Is it that certain attributes of pure womanliness run through the female of animals, or that every woman has a touch of the tigress about her? Jack felt incompetent to decide.

Dodo's dance came to an end. She accepted Prince Waldenech's arm, and went down to supper. As he advanced to her, Dodo dropped a curtsey, and he stooped and kissed her hand. "The brute," thought Jack, as he strolled out into the ballroom, where people were beginning to collect again. Many turned and looked at Dodo as she passed out with her handsome partner. The glow of exercise and excitement and success burned brightly in her cheeks, and no one accused Dodo of using rouge. The supper was spread on a number of small tables, laid for four or six each. The Prince led her to an empty one, and sat down by her side.

"I have seen many beautiful things," he said, in French, which permits a man to say more than he may in English, "but none so beautiful as what I have seen to-night."

Dodo was far too accomplished a coquette to pretend not to know what he meant. She made him a charming little obeisance.

"Politeness required that of your Highness," she said. "That is only my due, you know."

"I can never give you your due," said he.

"My due in this case is the knowledge I have pleased you."

Dodo felt suddenly a little uncomfortable. The forgotten picture flashed for a moment across her inward eye. She spoke of other things: praised the prettiness of the ballroom, the excellence of the band.

"Lady Bretton has given a fine setting to the diamond," said the Prince, "but the diamond is not hers."

Dodo laughed. He was a little ponderous, and he deserved to be told so.

"You Austrians have beautiful manners," she said, "but you are too serious. English are always accused of sharing that fault, but anyhow, when they pay compliments, they have at least the air of not meaning what they say."

"That is the fault of the English, or of the compliment."

"No one means what they say when they pay compliments," said Dodo. "They are only a kind of formula to avoid the unpleasantness of saying nothing."

"Austrians seldom pay compliments," said he; "but when they do, they mean them."

"Ouf," said Dodo; "that sounds homelike to you, doesn't it? All Austrians say 'ouf' in books—do they really say 'ouf,' by the way?—What a bald way of saying that I needn't expect any more to-night. Really, Prince, that's rather unflattering to you. No, don't excuse yourself; I understand perfectly. I'm not fishing for any more. Come, there's the *pas de quatre* beginning. That's the 'Old Kent Road' tune. It's much the best. What do you suppose 'Knocked 'em in the Old Kent Road' means? No foreigner has ever been able to translate it to me yet. This is your dance, isn't it? O dear me, half the night's gone, and I feel as if I hadn't begun yet. Some people are in bed now; what a waste of time, you know."

The ball went on and on, and Dodo seemed to gather fresh strength and brilliance with each hour. Extra dances were added and still added, and many who were tired with dancing stayed and watched her. The princes went away, and nobody noticed their departure. If Cleopatra herself had suddenly entered the ballroom, she would have found herself at a discount. It was the culmination of Dodo's successes. She seemed different in kind, as well as in degree, from the crowd around her. Pretty women seemed suddenly plain and middle-aged; well-dressed women looked dowdy beside her, and when at length, as the electric light began to pale perceptibly before the breaking day, Dodo asked her partner to take her to Lady Bretton, the dancers stopped, and followed Dodo and Prince Waldenech, for she was dancing with him, to where Lady Bretton was standing.

"It has been heavenly," said Dodo. "It's a dreadful bore to have people come and say how much they have enjoyed themselves, but

I've done it now. Tell Lucas I wish he would come of age every year; he really is a public benefactor."

She took Prince Waldenech's arm, and stood waiting with him, while her carriage detached itself from the others which lined the square, and drove up to the door. And, as they stood there, the crowd followed her slowly out of the ballroom, still silent, and still watching her, and lined the stairs, as she passed down to the front door.

Then, when she had got into her carriage, and had driven off, they looked at each other as if they had all been walking in their sleep, and no one knew exactly why they were there. And a quarter of an hour later the rooms were completely empty.

Meanwhile, as Dodo drove back through the still, cool, morning air, she threw down the windows of her carriage, and drew in deep satisfied breaths of its freshness. She thought of the crowds who had followed her down to the door, and laughed for pleasure. "It's life, it's life," she thought. "They followed me like sheep. Ah, how I love it!"

It was nearly six when she reached home. "Decidedly it would be too absurd to go to bed," she thought. "I shall go for a glorious gallop, and come back to breakfast with Chesterford. Tell them to saddle Starlight at once," she said to the footman: "I sha'n't want a groom. And tell Lord Chesterford, when he wakes, that I shall be back to breakfast."

12

Chesterford did not let Dodo see how strongly he had felt on the subject of the ball. He argued to himself that it would do no good. Dodo would not understand, or, understanding, would misunderstand the strength of his feeling, and he did not care that she should know that he thought her heartless. He was quite conscious that matters were a little strained between them, though Dodo apparently was sublimely unaware of it. She had a momentary nervousness when they met at breakfast, on the morning after the ball, that Chesterford was going to make a fuss, and she could not quite see what it would end in, if the subject was broached. But he came in looking as usual. He told her how matters had gone with him on the previous day, and had recounted, with a certain humour, a few sharp words which an old lady in his railway carriage had addressed to him, because he didn't help her to hand out two large cages of canaries which she was taking home.

Dodo welcomed all this as a sign of grace, and was only too happy to meet her husband half-way. He had been a trifle melodramatic on the previous evening, but we are all liable to make mountains out of molehills at times, she thought. Personally her inclination was to make molehills out of mountains, but that was only a difference in temperament; both implied a judgment at fault, and she was quite willing to forgive and forget. In a word, she was particularly nice to him, and when breakfast was over she took his arm, and led him away to her room.

"Sit down in that very big chair, old boy," she said, "and twiddle your thumbs while I write some notes. I'm going to see Mrs. Vivian this morning, and your lordship may come in my ladyship's carriage if it likes. Is lordship masculine, feminine, or neuter, Chesterford? Anyhow, it's wrong to say your lordship may come in your carriage, because lordship is the nominative to the sentence, and is in the third person— what was I saying? Oh, yes, you may come if it likes, and drop me there, and then go away for about half an hour, and then come back, and then we'll have lunch together at home."

"I've got to go to some stupid committee at the club," said Chesterford, "but that's not till twelve. I'll send your carriage back for you, but I sha'n't be able to be in at lunch."

"Oh, very good," remarked Dodo. "I'm sorry I married you. I might be a lone lorn widdy for all you care. He prefers lunching at his club," she went on, dramatically, addressing the black virgin, "to having his chop at home with the wife of his bosom. How sharper than a serpent's tooth to have a thankless Chesterford!"

Dodo proceeded to write her notes, and threw them one by one at her husband as he sat contentedly by the window, in the very big chair that Dodo had indicated.

Dodo's correspondence was as varied as the collection of photographs on her mantelpiece. The first note was to her groom at Winston, telling him to have another riding-horse sent up at once, as her own particular mare had gone lame. It missed Chesterford's head, and fell with an ominous clatter among some *bric-a-brac* and china.

"That'll be a bill for you to pay, darling," said Dodo sweetly. "Why didn't you put your silly old head in the light?"

The next was a slightly better shot, and fell right side upwards on to Chesterford's knee, but with the address upside down to him. He looked at it vaguely.

"His Serene Highness who?" he asked, spelling it out.

"That's not grammar," said Dodo. "It's only to Prince Waldenech. He is Serene, isn't he? He looks it, anyhow. He was at the Brettons' last night. Austrian but amiable."

Chesterford was fingering the envelope.

"He's an unmitigated blackguard," he said, after a little consideration. "I wish you'd let me tear it up, Dodo. What on earth have you got to say to him?"

"I shall have to write it again, dear, if you do," said she, conscious of bridling a rising irritation.

"He really is an awful brute," he repeated.

"Oh, my dear Chesterford, what does that matter?" asked Dodo, impatiently tapping the floor with the toe of her shoe. "It isn't my business to go raking up the character of people I'm introduced to."

"You mean you don't mind what a man's character is as long as he's agreeable."

"It isn't my business to be court inquisitor," she said. "Half of what one hears about people isn't true, and the other half—well, all you can say is, that it isn't exactly false."

Dodo could lose her temper very quickly on occasions, especially when she was in a hurry, as she was now.

"My dear Dodo, do you happen to know the story of—"

"No, I don't," she said vehemently. "Shall I seem rude if I say I don't want to? I really think you might find something better to do than tell scandalous stories about people you don't know."

"I know all I want to know about Prince Waldenech," said Chesterford, rising.

"You'll know more about him soon," remarked Dodo, "because I've asked him to stay at Winston. I suppose you think I wanted to make a secret about it. I have no such intention, I assure you."

"Is this note to ask him to come?" he inquired.

"Certainly it is," said Dodo defiantly.

"I may as well tear it up," said he. "I don't mean him to be asked, Dodo. I don't wish to have him in the house."

Dodo had lost her temper thoroughly.

"His being asked to Winston is immaterial," she said, with scorn in her voice. "You certainly have the power to prevent his coming to your house. Your power I must regard, your wishes I shall not. I can see him in London with perfect ease."

"You mean you attach no weight to my wishes in this matter?" said Chesterford.

"None."

"Will no knowledge of what the man is really like, stop you holding further intercourse with him?" he asked.

"None whatever, now!"

"I don't wish it to be known that my wife associates with such people," he said.

"Your wife does not regard it in that light," replied Dodo. "I have no intention of proclaiming the fact from the housetops."

To do Chesterford justice he was getting angry too.

"It's perfectly intolerable that there should be this sort of dispute between you and me, Dodo," he said.

"That is the first point on which we have not differed."

"You entirely decline to listen to reason?"

"To your reason, you mean," said Dodo.

"To mine or any honest man's."

Dodo burst out into a harsh, mirthless laugh.

"Ah, you're beginning to be jealous," she said. "It is very bourgeois to be jealous."

Chesterford coloured angrily.

"That is an insult, Dodo," he said. "Remember that there is a courtesy due even from a wife to her husband. Besides that, you know the contrary."

"Really, I know nothing of the sort," she remarked. "Your whole conduct, both last night and this morning, has been so melodramatic, that I begin to suspect all sorts of latent virtues in you."

"We are wandering from the point," said he. "Do you mean that nothing will deter you from seeing this Austrian?"

"He is received in society," said Dodo; "he is presentable, he is even amusing. Am I to tell him that my husband is afraid he'll corrupt my morals? If people in general cut him, I don't say that I should continue to cultivate his acquaintance. It is absurd to run amuck of such conventions. If you had approached me in a proper manner, I don't say that I mightn't have seen my way to meeting your wishes."

"I don't feel I am to blame in that respect," said he.

"That shows you don't know how far we are apart," she replied.

He was suddenly frightened. He came closer to her.

"Far apart, Dodo? We?"

"It seems to me that this interview has revealed some astonishing differences of opinion between us," she said. "I don't wish to multiply words. You have told me what you think on the subject, and I have told you what I think. You have claimed the power a husband certainly possesses, and I claim the liberty that my husband cannot deprive me of. Or perhaps you wish to lock me up. We quite understand one another. Let us agree to differ. Give me that note, please. I suppose you can trust me not to send it. I should like to keep it. It is interesting to count the milestones."

Dodo spoke with the recklessness of a woman's anger, which is always much more unwanton than that of a man. A man does not say cruel things when he is angry, because they are cruel, but because he is angry. Dodo was cruel because she wished to be cruel. He gave her the note, and turned to leave the room. Dodo's last speech made it impossible for him to say more. The only thing he would not sacrifice to his love was his honour or hers. But Dodo suddenly saw the horrible impossibility of the situation. She had not the smallest intention of living on bad terms with her husband. They had quarrelled, it was a pity, but it was over. A storm may only clear the air; it is not always the precursor of bad weather. The air wanted clearing, and Dodo determined that it should not be the prelude of rain and wind. To her, of course, the knowledge that she did not love her husband had long been a commonplace, but to him the truth was coming in fierce, blinding flashes, and by their light he could see that a great flood had come down into his happy valley, carrying desolation before it, and between him and Dodo stretched a tawny waste of water. But Dodo had no intention of quarrelling with him, or maintaining a dignified reserve in their daily intercourse. That would be quite unbearable, and she wished there to be no misunderstanding on that point.

"Chesterford," she said, "we've quarrelled, and that's a pity. I hardly ever quarrel, and it was stupid of me. I am sorry. But I have no intention of standing on my dignity, and I sha'n't allow you to stand on yours. I shall pull you down, and you'll go flop. You object to something which I propose to do, you exert your rights, as far as having him in the house goes, and I exert mine by going to see him. I shall go this afternoon. Your veto on his coming to Winston seems quite as objectionable to me, as my going to see him does to you. That's our position; accept it. Let us understand each other completely. *C'est aimer.*" As she spoke she recovered her equanimity, and she smiled serenely on him. Scenes like this left no impression on her. The tragedy passed over her head; and, though it was written in the lines of her husband's face, she did not trouble to read it. She got up from her chair and went to him. He was standing with his hands clasped behind him near the door. She laid her hands on his shoulder, and gave him a little shake.

"Now, Chesterford, I'm going to make it up," she said. "Twenty minutes is heaps of time for the most quarrelsome people to say sufficient nasty things in, and time's up. I'm going to behave exactly as usual. I hate quarrelling, and you don't look as if it agreed with you. Kiss me this moment. No, not on the top of my head. That's better. My carriage ought to be ready by this time, and you are coming with me as far as Prince's Gate."

13

Lord and Lady Chesterford were sitting at breakfast at Winston towards the end of September. He had an open letter in front of him propped up against his cup, and between mouthfuls of fried fish he glanced at it.

"Dodo."

No answer.

"Dodo," rather louder.

Dodo was also reading a letter, which covered two sheets and was closely written. It seemed to be interesting, for she had paused with a piece of fish on the end of her fork, and had then laid it down again. This time, however, she heard.

"Oh, what?" she said abstractedly. "Jack's coming to-day; I've just heard from him. He's going to bring his hunter. You can get some cub-hunting, I suppose, Chesterford? The hunt itself doesn't begin till the 15th, does it?"

"Ah, I'm glad he can come," said Chesterford. "Little Spencer would be rather hard to amuse alone. But that isn't what I was going to say."

"What is it?" said Dodo, relapsing into her letter.

"The bailiff writes to tell me that they have discovered a rich coal shaft under the Far Oaks." A pause. "But, Dodo, you are not listening."

"I'm sorry," she said. "Do you know, Jack nearly shot himself the other day at a grouse drive?"

"I don't care," said Chesterford brutally. "Listen, Dodo. Tompkinson says they've discovered a rich coal shaft under the Far Oaks. Confound the man, I wish he hadn't."

"Oh, Chesterford, how splendid!" said Dodo, dropping her letter in earnest. "Dig it up and spend it on your party, and they'll make you a duke for certain. I want to be a duchess very much. Good morning, your grace," said Dodo reflectively.

"Oh, that's impossible," said he. "I never thought of touching it, but the ass tells me that he's seen the news of it in the *Staffordshire Herald*. So I suppose everybody knows, and I shall be pestered."

"But do you mean to say you're going to let the coal stop there?" asked Dodo.

"Yes, dear, I can't possibly touch it. It goes right under all those oaks, and under the Memorial Chapel, close to the surface."

"But what does that matter?" asked Dodo, in real surprise.

"I can't possibly touch it," said he; "you must see that. Why, the chapel would have to come down, and the oaks, and we don't want a dirty coal shaft in the Park."

"Chesterford, how ridiculous!" exclaimed Dodo. "Do you mean you're going to leave thousands of pounds lying there in the earth?"

"I can't discuss it, dear, even with you," said he. "The only question is whether we can stop the report of it going about."

Dodo felt intensely irritated.

"Really you are most unreasonable," she said. "I did flatter myself that I had a reasonable husband. You were unreasonable about the Brettons' ball, and you were unreasonable about Prince Waldenech's coming here, and you are unreasonable about this."

Chesterford lost his patience a little.

"About the Brettons' ball," he said, "there was only one opinion, and that was mine. About the Prince's coming here, which we agreed not to talk about, you know the further reason. I don't like saying such things. You are aware what that officious ass Clayton told me was said at the club. Of course it was an insult to you, and a confounded lie, but I don't care for such things to be said about my wife. And about this—"

"About this," said Dodo, "you are as obstinate as you were about those other things. Excuse me if I find you rather annoying."

Chesterford felt sick at heart.

"Ah, Dodo," he said, "cannot you believe in me at all?" He rose and stood by her. "My darling, you must know how I would do anything for love of you. But these are cases in which that clashes with duty. I only want to be loved a little. Can't you see there are some things I cannot help doing, and some I must do?"

"The things that you like doing," said Dodo, in a cool voice, pouring out some more tea. "I don't wish to discuss this either. You know my opinion. It is absurd to quarrel; I dislike quarrelling with anybody, and more especially a person whom I live with. Please take your hand away, I can't reach the sugar."

Dodo returned to her letter. Chesterford stood by her for a moment, and then left the room.

"It gets more and more intolerable every day. I can't bear quarrelling; it makes me ill," thought Dodo, with a fine sense of irresponsibility. "And I know he'll come and say he was sorry he said what he did. Thank goodness, Jack comes to-day."

Chesterford, meanwhile, was standing in the hall, feeling helpless and bewildered. This sort of thing was always happening now, do what he could; and the intervals were not much better. Dodo treated him with a passive tolerance that was very hard to bear. Even her frank determination to keep on good terms with her husband had undergone considerable modification. She was silent and indifferent. Now and then when he came into her room he heard, as he passed down the passage, the sound of her piano or her voice, but when he entered Dodo would break off and ask him what he wanted. He half wished that he did not love her, but he found himself sickening and longing for Dodo to behave to him as she used. It would have been something to know that his presence was not positively distasteful to her. Dodo no longer "kept it up," as Jack said. She did not pat his hand, or call him a silly old dear, or pull his moustache, as once she did. He had once taken those little things as a sign of her love. He had found in them the pleasure that Dodo's smallest action always had for him; but now even they, the husk and shell of what had never existed, had gone from him, and he was left with that which was at once his greatest sorrow and his greatest joy, his own love for Dodo. And Dodo—God help him! he had learned it well enough now—Dodo did not love him, and never had loved him. He wondered what the end would be—whether his love, too, would die. In that case he foresaw that they would very likely go on living together as fifty other people lived—being polite to each other, and gracefully tolerant of each other's presence; that nobody would know, and the world would say, "What a model and excellent couple."

So he stood there, biting the ends of his long moustache. Then he said to himself, "I was beastly to her. What the devil made me say all those things."

He went back to the dining-room, and found Dodo as he had left her.

"Dodo, dear," he said, "forgive me for being so cross. I said a lot of abominable things."

Dodo was rather amused. She knew this would happen.

"Oh, yes," she said; "it doesn't signify. But are you determined about the coal mine?"

Chesterford was disappointed and chilled. He turned on his heel and went out again. Dodo raised her eyebrows, shrugged her shoulders imperceptibly, and returned to her letter.

If you had asked Dodo when this state of things began she could probably not have told you. She would have said, "Oh, it came on by degrees. It began by my being bored with him, and culminated when I no longer concealed it." But Chesterford, to whom daily intercourse had become an awful struggle between his passionate love for Dodo and his bitter disappointment at what he would certainly have partly attributed to his own stupidity and inadequacy, could have named the day and hour when he first realised how far he was apart from his wife. It was when he returned by the earlier train and met

Dodo in the hall going to her dance; that moment had thrown a dangerous clear light over the previous month. He argued to himself, with
fatal correctness, that Dodo could not have stopped caring for him
in a moment, and he was driven to the inevitable conclusion that
she had been drifting away from him for a long time before that;
indeed, had she ever been near him? But he was deeply grateful to
those months when he had deceived himself, or she had deceived him,
into believing that she cared for him. He knew well that they had
been the happiest in his life, and though the subsequent disappointment
was bitter, it had not embittered him. His love for Dodo had a sacred-
ness for him that nothing could remove; it was something separate
from the rest of his life, that had stooped from heaven and entered
into it, and lo! it was glorified. That memory was his for ever, nothing
could rob him of that.

In August Dodo had left him. They had settled a series of visits in
Scotland, after a fortnight at their own house, but after that Dodo
had made arrangements apart from him. She had to go and see her
mother, she had to go here and there, and half way through September,
when Chesterford had returned to Harchester expecting her the same
night, he found a postcard from her, saying she had to spend three
days with someone else, and the three days lengthened into a week,
and it was only yesterday that Dodo had come, and people were arriving
that very evening. There was only one conclusion to be drawn from
all this, and not even he could help drawing it.

Jack and Mr. Spencer and Maud, now Mrs. Spencer, arrived that
evening. Maud had started a sort of small store of work, and the worsted
and crochet went on with feverish rapidity. It had become a habit
with her before her marriage, and the undeveloped possibilities, that
no doubt lurked within it, had blossomed under her husband's care.
For there was a demand beyond the limits of supply for her woollen
shawls and comforters. Mr. Spencer's parish was already speckled with
testimonies to his wife's handiwork, and Maud's dream of being some
day useful to somebody was finding a glorious fulfillment.

Dodo, I am sorry to say, found her sister more unsatisfactory than
ever. Maud had a sort of confused idea that it helped the poor if
she dressed untidily, and this was a ministry that came without effort.
Dodo took her in hand as soon as she arrived, and made her presentable.
"Because you are a clergyman's wife, there is no reason that you
shouldn't wear a tucker or something round your neck," she said.
"Your sister is a marchioness, and when you stay with her you must
behave as if you were an honourable. There will be time to sit in
the gutter when you get back to Gloucester."

Dodo also did her duty by Mr. Spencer. She called him Algernon in the friendliest way, and gave him several lessons at billiards. This done, she turned to Jack.

The three had been there several days, and Dodo was getting impatient. Jack and Chesterford went out shooting, and she was left to entertain the other two. Mr. Spencer's reluctance to shoot was attributable not so much to his aversion to killing live animals, as his inability to slay. But when Dodo urged on him that he would soon learn, he claimed the higher motive. She was rather silent, for she was thinking about something important.

Dodo was surprised at the eagerness with which she looked forward to Jack's coming. Somehow, in a dim kind of way, she regarded him as the solution of her difficulties. She felt pretty certain Jack would do as he was asked, and she had made up her mind that when Jack went away she would go with him to see friends at other houses to which he was going. And Chesterford? Dodo's scheme did not seem to take in Chesterford. She had painted a charming little picture in her own mind as to where she should go, and whom she would see, but she certainly was aware that Chesterford did not seem to come in. It would spoil the composition, she thought, to introduce another figure. That would be a respite, anyhow. But after that, what then? Dodo had found it bad enough coming back this September, and she could not contemplate renewing this *tête-à-tête* that went on for months. And by degrees another picture took its place—a dim one, for the details were not worked out—but in that picture there were only two figures. The days went on and Dodo could bear it no longer.

One evening she went into the smoking-room after tea. Chesterford was writing letters, and Maud and her husband were sitting in the drawing-room. It may be presumed that Maud was doing crochet. Jack looked up with a smile as Dodo entered.

"Hurrah," he said, "I haven't had a word with you since we came. Come and talk, Dodo."

But Dodo did not smile.

"How have you been getting on?" continued Jack, looking at the fire. "You see I haven't lost my interest in you."

"Jack," said Dodo solemnly, "you are right, and I was wrong. And I can't bear it any longer."

Jack did not need explanations.

"Ah!"—then after a moment, "poor Chesterford!"

"I don't see why 'poor Chesterford,'" said Dodo, "any more than 'poor me.' He was quite satisfied, anyhow, for some months, for a year in fact, more or less, and I was never satisfied at all. I haven't got a particle of pride left in me, or else I shouldn't be telling you. I can't bear it. If you only knew what I have been through you would pity me as well. It has been a continual effort with me; surely that is something to pity. And one day I broke down; I forget when, it is immaterial. Oh, why couldn't I love him! I thought I was going to, and it was all a wretched mistake."

Dodo sat with her hands clasped before her, with something like tears in her eyes.

"I am not all selfish," she went on; "I am sorry for him, too, but I am so annoyed with him that I lose my sorrow whenever I see him. Why couldn't he have accepted the position sooner? We might have been excellent friends then, but now that is impossible. I have got past that. I cannot even be good friends with him. Oh, it isn't my fault; you know I tried to behave well."

Jack felt intensely uncomfortable.

"I can't help you, Dodo," he said. "It is useless for me to say I am sincerely sorry. That is no word between you and me."

Dodo, for once in her life, seemed to have something to say, and not be able to say it.

At last it came out with an effort.

"Jack, do you still love me?"

Dodo did not look at him, but kept her eyes on the fire.

Jack did not pause to think.

"Before God, Dodo," he said, "I believe I love you more than anything in the world."

"Will you do what I ask you?"

This time he did pause. He got up and stood before the fire. Still Dodo did not look at him.

"Ah, Dodo," he said, "what are you going to ask? There are some things I cannot do."

"It seems to me this love you talk of is a very weak thing," said Dodo. "It always fails, or is in danger of failing, at the critical point. I believe I could do anything for the man I loved. I did not think so once. But I was wrong, as I have been in my marriage."

Dodo paused; but Jack said nothing; it seemed to him as if Dodo had not quite finished.

"Yes," she said; then paused again. "Yes, you are he."

There was a dead silence. For one moment time seemed to Jack to have stopped, and he could have believed that that moment lasted for years—for ever.

"Oh, my God," he murmured, "at last."

He was conscious of Dodo sitting there, with her eyes raised to his, and a smile on her lips. He felt himself bending forward towards her, and he thought she half rose in her chair to receive his embrace.

But the next moment she put out her hand as if to stop him.

"Stay," she said. "Not yet, not yet. There is something first. I will tell you what I have done. I counted on this. I have ordered the carriage after dinner at half-past ten. You and I go in that, and leave by the train. Jack, I am yours—will you come?"

Dodo had taken the plunge. She had been wavering on the brink of this for days. It had struck her suddenly that afternoon that Jack was going away next day, and she was aware she could not contemplate the indefinite to-morrow and to-morrow without him. Like all Dodo's actions it came suddenly. The forces in her which had been drawing her on to this had gathered strength and sureness imperceptibly, and this evening they had suddenly burst through the very flimsy dam that Dodo had erected between the things she might do, and the things she might not, and their possession was complete. In a way it was inevitable. Dodo felt that her life was impossible. Chesterford, with infinite yearning and hunger at his heart, perhaps felt it too.

Jack felt as if he was waking out of some blissful dream to a return of his ordinary everyday life, which, unfortunately, had certain moral obligations attached to it. If Dodo's speech had been shorter, the result might have been different. He steadied himself for a moment, for the room seemed to reel and swim, and then he answered her.

"No, Dodo," he said hoarsely, "I cannot do it. Think of Chesterford! Think of anything! Don't tempt me. You know I cannot. How dare you ask me?"

Dodo's face grew hard and white. She tried to laugh, but could not manage it.

"Ah," she said, "the old story, isn't it? Potiphar's wife again. I really do not understand what this love of yours is. And now I have debased and humbled myself before you, and there you stand in your immaculate virtue, not caring—"

"Don't, Dodo," he said. "Be merciful to me, spare me. Not caring—you know it is not so. But I cannot do this. My Dodo, my darling."

The strain was too great for him. He knelt down beside her, and kissed her hand passionately.

"I will do anything for you," he whispered, "that is in my power to do; but this is impossible. I never yet did, with deliberate forethought, what seemed to me mean or low, and I can't now. I don't want credit for it, because I was made that way; I don't happen to be a blackguard by nature. Don't tempt me—I am too weak. But you mustn't blame me for it. You know—you must know that I love you. I left England last autumn to cure myself of it, but it didn't answer a bit. I don't ask more than what you have just told me. That is something—isn't it, Dodo? And, if you love me, that is something for you. Don't let us degrade it, let it be a strength to us and not a weakness. You must feel it so."

· · · · · · ·

There was a long silence, and in that silence the great drama of love and life, and good and evil, which has been played every day of every year since the beginning of this world, and which will never cease till all mankind are saints or sexless, filled the stage. Dodo thought, at any rate, that she loved him, and that knowledge made her feel less abased before him. All love—the love for children, for parents, for husband, for wife, for lover, for mistress—has something divine about it, or else it is not love. The love Jack felt for her was divine enough not to seek its own, to sacrifice itself on the altar of duty and loyalty and the pure cold gods, and in its tumultuous happiness it could think of others. And Dodo's love was touched, though ever so faintly, with the same divine spark, a something so human that it touched heaven.

Now it had so happened that, exactly three minutes before this, Maud had found that she had left a particularly precious skein of wool in another room. About ten seconds' reflection made her remember she had left it in the smoking-room, where she had sat with Dodo after lunch, who had smoked cigarettes, and lectured her on her appearance. The smoking-room had two doors, about eight yards apart, forming a little passage lighted with a skylight. The first of those doors was of wood, the second, which led into the smoking-room, of baize. The first door was opened in the ordinary manner, the second with a silent push. Maud had made this silent push at the moment when Jack was kneeling by Dodo's side, kissing her hand. Maud was not versed in the wickedness of this present world, but she realized that this was a peculiar thing for Jack to do, and she let the door swing quietly back, and ran downstairs, intending to ask her husband's advice. Chesterford's study opened into the drawing-room. During the time that Maud had been upstairs he had gone in to fetch Dodo, and seeing she was not there he went back, but did not close the door behind him. A moment afterwards Maud rushed into the drawing-room from the hall, and carefully shutting the door behind her, lest anyone should hear, exclaimed:—

"Algy, I've seen something awful! I went into the smoking-room to fetch my wool, and I saw Jack kissing Dodo's hand. What am I to do?"

Algernon was suitably horrified. He remarked, with much reason, that it was no use telling Dodo and Jack, because they knew already.

At this moment the door of Lord Chesterford's study was closed quietly. He did not wish to hear any more just yet. But they neither of them noticed it.

He had overheard something which was not meant for his ears, related by a person who had overseen what she was not meant to see; he hated learning anything that was not his own affair, but he had learned it, and it turned out to be unpleasantly closely connected with him.

His first impulse was to think that Jack had behaved in a treacherous and blackguardly manner, and this conclusion surprised him so much that he set to ponder over it. The more he thought of it, the more unlikely it appeared to him. Jack making love to his wife under cover of his own roof was too preposterous an idea to be entertained. He held a very high opinion of Jack, and it did not at all seem to fit in with this. Was there any other possibility? It came upon him with a sense of sickening probability that there was. He remembered the long loveless months; he remembered Dodo's indifference to him, then her neglect, then her dislike. Had Jack been hideously tempted and not been able to resist? Chesterford almost felt a friendly feeling for not being able to resist Dodo. What did all this imply? How long had it been going on? How did it begin? Where would it stop? He felt he had a right to ask these questions, and he meant to ask them of the proper person. But not yet. He would wait; he would see what happened. He was afraid of judging both too harshly. Maud's account might have been incorrect; anyhow it was not meant for him. His thoughts wandered on dismally and vaguely. But the outcome was, that he said to himself, "Poor Dodo, God forgive her."

He had been so long used to the altered state of things that this blow seemed to him only a natural sequence. But he had been used to feed his starved heart with promises that Dodo would care for him again; that those months when they were first married were only the bud of a flower that would some day blossom. It was this feeble hope that what he had heard destroyed. If things had gone as far as that it was hopeless.

"Yes," he repeated, "it is all gone."

If anything could have killed his love for Dodo he felt that it would have been this. But, as he sat there, he said to himself, "She shall never know that I know of it." That was his final determination. Dodo had wronged him cruelly; his only revenge was to continue as if she had been a faithful wife, for she would not let him love her.

Dodo should never know, she should not even suspect. He would go on behaving to her as before, as far as lay in his power. He would do his utmost to make her contented, to make her less sorry—yes, less sorry—she married him.

Meanwhile Dodo and Jack were sitting before the fire in the smoking-room. He still retained Dodo's hand, and it lay unresistingly in his. Dodo was the first to speak.

"We must make the best of it, Jack," she said; "and you must help me. I cannot trust myself any longer. I used to be so sure of myself, so convinced that I could be happy. I blame myself for it, not him; but then, you see, I can't get rid of myself, and I can of him. Hence this plan. I have been a fool and a beast. And he, you know, he is the best of men. Poor, dear old boy. It isn't his fault, but it isn't mine. I should like to know who profits by this absurd arrangement. Why can't I love him? Why can't I even like him? Why can't I help hating him? Yes, Jack, it has come to that. God knows there is no one more sorry than I am about it. But this is only a mood. I daresay in half an hour's time I shall only feel angry with him, and not sorry at all. I wonder if this match was made in heaven. Oh, I am miserable."

Jack was really to be pitied more than Dodo. He knelt by her with her hand in his, feeling that he would have given his life without question to make her happy, but knowing that he had better give his life than do so. The struggle itself was over. He felt like a chain being pulled in opposite directions. He did not wrestle any longer; the two forces, he thought, were simply fighting it out over his rigid body. He wondered vaguely whether something would break, and, if so, what? But he did not dream for a moment of ever reconsidering his answer to Dodo. The question did not even present itself. So he knelt by her, still holding her hand, and waiting for her to speak again.

"You mustn't desert me, Jack," Dodo went on. "It is easier for Chesterford, as well as for me, that you should be with us often, and I believe it is easier for you too. If I never saw you at all, I believe the crash would come. I should leave Chesterford, not to come to you, for that can't be, but simply to get away."

"Ah, don't," said Jack, "don't go on talking about it like that. I can't do what you asked, you know that, simply because I love you and am Chesterford's friend. Think of your duty to him. Think, yes, think of our love for each other. Let it be something sacred, Dodo. Don't desecrate it. Help me not to desecrate it. Let it be our safeguard. It is better to have that, isn't it? than to think of going on living, as you must, without it. You said so yourself when you asked me to be with you often. To-night a deep joy has come into my life; let us keep it from disgrace. Ah, Dodo, thank God you love me."

"Yes, Jack, I believe I do," said Dodo. "And you are right; I always knew I should rise to the occasion if it was put forcibly before me. I believe I have an ideal—which I have never had before—something to respect and to keep very clean. Fancy me with an ideal! Mother wouldn't know me again—there never was such a thing in the house."

They were silent for a few minutes.

"But I must go to-morrow," said Jack, "as I settled to, by the disgusting early train. And the dressing-bell has sounded, and the ideal inexorably forbids us to be late for dinner, so I sha'n't see you alone again."

He pressed her hand and she rose.

"Poor little ideal," said Dodo. "I suppose it would endanger its life if you stopped, wouldn't it, Jack? It must live to grow up. Poor little ideal, what a hell of a time it will have when you're gone. Poor dear."

Dinner went off as usual. Dodo seemed to be in her ordinary spirits. Chesterford discussed parochial help with Mrs. Vivian. He glanced at Dodo occasionally through the little grove of orchids that separated them, but Dodo did not seem to notice. She ate a remarkably good dinner, and talked nonsense to Mr. Spencer who sat next her, and showed him how to construct a sea-sick passenger out of an orange, and smoked two cigarettes after the servants had left the room. Maud alone was ill at ease. She glanced apprehensively at Jack, as if she expected him to begin kissing Dodo's hand again, and, when he asked her casually where she had been since tea, she answered, "In the smoking-room—I mean the drawing-room." Jack merely raised his eyebrows, and remarked that he had been there himself, and did not remember seeing her.

In the drawing-room again Dodo was in the best spirits. She gave Spencer lessons as to how to whistle on his fingers, and sang a French song in a brilliant and somewhat broad manner. The ladies soon retired, as there was a meet early on the following morning, and, after they had gone, Jack went up to the smoking-room, leaving Chesterford to finish a letter in his study. Shortly afterwards the latter heard the sound of wheels outside, and a footman entered to tell him the carriage was ready.

Chesterford was writing when the man entered, and did not look up.

"I did not order the carriage," he said.

"Her ladyship ordered it for half-past ten," said the man. "She gave the order to me."

Still Lord Chesterford did not look up, and sat silent so long that the man spoke again.

"Shall I tell her ladyship it is round?" he asked. "I came to your lordship, as I understood her ladyship had gone upstairs."

"You did quite right," he said. "There has been a mistake; it will not be wanted. Don't disturb Lady Chesterford, or mention it to her."

"Very good, my lord."

He turned to leave the room, when Lord Chesterford stopped him again. He spoke slowly.

"Did Lady Chesterford give you any other orders?"

"She told me to see that Mr. Broxton's things were packed, my lord, as he would go away to-night. But she told me just before dinner that he wouldn't leave till the morning."

"Thanks," said Lord Chesterford. "That's all, I think. When is Mr. Broxton leaving?"

"By the early train to-morrow, my lord."

"Go up to the smoking-room and ask him to be so good as to come here a minute."

The man left the room, and gave his message. Jack wondered a little, but went down.

Lord Chesterford was standing with his back to the fire. He looked up when Jack entered. He seemed to find some difficulty in speaking.

"Jack, old boy," he said at last, "you and I have been friends a long time, and you will not mind my being frank. Can you honestly say that you are still a friend of mine?"

Jack advanced towards him.

"I thank God that I can," he said simply, and held out his hand.

He spoke without reflecting, for he did not know how much Chesterford knew. Of course, up to this moment, he had not been aware that he knew anything. But Chesterford's tone convinced him. But a moment afterwards he saw that he had made a mistake, and he hastened to correct it.

"I spoke at random," he said, "though I swear that what I said was true. I do not know on what grounds you put the question to me."

Lord Chesterford did not seem to be attending.

"But it was true?" he asked.

Jack felt in a horrible mess. If he attempted to explain, it would necessitate letting Chesterford know the whole business. He chose between the two evils, for he would not betray Dodo.

"Yes, it is true," he said.

Chesterford shook his hand.

"Forgive me for asking you, Jack," he said. "Then that's done with. But there is something more, something which is hard for me to say." He paused, and Jack noticed that he was crumpling a piece of paper he held in his hand into a tight hard ball. "Then—then Dodo is tired of me?"

Jack felt helpless and sick. He could not trust himself to speak.

"Isn't it so?" asked Chesterford again.

Jack for reply held out both his hands without speaking. There was something horrible in the sight of this strong man standing pale and trembling before him. In a moment Chesterford turned away, and stood warming his hands at the fire.

"I heard something I wasn't meant to hear," he said, "and I know as much as I wish to. It doesn't much matter exactly what has happened. You have told me you are still my friend, and I thank you for it. And Dodo—Dodo is tired of me. I can reconstruct as much as is necessary. You are going off to-morrow, aren't you? I sha'n't see you again. Good-bye, Jack; try to forget I ever mistrusted you. I must ask you to leave me; I've got some things to think over."

But Jack still lingered.

"Try to forgive Dodo," he said; "and forgive me for saying so, but don't be hard on her. It will only make things worse."

"Hard on her?" asked Chesterford. "Poor Dodo, it is hard on her enough without that. She shall never know that I know, if I can help. I am not going to tell you what I know either. If you feel wronged that I even asked you that question, I am sorry for it, but I had grounds, and I am not a jealous man. The whole thing has been an awful mistake. I knew it in July, but I shall not make it worse by telling Dodo."

Jack went out from his presence with a kind of awe. He did not care to know how Chesterford had found out, or how much. All other feelings were swallowed up in a vast pity for this poor man, whom no human aid could ever reach. The great fabric which his love had raised had been shattered hopelessly, and his love sat among its ruins and wept. It was all summed up in that short sentence, "Dodo is tired of me," and Jack knew that it was true. The whole business was hopeless. Dodo had betrayed him, and he knew it. He could no longer find a cold comfort in the thought that some day, if the difficult places could be tided over, she might grow to love him again. That was past. And yet he had only one thought, and that was for Dodo. "She shall never know I know it." Truly there is something divine in those men we thought most human.

Jack went to his room and thought it all over. He was horribly vexed with himself for having exculpated himself, but the point of Chesterford's question was quite clear, and there was only one answer to it. Chesterford obviously did mean to ask whether he had been guilty of the great act of disloyalty which Dodo had proposed, and on the whole he would reconstruct the story in his mind more faithfully than if he had answered anything else, or had refused to answer. But Jack very much doubted whether Chesterford would reconstruct the story at all. The details had evidently no interest for him. All that mattered was expressed in that one sentence, "Dodo is tired of me." Jack would have given his right hand to have been able to answer "No," or to have been able to warn Dodo; but he saw that there was nothing to be done. The smash had come, Chesterford had had a rude awakening. But his love was not dead, though it was stoned and beaten and outcast. With this in mind Jack took a sheet of paper from his writing-case, and wrote on it these words:—

"Do not desecrate it; let it help you to make an effort."

He addressed it to Dodo, and when he went downstairs the next morning he slipped it among the letters that were waiting for her. The footman told him she had gone hunting.

"Is Lord Chesterford up yet?" said Jack.

"Yes, sir; he went hunting too with her ladyship," replied the man.

14

Dodo was called that morning at six, and she felt in very good spirits. There was something exhilarating in the thought of a good gallop again. There had been frost for a week before, and hunting had been stopped, but Dodo meant to make up all arrears. And, on the whole, her interview with Jack had consoled her, and it had given her quite a new feeling of duty. Dodo always liked new things, at any rate till the varnish had rubbed off, and she quite realised that Jack was making a sacrifice to the same forbidding goddess.

"Well, I will make a sacrifice, too," she thought as she dressed, "and when I die I shall be St. Dodo. I don't think there ever was a saint Dodo before, or is it saintess? Anyhow, I am going to be very good. Jack really is right; it is the only thing to do. I should have felt horribly mean if I had gone off last night, and I daresay I should have had to go abroad, which would have been a nuisance. I wonder if Chesterford's coming. I shall make him, I think, and be very charming indeed. Westley, go and tap at the door of Lord Chesterford's room, and tell him he is coming hunting, and that I've ordered his horse, and send his man to him, and let us have breakfast at once for two instead of one."

Dodo arranged her hat and stood contemplating her own figure at a cheval glass. It really did make a charming picture, and Dodo gave two little steps on one side, holding her skirt up in her left hand.

> "Just look at that,
> Just look at this,
> I really think I'm not amiss,"

she hummed to herself. "Hurrah for a gallop."

She ran downstairs and made tea, and began breakfast. A moment afterwards she heard steps in the hall, and Chesterford entered. Dodo was not conscious of the least embarrassment, and determined to do her duty.

"Morning, old boy," she said, "you look as sleepy as a d. p. or dead pig. Look at my hat. It's a new hat, Chesterford, and is the joy of my heart. Isn't it sweet? Have some tea, and give me another kidney—two, I think. What happens to the sheep after they take its kidneys out? Do you suppose it dies? I wonder if they put india-rubber kidneys in. Kidneys do come from sheep, don't they? Or is there a kidney tree? Kidneys look like a sort of mushroom, and I suppose the bacon is the leaves, Kidnonia Baconiensis; now you're doing Latin, Chesterford, as you used to at Eton. I daresay you've forgotten what the Latin for kidneys is. I should like to have seen you at Eton, Chesterford. You must have been such a dear, chubby boy with blue eyes. You've got rather good eyes. I think I shall paint mine blue, and we shall have a nice little paragraph in the *Sportsman.* 'Extraördinary example of conjugal devotion. The beautiful and fascinating Lady C. (you know I am beautiful and fascinating, that's why you married me), the wife of the charming and manly Lord C. (you know you are charming and manly, or I shouldn't have married you, and where would you have been then? like Methusaleh when the candle went out), who lived not a hundred miles from the ancient city of Harchester,' etc. Now it's your turn to say something, I can't carry on a conversation alone. Besides, I've finished breakfast, and I shall sit by you and feed you. Don't take such large mouthfuls. That was nearly a whole kidney you put in then. You'll die of kidneys, and then people will think you had something wrong with your inside, but I shall put on your tombstone, 'Because he ate them two at a time.'"

Chesterford laughed. Dodo had not behaved like this for months. What did it all mean? But the events of the night before were too deeply branded on his memory to let him comfort himself very much. But anyhow it was charming to see Dodo like this again. And she shall never know.

"You'll choke if you laugh with five kidneys in your mouth," Dodo went on. "They'll get down into your lungs and bob about, and all your organs will get mixed up together, and you won't be able to play on them. I suppose Americans have American organs in their insides, which accounts for their squeaky voices. Now, have you finished? Oh, you really can't have any marmalade; put it in your pocket and eat it as you go along."

Dodo was surprised at the ease with which she could talk nonsense again. She abused herself for ever having let it drop. It really was much better than yawning and being bored. She had no idea how entertaining she was to herself. And Chesterford had lost his hang-dog look. He put her hat straight for her, and gave her a little kiss just as he used to. After all, things were not so bad.

It was a perfect morning. They left the house about a quarter to seven, and the world was beginning to wake again. There was a slight hoar-frost on the blades of grass that lined the road, and on the sprigs of bare hawthorn. In the east the sky was red with the coming day. Dodo sniffed the cool morning air with a sense of great satisfaction.

"Decidedly somebody washes the world every night," she said, "and those are the soapsuds which are still clinging to the grass. What nice clean soap, all in little white crystals and spikes. And oh, how good it smells! Look at those poor little devils of birds looking for their breakfast. Poor dears, I suppose they'll be dead when the spring comes. There are the hounds. Come on, Chesterford, they're just going to draw the far cover. It is a sensible plan beginning hunting by seven. You get five hours by lunch-time."

None of Dodo's worst enemies accused her of riding badly. She had a perfect seat, and that mysterious communication with her horse that seems nothing short of magical. "If you tell your horse to do a thing the right way," she used to say, "he does it. It is inevitable. The question is, 'Who is master?' as Humpty Dumpty said. But it isn't only master; you must make him enjoy it. You must make him feel friendly as well, or else he'll go over the fence right enough, but buck you off on the other side, as a kind of protest, and quite right too."

Dodo had a most enjoyable day's hunting, and returned home well pleased with herself and everybody else. She found Jack's note waiting for her. She read it thoughtfully, and said to herself, "He is quite right, and that is what I mean to do. My young ideal, I am teaching you how to shoot."

She took up a pen, meaning to write to him, but laid it down again. "No," she said, "I can do without that at present. I will keep that for my bad days. I suppose the bad days will come, and I won't use my remedies before I get the disease."

The days passed on. They went hunting every morning, and Dodo began to form very high hopes of her new child, as she called her ideal. The bad days did not seem to be the least imminent. Chesterford behaved almost like a lover again in the light of Dodo's new smiles. He kept his bad times to himself. They came in the evening usually when the others had gone to bed. He used to sit up late by himself over his study fire, thinking hopelessly of the day that had gone and the day that was to come. It was a constant struggle not to tell Dodo all he knew. He could scarcely believe that he had heard what Maud had said, or that he ever had had that interview with Jack. He could not reconcile these things with Dodo's altered behaviour, and he gave it up. Dodo was tired of him, and he knew that he loved her more than ever. A more delicately-strung mind might almost have given way under the hourly struggle, but it is the fate of a healthy simple man to be capable of more continued suffering than one more highly developed. The latter breaks down, or he gets numbed with the pain; but Chesterford went on living under the slow ache, and his suffering grew no less. But through it all he looked back with deep gratitude to the chance that had sent Dodo in his way. He did not grow bitter, and realised in the midst of his suffering how happy he had been. He had only one strong wish. "Oh, God," he cried, "give me her back for one moment! Let her be sorry just once for my sake."

But there is a limit set to human misery, and the end had nearly come.

It was about a fortnight after Jack had gone. Maud and Mr. Spencer had gone too, but Mrs. Vivian was with them still. Dodo had more than once thought of telling her what had happened, but she could not manage it. When Mrs. Vivian had spoken of going, Dodo entreated her to stop, for she had a great fear of being left alone with Chesterford.

They had been out hunting, and Dodo had got home first. It was about three in the afternoon, and it had begun to snow. She had had lunch, and was sitting in the morning-room in a drowsy frame of mind. She was wondering whether Chesterford had returned, and whether he would come up and see her, and whether she was not too lazy to exert herself. She heard a carriage come slowly up the drive, and did not feel interested enough to look out of the window. She was sitting with her shoes off warming her feet at the fire, with a novel in her lap, which she was not reading, and a cigarette in her hand. She heard the opening and shutting of doors, and slow steps on the stairs. Then the door opened and Mrs. Vivian came in.

Dodo had seen that look in her face once before, when she was riding in the Park with Jack, and a fearful certainty came upon her.

She got up and turned towards her.

"Is he dead?" she asked.

Mrs. Vivian drew her back into her seat.

"I will tell you all," she said. "He has had a dangerous fall hunting, and it is very serious. The doctors are with him. There is some internal injury, and he is to have an operation. It is the only chance of saving his life, and even then it is a very slender one. He is quite conscious, and asked me to tell you. You will not be able to see him for half an hour. The operation is going on now."

Dodo sat perfectly still. She did not speak a word; she scarcely even thought anything. Everything seemed to be a horrible blank to her.

"Ah God, ah God!" she burst out at last. "Can't I do anything to

help? I would give my right hand to help him. It is all too horrible.
To think that I—" She walked up and down the room, and then suddenly opened the door and went downstairs. She paced up and down
the drawing-room, paused a moment, and went into his study. His
papers were lying about in confusion on the table, but on the top
was a guide-book to the Riviera. Dodo remembered his buying this
at Mentone on their wedding-tour, and conscientiously walking about
the town sight-seeing. She sat down in his chair and took it up. She
remembered also that he had bought her that day a new volume of
poems which had just come out, and had read to her out of it. There
was in it a poem called "Paris and Helen." He had read that among
others, and had said to her, as they were being rowed back to the
yacht again that evening, "That is you and I, Dodo, going home."

On the fly-leaf of the guide-book he had written it out, and, as
she sat there now, Dodo read it.

> As o'er the swelling tides we slip
> That know not wave nor foam,
> Behold the helmsman of our ship,
>   Love leads us safely home.
>
> His ministers around us move
> To aid the westering breeze,
> He leads us softly home, my love,
>   Across the shining seas.
>
> My golden Helen, day and night
> Love's light is o'er us flung,
> Each hour for us is infinite,
>   And all the world is young.
>
> There is none else but thou and I
> Beneath the heaven's high dome,
> Love's ministers around us fly,
>   Love leads us safely home.

Dodo buried her face in her hands with a low cry. "I have been
cruel and wicked," she sobbed to herself. "I have despised the best
that any man could ever give me, and I can never make him amends.
I will tell him all. I will ask him to forgive me. Oh, poor Chesterford,
poor Chesterford!"

She sat there sobbing in complete misery. She saw, as she had never
seen before, the greatness of his love for her, and her wretched, miserable return for his gift.

"It is all over; I know he will die," she sobbed. "Supposing he does
not know me—supposing he dies before I can tell him. Oh, my husband,
my husband, live to forgive me!"

She was roused by a touch on her shoulder. Mrs. Vivian stood by
her.

"You must be quick, Dodo," she said. "There is not much time."

Dodo did not answer her, but went upstairs. Before the bedroom door she stopped.

"I must speak to him alone," she said. "Send them all out."

"They have gone into the dressing-room," said Mrs. Vivian; "he is alone."

Dodo stayed no longer, but went in.

He was lying facing the door, and the shadow of death was on his face. But he recognised Dodo, and smiled and held out his hand.

Dodo ran to the bedside and knelt by it.

"Oh, Chesterford," she sobbed, "I have wronged you cruelly, and I can never make it up. I will tell you all."

"There is no need," said he; "I knew it all along."

Dodo raised her head.

"You knew it all?" she asked.

"Yes, dear," he said; "it was by accident that I knew it."

"And you behaved to me as usual," said Dodo.

"Yes, my darling," said he; "you wouldn't have had me beat you, would you? Don't speak of it—there is not much time."

"Ah, forgive me, forgive me!" she cried. "How could I have done it?"

"It was not a case of forgiving," he said. "You are you, you are Dodo. My darling, there is not time to say much. You have been very good to me, and have given me more happiness than I ever thought I could have had."

"Chesterford! Chesterford!" cried Dodo pleadingly.

"Yes, darling," he answered; "my own wife. Dodo, I shall see the boy soon, and we will wait for you together. You will be mine again then. There shall be no more parting."

Dodo could not answer him. She could only press his hand and kiss his lips, which were growing very white.

It was becoming a fearful effort for him to speak. The words came slowly with long pauses.

"There is one more thing," he said. "You must marry Jack. You must make him very happy—as you have made me."

"Ah, don't say that," said Dodo brokenly; "don't cut me to the heart."

"My darling," he said, "my sweet own wife, I am so glad you told me. It has cleared up the only cloud. I wondered whether you would tell me. I prayed God you might, and He has granted it me. Good-bye, my own darling, good-bye."

Dodo lay in his arms, and kissed him passionately.

"Good-bye, dear," she sobbed.

He half raised himself in bed.

"Ah, my Dodo, my sweet wife," he said.

Then he fell back and lay very still.

How long Dodo remained there she did not know. She remembered Mrs. Vivian coming in and raising her gently, and they left the darkened room together.

15

Picture to yourself, or let me try to picture for you, a long, low, rambling house, covering a quite unnecessary area of ground, with many gables, tall, red-brick chimneys, unexpected corners, and little bow windows looking out from narrow turrets—a house that looks as if it had grown, rather than been designed and built. It began obviously with that little grey stone section, which seems to consist of small rooms with mullion windows, over which the ivy has asserted so supreme a dominion. The next occupant had been a man who knew how to make himself comfortable, but did not care in the least what sort of appearance his additions would wear to the world at large; to him we may assign that uncompromising straight wing which projects to the right of the little core of grey stone. Then came a series of attempts to screen the puritanical ugliness of the offending block. Some one ran up two little turrets at one end, and a clock tower in the middle; one side of it was made the main entrance of the house, and two red-tiled lines of building were built at right angles to it to form a three-sided quadrangle, and the carriage drive was brought up in a wide sweep to the door, and a sun-dial was planted down in the grass plot in the middle, in such a way that the sun could only peep at it for an hour or two every day, owing to the line of building which sheltered it on every side except the north. So the old house went on growing, and got more incongruous and more delightful with every addition.

The garden has had to take care of itself under such circumstances, and if the house has been pushing it back in one place, it has wormed itself in at another, and queer little lawns with flower beds of old-fashioned, sweet-smelling plants have crept in where you least expect them. This particular garden has always seemed to me the ideal of what a garden should be. It is made to sit in, to smoke in, to think in, to do nothing in. A wavy, irregular lawn forbids the possibility of tennis, or any game that implies exertion or skill, and it is the home of sweet smells, bright colour, and chuckling birds. There are long borders of mignonette, wallflowers and hollyhocks, and many old-fashioned flowers, which are going the way of all old fashions. London pride, with its delicate spirals and star-like blossoms, and the red drooping velvet of love-lies-a-bleeding. The thump of tennis balls, the flying horrors of ring-goal, even the clash of croquet is tabooed in this sacred spot. Down below, indeed, beyond that thick privet hedge, you may find, if you wish, a smooth, well-kept piece of grass, where, even now—if we may judge from white figures that cross the little square, where a swinging iron gate seems to remonstrate hastily and ill-temperedly with those who leave these reflective shades for the glare and publicity of tennis—a game seems to be in progress. If you had exploring tendencies in your nature, and had happened to find yourself, on the afternoon of which I propose to speak, in this delightful garden, you would sooner or later have wandered into a low-lying grassy basin, shut in on three sides by banks of bushy rose-trees. The faint, delicate smell of their pale fragrance would have led you there, or, perhaps, the light trickling of a fountain, now nearly summer dry. Perhaps the exploring tendency would account for your discovery. There, lying back in a basket-chair, with a half-read letter in her hand, and an accusing tennis racquet by her side, you would have found Edith Staines. She had waited after lunch to get her letters, and going out, meaning to join the others, she had found something among them that interested her, and she was reading a certain letter through a second time when you broke in upon her. After a few minutes she folded it up, put it back in the envelope, and sat still, thinking. "So she's going to marry him," she said half aloud, and she took up her racquet and went down to the tennis courts.

Ten days ago she had come down to stay with Miss Grantham, at the end of the London season. Miss Grantham's father was a somewhat florid baronet of fifty years of age. He had six feet of height, a cheerful, high-coloured face, and a moustache, which he was just conscious had military suggestions about it—though he had never been in the army—which was beginning to grow grey. His wife had been a lovely woman, half Spanish by birth, with that peculiarly crisp pronunciation that English people so seldom possess, and which is almost as charming to hear as a child's first conscious grasp of new words. She dressed remarkably well; her reading chiefly consisted of the *Morning Post*, French novels, and small books of morbid poetry, which seemed to her very *chic*, and she was worldly to the tips of her delicate fingers. She had no accomplishments of any sort, except a great knowledge of foreign languages. She argued, with much reason, that you could get other people to do your accomplishments for you. "Why should I worry myself with playing scales?" she said. "I can hire some poor wretch" (she never could quite manage the English "r") "to play to me by the hour. He will play much better than I ever should, and it is a form of charity as well."

Edith had made great friends with her, and disagreed with her on every topic under the sun. Lady Grantham admired Edith's vivacity, though her own line was serene elegance, and respected her success. Success was the one accomplishment that she really looked up to (partly, perhaps, because she felt she had such a large measure of it herself), and no one could deny that Edith was successful. She had enough broadness of view to admire success in any line, and would have had a vague sense of satisfaction in accepting the arm of the best crossing-sweeper in London to take her in to dinner. She lived in a leonine atmosphere, and if you did not happen to meet a particular lion at her house, it was because "he was here on Monday, or is coming on Wednesday"; at any rate, not because he had not been asked.

Edith, however, felt thoroughly pleased with her quarters. She had hinted once that she had to go the day after to-morrow, but Nora Grantham had declined to argue the question. "You're only going home to do your music," she said. "We've got quite as good a piano here as you have, and we leave you entirely to your own devices. Besides, you're mother's lion just now—isn't she, mother?—and you're not going to get out of the menagerie just yet. There's going to be a big feeding-time next week, and you will have to roar." Edith's remark about the necessity of going had been dictated only by a sense of duty, in order to give her hosts an opportunity of getting rid of her if they wished, and she was quite content to stop. She strolled down across the lawn to the tennis courts in a thoughtful frame of mind, and met Miss Grantham, who was coming to look for her.

"Where have you been, Edith?" she said. "They're all clamouring for you. Mother is sitting in the summer-house wondering why anybody wants to play tennis. She says none of them will ever be as good as Cracklin, and he's a cad."

"Grantie," said Edith, "Dodo's engaged."

"Oh, dear, yes," said Miss Grantham. "I knew she would be. How delightful. Jack's got his reward at last. May I tell everyone? How funny that she should marry a Lord Chesterford twice. It was so convenient that the first one shouldn't have had any brothers, and Dodo won't have to change her visiting cards, or have new handkerchiefs or anything. What a contrast, though!"

"No, it's private at present," said Edith. "Dodo has just written to me; she told me I might tell you. Do you altogether like it?"

"Of course I do," said Miss Grantham. "Only I should like to marry Jack myself. I wonder if he asked Dodo, or if Dodo asked him."

"I suppose it was inevitable," said Edith. "Dodo says that Chesterford's last words to her were that she should marry Jack."

"That was so sweet of him," murmured Miss Grantham. "He was very sweet and dear and remembering, wasn't he?"

Edith was still grave and doubtful.

"I'm sure there was nearly a crash," she said. "Do you remember the Brettons' ball? Chesterford didn't like that, and they quarrelled, I know, next morning."

"Oh, *how* interesting," said Miss Grantham. "But Dodo was quite right to go, I think. She was dreadfully bored, and she will not stand being bored. She might have done something much worse."

"It seems to be imperatively necessary for Dodo to do something unexpected," said Edith. "I wonder, oh, I wonder—Jack will be very happy for a time," she added inconsequently.

Edith's coming was the signal for serious play to begin. She entirely declined to play except with people who considered it, for the time being, the most important thing in the world, and naturally she played well.

A young man, of military appearance on a small scale, was sitting by Lady Grantham in the tent, and entertaining her with somewhat unfledged remarks.

"Miss Staines does play so arfly well, doesn't she?" he was saying. "Look at that stroke, perfectly rippin' you know, what?"

Mr. Featherstone had a habit of finishing all his sentences with "what?" He pronounced it to rhyme with heart.

Lady Grantham was reading Loti's book of pity and death. It answered the double purpose of being French and morbid.

"What book have you got hold of there?" continued Featherstone. "It's an awful bore reading books, dontcherthink, what? I wish one could get a feller to read them for me, and then tell one about them."

"I rather enjoy some books," said Lady Grantham. "This, for instance, is a good one," and she held the book towards him.

"Oh, that's French, isn't it?" remarked Featherstone. "I did French at school; don't know a word now. It's an arful bore having to learn French, isn't it? Couldn't I get a feller to learn it for me?"

Lady Grantham reflected.

"I daresay you could," she replied. "You might get your man—tiger—how do you call him?—to learn it. It's capable of comprehension to the lowest intellect," she added crisply.

"Oh, come, Lady Grantham," he replied, "you don't think so badly of me as that, do you?"

Lady Grantham was seized with a momentary desire to run her parasol through his body, provided it could be done languidly and without effort. Her daughter had come up, and sat down in a low chair by her. Featherstone was devoting the whole of his great mind to the end of his moustache.

"Nora," she said, quietly, "this little man must be taken away. I can't quite manage him. Tell him to go and play about."

"Dear mother," she replied, "bear him a little longer. He can't play about by himself."

Lady Grantham got gently up from her chair, and thrust an exquisite little silver paper-knife between the leaves of her book.

"I think I will ask you to take my chair across to that tree opposite," she said to him, without looking at him.

He followed her, dragging the chair after him. Halfway across the lawn they met a footman bringing tea down into the ground.

"Take the chair," she said. Then she turned to her little man. "Many thanks. I won't detain you," she said, with a sweet smile. "So good of you to have come here this afternoon."

Featherstone was impenetrable. He lounged back, if so small a thing can be said to lounge, and sat down again by Miss Grantham.

"Fascinatin' woman your mother is," he said. "Arfly clever, isn't she? What? Knows French and that sort of thing. I can always get along all right in France. If you only swear at the waiters they understand what you want all right, you know."

Two or three other fresh arrivals made it possible for another set to be started, and Mr. Featherstone was induced to play, in spite of his protestations that he had quite given up tennis for polo. Lady Grantham finished her Loti, and moved back to the tea-table, where Edith was sitting, fanning herself with a cabbage leaf, and receiving homage on the score of her tennis-playing. Lady Grantham did not offer to give anybody any tea; she supposed they would take it when they wanted it, but she wished someone would give her a cup.

"What's the name of the little man and his moustache?" she asked Edith, indicating Mr. Featherstone, who was performing wild antics in the next court.

Edith informed her.

"How did he get here?" demanded Lady Grantham.

"Oh, he's a friend of mine. I think he came to see me," replied Edith. "He lives somewhere about. I suppose you find him rather trying. It doesn't matter; he's of no consequence."

"My dear Edith, between your sporting curate, and your German conductor, and your Roman Catholic curé, and this man, one's life isn't safe."

"You won't see the good side of those sort of people," said Edith. "If they've got rather overwhelming manners, and aren't as silent and bored as you think young men ought to be, you think they're utter outsiders."

"I only want to know if there are any more of that sort going to turn up. Think of the positions you put me in! When I went into the drawing-room yesterday, for instance, before lunch, I find a Roman Catholic priest there, who puts up two fingers at me, and says 'Benedicite.' "

Edith lay back in her chair and laughed.

"How I should like to have seen you! Did you think he was saying grace, or did you tell him not to be insolent?"

"I behaved with admirable moderation," said Lady Grantham. "I even prepared to be nice to him. But he had sudden misgivings, and said, 'I beg your pardon, I thought you were Miss Staines.' I saw I was not wanted, and retreated. That is not all. Bob told me that I had to take a curate in to dinner last night, and asked me not to frighten him. I suppose he thought I wanted to say 'Bo,' or howl at him. The curate tried me. I sat down when we got to the table, and he turned to me and said, 'I beg your pardon'—they all beg my pardon—'but I'm going to say grace.' Then I prepared myself to talk night schools and district visiting; but he turned on me, and asked what I thought of Orme's chances for the St. Leger."

"Oh, dear! oh, dear!" cried Edith; "he told me afterwards that you seemed a very serious lady."

"I didn't intend to encourage that," continued Lady Grantham; "so I held on to district visiting. We shook our heads together over dissent in Wales. We split over Calvinism—who was Calvin? We renounced society; and I was going to work him a pair of slippers. We were very edifying. Then he sang comic songs in the drawing-room, and discussed the methods of cheating at baccarat. I was a dead failure."

"Anyhow, you're a serious lady," said Edith.

"That young man will come to a bad end," said Lady Grantham; "so will your German conductor. He ordered beer in the middle of the morning, to-day—the second footman will certainly give notice—and he smoked a little clay pipe after dinner in the dining-room. Then this afternoon comes this other friend of yours. He says, 'Arfly rippin' what.' "

"He said you were arfly fascinatin' what," interpolated Miss Grantham, "when you went away to read your book. You were very rude to him."

Sir Robert Grantham had joined the party. He was a great hand at adapting his conversation to his audience, and making everyone conscious that they ought to feel quite at home. He recounted at some length a series of tennis matches which he had taken part in a few years ago. A strained elbow had spoiled his chances of winning, but the games were most exciting, and it was generally agreed at the time that the form of the players was quite first-class. He talked about Wagner and counterpoint to Edith. He asked his vicar abstruse questions on the evidence of the immortality of the soul after death; he discussed agriculture and farming with tenants, to whom he always said "thank ye," instead of "thank you," in order that they might feel quite at their ease; he lamented the want of physique in the English army to Mr. Featherstone, who was very short, and declared that the average height of Englishmen was only five feet four. As he said this he drew himself up, and made it quite obvious that he himself was six feet high, and broad in proportion.

A few more cups of tea were drunk, and a few more sets played, and the party dispersed. Edith was the only guest in the house, and she and Frank, the Oxford son, stopped behind to play a game or two more before dinner. Lady Grantham and Nora strolled up through the garden towards the house, while Sir Robert remained on the ground, and mingled advice, criticism, and approbation to the tennis players; Frank's back-handed stroke, he thought, was not as good as it might be, and Edith could certainly put half fifteen on to her game if judiciously coached. Neither of the players volleyed as well as himself, but volleying was his strong point, and they must not be discouraged. Frank's attitude to his father was that of undisguised amusement; but he found him very entertaining.

They were all rather late for dinner, and Lady Grantham was waiting for them in the drawing-room. Frank and his father were down before Edith, and Lady Grantham was making remarks on their personal appearance.

"You look very hot and red," she was saying to her son, "and I really wish you would brush your hair better. I don't know what young men are coming to, they seem to think that everything is to be kept waiting for them."

Frank's attitude was one of serene indifference.

"Go on, go on," he said; "I don't mind."

Edith was five minutes later. Lady Grantham remarked on the importance of being in time for dinner, and hoped they wouldn't all die from going to bed too soon afterwards. Frank apologised for his mother.

"Don't mind her, Miss Staines," he said, "they're only her foreign manners. She doesn't know how to behave. It's all right. I'm going to take you in, mother. Are we going to have grouse?"

That evening Miss Grantham and Edith "talked Dodo," as the latter called it, till the small hours.

She produced Dodo's letter, and read extracts.

"Of course, we sha'n't be married till after next November," wrote Dodo. "Jack wouldn't hear of it, and it would seem very unfeeling. Don't you think so? It will be odd going back to Winston again. Mind you come and stay with us at Easter."

"I wonder if Dodo ever thinks with regret of anything or anybody," said Edith. "Imagine writing like that—asking me if I shouldn't think it unfeeling."

"Oh, but she says she would think it unfeeling," said Miss Grantham. "That's so sweet and remembering of her."

"But don't you see," said Edith, "she evidently thinks it is so good of her to have feelings about it at all. She might as well call attention to the fact that she always puts her shoes and stockings on to go to church."

"There's a lot of women who would marry again before a year was out if it wasn't for convention," said Miss Grantham.

"That's probably the case with Dodo," remarked Edith. "Dodo doesn't care one pin for the memory of that man. She knows it, and she knows I know it. Why does she say that sort of thing to me? He was a good man, too, and I'm not sure that he wasn't great. Chesterford detested me, but I recognised him."

"Oh, I don't think he was great," said Miss Grantham. "Didn't he always strike you as a little stupid?"

"I prefer stupid people," declared Edith roundly. "They are so restful. They're like nice, sweet, white bread; they quench your hunger as well as *paté de foie gras,* and they are much better for you."

"I think they make you just a little thirsty," remarked Miss Grantham. "I should have said they were more like cracknels. Besides, do you think that it's an advantage to associate with people who are good for you? It produces a sort of rabies in me. I want to bite them."

"You like making yourself out worse than you are, Grantie," said Edith.

"I think you like making Dodo out worse than she is," returned Nora. "I always used to think you were very fond of her."

"I am fond of her," said Edith; "that's why I'm dissatisfied with her."

"What a curious way of showing your affection," said Miss Grantham. "I love Dodo, and if I was a man I should like to marry her."

"Dodo is too dramatic," said Edith. "She never gets off the stage; and sometimes she plays to the gallery, and then the stalls say, 'How cheap she's making herself.' She has the elements of a low comedian about her."

"And the airs of a tragedy queen, I suppose," added Miss Grantham.

"Exactly," said Edith; "and the consequence is that she is a burlesque sometimes. She is her own parody."

"Darling Dodo," said Grantie, with feeling. "I *do* want to see her again."

"All her conduct after his death," continued Edith, "that was the tragedy queen; she shut herself up in that great house, quite alone, for two months, and went to church with a large prayer-book every morning at eight. But it was burlesque all the same. Dodo isn't sorry like that. The gallery yelled with applause."

"I thought it was so sweet of her," murmured Grantie. "I suppose I'm gallery too."

"Then she went abroad," continued Edith, "and sat down and wept by the waters of Aix. But she soon took down her harp. She gave banjo parties on the lake, and sang coster songs."

"Mrs. Vane told me she recovered her spirits wonderfully at Aix," remarked Miss Grantham.

"And played baccarat, and recovered other people's money," pursued Edith. "If she'd taken the first train for Aix after the funeral, I should have respected her."

"Oh, that would have been horrid," said Miss Grantham; "besides, it wouldn't have been the season."

"That's true," said Edith. "Dodo probably remembered that."

"Oh, you sha'n't abuse Dodo any more," said Miss Grantham. "I think it's perfectly horrid of you. Go and play me something."

Perhaps the thought of Chesterford was in Edith's mind as she sat down to the piano, for she played a piece of Mozart's "Requiem," which is the saddest music in the world.

Miss Grantham shivered a little. The long wailing notes struck some chord within her, which disturbed her peace of mind.

"What a dismal thing," she said, when Edith had finished. "You make me feel like Sunday evening after a country church."

Edith stood looking out of the window. The moon was up, and the great stars were wheeling in their courses through the infinite vault. A nightingale was singing loud in the trees, and the little mysterious noises of night stole about among the bushes. As Edith thought of Chesterford she remembered how the Greeks mistook the passionate song of the bird for the lament of the dead, and it did not seem strange to her. For love sometimes goes hand-in-hand with death.

She turned back into the room again.

"God forgive her," she said, "if we cannot."

"I'm not going to bed with that requiem in my ears," said Miss Grantham. "I should dream of hearses."

Edith went to the piano, and broke into a quick, rippling movement. Miss Grantham listened, and felt she ought to know what it was.

"What is it?" she said, when Edith had finished.

"It is the scherzo from the 'Dodo Symphony,'" she said. "I composed it two years ago at Winston."

16

Dodo had written to Edith from Zermatt, where she was enjoying herself amazingly. Mrs. Vane was there, and Mr. and Mrs. Algernon Spencer, and Prince Waldenech and Jack. As there would have
been some natural confusion in the hotel if Dodo had called herself
Lady Chesterford, when Lord Chesterford was also there, she settled
to be called Miss Vane. This tickled Prince Waldenech enormously;
it seemed to him a capital joke.

Dodo was sitting in the verandah of the hotel one afternoon, drinking
black coffee and smoking cigarettes. Half the hotel were scandalised
at her, and usually referred to her as "that Miss Vane"; the other
half adored her, and went expeditions with her, and took minor parts
in her theatricals, and generally played universal second fiddle.

Dodo enjoyed this sort of life. There was in her an undeveloped
germ of simplicity, that found pleasure in watching the slow-footed
cows driven home from the pastures, in sitting with Jack—regardless
of her assumed name—in the crocus-studded meadows, or by the side
of the swirling glacier-fed stream that makes the valley melodious.
She argued, with great reason, that she had already shocked all the
people that were going to be shocked so much that it didn't matter
what she did; while the other contingent, who were not going to be
shocked, were not going to be shocked. "Everyone must either be
shocked or not shocked," she said, "and they're that already. That's
why Prince Waldenech and I are going for a moonlight walk next
week when the moon comes back."

Dodo had made great friends with the Prince's half-sister, a Russian
on her mother's side, and she was reading her extracts out of her
unwritten book of the *Philosophy of Life,* an interesting work, which
varied considerably according to Dodo's mood. Just now it suited Dodo
to be in love with life.

"You are a Russian by nature and sympathy, my dear Princess,"
she was saying, "and you are therefore in a continual state of complete
boredom. You think you are bored here, because it is not Paris; in
Paris you are quite as much bored with all your *fêtes,* and dances, and
parties as you are here. I tell you frankly you are wrong. Why don't
you come and sit in the grass, and look at the crocuses, and throw
stones into the stream like me."

The Princess stretched out a delicate arm.

"I don't think I ever threw a stone in my life," she said dubiously.
"Would it amuse me, do you think?"

"Not at first," said Dodo; "and you will never be amused at all if you think about it."

"What am I to think about then?" she asked.

"You must think about the stone," said Dodo decisively, "you must think about the crocuses, you must think about the cows."

"It's all so new to me," remarked the Princess. "We never think about cows in Russia."

"That's just what I'm saying," said Dodo. "You must get out of yourself. Anything does to think about, and nobody is bored unless they think about being bored. When one has the whole world to choose from, and only one subject in it that can make one feel bored, it really shows a want of resource to think about that. Then you ought to take walks and make yourself tired."

The Princess cast a vague eye on the Matterhorn.

"That sort of horror?" she asked.

"No, you needn't begin with the Matterhorn," said Dodo, laughing. "Go to the glaciers, and get rather cold and wet. Boredom is chiefly physical."

"I'm sure being cold and wet would bore me frightfully," she said.

"No, no—a big no," cried Dodo. "No one is ever bored unless they are comfortable. That's the great principle. There isn't time for it. You cannot be bored and something else at the same time. Being comfortable doesn't count; that's our normal condition. But you needn't be uncomfortable in order to be bored. It's very comfortable sitting here with you, and I'm not the least bored. I should poison myself if I were bored. I can't think why you don't."

"I will do anything you recommend," said the Princess placidly. "You are the only woman I know who never appears to be bored. I wonder if my husband would bore you. He is very big, and very good, and he eats a large breakfast, and looks after his serfs. He bores me to extinction. He would wear black for ten years if I poisoned myself."

A shade of something passed over Dodo's face. It might have been regret, or stifled remembrance, or a sudden twinge of pain, and it lasted an appreciable fraction of a second.

"I can imagine being bored with that kind of man," she said in a moment.

The Princess was lying back in her chair, and did not notice a curious hardness in Dodo's voice.

"I should so like to introduce you to him," said she. "I should like to shut you up with him for a month at our place on the Volga. It snows a good deal there, and he goes out in the snow and shoots animals, and comes back in the evening with a red face, and tells me all about it. It is very entertaining, but a trifle monotonous. He does not know English, nor German, nor French. He laughs very loud. He is devoted to me. Do go and stay with him. I think I'll join you when you've been there three weeks. He is quite safe. I shall not be afraid. He writes to me every day, and suggests that he should join me here."

Dodo shifted her position and looked up at the Matterhorn.

"Yes," she said. "I should certainly be bored with him, but I'm not sure that I would show it."

"He wouldn't like you at all," continued the Princess. "He would think you loud. That is so odd. He thinks it unfeminine to smoke. He has great ideas about the position of women. He gave me a book of private devotions bound in the parchment from a bear he had shot on my last birthday."

Dodo laughed.

"I'm sure you need not be bored with him," she said. "He must have a strong vein of unconscious humour about him."

"I'm quite unconscious of it," said the Princess. "You cannot form the slightest idea of what he's like till you see him. I almost feel inclined to tell him to come here."

"Ah, but you Russian women have such liberty," said Dodo. "You can tell your husband not to expect to see you again for three months. We can't do that. An English husband and wife are like two Siamese twins. Until about ten years ago they used to enter the drawing-room, when they were going out to dinner, arm-in-arm."

"That's very bourgeois," said the Princess. "You are rather a bourgeois race. You are very hearty, and pleased to see one, and all that. There's Lord Chesterford. You're a great friend of his, aren't you? He looks very distinguished. I should say he was usually bored."

"He was my husband's first cousin," said Dodo. Princess Alexandrina of course knew that Miss Vane was a widow. "I was always an old friend of his—as long as I can remember, that's to say. Jack and I are going up towards the Riffel to watch the sunset. Come with us."

"I think I'll see the sunset from here," she said. "You're going up a hill, I suppose?"

"Oh, but you can't see it from here," said Dodo. "That great mass of mountain is in the way."

The Princess considered.

"I don't think I want to see the sunset after all," she said. "I've just found the *Kreutzer Sonata*. I've been rural enough for one day, and I want a breath of civilised air. Do you know, I never feel bored when you are talking to me."

"Oh, that's part of my charm, isn't it?" said Dodo to Jack, who had lounged up to where they were sitting.

"Dodo's been lecturing me, Lord Chesterford," said the Princess. "Does she ever lecture you?"

"She gave me quite a long lecture once," said he. "She recommended me to live in a cathedral town."

"A cathedral town," said the Princess. "That's something fearful, isn't it? Why did you tell him to do that?" she said.

"I think it was a mistake," said Dodo. "Anyhow, Jack didn't take my advice. I shouldn't recommend him to do it now, but he has a perfect genius for being domestic. Everyone is very domestic in cathedral towns. They all dine at seven and breakfast at a quarter past eight—next morning, you understand. That quarter past is delightful. But Jack said he didn't want to score small successes," she added, employing a figure grammatically known as "hiatus."

"My husband is very domestic," said the Princess. "But he isn't a bit like Lord Chesterford. He would like to live with me in a little house in the country, and never have anyone to stay with us. That would be so cheerful during the winter months."

"Jack, would you like to live with your wife in a little house in the country?" demanded Dodo.

"I don't think I should ever marry a woman who wanted to," remarked Jack, meeting Dodo's glance.

"Imagine two people really liking each other better than all the rest of the world," said the Princess, "and living on milk, and love, and wild roses, and fresh eggs! I can't bear fresh eggs."

"My egg this morning wasn't at all fresh," said Dodo. "I wish I'd thought of sending it to your room."

"Would you never get tired of your wife, don't you think," continued the Princess, "if you shut yourselves up in the country? Supposing she wished to pick roses when you wanted to play lawn tennis?"

"Oh, Jack, it wouldn't do," said Dodo. "You'd make her play lawn tennis."

"My husband and I never thought of playing lawn tennis," said the Princess. "I shall try that when we meet next. It's very amusing, isn't it?"

"It makes you die of laughing," said Dodo, solemnly. "Come, Jack, we're going to see the sunset. Good-bye, dear. Go and play with your maid. She can go out of the room while you think of something, and then come in and guess what you've thought of."

Jack and Dodo strolled up through the sweet-smelling meadows towards the Riffelberg. A cool breeze was streaming down from the "furrow cloven alls" of the glacier, heavy with the clean smell of pine woods and summer flowers, and thick with a hundred mingling sounds. The cows were being driven homewards, and the faint sounds of bells were carried down to them from the green heights above. Now and then they passed a herd of goats, still nibbling anxiously at the wayside grass, followed by some small ragged shepherd, who brushed his long hair away from his eyes to get a better look at this dazzling, fair-skinned woman, who evidently belonged to quite another order of beings from his wrinkled, early-old mother. One of them held out to Dodo a wilted little bunch of flowers, crumpled with much handling, but she did not seem to notice him. After they had passed he tossed them away, and ran off after his straying flock. Southwards, high above them, stretched the long lines of snow spread out under the feet of the Matterhorn, which sat like some huge sphinx, unapproachable, remote. Just below lay the village, sleeping in the last rays of the sun, which shone warmly on the red, weathered planks. Light blue smoke curled slowly up from the shingled roofs, and streamed gently down the valley in a thin, transparent haze.

"Decidedly it's a very nice world," said Dodo. "I'm so glad I wasn't born a Russian. The Princess never enjoys anything at all, except telling one how bored she is. But she's very amusing, and I gave her a great deal of good advice."

"What have you been telling her to do?" asked Jack.

"Oh, anything. I recommended her to sit in the meadows, and throw stones and get her feet wet. It's not affectation at all in her, she really is hopelessly bored. It's as easy for her to be bored as for me not to be. Jack, what will you do to me if I get bored when we're married?"

"I shall tell you to throw stones," said he.

"As long as you don't look at me reproachfully," said Dodo, "I sha'n't mind. Oh, look at the Matterhorn. Isn't it big?"

"I don't like it," said Jack; "it always looks as if it was taking notice, and reflecting how dreadfully small one is."

"I used to think Vivy was like that," said Dodo. "She was very good to me once or twice. I wonder what I shall be like when I'm middle-aged. I can't bear the thought of getting old, but that won't stop it. I don't want to sit by the fire and purr. I don't think I could do it."

"One won't get old all of a sudden, though," said Jack; "that's a great consideration. The change will come so gradually that one won't know it."

"Ah, don't," said Dodo quickly. "It's like dying by inches, losing hold of life gradually. It won't come to me like that. I shall wake up some morning and find I'm not young any more."

"Well, it won't come yet," said Jack with sympathy.

"Well, I'm not going to bother my head about it," said Dodo, "there isn't time. There's Maud and her little Spencer. He's a dear little man, and he ought to be put in a band-box with some pink cotton-wool, and taken out every Sunday morning."

Dodo whistled shrilly on her fingers to attract their attention.

Mr. Spencer had been gathering flowers and putting them into a neat, little tin box, which he slung over his shoulders. He was dressed in a Norfolk jacket carefully buttoned round his waist, with knicker-bockers and blue worsted stockings. He wore a small blue ribbon in his top button-hole, and a soft felt hat. He carried his flowers home in the evening, and always remembered to press them before he went to bed. He and Maud were sitting on a large grey rock by the wayside, reading the Psalms for the seventeenth evening of the month.

Dodo surveyed her critically, and laid herself out to be agreeable.

"Well, Algy," she said, "how are the flowers going on? Oh, what a sweet little gentian. Where did you get it? We're going to have some theatricals this evening, and you must come. It's going to be a charade, and you'll have to guess the word afterwards. Jack and I are going to look at the sunset. We shall be late for dinner. What's that book, Maud?"

"We were reading the Psalms for the evening," said Maud.

"Oh, how dear of you!" said Dodo. "What a lovely church this makes. Algy, why don't you have service out of doors at Gloucester? I always feel so much more devotional on fine evenings out in the open air. I think that's charming. Good-bye. Jack and I must go on."

Dodo was a good walker, and they were soon among the pines that climb up the long steep slope to the Riffel. Their steps were silent on the carpet of needles, and they walked on, not talking much, but each intensely conscious of the presence of the other. At a corner high up on the slope they stopped, for the great range in front of them had risen above the hills on the other side of the valley, and all the snow was flushed with the sunset.

Dodo laid her hand on Jack's.

"How odd it is that you and I should be here together, and like this," she said. "I often used to wonder years ago whether this would happen. Jack, you will make me very happy? Promise me that."

And Jack promised.

"I often think of Chesterford," Dodo went on. "He wished for this, you know. He told me so as he was dying. Did you ever know, Jack—" even Dodo found it hard to get on at this moment—"did you ever know—he knew all? I began to tell him, and he stopped me, saying he knew."

Jack's face was grave.

"He told me he knew," he said; "at least, I saw he did. I never felt so much ashamed. It was my fault. I would have given a great deal to save him that knowledge."

"God forgive me if I was cruel to him," said Dodo. "But, oh, Jack, I did try. I was mad that night I think."

"Don't talk of it," said he suddenly; "it was horrible; it was shameful."

They were silent a moment. Then Jack said,—

"Dodo, let us bury the thought of that for ever. There are some memories which are sacred to me. The memory of Chesterford is one. He was very faithful, and he was very unhappy. I feel as if I was striking his dead body when you speak of it. Requiescat."

They rose and went down to the hotel; the sun had set, and it grew suddenly cold.

The theatricals that night were a great success. Dodo was simply inimitable. Two maiden ladies left the hotel the next morning.

17

Dodo's marriage was announced in September. It was to be celebrated at the beginning of December, and was to be very grand indeed. Duchesses were expected to be nothing accounted of. She was still in Switzerland when it was made known, and events had developed themselves. The announcement came out in the following manner. She had taken her moonlight walk, but not with Prince Waldenech. She had mentioned to him incidentally that Jack was coming as well, and after dinner the Prince found he had important despatches waiting for him. Dodo was rather amused at the inadequacy of this statement, as no post had come in that morning. The thought that the Prince particularly wished to take a romantic walk with her was entertaining. Next morning, however, while Dodo was sitting in her room, looking out over the wide, green valley, her maid came in and asked if Prince Waldenech might have permission to speak to her.

"Good morning," said Dodo affably, as he entered. "I wish you had been with us last night. We had a charming walk, but Jack was dreadfully dull. Why didn't you come?"

The Prince twisted his long moustaches.

"Certainly I had no despatches," he declared with frankness; "that was—how do you call it?—oh, a white lie."

"Did you expect me to believe it?" asked Dodo.

"Assuredly not," he returned. "It would have been an insult to your understanding. But such statements are better than the truth sometimes.

But I came here for another purpose—to say good-bye."

"You're not going?" said Dodo surprisedly.

"Unless you tell me to stop," he murmured, advancing to her.

Dodo read his meaning at once, and determined to stop his saying anything more.

"Certainly I tell you to stop," she said. "You mustn't break up our charming party so soon. Besides, I have a piece of news for you this morning. I ask for your congratulations."

"Ah, those despatches," murmured the Prince.

"No, it was not the fault of your despatches," said Dodo, laughing. "It was settled some time ago. I shall be Lady Chesterford again next year. Allow me to introduce the Marchioness of Chesterford elect to your Highness," and she swept him a little curtsey.

The Prince bowed.

"The Marquis of Chesterford is a very fortunate man," he said. "Decidedly I had better go away to-morrow."

Dodo felt annoyed with him. "I thought he was clever enough not to say that," she thought to herself.

"No, my dear Prince, you shall do nothing of the sort," she said. "You are very happy here, and I don't choose that you should go away—I tell you to stop. You said you would if I told you."

"I am a man of honour still," said he, with mock solemnity. He put both hands together and bowed. "I shall be the first to congratulate the Marquis," he said, "and may I hope the Marchioness will think with pity on those less fortunate than he."

Dodo smiled benignantly. He really had got excellent manners. The scene was artistic, and it pleased her.

"I should think you were too proud to accept pity," she said.

"Have you ever seen me other than humble—to you?" he asked.

"Take it then," said Dodo; "as much as your case requires. But I feel it is insolent of me to offer it."

"I take all the pity you have," said he, smiling gravely. "I want it more than any other poor devil you might think of bestowing it on."

He bowed himself gracefully out of the room. He and Dodo had been discussing English proverbs the day before, and Dodo asserted broadly that they were all founded on universal truths. The Prince thought that pity was quite a promising gift.

Dodo was a little uneasy after he had gone. She was always a trifle afraid of him, though, to do her justice, no one would have guessed it. He had acted the rejected lover in the theatricals of the week before, and his acting had been rather too good. The scene she had just gone through reminded her very forcibly of it. She had found that she could not get the play out of her head afterwards, and had had long waking dreams that night, in which the Prince appeared time after time, and her refusal got more faint as he pressed his suit. She felt that he was the stronger of the two, and such a scene as the last inspired her with a kind of self-distrust. "He will not make himself 'cheap,' " Dodo said to herself. She was very glad he was going to stop, and had been surprised to feel how annoyed she was when he said he had come to wish good-bye. But she felt he had a certain power over her, and did not quite like it. She would take Jack out for a walk and make things even. Jack had no power over her, and she thought complacently how she could turn him round her little finger. Dear old Jack! What a good time they were going to have.

She went downstairs and met the Prince and Jack on the verandah. The former was murmuring congratulatory speeches, and Jack was saying "Thanks awfully" at intervals. He had once said to Dodo that the Prince was "an oily devil," which was putting it rather strongly. Dodo had stuck up for him. "You only say he's oily," she said, "because he's got much better manners than you, and can come into the room without looking ridiculous, and I rather like devils as a rule, and him in particular, though I don't say he is one. Anyhow he is a friend of mine, and you can talk about something else."

Jack followed Dodo into the square, and sat down by her.

"What made you tell that chap that we were engaged?" he asked.

"Oh, I had excellent reasons," said Dodo.

The memory of the interview was still rather strong in her mind, and she felt not quite sure of herself.

"No doubt," said Jack; "but I wish you'd tell me what they were."

"Don't talk as if you were the inquisition, old boy," she said. "I don't see why I should tell you if I don't like."

"Please yourself," said Jack crossly, and got up to walk away.

"Jack, behave this minute," said Dodo. "Apologise instantly for speaking like that."

"I beg its little pardon," said Jack contentedly.

He liked being hauled over the coals by Dodo.

"That's right; now, if you'll be good, I'll tell you. Has he gone quite away?"

"Quite; thank goodness," said Jack.

"Well," said Dodo, "I told him because he was just going to propose to me himself, and I wanted to stop him."

"Nasty brute," said Jack. "I hope you gave it him hot."

"That's a very rude thing to say, Jack," said she. "It argues excellent taste in him. Besides, you did it yourself. Nasty brute!"

"What right has he got to propose to you, I should like to know?" asked Jack.

"Just as much as you had."

"Then I ought to be kicked for doing it."

Dodo applied the toe of a muddy shoe to Jack's calf.

"Now, I've dirtied your pretty stockings," she said. "Serves you right for proposing to me. How dare you, you nasty brute!"

Jack made a grab at her foot, and made his fingers dirty.

"Jack, behave," said Dodo; "there are two thousand people looking."

"Let them look," said Jack recklessly. "I'm not going to be kicked in broad daylight within shouting distance of the hotel. Dodo, if you kick me again I shall call for help."

"Call away," said Dodo.

Jack opened his mouth and howled. An old gentleman, who was just folding his paper into a convenient form for reading, on a seat opposite, put on his spectacles and stared at them in blank amazement.

"I told you I would," remarked Jack parenthetically.

"It's only Lord Chesterford," exclaimed Dodo, in a shrill, treble voice, to the old gentleman. "I don't think he's very well. I daresay it's nothing."

"Most distressin'," said the old gentleman, in a tone of the deepest sarcasm, returning to his paper.

"Most distressin'," echoed Dodo pianissimo to Jack, who was laughing in a hopeless internal manner.

Dodo led him speechless away, and they wandered off to the little, low wall that separates the street from the square.

"Now, we'll go on talking," said Jack, when he had recovered somewhat. "We were talking about that Austrian. What did you say to him?"

"Oh, I've told you. I simply stopped him asking me by telling him I was going to marry someone else."

"What did he say then?" demanded Jack.

"Oh, he asked me for sympathy," said Dodo.

"Which you gave him?"

"Certainly," she answered. "I was very sorry for him, and I told him so; but we did it very nicely and politely, without stating anything, but only hinting at it."

"A nasty, vicious, oily brute," observed Jack.

"Jack, you're ridiculous," said she; "he's nothing of the sort. I've told him to come and see us when we're in England, and you'll have to be very polite and charming to him."

"Oh, he can come then," said Jack, "but I don't like him."

They strolled down the street towards the church, and Dodo insisted on buying several entirely useless brackets, with chamois horns stuck aimlessly about them.

"I haven't got any money," she observed. "Fork up, Jack. Seven and eight are fifteen and seven are twenty-two. Thanks."

Dodo was dissatisfied with one of her brackets before they reached the hotel again, and presented it to Jack.

"It's awfully good of you," said he; "do you mean that you only owe me fifteen?"

"Only fourteen," said Dodo; "this was eight francs. It will be very useful to you, and when you look at it, you can think of me," she observed with feeling.

"I'd sooner have my eight francs."

"Then you just won't get them," said Dodo, with finality; "and you sha'n't have that unless you say, 'Thank you.'"

The verandah was empty, as lunch had begun; so Jack said, "Thank you."

The news of their engagement soon got about the hotel, and caused a much more favourable view to be taken of Dodo's behaviour to Jack, in the minds of the hostile camp. "Of course, if she was engaged to Lord Chesterford all along," said the enemy, "it puts her conduct in an entirely different light. They say he's immensely rich, and we hope we shall meet them in London. Her acting the other night was really extremely clever."

Mrs. Vane gave quite a number of select little teas on the verandah to the penitent, and showed her teeth most graciously. "Darling Dodo, of course it's a great happiness to me," she would say, "and the Marquis is such a very old friend of ours. So charming, isn't he? Yes. And they are simply devoted to each other." The speeches seemed quite familiar still to her.

Dodo regarded the sudden change in the minds of the "shocked section" with much amusement. "It appears I'm quite proper after all," she thought. "That's a blessing anyhow. The colonial bishop will certainly ask me to share his mitre, now he knows I'm a good girl."

"Jack," she called out to him as he passed, "you said the salon smelled like a church this morning. Well, it's only me. I diffuse an odour of sanctity, I find."

The Princess expressed her opinions on the engagement.

"I'm sorry that you can't marry my brother," she said. "You would have suited him admirably, and it would have been only natural for you to stay with your brother-in-law. What shall I give you for a wedding present? There's the bear-skin prayer-book, if you like. Waldenech is very cross about it. He says you told him he mightn't go away, so he has to stop. Are you going out on the picnic? Waldenech's getting up a picnic. He's ordered champagne. Do you think it will be amusing? They will drink the health of you and Lord Chesterford.

If you'll promise to reply in suitable terms I'll come. Why didn't you come and see me this morning? I suppose you were engaged. Of course my brother was proposing to you after breakfast, and then you had to go and talk to your young man. Come to the picnic, Dodo. You shall show me how to throw stones."

They were going to walk up to a sufficiently remote spot in the rising ground to the east of Zermatt, and find their lunch ready for them. The Prince had no sympathy with meat sandwiches and a little sherry out of a flask, and his sister had expressed her antipathy to fresh eggs; so he had told the hotel-keeper that lunch would be wanted, and that there were to be no hard-boiled eggs and no sandwiches, and plenty of deck-chairs.

The Princess firmly refused to walk as far, and ordered what she said "was less unlike a horse than the others"; and asked Dodo to wait for her, as she knew she wouldn't be in time. She was one of those people who find it quite impossible to be punctual at whatever time she had an engagement. She was always twenty minutes late, but, as Dodo remarked, "That's the same thing as being punctual when people know you. I think punctuality is a necessity," she added, "more than a virtue."

"Haven't you got a proverb about making a virtue of necessity?" said the Princess vaguely. "That's what I do on the rare occasions on which I am punctual. All my virtues are the result of necessity, which is another word for inclination."

"Yes, inclination is necessity when it's sufficiently strong," said Dodo; "consequently, even when it's weak, it's still got a touch of necessity about it. That really is a comfortable doctrine. I shall remember that next time I want not to go to church."

"My husband is a very devout Roman Catholic," remarked the Princess. "He's got an admirable plan of managing such things. First of all, he does what his conscience—he's got a very fine conscience—tells him he shouldn't. It must be very amusing to have a conscience. You need never feel lonely. Then he goes and confesses, which makes it all right, and to make himself quite safe he gives a hundred roubles to the poor. He's very rich, you know; it doesn't matter to him a bit. That gets him an indulgence. I fancy he's minus about six weeks' purgatory. He's got a balance. I expect he'll give it me. You have to be very rich to have a balance. He pays for his pleasures down in hard cash, you see; it's much better than running up a bill. He is very anxious about my spiritual welfare sometimes."

"Does he really believe all that?" asked Dodo.

"Dear me, yes," said the Princess. "He has a most childlike faith. If the priest told him there was an eligible building site in heaven going cheap, he'd buy it at once. Personally I don't believe all those things. They don't seem to me in the least probable."

"What do you believe?" asked Dodo.

"Oh, I've got plenty of beliefs," said the Princess. "I believe it's wiser being good than bad, and fitter being sane than mad. I don't do obviously low things, I am sorry for the poor devils of this world, I'm not mean, I'm not coarse, I don't care about taking an unfair advantage of other people. My taste revolts against immorality; I should as soon think of going about with dirty nails. If I believed what the priests tell me I should be a very good woman, according to their lights. As it is, though my conduct in all matters of right and wrong is identical with what it would be, I'm one of the lost."

"English people are just as irrational in their way," said Dodo, "only they don't do such things in cold blood. They appeal to little morbid emotions, excited by Sunday evening and slow tunes in four sharps. I went to a country church once, on a lovely summer evening, and we all sang, 'Hark, hark, my soul!' at the tops of our voices, and I walked home with my husband, feeling that I'd never do anything naughty any more, and Maud and her husband, and he and I, sang hymns after dinner. It was simply delicious. The world was going to be a different place ever afterwards, and I expected to die in the night. But I didn't, you know, and next morning all the difference was that I'd caught a cold sitting in a hayfield—and that was the end."

"No, it's no use," said the Princess. "But I envy those who have 'the religion,' as they say in our country. It makes things so much easier."

"What I couldn't help wondering," said Dodo, "was whether I should be any better if I had kept up the feeling of that Sunday night. I should have stopped at home singing hymns, I suppose, instead of going out to dinner; but what then? Should I have been less objectionable when things went wrong? Should I have been any kinder to—to anybody? I don't believe it."

"Of course you wouldn't," said the Princess. "You go about it the wrong way. We neither of us can help it, because we're not made like that. It would be as sensible to cultivate eccentricity in order to become a genius. People who have 'the religion' like singing hymns, but they didn't get the religion by singing hymns. They sing hymns because they've got it. What is so absurd is to suppose, as my husband does, that a hundred roubles at stated intervals produces salvation. That's his form of singing hymns, and the priests encourage him. I gave it up long ago. If I thought singing hymns or encouraging priests would do any good, I'd sell my diamonds and buy a harmonium, and give the rest away. But I don't think anything so absurd."

"David was so sensible," said Dodo. "I've got a great affection for David. He told his people to sing praises with understanding. You see you've got to understand it first. I wonder if he would have understood 'Hark, hark, my soul!' I didn't, but it made me feel good inside."

"Somebody said religion was morality touched with emotion," said the Princess. "My husband hasn't got any morality, and his emotions are those excited by killing bears. Yet the priests say he's wonderfully religious."

"There's something wrong somewhere," said Dodo.

The party were waiting for them when they came up. The Prince led Dodo to a place next him, and the Princess sat next Jack.

"I'm so sorry," said Dodo; "I'm afraid we're dreadfully late."

"My sister is never in time," said the Prince. "She kept the Emperor waiting half an hour once. His Imperial Majesty swore."

"Oh, you're doing me an injustice," said she. "I was in time the other day."

"Let us do her justice," said the Prince. "She was in time, but that was because she forgot what the time was."

"That's the cause of my being unpunctual, dear," remarked the Princess. "To-day it was also because the thing like a horse wouldn't go, and Dodo and I talked a good deal."

Mrs. Vane was eating her chicken with great satisfaction. A picnic with a Prince was so much capital to her.

"I can't think why we don't all go and live in the country always," she said, "and have little picnics like this every day. Such a good idea of your Highness. So original—*and* such a charming day."

The Prince remarked that picnics were not his invention, and that the credit for the weather was due elsewhere.

"Oh, but you said last night you were sure it was going to be fine," said Mrs. Vane, floundering a little. "Dodo, dear, didn't you hear the Prince say so?"

"Here's to the health of our Zadkiel," said Dodo, "may his shadow, etc. Drink to old Zadkiel, Jack, the founder of the feast, who stands us champagne. I'll stand you a drink when you come to see us in England. His Serenity," she said, emptying her glass.

"What a lot of things I am," murmured the Prince. "Don't forget I'm a poor devil whom you pity as well."

"Do you find pity a satisfactory diet?" asked Dodo saucily.

She was determined not to be frightened of him any more.

The Prince decided on a bold stroke.

"Pity is akin to love," he said below his breath.

But he had found his match, for the time being, at any rate.

"Don't mistake it for its cousin, then," laughed Dodo.

The conversation became more general. The Princess said the mountains were too high and large, and she didn't like them. Jack remarked that it was purely a matter of degree, and the Princess explained that it was exactly what she meant, they were so much bigger than she was. Mr. Spencer plunged violently into the conversation, and said that Mount Everest was twice as high as the Matterhorn, and you never saw the top. The Princess said, "Oh," and Jack asked how they knew how high it was, if the top was never seen, and Mr. Spencer explained vaguely that they did it with sextants. Maud said she thought he meant theodolites, and Dodo asked a bad riddle about sextons. On the whole the picnic went off as well as could be expected, and Dodo determined to have lunch out of doors every day for the rest of her natural life.

After lunch Mr. Spencer and Maud wandered away to pick flowers, presumably. Mrs. Vane moved her chair into the shade, in such a position that she could command a view of the mountain, and fell asleep. Jack smoked a short black pipe, chiefly because the Prince offered him a cigar, and Dodo smoked cigarettes and ate cherries backwards, beginning with the stalk, and induced the Princess to do the same, receiving two seconds' start. "It's a form of throwing stones," Dodo explained. The "most distressin'" old gentleman was sighted under a large white umbrella, moving slowly up the path a little below them, and Dodo insisted on inviting him to lunch, as it was certain that he had just left the *table d'hote*. "He thought it simply charming of me," she said, as she came back. "He's quite forgiven Jack for shouting. Besides, I took him the Princess's compliments. He's English, you know."

18

Edith had stayed on with the Granthams till nearly the end of August. She declined to have breakfast with the family, after she had been there about a week, because she said it spoiled her mornings, and used to breakfast by herself at seven or half-past, which gave her extra two hours at her music; and Lady Grantham complained of being wakened in the middle of the night by funeral marches. So Edith promised to play with the soft pedal down, which she never did.

At lunch Sir Robert used to make a point of asking her how she had got on, and described to her the admirable band in the Casino at Monte Carlo. He was always extremely genial to her, and, when she played to them in the evening, he would beat time with one hand.

Now and then he even told her that she was not playing staccato enough, or that he heard it taken rather quicker at Bayreuth.

Dodo had written to Edith saying that she was coming to stay with her in September, and that Edith must be at home by the second, because she would probably come that day or the third. Edith happened to mention this one night in the hearing of Lady Grantham, who had been firing off home-truths at her husband and son like a minute gun, in a low, scornful voice. This habit of hers was rather embarrassing at times. At dinner, for instance, that evening, when he had been airing his musical views to Edith as usual, she had suddenly said,—

"You don't know how silly you're making yourself, Bob. Everyone knows that you can't distinguish one note from another!"

Though Edith felt on fairly intimate terms with the family, there were occasions when she didn't quite know how to behave. She attempted to continue her conversation with the Baronet, but Lady Grantham would not allow it.

"Edith, you know he doesn't know 'God, Save the Queen' when he hears it. You'll only make him conceited."

"She's only like this when she's here, Miss Staines," remarked Frank, alluding to his mother in the third person. "She's awfully polite when she's in London; she was to you the first week you were here, you know, but she can't keep it up. She's had a bad education. Poor dear!"

"Oh, you are a queer family," said Edith sometimes. "You really ought to have no faults left, any of you, you are so wonderfully candid to each other."

"Some people think mother so charming," continued Frank. "I never yet found out what her particular charm is."

On this occasion, when Edith mentioned that Dodo was coming to stay with her, Lady Grantham sounded truce at once, and left her unnatural offspring alone.

"I wish you'd ask me to come and stay with you, too," said she presently. "Bob and Frank will be going off partridge shooting all day, and Nora and I will be all alone, and they'll be sleepy in the evening, and snore in the drawing-room."

"I'd make her promise to be polite, Miss Staines," remarked Frank.

"I want to meet Lady Chesterford very much," she continued. "I hear she is so charming. She's a friend of yours, isn't she, Nora? Why have you never asked her to stay here? What's the good of having friends if you don't trot them out?"

"Oh, I've asked her more than once, mother," said Miss Grantham, "but she couldn't ever come."

"She's heard about ma at home," said Frank.

"I'm backing you, Frank," remarked the Baronet, who was still rather sore after his recent drubbing. "Go in and win, my boy."

"Bob, you shouldn't encourage Frank to be rude," said Lady Grantham. "He's bad enough without that."

"That's what comes of having a mamma with foreign manners. There's no word for 'thank you' in Spanish, is there, mother? Were you here with Charlie Broxton, Miss Staines? She told him he didn't brush his hair, or his teeth, and she hated little men. Charlie's five feet three. He was here as my friend."

"Do come," said Edith, when this skirmishing was over. "Nora will come with you, of course. We shall be only four. I don't suppose there will be anyone else at home."

"Hurrah," said Frank, "we'll have a real good time, father. No nagging in the evenings. We won't dress, and we'll smoke in the drawing-room."

"I long to see Dodo again," remarked Miss Grantham. "She's one of the few people I never get at all tired of."

"I know her by sight," said Lady Grantham. "She was talking very loud to Prince Waldenech when I saw her. It was at the Brettons'."

"Dodo can talk loud when she wants," remarked Miss Grantham. "Did you see her dance that night, mother? I believe she was splendid."

"She was doing nothing else," replied Lady Grantham.

"Oh, but by herself," said Edith. "She took a select party away, and tucked up her skirts and sent them all into raptures."

"That's so like Dodo," said Miss Grantham. "She never does anything badly. If she does it at all, it's good of its kind."

"I should like to know her," said Lady Grantham. The remark was characteristic.

Lady Grantham returned to the subject of Dodo in the course of the evening.

"Everyone says she is so supremely successful," she said to Edith. "What's her method?"

All successful people, according to Lady Grantham, had a method. They found out by experience what *rôle* suited them best, and they played it assiduously. To do her justice, there was a good deal of truth in it with regard to the people among whom she moved.

"Her method is purely to be dramatic, in the most unmistakable way," said Edith, after some consideration. "She is almost always picturesque. To all appearance her only method is to have no method. She seems to say and do anything that comes into her head, but all she says and does is rather striking. She can accommodate herself to nearly any circumstances. She is never colourless; and she is not quite like anybody else I ever met. She has an immense amount of vitality, and she is almost always doing something. It's hopeless to try and describe her; you will see. She is beautiful, unscrupulous, dramatic, warm-hearted, cold-blooded, and a hundred other things."

"Oh, you don't do her justice, Edith," remarked Miss Grantham. "She's much more than all that. She has got genius, or something very like it. I think Dodo gives me a better idea of the divine fire than anyone else."

"Then the divine fire resembles something not at all divine on occasions," observed Edith. "I don't think that the divine fire talks so much nonsense either."

Lady Grantham got up.

"I expect to be disappointed," she said. "Geniuses are nearly always badly dressed, or they wear spectacles, or they are very short. However, I shall come. Come, Nora, it's time to go to bed."

Lady Grantham never said "good-night" or "good-morning" to the members of her family. "They all sleep like hogs," she said, "and they are very cheerful in the morning. They get on quite well enough without my good wishes. It is very plebeian to be cheerful in the morning."

Although, as I have mentioned before, Sir Robert was an adept at choosing his conversation to suit his audience, there was one subject on which he considered that he might talk to anyone, and in which the whole world must necessarily take an intelligent and eager interest. The Romans used to worship the bones and spirits of their ancestors, and Sir Robert, perhaps because he was undoubtedly of Roman imperial blood, kept up the same custom. Frank used irreverently to call it "family prayers."

To know how the Granthams were connected with the Campbells, and the Vere de Veres, and the Stanleys, and the Montmorencies, and fifty other bluest strains, seemed to Sir Robert to be an essential part of a liberal education.

To try to be late for family prayers was hopeless. They were at no fixed hour, and were held as many times during the day as necessary. Sometimes they were cut down to a sentence or two, suggested by the mention of some ducal name; sometimes they involved a lengthy, pious orgie in front of the portraits. Tonight Edith was distinctly to blame, for she deliberately asked the name of the artist who had painted the picture hanging over the door into the library.

Sir Robert, according to custom, seemed rather bored at the subject. "Let's see," he said; "I've got no head for names. I think that's the one of my great-grandfather, isn't it? A tall, handsome man in peer's robes?"

"Now he's off." This *sotto voce* from Frank, who was reading Badminton on Cover Shooting.

Sir Robert drew his hand over his beautiful moustache once or twice. "Ah, yes, how stupid of me. That's the Reynolds, of course. Reynolds was quite unknown when he did that portrait. Lord Linton, that was my great-grandfather—he was made an earl after that portrait was taken—saw a drawing in a little shop in Piccadilly, which took his fancy, and he inquired the name of the artist. The shopman didn't know; but he said that the young man came very often with drawings to sell, and he gave him a trifle for them. Well, Lord Linton sent for him, and gave him a commission to do his portrait, had it exhibited, and young Reynolds came into notice. The portrait came into possession of my grandfather, who, as you know, was a younger son; don't know how, and there it is."

"It's a beautiful picture," remarked Edith.

"Ah, you like it? Lord Sandown, my first cousin, was here last week, and he said, 'Didn't know you'd been raised to the Peerage yet, Bob.' He thought it was a portrait of me. It is said to be very like. You'd noticed the resemblance, no doubt?"

"A tall, handsome man," remarked Frank to the fire-place.

"I don't know as much as I ought about my ancestors," continued Sir Robert, who was doing himself a gross injustice. "You ought to get Sandown on the subject. I found a curious old drawing the other day in a scrapbook belonging to my father. The name Grantham is printed in the centre of a large folio sheet, with a circle round it to imitate the sun, and from it go out rays in all directions, with the names of the different families with which we have intermarried."

"I haven't got any ancestors," remarked Edith. "My grandfather was a draper in Leeds, and made his fortune there. I should think ancestors were a great responsibility; you have to live up to them, or else they live down to you."

"I'm always saying to Frank," said Sir Robert, "that you have to judge a man by himself, and not by his family. If a man is a pleasant fellow it doesn't matter whether his family came over with the Conqueror or not. Our parson here, for instance, he's a decent sensible fellow, and I'm always delighted to give him a few days' shooting, or see him to dinner on Sunday after his services. His father was a tobacconist in the village, you know. There's the shop there now."

Edith rose to go.

Sir Robert lighted her candle for her.

"I should like to show you the few portraits we've got," he said. "There are some interesting names amongst them; but, of course, most of our family things are at Langfort."

"My grandfather's yard measure is the only heirloom that we've got," said Edith. "I'll show it to Lady Grantham when she comes to stay with me."

Frank had followed them into the hall.

"Family prayers over yet, father?" he asked. "I shall go and smoke. I hope you've been devout, Miss Staines."

Edith left the Granthams two days after this, "to buy legs of mutton," she explained, "and hire a charwoman. I don't suppose there's anyone at home. But I shall have things straight by the time you come."

Sir Robert was very gracious, and promised to send her a short memoir he was writing on the fortunes of the family. It was to be bound in white vellum, with their arms in gilt upon the outside.

Edith found no one at home but a few servants on board wages, who did not seem at all pleased to see her. She devoted her evening to what she called tidying, which consisted in emptying the contents of a quantity of drawers on to the floor of her room, and sitting down beside them. She turned them over with much energy for about half an hour, and then decided that she could throw nothing away, and told her maid to put them back again, and played her piano till bed-time.

Lady Grantham and Nora followed in a few days, and Dodo was to come the same evening. They were sitting out in the garden after dinner, when the sound of wheels was heard, and Edith went round to the front door to welcome her.

Dodo had not dined, so she went and "made hay among the broken meats," as she expressed it. Travelling produced no kind of fatigue in her; and the noise, and shaking, and smuts, that prey on most of us in railway carriages always seemed to leave her untouched. Dodo was particularly glad to get to England. She had had rather a trying time of it towards the end, for Jack and the Prince got on extremely badly together, and, as they both wished to be with Dodo, collisions were frequent. She gave the story of her adventure to Edith with singular frankness as she ate her broken meats.

"You see, Jack got it into his head that the Prince is a cad and a brute," said Dodo. "I quite admit that he may be, only neither Jack nor I have the slightest opportunity for judging. Socially he is neither, and what he is morally doesn't concern me. How should it? It isn't my business to inquire into his moral character. I'm not his mother nor his mother confessor. He is good company. I particularly like his sister, whom you must come and see, Edith. She and the Prince are going to stay with us when we get back to Winston; and he knows how to behave. Jack has a vague sort of feeling that his morals ought to prevent him from tolerating the Prince, which made him try to find opportunities for disliking him. But Jack didn't interfere with me."

"No," said Edith; "I really don't see why private individuals shouldn't associate with whom they like. One doesn't feel bound to be friends with people of high moral character, so I don't see why one should be bound to dislike people of low ditto."

"That's exactly my view," said Dodo; "morals don't come into the question at all. I particularly dislike some of the cardinal virtues— and the only reason for associating with anybody is that one takes pleasure in their company. Of course one wouldn't go about with a murderer, however amusing, because his moral deficiencies might produce unpleasant physical consequences to yourself. But my morals are able to look after themselves. I'm not afraid of moral cut-throats. Morals don't come into the social circle. You might as well dislike a man because he's got a sharp elbow-joint. He won't use it on your ribs, you know, in the drawing-room. To get under the influence of an immoral man would be different. Well, I've finished. Where are the others? Give me a cigarette, Edith. I sha'n't shock your servants, shall I? I've given up shocking people."

Dodo and Edith strolled out, and Dodo was introduced to Lady Grantham.

"What an age you and Edith have been," said Miss Grantham. "I have been dying to see you, Dodo."

"We were talking," said Dodo, "and for once Edith agreed with me."

"She never agrees with me," remarked Lady Grantham.

"I wonder if I should always agree with you then," said Dodo. "Do things that disagree with the same thing agree with one another?"

"What did Edith agree with you about?" asked Miss Grantham.

"I'm not sure that I did really agree with her," interpolated Edith.

"Oh, about morals," said Dodo. "I said that a man's morals did not matter in ordinary social life. That they did not come into the question at all."

"No, I don't think I do agree with you," said Edith. "All social life is a degree of intimacy, and you said yourself that you wouldn't get under the influence of an immoral man—in other words, you wouldn't be intimate with him."

"Oh, being intimate hasn't anything to do with being under a man's influence," said Dodo. "I'm very intimate with lots of people. Jack, for instance, but I'm not under his influence."

"Then you think it doesn't matter whether society is composed of people without morals?" said Edith.

"I think it's a bad thing that morals should deteriorate in any society," said Dodo; "but I don't think that society should take cognisance of the moral code. Public opinion don't touch that. If a man is a brute, he won't be any better for knowing that other people disapprove of him. If he knows that, and is worth anything at all, it will simply have the opposite effect on him. He very likely will try to hide it; but that doesn't make it any better. A whited sepulchre is no better than a sepulchre unwhitened. You must act by your own lights. If an action doesn't seem to you wrong nothing in the world will prevent your doing it, if your desire is sufficiently strong. You cannot elevate tone by punishing offences. There are no fewer criminals since the tread-mill was invented and Botany Bay discovered."

"You mean that there would be no increase in crime if the law did not punish?"

"I mean that punishment is not the best way of checking crime, though that is really altogether a different question. You won't check immorality by dealing with it as a social crime."

There was a short silence, broken only by the whispering of the wind in the fir trees. Then on the stillness came a light, rippling laugh. Dodo got out of her chair, and plucked a couple of roses from a bush near her.

"I can't be serious any longer," she said; "not a single moment longer. I'm so dreadfully glad to be in England again. Really, there is no place like it. I hate the insolent extravagant beauty of Switzerland—it is like chromo lithographs. Look at that long, flat, grey distance over there. There is nothing so beautiful as that abroad."

Dodo fastened the roses in the front of her dress, and laughed again.

"I laugh for pure happiness," she continued. "I laughed when I saw the cliff of Dover to-day, not because I was sea-sick—I never am sea-sick—but simply because I was coming home again. Jack parted from me at Dover. I am very happy about Jack. I believe in him thoroughly."

Dodo was getting serious again in spite of herself. Lady Grantham was watching her curiously, and without any feeling of disappointment. She did not wear spectacles, she was, at least, as tall as herself, and she dressed, if anything, rather better. She was still wearing half-mourning, but half-mourning suited Dodo very well.

"Decidedly it's a pity to analyse one's feelings," Dodo went on, "they do resolve themselves into such very small factors. I am well, I am in England, where you can eat your dinner without suspicion of frogs, or caterpillars in your cauliflower. I had two caterpillars in my cauliflower at Zermatt one night. I shall sleep in a clean white bed, and I shall not have to use Keating. I can talk as ridiculously as I like, without thinking of the French for anything. Oh, I'm entirely happy."

Dodo was aware of more reasons for happiness than she mentioned.

She was particularly conscious of the relief she felt in getting away from the Prince. For some days past she had been unpleasantly aware of his presence. She could not manage to think of him quite as lightly as she thought of anyone else. It was a continual effort to her to appear quite herself in his presence, and she was constantly rushing into extremes in order to seem at her ease. He was stronger, she felt, than she was, and she did not like it. The immense relief which his absence brought more than compensated for the slight blankness that his absence left. In a way she felt dependent on him, which chafed and irritated her, for she had never come under such a yoke before. She had had several moments of sudden anger against herself on her way home. She found herself always thinking about him when she was not thinking about anything else; and though she was quite capable of sending her thoughts off to other subjects, when they had done their work they always fluttered back again to the same resting-place, and Dodo was conscious of an effort, slight indeed, but still an effort, in frightening them off. Her curious insistence on her own happiness had struck Edith. She felt it unnatural that Dodo should mention it, and she drew one of two conclusions from it; either that Dodo had had a rather trying time, for some reason or other, or that she wished to convince herself, by constant repetition, of something that she was not quite sure about; and both of these conclusions were in a measure correct.

"Who was out at Zermatt when you were there?" inquired Miss Grantham.

"Oh, there was mother there, and Maud and her husband, and a Russian princess, Waldenech's sister, and Jack, of course," said Dodo.

"Wasn't Prince Waldenech there himself?" she asked.

"The Prince? Oh yes, he was there; didn't I say so?" said Dodo.

"He's rather amusing, isn't he?" said Miss Grantham. "I don't know him at all."

"Oh, yes," said Dodo; "a little ponderous, you know, but very presentable, and good company."

Edith looked up suddenly at Dodo. There was an elaborate carelessness, she thought, in her voice. It was just a little overdone. The night was descending fast, and she could only just see the lines of her face above the misty folds of her grey dress. But even in that half light she thought that her careless voice did not quite seem a true interpretation of her expression. It might have been only the dimness of the shadow, but she thought she looked anxious and rather depressed.

Lady Grantham drew her shawl more closely round her shoulders, and remarked that it was getting cold. Edith got up and prepared to go in, and Miss Grantham nestled in her chair. Only Dodo stood quite motionless, and Edith noticed that her hands were tearing one of the roses to pieces, and scattering the petals on the grass.

"Are you going in, Dodo?" she asked; "or would you rather stop out a little longer?"

"I think I won't come in just yet," said Dodo; "it's so delightful to have a breath of cool air, after being in a stuffy carriage all day. But don't any of you stop out if you'd rather go in. I shall just smoke one more cigarette."

"I'll stop with you, Dodo," said Miss Grantham. "I don't want to go in at all. Edith, if you're going in, throw the windows in the drawing-room open, and play to us."

Lady Grantham and Edith went towards the house.

"I didn't expect her to be a bit like that," said Lady Grantham. "I always heard she was so lively, and talked more nonsense in half an hour than we can get through in a year. She's very beautiful."

"I think Dodo must be tired or something," said Edith. "I never saw her like that before. She was horribly serious. I hope nothing has happened."

The piano in the drawing-room was close to a large French window opening on to the lawn. Edith threw it open, and stood for a moment looking out into the darkness. She could just see Dodo and Nora sitting where they had left them, though they were no more than two pale spots against the dark background. She was conscious of a strange feeling that there was an undercurrent at work in Dodo, which showed itself by a few chance bubbles and little sudden eddies on the surface, which she thought required explanation. Dodo certainly was not quite like herself. There was no edge to her vivacity: her attempts not to be serious had been distinctly forced, and she was unable to keep it up. Edith felt a vague sense of coming disaster; slight but certain. However, she drew her chair to the piano and began to play.

Miss Grantham was conscious of the same sort of feeling. Since the others had gone in, Dodo had sat quite silent, and she had not taken her cigarette.

"You had a nice time then, abroad?" she remarked at length.

"Oh, yes," said Dodo, rousing herself. "I enjoyed it a good deal. The hotel was full of the hotel class, you know. A little trying at times, but not to matter. We had a charming party there. Algernon is getting quite worldly. However, he is ridiculously fond of Maud, and she'll keep him straight. Do you know the Prince?"

"Hardly at all," said Miss Grantham.

"What do you think of him, as far as you've seen?" asked Dodo.

"I think he is rather impressive," said Miss Grantham. "I felt I should do as he told me."

"Ah, you think that, do you?" asked Dodo, with the most careful carelessness. "He struck me that way, too, a little."

"I should think he was an instance of what Edith meant when she said that to be intimate with anyone was to be under their influence."

"Edith's awfully wrong, I think, about the whole idea," said Dodo, hastily. "I should hate to be under anyone's influence; yet, I think, the only pleasure of knowing people is to be intimate. I would sooner have one real friend than fifty acquaintances."

"Did you see much of him?" asked Miss Grantham.

"Yes, a good deal," she said, "a great deal, in fact. I think Edith's right about intimacy as regards him, though he's an exception. In general, I think, she's wrong. What's that she's playing?"

"Anyhow, it's Wagner," said Miss Grantham.

"I know it," said Dodo. "It's the 'Tannhauser' overture. Listen, there's the Venus motif crossing the Pilgrim's march. Ah, that's simply wicked. The worst of it is, the Venus part is so much more attractive than the other. It's horrible."

"You're dreadfully serious to-night, Dodo," said Miss Grantham.

"I'm a little tired, I think," she said. "I was travelling all last night, you know. Come, let's go in."

Dodo went to bed soon afterwards. She said she was tired, and a little overdone. Edith looked at her rather closely as she said good-night.

"You're sure it's nothing more?" she asked. "There's nothing wrong with you, is there?"

"I shall be all right in the morning," said Dodo, rather wearily. "Don't let them call me till nine."

Dodo went upstairs and found that her maid had unpacked for her. A heap of books was lying on the table, and from among these she drew out a large envelope with a photograph inside. It was signed "Waldenech."

Dodo looked at it a moment, then placed it back in its envelope, and went to the window. She felt the necessity of air. The room seemed close and hot, and she threw it wide open.

She stood there for ten minutes or more quite still, looking out into the night. Then she went back to the table and took up the envelope again. With a sudden passionate gesture she tore it in half, then across again, and threw the pieces into the grate.

19

Dodo slept long and dreamlessly that night; the deep, dreamless sleep which an evenly-balanced fatigue of body and mind so often produces, though we get into bed feeling that our brain is too deep in some tangle of unsolved thought to be able to extricate itself, and fall into the dim immensity of sleep. The waking from such a sleep is not so pleasant. The first moment of conscious thought sometimes throws the whole burden again on to our brain with a sudden start of pain that is almost physical. There is no transition. We were asleep and we are awake, and we find that sleep has brought us only a doubtful gift, for with our renewed strength of body has come the capability of keener suffering. When we are tired, mental distress is only a dull ache, but in the hard, convincing morning it strikes a deadlier and deeper pain. But sometimes Nature is more merciful. She opens the sluices of our brain quietly, and, though the water still rushes in turbidly and roughly, yet the fact that our brain fills by degrees makes us more able to bear the full weight, than when it comes suddenly with a wrenching and, perhaps, a rending of our mental machinery.

It was in this way that Dodo woke. The trouble of the day came to her gradually during the moments of waking. She dreamed she was waiting for Jack in the garden where she had been sitting the night before. It was perfectly dark, and she could not see him coming, but she heard a step along the gravel path, and started up with a vague alarm, for it did not sound like his. Then a greyness, as of dawn, began to steal over the night, and she saw the outline of the trees against the sky, and the outline of a man's figure near her, and it was a figure she knew well, but it was not Jack. On this dream the sense of waking was pure relief; it was broad day, and her maid was standing by her and saying that it was a quarter past nine.

Dodo lay still a few moments longer, feeling a vague joy that her dream was not true, that the helplessness of that grey moment, when she saw that it was not Jack, was passed, that she was awake again, and unfettered, save by thoughts which could be consciously checked and stifled. It was with a vast sense of satisfaction that she remembered her last act on the evening before, of which the scattered fragments in the grate afforded ocular proof. She felt as if she had broken a visible, tangible fetter—one strand, at any rate, of the cord that bound her was lying broken before her eyes. If she had been quite securely tied she could not have done that.

The sense of successful effort, with a visible result, gave her a sudden feeling of power to do more; the absence of bodily fatigue, and the presence of superfluous physical health, all seemed part of a different order of things to that of the night before. She got up and dressed quickly, feeling more like her own self than she had done for several days. The destruction of his photograph was really a great achievement. She had no idea how far things had gone till she felt the full effect of conscious effort and its result. She could see now exactly where she had stood on the evening before, very unpleasantly close to the edge of a nasty place, slippery and steep. Anyhow, she was one step nearer that pleasant, green-looking spot at the top of the slope—a quiet, pretty place, not particularly extensive, but very pleasing, and very safe.

The three others were half-way through breakfast when Dodo came down. Lady Grantham was feeling a little bored. Dodo flung open the door and came marching in, whistling "See the Conquering Hero comes."

"That's by Handel, you know, Edith," she said. "Handel is very healthy, and he never bothers you with abstruse questions in the scandalous way that Wagner does. I'm going to have a barrel-organ made with twelve tunes by Handel, you only have to turn the handle and out he comes. I don't mean that for a pun. Your blood be on your own head if you notice it. I shall have my barrel-organ put on the box of my victoria, and the footman shall play tunes all the time I'm driving, and I shall hold out my hat and ask for pennies. Some of Jack's tenants in Ireland have refused to pay their rents this year, and he says we'll have to cut off coffee after dinner if it goes on. But we shall be able to have coffee after all with the pennies I collect. I talked so much sense last night that I don't mean to make another coherent remark this week."

Dodo went to the sideboard and cut a large slice of ham, which she carried back to her place on the end of her fork.

"I'm going for a ride this morning, Edith, if you've got a horse for me," she said. "I haven't ridden for weeks. I suppose you can give me something with four legs. Oh, I want to take a big fence again."

Dodo waved her fork triumphantly, and the slice of ham flew into the milk-jug. She became suddenly serious, and fished for it with the empty fork.

"The deep waters have drowned it," she remarked, "and it will be totally uneatable for evermore. Make it into ham-sandwiches and send it to the workhouse, Edith. *Jambon au lait.* I'm sure it would be very supporting."

"It's unlucky to spill things, isn't it?" Dodo went on. "I suppose it means I shall die, and shall go, we hope, to heaven, at the age of twenty-seven. I'm twenty-nine really. I don't look it, do I, Lady Grant-

ham? How old are you, Edith? You're twenty-nine too, aren't you?
We're two twin dewdrops, you and I; you can be the dewdrops, and
I'll be the twin. I suppose if two babies are twins, each of them is a
twin. Twin sounds like a sort of calico. Two yards of twin, please,
miss. There was a horrid fat man in the carriage across France, who
called me miss. Jack behaved abominably. He called me miss, too,
and wore the broadest grin on his silly face all the time. He really is
a perfect baby, and I'm another, and how we shall keep house together
I can't think. It'll be like a sort of game."

Dodo was eating her breakfast with an immense appetite and alarming rapidity, and she had finished as soon as the others.

"I want to smoke this instant minute," she said, going to the door
as soon as she had eaten all she wanted. "Where do you keep your
cigarettes, Edith? Oh, how you startled me!"

As she opened the door two large collies came bouncing in, panting
from sheer excitement.

"Oh, you sweet animals," said Dodo, sitting down on the floor and
going off at another tangent. "Come here and talk at once. Edith, may
I give them the milky ham? Here you are; drink the milk first, and
then eat the ham, and then say grace, and then you may get down."

Dodo poured the milk into two clean saucers, and set them on the
floor. There were a few drops left at the bottom of the jug, and she
made a neat little pool on the head of each of the dogs.

"What are their names?" she asked. "They ought to be Tweedledum
and Tweedledee, or Huz and Buz, or Ananias and Sapphira, or Darby
and Joan, or Harris and Ainsworth. It ought to be Harris and Ainsworth.
I'm sure, no one man could have written all that rot himself. Little
Spencer is very fond of Harrison Ainsworth; he said it was instructive
as well as palatable. I don't want to be instructed, and it isn't palatable.
I hate having little bits of information wrapped up and given to me
to swallow, like a powder in jam. Did you have to take powders when
you were little, Lady Grantham?"

Dodo's questions were purely rhetorical; they required no answer,
and she did not expect one.

"It is much nicer being completely ignorant and foolish like me,"
she said. "Nobody ever expects me to know anything, or to be instructive on any subject under the sun. Jack and I are going to be a simple
little couple, who are very nice and not at all wise. Nobody dislikes
one if one never pretends to be wise. But I like people to have a
large number of theories on every subject. Everyone is bound to form
conclusions, but what I dislike are people who have got good grounds
for their conclusions, who knock you slap down with statistics, if you
try to argue with them. It's impossible to argue with anyone who

has reasons for what he says, because you get to know sooner or later, and then the argument is over. Arguments ought to be like Epic poems, they leave off, they don't come to an end."

Dodo delivered herself of these surprising statements with great rapidity, and left the room to get her cigarettes. She left the door wide open, and in a minute or two her voice was heard from the drawing-room, screaming to Edith.

"Edith, here's the 'Dodo Symphony'; come and play it to me this moment."

"There's not much wrong with her this morning," thought Edith, as she went to the drawing-room, where Dodo was playing snatches of dance music.

"Play the scherzo, Edith," commanded Dodo. "Here you are. Now, quicker, quicker, rattle it out; make it buzz."

"Oh, I remember your playing that so well," said Dodo, as Edith finished. "It was that morning at Winston when you insisted on going shooting. You shot rather well, too, if I remember right."

Lady Grantham had followed Edith, and sat down, with her atmosphere of impenetrable leisure, near the piano.

Dodo made her feel uncomfortably old. She felt Dodo's extravagantly high spirits were a sort of milestone to show how far she herself had travelled from youth. It was impossible to conceive of Dodo ever getting middle-aged or elderly. She had racked her brains in vain to try to think of any woman of her own age who could possibly ever have been as insolently young as Dodo. She had the habit, as I have mentioned before, of making strangely direct remarks, and she turned to Dodo and said:—

"I should so like to see you ten years hence. I wonder if people like you ever grow old."

"I shall never grow old," declared Dodo confidently. "Something, I feel sure, will happen to prevent that. I shall stop young till I go out like a candle, or am carried off in a whirlwind or something. I couldn't be old; it isn't in me. I shall go on talking nonsense till the end of my life, and I can't talk nonsense if I have to sit by the fire and keep a shawl over my mouth, which I shall have to do if I get old. Wherefore I never shall. It's a great relief to be certain of that. I used to bother my head about it at one time! and it suddenly flashed upon me, about ten days ago, that I needn't bother about it any more, as I never should be old."

"Would you dislike having to be serious very much?" asked Edith.

"It isn't that I should dislike it," said Dodo; "I simply am incapable of it. I was serious last night for at least an hour, and a feverish reaction has set in. I couldn't be serious for a week together, if I was going to be beheaded the next moment, all the time. I daresay it would be very nice to be serious, just as I'm sure it would be very nice to live at the bottom of the sea and pull the fishes' tails, but it isn't possible."

Dodo had quite forgotten that she had intended to go for a ride, and she went into the garden with Nora, and played ducks and drakes on the pond, and punted herself about, and gathered water-lilies. Then she was seized with an irresistible desire to fish, and caught a large pike, which refused to be killed, and Dodo had to fetch the gardener to slay it. She then talked an astonishing amount of perfect nonsense, and thought that it must be lunch-time. Accordingly, she went back to the house, and was found by Edith, a quarter of an hour later, playing hide-and-seek with the coachman's children, whom she had lured in from the stable-yard as she went by. The rules were that the searchers were to catch the hiders, and Dodo had entrenched herself behind the piano, and erected an impregnable barricade, consisting of a revolving bookcase and the music-stool. The two seekers entirely declined to consider that she had won, and Dodo, with a show of reason, was telling them that they hadn't caught her yet at any rate. The situation seemed to admit of no compromise and no solution, unless, as Dodo suggested, they got a pound or two of blasting powder and destroyed her defences. However, a *deus ex machina* appeared in the person of the coachman himself, who had come in for orders, and hinted darkly that maternal vengeance was brewing if certain persons did not wash their hands in time for dinner, which was imminent.

"There's a telegram for you somewhere," said Edith to Dodo, as she emerged hot and victorious. "I sent a man out into the garden with it. The messenger is waiting for an answer."

Dodo became suddenly grave.

"I suppose he's gone to the pond," she said; "that's where I was seen last. I'll go and get it."

She met the man walking back to the house, having looked for her in vain. She took the telegram and opened it. It had been forwarded from her London house. It was very short.

"I arrive in London to-day. May I call?—WALDENECH."

Dodo experienced, in epitome at that moment, all she had gone through the night before. She went to a garden-seat, and remained there in silence so long that the footman asked her: "Will there be an answer, my lady? The messenger is waiting."

Dodo held out her hand for the telegraph form. She addressed it to the caretaker at her London house. It also was very short:

"Address uncertain; I leave here to-day. Forward nothing."

She handed it to the man, and gave orders that it should go at once.

Dodo did not move. She sat still with her hands clasped in front of her, unconscious of active thought, only knowing that a stream of pictures seemed to pass before her eyes. She saw the Prince standing on her doorstep, learning with surprise that Lady Chesterford was not at home, and that her address was not known. She saw him turn away, baffled but not beaten; she saw him remaining in London day after day, waiting for the house in Eaton Square to show some signs of life. She saw—ah, she dismissed that picture quickly.

She had one sudden impulse to call back the footman and ask for another telegraph form; but she felt if she could only keep a firm hand on herself for a few moments, the worst would be passed; and it was with a sense of overwhelming relief that she saw the telegraph boy walk off down the drive with the reply in his hand.

Then it suddenly struck her that the Prince was waiting for the answer at Dover Station.

"How savage he will be," thought Dodo. "There will be murder at the telegraph office if he waits for his answer there. Well, somebody must suffer, and it will be the telegraph boys."

The idea of the Prince waiting at Dover was distinctly amusing, and Dodo found a broad smile to bestow on the thought before she continued examining the state of her feelings and position. The Prince's influence over her she felt was local and personal, so to speak, and now she had made her decision, she was surprised at the ease with which it had been made. Had he been there in person, with his courtly presence and his serene remoteness from anything ordinary, and had said, in that smooth, well-modulated voice, "May I hope to find you in to-morrow?" Dodo felt that she would have said "Come." Her pride was in frantic rebellion at these admissions; even the telegram she had sent was a confession of weakness. She would not see him, because she was afraid. Was there any other reason? she asked herself. Yes; she could not see him because she longed to see him.

"Has it come to that?" she thought, as she crumpled up the telegram which had fluttered down from her lap on to the grass. Dodo felt she was quite unnecessarily honest with herself in making this admission. But what followed? Nothing followed. She was going to marry Jack, and be remarkably happy, and Prince Waldenech should come and stay with them because she liked him very much, and she would be delightfully kind to him, and Jack should like him too. Dear old Jack, she would write him a line this minute, saying when she would be back in London.

Dodo felt a sudden spasm of anger against the Prince. What right had he to behave like this? He was making it very hard for her, and he would get nothing by it. Her decision was irrevocable; she would not see him again, for some time at any rate. She would get over this ridiculous fear of him. What was he that other men were not? What was the position, after all? He had wanted to marry her; she had refused him because she was engaged to Jack. If there had been no Jack—well, there was a Jack, so it was unnecessary to pursue that any further. He had given her his photograph, and had said several things that he should not have said. Dodo thought of that scene with regret. She had had an opportunity which she had missed; she might easily have made it plain to him that his murmured speeches went beyond mere courtesy. Instead of that she had said she would always regard him as a great friend, and hoped he would see her often. She tapped the ground impatiently as she thought of missed opportunities. It was stupid, inconceivably stupid of her. Then he had followed her to England, and sent this telegram. She did not feel safe. She longed, and dreaded to see him again. It was too absurd that she should have to play this gigantic game of hide-and-seek. "I shall have to put on a blue veil and green goggles when I go back to London," thought Dodo. "Well, the seekers have to catch the hiders, and he hasn't caught me yet."

Meanwhile the Prince was smoking a cigar at Dover Station. The telegram had not come, though he had waited an hour, and he had settled to give it another half-hour and then go on to London. He was not at all angry; it was as good as a game of chess. The Prince was very fond of chess. He enjoyed exercising a calculating long-sight-edness, and he felt that the Marchioness of Chesterford elect was a problem that enabled him to exercise this faculty, of which he had plenty, to the full.

He had a sublime sense of certainty as to what he was going to do. He fully intended to marry Dodo, and he admitted no obstacles. She was engaged to Jack, was she? So much the worse for Jack. She wished to marry Jack, did she? So much the worse for her, and none the worse, possibly the better, for him. As it was quite certain that he himself was going to marry Dodo, these little hitches were entertaining than otherwise. It is more fun to catch your salmon after a quarter of an hour's rather exciting fight with him than to net him. Half the joy of a possession lies in the act of acquisition, and the pleasure of acquisition consists, at least in half of the excitement attendant on it. To say that the Prince ever regarded anyone's feelings would be understating the truth. The fact that his will worked its way in opposition to, and at the expense of others, afforded him a distinct and appreciable pleasure. If he wanted anything he went straight for it, and regarded neither man, nor devil, nor angel; and he wanted Dodo.

His mind, then, was thoroughly made up. She seemed to him immensely original and very complete. He read her, he thought, like a book, and the book was very interesting reading. His sending of the telegram with "Reply paid," was a positive stroke of genius. Dodo had told him that she was going straight to London, but, as we have seen, she did not stop the night there, but went straight on to Edith's home in Berkshire. There were two courses open to her; either to reply "Yes" or "No" to the telegram, or to leave it unanswered. If she left it "unanswered" it would delight him above measure, and it seemed that his wishes were to be realised. Not answering the telegram would imply that she did not think good to see him, and he judged that this decision was probably promoted by something deeper than mere indifference to his company. It must be dictated by a strong motive. His calculations were a little at fault, because Dodo had not stopped in London, but this made no difference, as events had turned out, to the correctness of his deductions.

He very much wished Dodo to be influenced by strong motives in her dealings with him. He would not have accepted, even as a gift, the real, quiet liking she had for Jack. Real, quiet likings seemed to him to be as dull as total indifference. He would not have objected to her regarding him with violent loathing, that would be something to correct; and his experience in such affairs was that strong sympathies and antipathies were more akin to each other than quiet affection or an apathetic indifference were to either. He walked up and down the platform with the smile of a man who is waiting for an interesting situation in a theatrical representation to develop itself. He had no wish to hurry it. The by-play seemed to him to be very suitable, and he bought a morning paper. He glanced through the leaders, and turned to the small society paragraphs. The first that struck his eye was this: "The Marchioness of Chesterford arrived in London yesterday afternoon from the Continent."

He felt it was the most orthodox way of bringing the scene to its climax. Enter a newsboy, who hands paper to Prince, and exit. Prince unfolds paper and reads the news of—well, of what he is expecting.

He snipped the paragraph neatly out from the paper, and put it in his card-case. His valet was standing by the telegraph office, waiting for the message. The Prince beckoned to him.

"There will be no telegram," he said. "We leave by the next train."

The Prince had a carriage reserved for him, and he stepped in with a sense of great satisfaction. He even went so far as to touch his hat in response to the obeisances of the obsequious guard, and told his valet to see that the man got something. He soon determined on his next move—a decided "check," and rather an awkward one; and for the rest of his journey he amused himself by looking out of the window, and admiring the efficient English farming. All the arrangements seemed to him to be very solid and adequate. The hedges were charming.

The cart horses were models of sturdy strength, and the hop harvest promised to be very fine. He was surprised when they drew near London. The journey had been shorter than he expected.

He gave a few directions to his valet about luggage, and drove off to Eaton Square.

The door was opened by an impenetrable caretaker.

"Is Lady Chesterford in?" asked the Prince.

"Her ladyship is not in London, sir," replied the man.

The Prince smiled. Dodo was evidently acting up to her refusal to answer his telegram.

"Ah, just so," he remarked. "Please take this to her, and say I am waiting."

He drew from his pocket a card, and the cutting from the *Morning Post*.

"Her ladyship is not in London," the man repeated.

"Perhaps you would let me have her address," said the Prince, feeling in his pockets.

"A telegram has come to-day, saying that her ladyship's address is uncertain," replied the caretaker.

"Would you be so good as to let me see the telegram?"

Certainly, he would fetch it.

The Prince waited serenely. Everything was going admirably.

The telegram was fetched. It had been handed in at Wokingham station at a quarter to one. "After she had received my telegram," reflected the Prince.

"Do you know with whom she has been staying?" he asked blandly.

"With Miss Staines."

The Prince was very much obliged. He left a large gratuity in the man's hand, and wished him good afternoon.

He drove straight to his house, and sent for his valet, whom he could trust implicitly, and who had often been employed on somewhat delicate affairs.

"Take the first train for Wokingham to-morrow morning," he said. "Find out where Miss Staines lives. Inquire whether Lady Chesterford left the house to-day."

"Yes, your Highness."

"And hold your tongue about the whole business," said the Prince negligently, turning away and lighting a cigar. "And send me a telegram from Wokingham: 'Left yesterday,' or 'Still here.' "

The Prince was sitting over a late breakfast on the following morning, when a telegram was brought in. He read it, and his eyes twinkled with genuine amusement.

"I think," he said to himself, "I think that's rather neat."

20

If Dodo had felt some excusable pride in having torn up the
Prince's photograph, her refusal to let him know where she was gave
her a still more vivid sense of something approaching heroism. She
did not blame anyone but herself for the position into which she had
drifted during those weeks in Switzerland. She was quite conscious
that she might have stopped any intimacy of this sort arising, and
consequently the establishment of this power over her. But she felt
she was regaining her lost position. Each sensible refusal to admit
his influence over her was the sensible tearing asunder of the fibres
which enveloped her. It was hard work, she admitted, but she was
quite surprised to find how comfortable she was becoming. Jack really
made a very satisfactory background to her thoughts. She was very
fond of him, and she looked forward to their marriage with an eager
expectancy, which was partly, however, the result of another fear.

She was sitting in the drawing-room next day with Miss Grantham,
talking about nothing particular very rapidly.

"Of course, one must be good to begin with," she was saying; "one
takes that for granted. The idea of being wicked never comes into
my reckoning at all. I should do lots of things if I didn't care what I
did, that I shouldn't think of doing at all now. I've got an admirable
conscience. It is quite good, without being at all priggish. It isn't exactly
what you might call in holy orders, but it is an ecclesiastical layman,
and has great sympathy with the Church. A sort of lay-reader, you
know."

"I haven't got any conscience at all," said Miss Grantham. "I believe
I am fastidious in a way, though, which prevents me doing conspicuously beastly things."

"Oh, get a conscience, Grantie," said Dodo fervently, "it is such a
convenience. It's like having someone to make up your mind for you.
I like making up other people's minds, but I cannot make up my own;
however, my conscience does that for me. It isn't me a bit. I just give
it a handful of questions which I want an answer upon, and it gives
me them back, neatly docketed, with 'Yes' or 'No' upon them."

"That's no use," said Miss Grantham. "I know the obvious 'Yeses'
and 'Noes' myself. What I don't know are the host of things that
don't matter much in themselves, which you can't put down either
right or wrong."

"Oh, I do all those," said Dodo serenely, "if I want to, and if I
don't, I have an excellent reason for not doing them, because I am
not sure whether they are right. When I set up my general advice

office, which I shall do before I die, I shall make a special point of that for other people. I shall give decided answers in most cases, but I shall reserve a class of things indifferent, which are simply to be settled by inclination."

"What do you call indifferent things?" asked Miss Grantham, pursuing the Socratic method.

"Oh, whether you are to play lawn tennis on Sunday afternoon," said Dodo, "or wear mourning for second cousins, or sing alto in church for the sake of the choir; all that sort of thing."

"Your conscience evidently hasn't taken orders," remarked Miss Grantham.

"That's got nothing to do with my conscience," said Dodo. "My conscience doesn't touch those things at all. It only concerns itself with right and wrong."

"You're very moral this morning," said Miss Grantham. "Edith," she went on, as Miss Staines entered in a howling wilderness of dogs, "Dodo has discovered a conscience."

"Whose?" asked Edith.

"Why, my own, of course," said Dodo; "but it's no discovery. I always knew I had one."

"There's someone waiting to see you," said Edith. "I brought his card in."

She handed Dodo a card.

"Prince Waldenech," she said quietly to herself; "let him come in here, Edith. You need not go away."

Dodo got up and stood by the mantelpiece, and displayed an elaborate attention to one of Edith's dogs. She was angry with herself for needing this minute of preparation, but she certainly used it to the best advantage; and when the Prince entered she greeted him with an entirely natural smile of welcome.

"Ah, this is charming," she said, advancing to him. "How clever of you to find out my address."

"I am staying at a house down here," said the Prince, lying with conscious satisfaction as he could not be contradicted, "and I could not resist the pleasure."

Dodo introduced him to Edith and Miss Grantham, and sat down again.

"I sent no address, as I really did not know where I might be going," she said, following the Prince's lead. "That I was not in London was all my message meant. I did not know you would be down here."

"Lord Chesterford is in England?" asked the Prince.

"Oh, yes, Jack came with me as far as Dover, and then he left me for the superior attractions of partridge-shooting. Wasn't it rude of him?"

"He deserves not to be forgiven," said the Prince.

"I think I shall send you to call him out for insulting me," said Dodo lightly; "and you can kill each other comfortably while I look on. Dear old Jack."

"I should feel great pleasure in fighting Lord Chesterford if you told me to," said the Prince, "or if you told him to, I'm sure he would feel equal pleasure in killing me."

Dodo laughed.

"Duelling has quite gone out," she said. "I sha'n't require you ever to do anything of that kind."

"I am at your service," he said.

"I wish you'd open that window then," said Dodo; "it is dreadfully stuffy. Edith, you really have too many flowers in the room."

"Why do you say that duelling has gone out?" he asked. "You might as well say that devotion has gone out."

"No one fights duels now," said Dodo; "except in France, and no one, even there, is ever hurt, unless they catch cold in the morning air, like Mark Twain."

"Certainly no one goes out with a pistol-case, and a second, and a doctor," said the Prince; "that was an absurd way of duelling. It is no satisfaction to know that you are a better shot than your antagonist."

"Still less to know that he is a better shot than you," remarked Miss Grantham.

"Charming," said the Prince; "that is worthy of Lady Chesterford. And higher praise—"

"Go on about duelling," said Dodo, unceremoniously.

"The old system was no satisfaction, because the quarrel was not about who was the better shot. Duelling is now strictly decided by merit. Two men quarrel about a woman. They both make love to her; in other words, they both try to cut each other's throats, and one succeeds. It is far more sensible. Pistols are stupid bull-headed weapons. Words are much finer. They are exquisite sharp daggers. There is no unnecessary noise or smoke, and they are quite orderly."

"Are those the weapons you would fight Lord Chesterford with, if Dodo told you to?" asked Edith, who was growing uneasy.

The Prince, as Dodo once said, never made a fool of himself. It was a position in which it was extremely easy for a stupid man to say something very awkward. Lady Grantham, with all her talent for asking inconvenient questions, could not have formed a more unpleasant one. He looked across at Dodo a moment, and said, without a perceptible pause,—

"If I ever was the challenger of Lady Chesterford's husband, the receiver of the challenge has the right to choose the weapons."

The words startled Dodo somehow. She looked up and met his eye.

"Your system is no better than the old one," she said. "Words become the weapons instead of pistols, and the man who is most skilful with words has the same advantage as the good shot. You are not quarrelling about words, but about a woman."

"But words are the expression of what a man is," said the Prince. "You are pitting merit against merit."

Dodo rose and began to laugh.

"Don't quarrel with Jack, then," she said. "He would tell the footman to show you the door. You would have to fight the footman. Jack would not speak to you."

Dodo felt strongly the necessity of putting an end to this conversation, which was effectually done by this somewhat uncourteous speech. The fencing had become rather too serious to please her, and she did not wish to be serious. But she felt oppressively conscious of this man's personality, and saw that he was stronger than she was herself. She decided to retreat, and made a desperate effort to be entirely flippant.

"I hope the Princess has profited by the advice I gave her," she said. "I told her how to be happy though married, and how not to be bored though a Russian. But she's a very bad case."

"She said to me dreamily as I left," said the Prince, " 'You'll hear of my death on the Matterhorn. Tell Lady Chesterford it was her fault.' "

Dodo laughed.

"Poor dear thing," she said, "I really am sorry for her. It's a great pity she didn't marry a day labourer and have to cook the dinner and slap the children. It would have been the making of her."

"It would have been a different sort of making," remarked the Prince.

"I believe you can even get *blasé* of being bored," said Miss Grantham, "and then, of course, you don't get bored any longer, because you are bored with it."

This remarkable statement was instantly contradicted by Edith.

"Being bored is a bottomless pit," she remarked. "You never get to the end, and the deeper you go the longer it takes to get out. I was never bored in my life. I like listening to what the dullest people say."

"Oh, but it's when they don't say anything that they're so trying," said Miss Grantham.

"I don't mind that a bit," remarked Dodo. "I simply think aloud to them. The less a person says the more I talk, and then suddenly I see that they're shocked at me, or that they don't understand. The Prince is often shocked at me, only he's too polite to say so. I don't mean that you're a dull person, you know, but he always understands.

You know he's quite intelligent," Dodo went on, introducing him with a wave of her hand, like a showman with a performing animal. "He knows several languages. He will talk on almost any subject you wish. He was thirty-five years of age last May, and will be thirty-six next May."

"He has an admirable temper," said the Prince, "and is devoted to his keeper."

"Oh, I'm not your keeper," said Dodo. "I wouldn't accept the responsibility. I'm only reading extracts from the advertisement about you."

"I was only reading extracts as well," observed the Prince. "Surely the intelligent animal, who knows several languages, may read its own advertisement?"

"I'm not so sure about your temper," said Dodo, reflectively. "I shall alter it to 'is believed to have an admirable temper.' "

"Never shows fight," said the Prince.

"But is willing to fight if told to," said she. "He said so himself."

"Oh, but I only bark when I bite," said the Prince, alluding to his modern system of duelling.

"Then your bite is as bad as your bark," remarked Dodo, "which is a sign of bad temper. And now, my dear Prince, if we talk any more about you, you will get intolerably conceited, and that won't do at all. I can't bear conceited men. They always seem to me to be like people on stilts. They are probably not taller than oneself really, and they're out of all proportion, all legs, and no body or head. I don't want anyone to bring themselves down to my level when they talk to me. Conceited people always do that. They get off their stilts. If there's one thing that amuses me more than another, it is getting hold of their stilts and sawing them half through. Then, when they get up again they come down 'Bang,' and you say: 'Oh, I hope you haven't hurt yourself. I didn't know you went about on stilts. They are very unsafe, aren't they?' "

Dodo was conscious of talking rather wildly and incoherently. She felt like a swimmer being dragged down by a deep undercurrent. All she could do was to make a splash on the surface. She could not swim quietly or strongly out of its reach. She stood by the window playing with the blind cord, wishing that the Prince would not look at her. He had a sort of deep, lazy strength about him that made Dodo distrust herself—the indolent consciousness of power that a tiger has when he plays contemptuously with his prey before hitting it with one deadly blow of that soft cushioned paw.

"Why can't I treat him like anyone else?" she said to herself impatiently. "Surely I am not afraid of him. I am only afraid of being afraid. He is handsome, and clever, and charming, and amiable, and here am I watching every movement and listening to every word he says. It's all nonsense. Here goes."

Dodo plunged back into the room, and sat down in the chair next him.

"What a charming time we had at Zermatt," she said. "That sort of place is so nice if you simply go there in order to amuse yourself without the bore of entertaining people. Half the people who go there treat it as their great social effort of the year. As if one didn't make enough social efforts at home!"

"Ah, Zermatt," said the Prince, meditatively. "It was the most delightful month I ever spent."

"Did you like it?" said Dodo negligently. "I should have thought that sort of place would have bored you. There was nothing to do. I expected you would rush off as soon as you got there, and go to shoot or something."

"Like Lord Chesterford and the partridges," suggested Edith.

"Oh, that's different," said Dodo. "Jack thinks it's the duty of every English landlord to shoot partridges. He's got great ideas of his duty."

"Even when it interferes with what must have been his pleasure, apparently," said the Prince.

"Oh, Jack and I will see plenty of each other in course of time. I'm not afraid he will go and play about without me."

"You are too merciful," said the Prince.

"Oh, I sha'n't be hard on Jack. I shall make every allowance for his shortcomings, and I shall expect that he will make allowance for mine."

"He will have the best of the bargain," said the Prince.

"You mean that he won't have to make much allowance for me?" asked Dodo. "My dear Prince, that shows how little you really know about me. I can be abominable. Ask Miss Staines if I can't. I can make a man angry quicker than any woman I know. I could make you angry in a minute and a quarter, but I am amiable this morning, and I will spare you."

"Please make me angry," said the Prince.

Dodo laughed, and held out her hand to him.

"Then you will excuse my leaving you?" she said. "I've got a letter to write before the midday post. That ought to make you angry. Are you stopping to lunch? No? *Au revoir*, then. We shall meet again sometime soon, I suppose. One is always running up against people."

Dodo shook hands with elaborate carelessness and went towards the door, which the Prince opened for her.

"You have made me angry," he murmured, as she passed out, "but you will pacify me again, I know."

Dodo went upstairs into her bedroom. She was half frightened at her own resolution, and the effort of appearing quite unconcerned had given her a queer, tired feeling. She heard a door shut in the drawing-room below, and steps in the hall. A faint flush came over her face, and she got up quickly from her chair and ran downstairs. The Prince was in the hall, and he did not look the least surprised to see Dodo again.

"Ah, you are just off?" she asked.

Then she stopped dead, and he waited as if expecting more. Dodo's eyes wandered round the walls and came back to his face again.

"Come and see me in London any time," she said in a low voice. "I shall go back at the end of the week."

The Prince bowed.

"I knew you would pacify me again," he said.

21

Dodo was up again in London at the end of the week, as she had told the Prince. Jack was also staying in town, and they often spent most of the day together, riding occasionally in the deserted Row, or sitting, as they were now, in Dodo's room in the Eaton Square house. They were both leaving for the country in a few days' time, where they had arranged to come across one another at various houses, and Dodo, at least, was finding these few days rather trying. She and Jack had arranged to have them together, quite alone, while they were in Switzerland, and Dodo had overlooked the fact that they might be rather hard to fill up. Not that she was disappointed in Jack. He was exactly what she had always supposed him to be. She never thought that he was very stimulating, though never dull, and she was quite conscious of enough stimulus in herself for that. For the rest he was quite satisfactory. But she was distinctly disappointed in herself. She felt as if her taste had been vitiated by drinking brandy. Mild flavours and very good bouquets of vintages that had pleased her before, sent no message from her palate to her brain. It was like the effect produced by the touch of hot iron on the skin, that forms a hard numb surface, which is curiously insensitive to touch. Dodo felt as if her powers of sensation had been seared in this way. Her perceptions no longer answered quickly to the causes that excited them; a layer of dull, unresponsive material lay between her and her world. She thought that her nerves and tissues were sound enough below. This numbness was only superficial, the burn would heal, and her skin would become pliant and soft again; and if she was conscious of all this and its corresponding causes, it could hardly be expected that Jack would be unconscious of it and its corresponding effects.

On this particular morning Dodo was particularly aware of it. It was raining dismally outside, and the sky was heavy and grey. The road was being repaired, and a traction engine was performing its dismal office in little aimless runs backwards and forwards. The official with a red flag had found there were no vehicles for him to warn and he had sat down on a heap of stones, and was smoking. There was a general air of stagnation, a sense of the futility of doing anything, and no one was more conscious of it than Dodo. She felt that there was only one event that was likely to interest her, and yet, in a way, she shrank from that. It was the searing process over again.

She wondered whether it would do any good to tell Jack of the fact that the Prince was down at Wokingham. She found the burden of an unshared secret exceptionally trying. Dodo had been so accustomed to be before the footlights all her life, that anything of the nature of a secret was oppressive. Her conduct to her first husband she did not regard as such. It was only an admirable piece of by-play, which the audience fully appreciated. Did Dodo then never think of her late husband with tenderness? Well, not often.

A thought seldom remained long in Dodo's mind without finding expression. She turned round suddenly.

"Jack, Prince Waldenech was at Wokingham."

"What was he there for?" asked Jack quickly.

"I think he came to see me," remarked Dodo serenely.

"I hope you didn't see him," he replied.

Dodo felt a slight stimulus in this subject.

"I saw him," she said, "because he came to see me, as they say in the French exercise books. I couldn't hide my head under the hearthrug like an ostrich—not that they hide their heads under hearthrugs, but the principle is the same. He walked in as cool as a cucumber, and said, 'Howdy?' So we talked, and he said he'd be glad to call you out, and you'd be glad to call him out, and we generally chattered, and then I made him angry."

"Why did he propose to call me out?" asked Jack coldly.

"Oh, he said he wouldn't call you out," remarked Dodo. "He said nothing would induce him to. I never said he proposed to call you out. You're stupid this morning, Jack."

"That man is an unutterable cad."

Dodo opened her eyes.

"Oh, he's nothing of the kind," she said. "Besides, he's a great friend of mine, so even if he was a cad it wouldn't matter."

"How did you make him angry?" demanded Jack.

"I told him I was going away to write some letters. It was rather damping, wasn't it? I hadn't got any letters to write, and he knew it, and I knew he knew it, and so on."

Jack was silent. He had been puzzled by Dodo's comparative reserve during the last few days. He felt as if he had missed a scene in a play, that there were certain things unexplained. He had even gone so far as to ask Dodo if anything was the matter, an inquiry which she detested profoundly. She laid down a universal rule on this occasion.

"Nothing is ever the matter," she had said, "and if it was, my not telling you would show that I didn't wish for sympathy, or help, or anything else. I tell you all I want you to know."

"You mean something is the matter, and you don't want me to know it," said Jack, rather unwisely.

They had been riding together when this occurred, and at that point Dodo had struck her horse savagely with her whip, and put an end to the conversation by galloping furiously off. When Jack caught her up she was herself again, and described how a selection of Edith's dogs had kept the postman at bay one morning, until the unusual absence of barking and howling had led their mistress to further investigations, which were rewarded by finding the postman sitting in the boat-house, and defending himself with the punt pole.

Jack was singularly easy-going, and very trustful, and he did not bother his head any more about it at the time. But we have to attain an almost unattainable dominion over our minds to prevent thoughts suddenly starting up in front of us. When a thought has occurred to one, it is a matter of training and practice to encourage or dismiss it, but the other is beyond the reach of the general. And as Dodo finished these last words, Jack found himself suddenly face to face with a new thought. It was so new that it startled him, and he looked at it again. At moments like these two people have an almost supernatural power of intuition towards each other. Dodo was standing in the window, and Jack was sitting in a very low chair, looking straight towards her, with the light from the window full on his face, and at that moment she read his thought as clearly as if he had spoken it, for it was familiar already to her.

She felt a sudden impulse of anger.

"How dare you think that?" she said.

Jack needed no explanation, and he behaved well.

"Dodo," he said gently, "you have no right to say that, but you have said it now. If there is not anything I had better know, just tell me so, for your own sake and for mine. I can only plead for your forgiveness. It was by no will of mine that such a thought crossed my mind. You can afford to be generous, Dodo."

Something in his speech made Dodo even angrier.

"You are simply forcing my confidence," she said. "If it was something you had better know, do you suppose that——"

She stopped abruptly.

Jack rose from his chair and stood by her in the window.

"You are not very generous to me," he said. "We are old friends though we are lovers."

"Take care you don't lose my friendship, then," said Dodo fiercely. "It is no use saying 'auld lang syne' when 'auld lang syne' is in danger. It would be like singing 'God save the Queen' when she was dying. You should never recall old memories when they are strained."

Jack was getting a little impatient, though he was not frightened yet.

"Dodo, you really are rather unreasonable," he said. "To begin with, you quarrel with an unspoken thought, and you haven't even given me a definite accusation."

"That is because it is unnecessary, and you know it," said Dodo. "However, as you like. You think you have cause to be jealous or foolish or melodramatic about Prince Waldenech. Dear me, it is quite like old times."

Jack turned on her angrily.

"If you propose to treat me as you treated that poor man, who was the best man I ever knew," he said, "the sooner you learn your mistake the better for us both. It would have been in better taste not to have referred to that."

"At present that is beside the point," said Dodo. "Was that your unspoken thought, or was it not?"

"If I would not insult you by speaking my thought whether you are right or not," said Jack, "I shall not insult you by answering that question. My answer shall take another form. Listen, Dodo. The Prince is in love with you. He proposed to you at Zermatt. That passionless inhuman piece of mechanism, his sister, told me how much he was in love with you. She meant it as a compliment. He is a dangerous, bad man. He forces himself on you. He went down to Wokingham to see you; you told me so yourself. He is dangerous and strong. For God's sake keep away from him. I don't distrust you; but I am afraid you may get to distrust yourself. He will make you afraid of crossing his will. Dodo, will you do this for me? It is quite unreasonable probably, but I am unreasonable when I think of you."

"Oh, my dear Jack," said Dodo impatiently, "you really make me angry. It is dreadfully bad form to be angry, and it is absurd that you and I should quarrel. You've got such a low opinion of me; though

I suppose that's as much my fault as yours. Your opinion is fiction, but I am the fact on which it is founded, and what do you take me for? The Prince telegraphed from Dover to ask if I would see him, and I deliberately sent no answer. How he found out where I was I don't know. I suppose he got hold of the telegram I sent here to say my address was uncertain. Does that look as if I wanted to see him so dreadfully?"

"I never said you did want to see him," said Jack. "I said he very much wanted to see you, and what you say proves it."

"Well, what then?" said Dodo. "You wanted to see me very much when I was married. Would you have thought it reasonable if Chesterford had entreated me never to see you—to keep away for God's sake, as you said just now?"

"I am not the Prince," said Jack, "neither am I going to be treated as you treated your husband. Do not let us refer to him again; it is a desecration."

"You mean that in the light of subsequent events it would have been reasonable in him to ask me to keep away from you?"

"Yes," said he.

Jack looked Dodo full in the face, in the noble shame of a confessed sin. In that moment he was greater, perhaps, and had risen higher above his vague self-satisfied indifference than ever before. Dodo felt it, and it irritated her, it seemed positively unpardonable.

"Perhaps you do not see that you involve me in your confession," she said with cold scorn. "I decline to be judged by your standards, thanks."

Jack felt a sudden immense pity and anger for her. She would not, or could not, accept the existence of other points of view than her own.

"Apparently you decline to consider the fact of other standards at all."

"I don't accept views which seem to me unreasonable," she said.

"I only ask you to consider this particular view. The story you have just told me shows that he is anxious to see you, which was my point. That he is dangerous and strong I ask you to accept."

"What if I don't?" she asked.

"This," said he. "When a man of that sort desires anything, as he evidently desires you, there is danger. If you are alive to it, and as strong as he is, you are safe. That you are not alive to it you show by your present position; that you are as strong as he, I doubt."

"You assume far too much," said Dodo. "What you mean by my present position I don't care to know. But I am perfectly alive to the whole state of the case. Wait. I will speak. I entirely decline to be dictated to. I shall do as I choose in this matter."

"Do you quite realise what that means?" said Jack, rising.

Dodo had risen too; she was standing before him with a great anger burning in her eyes. Her face was very pale, and she moved towards the bell.

When a boat is in the rapids the cataract is inevitable.

"It means this," she said. "He will be here in a minute or two; I told him I should be in at twelve. I am going to ring the bell and tell the man to show him up. You will stay here, and treat him as one man should treat another. If you are insolent to him, understand that you include me. You will imply that you distrust me. Perhaps you would ring the bell for me, as you are closer to it."

She sat down by her writing-table and waited.

Jack paused with his hand on the bell.

"I will be perfectly explicit with you," he said. "If you see him, you see him alone. I do not wish to hear what he has to say to you. As he enters the door I leave it. That is all. You may choose."

He rang the bell.

"There is no reason for you to wait till then," said Dodo. "I am going to see him as soon as he comes. Tell Prince Waldenech that I am in," she said to the footman. "Show him up as soon as he comes."

Jack leant against the chimney-piece.

"Well?" said Dodo.

"I am making up my mind."

There was a dead silence. "What on earth are we quarrelling about?" thought Jack to himself. "Is it simply whether I stop here and talk to that cad? I wonder if all women are as obstinate as this."

It did seem a little ridiculous, but he felt that his dignity forbade him to yield. He had told her he did not distrust her; that was enough. No, he would go away, and when he came back to-morrow Dodo would be more reasonable.

"I think I am going," remarked he. "I sha'n't see you again till to-morrow afternoon. I am away to-night."

Dodo was turning over the pages of a magazine and did not answer. Jack became a little impatient.

"Really, this is extraordinarily childish," he said. "I sha'n't stop to see the Prince because he is a detestable cad. Think it over, Dodo."

At the mention of the Prince, if Jack had been watching Dodo more closely, he might have seen a sudden colour rush to her face, faint but perceptible. But he was devoting his attention to keeping his temper, and stifling a vague dread and distrust, which he was too loyal to admit.

At the door he paused a moment.

"Ah, Dodo," he said, with entreaty in his voice.

Dodo did not move nor look at him.

He left the room without more words, and on the stair he met the Prince. He bowed silently to his greeting, and stood aside for him to pass.

The Prince glanced back at him with amusement. "His lordship does **me** the honour to be jealous of me," he said to himself.

· · · · · · ·

Next day Jack called at Dodo's house. The door was opened by a servant, whose face he thought he ought to know; that he was not one of Dodo's men he felt certain. In another moment it had flashed across him that the man had been with the Prince at Zermatt.

"Is Lady Chesterford in?" he asked.

The man looked at him a moment, then, like all well-bred servants, dropped his eyes before he answered,—

"Her Serene Highness left for Paris this morning."

DODO THE SECOND

1

Nadine Waldenech's sitting-room in her mother's cottage at Meering in North Wales was a great square chamber on the ground floor with many windows. The cottage, considered as a cottage, was quite a large one, for it held some eighteen people, but Dodo was firm on this subject of its not being in any sense a house, because if undesirable guests proposed themselves, no one believed you if you said your house was full, whereas it was clearly credible that a cottage might be so crammed that people really were sticking out of the windows. In the days when the commodious cottage was built, this sitting-room of Nadine's had been the smoking-room, but since now-a-days everybody smoked in every room in the house, Nadine said that it was misleading, if not positively untrue, to call any room the smoking-room, and she wanted this particular room very much. It opened out of her bedroom on one side, which was convenient, and out of the drawing-room on the other. This, too, had its advantages, for it was thus an easy meeting-place for those who wished to drop in for a little more conversation after bed-time had been officially proclaimed. The official proclamation of bed-time, it may be remarked, was designed to get rid of bores, who, thereupon, if they had any sense of propriety, would proceed to immure themselves in their appointed resting-places. Just now Esther Sturgis shared Nadine's bedroom as people stuck out of most of the windows of the cottage.

The sitting-room at this period was completely black with regard to the colour of the carpet and the walls, and the ceiling, and to be alone in it was like being in a family vault, but practically speaking this never happened. This funeral colouring was Nadine's latest plan, and since it was her latest, it was necessarily a very recent one. She had observed that when it was all white people looked slightly discoloured, like London snow, whereas against a black background, they seemed to be of gem-like brilliance. But since she always looked brilliant herself even against yellow, the new colour was prompted by wholly altruistic motives. She liked her friends to look brilliant too, and she would have preferred even a brilliant enemy to a discoloured one. During this last week there had been a good many friends in her room, and bed-time having been already officially proclaimed, there were a certain number here now and she expected more. A peculiarly frank intimacy reigned among them, and collectively they were known as the clan.

Up one side of the room ran an enormous low settee, covered and piled with large black cushions so that you could fall down on to it instead of taking the trouble to seat yourself. At present it was occupied by only three people, she herself lying on the right of it. She had already taken off her dinner-dress, which she said made her feel burdened with respectability, and had on a remarkable dressing-gown of Oriental silk, which looked like a cheerful family of intoxicated rainbows. It left her arms bare to the elbows, but came down to her feet, so that only the tips of her pink satin shoes peeped out. In the middle of the settee was lying Esther Sturgis, and along the foot of it Bertie Arbuthnot the younger, who was twenty-one years old, and about the same number of feet in height. In consequence his head dangled over one end of it like a tired and sunburned flower, and his large feet projected over the other. He and his hostess were both smoking cigarettes as if against time, the ash of which they flicked on to the floor, relighting fresh ones from a silver box like a small portmanteau that lay to hand. They neither of them had any clear idea as to what happened to the smoked-out ends, but something must have. Esther Sturgis on the other hand was occasionally sipping camomile tea. What she did not sip she spilt.

"Heredity is such nonsense," said Nadine crisply, speaking with that precision that the English-born never quite attain. "Look at me for instance, and how nice I am, and then consider Mamma and Daddy."

Esther emotionally spilt a larger quantity of camomile tea than usual. It was difficult to drink lying down.

"You shan't say a word against Aunt Dodo," she said.

"My dear, I do not propose to. Mamma is the biggest duck that ever happened. But I don't inherit. She had such a lot of hearts—it sounds like Bridge—and here am I without any. First of all she married poor step-papa—is it a step-papa if he is already dead before you have begun? Anyhow, I mean the Lord Chesterford whom she married before she married Daddy. That is one heart, but I think that was only a little one, the three, perhaps. Then she married Daddy, which is another heart."

"The Knave," said Esther.

"Yes. Poor Daddy. She ran away with him, you know, *ventre à terre,* while she was engaged to the other Lord Chesterford who succeeded step-papa."

"Oh, Jack the Ripper," said Esther.

Bertie raised his head a little.

"Who?" he asked.

"Jack Chesterford, because he is such a ripper," said Nadine. "And he is coming here to-morrow. Isn't it a thrill? Mamma hasn't seen him except once in a taxi, since she didn't see him one day when he called, and found she had run away with Daddy."

"Did he rip anybody?" asked Bertie, who was famed for going on asking questions, until he completely understood.

"No, donkey. You are thinking of some criminal. Mamma was engaged to him, and she thought she couldn't—so *she* ripped—let her rip, is it not?—and got married to Daddy instead. Daddy was quite mad about darling Mamma, but recovered very soon. He made a very bad recovery. Don't interrupt, Berts. I was talking about heredity. Well, there's Mamma and Daddy, well, we all know what Daddy is, and let me tell you he is the best of the family, which is poor. He is a gentleman after all, whatever he has done. And he's done a lot. Indeed he has never had an idle moment, except when he was busy!"

Esther gave a great sigh: she always sighed when she appreciated, and appreciation was the work of her life. She never got over the wonderfulness of Nadine and was in a perpetual state of deep breathing. She admired Bertie too, and they often used to talk about getting engaged to each other some day, in a mild and sexless fashion. But they were neither of them in any hurry.

"Aren't your other people gentlemen?" he asked. "I thought in Austria you were always all right if you quartered yourself into sixteen parts."

Nadine threw an almost unsmoked cigarette on to the floor with a little show of impatience.

"Of course one has the ordinary number of great great grandparents," she said, "or you wouldn't be here at all, and you quarter anything you choose. Two of my great-grandfathers were hung and drawn, apart from their quarterings. But really I don't think you understand what I mean by gentlemen. I mean people who have brains, and who have tastes, and who have fine perceptions. English people think they know the difference between the bourgeoisie and the aristocrats. How wrong they are! As if living in a castle like poor Esther's parents had anything to do with it! Look at some of your marquises—Esther darling, I don't mean Lord Ayr—— What cads! Your barons! What Aunt Sallys, always making the float-face, don't you call it, the *bêtise*, the stupidity. Is that the aristocracy? Great solemn Aunt Sallys and the rest brewers! Show me an idea, show me a brain, show me somebody with the distinction that thought and taste alone bring! I do not want a mere busy prating monkey thinking it is a man. But I want people: somebody with a man or woman inside it. Ah—give me a grocer. That will do!"

Bertie put down his head again.

"Let us be calm," he said. "I'll find you a grocer to-morrow. There is sure to be one in the village."

Nadine laughed. She had a curiously unmelodious but wonderfully infectious laugh. People hearing it laughed too: they caught it. But there was no sound of silvery bells. She gave a sort of hiccup and then gurgled.

"I get too excited over such things," she said. "And when I get excited I forget my English and talk execrably. I will be calm again. I do not mean that a man is not a gentleman because he is stupid, but I do mean that quarterings cannot make him one. The whole idea is so obsolete, so Victorian, like the old mahogany sideboards. Who cares about a grandfather? What does a grandfather matter any more? They used to say 'Move with *The Times.*' Now we move instead with the '*Daily Mail.*' I am half foreign and yet I am much more English than you all. The world goes spinning on. If we do not wish to become obsolete we spin too. I hate the common people, but I do not hate them because they have no grandfathers, but just because they are common. I hate quantities of your de Veres for the same reason. Their grandfathers make them no less common. But also I hate your sweet people, with blue eyes, of whom there are far too many. Put them in bottles like lollipops and let them stick together with their own sugar. *Mon Dieu*, what a world of abhorences!"

There was a short silence. Bertie broke it.

"How old are you?" he asked.

"Going in twenty-two. I am as old as there is any need to be. There is only one person in the house younger than me, and that is darling Mamma. She is twenty."

Esther gave another huge sigh. She appreciated Nadine very much, but she was not sure that she did not appreciate Aunt Dodo more. It may be remarked that there was no sort of consanguinity between them: the relationship was one of mere affection. She had a mother already, so Dodo must be the next nearest relative. Frankly, she would have liked to change the relationship between the two. And yet you could say things to an aunt who wasn't an aunt more freely than to a woman who actually happened to be your mother. Apart from natural love, Esther did not care for her mother. She would not, that is to say, have cared for her if she had been somebody else's mother, and, indeed, there was very little reason to do so. She had a Roman nose and talked about the Norman Conquest, which in the view of her family, was a very upstart affair. She had not a kind heart, but she had an immense coronet in her own right, and had married another. Indeed she had married another twice: there was a positive triple crown on her head like the Pope; in other respects also she was like a pope, and was infallible with almost indecent frequency. Nadine loved to refer to her as Holy Mother. She felt herself perfectly capable of managing everybody's affairs, and instead of being as broad as she was long, was as narrow as she was tall, and resembled an elderly guardsman.

Her degenerate daughter finished her sigh.

"Go on about your horrible family," she said to Nadine. "I think it's so illustrious of you to see them as they are."

The door opened, and Tommy Freshfield entered with a large black cigar in his mouth. He was rather short, and had the misfortune to look extremely dissipated, whereas he was hopelessly almost pathetically incapable of anything approaching dissipation. He put down his bedroom candle, stepped over Bertie and lay down on the couch next Esther Sturgis.

"Have you been comforting Hughie?" she asked.

"Yes, until he went to play billiards with the bishdean. Portmanteau word. He used to be a bishop but subsequently became a dean. I think Aunt Dodo believes he is a bishop still. Lots of bishops do it now he told me; it is the same as putting a carriage-horse out to grass: there is no work, but less corn. Hughie's coming up here when he's finished his game."

The appreciative Esther sat up.

"It's too wonderful of him," she said. "Nadine, Hugh is coming up here soon. Do be nice to him."

Nadine sat up also.

"Of course," she said. "Hughie has such tact, and I love him for it. Berts has none: he would sulk if I had just refused to marry him, and very likely would not speak to me till next day."

"You haven't had the chance to refuse me yet," remarked Berts.

"That is mere scoring for the sake of scoring, Berts, darling," said she. "But Hugh——"

"O Nadine, I wish you would marry him," said Esther. "It would make you so gorgeously complete and golden. Did you refuse him absolutely? Or would you rather not talk about it?"

Nadine turned a little sideways on the couch.

"No, we will not talk of it," she said. "What else were we saying? Ah, my family! Yes, it is a wonder that I am not a horror. Daddy is the pick of the bunch, but such a bunch, *mon Dieu!* such wild flowers, and poor Daddy always gets a little drunk in the evening now; and to-night he was so more than a little. But he is such an original! Fancy his coming to stay with Mamma here only a year after she divorced him. I think it is too sweet of her to let him come, and too sweet of him to suggest it. She is so remembering, too: she ordered him his particular brandy, without which he is never comfortable, and it is most expensive as well as being strong. Well, that's Daddy: then there are my uncles: such histories. Uncle Josef murdered a groom (there is no doubt whatever about it) who tried to blackmail him. I think he was quite right; and I daresay the groom was quite right, but it is a horrible thing to blackmail: it is a cleaner thing to kill. Then there is Uncle Anthony who ought to have been divorced like Daddy, but he was so mean and careful and sly that they could not catch him. There was never anything careful about Daddy."

She was ticking off these agreeable relations on her white fingers. "Then Grandpapa Waldenech committed suicide," she said, "and Grandpapa Vane fell into a cauldron at his own iron-works and was utterly burnt. So ridiculous: they could not even bury him, there was nothing left, except the thick smoke, and they had to open the windows. Then the Aunts. There was Aunt Lispeth, who kept nothing but white rats in her house in Vienna, hundreds and hundreds there were, the place crawled with them. Daddy could not go near it: he was afraid of their not being real, whereas I was afraid because they were real. Then there is Aunt Eleanor, who stole many of Daddy's gold snuff boxes and said the Emperor had given them her. Of course it was a long time before she was ever suspected, for she was always going to church when she was not stealing; she made quite a collection. Aunt Julia is more modern: she only cares about the music of Strauss and appendicitis."

Berts gave a sympathetic wriggle.

"I had appendicitis twice," he said, "which was enough, and I went to 'Electra' once which was too much. How often did Aunt Julia have appendicitis?"

"She never had it," said Nadine. "That is why she is so devoted to it, an ideal she never attains. It is about the only thing she has never had, and the others fatigue her. But she always goes to the opera whenever there is Strauss, because she cannot sleep afterwards, and so lies awake and thinks about appendicitis. I go to the opera, too, whenever there is not Strauss, in order to think about Hugh."

"And then you refuse him?"

"Yes, but we will not talk of it. There is nothing to explain. He is like that delicious ginger-beer I drank at dinner in stone bottles. You can't explain! It is ginger-beer. So is Hugh."

"I had a bottle of it, too," said Bertie. "More than one, I think. I hate wine. Wine is only fit for old women who want bucking up. There's an old man in the village at home who's ninety-five, and he never touched wine all his life."

"That proves nothing," said Nadine. "If he had drunk wine he might have been a hundred by now. But I like wine: perhaps I shall take after Daddy."

A long ash off Tommy Freshfield's cigar here fell into Esther's camomile tea. It fizzed agreeably as it was quenched, and she looked enquiringly into the glass.

"Oh, that's really dear of you, Tommy," she said. "I can't drink any more. John always insists upon my taking a glass of it to go to bed with."

"Your brother John is a prig, perhaps the biggest," said Nadine.

Esther reached out across Tommy, who did not offer his assistance, and put down her glass on the small table at the end of the settee.

"I hope there's no doubt of that," she said. "John would be very much upset if he thought he wasn't considered a prig. He is a snob, too, which is so frightfully Victorian, and thinks about lineage. Of course he takes after mother. I found him reading Debrett once."

"What is that?" asked Nadine.

"Oh, a red book about peers and baronets," said Esther rather vaguely. "You can look yourself up, and learn all about yourself, and see who you are."

"Poor John," said Nadine. "He had his camomile tea brought into the drawing-room to-night while he was talking to the bishop about Gothic architecture and the morals of great cities. He was asking if confirmation was found to have a great hold on the masses. The bishop didn't seem to have the slightest idea."

"John would make that all right," said his sister. "He would tell him. Nadine, why does darling Aunt Dodo so often have a bishop staying with her?"

Nadine sighed.

"Nobody really understands Mamma, except me," she said. "I thought perhaps you did, Esther, but it is clear you don't. She is religious, that's why. Just as artistic people like artists in their house, so religious people like bishops. I don't say that bishops are better than other people, any more than R.A.'s are finer artists, but they are recognised professionals. It is so; you may think I am laughing or mocking. But I am not. Give me more pillow, and Berts, take your face a little further from my feet. Or I shall kick it if I get excited again without intending to, but it will hurt you just the same."

Bertie followed this counsel of commonsense.

"That seems a simple explanation," he said.

Esther frowned; she was not quite so well satisfied.

"But is darling Aunt Dodo quite as religious when a bishop doesn't happen to be here?" she asked. "I mean, does she always have family prayers?"

"No, not always, nor do you go to your slums if there is anything very amusing elsewhere."

"But what have they got to do with religion?" asked Bertie.

"Haven't they something to do with it? I thought they had. I know Esther looks good when she has been to the slums, though, of course, it's quite delicious of her to go. Still if it makes you feel good, it isn't wholly unselfish. There is nothing so pleasant as feeling good. I felt good the day before yesterday. But after all there are exactly as many ways of being religious as there are people in the world. No two mean quite the same. I feel religious if I drive home just at dawn after a ball when all the streets are clean and empty and pearl-coloured. Darling Daddy feels religious when he doesn't eat meat on Thursday or Friday, whichever it is, and he has his immediate reward because he has the most delicious things instead, truffles stuffed with mushrooms or mushrooms stuffed with truffles. Also he drinks a good deal of wine that day, because you may drink what you like, and he likes tremendously. He has a particular *chef* for the days of meagre, who has to sit and think for six days, like the creation, and then work instead."

Nadine gurgled again.

"I suppose I shock you all," she said, "but English people are so unexpected about getting shocked that it is no use being careful. But they never get shocked at what they do themselves. Whatever they do themselves they know must be all right, and they take hands and sing Rule Britannia. They are the *enfants terrible* of Europe. They put their big stupid feet into everything, and when they have spoiled it all, so that nobody cares for it any longer, they ask why people are vexed at them! And then they go and play golf! I am getting very English myself. Except when I talk fast you would not know I was not English."

Esther, since her camomile tea was quite spoiled took a cigarette instead, which she liked better.

"Well, darling, you know every now and then you are a shade foreign," she said. "Especially when you talk about nationalities. As a nation I believe you positively loathe us. But that doesn't matter. It's he and she who matter, not they."

Berts had sat up at the mention of golf and was talking to Tommy.

"Yes, I won at the seventeenth," he said. "I took it in three. Two smacks and one put."

"Gosh," said Tommy.

"I wish I hadn't mentioned that damned game," said Nadine very distinctly. "You will talk about golf now till morning."

"Yes, but you needn't. Go on about your Daddy," said Esther.

"Certainly he is more interesting than golf, and gets into just as many holes. He is a creature of Nature. He falls in love every year, when the hounds of spring——"

Esther and Tommy interrupted loudly.

"Are on winter's traces, the Mother of months——"

"O ripping!" said Berts, wriggling.

"Yes. How *chic* to have written that and to have lived at Putney," said Nadine. "Mamma once took me to see Mr. Swinburne, and told me to kiss his hand as soon as ever I got into the room. So when we got in, there was one little old man there, and I kissed his hand, but it was not Mr. Swinburne at all, but somebody who had come to see him just like Mamma and me."

Again the door opened, and a woman entered, big, beautiful, vital. There was no mistaking her. The others had not been lacking in vitality before, but she brought in with her a far more abundant measure. She was forty-five perhaps, but clearly her age was the last thing to be thought about with regard to her. You could as well wonder what was the age of a sunlit wave breaking on the shore, or of a wind that blew from the sea. Everybody sat up at once.

"Mamma, darling, come here," said Nadine, "and talk to us."

Princess Waldenech looked round her largely and brilliantly.

"I thought I should find you all here," she said. "Nadine dear, of course you know best, but is it usual for girls to have two young gentlemen lying about with them on one sofa? I suppose it must be, since you all do it. Berts, is that you Berts? Really one can hardly see for the smoke. But after all this used to be the smoking-room, and I suppose it has formed the habit. Berts, you fiend, you made me laugh at dinner just when Bishop Spenser was telling me about the crisis of faith he went through when he was a young man so that he nearly became a Buddhist instead of a Bishop. Or do Buddhists have bishops too? Wasn't it dreadful? He's a dear, and he gives all his money away to endow other bishops, both black and white, like chess. Of course he isn't a bishop any more, but only a dean, but he keeps his title, like me. Hugh is playing billiards with him now, and told me in a whisper that he marked three for every cannon he made. Of course Hughie couldn't tell him it only counted two. It would have seemed unkind. Hugh has such tact."

"What I was saying," said Nadine. "Mamma, he proposed to me again this evening, and I said no, as usual. Is he depressed?"

"No, dear, not in the least, except about the cannons. Probably you will say yes, sometime. And I want a cigarette and something to drink, and to be amused for exactly half-an-hour, when I shall take myself to pieces and go to bed. I hate going to bed, and it adds to the depression to know that I shall have to get up again. If only I could be a Christian Scientist I should know that there is no such thing as a bed, and that therefore you can't go there. On the other hand that would be fatiguing, I suppose."

Tommy gave her a cigarette, and Nadine fetched her mother her bedroom bottle of water, out of which she drank freely, having refused camomile tea with cigar ash in it.

"Too delicious!" she said. "Nadine, darling, do marry Hugh before you are twenty-two. Nowadays if girls don't marry before that they take a flat or something and read at the British Museum till they are thirty and have got spectacles, without even getting compromised——"

"Compromised? Of course not," cried Nadine. "You can't get compromised now. There is no such thing as compromise. We die in the ditch sooner, like poor Lord Halsbury. Being compromised was purely a Victorian sort of decoration, like—like crinolines. Oh, do tell us about those delicious Victorian days of 1890 when you were a girl and people thought you fast and were shocked."

"My dear, you wouldn't believe it," said Dodo, "you would think I was describing what happened in Noah's Ark. Berts and Tommy, for instance, would never have been allowed to come and lie about like this."

"Oh, why not?" asked Esther.

"Because you and Nadine are girls and they are boys. That sounds simple nonsense, doesn't it? Also because to a certain extent boys and girls then did as older people told them to, and other people would have told them to go away. You see we used to listen to older people because they were older, now you don't listen to them for identically the same reason. We thought they were bores and obeyed them; you are perfectly sweet to them, but they have learned never to tell you to do anything. You would never do what I told you, dear, unless you wanted to."

"No, Mamma, I suppose not. But I always do what you tell me, as it is, because you always tell me to do exactly what I want to."

Dodo laughed.

"Yes, that is just what education means now. And how nicely we get along. Nobody is shocked now in consequence, which is much better for them. You can die of shock, so doctors say, without any other injury at all. So it is clearly wise not to be shocked. I was shocked once, when I was eight years old, because I was taken to the dentist without being told. I was told that I was to go for an ordinary walk with my sister Maud. And then, before I knew where I was there was my mouth open as far as my uvula, and a dreadful man with a mirror and a pincer was looking at my teeth. I lost my trust in human honour, which I have since then regained. I think Maud was more shocked than me. I think it conduced to her death. You don't remember Auntie Maud, Nadine, do you? You were so little and she was so unrememberable. Yes: a quantity of worsted work. But that's why I always want the Bishop to come whenever he can."

"I don't see why even now," said Nadine.

"Darling, aren't you rather slow? Bishop Spenser you know, who was Auntie Maud's husband. Surely you've heard me call him Algie. Who ever called a Bishop by his Christian name unless he was a relative? Maud loved him when he was a curate. She fluffed herself up in him, just as she used to do in her worsted, and nobody ever saw her any more. But I loved Maud, and I don't think she ever knew it. Some people don't know you love them unless you tell them so, and it is so silly to tell your sister that you love her. I never say I love you, either, and I don't say I love Esther, and that silly Berts, and serious Tommy. But what's the use of you all unless you know it? Nadine, ring the bell, please. It all looks as if we were going to talk, and I had no dinner to speak of, because I was being anxious about Daddy. I thought he was going to talk Hungarian; he looked as if he was, and so I got anxious, because he only talks Hungarian when he is what people call very much on. Certainly he wasn't 'off' to-night; he is off to-morrow. And so I want food. If I am being anxious I want food immediately afterwards, as soon as the anxiety is removed. At least I suppose Daddy has gone to bed. You haven't got him here have you? Fancy me being as old as any two of you. You are all so delightful, that you mustn't put me on the shelf yet. But just think! I was nice the other day to Berts' sister, and she told her mother she had got a new friend, who was quite old. 'Not so old as Grannie,' she said, 'but quite old!' And all the time I thought we were being girls together. At least I thought I was: I thought she was rather middle-aged. How is your mother, Berts? She doesn't approve of me, but I hope she is quite well."

Bertie also was a nephew by affection.

"Aunt Dodo," he said, "I think mother is too silly for anything."

"I knew something was coming," said Dodo.

"Well, it is. She said she thought you were heartless."

"Silly ass," said Esther. "Go on, Berts."

Berts felt goaded.

"Of course mother is a silly ass," he said. "It's no use telling me that. Your mother is a silly ass, too, with her coronets and all that sort of fudge. But altogether there is very little to be said for people over forty, except Aunt Dodo."

"Beloved Berts," remarked Dodo. "Go on about Edith."

"But it is so. They're all antiques except you, battered antiques. Let's talk about mothers generally. Look at Esther's mother. She doesn't want me to marry Esther because my father is only an ordinary Mister. There's a reason! And I don't want to marry Esther because her father is a marquis. There's something comic about marquises. And after all my mother has done more than Esther's, who never did anything except cut William the Conqueror when he came over and tell him he was of very poor new family. But my mother wrote the 'Dodo Symphony' for instance. She's something: she was Edith Staines, and when she has her songs sung at the Queen's Hall, she goes and conducts them——"

"Bertie, in a short skirt and boots with enormous nails," said Esther. "And very likely an immense tiara."

"And why not? She may be a silly ass in some things, but she's done something."

Bertie uncoiled all his yards of height and stood up.

"You began," he said. "I'm only answering you back. Lady Ayr has never done anything at all except talk about her family. She doesn't think about anything but family; she's the most antiquated and absurd type of snob there is. And your ridiculous brother John is exactly the same. You're the most awful family, and make one long for grocers, like Nadine."

"Darling, what do you want a grocer for?" asked Dodo.

But Berts had not finished yet.

"And as for your brother Seymour, all that can be said about him is that he is a perfect lady," he said, "but he ought to have been drowned when he was a girl, like a kitten."

Esther shouted with laughter.

"Oh, Berts, I wish you would be roused oftener," she said. "I absolutely adore you when you are roused. But you aren't quite right about Seymour. He isn't a lady any more than he's a gentleman: he's—he's just a phenomenon. And after all he has got a real brain."

"Well, it takes all sorts to make a world," said Dodo, "and Esther dear, I'm often extremely grateful to Seymour. He will always come to dinner at the very last moment——"

"That's because nobody else ever asks him," said Bertie, still fizzing and spouting a little. "That's one of the objections to marrying you, Esther: you will always be letting him come to dinner."

"Be quiet, Berts. As I say, he never minds how late he is asked, and he invariably makes himself charming to the oldest and plainest women present. Here, for instance, he would be making himself pleasant to me."

"Poor chap!" said Berts, lighting another cigarette, and lying down again.

A tray with some cold ham, a plate of strawberries, and a small jug of iced lemonade which had been ordered by Nadine for her mother was here brought in by a perfectly impassive footman, and placed on the settee between her and Nadine. No servant in Dodo's house ever felt the smallest surprise at anything which was demanded of him, and if Nadine had at this moment asked him to wash her face, he would probably have merely said: "Hot or cold water, your Highness?"

Nadine had not contributed anything to the discussion on Seymour, because she was almost inconveniently aware that she did not know what she thought about him. Certainly he had brains, and for brains she had an enormous respect.

"Seeing things to eat always makes me feel hungry," said Nadine, absently taking strawberries, "just as the sight of a bed makes me very wide-awake. It is called suggestion, and acts exactly in the way you least expect. Really the chief use of going to bed is that you are alone and have time to think."

"And that is so exhausting that I instantly go to sleep," remarked Tommy.

"You improve at thinking, if you practise, Tommy," said Nadine. "People imagine that because they have a brain they can think. It isn't so: you have to learn to think. You have a tongue, but you must learn to talk; you have arms, and yet you must learn how to play your foolish golf."

"You don't learn it, darling," said Dodo.

"Mamma, you are eating ham and have not been attending. Really it is so. Most people can't think: if they try to think, they can only think about something else. Esther, for instance——"

"It's quite true," said Esther. "I felt full of ideas this morning, and so I went away all alone along the beach to think them out. But I couldn't. There were my ideas all right, and that was all. I couldn't think about them. There they were, ideas; just that, framed and glazed."

Tommy rose.

"I'm worse than that," he said. "I never have any ideas. In some ways it's an advantage, because if we all had ideas, I suppose we should want to express them. As it is, I am at leisure to listen."

Dodo took a long draught of lemonade.

"I have one idea," she said, "and that is that it's bed-time. I shall go and exhaust myself with thought. The process of exhaustion does not take long. Besides, if I sit up much later than twelve, my maid always pulls my hair, and whips my head with the brush instead of treating me kindly."

"I should dismiss her," said Nadine.

"I couldn't, dear. She's so imbecile that she would never get another situation. Ah, there's Hugh! Hugh, did poor Algie Balearic-isles beat you?"

A very large young man had just appeared in the doorway. He held in his hand a sandwich out of which he had just taken an enormous semi-circular bite. The rest of it was in his mouth, and he spoke with the mumbling utterance necessary to those who converse when their mouths are full. People ate when they were hungry at Dodo's cottage, which might occur at any time.

"Oh, is that where he comes from?" he asked.

"No, my dear that is where he went to, though of course since he is here now he did come from them in a sense. Dear me, if he had been Bishop there about seventy years earlier he might have confirmed Chopin. How thrilling! Fancy confirming Chopin!"

"Yes, the Isles won," said Hugh, his voice clearing as he swallowed. "Oh, Aunt Dodo"—this again was a relationship founded only on affection—"he said your price was beyond rubies, but you're his deceased wife's sister, aren't you? What a lot of people there seems to be here. I came to talk to Nadine. Oh, there she is. Or would it be better taste if I didn't? I shall go to bed instead."

"Then what you call taste is what I call peevishness," said Nadine succinctly.

"I don't understand. What is better peevishness, then?"

"You take me at the foot of the letter," said she. "You see what I mean?"

"Yes. I see that you mean 'literally.' But in any case there are too many people, chiefly upside down from where I am. That's Esther, isn't it, and Berts?"

Esther scrambled off the settee, and went to the door of the room where she and Nadine slept.

"Why, of course, if you want to talk to Nadine I will go," she said. "Nadine, if you and Hughie disagree on any point, tap at the door, and I will come and be referee."

Bertie gave a long sigh, but did not move.

"I shall lie here," he said, "like the frog-footman, on and off for days and days."

"Well, lie off now," said Hugh.

"Very good. But I don't want to go to bed. Mayn't I brush your hair for you, instead of your spanking maid, Aunt Dodo?"

"No, my dear. You had better brush your own. It needs it. Good night, you dears."

Hugh Graves went across to the windows as soon as they had gone, and threw several of them open.

"The room smells of stale smokes and epigrams," he said in explanation.

"That's not very polite, Hugh," said she, "since I have been talking most and not smoking least. But I suppose you will answer that you didn't come here to be polite."

In a moment, even as the physical atmosphere of the room altered, so also did the spiritual. It seemed to Nadine that she and Hugh took hands and dived through the surface foam and brightness in which they had been playing into some place which they had made for themselves, which was dim and subaqueous. The foam and brightness was all perfectly sincere, for she was never other than sincere, but it had no more than the sincerity of soap bubbles.

"No. I didn't come here to be polite," said Hugh, "though I didn't come here to be rude. I came to ask you a couple of questions."

Nadine had not moved from the settee, but she collected a load of cushions behind her, so that she was propped up by them. Her arms were clasped behind her head, and the folds of her rainbow dressing-gown fell back from them, leaving them bare nearly to the shoulder. The shaded light above her fell on to her hair, burnishing its gold, and her face below it was dim and suggested rather than outlined. The most accomplished of coquettes would, after thought, have chosen exactly that attitude and lighting, if she wanted to appear to the greatest advantage to a man who loved her, but Nadine had done it without motive. It may have been that it was an instinct with her to appear to the utmost advantage, but she would have done the same, without thought, if she was talking to a middle-aged dentist. Hugh had seated himself at some little distance from her, and the same light threw his face into strong line and vivid colour. He had still something of the softness of youth about him, but none of youth's indeterminateness, and he looked older than his twenty-five years. When he was moving, he moved with a boy's quickness; when he sat still he sat with the steadiness of strong maturity.

"You needn't ask them," she said. "I can answer you without that. The answer to them both is that I don't know."

"How do you know the questions yet?" said he.

"I do. You want to know whether my answer to you this evening is final. You want also to know why I don't say yes."

His eyes admitted the correctness of this: he need not have spoken.

"After all, there was not much divination wanted," he said. "I am as obvious as usual. And you understand me as well as usual."

She shook her head at this, not denying it, but only deprecating it.

"I always understand you too well," she said. "If only I didn't understand you, just as I don't understand Seymour! You have suggested a reason why I don't say yes. I think it is correct. Ah, don't quote silly proverbs about love being complete understanding. Most of the proverbs are silly, for Solomon was so old when he wrote them——"

His mouth uncurled from its gravity.

"That wasn't one of Solomon's," he said.

"Then it might have been. In any case exactly the opposite is true. If love is anything at all, and it quite certainly is, it is not understanding. It is the opposite, the not-understanding——"

"Mis-understanding?"

"No. The not-understanding, the mysterious, the unaccountable——"

Nadine gathered her legs up under her and sat clasping them round the knees, and her utterance grew most rapid. Her face, young and undeveloped, and white and exquisite, was full of eager animation.

"That is what I feel, anyhow," she said. "Of course I can't say 'this is love' and 'this is not love,' and label other people's emotions. There is one way of love and another way of love, and another and another. There are as many modes of love, I suppose, as there are people who are capable of it. But don't tell me everybody is capable of it. At least, tell me so if you like, but allow me to disagree. For myself, all I am certain of is that I look for something which you don't give me. Perhaps I am incapable of love. And if I was sure of that, Hughie, I would marry you. Do you see?"

She, as was always the case with her, made him forget himself. When he was with her, she absorbed his consciousness: his only desire was to follow her, not caring where she led. This desire to apprehend her corrugated his forehead into the soft wrinkles of youth, and narrowed his eyes.

"Tell me why that is not a bad reason," he said.

"Because I should know that I could never give anybody the highest," she said, "and then, oh, so willingly would I give you all the second-best. Look what quantities of people marry quite rightly without love. I don't refer to the obvious reason for marrying for position or wealth, but to the people who marry from admiration or from fear. Mamma, for instance; she married Daddy because she was afraid of him. Then she learned he was a——an amorous turnip-ghost with a brandy bottle, and so divorced him. She was not afraid any longer."

"I am neither," said he.

Nadine gave a little sigh, and he saw his stupidity.

"No; you never suggested that I was," he said.

"Well, you've given me one reason. And another is, isn't it, that I don't understand you?"

Somehow to Nadine this was unexpected, but almost instantly she recognised the truth of it.

"That is true," she said. "I want to be the inferior, mentally, spiritually, of the man I marry. I want to grovel, and, oh, Hughie, I can't grovel to you! I am just the opposite of those terrible people who want a vote, and say they are the equal of men. No woman who is a man's equal ought to marry him. How could a woman *stand* loving a man unless he was her superior? The superior women may be old maids, like Pallas Athene. If only it was you who were the incomprehensible, like the Athanasian Creed! I wish it was that way round."

"Oh, you do wish that?" he asked.

"Yes, of course, my dear."

"Then you have answered the other question. Your answer to me to-day is not final. I'll puzzle you yet."

"You speak of it all as if it was a conjuring trick," she said. "Don't make conjuring tricks. Don't let me see announced your approaching engagement to somebody else. That would not puzzle me at all. I shall simply see that it was meant to do so. Conjuring tricks don't mystify you: you know you have been cheated and don't care."

"No, I shan't make conjuring tricks," he said.

Nadine unclasped her knees, and got up, and began walking to and fro across the big room.

"Hugh, I wish I was altogether different," she said. "I wish I was like one of those simple girls whom you never by any chance meet outside the covers of six-shilling novels. They are quite human, only no human girl was ever like them. They like music and food and sentiment, and sea-bathing, and playing foolish games, just as we all do. But there is nobody behind them: they are tastes without character. If only one's character was nothing more than the sum total of one's tastes, how extraordinarily simple it would all be. We should spend our lives in making ourselves pleasant and enjoying ourselves. But there is something that sits behind all our tastes, and though those tastes express it, they do not express it all, nor do they express its essence. I am something beyond and back of the things I like, and the people I like. Something inside me says 'I want: I want.' I daresay it wants the moon, and has as much chance of getting it as I have of reaching up into the sky and pulling it down. And I want it because I can't get it, and because I can't understand it, and because it shines! Oh, because it shines! Hughie, I want the moon, and what will the moon be like? Will it be hard and cold or soft and warm? I don't care. I shall slip it between my breasts and hold it close."

She paused a moment opposite him.

"Am I talking damned rot?" she asked. "I daresay I am. I am a rotter then, because all I say is me. Another thing, too: morally, I am not in the least worthy of you. I don't know anyone who is. I don't really; and I'm not flattering you, because I don't rate the moral qualities very high. They are compatible with such low organisations. Earwigs, I read the other day, are excellent mothers. How that seems to alter one's conception of the beauty of the maternal instinct. But it does not alter my conception of earwigs in the least, and I shall continue to kill any excellent mothers that I find in my room."

Hugh laughed suddenly and uproariously, and then became perfectly grave again.

"Your moral organisation is probably extremely low," he said. "But I settled long ago to overlook that."

"Ah, there we are again," said Nadine. "You deliberately propose to misconceive me, with the kindest intentions I know, but with how wrong a principle. You shut your eyes to me, as if—as if I was a smut! You settle to overlook the fact that I have no real moral perception. Could you settle to overlook the fact if I had no nose and only one tooth? I assure you the lack of a moral nature is a more serious defect. But poor devil that I am, how was I to get one? We were talking about heredity before you came in——"

Nadine paused for a moment.

"As a matter of fact," she said, "I was telling them that there was no truth in heredity. I will now support the other side of the question. How was I, considering my family, to have moral perceptions?"

"Are you being quite consistent?" asked Hugh.

"Why should I be consistent? Who is consistent except those simple people of whom you buy so many for six shillings, and they are consistently tiresome. How, I said, was I to have got moral perception? There is Daddy! If I was a doctor I would certify anyone to be insane who said Daddy was a moral organism. There is darling Mamma! I would horsewhip anyone who said the same of her, for his gross stupidity and insolence. The result is me; I am more pagan than Heliogabalus. I do not think that anything is right or that anything is wrong. I want the moon, but I am afraid you are not the man in it."

"And now you are flippant."

"Flippant, serious, moral, immoral," cried Nadine. "Do not label me like luggage. You will tell me my destination next; shall we call it Abraham's bosom? Dear Hugh, you enrage me sometimes. Chiefly you enrage me because you have such an angelic temper yourself. I am not sure than an angelic temper is an advantage: it is always set fair, and there are no surprises. Ah, how it all leads round to that; there are no surprises; I understand you too well. I am very sorry.

Do me the justice to believe that. Really, I think that I am as sorry that
I can't marry you, as you are."

Hugh got up.

"I don't think I do quite believe that," he said. "And now as regards
the immediate future. I think I shall go away to-morrow."

This time he succeeded in surprising her.

"Himmel, but why?" she said.

"If you understood me as well as you say, you would know," he
said. "I don't find my own heart a satisfactory diet. Of course, if I
thought you would miss me——"

Nadine was quite silent for a moment.

"You shall go if you like, of course," she said. "But you do me
the most frightful injustice; you understand nothing about me if you
think I should not miss you. You cannot be so dull as not to know
that I should miss you more than if everybody else went, literally
everybody, leaving me alone. But go if you wish."

She walked across to the window, which Hugh had thrown open,
and leaned out. A moon rode high in mid-sky, and to the west a
quarter of a mile away and far below the sea glimmered like a shield
of dim silver. Below the window the ground sloped sharply away
down to the grey tumbled sand dunes that fringed the coast, and all
lay blurred and melted under the uncertain light. And when she turned
round again Hugh saw that her eyes were blurred and melted also.

"Do exactly as you please, Hughie," she said.

He laughed.

"Would you be surprised if I did not go?" he asked.

She came towards him with both hands out.

"Ah, that is dear of you," she said. "Look out of the window with
me a moment: how dim and mysterious. There is my moon which I
want so much, too. I will build altars and burn incense to any god
who will give it me. If only I knew what it was! My moon, I mean;
not anybody's moon. Now, perhaps, as it is nearly two o'clock, we
had better go to bed, Hughie. And I am so sorry that things are as
they are."

2

It had been said by Edith Arbuthnot, perhaps unkindly, but
with sufficient humour to neutralize the acidity, that there was always
somebody awake day and night in Dodo's house tending the flame
of egoistic introspection. Edith did not generally use long words, but
chose them carefully when she indulged in polysyllables. She had not

been so careful in the choice of her confidant, for she had fired this withering criticism at her son Berts, who, in the true spirit of an affectionate nephew, instantly repeated it to Dodo, who had roared with laughter and sent Edith an enormous telegram (costing nine shillings and a halfpenny, including sixpence for a paid reply in case Edith wanted to continue the discussion) describing a terrible accident that had just happened to herself.

"A most extraordinary and tragic affair" (this was all written out in full) "has just occurred at Meering in the house of Princess Waldenech. The unfortunate lady had just died of a sudden, though not unexpected attack of spontaneous egoism. Loud screams were heard from her room, and Mr. Bertie Arbuthnot, son of the celebrated Edith Arbuthnot, the musical composer, rushed in to find the princess enveloped in sheets of blue flame. The efforts made to quench her were of no avail, and in a few moments all that was left of her was a small handful of ashes, which, curiously enough, as they cooled, assumed the shape of the word 'Me.' Fear is felt that this outbreak may prove to be contagious, and all those who have been in contact with the combusted princess are busy disinfecting themselves by talking about each other. It is believed that Mrs. Arbuthnot has begun to write a funeral march for her friend, for whom she felt an adoring affection amounting almost to worship, in the unusual key of ten sharps and eleven flats. It is in brisk waltz time, and all the performers will blow their own trumpets. She is sending copies to nearly all the crowned heads of Europe."

Thus ran the telegram. Edith's reply was equally characteristic. "Dodo, I love you."

The truth in Edith's criticism was certainly exemplified on the night of which we are speaking, for Hugh did not leave Nadine's room, where she had been engaged on the self-analysis given in the last chapter till two o'clock, and at that precise moment Dodo, who had gone to bed more than an hour before, woke up and began thinking about herself with uncommon intensity. And indeed, there was sufficient to think about in the circumstances with which she had at this moment allowed herself to be surrounded. For the last two days the husband whom she had divorced with such extreme facility had been staying with her, and tomorrow, directly on his departure, Jack Chesterford, to whom she had been engaged when she ran away with the husband she had just divorced, was arriving. All her life Dodo had liked drama, as long as it occurred outside the walls of English theatres, but better than the theatres even of Paris were the dramas which came into real life, especially when you could not possibly tell (even though you were acting yourself) what was going to happen next. Best of all, she liked acting herself, having a part to play, without the slightest idea what she or anybody else was going to do or say.

Dodo's zest for life did not decrease with years, nor did her interest in it in the least diminish as the time of her youth began to recede into horizons far behind her. For all the time other horizons were getting closer to her, and she could imagine herself being quite old—"as old as Grannie," in fact—without any of the tragic envy of past years that so often makes wormwood of the present. She had indeed settled the mode of her procedure for those years, which were still far enough off, and was quite determined to have a mob cap with a blue riband in it, and tortoiseshell-rimmed spectacles. Also she would read Thomas à Kempis a great deal—she had read a little already, and was now deliberately keeping the rest till she was seventy—and walk about her garden with a tall cane and pick lavender. She had, moreover, promised herself to make no attempts at sprightliness or to have her hair dyed, since one of the few classes of women to whom she really objected were those whom she called grizzly kittens, who dabbed at you with their rheumatic old paws, and pretended that they had no need of spectacles, when it was quite clear they could not read the very largest print. But she fully intended to remain exceedingly happy when those years came, for happiness, so it seemed to her, was a gift that came from within and could not be taken from you by any amount of external calamities or accumulation of decades. Certainly in the years that had passed she had had her share of annoyances, and in support of her theory with regard to happiness it must be confessed that they had not deprived her of one atom of it. Her late husband's conduct, for instance, had for years been of the most disagreeable kind, and she had borne with it not in the least like a fearful lamb, but more like a cheerful lion. It had not in the least discouraged her with life in general, but only disgusted her with him. For the last two years before she got her divorce, he had been, as she expressed it, "too Bacchic for anything," and she had sent Nadine away from their homes in Austria, to live with a variety of old friends in England. Eventually Dodo had decided that she would waste no more time with her husband, and got her freedom, coupled with an extremely handsome allowance. She continued to call herself Princess Waldenech because it was still rather pleasant being a princess, and Waldenech told her that, as far as he was concerned, she might call herself Dowager-Empress Waldenech, or anything else she chose.

So for a year now she had been in England, and had stepped back, or rather jumped back into the old relations with almost all that numerous body of people who twenty years ago had helped to make life so enchanting. And with the same swiftness and sureness she had established herself in the hearts of the younger generation that had grown up since, so that the sons and daughters of her old friends became her nephews and nieces in affection. Nadine, with the beauty, the high spirits and power of enjoyment that was hers by birthright, had, so it seemed to her mother, succeeded to a place that was very like what her own had been rather more than twenty years ago. Of course, there was a tremendous difference in their modes, for the manners and outlook of one generation are as divergent from those of the last, as are the clothes they wear, but the same passionate love of life, the same curiosity and vividness inspired her daughter's friends, even as they had inspired her own. And since she herself had lost not one atom of her own vitality, it was not strange that the years between them and her were easily bridged over.

There were one or two voices that were silent in the chorus of welcome with which Dodo's reappearance had been hailed. One of these was Edith Arbuthnot, who, though she did not desire to put any restrictions on Berts' intimacy (which was lucky, since Berts was a young gentleman hideously gifted with the power of getting his way), loudly proclaimed that she could never be friends with Dodo again. But the answer she had sent to Dodo's remarkable telegram about combusted egoism a few days before seemed to indicate that she had surrendered, and though she had subsequently announced that Dodo was heartless, might be regarded as a convert, especially since Jack had at last yielded too, and had invited himself down here. Another fortress hitherto impregnable was Mrs. Vivian, for whom Dodo in days gone by had felt as solid an affection as she was capable of. Consequently she regretted that Mrs. Vivian was invariably unable to come and dine, and never manifested the slightest desire that Dodo should come to see her. Dodo's regret was slightly tempered by the fact that Mrs. Vivian had an ear-trumpet in these days, which she presented to people whose conversation she desired to hear rather in the manner that elephants at the Zoo hold out their trunks for chance refreshments. Somehow that seemed to make her matter less, and Dodo had not at present made any determined effort to beleaguer her. But she intended when she went back to town in July to capture what was now practically the only remaining stronghold of the disaffected.

When Dodo drowsily awoke that night, just at the time that Hugh and Nadine had finished their talk, it was the thought of Jack that first stirred in her mind. Instantly she was perfectly wide awake. During this last year, though he was great friends with Nadine, he had absolutely avoided coming into contact with herself. He never went to a house where Dodo was expected, and once, finding she was staying for a Saturday till Monday with the Granthams, had left within ten

minutes of his arrival there. Miss Grantham had conceived this misbe-
gotten plan of bringing them unexpectedly face to face, with the only
result that the party numbered thirteen, and her father was very uncomfortable for weeks afterwards. Once again they had been caught in a
block in taxi-cabs exactly opposite each other. Dodo, taking the bull
by the horns, had leaned impulsively towards him with both hands
outstretched and cried, "Ah, Jack, are we never to meet again?" On
which the bull, so to speak, paid his fare, and continued his journey
on foot. Dodo had been considerably disappointed by this rebuff: it
had seemed to her that no man should have resisted her direct appeal.
On the other hand, Jack, on seeing her, had nailed to his face so curiously icy a mask that his appearance became quite ludicrous. Also
he knocked his hat against the roof of the closed half of his cab,
and it fell into the road in the middle of an unusually deep puddle.
She noticed that he was not bald yet, which was a great relief, since
she detested the sight of craniums.

And now Jack had yielded, had walked out of his citadel without
any further assault being delivered, and was to arrive to-day. At the
thought, when she woke in this stillness of earliest morning, Dodo's
brain started into fullest activity, and, as always, as much interested
in the motives that inspired actions as in the actions themselves, she
set herself to ponder on the nature of the impulse which had caused
so complete a volte-face. But the action itself interested and charmed
her also: all this year she had wanted to see Jack again. He had understood her better than anyone, and in spite of the vile way in which
she had used him, she had more nearly loved him than either of the
men she had married. Her first husband had never been more to her
than "an old darling," and often something not nearly that. Of Waldenech she had simply been afraid: under the fascination of fear she
had done what he told her. But Jack——

Dodo felt for the switch of her electric light; the darkness was too
close to her eyes, and she wanted to focus them on something. Clearly
there were several possibilities, any of which would account for this
change in Jack. He might perhaps merely wish to resume ordinary
and friendly relations with her. But that did not seem a likely explanation, since, if that was all, he would more naturally have waited till
she returned to town again after this sojourn in the country. There
must have been in his mind a cause more potent than that. Naturally,
the more potent cause occurred to her, and she sat up in bed. . . .
"It is too ludicrous," she said to herself: "it cannot possibly be that."
And yet he had remained unmarried all these years, with how many
charming girls about who would have been perfectly willing to share
his wealth and title, not to speak of himself.

Dodo got out of bed altogether, and went across the room to where a big looking-glass set in the door of her wardrobe reflected her entire figure. She wished to be quite honest in her inspection of herself, to see there not what she wanted to see, but what there was to be seen. The room was brightly lit, and through her thin silk nightdress she could see the lines of her figure moulded in the soft swelling curves of her matured womanhood. Yet something of the slimness and firm elasticity of youth still dwelt there, even as youth still shone in the smooth, unwrinkled oval of her face and sparkled in the depths of her dark eyes. Right down to her waist hung the thick coils of her black hair, still untroubled by grey, and slim and shapely were her ankles, and soft and rosy from the warmth of her bed her exquisite feet. And at the sight of herself her mouth uncurled itself into a smile: the honesty of her scrutiny had produced no discouraging revelations. Then, frankly laughing at herself, she turned away again and wholly unconsciously and instinctively took half a dozen dance-steps across the Persian rugs that were laid down over the polished floor. She could no more help that impulse of her bubbling vitality than she could help the fact that she was five feet eight in height.

The coolness and refreshment of the two hours before dawn streamed in through her open window, and she put on the dressing-gown with its cascades of lace and blue ribands that lay on the chair by her dressing table. Supposing it was the case that Jack was coming for her, that he wanted her now as in the old days when she had thrown his devotion back at him like a pail of dirty water, what answer would she make him? Really she hardly knew. Neither of her marriages had been a conspicuous success, but for neither of her husbands had she felt anything of that quality of emotion which she had felt for the man she had treated so infamously. She gave a great sigh and began ticking off certain events on her fingers.

"First of all I refused him before I married poor darling Chesterford the first," she said to herself. "Secondly, having married Chesterford the first, I asked Jack to run away with me. But that was in a moment of great exasperation: it might have happened to anybody. Thirdly, as soon as Chesterford I. was taken I got engaged to Jack, which I ought to have done originally; and, fourthly, I jilted him and married Waldenech."

Dodo had arrived at her little finger, and held her other hand poised over it.

"What the devil is fifthly to be?" she said aloud.

She got out of her chair again.

"It is very odd, but I simply can't make up my mind," she thought, "and I usually can make it up without the slightest trouble; indeed, it is usually already made up, just as one used to find eggs ready boiled in that absurd machine that always stood by Chesterford at breakfast. I hate boiled eggs. But I wonder if I owe it to Jack to marry him if he wants me to? Supposing he says I have spoiled his life, and he wants me to unspoil it now? Is it my duty apart from whatever my inclination may be, and I wish I knew what that was?"

Dodo felt herself quite unable to make up her mind on this somewhat important point. She felt herself already embarked on an argument with Jack, as she had been so often embarked in the old days, and on how pleasant and summery a sea! She would certainly tell him that nobody ought to let his life be spoiled by anybody else, and she would point to herself as a triumphant instance of how she had refused to let her joy of life get ever so slightly tarnished by the really trying experiences in her partnership with Waldenech. Here was she positively as good as new. And then, unfortunately, it occurred to her that Jack might say, "But then you didn't love him." And the ingenious Dodo felt herself unable to frame any reply to this very bald suggestion. It really seemed unanswerable.

There was a further reason which might account for Jack's coming. Nadine. Dodo knew that the two were great friends; she had even heard it suggested that Jack had serious thoughts with regard to her. Very likely that was only invented by some friend who was curious to know how she herself would take the suggestion; but clearly this was not an improbable, far less an impossible contingency. But that Nadine had serious thoughts with regard to Jack was less likely. Dodo felt that her daughter took after herself in emotional matters, and was probably not at that age seriously thinking about anybody. Yet, after all, she herself had married at that age (though without serious thought), and the experiment, which seemed so sensible and promising, had been a distinct disappointment. Ought she to warn Nadine against marrying without love? Or would that look as if, for other reasons, she did not wish her to marry Jack? That would be an odious interpretation to put on it, and the worst of it was that she was not perfectly certain that there was not some sort of foundation for it. Something within her ever so faintly resented the idea of Jack's marrying Nadine.

Dodo's thought paused and was poised over this for a little, and she made an eager and conscious effort to root out from her mind this feeling, of which she was genuinely ashamed. Then suddenly all her meditations were banished, for from outside there came the first faint chirrupings of a waking bird. Deep down in her, below the trivialities and surface complications of life, below all her warm-heartedness and her egoism, there lay a strain of natural, untainted simplicity, and these first flutings of birds in the bushes roused it. She went to the window and drew up the blind.

The dusk still hovered over the sea and low-lying land, and in the sky, already turning dove-coloured, a late star lingered, remotely burning. The bird that had called her to look at the dawn had ceased again, and a pause holy and sweet and magical brooded over the virginal meeting of night and day. But far off to the right the hill-tops had got the earliest news of what was coming, and were flecked with pale Orient reflections and hints of gold and scarlet and faint crimson. But here below the dusk lay thick still, like clear, dark water.

Just below her window lay the lawn, garlanded round with sleeping and dew-drenched flower-beds, and the incense of their fragrant buds and folded petals still slept in the censer, till in the east should rise the gold-haired priest, and swing it, tossing high to heaven the sweetness of its burning. And then from out of the bushes beyond there scudded a thrush, perhaps the same which had called Dodo to the window. He scurried over the shimmering lawn with innumerable footfalls, and came so close underneath her window that she could see his eyes shining. Then he swelled his throat, and sang one soft phrase of morning, paused as if listening, and then repeated it. All the magic of youth and joy of life were there: there was also in Dodo's heart the indefinable yearning for days that were dead, the sense of the fathomless well of time into which for ever dropped beauty and youth and the soft, sweet days. But that lasted but a moment, for as long as the thrush paused. Another voice, and yet another, sounded from the bushes; there were other thrushes there, and in the ivy of the house arose the cheerful jangling of sparrows. Fresh feathered forms ran out on to the lawn, and the air was shrill with their pipings. Every moment the sky grew brighter with the imminent day, the last star faded in the glow of pink translucent alabaster, and in the green-crowned elms the breeze of morning awoke and stirred the tree-tops. Then it came lower, and began to move in the flower-beds, and the wine of the dew was spilled from the chalices of new-blown roses, and the tall lilies quivered. There was wafted up to her the indescribable odour of moist earth and opening flowers, and on the moment the first yellow ray of sunlight shot over the garden.

Dodo stood there dim-eyed, unspeakably and mysteriously moved. She thought of other dawns she had seen, when coming back perhaps from a ball where she had been the central and most brilliant figure all night long; she thought of other troubled dawns when she had woke from some unquiet dream and yet dreaded the day. But here was a perfect dawn, and it seemed to symbolize to her the beginning of the life that lay in front of her. She looked forward to it with eager anticipation, she gave it a rapturous welcome. She was in love with life still, she longed to see what delicious things it held in store for her. She felt sure that God was going to be tremendously kind to her. And in turn (for she had a certain sense of fairness) she felt most whole-heartedly grateful and determined to deserve these favours. There were things in her life she was very sorry for: such omissions and commissions should not occur again. She felt that the sight of this delicious dawn had been a sort of revelation to her. And with a great sigh of content she went back to bed, and without delay fell fast asleep, and did not awake till her maid came in at eight o'clock with a little tray of tea that smelt too good for anything, and a whole sheaf of attractive-looking letters, large stiff square ones, which certainly contained cards that bade her to delightful entertainments.

She always breakfasted in her room, and when she came downstairs about half-past ten, and looked into the dining-room, she found to her surprise that Waldenech was there, eating sausages one after the other. This was a very strange proceeding for him, since in general he adopted slightly snark-like hours and did not breakfast till at least lunch time. The years, or at any rate his habits and method of spending them, had not been so kind to him as to Dodo, and though they had not robbed him of that look of distinction which was always his, they had conferred upon him the look of being considerably the worse for wear. He seemed as much older than his years as Dodo appeared younger than hers, and she was no longer in the least afraid of him. Indeed, it struck her that morning as she came in, with a sense of wonder, that she had ever found him formidable.

"Good-morning, my dear," she said, "but how very surprising. Has everybody else finished and gone out? Waldenech, I am so glad you suggested coming here, and I hope you haven't regretted it."

"I have not enjoyed any days so much since you left me," he said.

"How dear of you to say that! Everyone thought it so extraordinary that you should want to come here, or that I should let you, but I am delighted you did."

He left his place and came to sit in a chair next to her. The remains of Nadine's breakfast were on a plate opposite: half a poached egg, some melon rind, marmalade, and a cigarette end. He pushed these rather discouraging relics away.

"It is not extraordinary that I should want to come here," he said, "for the simple reason that you are the one woman I ever really cared about. I always cared for you——"

"There are others who think you occasionally cared for them," remarked Dodo.

"That may be so. Why should one not care also for others? Now I should like to stop on. May I do so?"

"No, my dear, I am afraid that you certainly may not," she said. "Jack comes to-day, and the situation would not be quite comfortable, not to say decent."

"Do you think that matters?" he asked.

"It certainly is going to matter. You haven't really got a European mind, Waldenech. Your mind is probably Thibetan. Is it Thibet where you do exactly as you feel inclined? The place where there are llamas."

"I do as I feel inclined wherever I am," said he. "I am here."

Dodo remembered, again with wonder, the awful mastery that that sort of sentence as delivered by him used to have for her. Now it had none of any kind: his personality had simply ceased to be dominant with regard to her.

"But then you won't be here," said she. "You will go by that very excellent train that nevers stops at all: I have reserved a carriage for you."

He lit a cigarette.

"I must have been insane to behave to you as I did," he said. "It was most intensely foolish from a purely selfish point of view."

She patted his hand which lay on the table-cloth.

"Certainly it was," she said, "if you wanted to keep me. I told you so more than once. I told you that there were limits, but you appeared to believe there were not. That was quite like you, my dear. You always thought yourself a Czar of Czars. I do not think we need go into past histories."

He got up.

"Dodo, would you ever under any circumstances come back to me?" he said. "There is Nadine, you know. It gives her a better chance——"

Dodo interrupted him.

"You are not sincere when you say that. It isn't of Nadine that you think. As for your question, I have never heard of any circumstances which would induce me to do as you suggest. Of course, we cannot say that they don't exist, but I have never come across them. Don't let us think of it, Waldenech: it is quite impossible. If you were dying, I would come, but under the distinct understanding that I should go away again in case you got better, which I am sure I hope you would. I don't bear you the slightest ill-will. You didn't spoil my life at all, though it is true you often made me both angry and miserable. As regards Nadine, she has an excellent chance, as you call it, under the present arrangements. All my friends have come back to me except Mrs. Vivian."

"Mrs. Vivian?" said he. "Oh yes, an English type, earnest widow."

"With an ear-trumpet now," continued Dodo, "and I shall get her some day. And Jack comes this afternoon. *Voila*, the round table again! I take up the old life again, with the younger generation added, and not a penny the worse."

"You are a good many pennies the better," said he in self-justification. "As regards Lord Chesterford: why is he coming here?"

"I suppose because, like you, he wants to see me, or Nadine, or both of us."

"Do you suppose he wants to marry you?" he asked. "Will you marry him?"

Dodo got up, revelling in her sense of liberty. It was enormous to feel free in the presence of him who had bound her so long.

"Waldenech, you don't seem to realize that certain questions from you to me are impertinent," she said. "What I do now is none of your business. You have as much right to ask Mrs. Vivian whether she is thinking of marrying again. Realize, as I do, that you and I are apart. I have not the slightest idea if Jack wants to marry me now, as a matter of fact, and I have really no idea if I would marry him in case he did. It is more than twenty years since I spoke to him—oh, I spoke to him out of a taxi-cab the other day, but he did not answer—and I have no idea what he is like. In twenty years one may become an entirely different person. However, that is all my business, and no one else's; perhaps, least of all, yours. Now, if you have finished, let us take a stroll in the garden before your carriage comes round."

"I ask, then, a favour of you," he said.

"And what is that?"

"That you be yourself just for this stroll: that you be as you used to be when we met that summer at Zermatt."

Dodo was rather touched: she was also relieved that the favour was one so easy to grant. She took his arm as they left the dining-room and came out into the brilliant sunshine, and was her unembarrassed self.

"That is dear of you to remember Zermatt," she said. "Oh, Waldenech, think of those great mountains still standing there in their silly rows with their noses in the air. How frightfully fatiguing! And they all used to look as if they were cuts with each other, and there they'll be a thousand years hence, not having changed in the least. But I'm not sure we don't have the better time scampering about for a few more years shall roll, instead of thousands, and running in and out like mice, though we get uglier and older every day. Look, there is poor John Sturgis coming towards us: let us quickly go in the opposite direction. Ah, he has seen us! Dear John, Nadine was looking for you, I believe. I think she expected you to read something to her after breakfast about Goths and Goethe. Or was it Bishop Algie you were talking to last night about cathedrals and Gothic architecture? One or the other, I am sure. He said he so much enjoyed his talk with you."

Waldenech felt that Dodo was behaving exactly as she used to behave at Zermatt. Somehow in his sluggish and alcoholic soul there rose vibrations like those he had felt then.

"Talk to him or me, it doesn't matter," he said in German to her, "but talk like that. That is what I want. The babbling ridicules you."

Dodo gave him one glance of extraordinary meaning. This little muttered speech strangely reminded her of the paean in the thrush's song at dawn. It recalled a poignancy of emotion that belonged to days long past, but the same poignancy of feeling was hers still. She could easily feel and habitually felt, in spite of her forty and more years, the mere out-bubbling of life that expressed itself in out-bubbling speech. She also rather welcomed the presence of a third party: it was easier for her to babble to anybody rather than to Waldenech. She buttonholed the perfectly willing John.

"Bishop Algie is such a dear, isn't he?" she said. "He is accustomed not to talk at all, and so talking is a treat to him, and he loved you. He is taking a cinematograph show all about the Acts of the Apostles round the country next autumn to collect funds for Maud's orphanage. The orphanage is already built, but there are no orphans. I think the money he collects is to get orphans to go there—scholarships I suppose. He made all his friends group themselves for scenes in the Acts, and he is usually St. Paul, unless there is a better part of some kind. He did a delicious shipwreck, where they are tying up the boat with rug-straps and ropes. He had it taken in the bay here, and it was extremely rough, which made it all the more realistic, because dear Algy is a very bad sailor, and while he was being exceedingly unwell over the side, his halo fell off and sank."

"We did not talk about the Acts of the Apostles last night," said John firmly; "we talked about Gothic architecture, and Piccadilly, and Wagner."

"But how entrancing," said Dodo. "I particularly love Siegfried, because it is like a pantomime. Do you remember when the dragon comes out of his cave looking exactly like Paddington Station, with a red light on one side and a green one on the other, and a quantity of steam, and whistlings and some rails? Then afterwards a curious frosty female appears suddenly in the bole of a tree, and tells Wotan that his spear ought to be looked to before he fights. Waldenech, we went together to Bayreuth, and you snored, but luckily on the right note, and everybody thought it was Fafner. John, I was sitting in my window at dawn this morning, and all the birds in the world began to sing. It made me feel so common. Nobody ought to see the dawn except the birds, and I suppose the worms for the sake of the birds."

Waldenech turned to her, and again spoke in German.

"You are still yourself," he said. "After all these years you are still yourself."

Dodo's German was far more expressive than his, it was also ludicrously ungrammatical, and immensely rapid.

"There are no years," she said. "Years are only an expression used by people who think about what is young and what is old. Everyone has his essential age, and remains that age always. This man is about sixty, the age of his mother."

John Sturgis smiled in a kind and superior manner. "Perhaps I had better tell you that I know German perfectly," he said. "Also French and Italian, in case you want to say things that I shan't understand."

Dodo stared for a moment, then pealed with laughter.

"Darling John," she said, "I think that is too nice of you. If you were nasty you would have let me go on talking. Isn't my German execrable? How clever of you to understand it! But you are old, aren't you? Of course it is not your fault, nor is it your misfortune, since all ages are equally agreeable. We grow up into our ages if we are born old, and we grow out of them, like missing a train, if our essential age is young. When you are eighty, you will still be sixty, which will be delightful for you. I make plans for what I shall be when I am old, but I wonder if I shall be able to carry them out. When I am old, I shall be what I shall be, I suppose. The inevitable doesn't take much notice of our plans. It sits there like the princess on the top of the glass hill, while we all try, without the slightest success, to get at it. Ah, my dear Waldenech, there is the motor come round for you. You will have to start, because I have at last trained my chauffeur to give no one any time to wait at the station, and you must not jilt the compartment I have engaged you to. It will travel to London all alone: so bad for a young compartment."

He made no further attempt to induce her to let him stop, and Dodo with a certain relief of mind saw him drive off, and blew a large quantity of kisses after him.

"Waldenech was such a wonderful creature about the year you were born, John," she said, "but you are too old to remember that. Now I must be Martha, and see the cook, and all the people who make life possible. Then I shall become Mary again, and have a delicious bathe before lunch. Certainly the good part is much the pleasantest, as is the case always at private theatricals. I think we must act this evening: we have not had charades or anything for nearly two days."

John, like most prigs, was of a gregarious disposition, and liked his own superiority of intellect, of which he was so perfectly conscious, to be made manifest to others, and literally, he could not imagine that Dodo should seem to prefer burying herself in household affairs when he was clearly at leisure to converse with her. He did not feel himself quite in tune with the younger members of the party, and sometimes wondered why he had come here. That wonder was shared by others. His tediousness in ordinary intercourse was the tediousness of his genus, for he always wanted to improve the minds of his circle. Unfortunately he mistook quantity of information for quality of mind, and thought that large numbers of facts, even such low facts as dates, had in themselves something to do with culture. But since, at the present moment, Dodo showed not the smallest desire to profit by his leisure, he wandered off to the tennis courts, where he had reason to believe he should find companions. His faith was justified, for there was a rather typical party assembled. Berts and Hugh were playing a single, while Esther was admiringly fielding tennis-balls for them. They were both excellent performers, equally matched and immeasurably active. At the moment Esther standing, as before Ahasuerus, with balls ready to give to Berts, had got in his way and he had claimed a let.

"Thanks, Esther," he said, as he took a couple of balls from her, "but would you get a little further back? You are continually getting in my way."

"Oh Berts, I'm so sorry," she said. "You are playing so well!"

"I know. Esther was in the light, Hugh."

"Oh, rather; let, of course," said Hugh.

Nadine took no active share. She was lying on the grass at the side of the court with Tommy, and was reading "Pride and Prejudice" aloud. When Esther had a few moments to spare she came to listen. John joined the reading party, and wore an appreciative smile.

Nadine came to the end of a chapter.

"Yes, Art, oh great Art," she said, shutting the book, "but I am not enchained. It corresponds to Madame Bovary, or the Dutch pictures. It is beautifully done; none but an artist could have done it. But I find a great deal of it dull."

John's smile became indulgent.

"Ah, yes," he said, "but what you call dull, I expect I should call subtle. Surely, Nadine, you see how marvellous it all is."

Esther groaned.

"John, you make me feel sick," she began.

"Balls, please," said Hugh in an ill-used voice.

Esther sprang up.

"Yes, Hugh, I'll get them," she said. "Aren't those two marvellous?" she added to Nadine.

"John is more marvellous," said Nadine. "John, I wish you would get drunk or cheat at cards. It would do you a world of good to lose a little of your self-respect. You respect yourself far too much. Nobody is so respectable as you think yourself. We were talking of you last night: I wish you had been there to hear, but you had gone to bed with your camomile tea. Perhaps you think camomile tea subtle also, whereas I should only find it dull."

"I think you are quibbling with words," he said. "But I too wish I had heard you talking last night. I always welcome criticism so long as it is sincere."

"It was quite sincere," said Nadine. "You may rest assured. It was unanimous, too, we were all agreed."

John found this not in the least disconcerting.

"I am not so sure that it matters then," he said. "When several people are talking about one thing—you tell me you were talking about me—they ought to differ. If they all agree, it shows they only see one side of what they are discussing."

Nadine sat up, while Tommy buried his dissipated face in his hands.

"We only saw one side of you," she said, "and that was the obvious one. But it is the only one that you ever show; indeed, I don't believe there is another. And since you like criticism you shall know. We all thought you were a prig. Esther said you would be distressed if we thought differently. She said you like being a prig. Do tell me: is it pleasant? Or I expect what I call prig, you call cultured. Are you cultured?"

Tommy sat up.

"Come and listen, Esther," he shouted. "Those glorious athletes can pick up the balls themselves for a minute."

Esther emerged from a laurel bush triumphant with a strayed reveller.

"Oh, is Nadine telling John what she thinks?" she asked.

"Nadine is!" said Tommy.

Nadine meantime collected her thoughts. When she talked she ascertained for herself beforehand what she was going to say. In that respect she was unlike her mother, who ascertained what she thought when she found herself saying it. But the result in both cases had the spontaneous ring.

"John, somehow or other you are a dear," she said, "though we find you detestable. You think, anyhow. That gives you the badge. Anybody who thinks——"

Hugh, like Mr. Longfellow with his arrow, flung his racquet into the air, without looking where it went. He had a moment previously sent a fast drive into the corner of the court, which raised whitewash in a cloud, and won him the set.

"Nadine, are you administering the oath of the clan?" he said. "You haven't consulted either Berts or me."

Nadine looked pained.

"Did you really think I was admitting poor John without consulting you?" she said. "Though he complies with the regulations."

Hugh, streaming with the response that a healthy skin gives to heat, threw himself down on the grass.

"I vote against John," he said. "I would sooner vote for Seymour. And I won't vote for him. Also, it is surely time to go and bathe."

"I don't know what you are all talking about," said John. "I daresay it doesn't matter. But what is the clan?"

Hugh sat up.

"The clan is nearly prigs," he said, "but not quite. But you are quite. We are saved because we do laugh at ourselves——"

"And you are not saved because you don't," added Nadine.

"And is the whole object of the clan to think?" asked John.

"No, that is the subject. Also you speak as if we all had said 'Let there be a clan, and it was so,'" said Nadine. "You mustn't think that. There was a clan, and we discovered it, like Newton and the orange."

"Apple, surely," said John.

Nadine looked brilliantly round.

"I knew he would say that," she said. "You see you correct what I say, whereas a clansman would be content to understand what I mean."

"Bishop Algie is clan, by the way," said Hugh. "I went down to bathe before breakfast, and found him kneeling down on the beach saying his prayers. That is tremendously clannish."

"I don't see why," said John.

Esther sighed.

"No, of course you wouldn't see," she said.

"Try him with another," said Nadine.

Esther considered.

"Attend, John," she said. "When the last Stevenson letters came out Berts bought them and looked at one page. Then he took a taxi to Paddington and took a return ticket to Bristol."

"Swindon," said Berts.

"The station is immaterial, so long as it was far away. I daresay Swindon is quite as far as Bristol."

John smiled.

"There you are quite wrong," he said. "Swindon comes before Bath, and Bristol after Bath. No doubt it does not matter, though it is as well to be accurate."

Esther looked at him with painful anxiety.

"But don't you see why Berts went to Swindon or Bristol?" she said. "Poor dear, you do see now. That is hopeless. You ought to have felt. To reason out what should have been a flash is worse than not to have understood at all."

John, again like all other prigs, was patient with those not so gifted as himself.

"I daresay you will explain to me what it all amounts to," he said. "All I am certain of is that Berts wanted to read Stevenson's letters and so got into a train, where he would be undisturbed. Wouldn't it have answered the same purpose if he had taken a room at the Paddington Hotel?"

Nadine turned to Berts.

"Oh, Berts, that would have been rather lovely," she said.

"Not at all," said he. "I wanted the sense of travel."

John got up.

"Or, I should have recommended the Underground," he said. "You could have gone round and round until you had finished. It would have been much cheaper."

Nadine waved impotent arms of despair.

"Now you have spoiled it," she said. "There was a possibility in the Paddington Hotel, which sounds so remote. But the Underground! You might as well say, why do I bathe, I who cannot swim? I can get clean in a bath, though I only get dirty in the sea, and if I want the salt I can put Tiddle-de-wink salt, or whatever the name is, in my bath——"

"Tidman," said John.

"I am sure you are right, though who cares. I am knocked down by cold waves, I am cut by stones on my soles, I am pinched by crabs and *homards,* at least I think I am, the wind gnaws at my bones, and my hair is as salt as almonds. Between my toes is sand, and bits of seaweed make me a plaster, and my stockings fall into rock-pools; but do I go with rapture to have a bath in the bathroom? I hate washing. There is nothing so sordid as to wash my face, except to brush my teeth. But to bathe in the sea makes me think: it gives me romance. Poor John, you never get romance. You amass information, and make a Blue Book. But we all, we see blue mountains, which we never reach. If we reached them they would probably turn out to be green. As it is, they are always blue, because they are beyond. It is suggestion that we seek, not attainment. To attain is dull, to aspire is the sugar and salt of life. Don'ᵗ you see? To realize an ideal is to lose an ideal.

It is like a man growing rich: he never sees his sovereigns: when he has gained them he flings them forth again into something further. If he left them in a box, the real sovereigns, under his bed, what chance would there be for him to grow rich? But out they go, he never uses them, except that he makes them breed. It is the same with the riches of the mind. An idea or an ideal is yours. Do you keep it? Personally you do. But we, no. We invest it again. It is to our credit, at this bank of the mind. We do not hoard it, or spend it piecemeal. We put it into something else and never let it remain at home. But when I shall be a millionaire of the mind, what, what then? Yes, that makes me pause. Perhaps it will all be converted, as they convert bonds, is it not, and I shall put it all into love. Who knows? La-la."

Nadine paused a moment, but nobody spoke. Hugh was watching her with the absorption that was always his when she was there. But after a moment she spoke again.

"We talk what you call rot," she said. "But it is not rot. The people who always talk sense arrive at less. There are sparks that fly, as when you strike one flint with another. Your English philosophers—who are they—Mr. Chesterton I suppose, is he not a philosopher, or some Machiavelli or other? they sit down soberly to think, and when they have thought they wrap up their thought in paradox, as you wrap up a pill for your dog, so that he swallows it without thinking, and his inside becomes bitter and aches. That is not the way. You must start with pure enjoyment, and when a thought comes you must fling it into the air. It may hit a bird, or turn into a rainbow, or fall on your head; but what matter? You others sit and think, and when you have thought of something you put it in a beastly book, and have finished with it. You prigs turn the world topsy-turvy that way. You do not start with joy, and you finish in a slough of despondent information. Ah, yes: the child who picks up a match and rubs it against something, and finds it catches fire, realizes the romance of the match more than Mr. Bryant and May and Boots, is it, who made the match. Matches are made on earth, but the child who knows nothing about them and strikes one is the person who is in heaven. You are not content with the wonder and romance of the world, you prefer to explain the rainbow away instead of looking at it. It is a sort of murder to explain things away: you kill their souls, and demonstrate that they are only hydrogen."

She looked up at Hugh.

"We talked about it last night," she said. "We settled that it was a great misfortune to understand too well——"

A footman arrived at this moment with a telegram, which he handed to Berts, who opened it. He gave a shout of laughter and passed it to Nadine.

"What shall I say?" he asked.

"But of course yes," she said. "It is quite unnecessary to ask Mamma."

Berts scribbled a couple of words on the reply-paid form.

"It's only my mother," he said in general explanation. "She wants to come over for a day or two, and see Aunt Dodo again, but she doesn't feel sure if Aunt Dodo wants to see her. Are you sure there's a room, Nadine?"

"There always is some kind of room," said Nadine. "She can sleep in three-quarters of my bed, if not."

"I'm so glad she is tired of being a silly ass, as we settled she was last night," said Berts. "Perhaps I ought to ask Aunt Dodo, Nadine."

"Pish-posh," said Nadine.

John got up, and prig-like he had the last word.

"I see all about the clan," he said. "You have a quantity of vague enthusiasm, and a lack of information. You float about like jelly-fish without any sense of direction, and think each other very wonderful."

Nadine giggled.

"I *do* see what he means," she said candidly.

"I am glad of that," said John.

3

This sojourn at Meering in the month of June, when London and its diversions were at their mid-most, was Nadine's plan. Whatever Nadine was or was not, she was not a *poseuse*, and her contention that it was a waste of time to spend all day in talking to a hundred people who did not really matter, and in dancing all night with fifty of them, was absolutely genuine.

"As long as anything amuses you," she had said, "it is not waste of time, but when you begin to wonder if it really amuses you, it shows that it does not. Darling Mamma, may I go down to Meering for a week or ten days? I do not want anyone to come, but if anybody likes to come we might have a little cheerful party. Besides it is Coronation next week, and great *corvée!* I think it is likely that Esther would wish to escape and perhaps one or two others, and it would be enchanting at Meering now. It would be a rest cure: a very curious sort of rest, since we shall probably never cease bathing and talking and reading. But anyhow we shall not be tired over things that bore us. That is the true fatigue. You are never tired as long as you are interested, but I am not interested in the Coronation. I don't see how anybody possibly can be, except the King and Queen."

Nadine's solitary week had proved in quality to be populous, and in quantity to exceed the ten days, and it was already beginning to be doubtful if July would see any of them settled in London again. Dodo's house in Portman Square had been maintained in a state of habitableness with a kitchen-maid to cook, and a housemaid to sweep, and a footman to wait, and a chauffeur to drive, and an odd man to do whatever the other servants didn't, and occasionally one or two of the party made a brief excursion there for a couple of nights, if any peculiar attraction beckoned. The whole party had gone up for a Shakespeare ball at the Albert Hall, but had returned next day, and Dodo had hurried to St. Paul's Cathedral to attend a thanksgiving service, especially since she, on leaving London, had taken a season ticket, being convinced she would be continuously employed in rushing up and down. Subsequently she had defrauded the railway company by lending it, though strictly non-transferable, to any member of the party who wished to make the journey, with the result that Bertie had been asked by a truculent inspector whether he was really Princess Waldenech. His passionate denial of any such identity had led to a lesser frequency of these excursions.

Nadine with the same sincerity had mapped out for herself a course of study at Meering, and she read Plato every afternoon in the original Greek, with an admirable translation at hand, from three o'clock till five. During these hours she was inaccessible, and when she emerged rather flushed sometimes from the difficulty of comprehending what some of the dialogues were about, she was slightly Socratic at tea, and tried to prove, as Dodo said, that the muse of Mr. Harry Lauder was the same as the muse of Sir George Alexander, and that she ought to be rude to Hugh if she loved him. She was extremely clear-headed in her reasoning, and referred them to the Symposium and the dialogue on Lysis to prove her point. But as nobody thought of contradicting her, since the Socratic mood soon wore off, they did not attempt to find out the Hellenic equivalents for those amazing doctrines.

She was markedly Socratic this afternoon, when the whole party were having tea on the lawn. Esther and Bertie had been down to bathe after lunch, and since everybody was going to bathe again after tea, they had left their clothes behind different rocky screens above the probable high-water level on the beach, and were clad in bathing-dress, moderately dried in the sun, with dressing-gowns above. Berts had nothing in the shape of what is called foot-gear on his feet, since it was simpler to walk up barefoot, and he was wriggling his toes, one after the other, in order to divest them of an excess of sand.

"But pain and pleasure are so closely conjoined," said Nadine, in answer to an exclamation of his concerning stepping in a gorse-bush. "It hurts you to have a prickle in your foot, but the pleasure of taking it out compensates for the pain."

"That's cribbed from Socrates," said Hugh. "He said that when they took off his chains just before they hemlocked him. You didn't think of that, Nadine."

"I didn't claim to, but it is quite true. There is actual pleasure in the cessation of pain. If you are unhappy and the cause of your unhappiness is removed, your happiness is largely derived from the fact that you were unhappy. For instance, did you ever have a fish-bone stick in your throat, Hugh?"

"As a matter of fact never," said Hugh. "But as I am meant to say 'Yes,' I will."

"And did you cough?"

"Violently," said Hugh.

"Upon which the fish-bone returned to your mouth?"

"No," said Hugh. "I swallowed it. It never returned at all."

"It does not matter which way it went," said Nadine, "but your feeling of pleasure at its going was derived from the pain which its sticking gave you."

"Is that all," said Hugh.

"Does it not seem to you to be proved?"

"Oh, yes. It was proved long ago. But it's a pedantic point. The sort of point John would have made."

He absently whistled the first two lines of "Am Stillen Herde," and Nadine was diverted from her Platonisms.

"Ah, that is so much finer than the finished 'Preislied,' " she said. "He curled and oiled his verses like an Assyrian bull. He and Sachs had cobbled at it too much: they had brushed and combed it. It had lost something of springtime and sea-breeze. A finished work of art has necessarily less quality of suggestiveness. Look at the Leonardo drawings! Is the Gioconda ever quite as suggestive? I am rather glad it was stolen.* I think Leonardo is greater without it."

John drew in his breath in a pained manner.

"Mona Lisa was the whole wonder of the world," he said. "I had sooner the thief had taken away the moon. Do you remember—perhaps you didn't notice it—the painting of the circle of rock in which she sat?"

"You are going to quote Pater," said Nadine. "Pray do not: it is a deplorable passage, and though it has lost nothing by repetition, for

---

* Nadine forgot that La Gioconda was not stolen until August of this year.

there was nothing to lose, it shows an awful ignorance of the spirit of the Renaissance. The eyelids are not a little weary: they are a little out of drawing only."

Esther looked across at Berts.

"Berts is either out of drawing," she said, "or else his dressing-gown is. I think both are: he is a little too long, and also the dressing-gown is too short. It ought to proceed as far as the ankles, but Berts' dressing-gown got a little weary at his knees."

"I barked my knees on those foul rocks," said Berts, examining those injured joints.

"Barking them is worse than biting them," said Nadine.

"I never bite my knees," said he. "It is a greedy habit. Worse than doing it to your nails."

"If you are not careful you will talk nonsense," said Nadine.

"I don't agree. If you are not careful you can't talk nonsense. If you want to talk nonsense, you've not got to be not careful——"

"There are too many 'nots,' " remarked Nadine.

"I will make it easier. If you are careless some sort of idea creeps into what you say, and it ceases to be nonsense. There are lots of ideas creeping about like microbes, any of which spoil it. Hardly anybody can be really meaningless for five minutes. That is why the Mad tea-party is a supreme work of art: you can't attach the slightest sense to anything that is said in it."

"The question is what you mean by nonsense," said Nadine. "Is it what Mr. Bernard Shaw writes in his plays, or what Mrs. Humphry Ward writes in her books? They neither mean anything but they are not at all alike. In fact they are as completely opposed to each other as sense is to nonsense."

Berts threw himself back on the turf.

"True," he said, "but they are neither of them nonsense. The lame and the halt and the blind ideas creep into both. They both talk sense mortally wounded."

Esther gave her appreciative sigh.

"Oh, Berts, how true," she said. "I went to a play by Mrs. Humphry Ward the other day, or else I read a book by Bernard Shaw, I forget which, and all the time I kept trying to see what the sense of it had been before it had its throat cut. But no one ever tried to see what Alice in Wonderland meant, or what Aunt Dodo means."

"Mamma is wonderful," said Nadine. "She lives up to what she says, too. Her whole life has been complete nonsense. I do hope Uncle Jack will persuade her to do the most ridiculous thing of all, and marry him."

"Is that why he is coming?" asked Esther.

"Oh, I hope so. It would be *the* greatest and most absurd romance of the century."

Hugh was eating sugar meditatively out of the sugar basin.

"I don't see that you have any qualifications for laying down the law about nonsense, Nadine," he said. "You are constantly reading Plato, and making arguments, which are meant to be consecutive."

"I do that to relax my mind," said Nadine. "Berts is quite right. Nonsense is not the absence of sense, but the negative of sense, just as sugar is the negative of salt. To get non-salt with your egg, you must eat sugar with it, not only abstain from salt."

"You will get a remarkably nasty taste," remarked John.

"Dear John, nobody ever wronged you so much as to suggest that you would like nonsense. When was Leonardo born? And how old was he when he died? And how many golden crowns did Francis of France give him for the Gioconda? Your mind is full of interesting facts, and so is your mouth. That is why you are so tedious. You are like the sand they used to put on letters, which instantly made them dry."

Berts got up.

"We will go and bathe again," he said, "and John shall remain on the beach and look older than the rocks he sits among. The rocks by the way are old red sandstone. They will blossom as the rose when Granite John sits among them. His is the head on which all the beginnings of the world have come, and he is never weary. Dear me, if I was not a teetotaller I should imagine I was drunk. I think it is the sea. What a heavenly time, the man who stole the Gioconda must have had. He just took it away. I can imagine him going to the Abbey at the Coronation, and taking away the King's crown without anybody seeing. There is genius, and it is also nonsense. It is pure nonsense to imagine going to the Louvre and taking La Gioconda away."

"I wonder what he has done with it," said Nadine. "I think he must be a jig-saw puzzle maniac, and have felt compelled to cut it up. Probably the Louvre will receive little bits of it by registered post. The nose will come, and then some rocks, and then a rather weary eyelid. I think John stole it: he was absorbed in jig-saw puzzles all morning. Now that seems to me nonsense."

"Wrong again," said Berts. "When the puzzle is put together it is sense. If people cut up the picture and then threw the bits away, it might be nonsense. But they keep the pieces and they become the picture again."

"The process of cutting up is nonsense," said Nadine.

"Yes, and the process of putting it together is nonsense," said Esther.

"And the two make sense," said Berts. "Let's go and bathe. Nadine, take down some proper book, and read to us in the intervals."

"Pride and Prej?" said Nadine.

"Oh, do you think so? Not marine in spirit. Why not 'Poems and Ballads'?"

"John will be shocked," said Nadine.

"Not at all. He will be older than red sandstone. I know Aunt Dodo has a copy. I think Mr. Swinburne gave it her," said Esther.

"She may value it," said Nadine. "And it may fall into the sea."

"Not if you are careful. Besides, that would be rather suitable. Swinburne loved the sea, and also understood it. I think his spirit would like it if a copy was drowned."

"But Mamma's spirit wouldn't," said Nadine.

On the moment of her mentioned name Dodo appeared at the long window of the drawing-room that opened on to the lawn. Simultaneously there was heard the buzz of a motor-car stopping at the front door just round the corner.

"Oh, all you darlings," said Dodo, in the style of the 'Omnia opera,' "are you going to bathe, or have you bathed? Berts, dear, we know that above the knee comes the thigh, without your showing us. Surely there are bigger dressing-gowns somewhere? Of course it does not matter: don't bother, and you've got beautiful legs, Berts."

"Aren't they lovely?" said Esther. "They ought to be cast in plaster of Paris."

"But if you have bathed why not dress?" said Dodo, "and if you haven't why undress at present?"

"Oh, but it's both," said Berts, "and so is Esther. We have bathed, and are going to do it again, as soon as we've eaten enough tea."

Dodo looked appreciatively round.

"You refreshing children!" she said. "If I bathed directly after tea I should turn blue and green like a bruise. I have wasted all afternoon in looking at a box of novels from Melland's. I don't know what has happened to the novelists: their only object seems to be to tell you about utterly dull and sordid people. There is no longer any vitality in them; they are like leaders in the papers, full of reliable information. One instance shocked me; the heroine in No. 11 Lambeth Walk went to Birmingham by a train that left Euston at 2:30 P.M. and her ticket cost nine shillings and twopence halfpenny. An awful misgiving seized me that it was all true and I rang for an A.B.C. and looked out Birmingham. It was so; there was a train at that hour and the ticket cost exactly that."

"How wretched!" said Nadine in a pained voice.

"Darling, don't take it too much to heart. And one of those novels was about Home Rule and another about Soap, and another about Tariff Reform, and a fourth about Christianity, which was absolutely convincing. But one doesn't go to a novel in order to learn Christianity, or soap-making. One reads novels in order to be entertained and escape from real life into the society of imaginary and fiery people. No good novel ever resembles real life. Another one——"

Dodo stopped suddenly, as a man came out of the drawing-room window. Then she held both her hands out.

"Ah, Jack," she said. "Welcome, welcome!"

A very kind face, grizzled as to the hair and moustache looked down on her from its great height, a face that was wonderfully patient and reasonable and trustworthy. Jack Chesterford wore his years well, but he wore them all, he did not look to be on the summer side of forty-five. He was spare still; life had not made him the unwilling recipient of the most voluminous and ironic of its burdens, obesity, but his movements were rather slow and deliberate, as if he was tired of the senseless repetition of the days. But there seemed to be no irritation mingled with his fatigue; he but yawned and smiled, and turned over fresh pages.

But at the moment, as he stood there with both of Dodo's hands in his, there was no appearance of weariness, and indeed it would have been a man of dough who remained uninspired by the extraordinary perfection and cordiality of her greeting. It was almost as if she welcomed a lover: it was quite as if she welcomed the best of friends long absent. That she had thought out the manner of her salutation, said nothing against its genuineness, but she could have welcomed him quite as genuinely in other modes. She had thought indeed of putting pathos, penitence and shamefacedness into her greeting; she could with real emotion to endorse it have just raised her eyes to his, and let them fall again, as if conscious of the need of forgiveness. Or, (with perhaps a little less genuineness) she could have adopted the matronly and "too late" attitude, but this would have been less genuine because she did not feel at all matronly, or think that it was in the least "too late." But warm and unmixed cordiality with no consciousness of things behind, was perhaps the most genuine and least complicated of all welcomes, and she gave it.

She did not hold his hands more than a second or two, for Nadine and others claimed them. But after a few minutes he and Dodo were alone again together, for Jack declined the invitation to join the bathers, on the plea of senility and feeling cold like David. Then when the noise of their laughter and talk had faded seawards, he dropped the trivialities that till now had engaged them, and turned to her.

"I have been a long time coming, Dodo," he said. "Indeed, I meant never to come at all. But I could not help it. I do not think I need explain either why I stopped away, or why I have come now."

Apart from the perfectly authentic pleasure that Dodo felt in seeing her old friend again, there went through her a thrill of delight at Jack's implication of what she was to him. She loved to have that power over a man; she loved to know how potent over him still was the spell she wielded. In days gone by she had not behaved well to him; it would be truer to acknowledge that she had behaved just as outrageously as was possible for anybody not a pure-bred fiend. But he had come back. It was unnecessary to explain why.

And then suddenly with the rush of old memories revived, memories of his unfailing loyalty to her, his generosity, his unwearying lovingkindness, her eyes grew dim, and her hands caught his again.

"Jack, dear," she said, "I want to say one thing. I am sorry for all I did, for my—my treachery, my—my damnedness. I was frightened: I have no other excuse. And, my dear, I have been punished. But I tell you that what hurts most is your coming here. Your forgiveness."

She had not meant to say any of this, it all belonged to one of the welcomes of him which she had rejected. But the impulse was not to be resisted.

"It is so," she said, with mouth that quivered.

"Wipe it all out, Dodo," he said. "We start again to-day."

Dodo's power of rallying from perfectly sincere attacks of emotion was absolutely amazing and quite unimpaired. Only for five seconds more did her gravity linger.

"Dear old Jack," she said. "It is good to see you. Oh, Jack, the grey hairs. What a lot, but they become you, and you look just as kind and big as ever. I used to think it would be so dreadful when we were all over forty, but I like it quite immensely, and the young generation are such ducks, and I am not the least envious of them. But aren't some of them weird? I wonder if we were as weird: I was always weirdish, I suppose, and I am too old to change now. But I've still got one defect, though you would hardly believe it. I can't get enough into the day, and I haven't learned how to be in two places at once. But I have just had three telephone lines put into my house in town. Even that isn't absolutely satisfactory, because the idea was to talk to three people at once, and I quite forgot that I hadn't three ears. I really ought to have been one of the young women in the Central Exchange, who sniff and give you the wrong number. You must feel really in the swim, if you are the go-between of everybody who wants to talk to everybody else, but I should want to talk to them all. Have you had tea? Yes? Then let us go down to the sea

because I must have a bathe before dinner. Oh, by the way Edith is
coming to-night. I have not seen her yet. You and she were the remnant
of the old guard who wouldn't surrender, Jack, but went on sullenly
firing your muskets at me. I forgot Mrs. Vivian, but her ear-trumpet
seems to make her matter less."

They went together across the lawn, which that morning had been
so sweetly bird-haunted, and down the steep hill-side that led across
the dunes to the sea. Here a mile of sands was framed between two
bold headlands that plunged steeply into the sea, and Jack and Dodo
walked along the firm shining beach towards the huge boulders which
had in some remote cataclysm been toppled down from the cliff, and
formed the rocks than which John was so much older. Like brown
amphibious sheep with fleeces of seaweed they lay grazing on the
sands, and dotted about in the water, and from the end of them a
long reef of cruel-toothed rocks jutted out a couple of hundred yards
into the sea, while higher up on the beach were more monstrous fragments, as big as cottages behind which the processes of dressing and
undressing of bathers could discreetly and invisibly proceed. Dodo
had forgotten about this and talking rapidly was just about to proceed
round one of them when an agonised trio of male voices warned her
what sight would meet her outraged eyes. The tide was nearly at its
lowest and but a little way out at the side of the reef these rocks
ended altogether, giving place to the wrinkled sand, and in among
them were delectable rock-pools with torpid strawberry-looking anem-
ones, and sideways-scuttling crabs with a perfect passion for self-ef-
facement in the sand, who, if effacement was impossible, turned themselves into wide-pincered grotesques, and tried to make themselves
look tall. Bertie and Esther who were already prepared for the bathe
were pursuing marine excavations in one of these, and Dodo ecstatically
pulled off her shoes and stockings, one of which fell into the rock-
pool in question.

"Oh, Jack, if you won't bathe you might at least paddle," she said.
"Berts, *do* you see that very red-faced anemone? Isn't it like Nadine's
maid? Esther, do take care. There's an enormous crab crept under the
seaweed by your foot. Don't let it pinch you, darling. Isn't cancer
the Latin for crab? It might give you cancer if it pinched you. Here
are the rest of them, I must go and put on my bathing-dress. It's in
the tent. I put up a tent for these children, Jack, at great expense,
and they none of them ever use it. Nadine, you are going to read to
us all in the water. Do wait till I come. What book is it? 'Poems and
Ballads'? and so suspiciously like the copy Mr. Swinburne gave me.
Don't drop it into the water more often than is necessary. You shall

read us 'Dolores our lady of pain,' as we step on sharp rocks and are
pinched by crabs. How Mr. Swinburne would have liked to know
that we read his poems as we bathed. And there's that other delicious
one 'Swallow my sister, oh, sister swallow.' It sounds at first as if
her sister was a pill, and she had to swallow her. Jack dear, you make
me talk nonsense somehow. Come up with me as far as the tent, and
while I get ready you shall converse politely from outside. It is so
dull undressing without anybody to talk to."

· · · · · · · · ·

Jack, though cordially invited to take part in the usual Symposium
in Nadine's room that night at bedtime, preferred to go to his own,
though he had no intention of going to bed. He wanted to think, to
ascertain how he felt. He imagined that this would be a complicated
process; instead he found it extraordinarily simple. That there were
plenty of things to think about was perfectly true, but they all faced
one way, so to speak, one dominant emotion inspired them all. He
was as much in love with Dodo as ever. He did not, because he could
not, consider how cruelly she had wronged him: all that she had done
was but a rush-light in the midday sun of what she was. He was
amazed at his stupidity in letting a day, not to speak of a year, elapse
without seeing her, since she was free again; it had been a wanton
waste of twelve golden months to do so. Often during these last two
years, he had almost fancied himself in love with Nadine; now he
saw so clearly why. It was because in face and corporal presence no
less than in mind she reminded him so often of what Dodo had been
like. She reproduced something of Dodo's inimitable charm. But now
that he saw the two together, how utterly had the image of Nadine
faded from his heart! In his affection, in his appreciation of her beauty
and vitality she was still exactly where she was, but out of the book
of love her name had been quite blotted out. Blotted out too, were
the fires of his anger and the scars of a bleeding heart, and years of
indignant suffering. But he had never let them take entire possession
of him: in his immense soul there had ever been alight the still secret
flame that no winds or tempests could make to flicker. And to-day,
at the sight of her, that flame had shot up again, a beacon that reached
to heaven.

Hard work had helped him all these years to keep his nature un-
soured. His great estates were managed with a care and consideration
for those who lived on his land unequalled in England, and politically
he had made for himself a name universally respected for the absolute
integrity of which it was the guarantee. But all that, so it seemed to
him now had been his employment not his life. His life, all these
years, had lain like some enchanted and sleeping entity, waiting for

the spell that would awaken it again. Now the spell had been spoken.

For a moment his thought paused, wondering at itself. It seemed incredible that he should be so weak, so wax-like. Yet that seemed to matter not at all. He might be weak or wax-like, or anything else that a man should not be, but the point was that he was alive again.

For a little he let himself drift back on to the surface of things. He had passed a perfectly amazing evening. Edith Arbuthnot had arrived, bringing with her a violinist, a viola-player and a 'cellist, but neither maid nor luggage. Her luggage, except her golf-clubs, and a chest containing music (as she was only coming for a few days) was certainly lost, but she was not sure whether her maid had ever meant to come, for she could not remember seeing her at the station. So the violinist had her maid's room and the viola-player and 'cellist, young and guttural Germans, had quarters found for them in the village, since Dodo's cottage was completely crammed. But they had given positively the first performance of Edith's new quartette and at the end the violinist had ceremoniously crowned her with a wreath of laurels which he had picked from the shrubbery before dinner. Then they went into wild ecstacies of homage, and drank more beer than would have been thought possible, while Edith talked German even more remarkably than Dodo, and much louder. With her laurel wreath tilted rakishly over one ear, a mug of beer in her hand, and wearing an exceedingly smart dinner-gown belonging to Dodo, and rather large walking-boots of her own, since nobody else's shoes would fit her, she presented so astounding a spectacle, that Jack had unexpectedly been seized with a fury of inextinguishable laughter, and had to go outside followed by Dodo who patted him on the back. When they returned, Edith was lecturing about the music they had just heard. Apparently it was impossible to grasp it all at one hearing, while it was obviously essential that they must all grasp it without delay. In consequence it was performed all over again, while she conducted with her wreath on. There was more homage and more beer. Then they had had charades by Dodo and Edith, and Edith sang a long song of her own composition with an immense trill on the last note but one, which was "Shade"; and her band played a quantity of Siegfried music, while Dodo with a long white beard made of cotton-wool was Wotan, and Edith truculently broke her walking-stick, and that was "Spear," and they did whatever they could remember out of "Macbeth," which wasn't much, but which was Shakespeare.

It was all intensely silly, but Jack knew that he had not laughed so much during all those years which to-night had rolled away. . . .

Then he left the surface and dived down into his heart again. . . . There was no question of forgiving Dodo for the way in which she had treated him, the idea of forgiveness was as foreign to the whole question as it would have been to forgive the barometer for going down and presaging rain. It couldn't help it; it was made like that. But in stormy weather and fine, in tempest and in the clear shining after rain, he loved Dodo. What his chances were he could not at present consider, for his whole soul was absorbed in the one emotion.

Jack, for all his grizzled hair and his serious political years, had a great deal about him that was still boyish, and with the inconsistency of youth having settled that it was impossible to think about his chance, proceeded very earnestly to do so. The chance seemed a conspicuously outside one. Dodo had had more than one opportunity of marrying him before, and had felt herself unable to take advantage of it: it was very little likely that she should find him desirable now. Twice already she had embarked on the unaccountable sea; both times her boat had foundered. Once the sea was made, in her estimate, of cotton-wool, the second time, in anybody's estimate, of amorous brandy. It was not to be expected that she would experiment again with so unexpected a Proteus.

Meantime a Parliament of the younger generation in Nadine's room was talking with the frankness that characterised them about exactly the same subject as Jack was revolving alone, for Dodo had gone away with Edith in order to epitomise the last twenty years, and begin again with a fresh twenty to-morrow.

"It is quite certain that it is Mamma he wants to marry and not me," said Nadine. "I thought it was going to be me. I feel a little hurt, like when one isn't asked to a party to which one doesn't want to go."

"You don't want to go to any parties," said Hugh rather acidly, "but I believe you love being asked to them."

Nadine turned quickly round to him.

"That is awfully unfair, Hughie," she said in a low voice, "if you mean what I suppose you do. Do you mean that?"

"What I mean is quite obvious," he said.

Nadine got up from the window-seat where she was sitting with him.

"I think we had all better go to bed," she said. "Hugh is being odious."

"If you meant what you said," he remarked, "the odiousness is with you. It is bad taste to tell me that you feel hurt that the Ripper doesn't want you to marry him."

Nadine was silent a moment. Then she held out her hand to him.

"Yes, you are quite right, Hugh," she said. "It was bad taste. I am sorry. Is that enough?"

He nodded, and dropped her hand again.

"The fact is we are all rather cross," said Esther. "We haven't had a look in to-night. We haven't been a bit wonderful."

"Mother is quite overwhelming," said Berts. "She and Aunt Dodo between them make one feel exactly a hundred and two years' old; as old as John. Here we all sit, we old people, Nadine and Esther and Hugh and I, and we are really much more serious than they."

"Your mother is serious enough about her music," said Nadine. "And Jack is serious about Mamma. The fact is that they are serious about serious things."

"Do you really think of Mother as a serious person with her large boots and her laurel-crown?" asked Berts.

"Certainly; all that is nothing to her. She doesn't heed it, while we who think we are musical can see nothing else. I couldn't bear her quartette either, and I know how good it was. I really believe that we are rotten before we are ripe. I except Hugh."

Nadine got up, and began walking up and down the room as she did when her alert analytical brain was in grips with a problem.

"Look at Jack the Ripper," she said. "Why, he's living in high romance; he's like a very nice grey-headed boy of twenty. Fancy keeping fresh all that time! Hugh and he are fresh. Berts is a stale old man, who can't make up his mind whether he wants to marry Esther or not. I am even worse. I am interested in Plato, and in all the novels about social reform and dull people who live in sordid respectability, which Mamma finds so utterly tedious."

Nadine threw her arms wide.

"I can't surrender myself to anybody or anything," she said. "I can be cool and judge, but I can't get away from my mind. It sits up in a corner like a great governess. Whereas Mamma takes up her mind like one of those flat pebbles on the shore and plays ducks and drakes with it, throws it into the sea, and then really enjoys herself, lets herself feel. If for a moment I attempt to feel, my mind gives me a poke and says 'Attend to your lessons, Miss Nadine!' The great Judy! If only I could treat her like one, and take her out and throw brickbats at her. But I can't; I am terrified of her; also I find her quite immensely interesting. She looks at me over the top of her gold-rimmed spectacles, and though she is very hard and angular yet somehow I adore her. I loathe her you know, and want to escape, but I do like earning her approbation. Silly old Judy!"

Berts gave a heavy sigh.

"What an extraordinary lot of words to tell us that you are an intellectual egoist," he said "And you needn't have told us at all. We all knew it."

Nadine gave her hiccup-laugh.

"I am like the starling," she said. "I can't get out. I want to get out and go walking with Hugh. And he can't get in. For what a pack of miseries was *le bon Dieu* responsible when he thought of the world."

"I should have been exceedingly annoyed if He had not thought of me," said Berts.

Nadine paused opposite the window-seat, where Hugh was sitting silent.

"Oh, Hugh," she said, speaking very low. "There is a real me somewhere, I believe. But I cannot find it. I am like the poor thing in the fairy-tale, that lost its shadow. Indeed I am in the more desperate plight, I have got my shadow, but I have lost my substance, though not in riotous living."

"For God's sake find it," he said, "and then give it me to keep safe."

She looked at him with her dim smile that always seemed to him to mean the whole world.

"When I find it, you shall have it," she said.

"And last night it was the moon you wanted," said he, "not yourself."

Nadine shrugged her shoulders.

"What would you have?" she said. "That was but another point of view. Do not ask me to see things always from the same standpoint. And now, since my Mamma and Berts have made us all feel old, let us put on our night-caps and rub some cold cream on our venerable faces and go to bed. Perhaps to-morrow we shall feel younger."

4

Seymour Sturgis (who, Berts thought, ought to have been drowned when he was a girl), was employed one morning in July in dusting his jade. He lived in a small flat just off Langham Place, with a large capable middle-aged Frenchwoman, who worshipped the ground on which he so delicately trod with the cloth-topped boots which she made so resplendent. She cooked for him in the inimitable manner of her race, she kept his flat speckless and shining, she valetted him, she did everything in fact except dust the jade. Highly as Seymour thought of Antoinette he could not let her do that. He always alluded to her as "my maid," and used to take her with him, as valet, to country houses. It must, however, be added that he did this largely to annoy, and he largely succeeded.

The room which was adorned by his collection of jade, seemed somehow strangely unlike a man's room. A French writing table stood in the window with a writing-case and blotting book stamped with his initials in gilt; by the pen-tray was a smelling-bottle with a gold screw-top to it. Thin lace blinds hung across the windows, and the carpet was of thick, fawn-coloured fabric with remarkably good Persian rugs laid down over it. On the chimney-piece was a Louis Seize garniture of clock and candlesticks, and a quantity of invitation cards were stuck into the mirror behind. There were half a dozen French chairs, a sofa, a baby-grand, a small table or two, and a bookcase of volumes all in morocco dress-clothes. On the walls there were a few prints, and in glazed cabinets against the wall was the jade. Nothing, except perhaps the smelling-bottle suggested a mistress rather than a master, but the whole effect was feminine. Seymour rather liked that; he had very little liking for his own sex. They seemed to him both clumsy and stupid, and his worst enemies (of whom he had plenty) could not accuse him of being either the one or the other. On their side they disliked him because he was not like a man; he disliked them because they were.

But while he detested his own sex, he did not regard the other with the ordinary feeling of a man. He liked their dresses, their per-fumes, their hair, their femininity more than he liked them. He was quite as charming to plain old ladies, even as Dodo had said, as he was to girls, and he was perfectly happy, when staying in the country, to go a motor drive with aunts and grandmothers. He had a perfectly marvellous digestion; ate a huge lunch, sat still in the motor all after-noon, and had quantities of buttered buns for tea. He dressed rather too carefully to be really well-dressed, and always wore a tie and socks of the same colour, which repeated in a more vivid shade the tone of his clothes. He had a ruby ring, a sapphire ring, and an emerald ring; they were worn singly and matched his clothes. He spoke French quite perfectly.

All these depressing traits naturally enraged such men as came in contact with him, but though they abhorred him they could not openly laugh at him, for he had a tongue, when he chose, of quite unparalleled acidity, and was markedly capable of using it when required and taking care of himself afterwards. In matters of art, he had a taste that was faultless and his taste was founded on real knowledge and technique, so that really great singers delighted to perform to his accompaniment, and in matters of jewellry he designed for Grinelle. In fact, from the point of view of his own sex, he was detestable rather than ridiculous, while considerable numbers of the other sex did their very best to spoil him, for none could want a more amusing companion, and his good looks were quite undeniable. But somewhere in his nature there was a certain grit which quite refused to be ground into the pulp of a spoiled young man. In his slender frame, too, there were nerves of steel, and, most amazing of all, when not better employed in designing for Grinelle, or engaged on bloodless flirtations, he was a first-class golfer. But he preferred to go for a drive in the afternoon, and smoke a succession of rose-scented cigarettes, which could scarcely be considered tobacco at all. He was fond of food, and drank a good many glasses of port rather petulantly, after dinner, as if they were medicine.

This morning he was particularly anxious that his jade should show to advantage, for Nadine was coming to lunch with him, to ask his advice about something which she thought was old Venetian-point lace. He had taken particular pains also about the lunch; everything was to be *en casserole;* there were eggs in spinach, and quails, and a marvellous casseroled cherry tart. He could not bear that anything about him, whether designed for the inside or the outside, should be other than exquisite, and he would have been just as sedulous a Martha if that strange barbarian called Berts was coming. Only he would have given Berts an immense beef steak as well (which Berts detested), to show that he knew that it was manly to eat lumps of meat.

The bell of his flat rang, announcing Nadine. He did not like the shrill treble bells, and had got one that made a low bubbling note like the laugh of Sir Charles Wyndham, and Nadine came in.

"Enchanted!" he said. "How is Philistia?"

"Not being the least glad of you," she said. "I wish I could make people detest me, as Berts detests you. It shows force of character. Oh, Seymour, what jade! It is almost shameless! Isn't it shameless jade I mean? Is any one else coming to lunch?"

"Of course not. I don't dilute you with other people, I prefer Nadine neat. Now let's have the crisis at once. Bring out the lace."

Nadine produced a small parcel and unfolded it.

"Pretty," said he.

Then he looked at it more closely, and tossed it aside. "I hoped it was more like Venetian point than that," he said. "It's all quite wrong; the thread's wrong; the stitch is wrong; it smells wrong. Don't tell me you've bought it."

"No, I shan't tell you," she said.

He took it up again and pondered.

"You got it at Ducane's," he said. "I remember seeing it. Well, take it back to Ducane, and tell him if he sold it as Venetian, that he must give you back your money. My dear, it is no wonder these dealers get rich, if they can palm off things like that. *C'est fini.* Ah, but that is an exquisite aquamarine you are wearing. Those little diamond points round it throw the light into it. Why, I believe I designed the mount myself! How odd people usually are about jewellery. They think great buns of diamonds are sufficient to make an adornment. You might as well send up an ox's hind leg on the table. What makes the difference is the manner of its presentation. . . . Or it is like that lady who employs herself in writing passionate love-novels. She says on page one that he was madly in love with her, on page two that she was madly in love with him, on page three that they were madly in love with each other, and then come some asterisks. (How much more artistic by the way if they printed the asterisks and left out the rest! Then we should know what it really was like.) You can appreciate nothing until it is framed or cooked; then you can see the details. The poor lady presents us with chunks of meat and informs us that they are voluptuous men and women. I will write a novel some day, from the detached standpoint, observing and noting. Then I shall go away abroad. It is only bachelors who can write about love. Do you like my tie?"

Seymour had a trick of putting expression into what he said by means of his hands. He waved and dabbed with them; they fondled each other, and then started apart as if they had quarrelled. Sometimes one finger pointed, sometimes another, and they were all beautifully manicured. Antoinette did that, and as she scraped and filed and polished he talked his admirable French to her, and asked after the old home in Normandy, where she learned to make wonderful soup out of carrots and turnips and shin bones of beef. At the moment she came in to announce the readiness of lunch.

"Oh, is it lunch already?" said Nadine. "Can't we have it after half an hour? I should like to see the jade."

"Oh, quite impossible," said he. "She has taken such pains. It would distress her. For me, I should prefer not to lunch yet, but she is the artist now. There are fragile things, Nadine, eggs in spinach. You must come at once."

"How greedy you are," she said.

"For you that is a foolish thing to say. I am simply thinking of Antoinette's pride. It is as if I blew a soap bubble, all iridescent, and you said you would come to look at it in ten minutes. You shall tell me news; if you talk you can always eat. What has happened in Philistia?"

Nadine frowned.

"You think of us all as Philistines," she said, "because we like simple pleasures, and because we are enthusiastic."

"Ah, you mistake!" he said. "You couple two reasons which have nothing to do with each other. To be enthusiastic is the best possible condition, but you must be enthusiastic over what is worth enthusiasm. Is it so lovely really, that Aunt Dodo has settled to marry the Ripper?

Surely that is a *réchauffée*. You wrote me the silliest letter about it. Of course it does not matter at all. Much more important is that you look perfectly exquisite. Antoinette, the spinach is *sans pareil*; give me some more spinach. But it is slightly *bourgeois* in Jack the R. to have been faithful for so many years. It shows a want of imagination, also, I think, a want of vitality, only to care for one woman."

"That is one more than you ever cared for," remarked Nadine.

"I know. I said it was *bourgeois* to care for one. It is not the least *bourgeois* to care for none. But to care for one is rather like a troubadour. I am not in the least like a troubadour, thank God. But I think I shall get married soon. It gives one more liberty; people don't feel curious about one any more. English people are so odd; they think you must lead a life *à deux*, and if you don't lead the ordinary double life with a wife, they think you lead it with somebody else, and they get curious. I am not in the least curious about other people; they can lead as many lives as a piano has strings for all I care, and thump all the strings together, or play delicate arpeggios on them. Nadine, that hat-pin of yours is simply too divine. I will eat it pin and all if it is not Fabergé."

Nadine laughed.

"I can't imagine you married," she said. "You would make a very odd husband."

"I would make a very odd anything," said he. "I don't find any recognised niche that really fits me, whereas almost everybody has some sort of niche. Indeed, in the course of hundreds of years the manner of people's lives, which is what I mean by niches, has been evolved to suit the sort of types which nature produces. They live in rows and respect each other. But why it should be considered respectable to marry and have hosts of horrible children I cannot imagine. But it is, and I bow to the united strength of middle-class opinion. But neither you nor I are really made to live in rows. We are Bedouins by nature, and like to see a different sunrise every day. There shall be another tent for Antoinette."

That admirable lady was just bringing them their coffee, and he spoke to her in French.

"Antoinette, we start for the desert of Sahara to-morrow," he said. "We shall live in tents."

Antoinette's plump face wrinkled itself up into enchanted smiles.

"Bien, m'sieur," she said. "A quelle heure?"

Nadine crunched up her coffee sugar between her white teeth.

"You are as little fitted to cross the desert of Sahara as anyone I ever met," she said.

"I should not cross it; I should——"

"You would be miserable without your jade or your brocade and the sand would get into your hair, and you would have no bath," she said. "But everyone who thinks has a Bedouin mind; it always wants to go on and find new horizons and get nearer to blue mountains."

"The matter with you is that you want and you don't know what you want," said he.

Nadine nodded at him. Sometimes when she was with him she felt as if she was talking to a shrewd middle-aged man, sometimes to a rather affected girl. Then occasionally, and this had been in evidence to-day, she felt as if she was talking to some curious mixture of the two, who had a girl's intuition and a man's judgment. Fond as she was of the friends whom she had so easily gathered round her, gleeful as was the nonsense they talked, serious as was her study of Plato, she felt sometimes that all those sunny hours concerned but the surface of her, that, as she had said before, the individual, the character that sat behind was not really concerned in them. And Seymour, when he made mixture of his two types, had the effect of making her very conscious of the character that sat behind her tastes. He had described it just now in a sentence; it wanted, but knew not what.

"And I want it so frightfully," she said. "It is a pity I don't know what it is. Because then I should probably get it. One gets what one wants if one wants enough."

"A convenient theory," he said, "and if you don't get it, you account for it by saying you didn't want it enough. I don't think it's true. In any case the converse isn't, one gets a quantity of things which one doesn't want in the least, whereas you ought not to get, on the same theory, the things you passionately desire not to have."

Nadine finished her sugar and lit a cigarette.

"Oh, don't upset every theory," she said. "I am really rather serious about it."

He regarded her with his head on one side for a moment.

"What has happened is that somebody has asked you to do something, and you have refused. You are salving your conscience by saying that he doesn't want it enough, or you would not have refused."

She laughed.

"You are really rather uncanny sometimes," she said.

"Only a guess," he said.

"Guess again then; define," she said.

"The obvious suggestion is that Hugh has proposed to you again."

"You would have been burned as a witch two hundred years ago," said she. "I should have contributed faggots. Oh, Seymour, that was really why I came to see you. I didn't care two straws about the foolish lace. They all tell me I had better marry Hugh, and I wanted to find somebody to agree with me. I hoped perhaps you might. He is such a dear you know, and I should always have my own way; I could always convince him I was right."

"Most girls would consider that an advantage."

"In that case I am not like most girls; I often wish I was. He always thinks that all I do is admirable; it is such a pity. I wrote an article a month or two ago about Tolstoi, and read it to him, and he thought it quite wonderful. Well, it wasn't. It was silly rot; I wrote it, and so of course I know. It came out in a magazine."

"I read it," remarked Seymour in a strictly neutral voice.

"Well, wasn't it very poor stuff?" asked Nadine.

"To be quite accurate," said Seymour. "I only read some of it. I thought it very poor indeed. It was ignorant and affected."

Nadine gave him an approving smile.

"There you are, then! And with Hugh it would be the same in every-thing else. He would always think what I did was quite wonderful. They say love is blind, don't they? So much the worse for love. It seems to me a very poor sort of thing if, in order to love anybody, you must lose, with regard to her, any power of mind and judgment that you may happen to possess. I don't want to be loved like that. I want people to sing my praises with understanding, and sit on my defects also with discretion. If I was perfectly blind too, I suppose it would be quite ideal to marry him. But I'm not, and I'm not even sure that I wish I was. Again, if Hugh was perfectly critical about me, it would be quite ideal. It seems to me you must have the same quality of love on both sides, or, at any rate, the same quality of affection. People make charming marriages without any love at all, if they have affection and esteem and respect for each other."

They had gone back to the drawing-room, and Seymour was handing pieces of his most precious jade to Nadine, who looked at them ab-sently, and then gave them back to him, with the same incuriousness as people give tickets to be punched by the collector. This Seymour bore with equanimity, for Nadine was interesting on her own account, and he did not care whether she looked at his jade or not. But at this moment he screamed loudly, for she put a little round medallion of exquisitely carved yellow jade up to her mouth, as if to bite it.

"Oh, Seymour, I'm so sorry," she said. "I wasn't attending to your jade, which is quite lovely, and subconsciously this piece appeared like a biscuit. Tell me, do you like jade better than anything else? It is part of a larger question, which is 'Do you like things better than people?' Personally, I like people so far more than everything else in the world, but I don't like any particular person nearly as much. I like them in groups, I suppose. If I married at all, I should probably be a polyandrist. Certainly, if I could marry four or five people at once, I should marry them all. But I don't want to marry any one of them."

Seymour put the priceless biscuit back into its cabinet.

"Who," he asked, "are this quartet of fortunate swains?"

"Well, Hugh, of course, would be one," said she, "and I think Berts would be another. And if it won't be a shock to you, you would be the third, and Jack the R. would be the fourth. I should then have a variety of interests: there would be the world, and the flesh, and the devil, and a saint."

"St. Seymour," said he, as if trying how it sounded, like a Liberal peer selecting his title.

"I am afraid you are cast for the devil," said Nadine, candidly. "Berts is the world because he thinks he is cynical. And Jack is the flesh——"

"Because he is so thin?"

"Partly. But also because he is so rich."

Seymour turned the key on his jade. This interested him much more. But he had to make further inquiries.

"If every girl wanted four husbands," he said, "there wouldn't be enough men to go round."

"Round what?" asked Nadine, still entirely absorbed in what she was thinking.

"Round the marriageable females. Or does your plan include poly-womany, or whatever the word is, for men?"

"But, of course. There are such lots of bachelors who would marry if they could have two or three wives, just as there are such lots of girls who would marry if they could have two or three husbands. All those laws about one man one wife were made by ordinary people for ordinary people. And ordinary people are in the majority. There ought to be a small county set apart for ridiculous people, with a rabbit fence all round it, and anyone who could be certified to be ridiculous in his tastes should be allowed to go and live there unmolested. That would be much better than your plan of going to the Sahara with Antoinette. You would have to get five householders to certify you as ridiculous, in order to obtain admission. Then you would do what you chose within the rabbit fence, but when you wanted to be what they call sensible again you would come out, and be bound to behave like anybody else, as long as you were out, under penalty of not being admitted again."

Seymour considered this.

"There's a lot in it," he said, "and there would be a lot of people in the rabbit fence. I should go there to-morrow, and never come out at all. But a smaller county would be no use. I should start with Kent, not Rutlandshire, and be prepared to migrate to Yorkshire. I accept the position of one of your husbands."

"That is sweet of you. I think——"

He interrupted.

"I shall have some more wives," he said. "I should like a lunch wife and a dinner wife. I want to see a certain kind of person from about midday till tea-time."

"Is that a hint that it is time for me to go," asked Nadine.

"Nearly. Don't interrupt. But then, if one is not in love with anybody at all, as you are not, and as I am not, you want a perfectly different kind of person in the evening. To be allowed only one wife has evolved a very tiresome type of woman; a woman who is like a general servant, and can, so to speak, wait at table, cook a little, and make beds. People look for somebody who, on the whole, suits them. It is like buying a reach-me-down suit, which I have never done. It probably fits pretty well. But if it is to be worn every day until you die, it must fit absolutely. If it doesn't, there are fifty other suits that would do as well."

"Translate," said Nadine.

"Surely there is no need. What I mean is that occasionally two people are ideally fitted. But the fit only occurs intermittently: it is not common. Short of that, as long as people don't blow their noses wrong, or walk badly, or admire Carlo Dolci, or fail to admire Bach, so long, in fact, as they do not have impossible tastes, any phalanx of a thousand men can marry a similar phalanx of a thousand women, and be as happy, the one with the other, as with any other permutation or combination of the thousand. There is a possible high, big, tremulous, romantic attachment possible, and it occasionally occurs. Short of that, with the limitation about Carlo Dolci and Bach, anybody would be as happy with anybody else, as anybody would be with anybody. We are all on a level, except the highest of all, and the lowest of all. Life, not death, is the leveller!"

"Still life is as bad as still death," said she.

Seymour groaned and waved his hands.

"You deserve a good scolding, Nadine, for saying a foolish thing like that," he said. "You are not with your Philistines now. There is not Esther here to tell you how marvellous you are, nor Berts to wave his great legs and say you are like the moon coming out of the clouds over the sea. I am not in the least impressed by a little juggling with words such as they think clever. It isn't clever; it is a sort of parrot talk. You open your mouth and say something that sounds paradoxical, and they all hunt about to find some sense in it, and think they do."

Seymour got up and began walking up and down the room with

his little short-stepped waggling walk. "It is the most amazing thing to me," he said, "that you, who have got brains, should be content to score absurd little successes with your dreadful clan, who have the most ordinary intelligences. I love your Philistines, but I cannot bear that they should think they are clever. They are stupid, and though stupid people are excellent in their way, they become trying when they think they are wise. You are not made wise by bathing all day in the silly salt sea, and reading a book——"

"How did you know?" asked Nadine.

"I didn't; it is merely the sort of thing I imagine you do at Meering. Aunt Dodo is different; there is no rot about Aunt Dodo, nor is there about Hugh. But Esther, my poor sister, and the beautiful Berts!"

Nadine took up the cudgels for the clan.

"Ah, you are quite wrong," she said. "You do us no justice at all. We are eager, we are really; we want to learn, we think it waste of time to spend all day and night at parties and balls. We are critical, and want to know how and why. Seymour, I wish we saw more of you. Whenever I am with you, I feel like a pencil being sharpened. I can make fine marks afterwards."

"Keep them for the clan," he said. "No, I can't stand the clan, nor could they possibly stand me. When Esther squirms and says 'O, Nadine, how wonderful you are,' I want to be sick, and when I wave my hands and talk in a high voice, as I frequently do, I can see Berts turning pale with the desire to kill me. Poor Berts! Once I took his arm, and he shuddered at my baleful touch. I must remember to do it again. Really, I don't think I can be one of your husbands if Berts is to be another."

"Very well; I'll leave out Berts," said she.

"This is almost equivalent to a proposal," said Seymour, in some alarm.

She laughed.

"I won't press it," she said. "And now I must go. Thanks for sharpening me, my dear, though you have done it rather roughly. I am going down to Meering again to-morrow; London is a mere rabble of colonels and colonials. Come down if you feel inclined."

"God forbid!" said Seymour, piously.

Nadine had spent some time with him, but long after she had gone something of her seemed to linger in his room. Some subtle aroma of her, too fine to be purely physical, still haunted the room, and the sound of her detached crisp speech echoed in the chambers of his brain. He had never known a girl so variable in her moods; on one day she would talk nothing but the most arrant nonsense, on another, as to-day, there mingled with it something extraordinarily tender and wistful; on a third day she would be an impetuous scholar, on the fourth she threw herself heart and soul (if she had a heart) into the gay froth of this London life. Indeed "moods" seemed to be too superficial a word to describe her aspects; it was as if three or four different personalities were lodged in that slim body and directed affairs from the cool brain in that small, poised head. It would be scarcely necessary to marry other wives, according to their scheme, if Nadine was one of them, for it was impossible to tell even from minute to minute with which of her you were about to converse, or which of her was coming down to dinner. But all these personalities had the same vivid quality, the same exuberance of vitality, and in whatever character she appeared she was like some swiftly-acting tonic, that braced you up and, unlike mere alcoholic stimulant, was not followed by a reaction. She often irritated him, but she never resented the expression of his impatience, and above all things, she was never dull. And for once Seymour left incomplete the dusting of the precious jade, and tried to imagine what it would be like to have Nadine always here. He did not succeed in imagining it with any great vividness, but it must be remembered that this was the first time he had ever tried to imagine anything of the kind.

Edith had left Meering with Dodo two days before, and was going to spend a week with her in town, since she was rather tired of her own house. But she had seen out of the railway carriage window on the north coast of Wales, so attractive-looking a golf-links, that she had got out with Berts at the next station, to have a day or two golfing. The obdurate guard had refused to take their labelled luggage out, and it was whirled on to London to be sent back by Dodo on arrival. But Edith declared that it gave her a sense of freedom to have no luggage, and she spent two charming days there, and had arrived in London only this afternoon. She had gone straight to Dodo's house, and had found Jack with her, and there learned the news of their engagement, which had taken place only the day before. Upon which she sprang up and remorselessly kissed both Dodo and Jack.

"I can't help it if you don't like it," she said, "but that's what I feel like. Of course it ought to have happened more than twenty years ago, and it would have saved you both a great deal of bother. Dodo, I haven't been so pleased since my mass was performed at the Queen's Hall. You must get married at once, and have some children. It will be like living your life all over again without any of those fatal mistakes, Dodo. Jack—I shall call you Jack now—Jack, you have been more wonderfully faithful than anybody I ever heard of. You have seen all along what Dodo was, without being put off by what she did——"

Dodo screamed with laughter.

"Are these meant to be congratulations?" she said. "It is the very oddest way to congratulate a man on his engagement, by telling him that he is wise to overlook his future wife's past. It is also so pleasant for me."

Edith was still shaking hands with them both, as if to see whether their hands were fixtures or would come off if violently agitated.

"You know what I mean," she said. "It is useless my pretending to approve of most things you have done; it is useless for Jack also. But he marries the essential you, not a parcel of actions."

Jack kept saying "Thanks awfully" at intervals like a minute gun, and trying to get his hand away. Eventually Edith released it.

"I am delighted with you both," she said. "And to think that only a fortnight ago I was still not on speaking terms with you, Dodo. And Jack wasn't either. I love having rows with people if I know things are going to come straight afterwards, because then I love them more than ever. And I knew that some time I should have to make it up with you, Dodo, though if I was Jack I don't think I could have forgiven—well, you don't wish me to go on about that. Anyhow, you are ducks, and now I shall leave the young couple alone, and have a wash and brush-up. I have been playing golf quite superbly."

Edith banged the door behind her, and they heard her shrilly whistling as she went down the passages.

Then Dodo turned to Jack.

"Jack, dear, I thought I should burst when Edith kissed you," she said. "You half shut your eyes and screwed up your face like a dog that is just going to be whipped. But I love Edith. Now come and sit here and talk. I have hardly seen you since—well, since we settled that we should see a good deal more of each other in the future—I want you to tell me, oh, such lots of things. How often a month on the average have you thought about me during all these years? Jack, dear, I want to be wanted, so much."

"You have always been wanted by me," he said. "It is more a question of how many minutes in the month I haven't thought about you. They are more easily counted."

He sat down on the sofa by her, as her hand indicated.

"Dodo," he said, "I don't make demands of you, except that you should be yourself. But I do want that. We are all made differently; if we were not, the world would be a very stupidly simple affair. And you must know that in one respect anyhow I am appallingly simple. I have never cared for any woman except you. That is the fact. Let us have it out between us just once. I have never worn my heart on my sleeve, for any woman to pluck at, and carry away a mouthful of it. There are no bits missing, I assure you. It is all there, and it is all yours. It is in no way the worse for wear, because it has had no wear. I feel as if——"

Jack paused a moment; he knew the meaning of his thought, but found it not so easy to make expression of it.

"I feel as if I had been sitting all my life at a window in my heart," he said, "looking out, and waiting for you to come by. But you had to come by alone. You came by once with my cousin. You came by a second time with Waldenech. You were bored the first time, you were frightened the second time. But you were not alone. I believe you are alone now; I believe you look up to my window. Ah, how stupid all language is! As if you looked up to it!"

Dodo was really moved, and when she spoke her voice was unsteady.

"I do look up to it, Jack," she said. "Oh, my dear, how the world would laugh at the idea of a woman already twice married, having romance still in front of her. But there is romance, Jack. You see— you see you have run through my life just as a string runs through a necklace of pearls or beads; beads perhaps is better—yet I don't know. Chesterford gave me pearls, all the pearls. A necklace of pearls before swine shall we say? I was swine, if you understand. But you always ran through it all, which sounds as if I meant you were a spendthrift, but you know what I do mean. Really I wonder if anybody ever made a worse mess of her life than I have done, and found it so beautifully cleaned up in the middle. But there you were—I ought to have married you originally; I ought to have married you unoriginally. But I never trusted my heart. You might easily tell me that I hadn't got one, but I had. I daresay it was a very little one, so little that I thought it didn't matter. I suppose I was like the man who swore something or other on the crucifix, and when he broke his oath he said the crucifix was such a small one."

She paused again.

"Jack, are you sure?" she asked. "I want you to have the best life that you can have. Are you sure you give yourself the best chance with me? My dear, there will be no syllable of reproach on my lips, or in my mind, if you reconsider. You ought to marry a younger woman than me. You will be still a man at sixty, I shall be just a thing at fifty-eight."

Dodo took a long breath and stood up.

"Marry Nadine," she said. "She is so like what I was; you said it yourself. And she hasn't been battered like me. I think she would marry you. I know how fond she is of you, anyhow, and the rest will follow. I can't bear to think of you pushing my bath-chair. God knows, I have spoiled many of your years. But, God knows, I don't want to spoil more of them. She will give you all that I could have given you twenty years ago. Ah, my dear, the years! How cruel they are! How they take away from us all that we want most! You love children for instance, Jack. Perhaps I shall not be able to give you children. Nadine is twenty-one. That is a long time ago. You should consider. I said 'yes' to you yesterday, but perhaps I had not thought about it sufficiently. I have thought since. Before you came down to Meering I was awake so long one night, wondering why you came. I was quite prepared that it should be Nadine you wanted. And, oh, how gladly I would give Nadine to you, instead of giving myself! I should see; I should understand; at first I thought that I should not like it, that I should be jealous, to put it quite frankly, of Nadine. But somehow now that I know that your first desire was for me, I am jealous no longer. Take Nadine, Jack! I want you to take Nadine. It will be better. We know each other well enough to trust each other, and now that I tell you that there will be nothing but rejoicing left in my heart if you want Nadine, you must believe that I tell you the entire truth. I know very well about Nadine. She will not marry Hugh. She wants somebody who has a bigger mind. She wants also to put Hugh out of the question. She does not mean to marry him, and she would like it to be made impossible. Woo Nadine, dear Jack, and win her. She will give you all I could once have given you, all that I ought to have given you."

At that moment Dodo was making the great renunciation of her life. She had been completely stirred out of herself and she pleaded against her own cause. She was quite sincere, and she wanted Jack's happiness more than her own. She believed even while she renounced all claim on him, that her best chance of happiness was with him, for it had taken her no time at all to make up her mind when he proposed to her yesterday. And she had not exaggerated when just now she told him that he ran through her life like a string that keeps the beads of time in place. She had never felt for another man what she had felt for him, and her declaration of his freedom was a real renunciation, made impulsively but most generously and completely. She entirely meant it, and she did not pause to consider that the offer was one of which no man could conceivably take advantage. And Jack felt and knew her sincerity.

"You are absolutely free my dear," she said. "Absolutely! And I will come to your wedding, and dance at it if you like, for joy that you are happy."

He got up too.

"There will be no wedding unless you come to it," he said. "Dance at it, Dodo, but marry me. Nobody else will do."

Dodo looked him full in the face.

"Edith was quite right to remind you of—of what I have done," she said.

"And I am quite right to forget it," said he.

She shook her head, smiling a little tremulously.

"Oh, Jack," she said in a sigh.

He took her close to him.

"My beloved," he said, and kissed her.

5

Dodo's wedding, which took place at the end of July in Westminster Abbey, was a very remarkable and characteristic affair. In the first place she arrived so late that people began to wonder whether she was going to throw Jack over again, this time at the very last moment. Jack himself did not share these misgivings and stood at the west door rather hot and shy but quite serene, waiting till his bride should come. Eventually Nadine who was to have come with her mother appeared in a taxi going miles above the legal limit, with the information that Dodo was in floods of tears because she had been so horrible to Jack before, and wanted to be so nice now. She said she would stop crying as soon as she possibly could, but would Nadine ask Jack to be a dear and put off the wedding till to-morrow, since her tears had made her a perfect fright. On which the bridegroom took a card and wrote on it "I won't put off the wedding, and if you don't come at once, I shall go away. Do be quick; there are millions and millions of people all staring."

"Oh, Uncle Jack, what a brute you are," said Nadine, as she read it, "I don't think I can take it."

"You can and will," said he. "You will also take your mother by the hand and bring her here. Bring her, do you understand, whether she is crying or not. Tell her that in twenty minutes from now I shall go."

Somehow Dodo's marriage had seized the popular imagination, and the Abbey was crammed, so also for half a mile were the pavements. The traffic by the Abbey had been diverted, and all round the windows were clustered with sightseers. The choir was reserved for the more intimate friends, and Bishop Algy who was to perform the ceremony was endorsed by a flock of eminent clergy. The news that Dodo was in tears, but that Nadine had been sent by the bridegroom to fetch her, travelled swiftly up the Abbey, and a perfect babel of conversation broke out, almost drowning the rather Debussy-like wedding march which Edith had composed for the occasion. She had also written an

anthem "Thy wife shall be as the fruitful vine" and composed a highly
original hymn-tune, and two chants for the psalms written for full
orchestra with percussion and an eight-part choir. She had wanted
to conduct the whole herself, and expressed her perfect willingness
to wear a surplice and her music doctor's hood, and keep on her cap
or not exactly as the Dean preferred. But the Dean preferred that
she should take no part whatever beyond contributing the whole of
the music, which annoyed her very much, and several incisive letters
passed between them in which the topics of conventionalism, Pharisees
and cant were freely introduced. Edith had to give way, but consoled
herself by arranging that the whole of the "Marriage Suite" should
be shortly after performed at the Queen's Hall, where no Dean or
other unenlightened people could prevent her conducting in any cos-
tume she chose. But temporarily she had been extremely upset by
this ridiculous bigotry.

Dodo had arrived before the twenty minutes were over, and she
came up the choir on Jack's arm, looking quite superb and singing
Edith's hymn-tune very loud and occasionally incorrectly. She had
just come opposite Edith, who had, in default of conducting, secured
a singularly prominent position, when she sang a long bell-like B flat,
and Edith had said "B natural, Dodo," in a curdling sibilant whisper.
There were of course no bridesmaids, but Dodo's train was carried
by pages, both of whom she kissed when they arrived at the end of
their long march up the choir. Mrs. Vivian, who on Dodo's engagement
had finally capitulated, was next Edith, and Dodo said "Vivy, dear"
into her ear-trumpet, as she passed up the aisle. Miss Grantham alone
among the older friends was absent; she had said from the beginning
that it was dreadfully common of Dodo to marry Jack, as it was a
"lived happily ever afterwards" kind of ending to Dodo's unique experiences. She knew that they would both become stout and serene and
commonplace, instead of being wild and unhappy and interesting, and
to mark her disapproval, made an appointment with her dentist at
the hour at which the voice would be breathing over Eden in the
exceedingly up-to-date music which Edith had composed. But so far
from her dentist finding change and decay in all around he saw, he
dismissed her five minutes after she had sat down, and seized by a
sudden ungovernable fit of curiosity she drove straight off to the Abbey
to find that Dodo had not arrived, and it seemed possible that there
was a thrill coming, and everything might not end happily. But when
it became known that Dodo was only late for tearful reasons, she
left again in disgust, and ran into Dodo at the west door, and said "I
am disappointed, Dodo."

Dodo sang Edith's psalm with equal fervour, but thought it would be egoistic to join in the anthem, since it was about herself. But she whispered to Jack, "Jack dear; it's much the most delicious marriage I ever had. Hush, you must be grave because dear Algy is going to address us. I hope he will give us a nice long sermon."

The register was signed by almost everybody in the world, and there were so many royalties that it looked at first as if everybody was going to leave out their surnames. But the time of ambassadors and peers came at last, and then it looked as if the fashion was to discard Christian names. "In fact," said Dodo, "I suppose if you were much more royal than anybody else, you would lose your Christian name as well, your Royal Highness, and simply answer to 'Hie! or to any loud cry'—Oh, are we all ready again? We've got to go first, Jack. Darling, I hope you won't shy at the cinematographs. I hear the porch is full of them, like Gatling guns, and to-night you and I will be in all the music-halls of London. Where are my ducks of pages? That's right; one on each side. Now give me your arm, Jack. Here we go! Listen to Edith's wedding march! I wonder if it's safe to play as loud as that in anything so old as the Abbey. I should really be rather afraid of its falling down if Algy hadn't told me not to be afraid with any amazement."

It took the procession a considerable time to get down the choir, since Dodo had to kiss her bouquet (not having a hand to spare) to such an extraordinary number of people. But in course of time they got out, faced the battery of cameras and cinematograph machines, and got into their car. Jack effaced himself in a corner, but Dodo bowed and smiled with wonderful assiduity to the crowds.

"They have come to see us," she explained. "So it is essential that we should look pleased to see them. I should so like to be the Queen, say on Saturdays only, like the train you always want to go by on other days in the week. Darling, can't you smile at them? Or put out your tongue, and make a face. They would enjoy it hugely."

Eventually, as they got further away from the Abbey, it became clear to Dodo that the people in the street were concerned with their own businesses, and not hers and she leaned back in the carriage.

"Oh, Jack," she said. "It is you and I at last. But I can't help talking nonsense, dear. I only do it because I'm so happy. I am indeed. And you?"

"It is morning with me," he said.

They left town that afternoon, though Dodo rather regretted that they would not see themselves in the cinematograph to make sure that she had smiled and that Jack's hair was tidy, and went down to Winston, Jack's country place, where so many years ago Dodo had arrived before, as the bride of his cousin. He had wondered whether, for her sake, another place would not be more suitable as a honeymoon resort, but she thought the plan quite ideal.

"It will be like the renewal of one's youth," she said, "and I am going to be so happy there now. Jack, we were neither of us happy when you used to come to stay there before, and to go back like this will wipe out all that is painful in those old memories, and keep all that isn't. Is it much changed? I should so like my old sitting-room again if you haven't made it something else."

"It is exactly as you left it," said he. "I couldn't alter anything."

Dodo slipped her hand into his.

"Did you try to, Jack?" she asked.

"Yes. I meant to alter it entirely; I meant to put away all that could remind me of you. In fact I went down there on purpose to do it. But when I saw it, I couldn't. I sat down there, and——"

"Cried?" said Dodo softly and sympathetically.

"No, I didn't cry. I smoked a cigarette and looked round in a stupid manner. Then I took out of its frame a big photograph of myself that I had given you in order to tear it up. But I put it back in its frame again, and put the frame exactly where it was before."

Dodo gave a little moan.

"Oh, Jack, how you must have hated me!" she said.

"I hated what you had done: I hated that you could do it. But the other, never. And, Dodo, let us never talk about all those things again; don't let us even think of them. It is finished, and what is real is just beginning."

"It was real all along," she said, "and I knew it was real all along— you and me that is to say—but I chose to tell myself that it wasn't. I have been like the people who when they hear the scream of somebody being murdered, say it is only the cat. I have been a little brute all my life, and in all probability it is more than half over for me already, in fact it certainly is unless I am going to live to be ninety. I'm not sure that I want to, and yet I don't want to die one bit."

"I should be very much annoyed if you ventured to do anything of the sort," remarked Jack.

"Yes, and that is so wonderful of you. You ought to have wished me dead a hundred times. What's the phrase? Yes, she would be better dead. Just now I want to be better without being dead. I often think we all have a sort of half-time in our lives, like people in football matches, when they stop playing and eat lemons. The lemons, you understand, are rather sour reflections that we are no better than we might be, but a great deal worse. And somehow that gives us a sort of fresh start, and we begin playing again."

They arrived at Winston late in the afternoon; the village had turned out to greet them, flags and arches made rainbow of the grey street with its thatched houses and air of protected stability, and from the church tower the bells pealed welcome. Dodo, always impressionable and impulsive, was tremendously moved and with eyes brimming over, leaned out of one side of the carriage and then the other to acknowledge these salutations.

"Oh Jack, isn't it dear of them?" she said. "Of course I know it's all for you really, but you've endowed me with everything, and so this is mine too. Look at that little duck whom that nice-faced woman is holding up, waving a flag! Oh, it looked at me and then burst into tears! What a silly little idiot! Hark to the bells! Do you remember the poem by Browning, 'The air broke into a mist with bells'? This is a positive London fog of bells; can't you taste it? Is it the foghorns, in that case that make the fogs? And here we are at the lodge, and there's the lake, and the house! Ah, what a gracious thing a summer evening is. But how fragile, Jack, and how soon over."

That wistful underlying tenderness in her nature, almost melancholy, but wholly womanly, rose for the moment to the surface. It was not the less sincere because it was seldom in evidence. It was as truly part of her (and a growing part of her) as her brilliant enjoyment and insouciance. And the expression of it gleamed darkly in her soft brown eyes, as she leaned back in the carriage and took his hand.

"I will try to make you happy," she said.

He bent over her.

"Don't try to do anything, Dodo," he said. "Just—just be."

For a moment a queer little qualm came over her. Had she followed her immediate impulse, she would have said:

"I don't know how to love like that. I have to try: I want to learn."

But that would have done no good, and in her most introspective moments Dodo was always practical. The qualm lasted but a moment, as the door was opened, when they drew up. But it lasted long enough to cause her to wonder whether it would be the past that would be entered again instead of the future, entered, too, not by another door, but by the same.

On the doorstep she paused.

"Lift me over the threshold, Jack," she said, "it is such bad luck for a bride to stumble when she enters her home."

"My dear, what nonsense."

"Very likely, but let's be nonsensical. Let us propitiate all the gods and demons. Lift me, Jack."

He yielded to her whim.

"That is dear of you," she said. "That was a perfect entry. Aren't

I silly? But no Austrian would ever dream of letting his wife walk over the threshold for the first time. And—and that's all about Austria," she added rather hastily.

Dodo looked swiftly round the old, remembered hall. Opposite was the big open fireplace, round which they so often had sat, preferring its wide-flaring homely comfort to the more formal drawing-rooms. To-day, no fire burned there, for it was midsummer weather, but as in old times a big yellow collie sprawled in front of it, grandson perhaps, so short are the generations of dogs, to the yellow collies of the time when she was here last. He, too, gave good omen, for he rose and stretched and waved a banner of a tail, and came stately towards them with a thrusting nose of welcome. The same pictures hung on the walls; high up there ran round the palisade of stags' heads, and Dodo (with a conscious sense of most creditable memory) recognised the butler as having been her first husband's valet. She also remembered his name.

"Why, Vincent," she said, holding out her hand. "It is nice to see another old face. And you don't look one day older, any more than his lordship does. Tea: yes, let us have tea at once, Jack. I am so hungry: happiness is frightfully exhausting, and I don't mind how exhausted I am."

Suddenly Dodo caught sight of the portrait of herself which had been painted when this house was for the first time her home.

"Oh, Jack, look at that little brute smiling there!" she said. "I was rather pretty though, but I don't think I like myself at all. Dear me, I hope I'm not just the same now, with all the prettiness and youth removed. I don't think I am quite, and oh, Jack, there's the picture of poor dear old Chesterford. Ah, that hurts me; it gives me a bitter little heartache. Would you mind Jack, if——"

Jack felt horribly annoyed with himself for not having seen to this.

"My dear," he said, "it was awfully thoughtless of me. Of course, it shall go. It was stupid, but Dodo, I was so happy all this last month, that I have thought of nothing except myself."

Dodo turned away from the picture to him.

"And all the time I thought you were thinking about me!" she said. "Jack, what a deceiver!"

He shook his head.

"No: it is that you don't understand. You *are* me."

"Am I? I should be a much nicer fellow if I was. Jack, don't have that picture moved. It only hurt for a moment: it was a ghost that startled me merely because I did not expect it. It is a dear ghost: it is not jealous, it will not spoil things or come between us. It—it wants us to be happy, for he told me, you know, it was the last thing he said—that I was to marry you. It is a long time ago, oh, how long ago, though I say it to my shame. Besides, if you are to pull down or put away all that reminds me of that dreadful young woman"— Dodo put out her tongue and made a face at her own picture—"you will have to pull down the house and drink up the lake and cut down the trees. Ah, how lovely the garden looks! I was never here in the summer before: we only came for the shooting and hunting and the garden invariably consisted of rows of blackened salvias and decaying dahlias. But it is summer now, Jack."

There was no mistaking the figurative sense in which she meant him to understand the word "summer." It had been winter, winter of discontent—so the glance she gave him inevitably implied—when she was here before, and she rejoiced in and admired this excellent glory of summer time. And yet but a moment before the picture in the hall had "hurt" her, until she remembered that even on his death-bed her first husband had bidden her marry the man who had brought her back here to-day. She had neglected to do as she was told for about a quarter of a century and had married somebody else instead, and yet this amazing variety of topics that concerned her heart, any one of which you would have expected was of sufficient import to fill her mind to the exclusion of all else, but bowled across it, as the shadows of clouds bowl across the fields on a day of spring winds, leaving the untarnished sunshine after their passage. It was not because she was heartless that she touched on this series of somewhat tremendous things; it was rather that her vitality instantly reasserted itself: it was undeterred, impervious to discouraging or disturbing reflections.

Dodo ate what may be termed a good tea, and smoked several cigarettes. Then noticing that a small golf links had been laid out in the fields below the garden, she rushed indoors to change her dress, and played a game with her husband.

"It won't be much fun for you, darling," she said, "because my golf is a species of landscape gardening, and I dig immense hollows with my club and alter the lie of the country generally. Also I sometimes cheat, if nobody is looking, so admire the beauties of nature if you hear me say that I have a bad lie, because if you looked you would see me pushing the ball into a pleasanter place, and that would give you a low opinion of me. But a little exercise would be so good for us both after being married; the Abbey was terribly stuffy."

The fifth hole brought them near the little memorial chapel in the park, where her first husband was buried.

"Darling, that puts you five up," she said, "and would you mind waiting here a minute, while I go in alone? I don't want even you with me; I want to go alone and kneel for a minute by his grave, and say my prayers, and tell him I have come back again with you. Will you wait for a minute, Jack? I shan't be long."

Dodo wasn't long; she said her prayers with remarkable celerity, and came out again wiping her eyes.

"Oh, Jack," she said, "what a beautiful monument; it wasn't finished, you know, when I went away, and I hadn't seen it. And it's so touching to have just those three words, 'Lead kindly Light'; the dear old boy was so fond of that hymn. It's all so lovely and peaceful, and if ever there was a saint in the nineteenth century, it was he. Somehow I felt as if he knew about us and approved, and I remember he had 'Lead kindly Light' on the very last Sunday evening of all. I am so glad I went in."

Dodo gave a little sigh.

"Where are we?" she said. "Am I one hole up or two? Two, isn't it? Do let it be two! And what a lovely piece of marble. It looks like the most wonderful cold cream turned to stone. It must be Carrara. Oh, Jack, what a beautiful drive! It went much faster than the legal limit."

The flames of the summer sunset were beginning to fade in the sky when they got back to the house, and it was near dinner-time. Dodo's spirits and appetite were both of the most excellent order, and all the memories that this house brought back to her, so far from causing any aching resuscitation of past years, were, owing to the incomparable alchemy of her mind, but transformed into a soft and suitable background for the present. Afterwards, they sat on the terrace in the warm dusk.

"I must telegraph to Nadine to-morrow," she said, "and tell her how happy I am. Jack, sometimes Nadine seems to me exactly what I should expect a very attractive aunt to be. Do you know what I mean? I feel she could have warned me of all the mistakes I have made in my life, before they happened, if she had been born. And she approves of you and me; isn't it lucky? I wonder why I feel so young on the very day on which I should most naturally be thinking what a lot of life has passed. Jack, I don't want any more events. Some people reckon life by events, and that is so unreasonable. Events are thrust upon you, what counts is what you feel."

He moved his chair a little nearer to hers.

"I am satisfied with what I feel," he said. "And though I have felt it for very many years, it has never lost its freshness. I have always wanted, and now I have got."

Suddenly Dodo's mood changed.

"Oh, you take a great risk," she said. "Who is to assure you that I shan't disappoint you, disappoint you horribly? I can't assure you of that, Jack. It is easy to understand other people, but the silly proverb that tells you to know yourself, makes a far more difficult demand. If I disappoint you, what are we to do?"

"You can't disappoint me if you are yourself," he said.

"You say that! To me, too, who have outraged every sort of decency with regard to you?"

He was silent a moment.

"Yes, I say that to you," he said.

Dodo gave a little bubbling laugh.

"You are not very polite," she said. "I say that I have outraged every sort of decency, and you don't even contradict me."

"No. What you say is—is perfectly true. But the comment of you and me sitting here on our bridal night, is sufficient, is it not? Dodo, there is no use in your calling yourself names. Leave it all alone; we are here, you and I. And it is getting late, my darling."

The same night Lady Ayr was giving one of her awful dinner-parties. Her family, John, Esther, and Seymour were always bidden to them, and went in to dinner in exactly their proper places as sons and daughters of a marquis. Before now it had happened that Seymour had to take Esther in to dinner, and it was so to-night. But in the general way they saw so little of each other, that they did not very much object. They usually quarrelled before long, but made their differences up again by their unanimity of opinion about their mother. That had already happened this evening.

"Mother is bursting with curiosity about Aunt Dodo's wedding," said Esther. "She wasn't asked. I told her it was a very pretty wedding."

"I went," said Seymour, "and I am going to write an account of it for *The Lady*. If you will tell me how you were dressed, I will put it in, that is, supposing you were decently dressed. Mother asked me about it, too, and I think I said the bridesmaids looked lovely."

"But there weren't any," said Esther.

"Of course there weren't, but it enraged her. By the way, there is some awful stained glass put up in the staircase since I was here last. A ruby crown has apparently had twins, one of which is a sapphire crown and the other a diamond crown. I shouldn't mind that sort of thing happening, if it wasn't so badly done. I shall try to break it by accident after dinner. Did you design it? My dear, I forgot we had finished quarrelling. Let us talk about something else. Nadine came to see me the other day, and if you will not tell anybody, I think it quite likely that I shall marry her. She likes jade. And she looks quite pretty to-night, doesn't she?"

Esther had already alluded to Nadine, who was sitting opposite as the dream of dreams, and further appreciation was unnecessary.

"You don't happen to have asked her yet?" she said, with marked neutrality.

"No, one doesn't ask that sort of thing until one knows the answer," said he. "That is, unless you are one of the ridiculous people who ask for information. I hate the information I get by asking, unless I know it already."

"And then you don't get it."

"No. Esther, that is a charming emerald you are wearing, but it is atrociously set. If you will send it round to-morrow, I will draw a decent setting for it. Do look at Mother. She has got the family lace on, which is made of string. I think it is Saxon. Oh, of course, the coronets are about her. How foolish of me not to have guessed."

"It is more foolish of you to think that Nadine would look at you," said Esther.

"I didn't ask her to look at me, and I shan't ask her to look at me. I shall recommend her not to look at me. But I shall marry her or Antoinette. I don't see why you are so stuffy about it. Or, perhaps, you would prefer Antoinette for a sister-in-law."

"If she is to be your wife, dear, I think I should," said Esther.

Seymour laid his hand on hers. His smelt vaguely of wall-flowers.

"How disagreeable you are," he said. "I don't think I shall say anything about your dress in *The Lady*. I shall simply say that Lady Esther Sturgis was there looking very plain and tired. I shall describe my own dress instead. I had on an emerald pin, properly set, instead of its being set like that sort of cheese-cake you are wearing. No, it's not exactly a cheese-cake; it is as if you had split some *créme-de-menthe,* and put a little palisade of broken glass round it to prevent it spreading. What a disgusting dinner we are having, aren't we? I never know what to do before I dine with Mother, whether to eat so much lunch that I don't want any dinner, or to eat none at all, so that I can manage to swallow this sort of garbage. To-night I am rather hungry; won't you come away early with me and have some supper at home? Perhaps Nadine will come too."

"If Nadine will come, I will," said Esther. "I suppose we can chaperone each other."

"Certainly, if it amuses you. Shall we ask anybody else? I see hardly anybody here whom I know by sight. I think they must all be earls and countesses. It's funny how few of one's own class are worth speaking to. Look at Mamma! I know I keep telling you to look at Mamma, but she is so remarkable. She said 'sir' just now to the man next her. He must be a Saxon king. I wish she was responsible for the wine instead of father; teetotalers usually give one excellent wine, because they don't imagine they know anything about it, and tell the wine merchants just to send round some champagne and hock. So, of course they send the most expensive."

"I think we ought to talk to our neighbours," said Esther. "Mamma is making faces."

"That is because she has eaten some of this *entrée*, I expect. I make no face because I haven't. But I can't talk to my neighbour. I tried, but she is unspeakable to. I wish my nose would bleed, because then I should go away."

One of the frequent pauses that occurred at Lady Ayr's dinners was taking place at the moment, and Seymour's rather shrill voice was widely audible. A buzz of vacant conversation succeeded, and he continued.

"That was heard," he said, "and really I didn't mean it to be heard. I am sorry. I shall make myself agreeable. But tell Nadine we shall go away soon after dinner. If you will be ready, I shall not go up into the drawing-room at all."

Seymour turned brightly to the woman seated on his right.

"Have you been to 'The Follies'?" he asked. "I hope you haven't, because then we can't talk about them, since I haven't either. There are enough follies going about, without going to them."

"How amusin' you are," said his neighbour.

Seymour felt exasperated.

"I know I am," he said. "Do be amusing too; then we shall be delighted with each other."

"But I don't know who you are," said his neighbour.

"Well, that is the case with me," said he. "But my mother——"

His neighbour's face instantly changed from a chilly neutrality to a welcoming warmth.

"Oh, are you Lord Seymour?" she asked.

"I should find it very uncomfortable to be anybody else," said he. "I should not know what to do."

"Then *do* tell me, because, of course, you know all about these things. Are we all going to wear slabs of jade next year? And did you see me at Princess Waldenech's wedding this morning? And who manicures you? I hear you have got a marvellous person."

Seymour really wished to atone for the unfortunate remark that had broken the silence, and exerted himself.

"But, of course," he said, "it is Antoinette. She cooks for me and calls me; she dusts my rooms, and brushes my boots. She stirs the soup with one hand and manicures me with the other. Fancy not knowing Antoinette! She is fifty-two; by the time you are fifty-two you ought to be known anywhere. If she marries I shall die; if I marry, she will still live, I hope. Now, do tell me; do you recommend me to marry?"

"Doesn't it depend upon whom you marry?"

"Not much, do you think? But perhaps you are married, and so know. Are you married? And would you mind telling me who you are, as I have told you?"

"You never told me; I guessed. Guess who I am."

Seymour looked at her attentively. She was a woman of about fifty with a shrewd face, like a handsome monkey, and his millinerish eyes saw that she was dressed without the slightest regard to expense.

"I haven't the slightest idea," he said. "But please don't tell me, if you have any private reason for not wishing it to be known. I can readily understand you would not like people to be able to say that you were seen dining with Mamma. Of course you are not English."

"Why do you think that?"

"Because you talk it so well. English people always talk it abominably. But——"

He looked at her again, and a vague resemblance both in speech and in the shape of her head struck him.

"I will guess," he said, "you are a relation of Nadine's."

"Quite right; go on."

Seymour was suddenly agitated, and upset a glass of champagne that had just been filled. He took not the slightest notice of this.

"Is it too much to hope that you are the aunt who—who had so many snuff-boxes," he asked. "I mean the one to whom the Emperor gave all those lovely snuff-boxes? Or is it too good to be true?"

"Just good enough," she said.

"How wildly exciting! Will you come back to my flat as soon as we can escape from this purgatory, and Antoinette shall manicure you. Do tell me about the snuff-boxes; I am sure they were beauties, or you would not—I mean the Emperor would not have given you them."

"Of course not. But I am afraid I can't come to your flat to-night, as I am going to a dance. Ask me another day. I hear you have got some lovely jade, and are going to make it the fashion. Then I suppose you will sell it."

Seymour determined to insure his jade before Countess Eleanor entered his rooms, for fear of its subsequently appearing that the Austrian Emperor had followed up his present of snuff-boxes with a present of jade. But he let no suspicion mar the cordiality of his tone.

"Yes, that's the idea," he said. "You see no younger son can possibly live in the way he has been brought up unless he does something honest and commercial like that, or cheats at Bridge. But that is so difficult, I am told. You have to learn Bridge first, and then go to a conjuror, during which time you probably forget Bridge again. But otherwise you can't live at all unless you marry, and the only thing left to do is to take to drink and die."

"My brother took to it and lives," said she.

"I know, but you are a very remarkable family."

A footman had wiped up the greater part of the champagne that Seymour had spilt and now stood waiting till he could speak to him.

"Her ladyship told me to tell you that you seemed to have had enough champagne, my lord," he said.

Seymour paused a moment, and his face turned white with indignation.

"Tell her ladyship she is quite right," he said, "and that the first sip I took of it was more than enough."

"Very good, my lord."

"And tell her that the fish was stale," said Seymour shrilly.

"Yes, my lord."

"And tell her——" began Seymour again.

Countess Eleanor interrupted him.

"You have sent enough pleasant messages for one time," she said. "You can talk to your mother afterwards; at present talk to me. Did you go to the wedding this morning?"

"Yes."

Seymour rather frequently allowed himself to be ruffled, but he always calmed down again quickly.

"It is so like Mamma to send a servant in the middle of dinner to say I am drunk," he said, "but she will be sorry now. Look, she is receiving my message, and is turning purple. That is satisfactory. She looks unusually plain when she is purple. Yes; I am describing the wedding for a lady's paper. I shall get four guineas for it."

"You do not look as if that would do you much good."

"If you take four guineas often enough they—they purify the blood," said he, "though certainly the dose is homœopathic. It is called the gold cure. About the wedding. I thought it was very vulgar. And it was frightfully *bourgeois* in spirit. It is very early Victorian to marry a man who has waited for you since about 1820."

"But they will be very happy."

"So are the *bourgeoisie* who change hats. At least, I should have to be frightfully happy to think of putting on anybody else's hat. I recommend you not to eat that savoury unless you have a bad cold that prevents your tasting anything. Shall I send another message to Mamma about it?"

"Ah, my dear young man," said Countess Eleanor, "we are all common when we fall in love. You will find yourself being common too, some day. And the people who are least *bourgeois* become the most common of all. Nadine for instance; there is no one less *bourgeois* than Nadine, but if she ever falls in love she will be so common that she will be perfectly sublime. She will be the embodiment of humanity. But she is not in love with the great boy next her, who is so clearly in love with her. Dear me, what beautiful Sèvres dessert plates. I once collected Sèvres as well as snuff-boxes."

"Did you—did you get together a fine collection?" asked Seymour.

"Pretty well. It is easier to get snuff-boxes. My brother has some that used to be mine. Ah, they are all getting up. Let me come to see your jade some other day."

Nadine and Esther escaped very soon after dinner from this dreadful party, and went to Seymour's flat, where he had preceded them, and was busy cooking with Antoinette in the kitchen when they arrived. He opened the door for them himself with his shirt sleeves rolled up above his elbows, shewing an extremely white and delicate skin. Round one wrist he wore a gold bangle.

"I've left the kitchen door open," he said, "so that the whole flat shall smell as strong as possible of cooking. There is nothing so delicious when you are hungry. We will open the windows afterwards. You and Esther must amuse yourselves for ten minutes, and then supper will be ready."

"Oh, may I come and cook too, Seymour?" asked Nadine.

"Certainly not. Antoinette is the only woman in the world who knows how to cook. You would make everything messy. Go and rock the cradle or rule the world, or whatever you consider to be a woman's sphere, until we are ready."

Seymour disappeared again into the kitchen from which came rich cracklings and odours of frying, and Nadine turned to Esther with a sigh.

"My dear, I have got remorse and world yearnings to-night," she said. "I attribute it to your mother's awful party. But I daresay we shall all be better soon. You know, if I had asked Hugh to let me come and cook, he would have given me a golden spoon to stir with, and eaten till he burst because I cooked it. And I don't care! He was so dear and so utterly impossible this evening. I told him I wasn't going to the dance at the Embassy, and he said he should go in case I changed my mind. And if it had been Hugh cooking in there, I should have gone and cooked too, even if he hadn't wanted me to. It's no use, Esther; I can't marry Hugh. There's the end of it. Up till to-night I have always wondered if I could. Now I know I can't. I think I shan't see so much of him. I shall miss him—don't think I shan't miss him—but I want to be fair to him. As it is now, whenever I am nice to him, which I always am, he thinks it means that I am beginning to love him. Whereas it doesn't mean anything whatever. I wish people hadn't got into the habit of marrying each other, but bought their babies at a shop instead. And kissing is so disgusting. The only person I ever like kissing is Mamma, because her skin is so delicious and smells very faintly of raspberries. Hugh smells of cigarettes and soap——"

"Darling Nadine, you haven't been kissing Hugh, have you?" asked Esther.

"Yes, I kissed him this evening, when he was putting my cloak on, but there were ninety-five footmen there so it wasn't compromising; we were heavily chaperoned. And I would just as soon have kissed any of the other ninety-five. But he wanted me to, and so I did, and then suddenly I saw how unfair it was of me. It didn't mean anything: I kissed him just as I kiss my dog, because he is such a duck. Also because he wanted me to, which Tobias never does: he always cleans his face on the rug after I have kissed him, and sneezes."

"Did he ask you to?" said Esther. "Not Toby, Hugh."

"No; but I can see by a man's face when he wants. I saw one of the footmen wanted, too, and perhaps I ought to have kissed him as well, to show Hugh it did not mean anything."

Nadine sat down and spread her hands wide with a surprisingly dramatic gesture of innocence and despair.

"It isn't my fault," she said. "I am I. *Son io. Je suis moi. Ich bin Ich.* I would translate it into all the languages of the world, like the Bible, if that would make Hugh understand. People can't be different from what they are. It's a grand mistake to suppose otherwise. They can act and talk in accordance with what they are, or they can act and talk otherwise, but they, the personalities, are unchangeable except by miracles. I could act contrary to my own self and marry Hugh, but it would be no particle of good. I want him to understand that I can't love him, and I am too fond of him to marry him without. I wish to heaven he would marry somebody else."

"He won't do that," said Esther.

"I am afraid not. I think it is rather selfish. It is putting it all on me. I shall have to marry somebody else, I suppose, and that will be very unselfish of me, because I don't want to marry. Of course, one has to; I don't want to grow old, but I shall have to grow old. They are both laws of nature, and perhaps neither the one nor the other is so disagreeable really."

Esther gave her long appreciative sigh.

"It would be too wonderful of you to marry somebody else in order to make it clear to Hugh that you couldn't marry him," she said. "It would be the most illustrious thing to do, and would show that you are devoted to Hugh. But do you really think that people don't change, Nadine?"

"Not unless a moral earthquake happens, and earthquakes are not to be expected. Only an upheaval of that kind makes any difference in the essential things. Their tastes change, as their noses and hair change, but the thing that sits behind, like some beastly idol in a temple, never moves, and looks on at all that changes round it with the same wooden eyes. Oh, dear, I am so tired of myself, and I can't get out of sight of myself."

Nadine looked at herself in a Louis Seize mirror that hung above the fireplace, and pointed a contemplative finger at the reflection of her pale loveliness.

"I wish I was anything in the world except that thing," she said. "I am genuine when I say that; but, having said that, there is nothing else about me but what is intolerable. But I am aware that I don't really care about anybody in the world. The only thing that can be said for me is that I detest myself. I wish I was like you, Esther, because you care for me; I wish I was like Aunt Eleanor, because she cares for stealing. I wish I was like Daddy because he cares for old brandy. You are all better off than I. I envy anybody and everybody who cares for anybody with her heart. No doubt having a heart is often a very great nuisance, and often leads you to make a dreadful fool of yourself; but it gets tedious to be wise and cool all the time, like me."

Seymour entered at this moment carrying a little silver censer with incense in it.

"The smell of food is sufficiently strong," he said, "and supper is ready. Also, the smell of incense reminds me of stepping out of the blazing sunlight into St. Mark's at Venice. Nadine, you look too exquisite, but depressed. Has not the effect of Mamma worn off yet?"

"Oh, it's not your mother, it's me," said she.

"You think about yourself too much," observed Seymour. "I know the temptation so well, and generally yield to it. It is a great mistake; one occasionally has doubts whether one is the nicest person in the world, and whether it is worth while doing anything, even collecting jade. But such doubts never last long with me."

"Don't you ever wish you had a heart, Seymour?" she asked. "You and I have neither of us got hearts."

"I know, and I am so exceedingly comfortable without one, that I should be sorry to get one. If you have a heart, sooner or later you get into a state of drivel about somebody, who probably doesn't drivel about you. That must be so mortifying. Even if two people drivel mutually they are deplorable objects, but a solitary driveller is like a lonely cat on the tiles, and is a positive nuisance. Poor Hugh! Nadine, you suit my wall-paper quite exquisitely. Also it suits you. Don't let any of us go to bed to-night, but see the morning come. The early morning is the colour of a wood pigeon's breast, and looks frightfully tired, as if it had sat up all night too. Most people look perfectly hideous at that moment, but I really don't believe you would. Do sit up and let me see."

"I look the colour of an oyster at dawn," said Esther, "it is just as if I had gone bad."

Her brother looked at her thoughtfully.

"Yes, my dear, I can imagine your looking quite ghastly," he said. "You had better go away before dawn. It might make me seriously unwell."

"I shall. I shall go to the dance at the Embassy, I think. Madame Tavita is so hideous that she makes me feel good-looking for a week."

"You always behave as if you were pretty, which matters far more than being pretty," said Seymour. "It matters very little what people look like if they only behave as if they were Venuses, just as it does not matter how tall you are if you consistently look at a point rather above the head of the person you are talking to."

Nadine was recovering a little under the influence of food.

"That is quite true," she said. "And if you want to look really rich you must be shabby or not wash your face. Seymour, let us try to write a little book together, 'Fifty ways of appearing enviable.' You should eat a great deal in order to make it appear you have a good digestion, although you may be quite sick afterwards, and refuse a great many invitations to show what a wild social success you are, even though you dine all by yourself at home. My dear, what delicious food; did you cook it, or Antoinette?"

"Both. We each threw in what we thought would be good and stirred it together. I am sorry for people who are not greedy. I am told that when you are old food and saving money are the only pursuits that don't pall. At present food and spending money are particularly attractive, and a piquancy is added if you haven't got any money. And now we all feel better."

Seymour had a piece of needlework, which he often produced when he was staying with friends, in order to irritate them. He seldom worked at it when at home, but to-night he got it out in order to irritate his sister into going to the ball without delay, for Esther was always exasperated to a point almost beyond her control by the sight of her brother with his thimble and needle. So before long she took her departure,

leaving Nadine to follow (which was Seymour's design), and he put
the needlework back into its embroidered bag again.

"I am afraid my methods are a little obvious," he said, "but poor
Esther sees nothing but the most obvious hints. You have to say things
very loud and clear to her, like the man in 'Alice in Wonderland.' "

"Who was that?" asked Nadine absently. "And what did you want
Esther to do?"

"To go away, of course. I wanted to talk to you, Nadine. I have
never known you look so beautiful as to-night. You look troubled
too. Troubles make people feel plain but look beautiful."

Nadine shifted her position so that she faced him.

"Yes, do talk to me," she said. "See if you can distract me a little
from myself. My mind hurts me, Seymour. I wish I had a hard bright
mind, as some people have. Their minds are like ... I don't know
what they are like; I can't trouble to think to-night. How stupid are
all the jinkings and monkey-tricks we go through. I have worn an
inane smile all day, and when I tried to read my 'Plato,' it merely
bored me. Nothing seems worth while. And don't be commonplace,
and say that it is liver. It is nothing of the sort. Would you be surprised
if I burst into tears?"

"You have been thinking of the old 'un," remarked Seymour.

"Whom do you mean?"

"Hugh, of course. Do you know you are rather like a boy watching
the struggle of a butterfly he has impaled. You are sorry for it, but
you don't let it go."

"He impaled himself," said Nadine.

"Well, you gave him the pin. But, as you don't mean to marry
him, make that quite clear to him."

"But how?"

"Marry me," said Seymour.

6

Edith Arbuthnot had conceived the idea, an unhappy one
as regards her family and neighbours, that everyone who aspired to
the name of Musician (it is not too much to assert that her aspirations
tended that way) should be able to play every instrument in the band.
Just now she was learning the French horn and double-bass simultaneously. She kept her mind undistracted by the hideous noises she produced, and expected others to do so. Thus, unless she was practising
some instrument that required the exclusive use of the mouth, she
would talk (and did so) while she learned.

Just now she was seated on the terrace wall at Winston, which was of a convenient height for playing the double-bass, which rested on the terrace below, and conversing at the top of her voice to Dodo, who sat a yard or two away. These stentorian tones of course were necessary in order that she should be heard above the vibrating roar of the ill-played strings. She could not at present get much tone out of them; but for volume, it was as if all the bumble-bees in the world were swarming in all the threshing-machines in the world, which were threshing everything else in the world.

"I used to think you were heartless, Dodo," she shouted, "but compared to Nadine you are a sickly sentimentalist."

When Dodo did not feel equal to shouting back she spoke in dumb show. Now she concisely indicated "Rot" on her fingers.

"It isn't rot," shouted Edith. "Ah, what a wonderful thing a double-bass is; I shall write a Suite for the double-bass unaccompanied—I really mean it. If it is true that you are without a heart, Nadine would seem to have an organ which is all that a heart is not very highly developed. Probably she inherited a tendency from you, and has developed and cultivated it. What do you say?"

"I said, 'do stop that appalling noise, darling,'" screamed Dodo. "I shall burst a blood-vessel if I try to talk against it."

"Very well; I must just play just two or three scales," said Edith.

The hoarse clamour grew more and more vibrant and Dodo stopped her ears. Eventually the bow, as Edith brought it down on to the first note of a new scale, flew from her hands and, describing a parabola in the air, fell into a clump of sweet-peas in the flowerbed below the terrace.

"I must learn not to do that," she said. "It happened yesterday, and I shan't consider myself proficient until I am safe not to hit the conductor in the face. About Nadine. She is going to perpetrate the most horrible cruelty, marrying that dreadful young man, while Hugh is just dying for her. Hugh reminds me of what Jack was like, Dodo."

"Oh, do you think so?" said Dodo. "Except that Jack was once twenty-five, which is what Hugh is now, I don't see the smallest resemblance. Jack was so good-looking, and Hugh only looks good, and though Hugh is a darling, he is just a little slow and heavy, which Jack never was. You will be able to compare them, by the way, because Hugh is coming here this afternoon. I asked him not to, but he is coming just the same. I told him Nadine and Seymour were both here."

"Perhaps he means to kill Seymour," said Edith thoughtfully. "It certainly would be the obvious thing to do——"

"Hughie would always do the obvious thing," said Dodo.

"I will now finish my sentence," said Edith. "It certainly would be the obvious thing to do, provided that the public executioner would not hang him, and that Nadine would marry him. But things would probably go the other way about, which would not be so satisfactory for Hugh. Really the young generation is very bloodless; it talks more than we did, but it does absolutely nothing."

"We used to talk a good deal," remarked Dodo, "and we are not silent yet. At least you and I are not. Edith, has it ever struck you that you and I are middle-aged? Or is middle-age, do you think, not a matter of years but of inclination? I think it must be, for it is simply foolish to say that I am forty-five, though it would be simply untrue to say that I was anything else. That is by the way; we will talk of ourselves soon. Where had I got to? Oh yes, Hugh is coming down this afternoon though I implored him not to. Nadine says I was wrong. She wants me to be very nice to him, as she has been so horrid. They have not seen each other for a whole week, ever since her engagement was announced. I am sure Nadine misses him; she will be miserable if Hugh deserts her."

Edith plucked impatiently at the strings of the double-bass and aroused the bumble-bees again.

"That's what I mean by bloodless," she said. "They are all suffering from anaemia together. Their blood has turned to a not very high quality of grey matter in the brain. Nadine wants you to be kind to Hugh, because she has been so horrid! Dodo, don't you see how fish-like that is? And he, since he can't marry her, takes the post of *valet-de-chambre,* and looks on while Seymour gives her little butterfly kisses and small fragments of jade. I saw him kiss her yesterday, Dodo. It made me feel quite faint and weak, and I had to hurry into the dining-room and take half a glass of port. It was the most debilitated thing I ever saw. Berts is nearly as bad, and though he is nine feet high and plays cricket for his county, he is somehow lady-like. I can't think where he got it from; certainly not from me. And as for Hugh, I suppose he calls it faithfulness to hang about after Nadine, but I call it anaemia. I am surprised at Hugh; I should have thought he was sufficiently stupid to have more blood in him. He ought to box Nadine's ears, kick Seymour and instantly marry somebody else, and have dozens of great red-faced, white-toothed children. Bah!"

Dodo had subsided into hopeless giggles over this remarkable tirade against the anaemic generation, and Edith plucked at her double-bass again as she concluded with this exclamation of scorn.

"And I can't think how you allow Nadine to marry that—that jade," said Edith.

Dodo became momentarily serious.

"If you were Nadine's mother," she said, "you would be delighted at her marrying anybody. She is the sort of girl who doesn't want to marry, and afterwards wishes she had. I am not like that; I was continually marrying somebody and then wishing I hadn't. But Nadine doesn't make mistakes. She may do things that appear very odd, but they are not mistakes; she has thought things out very carefully first. You see quite a quantity of eligible youths and several remarkably ineligible ones have wanted to marry her, and she has never felt any—dear me, what is it a man with a small income always feels when a post with a large income is offered him—oh yes, a call; Nadine has never felt any call to marry any of them. There are many girls like that to whom the physical makes very little appeal. But what does appeal to Nadine very strongly is the mental, and Seymour however many times you call him a jade, is as clever as he can be. In him also, I should say, the physical side is extremely undeveloped, and so I think that he and Nadine may be very happy. Now Hugh is not clever at all; he has practically no intellect and that to Nadine is an insuperable defect. Now don't call her prig or blue stocking. She is neither the one nor the other. But she has a mind. So have you. So for that matter have I, and it has led me to do weird things."

Edith thrummed her double-bass again.

"Dodo, I can't tell you how I disapprove of you," she said, "and how I love you. You are almost entirely selfish, and yet you have charm. Most utterly selfish people lose their charm when they are about thirty. I made sure you would. But I was quite wrong. Now I am utterly unselfish: I live entirely for my husband and my art. I live for him by seldom going near him since he is much happier alone. But then I never had any charm at all. Now you have always lived, and do still, completely for your own pleasure——"

Dodo clapped her hands violently in Edith's face for it required drastic measures to succeed in interrupting her.

"Ah, that is an astonishingly foolish thing for you to say," she said. "If I lived for my pleasure, do you know what I should do? I should have a hot bath, go to bed and have dinner there. I should then go to sleep, and when I woke up I should go for a ride, have another hot bath and another dinner, and go to sleep again. There is nothing so pleasant as riding and hot baths and food and sleep. But I never have sought my pleasure. What I always have sought is my happiness. And that on the whole is our highest duty. Don't swear. There is nothing selfish about it, if you are made like me. Because the thing that above all others makes me happy is to contrive that other people should have their own way. That is why I never dream of interfering in what other people want. If they really want it, I do all I can to get it for them. I was not ever thus, as the hymn says, but I am so now. The longer I live the more clearly I see that it is impossible to understand why other people want what they want, but it seems to me that all that concerns me is that they do want. I can see how they want, but never why. I can't think, darling, for instance, why you want to make those excruciating noises, but I see how. Here's Jack: Jack, come and tell us about Utopia."

Edith had laid her double-bass down on the ground of the terrace.

"Yes, but I want to sit down," he said. "May I sit on it, Edith?"

Edith screamed. He took this as a sign that he might not, and sat on the terrace wall.

"Utopia?" he asked. "You've got to be a man to begin with and then you have to marry Dodo. It does the rest."

"What is It?"

"That which does it, your consciousness. Dodo, it would send up rents in Utopia if Seymour went to a nice girls' school. He is rather silly, and wants the nonsense knocked out of him."

"But there you make a mistake," said she. "Almost every one who is nice is nice because the nonsense has not been knocked out of him. People without heaps of nonsense are merely prigs. Indeed that is the best definition of a prig; one who has lost his capability for nonsense. Look at Edith! She doesn't know she's nonsensical, but she is. And she thinks she is serious all the time with her great boots and her great double-bass and her French horns. Oh me, oh me! The reasonable people in the world are the ruin of it; they spoil the sunshine. Look at the abominable Liberal party with terrible reasonable schemes for scullery-maids. They are all quite excellent, and it is for that reason they are so hopeless. It is, moreover, a great liberty to take with people to go about ameliorating them. I should be furious if anybody wanted to ameliorate me. Darling Bishop Algy, the other day, said he always prayed for my highest good. I begged him not to, because if his prayers were answered, Providence might think I should be better for a touch of typhoid. You can't tell what strange roundabout ways Providence may have. So he promised to stop praying for me, because he is so understanding, and knew what I meant. But when Lloyd George wants to give scullery-maids a happy old age with a canary in the window it is even worse. It is so sensible; I can see them sitting dismally in the room listening to their canary, when they would be much more comfortable in a nice workhouse, with Edith and me bringing them packets of tea and flannel. Don't let us talk politics; there is nothing that saps the intellect so much."

"Edith and I have not talked much yet," observed Jack.

"No, you are listening to Utopia, which as I said, consists largely of nonsense. If you are to be happy, you must play, you must be ridiculous, you must want everybody else to be ridiculous. But everybody must take his own absurdities quite seriously."

Dodo sat up, pulled Jack's cigarette case from his pocket and helped herself.

"The Greeks and Romans were so right," she said, "they had a slave class, though with them it was an involuntary slave-class. We ought to have a voluntary slave-class, consisting of all the people who like working for a cause. There are heaps of politicians who naturally belong to it, and clergymen and lawyers and financiers, all the people in fact who die when they retire, being devitalized when they have not got offices and churches to go to. You can recognise a slave the moment you see him. He always, socially, wants to open the door or shut the window, or pick up your gloves. The moment you see that look in a man's eye, that sort of itch to be useful, you should be able to give secret information and make him a slave at £200 a year, instead of making him a Cabinet Minister or a bishop or a director of a company. He wants work; let him have it. Edith, darling, you would be a slave instantly, and the State would provide you with double-basses and cornets. I haven't thought it all completely out, since it only occurred to me this minute, but it seems to me an almost painfully sound scheme now that I mention it. Think of the financiers you would get! There would be poor Mr. Carnegie and Rockefeller and the whole of the Rothschild house, and Barings and Speyers all quite happy because they are happy when they work. And all the millions they make—how they make it, I don't know, unless they buy gold cheap and sell it dear, which I believe is really what they do—all the millions they make would be at the disposal of those who know how to spend it. I suppose I am a Socialist."

Edith put her forehead in her hands.

"I don't know what you are talking about," she said.

"I have my doubts myself," said Dodo ingenuously. "It began about Nadine's marriage and then drifted. You get to all sorts of strange places if you drift, both morally and physically. It really seems very unfair, that if you don't ever resist anything you go to the bad. It looks as if evil was stronger than good, but Algy shall explain it to me. He can explain almost anything, including wasps. Jack, dear, do make me stop talking; you and the sunshine and Edith have gone to my head, and given me the babbles."

"I insist on your going on talking," said Edith. "I want to know how you can let Nadine marry without love."

"Because a great many of our unfortunate sex, dear, never fall in love, as I mean it, at all. But I would not have them not marry. They often make excellent wives and mothers. And I think Nadine is one of those. She is as nearly in love with Hugh as she has ever been with anybody, but she quite certainly will not marry him. Here she is; I daresay she will explain it all herself. My darling, come and talk matrimony shop to Edith; Jack and I are going for a short ride before lunch. Will you be in when Hugh comes?"

Nadine sat down in the chair from which Dodo had risen. She was dressed in a very simple linen dress of cornflower blue, that made the whites and pinks of her face look absolutely dazzling.

"Yes, I will wait for him," she said. "Seymour thought it would be kinder if he went to meet him at the station, so that Hughie could get rid of some of the hate on the way up. He has perception—*des apercus trés-fins.* And I will explain anything to anybody in the interval. I want to be married, and so does Seymour, and we think it will answer admirably if we marry each other. There is very little else to say. We are not foolish about each other——"

"I find you are extremely modern," interrupted Edith.

"You speak as if you did not like that," said Nadine, "but surely somebody has got to be modern if we are going to get on at all. Otherwise the world remains stock still, or goes back. I do not think it would be amusing to be Victorian again; indeed there would be no use in us trying. We should be such obvious forgeries, Seymour particularly. I consider it lucky that he was not born earlier; if he had grown up as he is in Victorian days, they would certainly have done away with him somehow. Or his mother would have exposed him in Battersea Park like Oedipus."

Edith leaned over the terrace wall, and took the double-bass bow out of the tall clump of sweet peas.

"There are exactly two things in the world worth doing," she said, "to love and to work. Certainly you don't work, Nadine, and I don't believe you love."

Nadine looked at her a moment in silence and hostility.

"That is a very comfortable reflection," she observed, "for you who like working better than anything else in the world except perhaps golf. I wonder you did not say there were three things in the world worth doing, making that damned game the third."

Edith had spoken with her usual cock-sure breezy enthusiasm, and looked up surprised at a certain venom and bitterness that underlay the girl's reply.

"My dear Nadine," she said. "What is the matter?"

Nadine glared at her a moment, and then broke into rapid speech.

"Do you think I would not give the world to be able to love?" she said. "Do you think I send Hugh marching through hell for fun? You say I am heartless, as if it was my fault! Would you go to a

blind man in the street and say 'You beast, you brute, why don't
you see?' Is he blind for fun? Am I like this for fun?"

She got up from her seat and came and stood in front of Edith,
flushed with an unusual colour, and continued more rapidly yet, em-
phasizing her points by admirable gesticulations of her hands. Indeed
they seemed to have speech on their own account; they were extraordinarily eloquent.

"Do you know you make me lose my temper?" she said. "That is
a rare thing with me; I seldom lose it, but when I do it is quite gone,
and I don't care what I say, so long as it is what I mean. For the
minute my temper is absolutely vanished, and I shall make the most
of its absence. Who are you to judge and condemn me? and give me
rules for conduct, how work and love are the only things worth doing?
What do you know about me? Either you are absolutely ignorant about
me, or so stupid that the very cabbages would seem clever by you.
And you go telling me what to do! And what do you know about
love? To look at you, as little as you know about me. Yes; no wonder
you sit there with your mouth open staring at me, you and your foolish
great fat-bellied bloated violin. You are not accustomed to be spoken
to like this. It never occurred to you that I would give the world to
be able to love as Jill and Polly and Mary and Minnie love. I do not
go about saying that any more than a cripple calls attention to his
defect: he tries to be brave and conceal it. But that is me, a dwarf, a
hunch-back, a *cretin* of the soul. That is the matter with me, and you
are so foolish that it never occurred to you that I wanted to be like
other people. You thought it was a pose of which I was proud, I think.
There! Now do not do that again."

Nadine paused, and then sighed.

"I feel better," she said, "but quite red in the face. However, I have
got my temper back again. If you like I will apologise for losing it."

Edith jumped up and kissed Nadine. When she intended to kiss
anybody she did it, whether the victim liked it or not.

"My dear, you are quite delightful," she said. "I thoroughly deserve
every word. I was utterly ignorant of you. But I am not stupid; if
you will go on, you will find I shall understand."

Suddenly Nadine felt utterly lonely. All she had said of herself in
her sudden exasperation was perfectly genuine, and now, when her
equanimity returned, she felt as if she must tell somebody about this
isolation, which for the moment, in any case, was sincerely and deeply
hers. That she was a girl of a hundred moods was quite true, but it
was equally true that each mood was authentically inspired from
within. Many of them, no doubt, were far from edifying, but none

could be found guilty of the threadbare tawdriness of pose. She nodded at Edith.

"It is as I say," she said. "I hate myself; but here I am, and here soon will Hugh be. It is a disease this heartlessness: I suffer from it. It is rather common too, but commoner among girls than boys."

Then, queerly and unexpectedly, but still honestly, her intellectual interest in herself, that cold egoism that was characteristic of another side of her, awoke.

"Yet it is interesting," she said, "because it is out of this sort of derangement that types and species come. For a million years the fish we call the sole had a headache, because one of its eyes was slowly travelling through its head. For a million years man was uncomfortable where the tail once came, because it was drying up. For a million years there will be girls like me, poor wretches, and at the end there will be another type of woman, a third sex, perhaps, who from not caring about those things which Nature evidently meant her to care about will have become different. And all the boys like Seymour will be approximating to the same type from the other side, so that eventually we shall be like the angels——"

"My dear, why angels?" asked Edith.

"Neither marrying nor giving in marriage. La, la! And I was saying only the other day to him that I wished to marry half a dozen men! What a good thing that one does not feel the same every day. It would be atrociously dull. But in the interval, it is lonely now and then for those of us who are not exactly and precisely of the normal type of girl. But if you have no heart, you have to follow your intelligence, to go where your intelligence leads you, and then wave a flag. Perhaps nobody sees it, or only the wrong sort of person, who says, 'What is that idiot-girl waving that rag for?' But she only waves it because she is lost, and hopes that somebody will see it."

Nadine laughed with her habitual gurgle.

"We are all lost," she said. "But we want to be found. It is only the stupidest who do not know they are lost. Well, I have—what is Hugh's word, ah yes—I have gassed enough for one morning. Ah, and there is the motor coming back from the station. I am glad that Hugh has not thrown Seymour out, and driven forwards and backwards over him."

The motor at this moment was passing not more than a couple of hundred yards off through the park which lay at the foot of the steep garden terraces below them. From there the road wound round in a long loop towards the house.

"I shall go to meet Hugh at once, and get it over," said Nadine;

and thereupon she whistled so shrilly and surprisingly on her fingers, that Hugh, who was driving, looked up and saw her over the terrace. She made staccato wavings to him, and he got out.

"You whistled the octave of B in alt," remarked Edith appreciatively.

"And my courage is somewhere about the octave of B in profundis," said Nadine. "I dread what Hugh may say to me."

"I will go and talk to him," said Edith. "I understand you now, Nadine. I will tell him."

Nadine smiled very faintly.

"That is sweet of you," she said, "but I am afraid it wouldn't be quite the same thing."

Nadine walked down the steep flight of steps in the middle of the terrace, and out through the Venetian gate into the park. Hugh had just arrived at it from the other side, and they met there. No word of greeting passed between them; they but stood looking at each other. He saw the girl he loved, neither more nor less than that, and did not know if she looked well or ill, or if her gown was blue or pink or rainbowed. To him it was Nadine who stood there. But she saw details, not being blinded: he was big and square, he looked a picture of health, brown-eyed, clear of skin, large-mouthed, with habit of smiling written strongly there. He had taken off his hat, as was usual with him, and as usual his hair looked a little disordered, as if he had been out on a windy morning. There was that slight thrusting outwards of his chin which suggested that he would meet argument with obstinacy, but that friendly and level look from his eyes that suggested an honesty and kindliness hardly met with outside the charming group of living beings known as dogs. He was like a big kind dog, polite to strangers, kind to friends, hopelessly devoted to the owner of his soul. But to-day his mouth did not indulge its habit: he was quite grave.

"Why did you kiss me the other night?" he said.

Nadine had already repented of that rash act. Being conscious of her own repentance, it seemed to her rather nagging of him to allude to it.

"I meant nothing," she said. "Hughie, are we going to stand like posts here? Shan't we stroll——"

"I don't see why: let us stand like posts. You did kiss me. Or do you kiss everybody?"

Nadine considered this for a moment.

"No, I don't kiss everybody," she said. "I never kissed a man before. It was stupid of me. The moment after I had done it I wanted to kiss some footmen to show you it didn't mean anything. You are like the Inquisition. My next answer is that I have kissed Seymour since. I—I don't particularly like kissing him. But it is usual."

"And you are going to marry him?"

Nadine's courage, which she had confessed was a B in profundis, sank into profundissima.

"Yes; I am going to marry him," she said.

"Why? You don't love him. And he doesn't love you."

"I don't love anybody," said Nadine quickly. "I have said that so often that I am tired of saying it. Girls often marry without being in love. It just happens. What do you want? Would you like me to go on spinstering just because I won't marry you? That I will not do. You know why. You love me, and I can't marry you unless I love you. Ah, *mon Dieu*, it sounds like Ollendorf. But I should be cheating you if I married you, and I will not cheat you. You would expect from me what you bring to me, and it would be right that I should bring it you, and I cannot. If you didn't love me like that, I would marry you to-morrow, and the trousseau might go and hang itself. Mamma would give me some blouses and stockings, and you would buy me a tooth-brush. Yes, this is very flippant, but when serious people are goaded they become flippant. Oh, Hughie, I wish I was different. But I am not different. And what is it you came down here about? Is it to ask me again to marry you, and to ask me not to marry my dear little Seymour?"

"Little?" he asked.

"It was a term of endearment. Besides, it is not his fault that he does not weigh fourteen stones——"

"Stone," said he, with the tremor of a smile.

"No, stones," said Nadine. "I choose that it should be stones: fourteen great square lumps. Hughie, don't catch my words up and correct me. I am serious and all you can answer is 'stone' instead of 'stones.' "

"I did it without thinking," he said. "I only fell back into the sort of speech there used to be between us. It was like that, serious one moment and silly the next. I spoke without thinking, as we used to speak. I won't do it again."

"And why not?" demanded Nadine.

"Because now that you tell me you really are going to marry Seymour, everything is changed between us. This is what I came to tell you. I am not going to hang about, a mixture between a valet and an *ami de la maison*. You have chosen now. When you refused me before, there was always in my mind the hope that some day you would give me a different answer. I waited long and patiently and willingly for that chance. Now the chance no longer exists. You have scratched me——"

Nadine drew her eyebrows together.

"Scratched you?" she said. "Oh, I see, a race; not nails."

"And I am definitely and finally out of it."

"You mean you are no longer among my friends?" asked Nadine.

"I shall not be with you so much or so intimately. We must talk over it just this once. We will stroll if you like. It is too hot for you standing in the sun without a hat."

"No, we will settle it here and now," said she quickly. "You don't understand. My marriage with Seymour will make no difference in the quality of affection I have always had for you. Why should I give up my best friend? Why should you?"

"Because you are much more than my best friend, and I am obliged to give up, at last, that idea of you. You have forced me to see that it is not to be realised. And I won't sit about your house, to have people pointing at me, and saying to each other, 'That's the one who is so frightfully in love with her.' It may sound priggish, but I don't choose to be quite so unmanly as that. Nor would you much respect me if I did so choose."

"But I never did respect you," said Nadine quickly. "I never thought of you as respectable or otherwise. It doesn't come in. You may steal and cheat at cards, and I shall not care. I like whom I like: I like you tremendously. What do you mean you are going to do? Go to Burmah or Bengal? I don't want to lose you, Hughie. It is unkind of you. Besides we shall not marry for a long time yet, and even then—Ah, it is the old tale, the old horror called 'Me' all over again—I don't love anybody. Many are delightful, and I am so fond of them. But the other, the absorption, the gorgeous foolishness of it all, it is away outside of me, a fairy-tale, and I am grown up now and say, 'For me it is not true.'"

Hugh came a step nearer her.

"You poor devil," he said gently.

Tears, as yet unshed, gathered in Nadine's eyes. They were fairly creditable tears: they were not, at any rate, like the weepings of the great prig-prince and compounded merely of "languor and self-pity," but sorrow for Hugh was one ingredient in them. Yet, in the main, they were for herself, since the only solvent for egoism is love.

"Yes, I am that," she said. "I'm a poor devil. I'm lost, as I said to that foolish Arbuthnot woman with her feet and great violin. Hark, she is playing it again: she is a big C major. She has been scolding me, though, if it comes to that, I gave it her back with far more *gamin* in my tongue. And now you say you will not be friends any longer, and Mamma does not like my marrying Seymour, though she does not argue, and there is no one left but myself, and I hate myself.

Oh, I am lost, and I wave my flags, and there is no one who sees or understands. I shall go back to Daddy, I think, and he and I will drink ourselves drunk, and I shall have the red nose. But you are the worst of them all, Hugh! It is a very strange sort of love you have for me, if all it can do is to desert me. And yet the other day I felt as you feel; I felt it would only be fair to you to see you less. I am a damned weather-cock. I go this way and that, but the wind is always cold. I am sorry for you, I want you to be happy, I would make you happy myself, if I could."

Nadine's eyes had quite overflowed, and as she poured out this remarkable series of lamentations, she dabbed at her moistened cheeks. Yet Hugh, though he was so largely to blame, as it seemed, for this emotion, and though all the most natural instincts in him longed to yield, knew that deep in him his determination was absolutely un-softened. It, and his love for Nadine were of the quality of nether millstones. But all the rest of him longed to comfort her.

"Oh, Nadine, don't cry," he said. "I'm not worth crying about to begin with."

"It is not you alone I cry about," said Nadine, with justice. "I cry a little for you, every third drop is for you. The rest is quite for myself."

"It is never worth while to cry for one's self," he said.

"Who wants it to be worth while? I feel like crying, therefore I cry. Hardly anything I do is worth while, yet I go on doing, and I get tired of it before it is done. Already I am tired of crying, and besides, it gives me the red nose without going to Daddy. Not you and I together are worth making myself ugly for. But you are so disagreeable, Hughie; first I wanted to stroll, and you said 'no,' and then when I didn't want to stroll you said 'yes,' and you aren't going to be friends with me, and I feel exactly as I used to feel when I was six years old, and it rained. Come, let us sit down a little, and you shall tell me what you mean to do, and how it will be between us. I will be very good; I will bless any plan you make like a bishop. It shall all be as you will. I owe you so much, and there is no way by which I can ever pay you. I don't want to be a curse to you, Hughie; I don't, indeed."

She sat down, leaning against a great beech trunk, and he lay on the coarse meadow grass beside her.

"I know you don't," he said.

He looked at her steadily, as she finished mopping her cheeks. Her little burst of tears had not made her nose at all red; it had but given a softness to her eyes. Never before had he so strongly felt her wayward irresistible charm, which it was so impossible to analyse or to explain. Indeed, if it came to analysis there were strange ingredients there;

there was egoism as complete, and yet as disarming as that of a Persian kitten; there was the unreasonableness of a spoilt child; there was the inconsiderateness and unreliability of an April day, which alternates its gleams of the saffron sun of spring with cold rain and plumping showers. Yet he felt that there was something utterly adorable, wholly womanly that lay sheathed in these more superficial imperfections, something that stirred within them conscious of the coming summer, just as the life embalmed within the chrysalis stirs, giving token of the time when the husk shall burst, and that which was but a brown mummied thing shall be wafted on wings of silver emblazoned with scarlet and gold. Then there was her beauty, too, which drew his eyes after the wonder of its perfection, and was worthy of the soul that he divined in her. And finally (and this, perhaps, to him was the supreme magnet) there was the amazing and superb quality of her vitality, that sparkled and effervesced in all she did and said, so that for him her speech was like song or light, and to be with her was to be bathed in the effulgence of her spirit. And Hugh looking at her now, felt, as always, that his self slipped from him, so that he was conscious of her only; she possessed him, and he lay like the sea with the dazzle of sunlight on it that both reflects the radiance and absorbs it.

Then he sat up, and half turned from her, for there were things to be said yet that he could scarcely say while he looked at her.

"I know you don't mean to be a curse to me," he said, "and you couldn't be if you tried. Whatever you did, and you are going to do a pretty bad thing now in marrying that chap, must be almost insignificant compared to the love which you have made exist in me."

He paused a moment.

"I have thought it all out," he said, "but it is difficult, and you must give me time. I'm not quick like you, as you know very well, but sometimes I get there. It is like this."

She was watching him and listening to him, with a curious intentness and nervousness, as a prisoner about to receive sentence may watch the judge. Her hands clasped and unclasped themselves, her breath came short and irregular. It seemed as if she, for once, had failed to understand him whom she had said she knew too fatally well. Just now, at any rate, and on this topic, it was clear she did not know what he was going to propose. Yet it was scarcely a proposal she waited for; she waited for his word, his ultimatum. Up till now she had dominated him completely with her quick wit, her far more subtle intelligence, her beauty, her vitality. But for once, now he was her master, she felt she had to bow to his simplicity and his uncomplicated strength, his brute virility. It was but faintly that she recognised it,

the recognition came to her consciousness but as an echo. But the
voice that made the echo came from within.

"I have received my dismissal from you," he said, "as head of your
house, as your possible husband. As I said, I won't take the place of
the tame cat instead. God knows I don't want to cut adrift from you,
and I can't cut adrift from you. But my aspiration is rendered impossible, and therefore both my mental attitude to you and my conduct
must be altered. I daresay Berts and Tommy and Esther and all the
rest of them will go lying about on your sofa, and smoking in your
bedroom just as before. Well, I can't be intimate in that sort of way
any longer. You said you never reckoned whether you respected me
or not, and that may be so. But without wanting to be heavy about
it, I have got to respect myself. I can't help being your lover, but I
can help tickling my love, so to speak, making it squirm and wriggle.
Whether I am respectable or not, it is, and I shan't—as I said—I shan't
tickle it. Also, though I would be hurt in any other way for your
sake, I won't be hurt like that. Don't misunderstand me. It is because
my love for you is not one atom abated, that I won't play tricks with
it. But when it says to me 'I can't bear it,' I shall not ask it to bear
it. You always found me too easy to understand; I think this is another
instance of it."

He paused a moment, and Nadine gave a little sobbing sigh.

"Oh, Hughie," she began.

"No, don't interrupt," he said. "I want to go through with it, without
discussion. There is no discussion possible. I wouldn't argue with God
about it. I should say 'You made me an ordinary human man, and
you've got to take the consequences.' In the same way you have chosen
Seymour, and I am telling you what is the effect. Now—you are tired
of hearing it—I love you. And therefore I want your happiness without
reservation. You have decided it will conduce to your happiness to
marry Seymour. Therefore, Nadine—this is quite simple and true—I
want you to do so. I may rage and storm on the surface, but essentially
I don't. Somewhere behind all I may say and do, there is, as you
once said to me, the essential me. Well, that says to you 'God bless
you.' That's all."

He unclasped his hands from round his knees, and stood up, big
and simple and strong.

"There's nothing more to be said," he went on. "I thought when I
came down it might take a long time to tell you this. But it has taken
ten minutes only. I thought perhaps you would have a lot to say about
it, and I daresay you have, but I find that it doesn't concern me. Don't
think me brutal, any more than I think you brutal. I am made like

this, and you are made otherwise. By all means, let us see each other often I hope, but not just yet. I've got to adjust myself you see, and you haven't. You never loved me, and so what you have done makes no difference in your feeling towards me. But I've got to get used to it."

She looked up at him, as he stood there in front of her with the green lights through the beech-leaves playing on him.

"You make me utterly miserable, Hugh," she said.

"No, I don't. There is no such thing as misery without love. You don't care for me in the way that could—could give you the privilege of being miserable."

For one half-second she did not follow him. But immediately the quickness of her mind grasped what came so easily and simply to him.

"Ah, I see," she said, her intelligence leading her away from him by the lure of the pleasure of perception. "When you are like that, it is even a joy to be miserable. Is that so?"

"Yes, I suppose that is it. Your misery is a—a wireless message from your love. Bad news, perhaps, but still a communication."

She got up.

"Ah, my dear," she said, "that must be so. I never thought of it. But I can infer that you are right. Somehow you are quickened, Hughie. You are giving me a series of little shocks. You were never quite like that before."

"I was always exactly like that," he said, "I have told you nothing that I have not always known."

Again her brilliant egoism asserted itself.

"Then it is I who am quickened," she said. "There is nothing that quickens one so much as being hurt. It makes all your nerves awake and active. Yes; you have hurt me, and you are not sorry. I do not mind being hurt, if it makes me more alive. Ah, the only point of life is to be alive. If life was a crown of thorns, how closely I would press it round my head, so that the points wounded and wounded me. It is so shallow just to desire to be happy. I do not care whether I am happy or not, so long as I feel. Give me all the cancers and consumptions and decayed teeth, and gout and indigestion and necrosis of the spine and liver if there is such a thing, so that I may feel. I *don't* feel: it is that which ails me. I have a sane body and a sane mind, and I am tired of sanity. Kick me, Hughie, strike me, spit at me, make me angry and disgusted, anything, oh anything. I want to feel, and I want to feel about you most particularly, and I can't, and there is Edith playing on her damned double-bass again. I hear it, I am conscious of it, and it is only the things that don't matter which

I am conscious of. I am conscious of your brown eyes, my dear, and your big mouth and your trousers and boots, and the cow that is wagging its tail and looking at us as if it was going to be sick. Its dinner, I remember, goes into its stomach, and then it comes up again, and then it becomes milk or a calf or something. It has nine stomachs, or is it a cat that has nine lives, or nine tails? I am sure about nine. Oh Hughie, I see the outside aspect of things, and I can't get below. I am a flat stone that you send to make chickens, is it—no, ducks and drakes over a pond; flop, flop, the foolish thing. And somehow you with your stupidity and simplicity, you go down below, and drown, and stick in the mud, and are so uncomfortable and miserable. And I am sorry for you; I hate you to be uncomfortable and miserable, and oh, I envy you. You suffer and are kind, and don't envy, and are not puffed up, and I envy your misery, and am puffed up because I am so desirable, and I don't really suffer—you are quite right—and I am not kind. Hugh, I can't bear that cow, drive it away, it will eat me, and make milk of me. And there, look, are Mamma and Papa Jack, coming back from their ride. Papa Jack loves her; his face is like a face in a spoon when he looks at her, and I know she is learning to love him. She no longer thinks when she is talking to him, as to whether he will be pleased. That is a sure sign. She is beginning to be herself, at her age too! She doesn't think about thinking about him any more: it comes naturally. And I am not myself; I am something else; rather, I am nothing else; I am nothing at all, just some intelligence, and some flesh and blood and bones. I am not a real person. It is that which is the matter. I long to be a real person, and I can't. I crawl sideways over other things like a crab; I wave my pincers and pinch. I am lost; I am nothing! And yet I know—how horribly I know it—there is something behind, more than the beastly idol with the wooden eye, which is all I know of my real self. If only I could find it! If only I could crack myself up like a nut and get to a kernel. For God's sake, Hughie, take the nut-crackers, and crack me. But it is idle to ask you to do it. You have tried often enough. You will have to get a stronger nut-cracker. Meantime I am a nut, just a nut, with its hard bright shell. Seymour is another nut. There we shall be."

Hugh caught her by the wrists.

"I can't stand it, Nadine," he said. "You feel nothing for him. He is nothing to you. How can you marry him? It's profane; it's blasphemous. You say you can give nothing to anybody. Well, make the best of yourself. I can give all I am to you. Isn't that better than absolute nil? You can't give, but let me give. It's worship, it's all there is——"

She stood there with her wrists in his hands, his strong fingers bruising and crushing them. She could have screamed for the pain of it.

"No, and a thousand times no," she said. "I won't cheat."

"I ask you to cheat."

"And I won't. Hughie dear, press harder, hurt me more, so that you may see I am serious. You may bite the flesh off me, you may strangle me, and I will stand quite still and let you do it. But I won't marry you. I won't cheat you. My will is stronger than your body, and I would die sooner."

"Then your marriage is a pure farce," said he.

"Come and laugh at it," she said.

7

Hugh's intention had been to stay several days, at the least, with the Chesterfords, and had brought down luggage that would last any reasonable person a fortnight. Unluckily he had not foreseen the very natural effect that the sight of Seymour would have on him, and as soon as lunch was over he took his hostess into a corner and presented the situation with his usual simplicity.

"It is like this, Aunt Dodo," he said. "I didn't realise exactly what it meant to me till I saw Seymour again. He drove me up from the station, and it got worse all the time. I thought perhaps since Nadine had chosen him, I might see him differently. I think perhaps I do, but it is worse. It is quite hopeless; the best thing I can do is to go away again at once."

Dodo had lit two cigarettes by mistake, and since, during their ride, Jack had (wantonly, so she thought) accused her of wastefulness, she was smoking them both, holding one in each hand in alternate whiffs. But she threw one of them away at this, and laid her hand on Hugh's knee.

"I know, my dear, and I am so dreadfully sorry," she said. "I was sure it would be so, and that's why I didn't want you to come here. I knew it was no good. I can see you feel really unwell whenever you catch sight of Seymour or hear anything he says. And about Nadine? Did you have a nice talk with her?"

Hugh considered.

"I don't think I should quite call it nice," he said. "I think I should call it necessary. Anyhow, we have had it and—and I quite understand now. As that is so, I shall go away again this afternoon. It was a mistake to come at all."

"Yes, but probably it was a necessary mistake. In certain situations mistakes are necessary; I mean whatever one does seems to be wrong. If you had stopped away you would have felt it wrong too."

"And will you answer two questions, Aunt Dodo?" he asked.

"Yes, I will certainly answer them. If they are very awkward ones I may not answer them quite truthfully."

"Well, I'll try. Do you approve of Nadine's marriage? Has it your blessing?"

"Yes, my dear; truthfully it has. But it is right to tell you that I give my blessings rather easily, and when it is clearly no use attempting to interfere in a matter, it is better to bless it than curse it. But if you ask me whether I would have chosen Seymour as Nadine's husband, out of all the possible ones, why, I would not. I thought at one time that perhaps it was going to be Jack. But then Jack chose me, and as we all know a girl may not marry her step-father, particularly if her mother is alive and well. But I should not have chosen you either, Hughie, if your question implies that. I used to think I would, but when Nadine explained to me the other day, I rather agreed with her. Of course, she has explained to you."

Hugh looked at her with his honest, trustworthy, brown eyes.

"Several times," he said. "But if I agreed, I shouldn't be worrying. Now another question. Do you think she will be happy?"

"Yes, up to her present capacity. If I did not think she would be happy, I would not bless it. Dear Edith, for example, thinks it is a shocking and terrible marriage. For her I daresay it would be, but then it isn't she whom Seymour proposed to marry. They would be a most remarkable couple, would they not? I think Edith would kill him, with the intention of committing suicide after, and then determine that there had been enough killing for one day. And the next day suicide would appear quite out of the question. So she would write a funeral march."

Dodo held the admirably sensible view that if discussion on a particular topic is hopeless, it is much better to abandon it, and talk as cheerfully as may be about something different. But this entertaining diversion altogether failed to divert Hugh.

"You said she would be happy up to her present capacity?" he reminded her.

"Yes: that is simple, is it not? As we develop our capacity for happiness, our misery also develops as well. Whether Nadine's capacity will develop much, I cannot tell. If it does, she may not be happy up to it. But who knows? We cannot spend our lives in arranging for contingencies that may never take place, and changes in ourselves that may never occur."

Dodo looked in silence for a moment at his grave reliable face, and felt a sudden wonder at Nadine for having chosen as she had done. And yet her reason for rejecting this extremely satisfactory youth was sound enough; their intellectual levels were such miles apart. But Dodo, though she did not express her further thought, had it very distinct in her mind. "If she does develop emotionally like a woman," she said to herself, "there will not be a superfluity of happiness about. And she will look at you and wonder how she could have refused you."

But necessarily she did not say this, and Hugh got up.

"Well then, at the risk of appearing a worse prig than John Sturgis," he said, "I may tell you that as long as Nadine is happy, the main object is accomplished. My own happiness consists so largely in the fact of hers. Dear me, I wonder you are not sick at my sententiousness. I am quite too noble to live, but I don't really want to die. Would it make Nadine happier, if I told Seymour I should be a brother to him?"

Dodo laughed.

"No, Hughie, it would make her afraid that your brain had gone, or that you were going to be ill. It would only make her anxious. Is the motor round? I am sorry you are going, but I think you are quite right to do so. Always propose yourself, Hughie, whenever you feel like it."

"I don't feel like it at present," said he. "But thanks awfully, Aunt Dodo."

Dodo felt extremely warmly towards this young man, who was behaving so very well and simply.

"God bless you, dear Hugh," she said, "and give you your heart's desire."

"At present my heart's desire appears to be making other plans for itself," said Hugh.

Esther had said once, in a more than usually enlightened moment, that Nadine's friends did her feeling for her, and she observed them, and put what they felt into vivacious and convincing language and applied it to herself. Certainly Hugh, when he drove away again this afternoon, was keenly conscious of what Nadine had talked about to Edith: he felt lost, and the flag he had industriously waved so long for her seemed to be entirely disregarded. He hardly knew what he had hoped would have come of this ill-conceived visit which had just ended so abruptly, but a vague sense of Nadine's engagement being too nightmare-like to be true had prompted him to go in person and find out. Also, it had seemed to him that when he was face to face with Nadine, asking her at point-blank range whether she was going to marry Seymour, it was impossible that she should say "yes." Something different must assuredly happen: either she would say it was a mistake or something inside him must snap. But there was no mistake about it, and nothing had snapped. The world proposed to proceed just as usual. And he could not decline to proceed with it; unless you died you were obliged to proceed, however intolerable the journey, however unthinkable the succession of days through which you were compelled to pass. Life was like a journey in an express train with no communication cord. You were locked in, and could not stop the train by any means. Some people, of course, threw themselves out of the window, so to speak, and made violent ends to themselves; but suicide is only possible to people of certain temperament, and Hugh was incapable of even contemplating such a step. He felt irretrievably lost, profoundly wretched, and yet, quite apart from the fact that he was temperamentally incapable of even wishing to commit suicide, the fact that Nadine was in the world (whatever Nadine was going to do) made it impossible to think of quitting it. That was the manner and characteristic of his love: his own unhappiness meant less to him than the fact of her.

Until she had suggested it the thought of travelling had not occurred to him: now, as he waited for his train at the station, he felt that at all costs he wanted to be on the move, to be employed in getting away from the "intolerable anywhere" that he might happen to be in. Wherever he was, it seemed that any other place would be preferable; and this he supposed was the essence of the distraction that travel is supposed to give. His own rooms in town he felt would be soaked in associations of Nadine, so too would be the houses where he would naturally spend these coming months of August and September. Not till October, when his duties as a clerk in the Foreign Office called him back to town, had he anything with which he felt he could occupy himself. An exceptional capacity for finding days too short and few, even though they had no duties to make the hours pass, had hitherto been his only brilliance; now all gift of the kind seemed to have been snatched from him; he could not conceive what to do with to-morrow or the next day or any of the days that should follow. An allowance of seven days to the week seemed an inordinate superfluity; he was filled with irritation at the thought of the leisurely march of interminable time.

He spent the evening alone, feeling that he was a shade less intolerable to himself than anybody else would have been; also, he felt incapable of the attention which social intercourse demands. His mind seemed utterly out of his control, as unable to remain in one place as his body. Even if he thought of Nadine, it wandered, and he would notice that a picture hung crooked, and jump up to straighten it. One such was a charming water-colour sketch by Esther of the beach at Meering, with a splash of sunlight low in the West that, shining through a chimney in the clouds, struck the sea very far out, and made there a little island of reflected gold. Esther had put in this golden islet with some reluctance: she had said that even in Nature it looked unreal, and would look even more unreal in Art, especially when the artist happened to be herself. But Nadine had voted with Hugh on behalf of the golden island, just because it would appear unreal and incredible. "It is only the unreal things that are vivid to us," she had said, "and the incredible things are just those which we believe in. Isn't that so, Hughie?"

How well he remembered her saying that; her voice rang in his ears like a haunting tune! And while Esther made this artistic sacrifice to the god of things as they are not, he and Nadine strolled along the firm sandy beach, shining with the moisture of the receding tide. She had taken his arm, and just as her voice now sounded in his ears so he could feel the pressure of her hand on his coat.

"You live among unrealities," she said, "although you are so simple and practical. You are thinking now that some day you and I will go to live on that golden island. But there is no island really; it is just like the rest of the sea, only the sun shines on it."

The bitter truth of that struck him now as applied to her and himself. Though she had refused him before, the sun shone on those days, and not until she had engaged herself to Seymour did the gold fade. Not until to-day, when he had definite confirmation of that from her own lips, had he really believed in her rejection of him. He well knew her affection for him; he believed, and rightly, that if she had been asked to name her best friend, she would have named none other than himself. It had been impossible for him not to be sanguine over the eventual outcome, and he had never really doubted that some day her affection would be kindled into flame. He had often told himself that it was through him that she would discover her heart. As she had suggested, he would some day crack the nut for her, and show her her own kernel, and she would find it was his.

And now all those optimisms were snuffed out. He had completely to alter and adjust his focus, but that could not be done at once. To-night he peered out, as it were, on to familiar scenes, and found that his sight of them was misty and blurred. The whole world had vanished in cold grey mists. He was lost, quite lost, and . . . and there was a letter for him on the table which he had not noticed. The envelope was obviously of cheap quality, and was of those proportions which suggest a bill. A bill it was, from a bookseller, of four shillings and sixpence incurred over a book Nadine had said she wanted to read. He had passed the bookseller's on his way home immediately afterwards, and of course he had ordered it for her. She had not cared for it; she had found it unreal. "The man is meant to arouse my sympathy," she had said, "and only arouses my intense indifference. I am acutely uninterested in what happens to him." Hugh felt as if she had been speaking of himself, but the moment after knew that he did her an injustice. Even now he could not doubt the sincerity of her affection for him. But there was something frozen about it. It was like sleet, and he, like a parched land, longed for the pity of the soft rain.

Hugh had a wholesome contempt for people who pity themselves, and it struck him at this point that he was in considerable danger of becoming despicable in his own eyes. He had been capable of sufficient manliness to remove himself from Nadine that afternoon, but his solitary evening was not up to that standard; he might as well have remained at Winston, if he was to endorse his refusal to dangle after her with nothing more virile than those drawling sentimentalities. She was not for him: he had made this expedition to-day in order to convince himself on that point, and already his determination was shewing itself unstable, if it suffered him to dangle in mind though not in body. And yet how was it possible not to? Nadine, physically and tangibly was certainly going to pass out of his life, but to eradicate her from his soul would be an act of spiritual suicide. Physically there was no doubt that he would continue to exist without her, spiritually he did not see how existence was possible on the same terms. But he need not drivel about her. There were always two ways of behaving after receiving a blow which knocked you down, and the one that commended itself most to Hugh was to get up again.

Lady Ayr at the end of the London season had for years been accustomed to carry out some itinerant plan for the improvement and discomfort of her family. One year she dragged them along the castles by the Loire, another she forced them, as if by pumping, through the picture galleries of Holland, and this summer she proposed to shew them a quantity of the English cathedrals. These abominable pilgrimages were made pompously and economically: they stayed at odious inns, where she haggled and bargained with the proprietors, but on the other hand she informed the petrified vergers and custodians whom she conducted (rather than was conducted by) round the cathedrals or castles in their charge, that she was the Marchioness of Ayr, was directly descended from the occupants of the finest and most antique tombs, that the castle in question had once belonged to her family, or that the gem of the Holbeins represented some aunt of hers in bygone generations. Here pomp held sway, but economy came into its own again over the small silver coin with which she rewarded her conductor. On English lines she had a third-class carriage reserved for her and beguiled the tedium of journeys by reading aloud out of guide-books an account of what they had seen or what they were going to visit. Generally they put up at temperance hotels, and she made a point of afternoon tea being included in the exiguous terms at which she insisted on being entertained. John aided and abetted her in those tours, exhibiting an ogreish appetite for all things Gothic and mental improvement, and her husband followed her with a white umbrella, and sat down as much as possible. Esther's part in them was that of a resigned and inattentive martyr, and she fired off picture postcards of the places they visited to Nadine and others with "This is a foul hole" or "The beastliest inn we have struck yet" written on them, while Seymour revenged himself for the discomforts inflicted on him by examining his mother as to where they had seen a particular rose-window or portrait by Rembrandt, and then by the aid of a guide-book proving she was wrong. Why none of them revolted and refused to go on these annual journeys, now that they had arrived at adult years, they none of them exactly knew, any more than they knew why they went, when summoned, to their mother's dreadful dinner-parties, and it must be supposed that there was a touch of the inevitable about such diversions: you might grumble and complain, but you went.

This year the tour was to start with the interesting city of Lincoln, and the party assembled on the platform at King's Cross at an early hour. The plan was to lunch in the train, so as to start sight-seeing immediately on arrival, and continue (with a short excursion to the hotel in order to have the tea which had been included in the terms) until the fading light made it impossible to distinguish ancestral tombs or Norman arches. Lady Ayr had not seen Seymour since his engagement, and as she ate rather gristly beef sandwiches, she gave him her views on the step. Though they were all together in one compartment the conversation might be considered a private one, for Lord Ayr was sleeping gently in one corner, John was absorbed in the account of the Roman remains at Lincoln (Lindun Colonia, as he had already announced), and Esther with a slightly leaky stylograph was writing a description of their depressing journey to Nadine.

"What you are marrying on, Seymour, I don't know," she said. "Neither your father or I will be able to increase your allowance, and Nadine Waldenech has the appearance of being an expensive young woman. I hope she realizes she is marrying the son of a poor man, and that we go third class."

"She is aware of all that," said Seymour, wiping his long white finger tips on an exceedingly fine cambric handkerchief, after swallowing a sandwich or two, "and we are marrying really on her money."

"I am not sure that I approve of that," said his mother.

"The remedy is obvious," remarked Seymour. "You can increase my allowance. I have no objection. Mamma, would you kindly let me throw the rest of that sandwich out of the window? It makes me ill to look at it."

"We are not talking about sandwiches. Why do you not earn some money like other younger sons?"

"I do. I earned four pounds last week, with describing your party and other things, and there is my embroidery as well, which I shall work at most industriously. I shall do embroidery in the evening, after dinner, while Nadine smokes."

Lady Ayr looked out of the window and pointed magisterially to the towers of some great church in the town through which the train was passing.

"Peterborough," she said, "We shall see Peterborough on our way back. Peterborough, John. Ayr and Esther, we are passing through Peterborough."

Esther looked out on to the mean backs of houses.

"The sooner we pass through Peterborough the better," she observed.

John turned rapidly over the leaves of his guidebook.

"Peterborough is seventy-eight miles from London, and contains many buildings of interest," he informed them.

Lady Ayr returned to Seymour.

"I hope you will insist on her leaving off smoking when you are married to her," she said. "I cannot say she is the wife I should have chosen for you."

"I chose her myself," observed Seymour.

"Tell me more about her. Certainly the Waldenechs are a very old family, there is that to be said. Is she serious? Does she feel her responsibilities? Or is she like her mother?"

Seymour brushed a few remaining sandwich-crumbs off his trousers.

"I think Aunt Dodo is one of the most serious people I know," he said. "She is serious about everything. She does everything with all her might. Nadine is not quite so serious as that. She is rather flippant about things like food and dress. However, no doubt my influence will make her more serious. But, as a matter of fact, I can't tell you about Nadine. A fortnight ago, when I proposed to her I could have. I could have given you a very complete account of her. But I can't any longer; I am getting blind about her. I only know that it is she. Not so long ago I told her a quantity of her faults with ruthless accuracy, but I couldn't now. I can't see them any more; there's a glamour."

Esther looked up.

"Oh, Seymour," she said, "are you talking about Nadine? Are you falling in love with her? How very awkward! Does she know?"

Seymour pointed a withering finger at his sister.

"Little girls should mind their own business," he said.

"Oh, but it is my business. Nadine matters far more than anyone else. She might easily think it not right to marry you if you were in love with her."

Lady Ayr turned a petrifying gaze from one to the other.

"She seems a very extraordinary young person," she said. "And in any case Esther has no business to know anything about it."

"Whether she thinks it right or not, she is going to marry me," said Seymour.

Esther shook her head.

"You are indeed blind about Nadine," she said, "if you think she would ever do anything she thought wrong."

"You might be describing John," said Seymour rather hotly. "Anyhow Nadine is not like John."

"I see no resemblance," said Lady Ayr. "But it is something to know she would not do anything she thought wrong."

"When you say it in that voice, mother," said Esther, "you make nonsense of it."

"The same words in any voice mean the same thing," said Lady Ayr.

Seymour sighed.

"I am on Esther's side for once," he said.

Esther turned to her brother:

"Seymour, you ought to tell Nadine you are falling in love with her," she said. "I really don't think she would approve. Why, you might become as bad as Hugh. Of course you are not so stupid as Hugh—ah, stupid is the wrong word—you haven't got such a plain kind of intellect as Hugh—which was Nadine's main objection——"

Seymour patted Esther's hand with odious superiority. "You are rather above yourself, my little girl," he said, "because just now I agreed with you. It has gone to your head, and makes you think yourself clever. Shut your eyes till we get to Lincoln. You will feel less giddy by degrees. And when you open them again, you can mind your own business, and Mamma will tell you about the Goths and Vandals who built the cathedral. You are a Vandal yourself; you will have a fellow feeling. Mamma dear, put down that window. I am going to see cathedrals to please you, but I will not be stifled to please anybody. The carriage reeks of your beef sandwiches. But I think I have some scent in my bag."

"I am quite sure you have," said Esther, scornfully. "I am writing to Nadine, by the way. I shall tell her you are falling in love with her."

"You can tell her exactly what you please," said Seymour, suavely. "Ah, here is some wall-flower scent. It is like a May morning. Yes, tell Nadine what you please, but don't bother me. What is this odious town we are coming to? I think it must be Lincoln. John, here is Lincoln, and all the people are ancient Romans."

Seymour obligingly sprayed the expensive scent about the carriage, even though they were so shortly to disembark.

"The river Witham," said John, pointing to a small and fetid ditch. "Remains of Roman villas——"

"The inhabitants of which died of typhoid," said Seymour. "Tell Nadine we are enjoying Lincoln, Esther. Had father better be allowed to sleep on, or shall I wake him? There is a porter; call him, mother—I won't carry my bag even to save you sixpence. But don't tell him we are Marchionesses and lords and ladies, because then he will expect a shilling. I perceive a seedy-looking bus outside. That is probably ours. It looks as if it came from some low kind of inn. I wish I had brought Antoinette. And yet I don't know. She would probably have given notice after seeing the degradation of our summer holiday."

"Seymour, you are making yourself exceedingly disagreeable," said his mother.

"It is intentional. You made yourself disagreeable to me; you began. As for you, Esther, you must expect to see a good deal less of Nadine after she and I are married. I will not have you mooning about the house, reminding her of all that damned—yes, I said damned—nonsense you and she and Berts and Hugh talked about the inequality of marriages where one person is clever and the other stupid, or where one loves and the other doesn't. You have roused me, you and mother between you, and I am here to tell you that I will manage my own affairs, which are Nadine's also, without the smallest assistance from you. Put that in—in your ginger-beer, or whatever we have for dinner, and drink it. You thought I was only a sort of thing that waved its hands and collected jade, and talked in rather a squeaky voice, and walked on its toes. Well, you have found out your mistake, and don't let me have to teach it you again. You can tell Nadine in your letter exactly what I have said. And don't rouse me again; it makes me hot. But mind your own business instead, and remember that when I want either your advice or mother's, I will ask for it. Till then you can keep it completely to yourselves. You needn't answer me; I don't want to hear anything you can have got to say. Let us go to the cathedral. I suppose it is that great cockshy on the top of the hill. I know it will prove to have been built by our forefathers. The verger will like to know about it. But bear in mind I don't want to be told anything about Nadine."

Seymour had become quite red in the face with the violence of the feelings that prompted these straightforward remarks, and before putting the spray of wallflower scent back in his bag, he shut his eyes and squirted himself in the face in order to cool himself, while Esther stared at him open-mouthed. She hardly knew him, for he had become exactly like a man, a transformation more unexpected than anything that ever happened at a pantomine, and she instantly and correctly connected this change in him with what he had been saying. For the reason of the change was perfectly simple and sufficient; during those last days at Winston, after the departure of Hugh, he had fallen in love with Nadine, and his nature, which had really been neither that of man or woman, had suddenly sexed itself. He had not in the least cast off his tastes and habits; to spray himself and a stuffy railway-carriage with wallflower scent was still perfectly natural to him, and no doubt, unless Nadine objected very much, he would continue to take Antoinette about with him as his maid, but he had declared himself a man, and found, even as his sister found, that the change in him was as immense as it was unexpected. He thought, with more than usual scorn, of Nadine's friends, such as Esther and Berts, who all played about together like healthy, but mentally anaemic, children, for he, the most anaemic of them all, had suddenly had live blood, as it were, squirted into him. Indeed, the only member of the clan whom he thought of with toleration was Hugh, with whom he felt a bond of brotherhood, for Hugh, like himself, loved Nadine like a man. Already, also, he felt sorry for him, recognising in him a member of his own sex. Hitherto he had disliked his own sex, because they were men, now he found himself detesting people like Berts, because they were not. For men, so he had begun to perceive, are essentially those who are aware of the fact of women; the rest of them, to which he had himself till so lately belonged, he now classified as more or less intellectual amoebae. And the corresponding members of the other sex were just as bad; Esther had no sense of sex, nor, perhaps, and here he paused, had Nadine.

That, it is true, gave him long pause. He knew quite well that Nadine had been no more in love with him, when they had got engaged, than had he been with her. They had both been (and she, so he must suppose, was still) quite undeveloped as regards those instincts. Hugh with all his devotion and developed manliness had awakened no corresponding flame in her, and Seymour was quite clear-sighted enough to see that there was no sign of his having succeeded where Hugh had failed. She belonged, as Dodo had remarked, to that essentially modern type of girl, which, unless she marries while quite young, will probably be spinster still at thirty. They had brains, they had a hundred intellectual and artistic interests, and studied mummies or logic, or Greek gems, or themselves, and lived in flats, eagerly and happily, and smoked and substituted tea for dinner. They knew of nothing in their natures that gave them any imperious call; on the other hand, they called imperiously, though unintentionally, to others. Nadine had called like that to Hugh, and was dismayed at the tumult she had roused, regretting it, but not comprehending it. And now she had called like that to Seymour. She was like the sleeping beauty in the wood, calling in her sleep. Hugh had answered her first, and had fought his way through thicket and briar, but his coming had not awakened her. Then she had called again, and this time Seymour stood by her. She had given him her hand, but her sleep had been undisturbed. She smiled at him, but she smiled in her sleep.

The seedy bus, of the type not yet quite extinct, with straw on the bottom of it, proved to be sent for them, and they proceeded over cobbled streets, half deafened by the clatter of ill-fitting windows. After a minute or two of this Seymour firmly declined to continue, for he said the straw got up his trousers and tickled his legs, and the drums of his ears were bursting. So he got delicately out, in order to take a proper conveyance, and promised to meet the rest of them at the west door of the cathedral. Here he sat very comfortably for ten minutes till they arrived, and entering in the manner of a storming party, they literally stumbled over an astonished Archdeacon, who was superintending some measurement of paving-stone immediately inside, and proved to be a cousin of Lady Ayr's. This fact was not elicited without pomp, for the cathedral was not open to visitors at this hour, as he informed them, on which Lady Ayr said: "I suppose there will be no difficulty in the way of the Marquis of Ayr—Ayr, this is an Archdeacon—and his wife and family seeing it." Upon which "an" Archdeacon said: "Oh, are you Susie Ayr?" Explanations of cousinship—luckily satisfactory—followed, and they were conducted round the cathedral by him free of all expense, and dined with him in the evening, at a quarter to eight, returning home at ten, in order to get a grip of all they were going to see next day, by a diligent perusal of the guide-books.

They were staying at an ancient hostelry called the "Goat and Compasses," a designation the origin of which John very obligingly explained to them, but Seymour, still, perhaps, suffering from the straw at the bottom of the bus, thought that the "Flea and Compasses" would be a more descriptive title. No room was on a level with any other room or with the passage outside it, and short, obscure flights of steps designed to upset the unwary communicated between them. A further trap was laid down for unsuspicious guests in the matter of doors and windows, for the doors were not quite high enough to enable the person of average height to pass through them without hitting his forehead against the jamb, and the windows, when induced to open, descended violently again in the manner of a guillotine. The floors were as wavy as the pavement of St. Mark's at Venice, the looking-glasses seemed like dusky wells, at the bottom of which the gazer darkly beheld his face, and the beds had feather mattresses on them. Altogether, it was quite in the right style, except that it was not a temperance hotel, for the accommodation of Lady Ayr on a tour of family culture, and she and John, after a short and decisive economical interview with the proprietor, took possession of the largest table in the public drawing-room, ejecting therefrom two nervous spinsters who had been looking forward to playing patience on it, and spreading their maps of the town over it, read to each other out of guide-books, while Lord Ayr propped himself up dejectedly in a corner, where he hoped to drop asleep unperceived. The troublesome interview with the proprietor had been on the subject of making a deduction from the agreed terms, since they had all dined out. He was finally routed by a short, plain statement of the case by Lady Ayr.

"If you can afford to take us in for so much, dinner included," she said, "you can afford to take us in for less without dinner. I think there is no more to be said on the subject. Breakfast, please, at a quarter past eight punctually, and I shall require a second candle in my bedroom. I think your terms, which I do not say are excessive, included lights? *Thank* you!"

Seymour had declined to take part in this guidebook conference, saying with truth that he felt sure it would all be very completely explained to him next day, and let himself out into the streets of the town, which were already growing empty of passengers. Above, the sky was lucent with many stars, and the moon, which had risen an hour before, cleared the house-roofs and shone down into the streets with a very white light, making the gas-lamps look red. Last night from the terrace at Winston they had all watched it rise, full-flaring, over the woods below the house. Then he and Nadine had strolled away together, and in that luminous solitude with her he had felt himself constrained and tongue-tied. He had no longer at command the gabble that usually rose so glibly to his lips, that gay, witty inconsequent talk that had truthfully represented what went on in his quick-discerning brain. His brain now was taken up with one topic only, and it was as hard for him to speak to her of that as it was for him to speak of anything else. He knew that she had entered into her engagement with him in the same spirit as he had proposed to her. They liked each other, each found the other a stimulating companion, by each, no doubt, the attraction of the other's good looks was felt.

She, he was certain, regarded him now as she had regarded him then, while for him the whole situation had undergone so complete a change that he felt that the very fortress of his identity had been stormed and garrisoned by the besieging host. And what was the host? That tall girl with the white slim hands, who without intention had picked up a key and, cursorily so it seemed, had unlocked his heart, so that it stood open to her. Honestly, he did not know that it was made to unlock; he had thought of it always as some toy Swiss chalet, not meant to be opened. But she had opened it, and gone inside.

The streets grew emptier, lights appeared behind blinds in upper windows, and only an occasional step sounded on the pavements. He had come to an open market place, and from where he paused and stood the western towers of the cathedral rose above the intervening roofs, and aspired whitely into the dark velvet of the night. Hitherto Seymour would have found nothing particular to say about moonlight, in which he took but the very faintest interest, except that it tended to provoke an untimely loquaciousness in cats. But to-night he found his mind flooded with the most hackneyed and commonplace reflections. It reminded him of Nadine: it was white, and chaste, and aloof, like her. . . . He wanted her, and he was going to get her, and yet would she really be his in the sense that he was hers? Then for a moment habit asserted itself, and he told himself he was being common, that he was dropping to the level of plain and barbarous Hugh. It was very mortifying, yet he could not keep off that level. He kept on dropping there, as he stared at the moonlit towers of the cathedral, unsatisfied and longing. But it may be doubted whether he would have felt better satisfied if he had known how earnestly Nadine had tried to drop, or rise, to the moonlit plane, or how sincerely, even with tears, she had deplored her inability to do so. For it was not he whom she had sought to join there.

8

Dodo was seated in her room in Jack's house in town, intermittently arguing with him and Miss Grantham and Edith and Berts, and in intervals ringing up on the telephone as many of her friends as she could remember the names of and asking them to her dance. The month was November, and the dance was for to-day week, which was the 1st of December, and as far as she had got at present it appeared that all her friends were in town and that they would all come. Nadine was similarly employed next door, and as they both asked anybody who occurred to them, the same people frequently got asked twice over.

"Which," said Dodo, "is an advantage, as it looks as if we really wanted them very much. Oh, is that Esther? Esther, we are having a dance on December the 1st, and will you all come? Yes: wasn't it a good idea? That is nice. Of course delighted if your mother cares to come too——"

"Then I shan't," said Berts.

"Berts, shut up," said Dodo in a penetrating whisper. "Yes, darling Esther, Berts said something, but I don't know what it was, as they are all talking together. Yes, a cotillion. Good-bye dear. . . . Look out the number of Hendrick's Stores, Grantie. But I really won't lead the cotillion with Berts. It is too ridiculous; a man may not lead the cotillion with his grandmother; it comes in the prayer-book."

"Three thousand and seven," said Miss Grantham. "Paddington."

"Three double o seven, Padd, please, miss," said Dodo briskly to the telephone. "I always say 'Please miss,' and then they are much pleasanter. I used to say 'I'm Princess Waldenech, please, miss'; but they never believed it, and said 'Garn!' But I was, darling Jack, I was! No, my days of leading the cotillion came to an end under William the Fourth. There is nothing so ridiculous as seeing an old thing— No, I'm not the Warwick Hotel! Do I sound like the Warwick Hotel?"

Dodo's face suddenly assumed an expression of seraphic interest.

"It's too entrancing," she whispered. "I'm sure it's a nice man, because he wants to marry me. He says I didn't meet him in the Warwick Hotel this morning. That was forgetful. Yes? Oh, he's rung off, he has jilted me. I wish I had said I was the Warwick Hotel: it was stupid of me. I wonder if you can be married by telephone with a clergyman taking the place of 'please miss.' Where had we got to? Oh yes, Hendrick's: three double o seven, you idiot. I mean please, miss. What? Thank you, miss. No, Nadine and Berts shall lead it."

"I would sooner lead with Lady Ayr," said Berts. "Nadine always forgets everything——"

"Oh, Hendrick's, is it?" said Dodo. "Yes, Lady Chesterford. I am really, and I want a band for the evening of December the 1st. No, not a waist-band. Music. Yes, send somebody round."

Dodo put down the ear-piece.

"Let us strive not to do several things together," she said. "For the moment we will concentrate on the cotillion. Jack, dear, why did you suggest I should lead? It has led to so much talking, of which I have had to do the largest part."

"I want you to," he said. "I'll take you to Egypt in the spring, if you will. I won't otherwise."

"Darling, you are too unfair for words. You want to make an ass of me. You want everybody to say, 'Look at that silly old grandmamma!'—I probably shall be a grandmamma quite soon, if Nadine is going to marry Seymour in January—'Silly old grandmamma,' they will say, 'capering about like a two-year old.' Because I shall caper: if I lead, I shan't be able to resist kicking up."

Jack came across the room and sat on the table by her.

"Don't you want to lead, Dodo?" he asked quietly.

"Yes, darling, I should love to. I only wanted pressing. Oh, my beloved Berts, what larks! We'll have hoops, and snow-balls, and looking-glass, and woolly-bear—don't you know woolly-bear?—and paper-bags and obstacles and balance. And then the very next day I shall settle down, and behave as befits my years and riches and honour. I am old and Jack is rich, and has endowed me with all his worldly goods, and we are both strictly honourable. But I feel it's a hazardous experiment. If I hear somebody saying, as no doubt I shall, 'Surely, Lady Chesterford is a little old?' I shall collapse in the middle of the floor, and burst into several tears. And then I shall wipe my eyes, both of them if both have cried, and if not one, and say 'Beloved Berts, come on!' And on we shall go."

"You haven't asked Hugh yet," said Miss Grantham, looking at the list.

"Nadine did," said Dodo. "He said he wasn't certain. They argued."

"They do," said Berts. "Aunt Dodo, may I come to dine this evening, and have a practice afterwards?"

"Yes, my dear. Are you going? Till this evening then."

Dodo turned to Jack, and spoke low.

"Oh, Jack," she said, "Waldenech's in town. Nadine saw him yesterday."

"Glad I didn't," said Jack.

"I'm sure you are, darling. But here we all are, you know. You can't put him out like a candle. About the dance, I mean. I think I had better ask him. He won't come, if I ask him."

"He won't come anyhow," said Jack.

"You can't tell. I know him better than you. He's nasty, you know, poor dear. If I didn't ask him, he might come. He might think he ought to have been asked, and so come instead. Whereas, if he was asked, he would probably think it merely insulting of me, and so stop at home."

"Don't whisper to each other," said Edith loudly. "I can't bear a husband and wife whispering to each other. It looks as if they hadn't got over the honeymoon. Dodo, I haven't had a single word with you yet——"

"Darling Edith, you haven't. If you only would go to the other end of the telephone, I would talk to you for hours, simply to thwart the 'please miss' who asks if we haven't done yet. The only comfortable conversation is conducted on the telephone. Then you can say 'hush' to everybody else, in the room. Indeed, it isn't usually necessary to say 'hush.' Anybody with a proper interest in the affairs of other people always listens to what you say, trying to reconstruct what the inaudible voice says. Jack was babbling down the telephone the other day, when I particularly wanted to talk, but when he said 'Never let him shave her again,' how could I interrupt?"

"Did he shave her again?" asked Miss Grantham. "Who was she?"

"You shouldn't have said that," said Dodo, "because now I have to explain. It was the poodle, who had been shaved wrong, and she had puppies soon after, and they probably all had hair in the unfashionable places. Please talk to each other, and not about poodles. Jack and I have a little serious conversation to get through."

"I will speak," said Edith, "because it matters to me. We've let our house, Dodo—at least Bertie let it, and has gone to Bath, because he is rheumatic. Berts can stay at the Bath Club, because he isn't, but I want to stay with you."

"This house is becoming like Basle railway-station," remarked Jack.

"Yes, dear. Every proper house in town is," said Dodo. "A house in London isn't a house, it is a junction. People dine and lunch, and sleep if they have time. I haven't. Yes, Edith, do come. Jack wants you to, too, only he doesn't say so, because he is naturally reticent."

Edith instantly got up.

"Then may I have some lunch at once?" she said. "Cold beef will do. But I have a rehearsal at half-past one."

The telephone bell rang and Dodo took up the ear-piece.

"No, Lady Chesterford is out," she said. "But who is it? No; she hasn't come in yet. What? No; she isn't expected at all. She is quite unexpected."

She replaced the instrument.

"I recognised his voice, Jack," she said, "it was Waldenech, and I oughtn't to have said I was unexpected, because perhaps he will guess. But he sounded a bit thick, don't they say? Yes, dear Edith, have some cold beef, because it is much nicer than anything else. I shall come and have lunch in one minute, too, as I didn't have any breakfast. Take Grantie away with you, and I will join you."

"I won't have cold beef, whatever happens," said Grantie.

Dodo turned round, facing Jack, as soon as the others had left the room, and laid her hand on his knee.

"Jack, I feel sure I am right," she said. "I don't want Waldenech here any more than you do. But, after all, he is Nadine's father. I wish Madge or Belle or somebody who writes about society would lay down for us the proper behaviour for re-married wives towards their divorced husbands."

"I can tell you the proper behaviour of divorced husbands towards re-married wives," said Jack.

"Yes, darling, but you must remember that Waldenech has nothing to do with proper behaviour. He always behaved most improperly. If he hadn't, I shouldn't be your wife now. I think that must be an instance of all things working together for good, as St. Peter says."

"Paul," remarked Jack.

"Very likely, though Peter might be supposed to know most about wives. Jack, dear, let us settle this at once, because I am infernally hungry, and the thought of Edith eating cold beef makes me feel home-sick. I think I had much better ask Waldenech to our dance. There he is: I've known him pretty well, and it's just because he is nothing more than an acquaintance now, that I wish to ask him. To ask him will show the—the gulf between us."

Jack shook his head.

"I prefer to show the gulf by not asking him," he said.

Dodo frowned, and tapped the skirt of her riding-habit with her whip. She was rather tired and very hungry, for she had been playing bridge till two o'clock the night before, and had got up at eight to go out riding, and, meaning to have breakfast afterwards, had found herself plunged in the arrangements for her ball, which had lasted without intermission till this moment. But she felt unwilling to give this point up, unless Jack absolutely put his foot down with regard to it.

"I think I am right," she said. "He is rather a devil."

"All the more reason for not asking him."

"Do you mean that you forbid me to invite him?" she asked.

He thought for a moment.

"Yes, I forbid you," he said.

Dodo got up at once, flicked him in the face with the end of her riding-whip, and before he had really time to blink, kissed him on exactly the same spot, which happened to be the end of his nose.

"That is finished, then," she said, in the most good-humoured voice. "And now I have both the whip and the whip-hand. If anything goes wrong, darling, I shall say, 'I told you so,' till you wish you had never been born."

He caught her whip and her hands in his.

"You couldn't make me wish that," he said.

Her whole face melted into a sunlight of adorable smiles.

"Oh, Jack, do you really mean that?" she asked. "And because of me?"

He pulled her close to him.

"I suppose I should mean in spite of you," he said. "Go and eat with that ogre Edith. And then, darling, will you rest a little? You look rather tired."

She raised her eyes to his.

"But I am tired," she said. "It would be a disgrace not to be tired every day. It would show you hadn't made the most of it."

"I don't like you to be tired," he said, "especially since it isn't lunch-time yet. You haven't got much more to do to-day, I hope."

"But lots, and all so jolly. Oh, my dear, the world is as full as the sea at high-tide. It would be wretched not to fling oneself into it. But it is only high-tide till after my dance. Then we go down to Meering, and snore, and sleep like pigs, and eat like kittens, and sprout like mushrooms."

"You've asked a houseful there," objected Jack.

"Yes, darling, but it's only people like you and Esther and Hugh. I shan't bother about you."

"Is Hugh coming there?" he asked.

"Yes. He goes abroad directly afterwards, as he has exchanged from the Foreign Office into the Embassy at Rome for six months. He is wise, I think. He doesn't want to be here when Nadine is married, nor for some time afterwards. But he wants to see her again first."

"The rest is wise," said Jack, "but that is abominably foolish."

"Perhaps it is, but how one hates a young man to be altogether wise. A wise young man is quite intolerable. In fact wisdom generally is intolerable. It would be intolerable of me to lie down after lunch, and not eat and drink what I chose. You would be intolerable if you didn't make yourself so utterly foolish about me. Oh, Jack, let us die if necessary, but don't let us be wise before that."

Jack had nothing to say to this remarkable aspiration, and Dodo went out to join Edith. But he sat still on the edge of the table after she had gone, not altogether at ease. During the last month or so, he had several times experienced impulses, not to be accounted for rationally, which had made him ask her if she felt quite well, and now that he collected these occasions in his mind, he could not recollect any very reassuring response on her part. She had told him not to fuss; she had stood before him, radiant, brilliant, and said, "*Do* I look particularly unwell? Why do you want to spoil the loveliest time of all my life?" But she did not seem to have given him any direct answer at all, and the cumulative effect of those possible evasions troubled him a little. But he soon told himself that such cloud was born of his imagination only, for it was impossible to conceive, when he let himself contemplate the memory of those days since last July, that there could be anything wrong behind them, in so serene a beneficence of happiness were they wrapped. He had never dreamed that the world held such store, and he had not ever so faintly realized how jejune and barren his life had been before. He, for all his fifty years, had not yet lived one half of them, for less than half himself had passed through the months that made them up. It was as if all his life he had dreamed, dreamed with God knew what shocks and catastrophes that Dodo was his, and last July only he had awoke to find that his arms were indeed about her, and that she herself was pressed close to him. And she, too, had told him that she was happy, not pleased merely, or excited or thrilled, but happy. Incredible as it seemed to his modest soul, her happiness was one with his. It seemed there was nothing left to ask God for; the only possible attitude was to stand up and praise and thank Him. Jack did that every day and night that passed.

Dodo, when she left her husband, had not gone straight to the dining-room to join Edith and the cold beef. For half-an-hour before, she had been conscious of a queer faintness and feeling of sickness that had made it an effort to continue enthusiastically telephoning and arguing. It seemed probable to her that it was merely the result of a rather strenuous morning without any food except the slice of bread and butter that had accompanied her early bedroom tea, but she thought that she would go upstairs and have her hot bath, and perhaps rest a little before she went downstairs again. Her bathroom, which opened out of her bedroom, was prepared for her, the water steaming and smelling of the delicious verbena-salts which her maid had put into it, and convinced that she would feel perfectly fit again after it, she quickly undressed, and went in with bare feet to enjoy herself. But even as she took off her dressing-gown, the sickness came on again with violent and overmastering qualms, unaccountable, rather alarming. But before long it passed off, and she was herself again, though still rather white and tremulous. It left her a little uneasy . . . she could not understand the suddenness of her indisposition. However, it had gone now, and instinctively obeying the habit of years, she swiftly turned her mind to contemplate the thoroughly delightful things that lay in front of her, rather than the disturbing moment that had passed now, leaving only a black patch in memory. But before she slipped into the hot, aromatic water, she wiped the sweat from her forehead. She splashed the steaming water over her back, wriggling a little at the touch of it.

"Oh, Lord, how nice," she said to herself, "and it's so hot that it's hardly possible to bear it. And that reminds me that I utterly forgot to say my prayers this morning, because I was in such a hurry. Anyone would have been on such a lovely morning, with such a lovely horse waiting at the door. But I am having the nicest time that anybody ever had, and I'll try not to be quite such a disgrace as I used to be."

Dodo gave a loud sigh of reverent content and splashed again. It must be understood that she was saying her forgotten prayers.

"And Jack's a perfect darling," she went on, "and I am so pleased to love somebody. I never really loved anybody before, if you know what I mean by love, except, perhaps, Nadine. It makes the most tremendous difference, and one doesn't think about one's self absolutely all the time, though I daresay very nearly. Of course I was always fond of people, but I think that was chiefly because they were mostly so nice to me. I must go to church next Sunday, which is to-morrow, and do all this properly, but it would have been much more convenient if it had been the day after to-morrow, as I think I promised Jack to play golf with him to-morrow. But I'll see what can be done. Now I've dropped the soap, and isn't everything extraordinarily mixed up? Oh, and I would much sooner not be so sick again, if it's all the same . . ."

Dodo dropped the soap which she had just rescued from the bottom of the cloudy water, and looked up with bright eyes. A sudden idea, wonderful, incredible, luminous, had dawned on her.

"Oh, my dear, can it be that?" she said aloud. "Is it possible?"

She recollected that she had said "my dear" when she was by way of saying her forgotten prayers, and so added "Amen" very loudly and piously. Then, quite revivified, she got out, dried herself with great speed, and went downstairs half-dressed with an immense fur-coat to cover deficiencies, since it was impossible to wait any longer for food. She felt no fatigue any more, but a sudden intense eagerness at the thought of what possibly her indisposition might mean. It seemed almost incredible, but she found herself longing for a return of that which had frightened her before.

It was impossible for her to cram any more engagements into that day, since they already fitted into each other like the petals of a rose not yet fully blown, but she made an appointment with her doctor for next morning. The interview was not a long one, but Dodo came out from it, wreathed in smiles, immensely excited, and hurried home, where she went straight up to Jack's room. She seized him with both hands, and kissed him indiscriminately.

"Oh, my dear, you can't possibly guess," she said, "because it is quite too ridiculous, and only a person like me could possibly have done anything of the kind, and you're Zecharias, but you needn't be dumb. Oh, Jack, don't you see. Yes; it's that. I'm gong to have a baby. There! I was—well—exceedingly Channel-steamer yesterday, and at first I didn't guess. I thought I was only being unwell. Did you ever hear anything so nice, and I am a very wonderful woman, aren't I, and pray God it will be a boy. Oh, Jack, think how bored I was with the bearing of my first child! I didn't deserve it, and you used to come and cheer me up. And then, poor little innocent, it was taken from me. Poor little chap; he would have been Lord Chesterford now instead of you, if he had lived. Won't it seem funny giving birth to the same baby, so to speak, twice? Ah, my dear, but it's not the same! It's your child this time, Jack, and I shan't be bored this time. You see, I didn't really become a woman at all till lately. I was merely a sprightly little devil, and so I suppose God is giving me another chance. Jack, it simply must be a boy; I shall love to hear Lord Harchester cry this time."

Jack, though informed that he needn't be like Zecharias, had been dumb because there was no vacant moment to speak in. The news had amazed and astounded him.

"Oh, Dodo!" he said. "Next to yourself, that is the best gift of all. But I'm not sure I forgive you, for suspecting you were ill, and not telling me."

"Then I shall get along quite nicely without your forgiveness," said she. "Forgiveness, indeed! Or will it be twins? Wouldn't that be exciting? But a boy anyhow; I've ordered him, and he shall have one blue eye because he's yours and one brown one because he's mine, and so he'll be like a Welsh collie, and everyone will say 'What a pretty little dog; does he bite?' Jack, I hope he'll be rather a rip when he grows up, and make love to other people's wives. I suppose I oughtn't to wish that, but I can't help it. I like a boy with a little dash in him. He shall be about as tall as you, but much better looking, and, oh, to think that I once had a boy before, and didn't care! My conscience! I care now, and only yesterday I said I should probably soon be a grandmother, and now I've got to leave out the grand, and be just a humble mother first. I'm not humble; I'm just as proud as I can stick together."

Suddenly this amazing flood of speech stopped, and Dodo grew dim-eyed, and laid her head on her husband's shoulder.

" 'My soul doth magnify the Lord!' " she whispered.

The night of Dodo's ball had arrived, and she was going to lead the cotillion, but not dance more than she felt to be absolutely necessary. She had told everybody what was going to happen to her, in strict privacy, which was clearly the best way of keeping it secret for the present. Since she was not going to dance more than a step or two she had put on all the jewels she could manage to attach to herself, including the girdle of great emeralds that Waldenech had given her. This was a magnificent adornment, far too nice to give back to him when she divorced him, and she meant to let Nadine have it, as soon as she could bear to part with it herself, which did not seem likely to happen in the immediate future. It consisted of large square stones set in brilliants, and long pear-shaped emeralds depended from it. Jack had once asked her how she could bear to wear it, and she had said "Darling, when emeralds are as big as that, they help you to bear a good deal. They make a perfect Spartan of me." In other respects she wore what she called the "nursery fender," which was a diamond crown so high that children would have been safe from falling over it into the fire, the famous Chesterford pearls, and a sort of breast-plate of rubies, like the high-priest.

"I suppose it's dreadfully vulgar to wear so many jewels," she said to Jack, as they took their stand at the top of the stairs, where Dodo intended to remain and receive her guests, as long as she could bear not being in the ball-room, "but most people who have got very nice stones like me, I notice, are vulgar. The truly-refined people are those who have got three garnets and one Oriental zircon. They also say that big pearls, great eggs like these, are vulgar, and seed-pearls tasteful. What a word 'tasteful'! And they talk of people being very simply and exquisitely dressed. Thank God, no one can say I'm simply dressed to-night. I'm not; I'm the most elaborate object for miles round. Jack, when my baby——Dear Lady Ayr, how nice to see you, and Esther and John. Seymour dined here, and he has been taking notes of our clothes for the new paper called 'Gowns.'"

As in the old days when Dodo piped, the world danced, and to-night she was as vital, as charged with that magnetism that spreads enjoyment round itself more infectiously than influenza, as ever. Her beauty too was like a rose, full-blown, but without one petal yet fallen; and she stood there, in the glory of her incomparable form, jewelled and superb, a Juno decked for a feast among the high gods. All the world of her friends streamed up the stairs to be welcomed by that wonderful smiling face, and many instead of going in to the ball-room waited round the balustrade at the stair-head watching her. By degrees the tide of arriving guests slackened, and she turned to Jack.

"Jack, dear, the band is turning all my blood into champagne, and I can't cork it," she said. "However, champagne oughtn't to be corked. Come and have one turn with me round the ball-room. Why are they all standing about, instead of going to dance? Do they want to be shewn how? Just once round, or perhaps twice, and then I will stop quiet until the cotillion."

Dodo suddenly knit her eyebrows, and looked sharply down into the hall below.

"I was right, and you were wrong," she said. "There's Waldenech just come in. He is not going to come upstairs. Wait here for me."

Jack stepped forward.

"No, that's for me to do," he said.

Dodo laid her hand on his arm.

"Do as I tell you, my dear," she said. "Wait here; it won't take me a minute."

She went straight down into the hall: all smiles and gaiety had left her face, but its vitality was quite unimpaired. The colour that was in her cheeks had left them, but it was not fear that had driven it away, but anger. He was just receiving a ticket for his hat and coat, and she went straight up to him.

"Waldenech, take your hat and coat, and go away," she said. "You must have come to the wrong house; you were not asked here."

He turned at the sound of her voice, and looked up at her.

"You incomparable creature," he said rather thickly. "You pearl!"

"Give the Prince his hat and coat," said Dodo. "Now go, Waldenech, before I disgrace you. I mean it; if you do not go quietly and at once, you shall be turned out."

His eyes wandered unsteadily from her face to her bosom, and down to her waist where the great girdle gleamed and shone.

"You still wear the jewels I gave you," he said.

Dodo instantly undid the clasp, and the girdle fell on to the carpet.

"I do not wear them any more," she said. "Take them, and go."

He stood there for a moment without moving, while the duel between their wills fought itself out. Then he bent down and picked the girdle up.

"I ask your pardon most humbly," he said. "I am a gentleman, really. Please let me see you put the girdle on again, before I go; and say you forgive me. Also, if your husband knows I am here, ask his pardon for me also."

Some great wave of pity came over Dodo, utterly quenching her anger.

"Oh, Waldenech, you have all my forgiveness, my dear," she said. "But take the jewels."

"I ask you to give me that sign of your forgiveness," he said.

Dodo smiled at him.

"Fasten it yourself, then," she said.

His fingers halted over this, but in a moment he had found and secured the clasp.

"Good-night," he said.

The whole scene had lasted not more than a minute, and scarcely half a dozen people had seen her speaking to him, or knew who he was. Berts, who had just arrived, was one of these. Dodo turned to him.

"Ah, there you are, Berts," she said. "We are going to begin the cotillion exactly at twelve. Yes, poor dear Waldenech looked in, but he couldn't stop. You might remember not to tell Nadine. And why wasn't Edith here for dinner? Or isn't she staying here now? Now I come to think of it, I haven't seen her all day."

"She left your house yesterday," said Berts, "and I've just left her at home eating a chop and correcting proofs of a part-song. She was also singing. She's coming though, and says she will lead the cotillion with me, as she's sure you oughtn't to. She didn't say why."

"What incomparable delicacy!" said Dodo. "Come upstairs, Bertino."

Dodo went up to Jack.

"He went like a lamb, poor dear," she said, "though I thought for a moment he was going to stop like a lion. It gave me a little heart-ache, Jack, for, after all, you know——Now we are going twice round the ball-room. It isn't much of a heart-ache, it's only a little one, and I expect it will soon stop."

This, it may be expected, was the case, for certainly Dodo did not behave as if she had any kind of ache, however little, anywhere, and, whether she danced or sat still, she was the sun and centre of the brilliant scene. Wall-flowers raised their heads on her approach, and were galvanized into vitality. She ordained that there should be a waltz in which nobody should take part who was not over forty, led off herself with Lord Ayr, who had not had a wink of sleep all evening, and was far too much surprised to be capable of resistance, and convinced him that his dancing days were not nearly over yet. All manner of women who hoped that nobody dreamed that they were more than thirty-five at the most followed her, reckless of the antiquity which they had publicly and irrevocably acknowledged, while Edith Arbuthnot, arriving in the middle of this, and being quite unable to find a disengaged gentleman of suitable years, pirouetted up and down the room all by herself, until she clawed hold of Jack, who was taking the breathless Lady Ayr to get some strictly unalcoholic refreshment.

"I don't know how I came to do it," said this lady to Esther, as she drank her lemonade. "I haven't danced for years. Somehow I feel as if it was Lady Chesterford's fault. She has got into everybody's head, it seems to me. We're all behaving like boys and girls. Fancy Ayr dancing, too! Ayr, I saw you dancing."

Lord Ayr had come in with Dodo, at the end of this, unutterably briskened up.

"And I saw you dancing, my dear," he said. "And I hope you feel all the better for it, because I do."

"We all do," said Dodo, "and we'll all do it again. Now I want everything at once, a cigarette and an ice and a glass of champagne and Berts. Esther, be angelic and fetch me Berts. Don't tell him only I want him, but fetch him. Oh Jack, isn't it fun; yes, darling, we're going to begin the cotillion immediately, and I'm going to be ever so quiet. Edith, it was dear of you to offer to take my place, but I wouldn't give it up to Terpsichore herself or even Salome. Jack dear, go and make everyone sit down in two rows round the ball-room, and if anybody finds a rather large diamond about, it's probably mine, though I never wrote my name on it. . . . Wasn't it careless? It resembles the Koh-i-noor. Oh, Berts, there you are. Now don't lose your head, but give all the plainest women the most favours. Then the pretty ones will easily see the plan, and the plain ones won't. It's the greatest happiness for the plainest number."

Certainly it was the most successful cotillion. As Dodo had arranged, all the more unattractive people got chosen first, and all the more attractive, as Dodo had foreseen, saw exactly what was happening. The style was distinctly anti-Leap-year and in the mirror figure men, instead of women, rejected the faces in the glass, and Lord Ayr had nothing whatever to say to his wife, who was instantly accepted by Jack. And at the end, a skirmishing section of the band preceding, they danced through the entire house, from cellar to garret. They waltzed through drawing-rooms and dining-room, and up the stairs, and through Dodo's bedroom, and through Jack's dressing-room, where his pyjamas were lying on his bed (Berts put them on, *en passant*), and into cul-de-sacs, and impenetrable servants' rooms. And somehow it was Dodo all the time who inspired these childish orgies; those near her saw her, those behind danced wildly after her to catch sight of her. There was no accounting for it, except in the fact that while she was enjoying herself so enormously, it was impossible not to enjoy too. Sometimes it was she shrieking "Yes, straight on," sometimes it was her laugh-choked voice, saying "No, don't go in there," but the fact that she was leading them, with her nursery fender, and her vitality, and her ropes of pearls, and her complete *abandon* to the spirit of dancing, with Berts for partner in Jack's pyjamas, made a magnet that it was impossible not to follow. They passed through bedroom and attic, they went twice round the huge kitchen, where the chef, at Dodo's imperious command, laid down his culinary implements (which at the moment meant, in short Saxon speech, an ice-pail) and joined the dance with the first kitchen-maid. Then Dodo saw a footman standing idle, and called to him "Take my maid, William," and William with a broad grin, embraced a perfectly willing French woman of great attractions, and joined in the dance. Like the fairies in Midsummer Night's Dream, they danced the whole house through, Dodo with Berts, the chef with the kitchen-maid, William with Dodo's maid, Lord Ayr with Nadine, Lady Ayr with somebody whom nobody knew by sight, and had probably come there intentionally by mistake, and the first twenty couples or so finished up in the cellar. This, though it seemed improvised, had been provided for, and there were cane-chairs to rest in, and bottles instantly opened. The rest, following the band, danced their way back to the supper-room, where they were almost immediately joined by the cellar-party, who were hungry as well as thirsty, and had nothing to eat down below.

It was between three and four o'clock that the last guests took their ways. As the dance had been announced to take place from ten till two, the cordial spirit of the invitation had been made good. And at length Dodo found herself alone with Jack.

"Lovely, just lovely," she said, as he unclasped her diamond collar. "Oh, Jack, what a darling world it is."

"Not tired?"

Dodo faced round, and her brilliance and freshness was a thing to marvel at.

"Look at me!" she said. "Tell me if I look tired!"

He laid the collar down on her table; her neck seemed to him so infinitely more beautiful than the gorgeous bauble with which it had been covered.

"Not very. Ah, Dodo, and this is the best of all, when they have all gone, and you are left."

She put her face up to his.

"Why, of course," she said. "Do you suppose I wasn't looking forward to this one minute alone with you all the evening? I was, my dear, though if I said I thought of it all the time, I should be telling a silly lie. But it was anchored firmly in my mind all the time. Oh, what pretty speeches for a middle-aged old couple to make to each other! But the fact is that we get on very nicely together. Good-night, old boy. It's all too lovely. Oh Daddy! Fancy becoming Daddy! Oh, by the way, did Hugh come? I didn't see him."

"Yes, he sat out a couple of dances with Nadine, and then went away."

"Poor old chap!" said Dodo.

As has been mentioned Dodo proposed to take her family and a great many other people as well to spend Christmas down at Meering, which at this inclement time of the year often had spells of warm and genial weather. Scattered through the same weeks there were to be several shooting-parties at Winston, but motorcars driven at a sufficiently high speed would make light of the difficulty of being in two places at the same time, and on the day after the dance she talked these arrangements over with Nadine.

"In any case," she said, "you can be hostess in one house and I in the other, so that we can be in two places at once quite easily, so Jack is wrong as usual. Jack, dear, I said, 'as usual.' "

Jack got up; it was he who had made the ill-considered remark that you can't be in two places at once.

"I heard," he said, "and you may hear, too, that I will not have you going up to North Wales every other day, and flying down again the next. Otherwise you may settle what you like. Personally I shall be at Winston almost all the time, as there's a heap of business to be done, and as Nadine hates shooting-parties——"

"Oh, a story!" said Nadine.

"Well, my dear, you always do your best to spoil them by making a large quantity of young gentlemen, who have been asked to shoot, sit round you and talk to you instead."

"Papa Jack, if you want to call me a flirt, pray do so. I will forgive you instantly. And to save you trouble, I will tell you what you are driving to——"

"At," said Jack.

"Driving to," repeated Nadine with considerable asperity, for she was aware she was wrong. "You want me to be at Meering, and Mamma to be at Winston. So why not say so without calling me a flirt?"

"This daughter of Eve——" began Jack.

"My name is Dorothea," interrupted Dodo, "but they call me Dodo for short. I was never called Eve either before, during, or after baptism."

"All I mean," said Jack, "is that Dorothea is not going to divide the week into week-ends, and be twenty-four hours at Meering and then twenty-four hours at Winston. The master of the house has spoken."

"What a bully!" said Nadine.

"Then I shan't give you a wedding-present," said Jack.

"Darling Papa Jack you are not a bully. Let's all go down to Meering in a few days, and stop there over Christmas. Then you and Dorothea shall go to Winston, and I shall be left all alone at Meering, and you shall have your horrid shooting parties and she shall do the flirting instead of me."

"Strictly speaking, will you be all alone at Meering?"

"Not absolutely. I have asked a few friends."

"Who is going to chaperone you all, darling?" said Dodo.

"We shall chaperone each other, as usual."

"That you and Dodo can settle," said Jack. "Good-bye: don't quarrel."

"Indeed that will be all right, Mamma," said Nadine, "or I daresay Edith would come. Anyhow, we were often all together before like that in the summer."

"Yes, my dear, but it's a little different now," said Dodo. "You are engaged to Seymour, and Hugh is going to be there, too."

"Yes, but that makes it all the simpler."

Dodo got up.

"I wonder if you realize that Seymour is in love with you," she said. "In love with you like Hugh is, I mean."

"Perfectly, and he is charming about it," said Nadine. "And I practise every morning being in love with him like that. I think I am getting on very well. I dreamed about him last night. I thought he gave me a great box of jade and when I opened it, there was a rabbit inside——"

"That shows great progress," said Dodo.

"Mamma, I think you are laughing at me. But what would you have? I am very fond of him, he is handsome and clever and charming. I expected to find it tiresome when he told me he was in love like that, but it is not the least so!"

Memories of the man she had married when she was even younger than Nadine, came unbidden into Dodo's mind; she remembered her first husband's blind dog-like devotion and her own *ennui* when he strove to express it, to communicate it to her.

"Nadine," she said, "treat it reverently, my dear. There is nothing in the world that a man can give a woman that is to be compared to that. It is better than a rabbit in a jade-box. When I was even younger than you Papa Jack's cousin gave it me, and—and I didn't reverence it. Don't repeat my irreparable error."

"Weren't you nice to him?" asked Nadine.

"I was a brute-beast to him, my darling."

"Oh, I shan't be a brute-beast to Seymour," said Nadine. "Besides I don't suppose you were. You didn't know; wasn't that all?"

Dodo wiped the mist from her eyes.

"No, that wasn't nearly all. But be tender with it, and pray, oh, my dear, pray that you may catch that—that noble fever. Who calls it that? It is so true. And Hughie? I never saw him last night."

Nadine made a little gesture of despair.

"Ah, dear Hughie," she said. "That is not very happy. That is so

largely why I wanted to marry Seymour quickly, in January instead
of later, so that it may be done, and Hughie will not fret any more.
I hate seeing him suffer. And I can't marry him. It would not be fair;
it would be cheating him, as I told him before."

"But are you not cheating Seymour?" asked Dodo.

"Not in the same way. He is not simple like Hugh. Hugh has only
one thought; Seymour has plenty of others. He has such a mind; it
is subtle and swift like a woman's. Hughie has the mind of a great
retriever dog, and the eyes of one. There is all the difference in the
world between them. Seymour knows what he is in for, and still wants
it. Hugh thinks he knows, but he doesn't. I understand Hugh so well;
I know I am right. And I would have given anything to be able to
be in love with him. It was a pity!"

There was something here that Dodo had not known and there was
a dangerous sound about it.

"Do you mean you wish you were in love with Hugh?" she asked.

"Oh, yes, Mamma, but I'm not. I used to practise trying to be for
months and months, just as I am practising for Seymour now. La, la,
what a world!"

Nadine paused a moment.

"Of course I've quite stopped practising being in love with Hugh
since I was engaged to Seymour," she said with an air of the most
candid virtue—"That *would* be cheating."

Nadine got up looking like a tall white lily.

"Seymour is so good for me," she said. "He doesn't think much of
my brain, you know, and I used to think a good deal of it. He doesn't
say I'm stupid, but he hasn't got the smallest respect for my mind. I
am not sure whether he is right, but I expect seeing so much of Hugh
made me think I was clever. I wonder if being in love makes people
stupid. He himself seems to me to be not quite so subtle as he was,
and perhaps it's my fault. What do you think, Mamma?"

9

It was the morning after Christmas Day, and Dodo and Jack
had just driven off from Meering on their way to Winston, where a
shooting party was to assemble that day, leaving behind them a party
that regretted their departure, but did not mean to repine. Edith Arbuthnot had promised to arrive two days before, to take over from Dodo
the duty of a chaperone, but she had not yet come, nor had anything
whatever been heard of her.

"Which shows," said Berts lucidly, "that nothing unpleasant can have happened to mother, or we should have heard."

Until she came Nadine had very kindly consented to act as regent, and in that capacity she appeared in the hall, a little while after Dodo had gone, with a large red contadina umbrella, a book or two, and an expressed determination to sit out on the hill-side till lunch-time.

"It is Boxing Day I know," she said, "but it is too warm to box, even if I knew how. The English climate has gone quite mad, and I have told my maid to put my fur coat in a box with those little white balls until May. Now I suppose you are all going to play the foolish game with those other little white balls till lunch."

Seymour was seated in the window-sill, stitching busily at a piece of embroidery which Antoinette had started for him.

"I am going to do nothing of the sort," he said. "It is much too fine a day to do anything. Besides, there is no one fit to play with. Nadine, will you be very kind and ring for my maid. I am getting in a muddle."

Berts, who was sitting near him, got up, looking rather ill. Also he resented being told he was not fit to play golf with.

"May I have my perambulator, please, Nadine?" he asked.

Seymour grinned.

"Berts, you are easier to get a rise out of than anyone I ever saw," he remarked. "It is hardly worth while fishing for you, for you are always on the feed. And if you attempt to rag I shall prick you with my needle."

Nadine lingered a little after the others had gone, and as soon as they were alone Seymour put down his embroidery.

"May I come and sit on the hill-side with you?" he asked. "Or is the—the box-seat already engaged?"

"Hugh suggested it," she said. "I was going out with him."

Seymour picked up his work again.

"It seems to me I am behaving rather nicely," he said. "At the same time I'm not sure that I am not behaving rather anaemically. I haven't seen you much since I came down here. And after all I didn't come down here to see Esther."

Nadine frowned, and laid her hand on his arm. But she did not do it quite instinctively. It was clear she thought it would be appropriate. Certainly that was quite clear to Seymour.

"Take that hand away," he said. "You only put it there because it was suitable. You didn't want to touch me."

Nadine removed her hand as if his coat-sleeve was red-hot.

"You are rather a brute," she said.

"No, I am not, unless it is brutal to tell you what you know already. I repeat that I am behaving rather nicely."

It was owing to him to do him so much justice.

"I know you are," she said, "you are behaving very nicely indeed. But it is only for a short time, Seymour. I don't mean that you won't always behave nicely, but that there are only a limited number of days on which this particular mode of niceness will be required of you, or be even possible. Hugh is going away next week, after that you and I will be Darby and Joan before he sees me again. You are all behaving nicely: he is too. He just wanted one week more of the old days, when we didn't think, but only babbled and chattered. I can't say that he is reviving them with very conspicuous success: he doesn't babble much, and I am sure he thinks furiously all the time. But he wanted the opportunity: it wasn't much to give him."

"Especially since I pay," said Seymour quickly.

He saw the blood leap to Nadine's face.

"I'm sorry," he said. "I oughtn't to have said that, though it is quite true. But I pay gladly: you must believe that also. And I'm glad Hugh is behaving nicely, that he doesn't indulge in—in embarrassing reflections. Also when does he go away?"

"Tuesday, I think."

"Morning?" asked Seymour hopefully.

Nadine laughed: he had done that cleverly, making a parody and a farce out of that which a moment before had been quite serious.

"You deserve it should be," she said.

"Then it is sure to be in the afternoon. Now I've finished being spitfire. I want to ask you something. You haven't been up to your usual form of futile and clannish conversation. You have been rather plaintive and windy——"

"Windy?" asked Nadine.

"Yes, full of sighs, and I should say it was Shakespeare. Are you worrying about anything?"

She looked up at him with complete candour.

"Why of course, about Hughie," she said. "How should I not?"

"I don't care two straws about that," said Seymour, "as long as your worrying is not connected with me. I mean I am sorry you worry, but I don't care. Of course you worry about Hugh. I understand that, because I understand what Hugh feels, and one doesn't like one's friends feeling like that. But it's not about you and me?"

Nadine shook her head and Seymour got up.

"Well, let us all be less plaintive," he said. "I have been rather plaintive too. I think I shall go and take on that great foolish Berts at golf. He will be plaintive afterwards, but nobody minds what Berts is. Will you give me a kiss, or would you rather not?"

"I don't mind," said Nadine.

Seymour very rudely put out his tongue at her. "Then, take, oh, take those lips away," he remarked.

Whatever plaintiveness there was about was certainly not shared by the weather, which, if it was mad, as Nadine had suggested, was possessed by a very genial kind of mania. An octave of spring-like days, with serene suns, and calm seas, and light breezes from the south-west had decreed an oasis in midwinter, warm halcyon days that made even in December the snow-drops and aconites to blossom humbly and bravely, and set the birds to busy themselves with sticks and straws as if nesting-time was already here. New grass already sprouted green among the greyness of last year's growth, and it seemed almost cynical to doubt that spring was not verily here. Indeed, where Hugh and Nadine sat this morning it was May, not March that seemed to have invaded and conquered December; there lay upon the hillside a vernal fragrance that set a stray bee or two buzzing round the honied sweetness of the gorse, with which the time of blossoming is never quite over, and to-day all the winds were still, and no breeze stirred in the bare, slender birches or set the spring-like stalks of the heather quivering. Only, very high up in the unplumbed blue of the zenith thin fleecy clouds lay stretched in streamers and combed feathers of white, shewing that far above rivers of air swept headlong and swift.

Nadine had a favourite nook on this steep hillside below the house, reached by a path that stretched out to the southern promontory of the bay. It was a little hollow, russet-coloured now with the bracken of the autumn and carpeted elsewhere by the short-napped velvet of the turf. Just in front the cliff plunged sheer on to the beach, where they had so often bathed in the summer, and where the reef of tumbled sandstone rocks stretched out on to the waveless sea like brown am-phibious monsters that were fish at high tide and grazing beasts at the ebb. Down there below a school of gulls hovered and fished with wheelings of white wings, but not a ripple lapped the edges of the rocks. Only the sea breathed softly as in sleep, stirring the fringes of brown weed that had gathered there, but no thinnest line of white shewed breaking water. Along the sandy foreshore of the bay there was the same stillness: heaven and earth and ocean lay under an en-chantment of quietude. The sand-dunes opposite and the hills beyond lay reflected in the sea, as if in the tranquility of some land-locked lake. There was a spell, a hush over the world, to be broken by God knew what gentle awakening of activity or catastrophic disturbance.

Hugh and she had walked to this withdrawn hollow of the hill almost in silence. He had offered to carry her books for her, but she had said that they were of no weight, and after a pause he had an-

nounced a fragment of current news to which she had no comment
to add, but had noticed the windless unnatural calm of the day. Something in this unusual stillness of weather had set her nerves a-quiver,
and perhaps the position she was in, bound as she was to Seymour,
not struggling against it, but quite accepting it, made ordinary intercourse difficult. For she had it all her own way; Hugh was behaving
with exemplary discretion, Seymour was behaving with admirable tolerance, and just because they both made her own part so easy for
her, she, womanlike, found the smoothed-out performance of it to
be difficult. Had she instructed each of them how to behave, her instructions were carried out to the letter's foot: they were impeccable as
lover and rejected lover, and therefore she wanted something different.
The situation was completely of her own making: her actors played
their parts exactly as she would have them play, and yet there was
something wanting. They were too well-drilled, too word-perfect, too
certain to say all she had designed for them from the right spot and
in the right voice. True, for a moment just now Seymour had shown
signs of individualism when he called attention to the fact that he
was behaving very nicely, and that he would be glad when the scene
was over, but Hugh had shown none whatever, except for the fact
that he had asked to be allowed a few days like the days of old before
he left England. He had assured her in the summer that he would
never seek to get back into the atmosphere of unthinking intimacy
again, but, poor fellow, when there were to be so few days left him
before the situation was sealed and made irrevocable his heart had
cried out against the edict of his will, and foolish though it might
be, he had asked for this week of Meering days. But from his point
of view, no less than from hers, they had been but a parody of what
he had hoped for, they had been frozen and congealed by the reserve
and restraint that he dared not break. Below that surface-ice he knew
how swiftly ran the torrent in his soul, but the ice quite stretched
from shore to shore. It was this which disappointed Nadine, for she
equally with Hugh had expected that he could realize the impossible,
and that he, loving her as he did, and knowing that she was so soon
to give herself to another man, could cast off the knowledge of that
and resume for a space the unshackled intimacy of old. The Ethiopian
and leopard would have found their appropriate feats far easier, for
it was Hugh's bones and blood he had to change, not mere skin and
hair, and the very strength of the bond that bound him to her made
the insuperableness of the barrier. He felt every moment the utter
failure of his attempt, while she, who thought she understood him
so well, had no notion how radical the failure was. Not loving, she
could not understand. He knew that now, and thought bitterly of

the little fireworks of words she had once lit for him on that same text, believing that by the light of those quick little squibs she could read his heart.

So, when they were settled in their nook, once again she tried to recapture the old ease. She pointed downwards over the edge of the cliff.

"Oh, Hughie, what a morning," she said. "Quiet sea and gulls, and bees and gorse. What a summer in December, a truce with winter, isn't it? I've brought a handful of nice books. Shall I read?"

"Oh, soon," said he. "But your summer in December isn't going to last long. There is a wind coming, and a big one. Look at the mares'-tails of clouds up above. Can't you smell the wind coming? I always can. And the barometer has dropped nearly an inch since last night."

He put back his head and sniffed, moving his nostrils rather like a horse.

"Oh, how fascinating," said Nadine. "If I do that shall I smell the wind?"

It made her sneeze instead.

"I don't think much of that," she said. "I expect you looked at the barometer before you smelt the wind. Besides, how is it possible to smell the wind before there is any wind to smell? And when it comes you feel it instead."

"It will be a big storm," said Hugh.

Even as he spoke some current of air stirred the surface of the sea below them, shattering the reflections. It was as if some great angel of the air had breathed on the polished mirror of the water, dimming it. Next moment the breath cleared away again, and the surface was as bright and unwavering as before. But some half-dozen of the gulls that had been hovering and chiding there rose into the higher air, leaving their feeding-ground, and after circling round once or twice, glided away over the sand-dunes inland. Almost immediately afterwards, another relay followed, and another, till the bay that had been so populous with birds was quite deserted. They did not pause in their flight, but went straight inland, in decreasing specks of white, till they vanished altogether.

"The gulls seem to think so, too," said Hugh.

"Then they are probably wrong," said Nadine. "The instincts Nature implants in animals are almost invariably incorrect. For instance, the Siberian tigers at the Zoo. For several years they never grew winter coats, and all the naturalists went down on their knees and said 'O wonderful Mother Nature: their instincts tell them this is a milder climate than Siberia.' But this winter, the mildest ever known, the poor things have grown the thickest winter coats ever seen. So all the naturalists had to get up again and dust their trousers where they had knelt down."

"Put your money on the gulls and me," said Hugh. "Look there again, far away along the sands."

To Nadine the most attractive feature about Hugh was his eyes. They had a far-away look in them that had nothing whatever spiritual or sentimental in it, but was simply due to the fact that he had extraordinarily long sight. She obediently screwed up her eyes and followed his direction, but saw nothing whatever of import.

"It's getting nearer; you'll see it soon," said Hugh.

Soon she saw. A whirlwind of sand was advancing towards them along the beach below, revolving giddily. As it came nearer they could see the loose pieces of seaweed and jetsam being caught up into it. It came forward in a straight line perhaps as fast as a man might run, getting taller as it approached and gyrating more violently. Then in its advance it came into collision with the wall of cliff on which they sat, and was shattered. They could hear, like the sound of rain, the sand and rubbish of which it was composed falling on the rocks.

"Oh, but did you invent that, Hughie?" she said. "It was quite a pretty trick. Was it a sign to this faithless generation, which is me, that you could smell the wind? Or did the gulls do it? Prophesy to me again!"

He lay back on the dry grass.

"Trouble coming, trouble coming," he said.

"Just the storm?" she asked. "Or is this more prophecy?"

"Oh, just the storm," he said. "I always feel depressed and irritated before a storm."

"Are you depressed and irritated?" she asked. "Sorry. I thought it was such a nice calm morning."

Hugh took up a book at random, which proved to be Swinburne's Poems and Ballads. At random he opened it, and saw the words:

> And though she saw all Heaven in flower above
>   She would not love.

"Oh, do read," said Nadine. "Anything; just where you opened it." Hugh sat up, a bitterness welling in his throat. He read:

> "And though she saw all Heaven in flower above
>   She would not love."

Nadine flushed slightly, and was annoyed with herself for flushing. She could not help knowing what must be in his mind, and tried to make a diversion.

"I don't think she was to be blamed," she said. "A quantity of flowers stuck all over the sky would look very odd, and I don't think would kindle anybody's emotions. That sounds rather a foolish poem. Read something else."

Hugh shut the book.

" 'Though all we fell on sleep, she would not weep,' is the end of another stanza," he said.

Nadine looked at him for a long moment, her lips parted as if to speak, but they only quivered; no words came. There was no doubt whatever as to what Hugh meant, but still, with love unwakened, and with her tremendous egotism rampant, she saw no further than that he was behaving very badly to her. He had come down here to renew the freedom and intimacy of old days; till to-day he had been silent, stupid, but when he spoke like this, silence and stupidity were better. She was sorry for him, very sorry, but the quiver of her lips half at least consisted of self-pity that he made her suffer too.

"You mean me," she said, speaking at length and speaking very rapidly. "It is odious of you. You know quite well I am sorry; I have told you so. I cried; I remember I cried when you made that visit to Winston, and the cow looked at me. I daresay you are suffering damned torments, but you are being unfair. Though I don't love you—like that, I wish I did. Do you think I make you suffer for my own amusement? Is it fun to see my best friend like that? Is it my fault? You have chosen to love this heartless person, me. If I had no liver, or no lungs, instead of no heart, you would be sorry for me. Instead you reproach me. Oh, not in words, but you meant me, when you said that. Where is the book out of which you read? There, I do that to it; I send it into the sea, and when the gulls come back they will peck it, or the sea will drown it first, and the wind which you smell will blow it to America. You don't understand; you are more stupid than the gulls."

She made one swift motion with her arm, and Poems and Ballads flopped in the sea as the book dived clear of the cliff into the water below.

More imminent than the storm which Hugh had prophesied was the storm in their souls. He, with his love baffled raged at the indifference with which she had given herself to another; she, distrusting for the first time, the sense and wisdom of her gift, raged at him for his rebellion against her choice.

"Don't speak," she said, "for I will tell you more things first. You are jealous of Seymour——"

Hugh threw back his head and laughed.

"Jealous of Seymour?" he cried. "Do you really think I would marry you if you consented in the spirit in which you are taking him? Once it is true, I wanted to. You refused to cheat me—those were your words—and I begged you to cheat me, I implored you to cheat me, so long as you gave me yourself. I didn't care how you took me, so long as you took me. But now I wouldn't take you like that. Now, for this last week, I have seen you and him together, and I know what it is like."

"You haven't seen us together much," said Nadine.

"I have seen you enough. I told you before that your marriage was a farce. I was wrong. It's much worse than a farce. You needn't laugh at a farce. But you can't help laughing, at least I can't, at a tragedy so ludicrous."

Nadine got up. The situation was as violent and sudden as some electric storm. What had been pent up in him all this week, had exploded; something in her exploded also.

"I think I hate you," she said.

"I am sure I despise you," said he.

He got up also, facing her. It was like the bursting of a reservoir; the great sheet of quiet water was suddenly turned into torrent and foam.

"I despise you," he said again. "You intended me to love you; you encouraged me to let myself go. All the time you held yourself in, though there was nothing to hold in; you observed, you dissected. You cut down with your damned scalpels and lancets to my heart, and said, 'How interesting to see it beating!' Then you looked coolly over your shoulder and saw Seymour, and said, 'He will do: he doesn't love me, and I don't love him!' But now he does love you, and you probably guess that. So, very soon, your lancet will come out again, and you will see his heart beating. And again you will say, 'How interesting!' But there will be blood on your lancet. You are safe, of course, from reprisals. No one can cut into you, and see your blood flow, because you haven't got any blood. You are something cold and hellish. You often said you understood me too well. Now you understand me even better. Toast my heart, fry it, eat it up! I am utterly at your mercy, and you haven't got any mercy. But I can manage to despise you; I can't do much else."

Nadine stood quite still, breathing rather quickly, and that movement of the nostrils, which she had tried to copy from him, did not make her sneeze now.

"It is well we should know each other," she said with an awful cold bitterness, "even though we shall know each other for so little time more. It is always interesting to see the real person——"

"If you mean me," he said hotly, "I always showed you the real person. I have never acted to you, nor pretended. And I have not changed. I am not responsible if you cannot see!"

Nadine passed her tongue over her lips. They seemed hard and dry, not flexible enough for speech.

"It was my blindness then," she said. "But we know where we are now. I hate you, and you despise me. We know now."

Then suddenly an impulse, wholly uncontrollable, and coming from she knew not where, seized and compelled her. She held out both her hands to him.

"Hughie, shake hands with me," she said. "This has been nightmare talk, a bad thing that one dreams. Shake hands with me, and that will wake us both up. What we have been saying to each other is impossible; it isn't real or true. It is utter nonsense we have been talking."

How he longed to take her hands and clasp them and kiss them! How he longed to wipe off all he had said, all she had said. But somehow it was beyond him to do it. It was by honest impulse that the words of hate and contempt had risen to their lips; the words might be cancelled, but what could not be quenched, until some mistake was shown in the workings of their souls, was the thought-fire that had made them boil up. She stood there, lovely and welcoming, the girl whom his whole soul loved, whose conduct his whole soul despised, eager for reconciliation, yearning for a mutual forgiveness. But her request was impossible. God could not cancel the bitterness that had made him speak. He threw his hands wide.

"It's no good," he said. "I am sorry I said certain things, for there was no use in saying them. But I can't help feeling that which made me say them. Cancel the speeches by all means. Let the words be unsaid with all my heart."

"But let us be prepared to say them again," said Nadine quietly. "It comes to that."

"Yes, it comes to that. I am not jealous of Seymour. I laughed when you suggested it; and I am not jealous because you don't love him. If you loved him, I should be jealous, and I should say, 'God bless you!' As it is——"

"As it is, you say 'Damn you!'" said Nadine.

Hugh shook his head.

"You don't understand anything about love," he said. "How can you until you know a little bit what it means? I could no more think or say 'Damn you,' than I could say 'God bless you.'"

Nadine had withdrawn from her welcome and desire for reconciliation.

"Neither would make any difference to me," she said.

"I don't suppose they would, since I make no difference to you," said he. "But there is no sense in adding hypocrisy to our quarrel."

Nadine sat down again on the sweet turf.

"I cancel my words then, even if you do not," she said. "I don't hate you. I can't hate you, any more than you can despise me. We must have been talking in nightmare."

"I am used to nightmare," said Hugh. "I have had six months of nightmare. I thought that I could wake; I thought I could—could pinch myself awake by seeing you and Seymour together. But it's still nightmare."

Nadine looked up at him.

"Oh, Hughie, if I loved you!" she said.

Hugh looked at her a moment, and then turned away from her. Outside of his control certain muscles worked in his throat; he felt strangled.

"I can say 'God bless you' for that, Nadine," he said huskily. "I do say it. God bless you, my darling."

Nadine had leaned her face on her hands when he turned away. She divined why he turned from her; she heard the huskiness of his voice, and the thought of Hughie wanting to cry gave her a pang that she had never yet known the like of. There was a long silence, she sitting with hand-buried face, he seeing the sunlight swim and dance through his tears. Then he touched her on the shoulder.

"So we are friends again in spite of ourselves," he said. "Just one thing more then, since we can talk without hatred and contempt. Why did you refuse to marry me, because you did not love me, and yet consent to marry Seymour like that?"

She looked up at him.

"Oh, Hughie, you fool," she said. "Because you matter so much more."

He smiled back at her.

"I don't want to wish I mattered less," he said.

"You couldn't matter less."

He had no reply to this, and sat down again beside her. After a little Nadine turned to him.

"And I said I thought it was such a calm morning," she said.

"And I said that storm was coming," said he.

She laid her hand on his knee.

"And will there be some pleasant weather now?" she said. "Oh, Hughie, what wouldn't I give to get two or three of the old days back again, when we babbled and chattered and were so content?"

"Speak for yourself, Miss," said Hugh. "And for God's sake don't let us begin again. I shall quarrel with you again, and—and it gives me a pain. Look here, it's a bad job for me all this, but I came here to get an oasis; also to pinch myself awake: metaphors are confusing things. Bring on your palms and springs. They haven't put in an appearance yet. Let's try anyhow."

Nadine sat up.

"Talking of the weather——" she began.

"I wasn't."

"Yes you were, before we began to exchange compliments."

She broke off suddenly.

"Oh, Hughie, what has happened to the sun?" she said.

"I know it is the moon," said Hugh.

"You needn't quote that. The shrew is tamed for a time. Is a shrew-mouse a lady mouse with a foul temper, do you think? About the sun—look."

It was worth looking at. Right round it, two or three diameters away, ran a complete halo, a pale white line in the abyss of the blue sky. The little feathers of wind-blown clouds had altogether vanished, and the heavens were untarnished from horizon to zenith. But the heat of the rays had sensibly diminished, and though the sunshine appeared as wholehearted as ever, it was warm no longer.

"This is my second conjuring-trick," said Hugh. "I make you a whirlwind, and now I make you a ring round the sun, and cut off the heating apparatus. Things are going to happen. Look at the sea, too. My orders."

The sea was also worth looking at. An hour ago it had been turquoise blue, reflecting the sky. Now it seemed to reflect a moonstone. It was grey-white, a corpse of its previous self. Then even as they looked, it seemed to vanish altogether. The horizon line was blotted out, for the sky was turning grey also, and both above and below, over the cliff-edge, there was nothing but an invisible grey of clear emptiness. The sun halo spread both inwards and outwards, so that the sun itself peered like a white plate through some layer of vapour that had suddenly formed across the whole field of the heavens. And still not a whistle or sigh of wind sounded.

Hugh got up.

"As I have forgotten what my third conjuring trick is," he said, "I think we had better go home. It looks as if it was going to be a violent one."

He paused a moment, peering out over the invisible sea. Then there came a shrill faint scream from somewhere out in the dim immensity.

"Hold on to me, Nadine," he cried. "Or lie down."

He felt her arm in his, and they stood there together.

The scream increased in volume, becoming a maniac bellow. Then like a solid wall the wind hit them. It did not begin out of the dead calm as a breeze; it did not grow from breeze to wind, it came from seawards, like the waters of the Red Sea on the hosts of Pharaoh, an overwhelming wall of riot and motion. Nadine's books, all but the one she had cast over the cliff's edge, turned over, and lay with flapping pages, then like wounded birds they were blown along the hill-side. The hat she had brought out with her, but had not put on, rose straight in the air and vanished. Hugh, with Nadine on his arm, had leaned forward against this maniac blast, and the two were not thrown down by it. The path to the house lay straight up the steep hillside behind them, and turning they were so blown up it that they stumbled in trying to keep pace to that irresistible torrent of wind that hurried them along. It took them but five minutes to get up the steep brae, while it had taken them ten minutes to walk down, and already there flew past them seaweed and sand and wrack, blown up from the beach below. Above, the sun was completely veiled, a web of cloud had already obscured the higher air, but below all was clear, and it looked as if a stone could be tossed on to the hills on the further side of the bay.

They had to cross the garden before they came to the house. Already two trees had fallen before this hurricane-blast and even as they hurried over the lawn, an elm, screaming in all its full-foliaged boughs, leaned towards them and cracked and fell. Then a chimney in the house itself wavered in outline, and next moment it crashed down on to the roof, and a covey of flying tiles fell round them.

It required Hugh's full strength to close the door again after they had entered, and Nadine turned to him, flushed and ecstatic.

"Hughie, how divine," she said. "It can't be measured, that lovely force. It's infinite. I never knew there was strength like that. Why have we come in? Let's go out again. It's God; it's just God."

His eyes too were alight with it and his soul surged to his lips.

"Yes," he said. "And that's what love is like."

And then for the first time, Nadine understood. She did not feel, but she was able to understand.

"Oh, Hughie," she said, "I am an unlucky wretch."

10

The section of the party which had gone to play golf, fought their way home a few minutes later, and they all met at lunch. Edith Arbuthnot had arrived before any of them got back, and asked if the world had been blown away. As it had not, she expressed herself ready to chaperone anybody.

"And Berts is happy too," said Seymour, when he came in very late for lunch, since he wished to change all his clothes first, as they smelt of wind, "because Berts has at last driven a ball two hundred yards. Don't let us mention the subject of golf. It would be tactless. There was no wind when he accomplished that remarkable feat, at least not more wind than there is now. What there was was behind him, and he topped his ball heavily. I said 'Good shot.' But I have tact. Since I have tact, I don't say to Nadine that it was a good day to sit out on the hill-side and read. I would scorn the suggestion."

A sudden sound as of drums on the window interrupted this tactful speech, and the panes streamed.

"Anyhow I shall play golf," said Edith. "What does a little rain matter? I'm not made of paper."

"Yes, you are; music paper," said Berts.

"If you want to win a match, play with Berts," said Seymour pensively. "But if you only want to be blown away and killed, anybody will do. I shall get on with my embroidery this afternoon, and my maid will sit by me and hold my hand. Dear me, I hope the house is well built."

For the moment it certainly seemed as if this was not the case, for the whole room shook under a sudden gust more appalling than anything they had felt yet. Then it died away again, and once more the windows were deluged with sheets of rain flung, it seemed, almost horizontally against them. For a few minutes only that lasted, then stopped as if a tap had been turned, and the wind settled down to blow with a steady uniform violence.

Nadine had finished lunch and went across to the window. The air was perfectly clear, and the hills across the bay, ten miles distant, seemed again but a stone's throw away. Overhead, straight across the sky, stretched a roof of hard grey cloud, but away to the west, just above the horizon line, there was an arch of perfectly clear sky, of pale duck's-egg green, and out of this it seemed as out of a funnel the fury of the gale was poured. The garden was strewn with branches and battered foliage, and the long gravel path flooded by the tempest of rain was discharging itself on to the lawn, where pools of bright yellow water were spreading. Across the grass lay the wreck of the fallen trees, the splintered corpses of what but an hour ago had been secure and living things, waiting, warm and drowsy for the tingle of spring-time and rising sap. Like the bodies of young men on a battle-field, with their potentialities of love and life unfulfilled, there, by the blast of the insensate fury of the wind, they lay stricken and dead, and the birds would no more build in their branches, nor make their shadowed nooks melodious with love-songs. No more would summer clothe them in green, nor autumn in their liveries of gold, they were dead things and at the most would make a little warmth on the hearth, before the feathery ash, all that was left of them, was dispersed on the homeless winds.

But the pity of this blind wantonness of destruction was more than compensated for in Nadine's mind by the glorious savagery and force of the unlooked-for hurricane, and she easily persuaded Hugh to come out with her and be beaten and stormed upon. Always sensitive to the weather, this portentous storm had aroused in her a sort of rapture of restlessness; she rejoiced in it, and somehow feared it for its ruthlessness and indifference.

They took the path that led downward to the beach, for it was the tumult and madness of the sea that Nadine especially wished to observe. Though as yet the gale had been blowing only an hour or two, it had raised a monstrous sea, and long before they came down within sight of it they heard the hoarse thunder and crash of broken waters penetrating the screaming bellow of the gale, and the air was salt with spray and flying foam. To the west there was still that clear arch of open sky through which the wind poured; somewhere behind the clouds to the left of it the sun was near to its setting, and a pale livid light shone out of it catching the tops of the breakers as they streamed landwards. Between these foam-capped tops lay huge hollows and darknesses, out of which would suddenly boil another crest of mountainous water. The tide was only at half flood, but the sea packed by this astounding wind was already breaking at the foot of the cliffs themselves, while in the troughs of the waves as they rode in there appeared and disappeared again the big scattered rocks from some remote cliff-fall that were strewn about the beach. Sometimes a wave would strike one of these full, and be shattered against it, spouting heavenwards in a column of solid water; oftener the breakers swept over them unbroken, until with menace of their toppling crests they flung themselves with long tongues of hissing water on the rocks at the foot of the cliffs. Then, with the scream of the withdrawn shingle, the spent water was furiously dragged back to the base of the next incoming wave, and was caught up again to hurl itself against the land. Sometimes a sudden blast of wind would cut off the crest of the billow even as it curled over, and fling it a monstrous riband of foam through the air, sometimes two waves converging rose up in a fountain of water and fell back without having reached the shore. This way and that, rushing and rolling, in hills and valleys of water, the maddened sea crashed and thundered, and every moment the spray rose more densely from the infernal cauldron. Then as the tide rose higher, the waves came in unbroken and hurled their tons of water against the face of the cliff itself. Above, continuous as a water-fall, rose the roar and scream of the gale, ominous, insensate, bewildering; it was as if the elements were being transmuted back into the chaos out of which they came.

Nadine and Hugh, clinging together for support, stood there for some minutes, half way down the side of the cliff, watching the terror and majesty of the spectacle, she utterly absorbed in it, and cruelly unconscious of him. Then, since they could no longer get down to the base of the cliff, they skirted along it till they came to the sandy foreshore of the bay. There from water-level they could better see the immensity of the tumult, the strange hardness and steepness of the wave-slopes. It was as if a line of towers and great buildings were throwing themselves down on to the sands, and breaking up into sheets and eddies of foam-sheeted water, while behind them there rose again another street of toppling buildings, which again shattered itself on the beach. Great balls of foam torn from the spent water trundled by them on the sands, and bunches of brown seaweed torn from the rocks were flung in handfulls at their feet. Once from the arch in the sky westwards a dusky crimson light suddenly burned, reddening the wave crests to blood, and then as the darkness of the early winter sunset gathered, they turned, and were blown up the steep cliff-path again, wet and buffeted. Conversation had been altogether impossible, and they could but communicate with pointing finger and nodding head. Yet, somehow, to be together thus, cut off by the riot of winds and waves, from all sense of the existence of others, in that pandemonium of tempest, gave to Hugh, at least, a closer feeling of intimacy with Nadine than he had ever yet known. She clung to him, she sheltered under his shoulder unconsciously, instinctively, as an animal trusts his master without knowing it is trusting. And that to his aching hunger for her was some thing. . . .

But the gale was to bring them closer together yet.

11

All the evening and all night long the gale continued. Now and then the constant scream of it would leap upwards a couple of octaves as a shriller blast struck the house, and again for a moment the mad chant, as of all the devils in hell intoning together, would drop into silence. From time to time, like a tattoo of drums, the rain battered at the window panes, but through it all whether in hushes of the wind, or when its fiercest squall descended, the beat of the surf sounded ever louder. And all through the night (the result perhaps of his agitated talk with Nadine in the morning, or of his intimate gale-encompassed isolation with her in the afternoon) Hugh turned and tossed midway between sleeping and waking. Sometimes he seemed to himself to be yelling round the house among the spirits of the air, seeking admittance, sometimes it seemed to him that he was anvil to the hammer of the surf, and whether he was homelessly wandering outside among the spirits of the wind, or was being done to death by those incessant blows of the beating waves, it was Nadine that he sought. And as the night went on the anguish of his desire grew ever more acute, and the beating of the waves a more poignant torture, until, while yet no faintest lightening of winter's dawn had broached the gross blackness of the night, he roused himself completely and sat up in bed and turned on his light.

To him awake the riot outside was vastly magnified compared with the dimmer trouble of his dream, so too was his yearning for Nadine. His windows looked eastwards away from the quarter of the gale, and, getting out of bed, he lifted a sash and peered out. Nothing whatever could be seen; it was as if he gazed into the darkness of the nethermost pit, out of which, blown by the blast of the anger of God, came the shrieks of souls that might not rest, driven for ever along, drenched by the river of their own unavailing tears. Even though he was awake, the strange remote horror of nightmare was on him, and it was in vain that he tried to comfort himself by saying, like some child repeating a senseless lesson, "A deep depression has reached us travelling eastwards from the Atlantic." He tried to read, but still the nightmare sense possessed him, and he fancied he had to read a whole line, neither more nor less, between the poundings of the waves. Then, as usually happens towards the ends of these witch-ridden Walpurgis nights, he got back to bed again and slept calmly and dreamlessly.

He and Seymour alone out of the party put in an appearance at breakfast time; it seemed probable that the others were compensating themselves for a disturbed night by breakfasting upstairs, and afterwards the two went out together to look at the doings of the darkness. By this time the wind had considerably moderated, the rain had ceased altogether, and the thick pall of cloud that had last night overlain the sky was split up into fragments and islands and flying vapours, so that here and there pale shafts of sunlight shone on to land and sea. But the thunder of the surf had immeasurably increased, and when they went to the cliff-edge which he and Nadine had passed down yesterday afternoon, they looked on to an indescribable confusion of tremendous waters. The tide was just beginning to flow, but the bay was still packed with the sea heaped up by the wind, and the end of the reef with its big scattered rocks was out beyond the walls of breaking water. The sea appeared to have been driven distraught by the stress of the night; cross currents carried the waves in all directions; it almost seemed that some, shrinking from the wall of cliff in front, were trying to beat out to sea again. Quite away from land they jousted and sparred with each other, not jestingly, but, it seemed, with some grim purpose, as if they were practising their strength for deeds of earnest violence, as for some civil war among themselves. It was round the outermost rocks that this sport of billowy giants most centred; right across the bay ran some current that set on to the end of the reef, and there it met with the waves coming straight in-shore from the direction of the blowing of the gale. There they spouted and foamed together, yet not in play; some purpose, so regular were these rounds of combat, seemed to underlie their wrestlings.

Hugh threw away a charred peninsula of paper, once a cigarette, which the wind had smoked for him. He never had felt much sense of comradeship in the presence of Seymour, and their after-breakfast stroll had no more virtue than was the reward of necessary politeness.

"There is something rather senseless in this display of wasted energy," said Seymour. "Each of those waves would probably cook a dinner, if its force was reasonably employed."

Hugh, in spite of his restless night, had something of Nadine's thrilled admiration for the turmoil, and felt slightly irritated.

"They would certainly cook your goose or mine," he remarked.

Seymour wondered whether it would be well to say "Do you allude to Nadine as our goose?" but, perhaps wisely, refrained.

"That would be to the good," he said. "Goose is a poor bird at any time, but uneatable unless properly roasted."

Hugh did not attend to this polite rejoinder, for he had caught sight of something incredible not so far out at sea, and he focussed his eyes instantly on it. For the moment, what he thought he had seen completely vanished; directly afterwards he caught sight of it again, a fishing-boat with mast broken, reeling drunkenly on the top of a huge wave. His quick long-sighted eyes told him in that one moment of slewing deck that it presented to them, before it was swallowed from sight in the trough of the next wave, that there were two figures on it, clinging to the stump of the broken mast.

"Look," he said, "there is a boat out there."

It rose again to the crest of a wave and again plunged giddily out of sight. The incoming tide was bearing it swiftly shorewards, swiftly also the cross-current that set towards the end of the reef was bearing it there.

Hugh did not pause. He laid hold of Seymour by the shoulder.

"Run up to the house," he said, "and fetch a couple of men. Bring down with you as much rope as you can find. Don't say anything to Nadine and the women. But be quick."

He ran down to the beach himself, as Seymour went on his errand, seeing at once that there were two things that might happen to this stricken cripple of a ship. In one case, the incoming tide with its following waves might bear it straight on to the sandy beach; in the other the cross-current, in which now it was labouring, might carry it across to the reef where the waves were roaring and wrestling together. It was in case of this first contingency that he ran down on to the sands to be ready. The beach was steep there; the boat would ride in until it was flung down by that fringe of toppling, hard-edged breakers. In that tumble and scurry of surf it might easily be that strong arms could drag out of the fury of the backwash whatever was cast there. The boat, a decked fishing boat, would be dumped down on the sand; there would be a half-minute, or a quarter-minute when something might be done. On the other hand this greedy sucking current might carry it on to the reef. Then, by the mercy of God, a rope might be of some avail, if a man could reach the ship before it got there.

As he ran down the cliff, a sudden splash of sunlight broke through the clouds, making a bright patch of illumination round the boat as it swung over another breaker. There was only one figure there now, lying full length on the deck, and clinging with both hands to the stump of the mast. Then once again the water broke over it, lucidly green in the sunlight, and all Hugh's heart went out to that solitary prone body, lying there helpless in the hands of God and the gale. His heart stood still to see whether when next the drifting boat reappeared it would be tenantless, and with a sob in his throat, "Oh thank God," he said, when he saw it again, for the figure still lay there.

It was doubtful whether the current or the tide would win, and Hugh pulled off his coat and waistcoat, and threw them on the beach, in order to be able to rush in unimpeded of arm and muscle. Then with a strange sickness of heart, he saw that as the boat was getting in nearer, it was visibly moving sideways across to the left, where the reef lay. And he waited, in the suspense of powerlessness.

The wind now had quite abated; it was as if it had done its work, in making ready the theatre of plunging waters, and now waited to observe what drama should be moving across the stage of billows.

Soon from behind, he heard across the shingle at the top of the beach the approach of the others. Seymour had brought Berts and two men with him, and they carried with them half a dozen long coils of rope, part of the fire-rescue apparatus of the house. While watching and waiting for them, Hugh's mind had been uncommonly busy, and he found now that his plan was quite made. It was no longer possible to hope that the boat would come to land on the sandy beach, where without doubt two or three able-bodied men could rescue anyone cast up, but was driving straight on to the rocks. Once there, rescue was all but impossible; the only chance lay in reaching it before it was smashed to atoms on the immense boulders and sharp-toothed fangs. Quickly he tied three of the ropes together, and fastened the end round his body just below the shoulders, and took off his boots.

"I'm going in;" he said, "you all hold the rope and pay it out. If I come near the end of it, tie a fresh piece on——"

Suddenly across the shingle came footsteps, and a cry. Nadine ran down the beach towards them. She was clad only in a dressing-gown, that rainbow-hued one in which one night last June she had entertained a company in her room, and slippers, so that her ankles showed white and bare. She saw what Hugh intended, and something within her, some denizen of her soul, which till that moment had been unknown to her, took possession of her.

"No, Hughie, not you, not you," she screamed. "Seymour, anybody, but not you."

The cry had come from her very heart; she could no more have stifled it than she could have stopped the beating of it. Then suddenly, she realized what she had said, and sank down on the beach burying her face in her hands.

"Take care of her, Seymour," said Hugh, and there was more heroism required for these few little words than for the desperate feat he was about to attempt. He did not look round again, nor wish to say anything more, and there was no time to lose.

"Now you chaps," he called out, and ran forward to the edge of the water.

At the moment an immense billow poised and curled just in front of him. The wash of it covered him waist-deep and he floundered and staggered as the rush of water went by him. Then as the spent water drew out to sea again he ran with it, to where another breaker was toppling in front of him. With a low outward spring he dived into the hollowed vault head foremost and passed through it.

The beach was very steep here, and coming up again through and beyond the line of surf, he found himself in deep water. Behind him lay the breaking line of billows, but in front the huge mountains of water rose and fell unbroken. As he was lifted up on the first of these, swimming strongly against it, he saw not a hundred yards from him his helpless and drifting goal. He could see, too, who it was who lay there, desperately clinging to the stump of the mast with white slender wrists; it was quite a young boy. And at that sight, Hugh's pity and determination were strung higher than ever. Here was a young creature, in desperate plight among these desperate waterways, one who should not yet have known what peril meant. And at the risk of spending a little strength, when strength was so valuable, Hugh gave a great shout of notice and encouragement. Then he was swallowed up in the trough of a wave again. But when he rose next, he saw that the boy had raised his head, and that he saw him.

The current that swept towards the rocks, swept also a little shorewards, and Hugh, measuring the distance between the boat and the fatal breakers with his eye, and measuring again the distance between the boat and himself, knew that he must exert himself to the point of exhaustion to get to the boat before it was drifted to its final destruction. But as he swam, he knew he had made a mistake in not taking off his shirt and trousers also, and giving himself an unimpeded use of his limbs. His trousers particularly dragged and hampered him; then suddenly he remembered a water-game at which he used to be expert at school, namely, of taking a header into the bathing-place in flannels and undressing in the water. It seemed worth while to sacrifice a few seconds to accomplish that, and, as cool and collected as when he was doing it for mere sport at school, he trod water, slipped his legs out of his trousers, and saw them float away from him. Then twice as vigorous he struck out again. His shirt did not bother him; besides, the rope was tied round his chest, and there was not time for more disencumbrances.

For the next five minutes, for he was fighting the tide, he just swam and swam. Occasionally rising to a wave it seemed to him that he was making no way at all, but somehow that did not discourage him. The only necessity that concerned him was that he must go till he could go no longer. And all the time like a dream and yet like a draught of wine to him was Nadine's involuntary cry "No, Hughie, not you." He did not trouble to guess what that meant. He was only conscious that it invigorated and inspired him.

The minutes passed; once the rope seemed to jerk him back, and he found himself swearing underneath his breath. Then, though it was terribly heavy, he realized that it was free again, and that he was not being hampered. Then he suddenly found himself much closer to the boat than he had any idea of, and this, though he was getting very tired, gave him a new supply of nervous force. He swam into three valleys more, he surmounted three ridges of water, and lo, the boat was on the peaks directly opposite to him, and from opposite sides they plunged into the same valley together. Not fifty yards off to the left, incredible fountains of foam spouted and aspired.

Then, oh, blessed moment, he caught hold of the side of the lurching fishing-smack, and a pale little boyish frightened face was close to his. He clung for a second to the side, and they went up and down two big billows together. Then he got breath enough to speak.

"Now, little chap," he said, "don't be frightened, for we're all right. Catch hold of the rope here, close to my body, and just jump in. Yes, that's right. Plucky boy! Take hold with both hands of the rope. Not so cold, is it?"

Once again, before he let go of the boat, they rose to an immense wall of water, and Hugh saw the figures on the beach, four of them standing in the wash of the sea, paying out the rope, and one standing there also a little apart waving seawards, clapping her hands. And what she said came to him clear and distinct across the hills and valleys of destruction.

"Oh, Hughie, well done, well done!" she cried. "Now pull, all of you, pull him in!"

He was glad she added that, for in the hurry of the moment he had given no instructions as to what they were to do when he reached the boat, and what seemed so obvious out here, might not have seemed so obvious to those on the beach, and he was not sure that there was enough power left in him to shout to them. But Nadine understood; once she had said she understood him too well. It was enough now that she understood him enough.

He let go of the boat. For a moment it seemed inclined to follow them, and he thought the bowsprit was going to hit him. Then he felt a little pull on the rope under his shoulders, and the boat made a sort of bow of farewell, and slid away towards the spouting towers of foam. Hugh was utterly exhausted; he could just paddle with a hand or kick downwards to keep his head above water, but he gave away one breath yet.

"Nothing to be frightened at," he said. "We're all right now."

The buoyant water, for all the wickedness of its foam and savage hunger, sustained him sufficiently. He turned round seawards in the water so that the great surges did not overwhelm him from behind, and put an arm on the rope underneath the boy's neck, so as to support them both. He forced himself even in his utter weariness to be collected, and to remember that for several minutes yet there was nothing whatever to be done except with the minimum possible of exertion to keep afloat, while the rope towed them back towards that line of steep towers and curling precipices beyond which lay the shore, and those who stood on the shore. Sometimes the crest of a wave broke over them, almost smothering him, but then again they found themselves on a downward hillside of water, where the panting lungs could be satisfied, and the labouring heart supplied. Somewhere, inside of him, he wanted to know where this poor foundered fishing-smack had come from and how this young boy had managed to cling to it, but he had not sufficient strength to give voice to his desire, for all that he had must be husbanded to meet that final assault of the row of breakers through which they had to pass.

And as they got nearer, he began to form his plan. This young, unknown life, precious to him now as an unborn baby to a woman, was given into his charge. It seemed to him that, as a woman has to bring to birth the life within her whatever it costs her, so he had to save the life of this unknown little fisher-boy, and take all risks himself. Whatever lay beyond that line of breakers, his business was here, and he did not for one second argue the values. He did not forget Nadine nor her last cry to him as he set forth on his peril, but for the moment there was something that concerned him even more than Nadine, and he had to make the best plans he could for saving this young life that had been put in his hands, even if he fought God over it. The only question was how to devise the best chance of saving it.

They were close in now, and this three-minute pause of floating had restored him. He was just conscious of bitter cold, even as he was conscious of the group on the edge of the sand, and of the hissing waters. But none of these things seemed to have anything to do with him; they were but external phenomena. Between him and the shore were still three towering lines of breakers, sharp-edged, steep as roofs. The third of them suddenly tumbled and disappeared with a thick thud, and an uprising of shattered spray. And suddenly his plan presented itself, fully finished in his mind.

He had been swimming for not more than a quarter of an hour, and the minutes of that fierce outward struggle which had seemed so long to him, had to Nadine passed in a flash. For once she had got completely outside herself, and, concentrated and absorbed in another, the time had gone by in one flare of triumphant expectation. For a moment after that heart's cry had been flung out of her, she had sat dazed and bewildered by the consciousness that it seemed to have revealed to her, for until she had cried out that Seymour, that anybody but Hugh must make the desperate attempt, she had not known her own heart, nor could she have, for it was not till then that it was unlocked to herself. When she looked up again Hugh had already plunged through the breakers, and was swimming, and instantly her soul was with him there in the inhuman sea, glorying in his strength, proud of his splendid and desperate adventure, and not for one moment doubting of its success. None but he, she felt, could do it, and it was impossible that he should fail. She would not have had him back by her side, saying that the attempt was mere suicide, for all the happiness that the world contained, and had she been able to change places with the boy who clung to the helpless boat, she would have sprung ecstatic to the noble risk, for the sake of having Hugh battle the seas on his way to rescue her. Failing that, it had been gloriously ordained that he should do this, and that she should stand with heart uplifted, and be privileged to see the triumphant venture. She saw him reach the boat, knowing that he would, and clapped her hands and called to him, and with bright eyes and laughing mouth she eagerly watched him getting nearer. Then, just as the moment when Hugh made his plan, she realised that between him and her there lay that precipice of water that kept flinging itself down in thunder on the shore, and ever reforming again. And the light died out of her face, and she grew ashen grey to the lips and watched.

Hugh had been floating with his face seawards. Now he turned round to the shore again. She saw him smile at the boy, as they rose on the crest of a wave, and she saw him speak.

"Now, we're all right," was what he said. "Get on my back, and hold on to my shoulders."

The rope had ceased to pull. The men in control of it just held it taut, waiting to pull when the exact moment came. The boy did as Hugh told him, and next moment the two rose up on the crest of the line of breakers. Twenty feet below him as they topped it, Hugh looked over on to the backwash of the preceding wave, being dragged into the rampart of water which bore them, and was growing higher as it rose to its ruin. But the boy's fall would be broken, if they were to be pounded on the beach by the toppling billow: at any rate, Hugh could not contrive a better plan.

Then the wave curled, and he was flung forwards, twisting as he fell. He saw the slim little figure he had been carrying shot over his shoulder, lifted from behind by the wave, and flung clear of its direct impact on the beach, and he heard his mind say, "That won't hurt him."

Then he felt something stupendous, as heavy as the world, strike him on the back. After that he felt nothing more at all.

· · · · · · ·

As dusk was closing in Nadine sat in the window of her big black-painted sitting-room, where so many well-attended sessions had been held. Hugh had been in the surgeon's hands since they carried him in, and all that could be done had been done. Afterwards, Nadine had seen the surgeon, and learned from him all there was to fear and the little there was to hope for. It was possible that Hugh might not live till the morning, but simply pass away from the shock of his injuries. On the other hand, his splendid constitution might pull him through that. But given that he lived through the immediate danger, it was doubtful if he could ever lead an active life again. The boy he had saved was practically unhurt, and was fast asleep.

Nadine sat there very quiet both in mind and body. She did not want to rave or rebel, she merely let her mind sit as it were, in front of these things, and contemplate them, like a picture, until they became familiar. She felt they were not familiar yet; though she knew them to be true, they were somehow unreal and incredible. She did not yet grasp them; it seemed to her that her mind was stunned and was incapable of apprehending them. So she had to keep her attention fixed on them, until they became real. Yet she found it difficult to control her mind; it kept wandering off into concentric circles round the centre of the only significant thing in the world. . . .

Out on the sea the sun had set, and there were cloud-bars of fading crimson on the horizon level across a field of saffron yellow. This yellow toned off into pale watery green, and high up in the middle of that was one little cloud like an island that still blazed in the sunlight of the upper air. Somehow that aroused a train of half-forgotten reminiscences. There had been a patch of sunlight once like an island, on the grey of the sea—it was connected with a picture—yes, it was a sketch which Esther had made for Hugh, and she had put in the island reluctantly, saying it looked unreal in nature and would be worse in art. But Hugh had wanted it there, and as Esther worked, she herself had walked with him along the beach from which he had been carried up to-day, and she had told him that he lived in unrealities, and pictured to himself that some day he and she would live on some golden sunlit island together. She remembered it all now——

Her mind came back to the centre, and started off again on that splendid deed of the morning. She had quite lost her head when she called out, "No, Hughie, not you!" It must have been Hugh to do it, no one else could have done it. The idea of Berts or Seymour wrestling with and overcoming that mountainous and maddened sea was unthinkable. Only Hugh could have done it, and the deed was as much part of him as his brown eyes or his white strong teeth. And if at the end the sea had flung him down and broken him, that was after he had laughed at the peril and snatched its prey out of its very jaws of death. Even as things were now with him, Nadine could not regret what he had done, and if time had run back, and she saw him again plunging into that riot and turmoil, she felt that she would not now cry out to him like that. She would have called God-speed to him instead.

Once again her mind rippled away from its centre. She had called out to Seymour or Berts to go. At the time it had been quite instinctive, but she saw now what had prompted her instinct. She meant—though then she did not know she meant it—that she could spare anyone but Hugh. That was what it came to, and she wondered if Hugh had understood that. Seymour, without doubt, must have done so; he was so clever. Probably he would tell her he understood, and ask her if it was not that which was implied. But all such considerations seemed to her to matter very little. There was only one thing that mattered, and that was not whether Hugh lived or died even, but simply the fact of Hugh.

Her mother had telegraphed that she was coming at once; and Nadine remembering that she had not told the servants, got up and rang the bell. But before it was answered there came an interruption for which she had been waiting. One of the two nurses whom the surgeon from Chester had brought with him, knocked at her door. She had been tidying up, and removing all traces of what had been done.

"The room is neat again now," she said, "and you may come and just look at him."

"Is he conscious or in pain?" asked Nadine.

"No; but he may regain consciousness at any time, though I don't think he will have any pain."

They went together up the long silent passages in which there hung that curious hush which settles down on a house when death is hovering by it, and came to his door which stood ajar. Then from some sudden qualm and weakness of flesh, Nadine halted, shrinking from entering.

"Do not come unless you feel up to it," said Nurse Bryerley. "But there is nothing that will shock you."

Nadine hesitated no more, but entered.

They had carried him, not to his own room, but to another with a dressing-room adjoining. His bed stood along the wall to the left of the door, and he lay on his back with his head a little sideways towards it. There was nothing in the room that suggested illness, and when Nadine looked at his face there was nothing there that suggested it either. His eyes were closed, but his face was as untroubled as that of some quiet sleeper. In the wall opposite were the western-looking windows and the room was lit only by that fast-fading splendour. The cloud-island still hung in the sky, but it had turned grey as the light left it.

Then even as Nadine looked at him, his eyes opened and he saw her.

"Nadine," he said.

The nurse stepped to the bedside.

"Ah, you are awake again," she said. "How do you feel?"

"Rather tired. But I want to speak to Nadine."

"Yes, you can speak to her," she said, and signed to the girl to come.

Nadine came across the room to him, and knelt down.

"Oh, Hughie," she said, "well done!"

He looked at her, puzzled for the moment, with troubled eyes.

"You said that before," he said. "It was the last thing you said. Why did you—oh, I remember now. Yes, what a bang I came. How's the little fellow, the one on my back?"

"Quite unhurt, Hughie. He is asleep."

"I thought he wouldn't be hurt. It was the best plan I could think of. I say, why did you call to me not to go at first? I had to."

"I know now you had to," said she.

"I want to ask you something else. How badly am I hurt?"

Nadine looked up at the nurse a moment, who nodded to her. She understood exactly what that meant.

"You are very badly hurt, dear Hughie," she said, "but, but it is worth it fifty times over."

Hugh was silent a moment.

"Am I going to die?" he asked.

Nadine did not need instruction about this.

"No, a thousand times, no," she said. "You're going to get quite well. But you must be patient and rest and sleep."

Nadine's throat grew suddenly small and aching, and she could not find her voice for a moment.

"You are quite certainly going to live," she said. "To begin with I can't spare you."

Hugh's eyelids fluttered and quivered.

"By Jove!" he said, and next moment they had quite closed.

The nurse signed to Nadine to get up and she rose very softly and tiptoed away. At the door she looked round once at Hugh, but already he was asleep. Then still softly she came back and kissed him on the forehead and was gone again.

She had been with him but a couple of minutes, but as she went back to her room, she heard the stir of arrival in the hall, and went down. Dodo had that moment arrived.

"Nadine, my dear," she said, "I started the moment I got your telegram. Tell me all you can. How is he? How did it happen? You only said he had had a bad accident, and that you wanted me."

Nadine kissed her.

"Oh Mamma," she said. "Thank God it wasn't an accident. It was done on purpose. He meant it just like that. But you don't know anything, I forgot. Will you come to my room?"

"Yes, let us go. Now tell me at once."

"We have had a frightful gale," she said, "and this morning Hughie saw a fishing boat close in land, driving on to the reef. There was just one shrimp of a boy on it, and Hughie went straight in, like a duck to water, and got him off and swam back with him. There was a rope and Seymour and Berts pulled him in. And when they got close in, Hughie put the boy on his back—oh Mamma, thank God for men like that—and the breakers banged him down on the beach, and the boy was unhurt. And Hughie may die very soon, or he may live——"

Nadine's voice choked for a moment. All day she had not felt a sob rise in her throat.

"And if he lives," she said, "he may never be able to walk again, and I love him."

Then came the tempest of tears, tears of joy and sorrow, a storm of them, fruitful as autumn rain, fruitful as the sudden deluges of April, with God knows what warmth of sun behind. The drought of summer in her, the ice of winter in her had broken up in the rain that makes the growth and the life of the world. The frozen ground melted under it, the soil cracked with drought drank it in; the parody of life that she had lived became the farce that preceded sweet serious drama, tragedy it might be, but something human. . . . And Dodo, woman also, understood that; she too had lived years that parodied herself, and knew what the awakening to womanhood was, and the immensity of that unsuspected kingdom. It had come late to her, to Nadine early: some were almost born in consciousness of their birthright, others died without realizing it. So, mother and daughter, they sat there in silence, while Nadine wept her fill.

"It was the splendidest adventure," she said, at length lifting her head. "It was all so gay. He shouted to that little boy in the boat to encourage him to cling on, and oh, those damned reefs were so close. And when they rode in, Hughie like a horse with a child on his back over that—that precipice, he said something again to encourage him."

Nadine broke down again for a moment.

"Hughie has never thought about himself at all," she said. "He used always to think about me. But when he went on his adventure he didn't think about me. He thought only of that little stupid boy, God bless him. And, oh Mamma, I gave myself away—I got down to the beach just before Hughie went in, and I lost my head and I screamed out: 'Not you, Hughie; Seymour, Berts, anybody, but not you.' It wasn't

I who screamed; something inside me screamed, and that which screamed was—was my love for Hughie, and I never knew of it. But inside me something swelled, and it burst. Yes; Hughie heard, I am sure, and Seymour heard, and I don't care at all."

Nadine sat up, with a sort of unconscious pride in her erectness.

"I saw him just now," she said, "and he quite knew me, and asked if he was going to die. I told him he certainly was not, as I couldn't spare him."

Nadine gave her little croaking laugh.

"And he instantly went to sleep," she said.

The veracious historian is bound to state that this was an adventure absolutely after Dodo's heart. All her life she had loved impulse, and disregarded its possibly appalling consequences. Never had she reasoned before she acted, and she could almost have laughed for joy at those blind strokes of fate. Hugh's splendid venture thrilled her, even as it thrilled Nadine, and for the moment the result seemed negligible. A great thing had "got done" in the world; now by all means let them hope for the best in its sequel, and do their utmost to bring about the best, not with a fainting or regretful heart, but with a heart that rejoiced and sang over the glory of the impetuous deed that brought about these dealings of love and life.

Dodo's eyes danced as she spoke, danced and were dim at the same time.

"Oh, Nadine, and you saw it!" she said. "How glorious for you to see that, and to know at the same moment that you loved him. And, my dear, if Hughie is to die, you must thank God for him without any regret. There is nothing to regret. And if he lives——"

"Oh, Mamma, one thing at a time," said Nadine. "If he only lives, if only I am going to be allowed to take care of him, and to do what can be done."

She paused a moment.

"I am so glad you have come," she said, "it was dear of you to start at once like that. Did Papa Jack want you not to go?"

"My dear, he hurried me off to that extent that I left behind the only bag that mattered."

"That was nice of him. They have been so hopeless, all of them here, because they didn't understand. Berts has been looking like a funeral all day, the sort with plumes. And Edith has been running in and out with soup for me, soup and mince and glasses of port. I think—I think Seymour understood though, because he was quite cheerful and normal. Oh Mamma, if Hughie only lives, I will marry Seymour as a thank-offering."

Dodo looked at her daughter in amazement.

"Not if Seymour understands," she said.

Nadine frowned.

"It's the devil's own mess," she observed.

"But the devil never cleans up his messes," said Dodo. "That's what we learn by degrees. He makes them, and we clean them up. More or less that is to say."

She paused a moment, and flung the spirit of her speech from her.

"I don't mean that," she said. "The opposite is the truth, for God makes beautiful things, and we spoil them. And then He makes them beautiful again. It is only people who can't see at all, that see the other aspect of it. I think they call them realists—I know it ends in 'ist.' But it doesn't matter what you call them. They are wrong. We have got to hold our hearts high, and let them beat, and let ourselves enjoy and be happy and taste things to the full. It is easier to be miserable, my dear, for most people. We are the lucky ones. Oh, if I had been a charwoman, like that thing in the play, with a husband who stole and was sent to prison, I should have found something to be happy about. Probably a large diamond in the grate, which I should have sold without being traced."

These remarkable statements were not made without purpose. Dodo knew quite well that courage and patience and cheerfulness would be needed by Nadine, and she was willing to talk the most outrageous nonsense to give the sense of vitality to her, to make her see that no great happening like this, whatever the end, was a thing to moan and brood over. It must be taken with much more than resignation—a quality which she despised—and with hardly less than gaiety. Such at any rate was her private human gospel, which she found had not served her so badly.

"I have quite missed my vocation," she said. "I ought to have been born in poverty-stricken and criminal classes to show the world that being hungry does not make you unhappy any more than having three diamond tiaras makes you happy. You've got the birthright of happiness, Nadine; don't sell it for any sort of pottage. Never anticipate trouble, but if it comes embrace and welcome it; it is part of life, and thus it becomes your friend. Oh, I wish I had been here this morning! I would have shouted for glee to see that darling Hughie go churning out to sea. I am jealous of you. Just think; if Papa Jack had come a-wooing of you, as I really thought he might be doing in the summer, you would have married him, and I should be looking after Hughie. Isn't that like me? I want everybody's good times myself."

These amazing statements were marvellously successful.

"I won't give my good time away even to you," said Nadine.

"No, you are sharper than a serpent's tooth. Now, darling, we will go very quietly along the passage, and just see if Hughie is asleep. I should so like to wake him up—I know he is asleep—in order to tell him how splendid it all is. Don't be frightened; I'm not going to. We will just go to the door, and that enormous nurse, whom I saw peering over the banisters, will tell us to go away. And then I shall go to dress for dinner, and you will too——"

"Oh Mamma, I can't come down to dinner," said Nadine.

"Yes, dear, you can and you will. There's going to be no sadness in my house. If you don't, I shall send Edith up to you with mince and her 'cello and soup. Oh, Nadine, and it was all just for a little stupid boy, who very likely would have been better dead. He will now probably grow up, and be an anxiety to his parents, if he's got any—they usually haven't—and came to a bad and early end. What a great world!"

12

Nadine enquired at Hugh's door again that night before she went to bed, and found that he was still asleep. She had promised her mother not to sit up, but as she undressed she almost smiled at the uselessness of going to bed, so impossible did it seem that sleep should come near her. Besides, it was quite possible, she knew, that before morning she would be called to see Hugh once more, and for the last time. . . . After her one outburst of crying, she had felt no further agitation, for something so big and so quiet had entered her heart that all poignancy of anxiety and suspense were powerless to disturb it. As has been said, it was scarcely even whether Hugh lived or died that mattered; the only thing that mattered was Hugh. Had she been compelled to say whether she believed he would live or not, she would have given the negative. And yet there was a quality of peace in her that could not be shaken. It was a peace that humbled and exalted her. It wrapped her round very close, and yet she looked up to it, as to a mountain-peak on which dawn has broken.

Despite her conviction that sleep was impossible, she had hardly closed her eyes, when it embraced and swallowed up all her consciousness. This cyclone of emotion, in the centre of which dwelt the windless calm, had utterly tired her out, though she was unaware of fatigue, and her rest was dreamless. Then suddenly she knew that there was light in the room, and that she was being spoken to, and she passed from unconsciousness back to the full possession of her faculties, as swiftly as they had been surrendered. She found Dodo bending over her.

"Come, my darling," she said.

Nadine had no need to ask any question, but as she put on her slippers and dressing-gown Dodo spoke again.

"He has been awake for an hour and asking for you," she said. "The nurse and the doctor are with him; they think you had better come. It is possible that if he sees you there, he may go off to sleep again. But it is possible—you are not afraid, darling?"

Nadine's mouth quivered into something very like a smile.

"Afraid of Hughie?" she asked.

They went up the stairs, and along the passage together. The moon that last night had been hidden by the tempest of storm-clouds, or perhaps blown away from the sky by the hurricane, now rode high and cloudlessly amid a multitude of stars. No wind moved across those ample floors; only from the beach they heard the plunge and thunder of the sea that could not so easily resume its tranquility. The moonlight came through the window of Hugh's room also, making on the floor a shadow-map of the bars.

He was lying again with his face towards the door, but now his eyes were vacantly open, and his whole face had changed. There was an agony of weariness over it, and from his eyes there looked out a dumb unavailing rebellion. Before they had got to the door they had heard a voice inside speaking, a voice that Nadine did not recognise. It kept saying over and over again: "Nadine, Nadine."

As she came across the room to the bed, he looked straight at her, but it was clear he did not see her, and the monotonous unrecognisable voice went on saying: "Nadine, Nadine."

The doctor was standing by the head of the bed, looking intently at Hugh, but doing nothing; the nurse was at the foot.

He signed to Nadine to come, and took a step towards her.

"You've got to make him feel you are here," he said. Then with his hand he beckoned to the nurse and to Dodo, to stand out of sight of Hugh, so that by chance he might think himself alone with the girl.

Nadine knelt down on the floor, so that her face was close to those unseeing eyes, and the mouth that babbled her name. And the great peace was with her still. She spoke in her ordinary natural voice without tremor.

"Yes, Hughie, yes," she said. "Don't go on calling me. Here I am. What's the use of calling now? I came as soon as I knew you wanted me."

"Nadine, Nadine," said Hughie, in the same unmeaning monotone.

"Hughie, you are quite idiotic!" she said. "As if you didn't know in your own heart that I would always come when you wanted me. I always would, my dear. You need never be afraid that I shall leave you. I am yours, don't you see?"

"Nadine, Nadine," said Hugh.

Nadine's whole soul went into her words.

"Hughie, you are not with me yet," she said. "I want you, too, and I mean to have you. I didn't know till to-day that I wanted you, and now I can't do without you. Hughie, do you hear?" she said.

There was dead silence. Then Hugh gave a great sigh.

"Nadine!" he said. But it was Hugh's own voice that spoke.

She bent forward.

"Oh, Hughie, you have come then," she said. "Welcome. You don't know how I wanted you."

"Yes; I'm here all right," said Hugh, in a voice scarcely audible. "But I'm so tired. It's horrible; it's like death!"

Nadine gave her little croaking laugh.

"It isn't like anything of the kind," she said. "But, of course, you are tired. Wouldn't it be a good thing to go to sleep?"

"I don't know," said Hugh.

"But I do. I'm tired too, Hughie, awfully tired. If I leaned my head back against your bed I should go to sleep too."

"Nadine, it is you?" said Hugh.

"Oh, my dear! What other girl could be with you?"

"No, that's true. Nadine, would it bore you to stop with me a bit? We might talk afterwards, when—when you've had a nap."

"That will be ripping," said Nadine, assuming a sleepy voice.

There was silence for a little. Then once again, but in his own voice Hugh spoke her name. This time she did not answer, and she felt his hand move till it rested against her hair.

Then in the silence Nadine became conscious of another noise regular and slow as the faint hoarse thunder of the sea, the sound of quiet breathing. After a while the doctor came round the head of the bed.

"We can manage to wrap you up, and make you fairly comfortable," he whispered. "I think he has a better chance of sleeping if you stop there."

The light and radiance in Nadine's eyes was a miracle of beauty, like some enchanted dawn rising over a virgin and unknown land. She smiled her unmistakable answer, but did not speak, and presently Dodo returned with pillows and blankets, which she spread over her and folded round her.

"The nurse will be in the next room," said the doctor, "call her if anything is wanted."

Dodo and the doctor went back to their rooms, and Nadine was left alone with Hugh. That night was birth-night and bridal-night of her soul; there was it born, and through the long hours of the winter night it watched beside its lover and its beloved, in that stillness of

surrender to and absorption in another that lies beyond and above
the unrest of passion, amid the snows and sunshine of the most ultimate
regions to which the human spirit can aspire. She knew nothing of
the passing of the hours, nor for a long time did any thought or desire
of sleep come near her eyelids, but the dim moon became to her the
golden island of which once, in uncomprehending mockery she had
spoken to Hugh. She knew it to be golden now, and so far from being
unreal, there was nothing in her experience so real as it.

She could just turn her head without disturbing Hugh's hand that
lay on her plaited hair, and from time to time she looked round at
him. His face still wore the sunken pallor of exhaustion, but as his
sleep, so still and even-breathing, began to restore the low ebb of
his vital force, it seemed to Nadine that the darkness of the valley
of the shadow to the entrance of which he had been so near, cleared
off his face as eclipse passes from the moon. How near he had been,
she guessed, but it seemed to her that for the present his face was
set the other way. She knew, too, that it was she who had had the
power to make him look lifewards again, and the knowledge filled
her with a thrill of abasing pride. He had answered to her voice when
he was past all other voices, and had come back in obedience to it.

She did not, and she could not be troubled with the thought of
anything else besides the fact that Hugh lived. As far as was known
yet, he might never recover his activity and movement again, and
years of crippled life might be all that lay in front of him, but in
the passing away of the immediate imminent fear, she could not weigh
or even consider what that would mean. Similarly the thought of Seymour lay for the present outside the focus of her mind; everything
but the fact that Hugh lived was blurred and had wavering outlines.
As the hours went on the oblongs of moonshine on the floor moved
across the room, narrowing as they went. Then the moon sank and
the velvet of the cloudless sky grew darker, and the stars more luminous. One great planet, tremulous and twinkling made a glory beside
which all the lesser lights paled into insignificance. No wind stirred
in the great halls of the night, the moans and yells of its unquiet
soul were still, and the boom of the surf grew ever less sonorous,
like the thunder of a retreating storm. Occasionally the night-nurse
appeared at the door-way of the room adjoining, and as often Nadine
looked up at her smiling. Once very softly, she came round the head
of the bed, and looked at Hugh, then bent down towards the girl.

"Won't you get some sleep?" she said, and Nadine made a little
gesture of raised eyebrows and parted hands that was characteristic
of her.

"I don't know," she whispered. "Perhaps not. I don't want to."

Then her solitary night vigil began again, and it seemed to her that she would not have bartered a minute of it for the best hour that her life had known before. The utter peace and happiness of it grew as the night went on, for still close to her head there came the regular uninterrupted breathing, and the weight, just the weight of a hand absolutely relaxed lay on her hair. Not the faintest stir of movement other than those regular respirations came from the bed, and all the laughter and joy of which her days had been full, was as the light of the remotest of stars compared to the glorious planet that sang in the windless sky, when weighed against the joy that that quiet breathing gave her. She did not colour her consciousness with hope, she did not illuminate it by prayer; there was no room in her mind for anything except the knowledge that Hugh slept and lived.

It was now near the dawning of the winter day; the stars were paling, and the sky grew ensaffroned with the indescribable hue that heralds day. Footfalls, muffled and remote began to stir in the house, and far away there came the sound of crowing cocks, faint but exultant, hailing the dawn. About that time, Nadine looked round once more at Hugh, and saw in the pallid light of morning that the change she had noticed before was more distinct. There had come back to his face something of the firm softness of youth, there had been withdrawn from it the droop and hardness of exhaustion. And turning again, she gave one sigh and fell fast asleep.

Lover and beloved they lay there sleeping, while the dawn brightened in the sky, she leaning against the bed where he was stretched, he with his hand on her hair. And strangely, the moment that she slept, their positions seemed to be reversed, and Hugh in his sleep appeared unconsciously to keep watch and guard over her, though all night she had been awake for him. Once her head slipped an inch or two, so that his hand no longer lay on her hair, but it seemed as if that movement reached down to him fathom-deep in his slumber and immediately afterwards his hand, which had lain so motionless and inert all night, moved, as if to a magnet, after that bright hair, seeking and finding it again. And dawn brightened into day, and the sun leaped up from his lair in the East, and still Nadine slept, and Hugh slept. It was as if until then the balance of vitality had kept the girl awake to pour into him of her superabundance; now she was drained, and sleep with the level stroke of his soft hand across the furrows of trouble and the jagged edges of injury and exhaustion comforted both alike.

It had been arranged after these events of storm that the party should disperse, and Dodo went to early breakfast downstairs with her departing guests, who were leaving soon after. But first she went into the nurse's room, next door to where Hugh lay, to make enquiries, and was taken by her to look into the sick-room. With daylight their sleep seemed only to have deepened; it was like the slumber of lovers who have been long awake in passion of mutual surrender, and at the end have fallen asleep like children, with mere effacement of consciousness. Nadine's head was a little bowed forward, and her breath came not more evenly than his. It was the sleep of childlike content that bound them both, and bound them together.

Dodo looked long, and then with redoubled precaution moved softly into the nurse's room again, with mouth quivering between smiles and tears.

"My dear, I never saw anything so perfectly sweet," she said. "Do let them have their sleep out, nurse. And Nadine has slept in Hugh's room all night! What ducks! Please God it shall so often happen again!"

Nurse Bryerley was not unsympathetic, but she felt that explanations were needed.

"I understood the young lady was engaged to someone else," she said.

Dodo smiled.

"But until now no one has quite understood the young lady," she said. "Least of all, has she understood herself. I think she will find that she is less mysterious now."

"Mr. Graves will have to take some nourishment soon," said Nurse Bryerley.

Dodo considered.

"Then could you not give him his nourishment very cautiously, so that he will go to sleep again afterwards?" she asked. "I should like them to sleep all day like that. But then, you see, nurse, I am a very odd woman. But don't disturb them till you must. I think their souls are getting to know each other. That may not be scientific nursing, but I think it is sound nursing."

"Certainly the young lady was awake till nearly dawn," said Nurse Bryerley. "It wouldn't hurt her to have a good rest."

Dodo beamed.

"Oh, leave them as long as possible," she said. "You have no idea how it warms my heart. There will be trouble enough when they wake."

Seymour was among those who were going by the early train, and when Dodo came down he had finished breakfast. He got up just as she entered.

"How is he?" he asked.

Dodo's warm approbation went out to him.

"It was nice of you to ask that first, dear Seymour," she said. "He is asleep; he has slept all night."

Seymour lit a cigarette.

"I asked that first," he said, "because it was a mixture of politeness and duty to do so. I suppose you understand."

Dodo took the young man by the arm.

"Come out and talk to me in the hall," she said. "Bring me a cup of tea."

The morning sunshine flooded the window-seat by the door, and Dodo sat down there for one moment's thought before he joined her. But she found that no thought was necessary. She had absolutely made up her mind as to her own view of the situation, and with all the regrets in the world for him, she was prepared to support it. In a minute Seymour joined her.

"Nadine came down to the beach just before Hugh went in yesterday morning," he said, "and she called out—called?—shouted out: 'Not you Hughie; Seymour, Berts, anybody, but not you.' There was no need for me to think what that meant."

Dodo looked at him straight.

"No, my dear, there was no need," she said.

"Then I have been a—a farcical interlude," said he, not very kindly. "You managed that farcical interlude, you know. You licensed it, so to speak, like the censor of plays."

"Yes, I licensed it; you are quite right. But, my dear, I didn't license it as a farce; there you wrong me, I licensed it as what I hoped would be a very pleasant play. You must be just, Seymour; you didn't love her then, nor she you. You were good friends, and there was no shadow of a reason to suppose that you would not pass very happy times together. The great love, the real thing, is not given to everybody. But when it comes, we must bow to it. . . . It is royal."

All his flippancy and quickness of wit had gone from him. Neat conversation remained only because it was a habit.

"And I am royal," he said. "I love Nadine like that."

"Then you know that when that regality comes," she said quickly, "it comes without your control. It is the same with Nadine; it is by no wish of her that it came."

"I must know that from Nadine," he said. "I can't take your word for it, or anybody's except hers. She made a promise to me."

"She cannot keep it," said Dodo. "It is an impossibility for her. She made it under different conditions, and you put your hand to it under the same. And Nadine said you understood, and behaved so delightfully yesterday. All honour to you, since behind your behaviour there was that knowledge, that royalty."

"I had to. But don't think I abdicated. But she was in terrible distress, and really, Aunt Dodo, the rest of your guests were quite idiotic. Berts looked like a frog; he had the meaningless pathos of a frog on his silly face——"

"Nadine said he looked like a funeral with plumes," Dodo permitted herself to interpolate.

"More like a frog. Edith kept pouring out glasses of port to take to Nadine, but I think she usually forgot and drank them herself. It was a lunatic asylum. But Nadine felt."

"Ah, my dear," said Dodo, with a movement of her hand on to his.

Seymour quietly disengaged his own.

"Very gratifying," he said: "but as I said, I take nobody's word for it, except Nadine's. She has got to tell me herself. Where is she? I have to go in five minutes, but to see her will still leave me four to spare."

Dodo got up.

"You shall see her," she said. "But come quietly because she is asleep."

"If she is only to talk to me in her sleep"—began he.

"Come quietly," said Dodo.

But all her pity was stirred, and as they went along the passage to Hugh's room, she slipped her arm into his. She knew that her *coup* was slightly theatrical, but there seemed no better way of showing him. It might fail: he might still desire explanations, but it was worth trying.

"And remember I am sorry," she said, "and be sure that Nadine will be sorry."

"Riddles," said Seymour.

"Yes, my dear, riddles if you will," said she. "But you may guess the answer."

Dodo quietly turned the handle of the door into the nurse's room, and entered with her arm still in his. She made a sign of silence, and took Seymour straight through into the sick-room. All was as she had left it a quarter-of-an-hour ago; Nadine still slept and Hugh, in that same attitude of security and love. Her head was drooped, she slept as only children and lovers sleep. But Dodo with all her intuition did not see as much as Seymour, who loved her, saw. The truth of it was branded into his brain, whereas it only shone in hers. She saw the situation; he felt it.

Then with a signal of pressure on his arm, she led him out again.

"She has been there all night," she said. "She only fell asleep at dawn."

They were in the passage again before Seymour spoke.

"There is no need for me to awake her or talk to her," he said. "You were quite right. And I congratulate you on your ensemble. I should have guessed that it required most careful rehearsal. And I should have been wrong. And now, for God's sake, don't be kind and tender——"

He took his arm away from hers, feeling for her the mere resentment that he might feel against the footman who conveyed cold soup to him. He did not want the footman's sympathy nor did he want Dodo's.

"And spare me your optimism," he said. "If you tell me it is all for the best, I shall scream. It isn't for the best, as far as I am concerned. It is damned bad. I was a Thing, and Nadine made a man of me. Now she is tired of her handiwork, and says that I shall be a Thing again. And don't tell me I shall get over it. The fact that I know I shall makes your information, which was on the tip of your tongue, wanton and superfluous. But if you think I shall love Hugh, because he loves Nadine, you are utterly astray. I am not a child in a Sunday school, letting the teacher smack both sides of my face. I hate Hugh, and I am not the least touched by the disgusting spectacle you have taken me on tiptoe to see. They looked like two amorous monkeys in the monkey-house——"

Seymour suddenly paused and gasped.

"They didn't," he said. "At any rate Nadine looked as I have often pictured her looking. The difference is that it was myself, not Hugh, beside whom I imagined her falling asleep. That makes a lot of difference if you happen to be the person concerned. And now I hope the motor is ready to take me away, and many thanks for an absolutely damnable visit. Don't look pained. It doesn't hurt you as much as it hurts me. There is a real *cliché* to finish with."

Dodo's *coup* had been sufficiently theatrical to satisfy her, but she had not reckoned with the possible savageness that it might arouse. Seymour's temper, as well as his love, was awake, and she had not thought of the two as being at home simultaneously, but had imagined they played Box and Cox with each other in the minds of men. Here Box and Cox met, and they were hand-in-hand. He was convinced and angry; she had imagined he would be convinced and pathetic. With that combination she had felt herself perfectly competent to deal. But his temper roused hers.

"You are at last interesting," she said briskly, "and I have enjoyed what you call your damnable visit as much as you. You seem to have behaved decently yesterday, but no doubt that was Nadine's mistake."

"Not at all; it was mine," he said.

"Which you now recognise," said she. "I am afraid you must be off, if you want to catch your train. Good-bye."

"Good-bye," said he.

He turned from her at the top of the stairs, and went down a half-dozen of them. Then suddenly he turned back again.

"Don't you see I'm in hell?" he said.

Dodo entirely melted at that, and ran down the stairs to him.

"Oh, Seymour, my dear," she said. "A woman's pity can't hurt you. Do accept it."

She drew that handsome tragical face towards hers and kissed him.

"Do you mind my kissing you?" she said. "There's my heart behind it. There is, indeed."

"Thanks, Aunt Dodo," he said. "And—and you might tell Nadine I saw her like that. I am not so very stupid. I understand; good-bye."

"And Hugh?" she asked, quite unwisely, but in that optimistic spirit that he had deprecated.

"Don't strain magnanimity," he said. "Its quality is *not* strained. I said good-bye. Say good-bye to Nadine for me. Say I saw her asleep, and didn't disturb her. I never thought much of her intelligence, but she may understand that. She will have to tell me what she means to do. That I require. At present our wedding-day is fixed."

Seymour broke off suddenly and ran downstairs without looking back.

Dodo was quite sincerely very sorry for him, but almost the moment he had gone she ceased altogether to think about him, for there was so many soul-absorbing topics to occupy her, and forgetting she had had no breakfast, she went to Edith's room (Edith alone had not the slightest intention of going away) to discuss them. Her optimism was quite incurable: she could not look on the darker aspect of affairs for more than a minute or two. She found Edith breakfasting in bed, with a large fur-cape flung over her shoulders. Her breakfast had been placed on a table beside her, but for greater convenience she had disposed the plates round her, on her counterpane. There were also disposed there sheets of music-paper, a pen and ink-bottle, and a box of cigarettes. The window was wide open, and as Dodo entered the draught caused the music paper to flutter, and Edith laid hasty restraining hands on it, and screamed with her mouth full.

"Shut the door quickly!" she cried. "And then come and have some breakfast, Dodo. I don't think I shall get up to-day. I have been composing since six this morning, and if I get up the thread may be entirely broken. Beethoven worked at the C Minor Symphony for three days and nights without eating, sleeping or washing."

"I see you are eating," remarked Dodo. "I hope that won't prevent your giving us another C minor."

"The C minor is a much over-rated work," said Edith, "it is common-place melodically, and clumsily handled. If I had composed it, I should not be very proud of it."

"Which is a blessing you didn't, because then you would have composed something of which you were not proud," said Dodo, ringing the bell. "Yes, I shall have some breakfast with you. Oh, Edith, everything is so interesting, and Hughie has slept all night, and Nadine with him. They are sleeping now, Nadine on the floor, half-sitting up with her head against the bed, looking too sweet for anything. And poor dear Seymour has just gone away. I took him in to see them by way of breaking it to him. Who could have guessed that he would fall in love with her? It is very awkward, for I thought it would be such a nice, sensible marriage. And now, of course, there will be no marriage at all."

At this moment the bell was answered, and Edith in trying to prevent her music-paper from practising aviation, upset the ink-bottle. Several minutes were spent in quenching the thirst of sheets of blotting paper at it, as you water horses when their day's work is over.

"One of the faults of your mind, Dodo," said Edith, as this process was going on, "is that you don't concentrate enough. You have too many objects in focus simultaneously. Now my success is due to the fact that I have only one in focus at a time. For instance, this Stygian pool of ink does not distress me in the slightest——"

"No, darling, it's not your counterpane," said Dodo.

"It wouldn't distress me if it was. But if I opened your mind I should find Hugh's recovery, Nadine's future, and your baby in about equally vivid colours, and all in sharp outline. Also you make too many plans for other people. Do leave something to Providence now and then."

"Oh, I leave lots," said Dodo. "I only try to touch up the designs now and then. Providence is often rather sketchy and unfinished. But yesterday's design was absolutely wonderful. I can hardly even be sorry for Hugh."

Edith shook her head.

"You are quite incorrigible," she said. "Providence sent what was clearly intended to be a terrible event, but you see all sorts of glories in it. I don't think it is very polite. It is like laughing at a ghost story instead of being terrified."

Dodo's breakfast had been brought in, and she fell to it with an excellent appetite.

"There is nothing like scenes before breakfast to make one hungry," she said. "Think how hungry a murderer would be if he was taken out to be hanged before breakfast, and then given his breakfast afterwards. I had a scene with Seymour, you know. I am very sorry for him, but somehow he doesn't seem to matter. He lost his temper, which I rather respected, and showed me he had an ideal. That I respect too. I remember the struggles I used to go through in order to get one."

"Were they successful?" asked Edith.

"Only by a process of elimination. I did everything that I wanted, and found it was a mistake. So, last of all, I married Jack. What a delightful life I have led, and how good this bacon is. Don't you think David is a very nice name? I am going to call my baby David."

"It may be a girl," said Edith.

"Then I shall call it Bathsheba," said Dodo without pause. "Or do I mean Beersheba? Bath, I think. Edith, why is it that when I am most anxious and full of cares, I feel it imperative to talk tommy-rot? I'm sure there is enough to worry me into a grave if not a vault, between Seymour and Nadine and Hugh. But after all, one needn't worry about Nadine. It is quite certain that she will do as she chooses, and if she wants to marry Hugh with both arms in slings, and two crutches, and a truss and one of those sort of scrapers under one foot, she certainly will. I brought her up on those lines, to know her own mind, and then do what she wanted. It has been a failure hitherto, because she has never really wanted anything. But now I think my system of education is going to be justified. I am also suffering from reaction. Last night I thought our dear Hughie was dying, and I am perfectly convinced this morning that he isn't. So too, I am sure, is Nadine: otherwise she couldn't have fallen asleep like that. And what Hughie did was so splendid. I am glad God made men like that, but it doesn't prevent my eating a huge breakfast and talking rot. I hope you don't mean to go away. It is so dull to be alone in the house with two young lovers, even when one adores them both."

"Aren't you getting on rather quick, Dodo?" asked Edith.

"Probably: but Seymour is *congedié*—how do you say it—spun, dismissed, and quite certainly Nadine has fallen in love with Hugh. There isn't time to be slow, nowadays. If you are slow you are left gasping on the beach like a fish. I still swim in the great water thank God."

Dodo got up, and her mood changed utterly. She was never other than genuine, but it had pleased Nature to give her many facets, all brilliant, but all reflecting different-coloured lights.

"Oh, my dear, life is so short," she said, "and every moment should be so precious to everybody. I hate going to sleep, for fear I may miss something. Fancy waking in the morning and finding you had missed something, like an earthquake or a suffragette riot! My days are reasonably full, but I want them to be unreasonably full. And just now Jack keeps saying 'Do rest; do lie down; do have some beef-tea.' Just as if I didn't know what was good for David! Edith, he is going to be such a gay dog! All the girls and all the women are going to fall desperately in love with him. He is going to marry when he is thirty, and not a day before, and he will be absolutely simple and unspoiled and a wicked little devil on his marriage morning. And then all his energies will be concentrated on one point, and that will be his wife. He will utterly adore her, and think of nobody else except me. I shall be seventy-five, you perceive, at that time, and so I shall be easy to please. The older one gets the easier one is to please. Already little things please me quite enormously, and big ones, as you also perceive, make me go off my head. Oh, I am sure heaven will be extremely nice, if I ever die, which God forbid, but however nice it is, it won't be the same as this. You agree there I know; you want to make all the music you can first——"

"As a protest against what seems to be the music of heaven," said Edith firmly. "If we may judge by hymn tunes and chants, and the first act of Parsifal, and I suppose the last of Faust, and Handel's oratorios, it is very degrading stuff; harmonically it is childishly simple, and the proportion of full closes is nearly indecent. The idea of putting on a golden crown and playing that sort of nursery-rhyme for ever and ever is most depressing. And I want another ink-bottle."

Edith whistled a short phrase on her teeth, as a gentle hint to her hostess.

"It's for the flutes," she said, "and the 'cellos take it up two octaves lower."

She grabbed at her music paper.

"Then the horns start it again in the subdominant," she said, "and all the silly audience will think they are merely out of tune. That's because they got what they didn't expect. To be any good, you must surprise the ear. I'll surprise them. But I want another ink-bottle. And may I have lunch in my room, Dodo, if necessary? I don't know when I shall be able to get up."

Dodo was not attending in any marked manner.

"We will all do what we choose," she said genially. "We will be a sort of harmless Medmenham Abbey. You shall spill all the ink you please, and Nadine shall marry Hugh, who will get quite well, and I shall go and order dinner and see if Nadine is awake. I am afraid I am rather fatuously optimistic this morning, like Mr. Chesterton, and that is always so depressing, both to other people at the time, and to oneself subsequently. Dear me, what a charming world if there was no such thing as reaction. As a matter of fact I do not experience much of it."

Edith gave a great sigh of relief as Dodo left the room, and concentrated herself with singular completeness on the horn-tune in the sub-dominant. She was quite devoted to Dodo, but the horn-tune was in focus just now, and she knew if Dodo had stopped any longer, she would have become barely tolerant of her presence. Shortly afterwards the fresh supply of ink came also, and Edith proceeded straight up into the seventh heaven of her own compositions.

Dodo found a packet of letters waiting for her and among them a telegram from Miss Grantham saying "Deeply grieved. Can I do any-thing?" This she swiftly answered, replying "Darling Grantie. Nothing whatever." and went to Nadine's room, where she found Nadine, half-dressed, rosy from her bath, and radiant of spirit.

"Oh, Mamma, I never had such a lovely night," she said. "How delicious it must be to be married! I didn't wake till half-an-hour ago, and simultaneously Hughie woke, which looks as if we suited each other, doesn't it? And then the doctor came in, and looked at him, and said he was much stronger, much fuller of vitality for his long sleep, and he congratulated me on having made him sleep. And the nurse told me the first great danger, that he would not rally after the shock of the operation, was over. As far as that goes he will be all right."

Nadine kissed her mother, and clung round her neck, dewy-eyed.

"I'm not going to think about the future," she said. "Sufficient unto the day is the good thereof. It is enough this morning that Hughie has got through the night and is stronger. If I had been given any wish to be fulfilled I should have chosen that. And if on the top of that I had been given another, it would have been that I should have helped towards it, which I suppose is the old Eve coming in. I think I had better finish dressing, Mamma, instead of babbling. Have you had breakfast?"

"Yes, dear, I had it with Edith. She is in bed making tunes and pouring ink over the counterpane, and not minding."

Nadine's face clouded for a moment, in spite of the accomplishment of her wishes.

"And then I must see Seymour," she said. "It is no use putting that off. But, oh, Mamma, to think that till yesterday I was willing to marry him, with Hugh in the world all the time. Whatever happens to Hugh, I can't marry him, Seymour, I mean, if the ridiculous English pronouns admit of any meaning, and I must tell him."

"Seymour left half-an-hour ago," said Dodo. "But there's no need for you to tell him. I took him into Hugh's room and he saw you asleep. He understands. He couldn't very well help understanding, darling—he told me he understood before, when you called out to Hugh not to attempt the rescue. But he only understood it pretty well, as the ordinary person says he understands French. But when he saw you asleep, not exactly in Hugh's arms, but sufficiently close, he understood it like a real native, poor boy!"

"What did he do?" asked Nadine.

"He behaved very rightly and properly, and lost his temper with me, just as I lose my temper with the porter at the station if I miss my train. I had been just porter to him. He thanked me for a horrid visit, only he called it damnable, and so I lost my temper, too, and we had a few flowers of speech on the staircase, not big ones, but just promising buds. And then, poor chap, he came back to me, and told me he was in hell, and I kissed him, and he didn't seem to mind much, and I suppose he caught his train. Otherwise he would have been back by now. I'm exceedingly sorry for him, Nadine, and you must write him a sweet little letter, which won't do any good at all, but it's one of the things you have to do. Darling, I wonder if jilting runs in families like consumption and red faces. You see I jilted my darling Jack, to marry into your family. But you must write the sweet little letter I spoke of, because you are sorry, only you couldn't help it."

"Did you write a sweet little letter under—under the same circumstances to Papa Jack?" asked Nadine.

"No, dear, because I hadn't got anybody exceedingly wise to give me that good advice," said Dodo. "Also because I was a little brute, there is no reason why you should be."

"Perhaps it runs in the family, too," suggested Nadine.

"Then the quicker it runs out of the family the better. Besides you are sorry for Seymour."

Nadine opened her hands wide.

"Am I? I hope so," she said. "But if you are quite full of gladness for one thing, Mamma, it is a little difficult to find a corner for anything else."

Dodo turned to leave the room.

"Anywhere will do. Just under the stairs," she said. "I don't want you to put it in the middle of the drawing-room. After all, darling, you propose to jilt him."

"There's something in that," said Nadine. "Oh, Mamma, I used not to have any heart at all and now I've got one, it doesn't belong to me."

"No woman's heart belongs to her," said Dodo. "If it belongs to her, it isn't a heart."

"I should have thought that nonsense yesterday," said Nadine. "Oh, wait while I finish dressing, I shan't be ten minutes. What meetings we have had in my lovely black room! One I remember so particularly.

You and Esther and Berts all lay on the settee like sardines in evening dresses, and I had just refused to marry Hugh, who was playing billiards with Uncle Algy. Somehow the things like love and devotion seemed to me quite old-fashioned, or anyhow they seemed to me signs of age. They did indeed. I thought a clear brain was infinitely preferable to a confused heart, especially if it belonged to somebody else. I'm not used to it now, Mamma; it still seems to me very odd like a hat that doesn't fit. But it's a fact, and I suppose I shall grow into it, not that anyone ever grew into a hat. But when Hugh swam out yesterday morning, something came tumbling down inside me. Or was it that only something cracked, like the shell of a nut? It does not much matter, so long as it is not mended again. But how queer that it should happen in a second, like that. I suppose time has nothing to do with what concerns one's soul. I believe Plato says something about it. I don't think I shall look it up. He wrote wonderfully, but when a thing happens to oneself, that seems to matter more than Plato's reflections on the subject."

There was a short pause as Nadine brushed her teeth, but Dodo sitting on the unslept-in bed, did not feel inclined to break it. She wondered whether a particular point in the situation would occur to Nadine, whether her illumination as regards a woman's heart threw any light on that very different affair, a man's heart. She was not left long in doubt. The question of a man's heart was altogether unilluminated, and to Dodo there was something poignantly pathetic about Nadine's blissful ignorance. She came and sat down on the bed close to her mother.

"Hughie will see I love him," she said, "because he won't be able to help it. I shall just wait, oh, so happily, for him to say again what he has so often said before. He will know my answer, before I give it him. I hope he will say it soon. Then we shall be engaged, and people who are engaged are a little freer, aren't they, Mamma?"

Dodo felt incapable of clouding that radiant face, for she knew in the days that were coming, all its radiance would be needed: not a single sparkle of light must be wasted. But it did not seem to her very likely that Hugh, whose joyous strength and splendid activity had been so often rejected by Nadine, would be likely to offer again what would be, in all probability, but a crippled parody of himself. But her sense of justice told her that Nadine owed him all the strength and encouragement her eager vitality could give him. It was only fair that she should devote herself to him, and let him feel all the inspiration to live that her care of him could give him. But it seemed to her very doubtful if Hugh would consent, even if he perceived that it was love not warm friendship that she gave him, to let himself and his crippled body appeal to her. In days gone by, she would not marry him for love, and it seemed to Dodo that a real man, as Hugh was, would not allow her to marry him for pity. He had offered her his best, and she had refused it; it would not be surprising if he refused to offer her his worst. The joy that had inspired Dodo so that she had softly melted over the sight of Nadine asleep by Hugh, and had exultantly mopped up the spilt ink with Edith suddenly evaporated, leaving her dry and cold.

"You must wait, Nadine," she said. "You must make no plans. Give Hughie your vitality, and don't ask more."

She got up.

"Now, my darling, I shall go downstairs," she said, "and order your breakfast. You must be hungry. And then you can say your prayers, and breakfast will be ready."

Nadine, absorbed in her own thoughts, felt nothing of this.

"Prayers?" she said. "Why I was praying all night till dawn. At least, I was wanting, just wanting, and not for myself. Isn't that prayers?"

Dodo loved that: it was exactly what she meant in her inmost heart by prayers. She drew Nadine to her and kissed her.

"Darling, you have said enough for a week," she said, "if not more. And you said them because you must, which is the only proper plan. If you don't feel you must say your prayers, it is just as well not to say them at all. But you shall have breakfast, whether you feel you must or not. I say you must."

13

One morning a fortnight later, Jack, Dodo, and Edith were sitting together on the cliff above the bay, looking down on to the sandy foreshore. Jack, finding that Dodo was obliged to stop at Meering with Nadine, had personally abandoned his third shooting-party, leaving Berts, whom he implicitly trusted to make himself and everybody else quite comfortable, in charge. Among the guests was Berts' father, whom Berts apparently kept in his place. Jack had just told Dodo and Edith the contents of Berts' letter, received that morning. All was going very well, but Berts had arranged that his father should escort two ladies of the party to see the interesting town of Lichfield one afternoon, instead of shooting the Warren beat, where birds came high and Berts' father was worse than useless. But it was certain that he would enjoy Lichfield very much, and the shoot would be more satisfactory without him. If his mother was still at Meering, Berts sent his love, and knew she would agree with him.

Edith just now, working her way through the entire orchestra, was engaged on the *cor anglais* which, while Hugh was still so ill, Dodo insisted should not be played in the house. It gave rather melancholy notes, and was productive of moisture. But she finished a passage which seemed to have no end, before she acknowledged these compliments. Then she emptied the *cor anglais* into the heather.

"Poor Bertie is a drone," she said, "he never thinks it worth while to do anything well. Berts is better: he thinks it worth while to sit on his father really properly. I thought my energy might wake Bertie up, and that was chiefly why I married him. But it only made him go to sleep. Lichfield is about his level. I don't know anything about Lichfield, and I don't know much about Bertie. But they seem to me rather suitable. And much more can be done with the *cor anglais* than Wagner ever imagined. The solo in *Tristan* is absolute child's play. I could perform it myself with a week's practice."

Dodo had been engaged in a small incendiary operation among the heather, with the match with which she had lit her cigarette. For the moment it seemed that her incendiarism was going to fulfil itself on larger lines than she had intended.

"Jack, I have set fire to Wales, like Lloyd George," she cried. "Stamp on it with your great feet. What great large strong feet! How beautiful are the feet of them that put out incendiary attempts in Wales! About Bertie, Edith, if you will stop playing that lamentable flute for a moment——"

"Flute?" asked Edith.

"Trombone if you like. The point is that your vitality hasn't inspired Bertie; it has only drained him of his. You set out to give him life, and you have become his vampire. I don't say it was your fault: it was his misfortune. But Berts is calm enough to keep your family going. The real question is about mine. Yes, Jack, that was where Hughie went into the sea, when the sea was like Switzerland. And those are the reefs, before which, though it's not grammatical, he had to reach the boat. He swam straight out from where your left foot is pointing. A Humane Society medal came for him yesterday, and Nadine pinned it on to his bed-clothes. He says it is rot, but I think he rather likes it. She pinned it on while he was asleep, and he didn't know what it meant. He thought it was the sort of thing that they give to guards of railway trains. The dear boy was rather confused, and asked if he had joined the station-masters."

Jack shaded his eyes from the sun.

"And a big sea was running?" he asked.

"But huge. It broke right up to the cliffs at the ebb. And into it he went like a duck to water."

Edith got up.

"I have heard enough of Hugh's trumpet blown," she said.

"And I have heard enough of the *cor anglais*," said Dodo. "Dear Edith, will you go away and play it there? You see, darling, Jack came out this morning to talk to me, and I came out to talk to him. Or we will go away if you like: the point is that somebody must."

"I shall go and play golf," said Edith with dignity. "I may not be back for lunch. Don't wait for me."

Dodo was roused to reply to this monstrous recommendation.

"If I had been in the habit of waiting for you," she said, "I should still be where I was twenty years ago. You are always in a hurry, darling, and never in time."

"I was in time for dinner last night," said Edith.

"Yes, because I told you it was at eight, when it was really at half-past."

Edith blew a melancholy minor phrase.

"Leit-motif," she said, "describing the treachery of a friend."

"Tooty, tooty, tooty," said Dodo cheerfully, "describing the gay impenitence of the same friend."

Edith exploded with laughter, and put the *cor anglais* into its green-baize bag.

"Goodbye," she said, "I forgive you."

"Thanks, darling. Mind you play better than anybody ever played before, as usual."

"But I do," said Edith passionately.

Dodo leaned back on the springy couch of the heather as Edith strode down the hillside.

"It's not conceit," she observed, "but conviction and it makes her so comfortable. I have got a certain amount of it myself, and so I know what it feels like. It was dear of you to come down, Jack, and it will be still dearer of you if you can persuade Nadine to go back with you to Winston."

"But I don't want to go back to Winston. Anyhow, tell me about Nadine. I don't really know anything more than that she has thrown Seymour over, and devotes herself to Hugh."

"My dear, she has fallen head over ears in love with him."

"You are a remarkably unexpected family," Jack allowed himself to say.

"Yes: that is part of our charm. I think somewhere deep down she was always in love with him, but, so to speak, she couldn't get at it.

355

It was like a seam of gold: you aren't rich until you have got down through the rock. And Hugh's adventure was a charge of dynamite to her: it sent the rock splintering in all directions. The gold lies in lumps before his eyes, but I am not sure whether he knows it is for him or not. He can't talk much, poor dear, he is just lying still, and slowly mending, and very likely he thinks no more than that she is only very sorry for him, and wants to do what she can. But in a fortnight from now comes the date when she was to have married Seymour. He can't have forgotten that."

"Forgotten?" asked Jack.

"Yes, he doesn't remember much at present. He had severe concussion as well as that awful breakage of the hip."

"Do they think he will recover completely?" asked Jack.

"They can't tell yet. His smaller injuries have healed so wonderfully that they hope he may. They are more anxious about the effects of the concussion than the other. He seems in a sort of stupor still; he recognises Nadine of course, but she hasn't except on that first night seemed to mean much to him."

"What was that?"

"He so nearly died then. He kept calling for her in a dreadful strange voice, and when she came he didn't know her for a time. Then she put her whole soul into it, the darling, and made him know her, and he went to sleep. She slept, or rather lay awake, all night by his bed. She saved his life, Jack; they all said so. She went into the valley of death after him, and led him back."

"It seems rather perverse to refuse to marry him when he is sound, and the moment he is terribly injured to want to," said Jack.

"My darling, it is no use criticising people," said Dodo, "unless by your criticism you can change them. Even then it is a great responsibility. But you could no more change Nadine by criticising her, than you could change the nature of the wild cat at the Zoo by sitting down in front of its cage, and telling it you didn't like its disposition, and that it had not a good temper. You may take it that Nadine is utterly in love with him."

"And as he has always been utterly in love with her, I don't know why you want me to take Nadine away. Bells and wedding-cake as soon as Hugh can hobble to church."

"Jackino, you don't see," she said. "If I know Hughie at all, he won't dream of offering himself to Nadine until it is certain that he will be an able-bodied man again. And she is expecting him to, and is worrying and wondering about it. Also, she is doing him no good now. It can't be good for an invalid to have continually before him the girl to whom he has given his soul, who has persistently refused to accept it. It is true that they have exchanged souls now—as far as that goes my darling Nadine has so much the best of the bargain—but Hugh has to begin the—the negotiations, and he won't, even if he sees that Nadine is a willing Barkis, until he knows he has something more than a shattered unmendable thing to offer her. Consequently he is silent, and Nadine is perplexed. I will go on saying it over and over again if it makes it any clearer, but if you understand, you may signify your assent in the usual manner. Clap your great hands and stamp your great feet; oh, Jack, what a baby you are!"

"Do you suppose she will consent to come away?" said Jack, coughing a little at the dust his great feet had raised from the loose soil.

"Yes, if you can persuade her that her presence isn't good for Hugh. So you will try: that's all right. Nadine has a great respect for Papa Jack's wisdom, and I can't think why. I always thought a lot of your heart, dear, but very little of your head. You mustn't retort that you never thought much of either of mine, because it wouldn't be manly, and I should tell you you were a coward as the Suffragettes do when they hit policemen in the face."

"And why should it be I to do all this?" asked Jack.

"Because you are Papa Jack," said Dodo, "and a girl listens to a man when she would not heed a woman. Oh, you might tell her, which is probably true, that you want somebody to take care of you at Winston. You could use that to help to preach down a step-daughter's heart. You must think of these things for yourself, though, because in my heart I am really altogether on Nadine's side. I think it is wonderful that she should now be waiting so eagerly and humbly for Hugh, poor crippled Hugh, as he at present is, to speak. She has chosen the good part like Mary, and I want you for the present to take it away from her. It's wiser for her to go, but am I," asked Dodo dramatically, "to supply the ruthless foe, which is you, with guns and ammunition against my daughter?"

"You can't take both sides," remarked Jack.

"Jack, I wish you were a woman for one minute, just to feel how ludicrous such an observation is. Our lives—not perhaps Edith's—are passed in taking both sides. My whole heart goes out to Hugh, who has been so punished for his gallant recklessness, and then the moment I say 'punished' I think of Nadine's awakened love and shout 'No, I meant rewarded.' Then I think of Nadine, and wonder if I could bear her being married to a cripple, and simultaneously, now that she has shown she can love, I cannot bear the thought of her being married to anybody else. After all Nelson had only one eye and one arm, and though he wasn't exactly married to Lady Hamilton, I'm sure she was divinely happy. But then, best of all, I think of Hugh making a complete recovery, and once more coming to Nadine with his great brown doggy eyes, and telling her. . . . Then for once I don't take both sides, but only one, which is theirs, and if it would advance their happiness, I would even take away from poor little Seymour his jade and his Antoinette, which is all that Nadine left him with, without a single qualm of regret."

"After all she has left him where she found him," said Jack, who had rather taken Edith's view about their marriage. "He had only his Antoinette and his jade when she accepted him, and until you make a further raid, he will have them still."

Dodo shook her head.

"Jack, it is rather tiresome of you," she said. "You are making me begin to have qualms for Seymour. She found his heart for him, you see, and now having taken everything out of it, she has gone away again, leaving him a cupboard as empty as Mother Hubbard's."

"He will put the jade back. And Antoinette," said Jack hopefully.

Dodo got up.

"That is what I doubt," she said. "Until we have known a thing, we can't miss it. We only miss it when we have known it, and it is taken away leaving the room empty. Then old things won't always go back into their places again: they look shabby and uninteresting, and the room is spoiled. It is very unfortunate. But what is to happen when a girl's heart is suddenly awakened? Is she to give it an opiate? What is the opiate for heartache? Surely not marriage with somebody different. Yet jilt is an ugly word."

Dodo looked at Jack with a sort of self-deprecation.

"Don't blame Nadine, darling," she said. "She inherited it; it runs in the family."

Jack jumped up, and took Dodo's hands in his.

"You shall not talk horrible scandal about the woman I love," he said.

"But it's true," said Dodo.

"Therefore it is the more abominable of you to repeat it," said he.

But there was a certain obstinacy about Dodo that morning.

"I think it's good for me to keep that scandal alive in my heart," she said. "Usen't the monks to keep peas in their boots to prevent them getting too comfortable?"

"Monks were idiots," said Jack loudly, "and any one less like a monk than you, I never saw. Monk, indeed! Besides I believe they used to boil the peas first."

Dodo's face, which had been a little troubled, cleared considerably.

"That showed great commonsense," she said. "I don't think they can have been such idiots. Jack, if I boil that pea, would you mind my still keeping it in my boot?"

"Rather messy," said he. "Better take it out. After all, you did really take it out when you married me."

Dodo raised her eyes to his.

"David shall take it out," she said.

Jack had not at present heard of this nomenclature. In fact it did him credit that he instantly guessed to whom allusion was being made.

"Oh, that's settled, is it?" he said. "And now, David's mother, give me a little news of yourself. Is all well?"

Dodo's mouth grew extraordinarily tender.

"Oh, so well, Jesse," she said, "so well."

She was standing a foot or so above him, on the steep hillside, and bending down to him, kissed him, and was silent a moment. Then she decided swiftly and characteristically that a few words like those that had just passed between them were as eloquent as longer speeches, and became her more usual self again.

"You are such a dear, Jack," she said, "and I will forgive your dreadful ignorance of the name of David's mother. Oh, look at the sea-gulls fishing for their lunch. Oh, for the wings of a sea-gull, not to fly and be at rest at all, but to take me straight to the dining-room. And I feel certain Nadine will listen to you, and it would be a good thing to take her away for a little. She is living on her nerves, which is as expensive as eating pearls, like Cleopatra."

"Drinking," said Jack. "She dissolved them——"

"Darling, vinegar doesn't dissolve pearls: it is a complete mistake to suppose it does. She took the pearl like a pill and drank some vinegar afterwards. Jack, pull me up the hill, not because I am tired but because it is pleasanter so. I am sorry you are going to-morrow, and I shall make love to Hughie after you've gone and pretend it's you. I do pray Hughie may get quite well, and he and Nadine, and you and I may all have our heart's desire. Edith too: I hope she will write a symphony so beautiful that by common consent we shall throw away all the works of Beethoven and Bach and Brahms just as we throw away antiquated Bradshaws."

She was rather out of breath after delivering herself of this series of remarkable statements, and Jack got in a word.

"And what was the name of David's mother?" he asked, with a rather tiresome reversion to an abandoned topic.

"I don't know or care," said Dodo with dignity. "But I'm going to be."

It required all Jack's wisdom to persuade Nadine to go away with him, at the first opening of the subject. But in the end she yielded, for during this last fortnight she had felt (as by the illumination of her love she could not help doing) that at present she "meant" very little to Hugh. Her presence, which on that first critical night had not done less than set his face towards life instead of death, had, she felt, since then, dimly troubled and perplexed him. Every day she had thought that he would need her, but each day passed and he still lay there with a barrier between him and her. Yet any day he might want her, and she was loth to go. But she knew how tired and overstrained she felt herself, and the ingenious Papa Jack made use of this.

"You have given him all you can, my dear, for the present," he said. "Come away and rest, and—what is Dodo's phrase?—and fill your pond again."

"And I may come back if Hughie wants me?" she asked.

That was easy to answer. If Hugh really wanted her, the difficult situation solved itself. But there was one thing more.

"I don't suppose I need ask it," said Nadine, "but if Hughie gets worse, much worse, then I may come? I—I could not be there then."

Jack kissed her.

"My dear girl," he said, "what do you take me for? An ogre? But we won't think about that at all. Please God, you will not come back for that reason."

Nadine very rudely dried her eyes on his rough homespun sleeve.

"You are such a comfort, Papa," she said. "You're quite firm and strong, like—like a big wisdom-tooth. And when we are at Winston will you let Seymour come down and see me if he wants to. And—and if he comes will you come and interrupt us in half an hour? I've behaved horribly to him, but I can't help it, and it—that we aren't to be married, I mean—was in the *Morning Post* to-day, and it looked so horrible and cold. But whatever he wants to say to me I think half an hour is sufficient. I wonder—I wonder if you know why I behaved like such a pig?"

"I think I might guess," said Jack.

"Then you needn't, because there's only one possible guess. So we'll assume that you know. What a nuisance women are to your poor long-suffering sex. Especially girls."

Jack laughed.

"They are just as much a nuisance afterwards," said he. "Look at your mother, how she is making life one perpetual martyrdom to me."

"But she used to be a nuisance to you, Papa Jack," said Nadine.

"There again you are wrong," he said. "I always loved her."

"And does that prevent one's being a nuisance?" asked Nadine. "Are you sure? Because if you are you needn't interrupt Seymour quite so soon. I said half an hour because I thought that would be time enough for him to tell me what a nuisance I was——"

"You're a heartless little baggage," observed Jack.

"Not quite," said Nadine.

"Well, you're an April day," said he, seeing the smile break through.

"And that is a doubtful compliment," said she. "But you are wrong if you think I am not sorry for Seymour. Yet what was I to do, Papa Jack, when I made The Discovery?"

"Well, you're not a heartless little baggage," conceded Jack, "but you have taken your heart out of one piece of the baggage, and packed it in another."

"Oh, la, la," said Nadine. "We mix our metaphors."

Nadine left with Jack in the motor soon after breakfast next morning. It had been settled that she should not tell Hugh she was going, until she said goodbye to him, and when she went to his room next morning to do so she found him still asleep, and the tall nurse entirely refused to have him awakened.

"Much better for him to sleep than to say goodbye," said this adamantine woman. "When he wakes, he shall be told you have gone, if he asks."

"Of course he'll ask," said Nadine.

She paused a moment.

"Will you let me know if he doesn't?" she added.

Nurse Bryerly's grim capable face relaxed into a smile. She did not quite understand the situation, but she was quite content to do her best for her patient according to her lights.

"And shall I say that you'll be back soon?" she asked.

Nadine had no direct reply to this.

"Ah, do make him get well," she said.

"That's what I'm here for. And I will say that you'll be back soon, shall I, if he wants you?"

"Soon?" said Nadine. "That minute."

Hugh slept long that morning, and Dodo was not told he was awake and ready to receive a morning call till the travellers had been gone a couple of hours. She had spent them in a pleasant atmosphere of conscious virtue, engendered by the feeling that she had sent Jack away when she would much have preferred his stopping here. But as Dodo explained to Edith it took quite a little thing to make her feel good, whereas it took a lot to make her feel wicked.

"A nice morning, for instance," she said, "or sending my darling Jack away because it's good for Nadine, or getting a postal order. Quite little things like that make me feel a perfect saint. Whereas the powers of hell have to do their worst as the hymn says, to make me feel wicked."

Edith gave a rather elaborate sigh. She had to sigh carefully because she had a cigarette and a pen in her mouth while she was scratching out a blot she had made on the score she was revising. So care was needed, otherwise cigarette and pen might have been shot from her mouth. When she spoke her utterance was indistinct and mumbling.

"I suppose you infer that you are more at home in heaven than hell," she said, "since just a touch makes you feel a saint. I should say it was the other way about. You are so at home in the other place that the most abysmal depths of infamy have to be presented to you before you know they are wicked at all, whereas you hail as divine the most infinitesimal distraction that breaks the monotonous round of vice. Perhaps I am expressing myself too strongly, but I feel strongly. The world is more high-coloured to me than to other people."

"Darling, I never heard such a moderate and well-balanced statement," said Dodo. "Do go on."

"I don't want to. But I thought your optimism about yourself was sickly, and wanted a—a dash of discouragement. But you and Nadine are both the same: if you behave charmingly you tell us to give the praise to you, if you behave abominably you say 'I can't help it; it was Nature's fault for making me like that.' Now I am not that sort of shuffler; whatever I do I take the responsibility, and say 'I am I. Take me or leave me.' But I have no doubt that Nadine believes it has been *too* wonderful of her to fall in love with Hugh. And when she jilts Seymour, she says 'Enquire at Nature's Workshop; this firm is entirely independent.' Bah!"

Dodo laughed, but her laugh died rather quickly.

"Ah, don't be hard, Edith," she said. "We most of us want encouragement at times, and we have to encourage ourselves by making ourselves out as nice as we can. Otherwise we should look on the mess we make of things as a hopeless job. Perhaps it is hopeless, but that is the one thing we mustn't allow. We are like"—Dodo paused for a simile—"we are like children to whom is given a quantity of lovely little squares of mosaic, and we know, our souls know, that they can be put together into the most beautiful patterns. And we begin fairly well, but then the devil comes along and jogs our elbow, and smashes it all up. Probably it is our own stupidity, but it is more encouraging to say it is the devil or nature, something not ourselves. Good heavens, my elbow has been jogged often enough! And when the pattern gets on well, we encourage ourselves by saying: 'This is clever and good and wise Me doing it now!' And then perhaps something very big and solemn comes our way, and we bow our heads, and know it isn't ourselves at all."

Edith had finished erasing her blot, and was gathering her sheets together. She tapped them dramatically with an inky-forefinger.

"This is big and solemn," she said. "But it's Me. The artist's inspiration never comes from outside: it is always from within. I'm going to send it to have the band parts copied to-day."

At the moment the message came that Hugh received, and Dodo got up. He had received Edith one morning, but the effect was that he had eaten no lunch and had dozed uneasily all the afternoon. Edith had been content with the explanation that her vitality was too strong for him, and, while ready to give him another dose of it, did not press the matter.

He lay propped up in bed, with a wad of pillows at his back. He looked far more alert and present than he had yet done. Hitherto, he had been slow to grasp the meaning of what was said to him, and he hardly ever volunteered a statement or question, but this morning he smiled and spoke with quite unusual quickness.

"Morning, Aunt Dodo," he said. "I'm awfully brisk to-day."

Nurse Bryerley put in a warning word.

"Don't be too brisk," she said. "Please don't let him be too brisk," she added looking at Dodo.

"Hughie dear, you do look better," she said, "but we'll all be quite calm and self-contained, like flats."

Hugh frowned for a moment; then his face cleared again.

"I see," he said. "Bright, aren't I? Aunt Dodo I have certainly woke up this morning. You look real, do you know; before I was never quite certain about you. You looked as if you might be a good forgery, but spurious. Have a cigarette, and why shouldn't I?"

"Wiser not," said Nurse Bryerley laconically.

Hugh's briskness did not seem to be entirely good-natured.

"How on earth could a cigarette hurt me?" he said. "Perhaps it would be wiser for Lady Chesterford not to smoke either. Aunt Dodo, you mustn't smoke. Wiser not."

Nurse Bryerley smiled with secret content.

"That's right, Mr. Graves," she said. "I like to see my patients irritable. It always shows they are getting better."

"I should have thought you might have seen that without annoying me," said Hugh.

"Well, well, I don't mind your having one cigarette to keep Lady Chesterford company," said the nurse. "But you'll be disappointed."

Dodo took out her case as Nurse Bryerley left the room. "Here you are, Hughie," she said.

Hugh lit one, and blew a cloud of smoke through his nostrils.

"Are they quite fresh, Aunt Dodo?" he said.

"Yes, dear, quite. Doesn't it taste right?"

"Yes, delicious," said Hugh, absolutely determined not to find it disappointing. "I say, what a sunny morning!"

"Is it too much in your eyes?"

"It is rather. Will you ask Nurse Bryerley to pull the blind down."

Dodo pulled down the blind too far on the first attempt to be pleasing, not far enough on the second. Hugh felt she was very clumsy.

"Isn't Nadine coming to see me this morning?" he asked. "But I daresay she is tired of sitting with me every day."

Dodo came back to her chair by the bed again.

"She went off with Jack to Winston this morning," she said. "Just for a change. She was very much tired and overdone. You've been a fearful anxiety to her, the dear bad boy."

Hugh put his cigarette down and shut his mouth, as if firmly determined never to speak again.

"She came in to say good-bye to you," she said, "but you were asleep and they didn't want to wake you."

There was still dead silence on Hugh's part.

"It was only settled she should go yesterday," she continued, "and she had to be persuaded. But Jack wanted one of us, and, as I say, she was very much overdone. Now I'm not the least overdone. So I stopped. But I wish she could have seen how much more yourself you were when you woke to-day."

At length Hugh spoke.

"What is the use of telling me that sort of tale?" he said. "She is going to be married to Seymour in a few days. She has gone away for that. I suppose in some cold-blooded way she thought it better to sneak off without telling me. No doubt it was very tactful of her."

Dodo turned round towards him.

"No, Hughie, you are quite wrong," she said. "Nadine is not going to marry Seymour at all."

Hugh lifted his right hand, and examined it cursorily. A long cut, now quite healed, run up the length of his forefinger.

"I see," he said. "She said she would marry Seymour in order to get rid of me, and now that I have been got rid of in other ways, she has no further use for him. Isn't that it?"

His face had become quite white, and the hand with the healed wound trembled so violently that the bed shook.

"No, that is not it," said Dodo quietly. "And don't be so nervous and fidgetty, my dear."

Suddenly the trembling ceased.

"Aunt Dodo, if it is not that, what is it?" he asked, in a voice that would have melted Rhadamanthus.

She turned a shining face on him, and laid her hand on his.

"Oh, Hughie, lie still and get well," she said. "And then ask Nadine herself. She will come back when you want her. She told Nurse Bryerley to tell you so, if you asked."

Hugh moved across his other hand, so that Dodo's lay between his.

"I must ask you one more thing," he said. "Is it because of me in any way that she chucked Seymour? I entreat you to say 'no,' if it is 'no.' "

"I can't say 'no,' " said Dodo.

Hugh drew one long sobbing breath.

"It's mere pity then," he said. "Nadine always liked me, and she always was impulsive like that. I daresay she won't marry him till I'm better, if I am ever better. She will wait till I am strong enough to enjoy it thoroughly."

Dodo interrupted him.

"Hughie, don't say bitter and untrue things like that," she said. "And don't feel them. She is not going to marry Seymour, either now or afterwards."

Once again Hugh was silent, and after an interval Dodo spoke, divining exactly what was in his irritable convalescent mind.

"I have never deceived you before, Hughie," she said, "and you have no right to distrust me now. I am telling you the truth. I also tell you the truth when I say you must get bitter thoughts out of your mind. Ah, my dear, it is not always easy. There's a beast within each of us."

"There's a beast within me," said Hugh.

"And there's a dear brave fellow whom I am so proud of," said Dodo.

Hugh's lips quivered, but there was a quality in his silence as different from that which had gone before, as there was between his callings of Nadine on the night when she fought death for him.

"And now that's enough," said Dodo. "Shall I read to you, Hughie, or shall I leave you for the present?"

He held her hand a moment longer.

"I think I will lie still and—and think," he said.

"Good luck to your fishing, dear," said she rising.

"Good luck to your fishing?" he asked. "It's in a picture. Small boy fishing, kneeling on the waves."

Dodo beat a strategic retreat.

"Is it?" she said.

But it seemed to Hugh that her voice lacked the blank-inquiry tone of ignorance.

Hugh settled himself a little lower down on his backing of pillows, after Dodo had left him, and tried to arrange his mind, so that the topics that concerned it stood consecutively. But Dodo's last remark, which certainly should have stood last also in his reflections, kept on shouldering itself forward. She had wished him "good luck to his fishing," and he could not bring himself to believe that, consciously or unconsciously, there was not in her mind a certain picture, of a little winged boy, kneeling in the waves, who dropped a red line into the unquiet sea. He could not, and did not try to remember the painter, but certainly the picture had been at some exhibition which he and Nadine had attended together. A little winged boy. . . . The title was printed after the number in the catalogue.

Nadine was not to marry Seymour now or afterwards. . . . There came a black speck again over his thoughts. He himself had been got rid of by this crippling accident, and now she had expunged Seymour also. "And though she saw all heaven in flower above, she would not love." The lines came into his mind without any searching for them; for the moment he could not remember where he had heard them. And then memory began to awake.

Hitherto, he had not been able to recall anything of the day or two that preceded his catastrophe, though he could remember a few of the events immediately before it. He remembered Nadine calling out "No, Hugh, not you," he remembered her cry of "Well done"; he remembered that he had floated in on that line of toppling waters with a small boy on his back. But now a fresh thread of memory had been awakened: some connection in his brain had been restored, and he remembered their quarrel and reconciliation on the day the gale began, how she had said, "Oh, Hughie, if only I loved you!" Soon after came the portentous advent of the wind, with the blotting out of the sun, and the transformation of the summer sea.

He heard with unspeakable irritation the entry of Nurse Bryerley. That seemed an unwarrantable intrusion, for he felt as if he had been alone with Nadine, and now this assiduous grenadier broke in upon them with a hundred fidgetty offices to perform. She restored to him a fallen pillow, she closed a window through which a breeze was blowing rather freely, she brought him a cup of chicken broth. It seemed an eternity before she asked him if he was comfortable, and made her long delayed exit. Even then she reminded him that the doctor was due in half an hour.

But for half an hour he would be alone now, and for the first time since his accident he found that he wanted to think. Hitherto his mind had sat vacant, like an idle passenger who sees without observation or interest the transit of the country. But Dodo's visit this morning, and her communications to him had made life appear a thing that once more concerned him: up till now it was but a manoeuvre taking place round him, but outside him. Now the warmth of it reached him again, and began to circulate through him. And what she had told him was being blown out, as it were, in his brain, even as a lather of soapsuds is blown out into an iridescent bubble, on which gleam all the hues of sunset and moonrise and rainbow. That rainbow was not one of the vague dreams in which, lately, his mind had moved, it was a real thing, not receding but coming nearer to him, blown towards him by some steady breeze, not idly vagrant in the effortless air. Should it break on his heart, not into nothingness, but into the one white light out of which the sum of all lights and colours is made?

He could not doubt that it was this which Dodo meant. Nadine had thrown over Seymour and that event concerned him. And then swift as the coming of the storm which they had seen together, came the thought, clear and precise as the rim of thunder-clouds, that, for all he knew, a barrier for ever impenetrable, lay between them. For he could never offer to her a cripple; the same pride that had refused to let him take an intimate place beside her after she, by her acceptance of Seymour, had definitely rejected him, forbade him, without possibility of discussion, to let her tie herself to him, unless he could stand sound and whole beside her. He must be competent in brain and bone and body to be Nadine's husband. And for that as yet he had no guarantee.

Since his accident he had not up till now cared to know precisely what his injuries were, nor whether he could ever completely recover from them. The concussion of the brain had quenched all curiosity and interest not only in things external to him, but in himself, and he had received the assurance that he was going on very well with the unconcern that we feel for remote events. But now his thoughts flew back from Nadine and clustered round himself. He felt that he must know his chances, the best or the worst . . . and yet he dreaded to know, for he could live for a little in a paradise by imagining that he would get completely well, instead of in the shattered ruin, which the knowledge of the worst would strew round him.

But this morning the energy of life which for those two weeks had lain dormant in him, began to stir again. He wanted. It seemed to him but a few moments since his nurse left him that Dr. Cardew came in. He saw the flushed face and brightened eyes of his patient, and after an enquiry or two took out the thermometer he had not used for days, and tested Hugh's temperature. He put it back again in its nickel case with a smile.

"Well, it's not any return of fever, anyhow," he said. "Do you feel different in any way this morning?"

"Yes. I want to get well."

"Highly commendable," said Dr. Cardew.

Hugh fingered the bed-clothes in sudden agitation.

"I want to know if I shall get well," he said. "I don't mean half well, in a Bath chair, but quite well. And I want to know what my injuries were."

Dr. Cardew looked at him a moment without speaking. But it was perfectly clear that this fresh colour and eagerness in Hugh's face, was but the lamp of life burning brighter. There was no reason that he should not know what he asked, now that he cared to know.

"You broke your hip-bone," he said. "You also had very severe concussion of the brain. There were a quantity of little injuries."

"Oh, tell me the best and the worst of it quickly," said Hugh with impatience.

"I can tell you nothing for certain for a few days yet about the fracture. There is no reason why it should not mend perfectly. And to-day for the first time I am not anxious about the other."

Quite suddenly Hugh put his hands before his face and broke into a passion of weeping.

14

A week later, Dodo was interviewing Dr. Cardew in her sitting-room at Meering. He had just spoken at some length to her, and she had time to notice that he looked like a third-rate actor, and recorded the fact also that Edith seemed to have gone back to scales and the double-bass. This impression was conveyed from next door. He spoke like an actor too, and said things several times over, as if it was a play. He talked about fractures and conjunctions, and X-ray photographs, and satisfaction, and the recuperative power of youth and satisfaction and X-rays. Eventually Dodo could stand this harangue no longer.

"It is all too wonderful," she said, "and I quite see that if science hadn't made so many discoveries, we couldn't tell if Hughie would have a bath chair till doomsday or not. But now, Dr. Cardew, he is longing to hear, and dreading to hear, poor lamb, and won't you let me be the butcher, or I suppose I should say Mary? You've been such a clever butcher, if you understand, and I do want to be Mary, who *had* a little lamb,"—she added in desperation, lest he should never understand her allusive conversation. "Of course he's not my little lamb, but my daughter's, and he wants to know so frightfully—Yes: I understand about his intellect too. It seems to me as bright as it ever was, and I notice no change whatever. He always spoke as if he was excited. May I go?"

Dodo intended to go, whether she might or not, but just at the door, she seemed to herself to have treated this distinguished physician with some abruptness. She unwillingly paused.

"Do stop to lunch," she said, "it will be lunch in ten minutes, and you will find me not so completely distracted. I shall be quite sensible, and would you ring the bell and tell them you are stopping? Don't mind the scales and the double-bass, dear Dr. Cardew: it is only Mrs. Arbuthnot, of whom you have heard. She will not play at lunch. I know you think you have come to a mad-house, but we are all quite sane. And I may go and tell Hughie what you have told me? If you hear loud screams of joy, it will only be me, and you needn't take any notice."

Dodo slid along the passage, upset a chair in Nurse Bryerley's room, and knelt down on the floor by Hugh's bed. She clawed at something with her eager hands, and it was chiefly bed-clothes.

"Oh, praise God, Hughie," she said. "Amen. There! Now you know, and there won't be any crutches, my dear, or the shadow of a bath-chair, whatever that is like. You won't have chicken-broth, and a foolish nurse, not you, dear Nurse Bryerley, I didn't mean you, and you will walk again and run again, and play the fool, just like me for a hundred years more. I told Dr. Cardew you weren't ever very calm or unexcited, and your poor broken hip has mended itself, and your kidneys aren't mixed up with your liver and lights, and you've—you've got your strong young body back again, and your silly young brain. Oh Hughie!"

Dodo leaned forward and clutched a more satisfactory handful of Hugh's shoulders.

"I couldn't let anybody but myself tell you," she said. "I had to tell you. But nobody else knows. You can tell anybody else you want to tell."

Hugh was paying but the very slightest attention to Dodo.

"Telegraph-form," he said rather rudely to Nurse Bryerley.

Dodo loved this inattention to herself. There was nothing *banal* about it. He had no more thought of her than he would have had for a newspaper that contained ecstatic tidings. He did not stroke or kiss or shake hands with a mere newspaper that told him such great things.

"It's so funny not to have telegraph-forms handy," he said.

"I know, dear. They ought always to be in every room. But servants are so forgetful. Talk to me until Nurse Bryerley gets one."

Hugh looked at her with shining eyes.

"How can I talk?" he said. "There's nothing to say. I want that telegraph-form."

Dodo, human and practical and explosive, yearned for the statement of what she knew.

"Whom are you going to telegraph to?" she asked.

Hugh had time for one contemptuous glance at her.

"Oh, Aunt Dodo, you ass!" he said. "Oh, by Jove, how awfully rude of me, and I haven't thanked you for coming to tell me. Thanks so much; I am so grateful to you for all your goodness to me—ah."

He took a telegraph-form and scribbled a few words.

"May it go now?" he said.

Dodo was almost embarrassingly communicative at lunch, at which meal Edith did not appear, and the continued booming of the double-bass indicated that Art was being particularly long that morning. Consequently Dodo found herself alone with an astonished physician.

"If only a man could be a clergyman and a doctor," she said, "you could tell him everything, because clergy know all about the soul and doctors all about the body, and when you completely understand anything, you can't be shocked at it. I think I should have poisoned you, Dr. Cardew, if you had said that Hughie would never be the same man again; anyhow I shouldn't have asked you to lunch. Ah, in that case I couldn't have poisoned you. How difficult it must be to plan a crime really satisfactorily. I always have had a great deal of sympathy with criminals, because my great-grandfather was hanged for smuggling. Do have some more mutton, which calls itself lamb. I certainly shall. I'm going to have a baby you know, or perhaps you didn't. Isn't it ridiculous at my age, and he's going to be called David."

"In case——" began Dr. Cardew.

"No, in any case," said Dodo. "I mean it certainly is going to be a boy. You shall see. What a day for January, is it not? The year has turned, though I hope that doesn't mean it will go bad. I wish you had seen Hughie's face when I told him he wasn't going to have a bath-chair. He looked like one of Sir Joshua Reynolds' angels with a three weeks' beard, which I shouldn't wonder if he was shaving now since, as I said, there aren't going to be any bath-chairs."

"I don't quite follow," said Dr. Cardew politely.

"I'm sure I don't wonder," said Dodo cordially, "although it's so clear to me. But you see, he's going to propose to my daughter now that it's certain he will be the same man again and not a different one, and no eligible young man ever has a beard. What a good title for a sordid and tragic romance 'Beards and Bath-chairs' would be. Of course Hughie instantly called for a telegraph-form, and when I asked him who he was telegraphing to, he called me an ass, in so many words, or rather so few. After all I had done for him, too! Oh, here's Edith! Edith, Dr. Cardew and I have not been listening to your playing but we're sure it has been lovely. Do you know Dr. Cardew, and it's Mrs. Arbuthnot, or ought I to say 'she's Mrs. Arbuthnot.' Edith, if you don't mind our smoking, Dr. Cardew and I will wait and talk to you for a little, but if you do, we won't."

Edith shook hands so warmly with the doctor, that he felt he must have been an old friend of hers, and that the fact had eluded his memory. But it was only the general zeal which a long musical morning gave her.

"I'm sure you came to see our poor Hugh," she said. "Do tell me, is there the slightest chance of his ever walking again?"

"Not the smallest," said Dodo. "I've just been to break the news to him, and he has telegraphed to Nadine to come at once. I can't keep it up. Edith, he is going to be perfectly well again, and he has telegraphed to Nadine just the same."

Edith looked a little disappointed.

"Then I suppose we must resign ourselves to a perfectly conventional and Philistine ending," she said. "There was all the makings of a twentieth century tragedy about the situation, and now I am afraid it is going to tail off and be domestic and happy and utterly inartistic. I had better hopes for Nadine, she always looked as if there might be some wild destiny in store for her, and when she engaged herself to Seymour without caring two straws for him, I thought I heard a great fate knocking at the door——"

This was too gross an inconsistency for even Dodo to pass over.

"And you said at the time you thought the engagement was horrible and unnatural, and me a wicked mother for permitting it," she cried.

"Very possibly. No doubt then I was being a woman, now I am talking as an artist. You always confuse the two, Dodo, for all your general acumen. When I have been playing all morning——"

"Scales," said Dodo.

"A great deal of the finest music in the world is based on scale passages, and the second movement of my symphony is based on them too. When I have been playing all morning, I see things as an artist. I know Dr. Cardew will agree with me: sometimes he sees things as a surgeon, sometimes as a man. As a surgeon if a hazardous operation is in front of him, he says to himself, 'This is a wonderful and dangerous thing, and it thrills me.' As a man he says 'Poor devil, I am afraid he may die under the knife.' As for you Dodo, artistically speaking, you spoiled a situation as lurid as a play by Webster. 'Princess Waldenech' might have been as classical in real life, as the 'Duchess of Malfi.' Artistically an atmosphere as stormy as the first act of the Valkyrie surrounded you. And now instead of the Gotterdammerung you are going to give us Hansel and Gretel, with flights of angels."

Dodo exploded with laughter.

"And while I was still giving you 'Princess Waldenech,' " she said, "you cut me for a year."

"As a woman," cried Edith; "as an artist I adored you. You were as ominous as Faust's black poodle. Of course your first marriage to a man who adored you, for whom you did not care one bar of the Hallelujah chorus, was a thing that might have happened to anybody, but when, as soon as he was mercifully delivered, you got engaged to Jack and at the last moment jilted him for that melodramatic drunkard, I thought great things were going to happen. Then you divorced him, and I waited with a beating heart. And now, would you believe it, Dr. Cardew," cried Edith pointing a carving fork, with a slice of ham on the end of it, at him. "She has married Lord Chesterford, as you know, and is going to have a baby. And all that wealth of potential tragedy is going to end in a silver christening mug. The silly suffragette with her hammer and a plate-glass window has more sense of drama than you, Dodo. And now Nadine is going to take after you and marry the man she loves. Hugh is just as bad: instead of dying for the sake of that blear-eyed child who comes up to enquire after him every day, he is going to live for the sake of Nadine. Drama is dead. Of course it has long been dead in literature, but I hoped it survived in life."

Dodo turned anxiously to Dr. Cardew.

"She isn't mad," she said reassuringly. "You needn't be the least frightened. She will play golf immediately after lunch."

Edith had been brought her large German pewter beer-mug, and for the moment she had put her face into it, like old-fashioned gentlemen praying into their hats on Sunday morning before service. There was a little froth on the end of her rather long nose when she took it out.

"Why not?" she said. "All artistic activity is a sort of celestial disease, and its antidote is bodily activity which is a material disease. A perfectly healthy body like mine does not need exercise, except in order to bring down the temperature of the celestial fever. When I am playing golf, my artistic soul goes to sleep and rests. And when I am composing, I should not know a golf-ball from an egg. That is me. You might think I am being egoistic, but I only take myself as an instance of a type. I speak for the whole corporate body of artists."

"Militant here on earth," remarked Dodo.

"Militant? Of course all artists are militant, and they fight against blind eyes and deaf ears. They thunder and lighten, and hope to shake this dull world into perception. But it is fighting against prodigious odds. The drama that seems to interest the world now is a presentation of the hopeless lives of surburban people. Any note of romance or distinction is sufficient to secure a failure. It's the same in music: Debussy, when he tells us of rain in the garden, makes the rain fall into a small back yard with sooty blighted plants growing in it, out of a foggy sky. When he gives us *reflêts sur l'eau* the water is in a little cement basin in the same back-yard, with anaemic gold-fish swimming about in it. As for Strauss, he began and finished with that terrible domestic symphony. It went from the kitchen into the scullery, and back again. Fiction is the same. Any book that deals with entirely dull people, provided that they none of them ever show a spark of real fire, or are touched by romance or joy or beauty, makes success. They must have the smell of oilcloth and Irish stew around them, and then the world says 'This is art' or 'This is reality.' There's the mistake! Art is never real: it is a fantasy, a fairy story, a soap bubble sailing into the sunset. It is art because it takes you out of reality. Of course artists are militant; they fight against dullness, and they will fight for ever, and they will never win. As for their being militant here on earth, you must be militant somewhere. I shall be militant in heaven by-and-by. I wonder if you understand. As I said I was disappointed in Nadine artistically, but I am enraptured with her humanly. On that same plane I was enraptured with you, Dodo. Humanly speaking, I have watched you with sobs in my throat, battling perilously on the great seas. And now you are like a battered ship, having weathered all storms, and putting into port, with all the piers and quays shouting congratulation. Artistically speaking, you are a derelict, and I should like to have you blown up. Hullo, what has happened to Dr. Cardew?"

Dodo looked quickly round. The thought just crossed her mind that he might be asleep or having a fit. But there was no Dr. Cardew there.

"He has gone away while we weren't attending, just as a conjurer changes a rabbit into an omelette while you aren't attending," she said, "and I'm sure I don't wonder. Oh, Edith, at last the Hunting of the Snark has come true. I see now that we are Boojums. People softly and silently vanish away when you and I are talking, poor dears. They can't stand it, and I've noticed it before. Dear old Chesterford used to vanish sometimes like that, and I never knew until I saw he wasn't there. I'm sure Bertie vanishes too sometimes. I suppose we ought to vanish also, as the table must be laid again for dinner to-night."

Edith finished her beer.

"I had breakfast, lunch and dinner on the same cloth once," she said. "I was composing all day, and at intervals things were stuck in front of me which I ate or drank. I didn't move from nine in the morning till half-past eight in the evening, and I wrote forty pages of full score, and the inspiration never flagged for a moment. I wonder why artists are so fond of writing what they call 'My memories'; they ought to be content, as I am, to stand or fall by what they have done. Thank God, I have never had any doubts about my standing. Oh, I see a telegraph boy coming up the drive. It is sure to be for me. I am expecting a quantity."

This particular one happened to be for Dodo. Edith was disposed to take it as a personal insult.

Nadine, during the days she had spent at Winston, had not done much looking after Papa Jack, which had been the face-reason of her going there, and it is doubtful whether the real reason had found itself fulfilled, since there was substituted for the strain of seeing Hugh daily the strain of wanting to see him. Dodo, with her own swift recuperative powers, and the genius she had for being absorbed in her immediate surroundings, had not reckoned with Nadine's inferior facility in this respect, nor had she realized how completely the love which had at last touched Nadine drained and dominated her whole nature. All her zest for living, all her sensitiveness and intelligence, seemed to have been, as by some alchemical touch, transformed into the gold which all her life had been missing from her. She explained this to Esther, who, with an open-mindedness that might have appeared rather unsisterly, ranged her sympathies in opposition to Seymour.

"How long I shall be able to stop here," she said, "I don't know. I promised Mamma I would go away for at least a week, unless Hughie wanted me; but after that I think I shall go back, whether he wants me or not. I can't attend to anything else, and last night when I was playing billiards I carefully put the chalk into my coffee, which is not at all the sort of thing I usually do. It is very odd; all my life I have been quite unaware of this one thing, now I am not really aware of anything else. You are rather dream-like yourself to me; I am not quite sure if you have really happened or are part of a general background——"

"I am not part of any back-ground," said Esther firmly.

"No, so you say; but perhaps it is only the background that tells me so. And I suppose I ought to think a great deal about Seymour. I try to do that, but when I've thought about him for about a minute and a quarter I find my thoughts wander, and I wonder if Hughie has had his beef-tea or not. I do hope that Seymour is not unhappy; but having hoped it, I have finished with that, and remember that just at this moment Hughie is being made comfortable for the night. But do pin me down to Seymour. Did you see him in town, and does he mean to tell me what he thinks?"

"Yes, I saw him. He was exceedingly cross, but I don't think his crossness came from temper; it came from his mind hurting him. He told me he had meant to come down here and have it out with you, but presently he said you weren't worth it. So I took your side."

"That was darling of you," said Nadine, "but I am not sure that Seymour is not right."

"How can he be right? You haven't changed towards him!"

"Oh, doesn't jilting him make a change?" asked Nadine hopefully.

"No, that is an accident, as I told him. You didn't do it on purpose. You might as well say that to be knocked down by a motor-car is done on purpose. You got knocked down by Hughie. You hadn't ever loved Seymour at all, and really you said you would marry him largely because you wanted Hughie to stop thinking about you. It was chiefly for Hughie's sake you said you would marry Seymour, and it was so wonderful of you. Then came another accident, and Seymour fell in love with you. I warned him when we were on the family improvement tour in the summer that he was doing rather a risky thing——"

Nadine got up.

"Risky?" she said. "Oh, how risky it is. It is that which makes it so splendid. You risk everything: you go for it blind. Do you think Seymour went for it blind? I don't believe he did: I think he had one eye open all the time. He couldn't be quite blind, I think; his intelligence would prevent it. And I don't think he would be cross now if he had been quite blind. So I am not properly sorry for him."

"I went to lunch with him," said Esther. "He ate an enormous lunch, which I suppose is a consoling sign. But then Seymour would eat an enormous breakfast on the morning he was going to be hung. He would feel that he would never have any more breakfasts, so he would eat one that would last for ever. I think we have given enough time to Seymour. It is much more important that you shouldn't think of me as a background."

Nadine apparently thought differently.

"But I want to be nice to Seymour," she said, "and I don't see how to begin. And—and he's part of the background, too. He doesn't seem really to matter. But if he was really fond of me, like that it's hateful of me not to care. But how can I care? I've tried to care every day, and often twice a day, but—oh, a huge 'but.' "

The two were talking in Dodo's sitting-room, which Nadine had very wisely appropriated. At this moment the door opened and Seymour stood there.

"I made up my mind not to come and see you," he said to Nadine, "and then I changed it."

Esther sprang up.

"Oh, Seymour, how mean of you," she said, "not to ask Nadine if you might come."

"Not at all. She was bound to see me. But I didn't come to see you. You had better go away."

"If Nadine wishes—" she began.

"It does not matter what Nadine wishes. Nadine, please tell her to go."

Seymour spoke quite quietly, and having spoken he turned aside and lit a cigarette he held in his hand. By the time he had finished doing that the door had closed behind Esther. He looked round.

"What a charming room," he said. "But if you are going to sit in a room like this you ought to dress for it."

Nadine felt that all the sorrow she had been conscious of for him was being squeezed out of her. He tiptoed about, looking now at a picture, and now fingering an embroidery. He stopped for a moment opposite a Louis Seize tapestry chair, and gently flicked off it the cigarette ash that he had let drop there. He looked at the faded crimson of the Spanish silk on the walls, and examined with extreme care a Dutch picture of a frozen canal with peasants skating that hung above the mantel-piece. There was an Aubusson carpet on the floor, and after one glance at it he went softly off it and stood on the hearth-rug.

"I should put three-quarters of this room into a museum," he said, "and the rest into a dust-bin. You are going to ask me what I should put into the dust-bin. I should put that sham Watteau picture there, and that bureau that thinks it is Jacobean."

"And me?" asked Nadine.

"I am not sure. No: I am sure. I don't put you anywhere. I want to know where you put yourself. Perhaps you think you don't owe me an explanation. But I disagree with you. I think you owe it me. Of course I know you haven't got an explanation. But I should like to hear your idea of one."

Standing on the hearth-rug he pointed his toe as he spoke, looking at the well-polished shoe that shod it. Nadine was just on the point of telling him that he was thinking not about her, but about his shoe, but he was too quick for her.

"Of course I'm thinking about my shoe," he said. "I was wondering how it is that Antoinette polishes shoes better than anyone in the world."

"Is that what you have come to talk about?" asked Nadine.

"That is a very foolish question, Nadine. You have quibbled and chattered so incessantly that sometimes I think you can do nothing else. You might retort with a *tu quoque,* but it would not be true. I was capable anyhow of falling in love with you, I regret to say."

Seymour paused a moment, and then raised his eyes, which had been steadily regarding the masterpieces of Antoinette, to Nadine.

"I am wrong: I don't regret it," he said.

Suddenly his sincerity and his reality reached and touched Nadine. He stepped out of the background, so to speak, and stood firmly and authentically beside her.

"I regret it very much," she said, "and I am as powerless to help you, as I am to help myself."

"You seem to have been helping yourself pretty freely," said he in sudden exasperation. But she, usually so quick to flare into flame, felt no particle of resentment.

"There is no good in saying that," she said.

"I did not mean there to be. Good? I did not come down here to do you good."

"Why did you come? Just to reproach me?"

"Partly."

Again Seymour paused.

"I came chiefly in order to look at you," he said at length. "You are quite as beautiful as ever, you may like to know."

It was as if a further light had been turned on him, making him clearer and more real. She had confessed to Esther her inability to be "properly sorry" for him, but now she found herself not so incapable.

"I can't help either you or myself," she said again. "We have both been taken in control by something outside ourselves which never happened to either of us before. You feel that I have behaved atrociously to you, and anyone you ask would agree with you. But the atrocity was necessary. I couldn't help it. Only you must not think that I am not sorry for the effect that such necessity has had on you. I regret it very much. But if you ask me whether I am ashamed of myself, I answer that I am not."

She went on with growing rapidity and animation.

"If you have been in love with me, Seymour," she said, "you will understand that, for you will know that compulsion has been put upon me. How was it any longer possible for me to marry you, when I fell in love with Hughie? I jilted you: it is a word quite hideous, like flirt, but just as never in my life did I flirt, so I have not jilted you in the hideous sense. It was not because I was tired of you, or had a fancy for someone else. There was no getting away from what happened. Hughie enveloped me. My walls fell down, and went to Jericho. It wasn't my fault. The trumpets blew, just that."

"And in walked Hugh," said Seymour.

"I am not sure about that," said Nadine. "I think he was there all the time, walled up."

Seymour was silent a moment.

"How is he?" he asked.

"He is going on well. They do not know more than that yet. He is getting over the concussion, but they cannot tell yet whether he will be able to walk again."

"And are you going to marry him in any case if he is a cripple, I mean?" he asked.

"If Hughie will have me. I daresay I shall propose to him, and be refused, and propose again and be refused, just as used to happen the other way round in the old days. Oh, I know what his soul is like so well! He will say that he will not let me spend all my life looking after a cripple. But I shall have my way in the end. I am much stronger than he."

Seymour saw and understood the change in her face when she spoke of Hugh. Admirable as her beauty always was he had not dreamed that such tender transfiguration could come to it, or that it was capable of assuming so inward-burning and devoted a quality, and yet shine with its habitual brilliance uneclipsed. The love which he had dreamed would some day awaken there for him he saw now in the first splendour of its dawning, and from it he could guess what would be the glory of its full noonday, and with how celestial a ray she would shine on her lover. For the moment it seemed to him not to matter that it was another, not he, on whom that dawn should break, for whom it should grow to noonday, and sink at last in the golden west of a life truly and lovingly lived without fear of the lengthening shadows and the night that must inevitably close as it had preceded it, for by the power of his own love he could detach himself from himself, and though only momentarily reach that summit of devotion far below which, remote and insignificant, lies the mere husk and shell of the world that spins through the illimitable azure. So Dante saw the face of Beatrice when he had passed into the sweetness of the Earthly Paradise, and there came to him she whom the chariot with its harnessed griffins drew. And not otherwise, in his degree and hers, Seymour looked now at Nadine's face, glorified and made tender by her love, and in the perception that his own love gave him, he hailed and adored it. . . .

"I came to scold and reproach," he said, "but I also came to see you, to look at you. There is no harm in that. And if there is I can't help it. Nadine, I used to wonder what you would look like when you loved. You have shown me that. I—I didn't guess. There's a poem by Browning which ends: 'Those who win heaven blest are they.' The man who speaks was just in my case. But he managed to say that. I say it too, very quickly, because I know this unnatural magnanimity won't last. I agree with all you have said: it wasn't your fault. I hope you won't be tied to a cripple all your life, or, if he has to be a cripple, I hope you will be tied to him. There! I've said it, and it is true, but it rather reminds me of holding my breath. Give me a kiss, please, and then I'll climb swiftly down out of this rarefied atmosphere."

He kissed her on the mouth, as his right had been, and for a moment held her to him in an embrace more intimate than he had ever yet claimed from her. Edith, it may be remembered, had once seen him kiss her, and had pronounced it an anaemic salutation. But it was not anaemic now: his blood was alert and virile: its quality was not inferior to that which, one day in the summer, made Hugh seize her wrists, demanding the annulment of the profanation of her marriage with Seymour. In both, too, was the same fierceness of farewell.

For a few seconds Seymour held her close to him, and felt her neither shrink from him nor respond. Her willing surrender to his right was the utmost she could give, and he knew there was nothing else for him.

And then he proceeded to descend from what he had called the rarefied atmosphere with the speed of a yet-unopened parachute.

"Damn Hugh!" he said. "Yes, damn him! For God's sake don't tell him I asked after him, or hoped he was getting better. I don't want him to die, since I don't suppose that would do me any good, nor do I want him to be crippled for life, since that also would be quite useless after what you have told me. But if you said to him that I had asked after him, I should sink into the earth for shame. He would think it noble and nice of me, and I'm not noble or nice. I should hate to be thought either. His good opinion of me would make me choke and retch. I should not be able to sleep if I thought Hugh was thinking well of me. So hold your tongue."

Nadine had never been able quite to keep pace with Seymour: she always lagged a little behind, just as Hugh lagged so much more behind her. She was still gasping from the violence of his seizure of her, when he had descended, so to speak, a thousand feet or so. Tenderness still clung about her like soaked raiment.

"Oh, Seymour," she said, "I didn't realize you felt like that: I didn't really. What are you going to do?"

His clever handsome face wore an uncompromising look, but there was humour in his eyes.

"I may take to drink," he said, "like your angelic father. Very likely

I shan't, because I notice that it spoils your breakfast, if you are intoxicated the evening before. I shall certainly try to get some more jade, and I shan't marry Antoinette, because she is buxom. If I marry, I shall marry some girl who reminds me of asparagus, like you. Not the stout French asparagus, of course, but the lean English variety. I should not wonder if I came to your wedding, and wrote an account of it to a ladies' newspaper. I shall say you were looking hideous. I haven't got any other plans, except to go away from this place. You are a sort of chucker-out, Nadine, at Winston. You chucked out Hugh in the summer, and now in the winter you chuck out me. You are a vampire, I think. You suck people dry, and then you throw them away like orange skins. Don't argue with me: if you argued I should become rude. I was rude to Aunt Dodo the other day, when she showed me you sleeping on the floor by Hugh's bed. It was a sickening spectacle: I told her so at the time, and I tell you so now."

Poor complicated Nadine! Her complications had been cancelled like vulgar fractions, and she was left in a state of the most deplorable simplicity. There was a numerator, and that was Hugh; there was a nought below, and that was she. The simplest arithmetician could see that the nought "went into" the numerator an infinite number of times. The result was that there was Hugh and nothing else at all. Her surrendered reply indicated this: it indicated also her knowledge of it.

"But it was Hughie there," she said.

And then suddenly Seymour's unexpanded parachute opened, and he floated in liquid air, with the azure encompassing him.

"Your Hughie," he said.

"Mine," said Nadine.

There came an interruption. A footman entered with a telegram which he gave to Nadine. And once again the ineffable light came into her face, coming from below, transfiguring it.

"That's from the cripple," said Seymour unerringly.

She passed him the words Hugh had written that morning. They could not have been simpler, nor could he, by any expenditure of separate half-pennies have said more.

"Come back," he had written, "important. Good news."

Seymour got up.

"So you are going?" he said.

Nadine did not seem to hear this. She addressed the footman.

"Tell them to send round the Napier car at once," she said.

"His lordship ordered the Napier to meet the shooters——"

"Has it gone?"

"No, your Highness: it was to pick up Lady Esther——"

"Then I want it at once, instead. I am going to start instantly. Tell them to send it round at once. And tell my maid to pack a bag for me, and follow with the rest of my luggage."

"Yes, your Highness. Where to, shall I say?"

"Meering, of course. She will go by train."

She turned her unclouded radiance to Seymour again, and held out both her hands.

"Oh, Seymour," she said, "I feel such a brute, such a brute. But it's my nature to."

"Clearly. Go and put on your hat."

"Will you let me hear of you sometimes?" she asked.

"I don't see why I should write to you, if you mean that," he said.

"Nor do I, now I come to think of it. I made a conventional observation. Will you let them know if you want lunch, or want to be taken to the station?"

"Yes. Thanks. Good-bye. And good luck."

She lingered one moment more.

"Thank you," she said. "And don't think of me without remembering I am sorry."

It was still an hour short of sunset when the car emerged from the mountainous inland on to the coast. The plain and the line of sand-dunes that bordered the sea slept under a haze of golden winter sun; a few wisps of light cloud hung round the slopes of Snowdon, but otherwise the sky was of pale unflecked blue, from rim to rim, and the sea was as untroubled as the turquoise vault which it reflected. Though January had still a half-dozen of days to run, a hint and promise of spring were in the air, and Nadine sat in the open car unchilled by its headlong passage. They had taken but five hours to come from the midlands, and they seemed to have passed for her in one throb of eager consciousness, so that she looked round bewildered to find that the familiar landmarks of home were close about her, and that they were already close to their journey's end. Soon they began to climb out of the plain again up the outlying flank of hill that formed the south end of the bay, and culminated in the steep bluff of rock at the top of which she and Hugh had sat and quarrelled, and been reconciled on the morning of the gale. To-day no tumult of maddened water beat at the base of it, nor did thunder of surges break into spray and flying foam, and the line of reef that ran out from it lay, with its huge scattered rocks, as quiet as a herd of sea-beasts grazing. As they got higher she could see over the sand-dunes on to the beach itself; no ramparts and towers of surf or ruins of shattered billows fringed it now, a child could have played on that zone of sounding and resistless forces. Of its dangers and menaces nothing was left; the great gift that it had brought to Nadine's heart alone remained, and flowered there like the rose-pink almonds blossom in spring. Nature had healed where she had hurt, and what had seemed but a blind and wanton stroke, had proved to be the smiting of the rock, so that the spring burst forth, and the rivers ran in the dry places. . . .

The house, grey and welcoming, stood dozing in the afternoon sun, and Nadine, suddenly conscious that they had arrived without a halt, said a contrite word to the chauffeur on the subject of lunch. She recollected also that she had sent no reply to Hugh's telegram, and that her arrival would be unexpected. Unexpected it certainly was, and Dodo who had just seen Edith off to play golf better than anybody else had ever done, jumped up with a scream as she entered.

"But my darling, is it you?" she cried. "We have been expecting to hear from you, but seeing is better than hearing. Oh, Nadine, such news! Of course you guess it, so I shall not tell you, as it is unnecessary, and besides Hughie must do that. He has been shaved, and looks quite clean and young again. Will you go up to see him at once? Perhaps it is equally unnecessary to ask that. Shall I come up with you? My darling, there's a third unnecessary question. Of course I shall do nothing of the kind. Ask the great grenadier if you may go in to him without his being told you are coming. It might be rather a shock, but personally I believe shocks of joy are always good for one. At least they have never hurt me, and I've had lots of them. Go upstairs, dear, and after an unreasonable time you might ring for me."

The nurse's room was a dressing-room attached to the bedroom where Hugh lay. Nadine went in through this, and the door into the room beyond being open, she saw that Nurse Bryerley was in there. At this moment she looked up and saw Nadine. She turned towards Hugh's bed.

"Here's a visitor for you," she said, and beckoned to Nadine to enter. She heard Hugh ask "Who?" in a voice that sounded somehow expectant, and she went in. In the doorway she passed Nurse Bryerley coming out, and the door closed behind her.

Hugh had raised himself on his elbow in bed, and the light in his eyes showed that, though he had asked who his visitor was, his heart knew. He neither spoke nor moved while Nadine came across the room to his bedside. Then in a whisper:

"It is Nadine," he said.

She knelt down by the bed.

"Yes, Hughie. You wanted me," she said.

"I always want you," he answered.

For a moment Nadine hid her face in her hands without replying. Then she raised it again to him.

"Hughie, you have always got me," she said.

She drew that beloved head down to hers.

"And the news?" she said presently.

"Oh, that!" said Hugh. "It's only that I am going to get quite well and strong again. That's all."

15

Dodo was sitting in her room in Jack's house in Eaton Square, one morning towards the end of May, being moderately busy. She was trying to engage in a very intimate conversation with her husband, and simultaneously to conduct communication through the telephone, to smoke a cigarette and to write letters. Considering the complicated nature of the proceeding viewed as a whole, she was getting on fairly well, but occasionally became a little mixed up in her mind, and spoke of intimate things to Jack in the determined telephone voice, habitually used, or puffed cigarette smoke violently into the receiver. She had just done this and apologised to the Central exchange.

"I never knew you could send smoke down a telephone," remarked Jack.

"Double one two four Gerrard," said Dodo. "In these days of modern science you can't tell what is going to happen, and it's well to anticipate anything. No, I said double one two four, eleven hundred and twenty-four if that makes it simpler. As I was saying, Jack, I don't see why I shouldn't stop in town, and have my baby here. You can put lots of straw down, like Margery Daw, and that always looks so interesting. I should like to have straw down permanently, why don't we? Darling, how are you, and as Jack's going out to lunch, and I shall be quite alone, do come round——"

Dodo's face suddenly became seraphically blank.

"Oh, are you?" she said. "Then will you tell Mrs. Arbuthnot that I hope she will come round to lunch with Lady Chesterford. Jack, I said all that to Edith's footman, who always smiles at me. I wonder if he will come to lunch instead, and say I asked him, which after all is quite true. But Edith talks so much like a man, that of course I thought it was she, whereas it was he. Yes, I don't see why I should go down to Winston for it. Babies born in London are just as healthy as babies born in Staffordshire, and people will drop in more easily afterwards. Besides I must go to Nadine's wedding if I possibly can. Not to go would be like reading a story that you know quite well is going to end happily, and finding that the last chapter of all, which you have been saving up for, so to speak, is torn out. I shall have the most enormous lump in my throat when I see her and Hughie go up to the altar-rails together, and I love lumps in the throat. Don't you? I don't mean quinzy."

"I'll tell you all about the last chapter," said Jack.

"That would be very dear of you, but it wouldn't be the same thing at all. I want to see it, to see Hugh walking as if he had never been smashed into ten thousand smithereens, and Nadine, as if she had never thought about anybody else since her cradle. Oh, by the way, they have settled at last that they would like to go on the yacht for their honeymoon. They are both bad sailors, but I suppose there are lots of harbours or breakwaters about, and they think it is the only plan by which they can be certain of being undisturbed. If it is rough, they will find a sort of pleasure in being sick into one basin: I really think they will. They are in that state of foolishness, that whatever they do together will be in the garden of Eden. And they are just forty-five years old between them, which is exactly what I am all by myself. It seems quite a coincidence, though I have no idea what it coincides with. So let them have the yacht, Jack, as you suggested, and the moon will be lovely honey, and they will be exceedingly unwell!"

Dodo finished her letter, and having telephoned enough for the present, came and sat in a chair by her husband, in order to continue the intimate conversation.

"Jack, dear," she said. "I never do behave quite like anybody else, as you have known, poor wretch, for I don't know how many years. So you must be prepared for surprises when I give you that darling David. Something ridiculous will happen. There'll be two or three of them, and the papers will say I have had a litter, or I shall die, or David will arrive quite unexpectedly like a flash of lightning, and I shall say 'Good heavens, David, is it you?' I should be exceedingly annoyed if I died."

"So should I," said Jack.

"I really believe you would. But it would be more annoying for me, because however nice the next world is going to be, I haven't had enough of this. I want years and years more, because eternity is there just the same, and if I live to be a hundred there won't be anything the less of that. Eternity is safe, so to speak: it is invested in the bank, but time is just pocket-money, of which you always say I want such a lot. Eternity will always be on tap, or else it wouldn't be eternal. But this particular brew will come to an end, and I shall be so sorry when the last gurgle sounds, and one knows there is no more. It couldn't come more nicely, if when it sounded I had given you a son. I can't imagine any nicer way to die."

Jack put a great hand on her arm.

"Dodo, if you talk about dying, I shall be—shall be as sick as Hughie and Nadine together," he said.

"Oh, don't. But you see, since we are us—is that right—there is nothing I can't say to you, because I am only talking to myself. I wonder if I had better write a quantity of letters to my son, as some woman, I believe a perfectly blameless spinster, did. David shall read them when he has learned how to read. Oh, I could tell him so well how to make love, I know exactly what women like a man to be. Luckily so few men really know it, otherwise the world would go round much quicker, and we should all be blown off it."

Dodo paused a moment. "But to be a mother," she said. "It is so holy; so holy. Once it wasn't holy to me; it was merely a bore. Then, when Nadine was born, it was not holy, but very exciting, and hugely delightful. But now it is holy. It's yours, as well as mine, you see. Poor, dear, holy Jack. But I love you; that makes such a difference."

She paused a moment.

"I don't want you to be as sick as Nadine and Hughie combined," she said, "but I should like to make a few cheerful remarks about dying. We've all got to do it, and it doesn't make it any nearer to talk about it. It's a pity we can't practise it, so as to be able to do it nicely, but it's one performance only, without rehearsals, unless you die daily like St. Paul. I don't think I shall do it at all solemnly or tragically, Jack, for it would not be the least in keeping with my life to have one tragic scene at the end. Nor would it suit the rest of my life to be frightened at it. You see if we all held hands and stood in a row and said, 'One, two, three, now we'll die,' it wouldn't be at all alarming. And then you see from a religious point of view, God has been such a brick—is that profane?—I don't think it is—such a brick to me all my life that it seems most unlikely that He won't see me through. Jack, dear, you look depressed. I won't talk about it any more. I shall very likely outlive you, and I shall be such a comfort to you when you are dying. I shall be exceedingly annoyed, just as you said you would be if I did it, but, oh, my dear, I shall say *au revoir* to you with such a stout heart, and when I pass through the valley of the shadow myself, how I shall look for your dear blue eyes to welcome me. It will be interesting! And now, as they say at the end of sermons, I must get ready to go out with Nadine. I promised to go out with her for an hour before lunch. Pull me up, and give me a chaste salute on my marble brow. What a good invention you are! It would be worse than going back to the days of hansoms and four-wheelers to be without you. Without undue flattery, it would!"

Dodo's slight attack of seriousness evaporated completely, and having tried the effect of her hat—which comprised, so she said, the entire flora and fauna of Brazil—on Jack's head, put it on her own, and sent a message to Nadine that she had been waiting an hour and a half.

"But Hughie shall not come out with us," she said, "since he and Nadine don't pay the smallest attention to me, when they are together, and I feel alone in London. Besides Nadine has to buy things that young gentlemen don't know anything about, and here you are at last, my darling Nadine, but I'm not going to take your darling with us, any more than he takes you to his haberdasher, or whoever it is sells that sort of thing. Don't look cross, Hughie, because Jack's going to let you have the yacht, and you and Nadine can be unwell to your heart's content. Go and sulk at your club, dear, for an hour, and then you can come back to lunch, and stop for tea and dinner if you like. But the obduracy of your esteemed mother-in-law elect on the subject of the drive is quite invincible. Dear me, what beautiful language!"

Nadine and her mother did their errands, and as only Edith was going to lunch with them, who was almost invariably half-an-hour late, but who, if she arrived in time, would be quite certain to begin lunch without them, they prolonged their outing by a turn in the Park. The morning was of that exquisite tempered heat that lies midway between the uncertain warmth of spring, and the fierceness of true midsummer weather, and, following, as it did, on a week of rainy days it had brought out both crowds and flowers. The little green seats and shady alleys were full of kaleidoscopic colour from hats and parasols and summer dresses, and more stable than these, but hardly less brilliant, were the clumps of full-flowered rhododendrons and beds of blossomings. The dust had been laid on the roads, and washed from the angled planes, and summer sat in the lap of spring. Summer and spring too, as it were, sat side by side in Dodo's motor, and who could say which was the more glorious, the mother in the splendour of her full-blown life, or Nadine, that exquisite opening bud, still dewy in the morning of her days, no wild-flower, but more like an orchid, fragrant and subtle and complex. All that still remained to her: she would never be wild-rose or honeysuckle, in spite of the big simple human love which had come to her, and daily sprang higher, flame-like.

To-day neither paid much attention to the crowd that contained so many friends. Occasionally Dodo blew a sudden gale of kissed finger-tips at some especially beloved face, but the smile that never left her face, though it did duty for general salutations, was really inspired from within.

"You and Hughie and Jack and I ought to be stuffed and put in the South Kensington Museum, darling," she said, "as curious survivals of absolutely happy people, who are getting exceedingly rare. I should utter a few words of passionate protest when the executioner and the taxidermist arrived, but I think I should consent for the good of the nation in general."

Nadine disagreed altogether.

"We are much more useful alive," she said, "because we're infectious. Or would our broad, fatuous grins be infectious when we were stuffed? Oh, there's Seymour, Mamma. Do kiss your hand violently, because it wouldn't be suitable for me to. I can only smile regretfully."

"But you don't regret," said Dodo after giving him a perfect volley of salutes.

"No, but only because I can't. My will regrets. He has sent me a lovely necklace of jade, with a little label 'Jade for the jade,' on it. So I think he must feel better, as it's a sort of joke. I wrote him quite a nice little note, and said how dear it would be of him to come to my wedding, if he felt up to it."

Dodo giggled.

"My dear, that is exactly what I should have done at your age," she said. "But I think I should have kissed my hand to him just now, and people would certainly have thought you heartless, if you had, just because they have got great wooden hearts themselves, accurately regulated, that pump exactly sixty times in a minute, neither more nor less. You do feel kindly and warmly to poor Seymour, and you trust he is getting over it. About stuffing us now, I'm not quite sure I should stuff Papa Jack. He's anxious about me, poor old darling, as if at my age I didn't know how to have a baby properly. I talked about dying a little, which upset him, I'm afraid, though it wasn't in the least meant to. My dear, to think that in ten days from now you'll be married! Nadine, I do look forward to being a grandmamma: I want to be lots of grandmammas, if you see what I mean. Then there'll be Papa Hughie, and Papa Jack, and look, there's Papa Waldenech. I never knew he was in town. We must stop a moment: I have not seen him since he came uninvited to my ball in the autumn, a little bit on. Ah, what a fool I am: I meant not to tell you, so bear in mind that I haven't. Waldenech, my dear, what a surprise."

They drew up at the kerb, and he came to the carriage-door, hat in hand, courteous, distinguished and evil.

"I have just come from Paris," he said. "It is charming of you to welcome me. Nadine, too. Nadine, is your father to be allowed to come to your wedding? May I——"

Dodo had half-risen to greet him, and he saw the lines of her figure. He broke off short.

"You are going to be a mother again?" he said.

"Yes, my dear, but you needn't tell the Albert Memorial about it," said she. "And of course you may come to Nadine's wedding. I had no notion you would be in England."

He appeared to pay not the slightest attention to this, but looked at her eagerly, hungrily, at those wonderful brown eyes, at the still youthful oval of her face, at the mouth he had so often kissed.

"My God, you are a beautiful woman!" he said, "and you used to be mine!"

Then he turned abruptly, and walked straight away from them without another glance. Dodo looked after him in silence for a moment, frowning and smiling together.

"Poor old chap: it was a shock to him somehow," she said. "But he'll go back to the Ritz and steady himself. How old he has got to look, Nadine."

But Nadine had the frown without the smile.

"I didn't like the way he went off," she said. "He didn't give another thought to my wedding, Mamma, after he saw. He looked hungry for you, and he looked horrible. He admired you so enormously. He was thinking of what he had lost and what Papa Jack had gained. And I felt frightened of him, just as I felt frightened one night when I was very little, and he came stumbling into the nursery, and wanted to say good-night to me. I remember my nurse tried to turn him out, and he looked as if he would have murdered her. Poor Daddy isn't a nice man, you know."

Dodo's frown had quite cleared away. She was far too essentially happy to mind about little surface disturbances.

"Poor old Daddy," she said. "He was startled, darling, and when people are startled they look like themselves, that is all, and Daddy isn't quite nice, any more than the rest of us are. But it was rather sweet of him to want to go to your wedding. I hope he will be sober. He will probably want to kiss us all in the vestry, all of us except Jack. I shall certainly kiss him if he shows the slightest wish that I should do so. But he might be nasty to Jack. Perhaps we had better not tell Jack he is here. It might make him anxious again, as when I talked about death this morning. Oh, Nadine, look at those delicious horses cantering along, and praising God because they feel so strong and young! What a rotten seat that man has: oh, of course he has, because he's Berts. How he fidgets his horse. Berts, dear——"

And Dodo blew a shower of kisses on the end of her fingers.

Nadine's enjoyment in this liquid air had been suddenly extinguished. She herself hardly knew why, but her lowered pleasure she felt to be connected with her father. She tried very sensibly to get

rid of it by speech, for the unreal thing when spoken becomes fantasti-
cally absurd.

"Was Daddy ever very jealous about you?" she asked.

Dodo recalled her mind from the tragedy of Berts riding so badly.

"But violently pea-green with it," she said, "so that sometimes I
didn't know if I could say good-morning to the butler in safety. That
was in the early days, and I am bound to confess that he got over it.
After that came my turn to be jealous, but I never took my turn, for
between the particular old brandy and Mademoiselle Chose, if you
understand, poor Daddy became entirely impossible. But for auld lang
syne, I shall certainly kiss him in the vestry after your wedding, and
he shall sign his name if he feels up to it."

Dodo's face recovered all its radiance.

"And he was the father who begot you," she said. "How can I
ever forget that, you joy of mine? I should be a beast if I wanted to.
But he did look rather wicked just now. I think we had better turn,
or Edith will have finished lunch and gone away."

Waldenech's appearance did not belie him: he both looked and felt
very wicked indeed. The sight of Dodo so soon to become the mother
of another man's child had caused to break out into hideous activity
a volcano that had long smouldered under the slag and ashes of his
drunken and debauched days, and he flamed with a jealousy the more
passionate because it had so long slumbered. He felt confused and
bewildered by the violence of this unexpected passion, and, as Dodo
had said, he felt he must steady himself. He wanted to think clearly
and constructively, to determine exactly what he must do and how
he must do it. At present he knew only of one necessity, that, even
as he had taken Dodo away from Jack years ago, so now he must
take Jack away from Dodo. The particular old brandy, imbibed in
sufficient quantities, would clear his head and enable him to think
out ways and means.

He shut himself into his sitting-room at the Ritz, and by degrees
the monstrous nightmare-like lucidity that alcohol brings to heavy
drinkers brightened in his brain, and he sat there emancipated from
all moral laws, and thought clearly and connectedly, seeing himself
and his desires as the legitimate centre of all existence; nothing else
and nobody else could be reckoned with. His jealousy that had shot
flaming up no longer flared and flickered, it shone with a steady and
tremendous light, a beacon to guide him and show him the way he
must follow. What should happen to himself he did not care, nor
did it enter into his calculations: most likely it would be better when
he had accounted for Jack to account for himself also. That would

arrange itself: he would see, when the time came, how he felt about it. And the time had better be soon, for there was no reason for delay. But he pushed away from him a glass which he had just refilled: he had drunk himself steady, and knew that if he went on he would drink himself maudlin and confused again. It would have been strange if by this time, he did not know the stages, even as a man knows the stairs in his own house.

He sat still a moment longer, rehearsing in his mind what he had taken so long to construct. He would go to the house in Eaton Square, so that Dodo would be there, and he would see her look on what he had done. To make the picture complete that touch was necessary, though he did not want to hurt her. Then he would have finished with them, and would finish with himself, instead of waiting for the farce of a trial and the ignominy of what must follow.

The afternoon had already waned, and looking at his watch he saw that it was after seven. That was a suitable hour to go on his errand, for it was probable that Jack would be at home now, soon to dress for dinner. As he got up to get from his despatch-box the revolver that he knew was there, he saw the glass of brandy which a little while ago he had pushed away from him still standing there, and from habit merely he drank it off. Then he put the weapon, completely loaded into his pocket, and took one more look round before leaving the room. Somewhere deep down in him, smothered, shadowed, was some vague repugnance for what he was going to do, and once more, forgetful of his resolution not to trespass on the steadiness of nerves the spirit had brought him, he refilled and emptied his glass. That he felt sure would soon stifle conflicting voices within him.

He had been indoors all the afternoon, and an instinct for fresh air and the evening breeze caused him to go on foot across the Green Park. The air was fresh, and it or the extra brandy he had just taken seemed quickly to harmonize and quiet that vague jangle of repugnance that twanged discordantly in his mind, and he became reconciled to himself again. But the wish not to hurt Dodo became rather more pronounced in his poor fuddled brain. He had to kill Jack, but he hoped she would not mind very much: he could make her understand surely that he was obliged to do it. He had always been devoted to her, even when he most outraged the merest decencies of their married life, and this morning the sight of her glorious beauty had awoke not jealousy only. She was superb in her wonderful womanhood; she was more beautiful now than she had ever been, and Nadine was not fit to sit beside her.

It was with surprise that he saw he had come to the house. A motor

was at the door which stood open. On the pavement there was a
footman wearing a coat and hat, holding a rug in his hand; another,
bareheaded, stood by the door. Waldenech told himself that he had
come very opportunely, for it was clear that they would soon come
out.

He hesitated a moment, swaying a little where he stood, not certain
whether he should just wait for them or go into the house. Soon he
decided to take this latter course, for it was possible that Dodo or
Nadine might be going out without Jack, and seeing him standing
there would ask him what he wanted. That risked his whole plan:
they might suspect something, and with one hand in his coat pocket,
where his fingers grasped that which he had brought with him, he
went up the three steps that led to the front door.

"Is Lord Chesterford in?" he asked.

"Yes, sir. But his lordship is just going out," said the man.

"Please tell him that Prince Waldenech would like to speak to him.
I shall not detain his lordship more than a moment!"

Dodo and her husband had dined early, for they were going to
the opera, which began at eight, and at this moment the dining-room
door which opened on to the back of the hall opposite the staircase
was thrown open, and Waldenech heard Dodo's voice.

"Come on, Jack," she said, "or we shall miss the overture, which
is the best part, and you will say it is my fault."

She came quickly round the corner, resplendent and jewelled, and
saw Waldenech's figure with his back to the light that came in through
the open door, so that for half-a-second she did not recognise him.
Simultaneously, Jack came out of the dining-room just behind her.
As he came out he turned up the electric light in the hall which had
not been lit, and she saw Waldenech's face. And at the moment he
took out of his pocket what his right hand was fingering.

"Stand aside, Dodo," he said rather thickly. "It is not for you."

Not more than half a dozen paces separated them, and for answer
Dodo, without the smallest hurry or hesitation walked straight up to
him, with arms outstretched so that he could not pass her, screening
Jack. She was as menacing as a Greek fury, beautiful as the dawn,
dominant as the sun. All depended on her not faltering, on her complete
self-assurance; and never in her life had she felt more entirely mistress
of herself and of the occasion than when she marched up to this drunkard with the loaded revolver.

"You coward and murderer," she said. "Give me that."

For one half-second he stood nerveless and irresolute, his poor sodden
wits startled into sobriety by the power and glory of her, and without
a moment's hesitation she seized the revolver that was pointed straight

at her, and tore it from his hand. By a miracle of good luck it did not go off.

"Out of the house," she cried, "for I swear to you by God that in another second I will shoot you like a dog. Did you think you would frighten me? Frighten me, you drunken brute?"

She stood there like some splendid wild animal at bay, absolutely fearless and irresistible. Without a single word, he turned, and shuffled out into the street again.

"Shut the door," said Dodo to the footman.

Then suddenly and unmistakably she felt the life within her stir, and a stab of blinding pain shot through her. So short had been the whole scene that Jack hurrying after her had only just reached her side, when she dropped the revolver, and laid her arms on his shoulders, leaning on him with all her weight.

"Jack, my time has come," she said. "Oh glory to God, my dear."

Just as dawn began to brighten in the sky, Dodo's baby was born, and soon made a lusty announcement that he lived. Presently after Jack was admitted for a moment just to see his son, and then went out again to wait. It was but a couple of hours afterwards that he was again sent for by a well-pleased nurse.

"I never saw such vitality," said this excellent woman. "It's like what they tell about the gipsies."

Dodo was lying propped up in bed, and her baby was at her breast. She gave Jack a brilliant smile of welcome.

"Oh, Jack, you and David and I!" she said. "Was there ever such a family? I may talk to you for five minutes, and then David and I are going to sleep. But about last night. Waldenech came here to shoot you. He was drunk, poor wretch, he couldn't face me for a moment. It was such a deplorable failure that I feel sure he won't try it again, but I should be happier if he left England. See your solicitor about it; have him threatened if he doesn't go. Do that this morning, dear, and when I wake be able to tell me he has gone. And now, oh, you and David and I! I told you I should behave in some unusual manner, but I didn't think Waldenech would be concerned in it. Jack, kiss the top of David's adorable head, but don't disturb him. And then, my dearest, kiss me, and I shall instantly go to sleep. And neither Waldenech nor I will be able to go to Nadine's wedding, but my reason for not going is much the nicest. Isn't it, oh my David?"

About ten o'clock Jack went out to do as Dodo had bidden him, and preferring to walk, crossed the Green Park, and went through the arcade fronting the Ritz Hotel. He had forgotten to ask Dodo where Waldenech was staying, but fancied that when he was in England last winter, he had stopped here. So he went through the revolving door, and into the Bureau.

"Is Prince Waldenech stopping here?" he asked.

The clerk looked down to consult the register of guests before he answered:

"His Serene Highness left for Paris this morning."

BOOK 3

DODO
WONDERS-

1

Dodo was so much interested in what she had herself been saying, that having just lit one cigarette, she lit another at it, and now contemplated the two with a dazed expression. She was talking to Edith Arbuthnot, who had just returned from a musical tour in Germany, where she had conducted a dozen concerts consisting entirely of her own music with flaring success. She had been urged by her agent to give half a dozen more, the glory of which, he guaranteed, would completely eclipse that of the first series, but instead she had come back to England. She did not quite know why she had done so: her husband Bertie had sent the most cordial message to say that he and their daughter Madge were getting on quite excellently without her—indeed that seemed rather unduly stressed—but . . . here she was. The statement of this, to be enlarged on no doubt later, had violently switched the talk on to a discussion on free will.

Edith, it may be remarked, had arrived at her house in town only to find that her husband and daughter had already gone away for Whitsuntide, and being unable to support the idea of a Sunday alone in London, had sent off a telegram to Dodo, whom she knew to be at Winston, announcing her advent, and had arrived before it. On the other hand, her luggage had not arrived at all, and for the present she was dressed in a tea-gown of Dodo's, and a pair of Lord Chesterford's tennis-shoes which fitted her perfectly.

"I wonder," said Dodo. "We talk glibly about free will and we haven't the slightest conception what we really mean by it. Look at these two cigarettes! I am going to throw one away in a moment, and smoke the other, but there is no earthly reason why I should throw this away rather than that, or that than this: they are both precisely alike. I think I can do as I choose, but I can't. Whatever I shall do, has been written in the Book of Fate; something comes in—I don't know what it is—which will direct my choice. I say to myself, 'I choose to smoke cigarette A and throw away cigarette B,' but all the time it has been already determined. So in order to score off the Book of Fate, I say that I will do precisely the opposite, and do it. Upon which Fate points with its horny finger to its dreadful book, and there it has all been written down since the beginning of the world if not before. Don't let us tak about free will any more, for it makes one's brain turn round like a Dancing Dervish, but continue to nurse our illusion on the subject. You could have stayed in Germany, but you chose not to. There!"

Edith had not nearly finished telling Dodo about these concerts, in fact, she had barely begun, when the uncomfortable doctrine of free will usurped Dodo's attention and wonder.

"The first concert, as I think I told you, was at Leipsic," she said. "It was really colossal. You don't know what an artistic triumph means to an artist."

"No, dear; tell me," said Dodo, still looking at her cigarettes.

"Then you must allow me to speak. It was crammed, of course, and the air was thick with jealousy and hostility. They hated me and my music, and everything about me, because I was English. Only, they couldn't keep away. They had to come in order to hate me keenly at close quarters. I'm beginning to think that is rather characteristic of the Germans; they are far the most intense nation there is. First I played——"

"I thought you conducted," said Dodo.

"Yes; we call that playing. That is the usual term. First I played the 'Dodo' symphony. I composed one movement of it here, I remember—the scherzo. Well, at the end of the first movement, about three people clapped their hands once, and there was dead silence again. At the end of the second there was a roar. They couldn't help it. Then they recollected themselves again, having forgotten for a moment how much they hated me, and the roar stopped like turning a tap off. You could have heard a pin drop."

"Did it?" asked Dodo.

"No: I dropped my baton, which sounded like a clap of thunder. Then came the scherzo, and from that moment they were Balaams. They had come to curse and they were obliged to bless. What happened to their free will then?"

"Yes, I know about Balaam," said Dodo, "he comes in the Bible. Darling, how delicious for you. I see quite well what you mean by an artistic triumph: it's to make people delight in you in spite of themselves. I've often done it."

Dodo had resolved the other problem of free will that concerned the cigarettes by smoking them alternately. It seemed very unlikely that Fate had thought of that. They were both finished now, and she got up to pour out tea.

"If I could envy anybody," she said, "which I am absolutely incapable of doing, I should envy you, Edith. You have always gone on doing all your life precisely what you meant to do. You've got a strong character, as strong as this tea, which has been standing. But all my remarkable feats have been those which I didn't mean to do. They just came along and got done. I always meant to marry Jack, but I didn't do it until I had married two other people first. Sugar? That's how I go on, you know, doing things on the spur of the moment, and trusting that they will come right afterwards, because I haven't really meant them at all. And yet 'orrible to relate, by degrees, by degrees as the years go on, we paint the pictures of ourselves which are the only authentic ones, since we have painted every bit of them ourselves. Everything I do adds another touch to mine, and at the end I shall get glanders or cancer or thrush, and just the moment before I die I shall take the brush for the last time and paint on it 'Dodo fecit.' Oh, my dear, what will the angels think of it, and what will our aspirations and our aims and our struggles think of it? We've gone on aspiring and perspiring and admiring and conspiring, and then it's all over. Strawberries! They're the first I've seen this year; let us eat them up before Jack comes. Sometimes I wish I was a canary or any other silly thing that doesn't think and try and fail. All the same, I shouldn't really like to be a bird. Imagine having black eyes like buttons, and a horny mouth with no teeth, and scaly legs. Groundsel, too! I would sooner be a cannibal than eat groundsel. And I couldn't possibly live in a cage; nor could I endure anybody throwing a piece of green baize over me when he thought I had talked enough. Fancy, if you could ring the bell now this moment, and say to the footman, 'Bring me her ladyship's baize!' It would take away all spontaneousness from my conversation. I should be afraid of saying anything for fear of being baized, and every one would think I was getting old and anæmic. I won't be a canary after all!''

Edith shouted with laughter.

"A mind like yours is such a relief after living with orderly German minds for a month," she said. "You always were a holiday. But why these morbid imaginings!''

"I'm sure I don't know. I think it's the effect of seeing you again after a long interval, and hearing you mention the time when you composed that scherzo. It's so long ago, and we were so young, and so exactly like what we are now. Does it ever strike you that we are growing up? Slowly, but surely, darling, we are growing up. I'm fifty-five: at least, I'm really only fifty-four, but I add one year to my age instead of taking off two, like most people, so that when the next birthday comes, I'm already used to being it, if you follow me, and so there's no shock.''

"Shock? I adore getting older," said Edith.

"It will be glorious being eighty. I wish I hadn't got to wait so long. Every year adds to one's perceptions and one's wisdom."

Dodo considered this.

"Yes, I daresay it is so up to a point," she said, "though I seem to have seen women of eighty whose relations tell me that darling granny has preserved all her faculties, and is particularly bright this morning. Then the door opens and in comes darling granny in her bath-chair, with her head shaking a little with palsy, and what I should call deaf and blind and crippled. My name is shouted at her, and she grins and picks at her shawl. Oh, my dear! But I daresay she is quite happy, which is what matters most, and it isn't that which I'm afraid of in getting old!"

"But you're not afraid of dying?" asked Edith incredulously.

"Good gracious, no. I'm never afraid of certainties; I'm only afraid of contingencies like missing a train. What I am afraid of in getting old is continuing to feel hopelessly young. I look in vain for signs that I realise I'm fifty-five. I tell myself I'm fifty-five——"

"Four," said Edith; "I'm six."

"And that I was young last century and not this century," continued Dodo without pause. "We're both Victorians, Edith, and all sorts of people have reigned since then. But I don't feel Victorian. I like the fox-trot, and going in an aeroplane, and modern pictures which look equally delicious upside down, and modern poetry which doesn't scan or rhyme or mean anything, and sitting up all night. And yet all the time I'm a grandmother, and even that doesn't make any impression on me. Nadine's got three children, you know, and look at Nadine herself. She's thirty, the darling, and she's stately—the person who sees everybody in the Park walking briskly and looking lovely, always says that Nadine is stately. I read his remarks in the paper for that reason, and cut that piece out and sent to Nadine. But am I a proper mother for a stately daughter? That dreadful thought occurs to Nadine sometimes, I am sure. Would you guess I had a stately daughter?"

It certainly would have seemed a very wild conjecture. Dodo had preserved up to the eminently respectable age of which she felt so unworthy, the aspect as well as the inward vitality of youth, and thus never did she appear to be attempting to be young, when she clearly was not. She was still slender and brisk in movement, her black hair was quite untouched with grey, the fine oval of her face was still firm and unwrinkled, and her eyes, still dancing with the fire that might have been expected to smoulder nowadays, were perfectly capable of fulfilling their purposes unaided. She had made an attempt a few years ago to wear large tortoise-shell spectacles, and that dismal failure occurred to her now.

"I have tried to meet old age halfway," she said, "but old age won't come and meet me! I can't really see the old hag on the road even yet. Do you remember my spectacles? That was a serious expedition in search of middle-age, but it did no good. I always forgot where they were, and sat down on them with faint fatal crunches. Then Jack didn't like them; he said he would never have married me if he had known I was going to get old so soon, and he always hid them when he found them lying about, and he gave me an ear-trumpet for a birthday present. David used to like them; that was the only purpose they served. He used to squeal with delight if he got hold of them, and run away and come back dressed up like Mummie."

"I am lost without spectacles," said Edith.

"But I'm not; it was my spectacles that were always lost. And then I like rainbows and conjuring-tricks and putting pennies on the line for the train to go over, and bare feet and chocolates. I *do* like them; there's no use in pretending that I don't. Besides, David would find me out in no time. It would be a poor pretence not to be excited when we have put our pennies on the line, and hear the Great Northern Express whistle as it passes through Winston on the way to our pennies. That's why it rushes all the way from London to Edinburgh, to go over our pennies. And we've got a new plan: you would never guess. We gum the pennies on the line and so they can't jump off, but all the wheels go over them, and they get hot and flat like pancakes. I like it! I like it!" cried Dodo.

Edith had finished tea, and was waiting, rather severely, for a pause.

"But that's not all of you, Dodo," she said; "there is a piece of you that's not a child. I want to talk to that."

Dodo nodded at her.

"Yes, I know it's there," she said, "and we shall come to it in time. Of course, if I only thought about pennies on the line and conjuring tricks I should be in my second childhood, and well on the way to preserving all my faculties like the poor things in the bath-chairs. You see, David is mixed up so tremendously in these games: I don't suppose I should go down to the line five minutes before the six o'clock express passed through and put pennies there if it wasn't for him. I was forty-five when he was born, so you must make allowances for me. You don't know what that means any more than I know what artistic triumphs mean. Oh, I forgot: I did know that. David's away, did I tell you? He went away to-day to pay a round of visits with his nurse. He is going to visit the dentist first and then the bootmaker, and then he's 'going on' to stay with Nadine for the night. That's the round, and he comes back to-morrow, thank God. Where were we when you got severe? Oh, I know. You said there was a piece of me which wasn't entirely absurd, and you wanted to talk to that. But it's ever so difficult to disentangle one piece of you from all the rest."

"Drawers!" said Edith relentlessly. "You must have drawers in your mind with handles and locks. You can unlock one, if you want what's inside it, and pull it out by its handle. When you've finished, push it back and lock it again. That certainly is one of the things we ought to have learned by this time. I have, but I don't think you have. All your drawers are open simultaneously, Dodo. That's a great mistake, for you go dabbing about in them all, instead of being occupied with one. You don't concentrate!"

She suddenly relented.

"Oh, Dodo, go on!" she said. "I'm having a delicious holiday. You always appear to talk utter nonsense, but it suits me admirably. I often think your activity is a fearful waste of energy, like a fall in a salmon-river which might have been making electricity instead of running away. And then quite suddenly there appears a large fat salmon leaping in the middle of it all, all shiny and fresh from the sea. Don't let us concentrate: let's have all the drawers open and turn out everything on to the floor. I don't grow old any more than you do inside, in spite of my raddled, kippered face, and bones sticking out like hat-pegs. I am just as keen as ever, and just as confident that I'm going to make Bach and Brahms and Beethoven turn in their graves. I hear there was a slight subsidence the other day over the grave of one of them: it was probably my last concert in Berlin that was the real cause of it. But I've kept young because all my life I have pursued one thing with grim persistence, and always known I was going to catch it. I haven't had time to grow old, let alone growing middle-aged, which is so much more tragic!"

"Oh, middle-age is rapidly growing extinct," said Dodo, "and we needn't be afraid of catching it nowadays. When we were young, people of our age were middle-aged. They wouldn't drain life to the dregs and then chuck the goblet away and be old. They kept a little wine in it still and sipped it on special occasions. They lay down afer lunch and took dinner-pills to preserve their fading energies. Now, we don't do that; as long as we have an ounce of energy left we use it, as long as there is a drop of wine left we drink it. The moment I cease to be drunk with any spoonfuls of youth that remain to me," said she with great emphasis, "I shall be a total abstainer. As long as the sun is up it shall be day, but as soon as it sets it shall be night. There shall be no long-drawn sunsets and disgusting after-glows with me. When I've finished I shall go 'pop,' and get into my bath-chair till I'm wheeled away into the family-vault. And all the time at the back of my atrophied brain will be the knowledge of what a lovely time I have had. That's my plan, anyhow."

Dodo had got quite serious and absently dipped the last two or three strawberries into her teacup, imagining apparently that it contained cream.

"You're different," she said; "you can achieve definite projections of yourself in music; you can still create, and as long as anybody creates she is not old. Stretching out: that's what youth means. I daresay you will write some new tunes and go to play them in Heligoland in the autumn. That's your anchor to youth, your power of creation. I've got no anchor of that kind; I've only got some fish-hooks, so to speak, consisting of my sympathy with what is young, and my love of what is new. But when you blame me for having all my drawers open, there I disagree. It is having all my drawers open that stands between me and the bath-chair. But, my dear, what pitfalls there are for us to avoid, if we are to steer clear of being terrible, grizzly kittens."

"Such as?" asked Edith.

"The most obvious is one so many sprightly old things like us fall into, namely, that of attaching some young man to their hoary old selves. There's nothing that makes a woman look so old as to drag about some doped boy, and there's nothing that actually ages her so quickly. I never fell into that mistake, and I'm not going to begin now. It is so easy to make a boy think you are marvellous: it's such a cheap success, like spending the season at some second-rate watering-place. No more flirting for us, darling! Of course every girl should be a flirt: it is her business to attract as many young men as possible, and then she chooses one and goes for him for all she's worth. That is Nature's way: look at the queen-bee."

"Where?" said Edith, not quite following.

"Anywhere," continued Dodo, not troubling to explain. "And then again every right-minded boy is in love with several girls at once, and he chooses one and the rest either go into a decline or marry somebody else, usually the latter. But then contrast that nice, clean way of doing things with the mature, greasy barmaids of our age, smirking over the counter at the boys, and, as I said, doping them. What hags! How easy to be a hag! I adore boys, but I won't be a hag."

Dodo broke off suddenly from these remarkable reflections, and adjusted her hat before the looking glass.

"They are older than the rocks they sit among, as Mr. Pater said," she remarked. "Let us go out, as Jack doesn't seem to be coming. His tennis-shoes fit you beautifully and so does my tea-gown. Do you know, it happens to be ten minutes to six, so that if we walk down across the fields, on to the railway-cutting, we shall get there in time for the express. One may as well go there as anywhere else. Besides,

David put the gum-bottle and our pennies inside the piano, and thought
it would be lovely if I gummed them down to-night, as if he was
here. That's really unselfish: if I was away and David here, I should
like him not to put any pennies down till I came home. But David
takes after Jack. Come on!"

The roses round the house were in full glory of June, but the hayfields down which they skirted their way were more to Dodo's mind.
She had two selves, so Jack told her, the town-self which delighted
in crowds and theatres and dances and sniffed the reek of fresh asphalt
and hot pavement with relish, and the country self which preferred
the wild-rose in the hedge and the ox-eyed daisies and buttercups
that climbed upwards through the growing grasses to the smooth lawn
and the garden-bed. She carried David's gum-bottle and the pennies,
already razor-edged from having been flattened out under train-wheels,
and ecstatically gummed them to the rails.

"And now we sit and wait as close as we dare," she said. "Waiting,
really is the best part. I don't think you agree. I think you like achievement better than expectation."

"Every artist does," said Edith. "I hated going to Germany, not because I thought there was any chance of my not scoring a howling
success, but because I had to wait to get there. When I want a thing
I want it now, so as to get on to the next thing."

"That's greedy," remarked Dodo.

"Not nearly so greedy as teasing yourself with expectation. The
glory of going on! as St. Paul said."

"And the satisfaction of standing still. I said that."

"But great people don't stand still, nor do great nations," said Edith.
"Look at Germany! How I adore the German spirit in spite of their
hatred of us. That great, relentless, magnificent machine, that never
stops and is never careless. I can't think why I was so glad to get
away. I had a feeling that there was something brewing there. There
was a sort of tense calm, as before a thunderstorm——"

The train swept round the corner and passed them with a roar and
rattle, towering high above them, a glory of efficiency, stirring and
bewildering. But for once Dodo paid no attention to it.

"Darling, there has been a lull before the storm ever since I can
remember," she said, "but the storm never breaks. I wonder if the
millennium has really come years ago, and we haven't noticed it. How
dreadful for the millennium to be a complete fiasco! Oh, there's Jack
going down to the river with his fishing-rod. Whistle on your fingers
and catch his attention. I want to show him your tennis-shoes. Now,
the fisherman is the real instance of the type that lives on expectation.
Jack goes and fishes for hours at a time in a state of rapt bliss, because

he thinks he is just going to catch something. He hasn't heard: I suppose he thought it was only the express."

"I want to fish too," said Edith. "I adore fishing because I do catch something, and then I go on and catch something else. Besides nobody ever fished in a tea-gown before."

"Very well. We'll go back and get another rod for you. Gracious me! I've forgotten the pennies and the gum-bottle. David would never forgive me, however hard he tried. Go on about Germany."

"But you don't believe what I say," said Edith. "Something is going to happen, and I hate the idea. You see, Germany has always been my mother: the whole joy of my life, which is music, comes from her, but this time she suddenly seemed like some dreadful old step-mother instead. I suppose that was why I came back. I wasn't comfortable there. I have always felt utterly at home there before, but this time I didn't. Shall I go back and give some more concerts after all?"

"Yes, darling, do: just as you are. I'll send your luggage back after you. Personally I rather like the German type of man. When I talk to one I feel as if I were talking to a large alligator, bald and horny, which puts on a great, long smile and watches you with its wicked little eyes. It would eat you up if it could get at you, and it smiles in order to encourage you to jump over the railings and go and pat it. Jack had a German agent here, you know, a quite terribly efficient alligator who never forgot anything. He always went to church and sang in the choir. He left quite suddenly the other day."

"Why?" asked Edith.

"I don't know; he went back to Germany."

Edith came back from her fishing a little after dinner-time rosy with triumph and the heat of the evening, and with her arms covered with midge-bites. Dodo had dressed already, and thought she had never seen quite so amazing a spectacle as Edith presented as she came up the terrace, with a soaked and ruined tea-gown trailing behind her, and Jack's tennis-shoes making large wet marks on the paving-stones.

"Six beauties," she said, displaying her laden landing-net, "and I missed another which must have been a three-pounder. Oh, and your tea-gown! I pinned it up around my knees with the greatest care, but it came undone, and, well—there it is. But I hear my luggage has come, and do let us have some of these trout for dinner. I have enjoyed myself so immensely. Don't wait for me: I must have a bath!"

Jack who had come in a quarter of an hour before, and had not yet seen Edith, came out of the drawing-room window at this moment. He sat down on the step, and went off into helpless laughter. . . .

Edith appeared at dinner simultaneously with the broiled trout. She had a garish order pinned rather crookedly on to her dress.

"Darling, what's that swank?" asked Dodo instantly.

"Bavarian Order of Music and Chivalry," she said. "The King gave it me at Munich. It has never been given to a woman before. There's a troubadour one side, and Richard Wagner on the other."

"I don't believe he would have been so chivalrous if he had seen you as Jack did just before dinner. Jack, would your chivalry have triumphed? Your tennis-shoes, my tea-gown, and Edith in the middle."

"What! My tennis-shoes?" asked Jack.

"Dodo, you should have broken it to him," said Edith with deep reproach.

"I didn't dare to. It might have made him stop laughing, and suppressed laughter is as dangerous as suppressed measles when you get on in life. There's another thing about your Germans. I thought of it while I was dressing. They only laugh at German jokes."

"There is one in *Faust*," said Jack with an air of scrupulous fairness. "At least there is believed to be: commentators differ. But when *Faust* is given in Germany, the whole theatre rocks with laughter at the proper point."

Edith rose to this with the eagerness of the trout she had caught.

"The humour of a nation doesn't depend on the number of jokes in its sublimest tragedy," she said. "Let us judge English humour by the funny things in *Hamlet*."

Dodo gave a commiserating sigh.

"That wasn't a very good choice," she said. "There are the grave-diggers, and there's Polonius all over the place. The most serious people see humour in Polonius. Why didn't you say Milton? Now it's too late."

"I beg your pardon," said he; "I wasn't thinking about Milton at all, but a vision of Dodo's tea-gown appeared to me, as I last saw it. Yes. Take Milton, Edith. Dodo can't give you a joke out of Milton because she has never read him. Don't interrupt, Dodo. Or take Dante. Ask me for a joke in Dante, and you win all down the line. Take Julius Cæsar: take any great creature you like. What you really want to point out is that great authors are seldom humorous. I agree: one up to you. Take a trout—I didn't catch any."

Edith did precisely as she was told.

"I hate arguing," she said. "Dodo insisted on arguing about middle-age all the afternoon. In the intervals she talked about putting pennies on the line. She said it was enormous fun, but she forgot all about them when she had put them there."

"Don't tell David, Jack," said Dodo, aside.

"All right. Dodo's got middle-age on her mind. She bought some spectacles once."

"My dear, we've had all that," said Dodo. "What we really want to know is how you are to get gracefully old, while you continue to feel young. We're wanting not to be middle-aged in the interval. There is no use in cutting off pleasures, while they please you, because that makes you not old but sour, and who wants to be sour? What a poor ambition! It really is rather an interesting question for us three, who are between fifty-four and sixty, and who don't feel like it. Jack, you're really the oldest of us, and more really you're the youngest."

"I doubt that," said Edith loudly.

"This is German scepticism then. Jack is much more like a boy than you are like a girl."

"I never was like a girl," said Edith. "Ask Bertie, ask anybody. I was always mature and feverish. Dodo was always calculating, and her calculations were interrupted by impulse. Jack was always the devout lover. The troubadour on my medal is extremely like him."

Jack passed his hand over his forehead.

"What are we talking about?" he said.

"Getting old, darling," said Dodo.

"So we are. But the fact is, you know, that we're getting old all the time, but we don't notice it till some shock comes. That crystallises things. What is fluid in you takes shape."

Dodo got up.

"So we've got to wait for a shock," she said.

"Is that all you can suggest? Anyhow, I shall hold your hand if a shock comes. What sort of a shock would be good for me, do you think? I know what would be good for Edith, and that would be that she suddenly found that she couldn't help writing music that was practically indistinguishable from the *Messiah*."

"And that," said Edith, "is blasphemy."

Jack caught on.

"Hush, Dodo," he said, "an inspired, a sacred work to all true musicians."

Edith glanced wildly round.

"I shall go mad," she said, "if there is any more of this delicious English humour. Handel! Me and Handel! How dare you? Brutes!"

2

Unlike most women Dodo much preferred to breakfast downstairs in a large dining-room, facing the window, rather than mumble a private tray in bed. Jack, in consequence, was allowed to be as grumpy as he pleased at this meal, for Dodo's sense of fairness told her that if she was so unfeminine as to feel cheerful and sociable at half-past nine in the morning, she must not expect her husband to be so unmasculine as to resemble her.

"Crumbs get into my bed," she had said to Edith the evening before, when the morning *venue* was debated, "and my egg tastes of blankets. And I hate bed when I wake: I feel bright and brisk and fresh, which is very trying for other people. Jack breakfasts downstairs, too, though if you asked him to breakfast in your bedroom, I daresay he would come."

"I hate seeing anybody till eleven," said Edith, "and many people then."

"Very well, Jack, as usual, will be cross to me, which is an excellent plan, because I don't mind, and he works off his morning temper. Don't come down to protect me: it's quite unnecessary."

This was really equivalent to an invitation to be absent, and as it coincided with Edith's inclination, the hour of half-past nine found Dodo reading her letters, and Jack, fortified against intrusive sociability by a copy of the *Times* propped against the tea-kettle.

The room faced south, and the sun from the window struck sideways across Dodo's face, as she exhibited a pleasant appetite for correspondence and solid food, while Jack sat morose in the shadow of the *Times*. This oblique light made the black ink in which Dodo's correspondents had written to her appear to be a rich crimson. She had already remarked on this interesting fact, with an allusion to the spectacles which had been finally lost three years ago, and as a test question to see how Jack was feeling, she asked him if he had seen them. As he made no answer whatever, she concluded that he was still feeling half-past ninish.

Then she got really interested in a letter from Miss Grantham, an old friend who had somehow slipped out of her orbit. Miss Grantham was expected here this afternoon, but apparently had time to write a long letter, though she could have said it all a few hours later.

"Grantie is getting poorer and poorer," she said. "A third aunt has died lately, and so Grantie had to pay three thousand pounds. I had no idea funerals were so expensive. Isn't it miserable for her?"

She turned over the page.

"Oh! There are compensations," she said, "for the third aunt left her twenty-five thousand pounds, so she's up on balance. Three from twenty-five. . . . Not funerals: duties. But she sold a picture by Franz Hals to make sure. How like Grantie: she would run no risks! She never did; she always remained single and lived in the country away from influenza and baccarat. Oh, Jack, the Franz Hals fetched eight thousand pounds, so her poverty is bearable. Wasn't that lovely?"

"Lovely!" said Jack.

Dodo looked up from Grantie's letter, and ran her eyes round the walls.

"But those two pictures there are by Franz Hals," she said. "Do let us sell one, and then we shall have eight thousand pounds. You shall have the eight, darling, because the picture is yours, and I shall have the thousands because I thought of it."

Jack gave a short grunt as he turned over his paper. He had not quite got over the attack of the morning microbe, to which males are chiefly subject.

"All right," he said. "And what shall we buy with the eight thousand pounds? Some more boots or bacon?"

Dodo considered this oracular utterance.

"That's a wonderfully sensible question," she said. "I don't really know what we should buy with it. I suppose we shouldn't buy anything, and the picture would be gone. I would certainly rather have it than nothing! What a mine of wisdom you are! I suppose it was my mercantile blood that made me think of selling a picture. Blood's thicker than paint. . . . It always shows through."

A fatal brown spot had appeared in the middle of Jack's paper just opposite the spirit-lamp of the tea-kettle against which it leaned. As he was considering this odd phenomenon, it spread and burst into flame.

"Fire!" cried Dodo. "Edith will be burned in her bed. Put—put a rug round it! Lie down on it, Jack! Turn the hot water on to it! Put some sand on it! Why aren't we at the seaside?"

Jack did none of these brilliant maneuvres. In an extraordinarily prosaic manner he took the paper up, dropped it into the grate and stamped on it. But the need for prompt action had started his drowsy mechanisms.

"Well, it's morning," he said as he returned to the table, "so let us begin. No: I think we won't sell a Franz Hals, Dodo. And then came Grantie and her auntie, and then you with your mercantile blood. Which shall we take first?"

"Oh, blood, I think," said Dodo, "because there's a letter from Daddy. He would like to come down this afternoon for the Sunday, and will I telephone? He put a postal order for three-and-sixpence in his letter, to pay for a trunk-call: isn't that rather sweet of him? Daddy is rich, but honest. Epigram. Put up a thumb, darling, to show you recognize it. Jack, shall I say that Daddy may come, and we should love it? I like people of eighty to want things. And really if we can give pleasure to a person of eighty hadn't we better? Eighty minus fifty-four: that leaves twenty-six. It would be pathetic if in twenty-six years from now you no longer cared about giving me pleasures. What has happened to the postal order for three-and-six? He did enclose it, I saw it. I believe you've burned it with the *Times*, Jack. Can we claim from the fire-insurance?"

Jack formed a mental picture of old Mr. Vane, contemplated it and dismissed it.

"Of course he shall come if you want him to," he said. "Send him my love."

"That's dear of you. I do want him to come because he wants to, which after all is a very good reason. Otherwise I think—I think I should have liked him to come perhaps another day, when there weren't twenty-five million other people. On the other hand Daddy will like that: he's getting tremendously smart, and 'goes on' to parties after dinner. My dear, do you think he will bring another large supply of his patent shoe-horns with him this time? I think we must examine his luggage, like a customhouse."

This was an allusion to a genteel piece of advertising which Mr. Vane had indulged in last time he stayed with them. On that occasion Dodo had met him at the door, and without any misgivings at all had seen taken down from the motor an oblong wooden box about which he was anxious, and which, so he mysteriously informed her, contained "presents." This she naturally interpreted to mean something nice for her. It subsequently appeared, however, that the presents were presents for everybody in the house, for Mr. Vane had instructed his valet to connive with the housemaids and arrange that on the dressing-table of every guest in the house there should be placed one of Vane's patent shoe-horns with a small paper of instructions. This slip explained how conveniently these shoe-horns fitted the shape of the human heel, and entailed no stamping of the human foot nor straining of leather. . . .

"That's what I mean by blood coming out," continued Dodo, "when I want to sell a Franz Hals. I think I must be rather like Daddy over that. He doesn't want any more money, any more than I do, but he cannot resist the opportunity of doing a little business. After all why not? A shoe-horn doesn't hurt anybody."

"It does: it hurt me!" said Jack. "It bruised my heel."

"Did it? Who would have thought Daddy was such a serpent? I didn't use mine: my maid threw it into the fire the moment she saw it. She observed, with a sniff, that she wouldn't have any of those nasty cheap things. I remonstrated: I told her it was a present from Daddy, and she said she thought he would have given me something handsomer than that."

"They weren't very handsome," remarked Jack. "Nothing out of the way, I mean. Not raging beauties."

"Daddy went on to Harrogate afterwards," said Dodo. "He flooded the hotel with them. He used to sit in the velvet place which they call a lounge, and make himself agreeable to strangers, and lead the conversation round to the fact that he was my father. Then as soon as they were getting on nicely, he produced a shoe-horn. Bertie Arbuthnot told me about it: Daddy worked the shoe-horn stunt on him."

"Priceless!" said Jack grinning. "Go on."

"Quite priceless: he gave them away free, gratis. Well, Daddy came in one day when Bertie was sitting in the lounge, and asked him if he knew me. So they got talking. And then Daddy looked fixedly at the heel of Bertie's shoe which was rather shabby, as heels usually are, and out came the shoe-horn. 'Take one of these, young man,' said he, 'and then you'll make no more complaints about the bills for the cobbling of the heels of your shoes. Vane's patent, you mark, and it's that very Vane who's addressing you!'"

Dodo burst out laughing.

"I adore seeing you and Daddy together," she said. "You find him so dreadfully trying, and I'm sure I don't wonder, and you bear it with the fortitude of an early Christian martyr. What was the poem he made about the shoe-horn which was printed at the top of the instructions?"

Jack promptly quoted it:

> "As I want to spare you pains
> Take the shoe-horn that is Vane's."

"Yes, that's it," said Dodo. "And what a gem! He told me he lay awake three nights making it up, like Flaubert squirming about on the floor and tearing his hair in the struggle to get the right word."

Dodo got up, looked for the *Times*, and remembered that it was burned.

"That's a relief anyhow," she said. "I think it's worth the destruction of the three-and-six-penny postal order. If it hadn't been burned I should have to read it to see what is going on."

"There's nothing."

"But one reads it all the same. If there's nothing in the large type, I read the paper across from column to column, and acquire snippets of information which get jumbled up together and sap the intellect. People with great minds like Edith never look at the paper at all. That's why she argues so well: she never knows anything about the subject, and so can give full play to her imagination."

Dodo threw up the window.

"Oh, Jack, it is silly to go to London in June," she said. "And yet it doesn't do to stay much in the country, unless you have a lot of people about who make you forget you are in the country at all."

"Who is coming to-day?" asked he.

"Well, I thought originally that we would have the sort of party we had twenty-five years ago, and see how we've all stood them; and so you and I and Edith and Grantie and Tommy Ledgers represent the old red sandstone. Then Nadine and Hughie and young Tommy Ledgers and two or three of their friends crept in, and then there are Prince and Princess Albert Allenstein. They didn't creep in: they shoved in."

"My dear, what a menagerie," said Jack.

"I know: the animals kept on coming in one by one and two by two, and we shall be about twenty-five altogether. Princess Albert is opening a bazaar or a bank or a barracks at Nottingham on Tuesday, that's why she is coming!"

"Then why have you asked her to come to-day?"

"I didn't: she thought it would be nice to come on Saturday instead of Monday, and wrote to tell me so—remind me to give Daddy the autograph: he has begun collecting autographs— However, he will look after her: he loves Princesses of any age or shape. As for Albert he shall have trays of food brought him at short and regular intervals, so he'll bother nobody. But best of all, beloved David is coming back to-day. He and his round of visits! I think I'll send a paragraph to the *Morning Post* to say that Lord Harchester has returned to the family seat after a round of visits. I won't say it was the dentist and the bootmaker."

"Oh, for goodness' sake don't teach David to be a snob!" said Jack.

"Darling, you're a little heavy this morning," said Dodo. "That was a joke."

"Not entirely," said Jack.

Dodo capitulated without the slightest attempt at defence.

"Quite right!" she said. "But you must remember that I was born, so to speak, in a frying-pan in Glasgow, enamelled by the Vane process, or at least that was my cradle, and if you asked me to swear on my bended knees that I wasn't a snob at all, I should instantly get up and change the subject. I do still think it's rather fun being what I have become, and having Royal Families staying with me——"

"And saying it's rather a bore," put in Jack.

"Of course. I like being bored that way, if you insist on it. I haven't ever quite got over my rise in life. Very nearly, but not quite."

"You really speak as if you thought it mattered," said Jack.

"I know it doesn't really. It's a game, a rather good one. Kind hearts are more than coronets, but I rather like having both. Most people are snobs, Jack, though they won't say so. It's distinctly snobbish of me to put my parties in the paper, and after all you read it in the morning, which is just as bad. The Court Circular too! Why should it be announced to all the world that they went to the private chapel on Sunday morning and who preached? It has to be written and printed and corrected. That wouldn't be done unless a quantity of people wanted to read it. I wonder if it's read up in heaven, and if the angels say to each other how pleasant it all is."

Dodo bubbled with laughter.

"Oh, my dear, how funny we all are," she said. "Just think of our pomposity, we little funny things kicking about together in the dust! We all rather like having titles and orders; otherwise the whole thing would have stopped long ago. Here's Edith: so it must be eleven."

Edith had taken to smoking a pipe lately, because her doctor said it was less injurious than cigarettes, and she wanted to hurt herself as little as possible. She found it difficult to keep it alight, and half-away across the room she struck a match on the sole of her shoe, and applied it to the bowl, from which a cracking noise issued.

"Dodo, is it true that the Allensteins are coming to stay here to-day?" she asked. "I saw it in the *Daily Mail.*"

Jack opened his mouth to speak, but Dodo clapped her hands in his face.

"Now, Jack, I didn't put it there," she said, "so don't make false accusations. Of course they did it themselves, because you and I—particularly I—are what people call smart, and the Allensteins aren't. That proves the point I was just going to make: in fact, that's the best definition of snob. Snobs want to show other people how nicely they are getting on."

Edith sat down in the window seat between Dodo and Jack, who shied away from the reek of her pipe, which an impartial breeze, coming in at the window, wafted this way and that.

"But who's a-deniging of it, Saireh Gamp?" she asked. "The snob's main object is not actually having the King or the Pope or the Archbishop of Canterbury to dinner; what he cares about is that other people should know that he has done so. Snobbishness isn't running after the great ones of the earth, but letting the little ones know you have caught the great ones."

"You hopeless women!" said Jack.

Dodo shook her head.

"He can't understand," she said, "for with all his virtues Jack isn't a snob at all, and he misses a great deal of pleasure. We all want to associate with our superiors in any line. It is more fun having notable people about than nonentities. When it comes to friends it is a different thing, and I would throw over the whole Almanack of Gotha for the sake of a friend——"

Jack turned his eyes heavenwards.

"What an angel!" he said. "Was ever such nobility and unworldliness embodied in a human form? What have I done to deserve——"

Dodo interrupted.

"*And* we like other people to know it," she said. "Poor Jack is a *lusus naturae;* he is swamped by the normal. You must yield, darling."

Jack made an awful face as the smoke from Edith's pipe blew across him, and got up.

"I yield to those deathly fumes," he said.

Dodo's guests arrived spasmodically during the afternoon. A couple of motors went backwards and forwards between the station and the house, meeting all probable trains, sometimes returning with one occupant, sometimes with three or four, for nobody had happened to say what time he was arriving. About five an aeroplane alighted in the park, bearing Hugh Graves as pilot, and his wife Nadine as passenger, and while Dodo, taking her daughter's place, succeeded in getting Hugh to take her up for a short flight, Prince and Princess Albert arrived in a cab with Nadine's maid, having somehow managed to miss the motor. Jack was out fishing at the time, and Prince Albert expressed over and over again his surprise at the informality of their reception. He was a slow, stout, stupid man of sixty, and in ten years' time would no doubt be slower, stouter, stupider and seventy. He had a miraculous digestion, a huge appetite for sleep, and a moderate acquaintance with the English language. They spent four months of the year in England in order to get away from their terrible little Court at Allenstein, and with a view to economy, passed most of those months in sponging on well-to-do acquaintances.

"Also this is very strange," he said slowly. "Where is Lady Chesterford? Where is Lord Chesterford? Where are our hosts? Where is tea?"

Princess Albert, brisk and buxom and pleasant and pleased, waddled through the house into the garden, where she met Nadine, leaving her husband to follow still wondering at the strangeness of it all. She talked voluble, effective English in a guttural manner.

"So screaming!" she said. "Nobody here, neither dearest Dodo nor her husband to receive us, so when they come we will receive them. Where is she?"

Nadine pointed to an aeroplane that was flying low over the house.

"She's there just now," she said.

"Flying? Albert, Dodo is flying. Is that not courageous of her?"

"But Lady Chesterford should have been here to receive us," said
he. "It is very strange, but we will have tea. And where is my evening
paper? I shall have left it in the cab, and it must be fetched. You
there: I wish my evening paper."

The person he had thus addressed, who resembled an aged but extremely respectable butler, took off his hat, and Princess Albert instantly recognised him.

"But it is dear Mr. Vane," she said. "How pleasant! Is it not amusing
that we should arrive when Dodo is flying and Lord Chesterford is
fishing? So awkward for them, poor things, when they find we are
here."

Prince Albert looked at him with some mistrust, which gradually
cleared.

"I remember you!" he said. "You are Lady Chesterford's father. Let
us have tea and my evening paper."

Once at the tea-table there was no more anxiety about Prince Albert.

"There are sandwiches," he said. "There is toast. There is jam. Also
these are caviare and these are bacon. And there is iced coffee. I will
stay here. But it is very strange that Lady Chesterford is not here.
Eat those sandwiches, Sophy. And there are cakes. Why is not Lady
Chesterford——"

"She is flying, dearest," said she. "Dodo cannot give us tea while
she is flying. Ah, and here is dearest Edith and Lord Ledgers."

The news of the august arrivals had spread through the house, and
such guests as were in it came out on to the terrace. Dodo's father
took up an advantageous position between the Prince and the Princess,
and was with difficulty persuaded to put on his hat again. He spoke
with a slight Scotch accent that formed a pleasant contrast to the German inflection.

"My daughter will be much distressed, your Highness," he said,
"that she has not been here to have the honour to receive you. And
so, your Highness, the privilege falls on me, and honoured I am
——"

"So kind of you, Mr. Vane," said that genial woman. "And your
children, Nadine? They are well. And, dearest Edith, you have been
in Berlin, I hear. How was my cousin Willie?"

Mr. Vane gave a little gasp; he prevented himself with difficulty
from taking off his hat again.

"The Emperor came to my concert there, ma'am," said Edith.

"He would be sure to. He is so musical: such an artist. His hymn
of Aegir. You have heard his hymn? What do you think about it?"

Edith's honesty about music was quite incorruptible.

"I don't think anything at all about it," she said. "There's nothing to think about."

Princess Albert choked with laughter.

"I shall tell Willie what you say," she said. "So good for him. Albert dearest, Mrs. Arbuthnot says that Willie's Aegir is nothing at all. Remind me to tell Willie that, when I write."

"Also, I will not any such thing remind you," said her husband. "It is not good to anger Willie. Also it is not good to speak like that of the Emperor. When all is said and done he is the Cherman Emperor. My estate, my money, my land, they are all in Chermany. No! I will have no more iced coffee. I will have iced champagne at dinner."

Mr. Vane already had his hand on the jug.

"Not just a wee thimbleful, sir?" he asked.

"And what is a thimbleful? I do not know a thimbleful. But I will have none. I will have iced champagne at dinner, and I will have port. I will have brandy with my coffee, but that will not be iced coffee: it shall be hot coffee. And I will remind you, Sophy, not to tell the Emperor what that lady said of his music. Instead I will remind you to say that she was gratified and flattified—is it not?—that he was so *leutselig* as to hear her music. Also I hear a flying-machine, so perhaps now we shall learn why Lady Chesterfield was not here—"

"Dearest, you have said that ten times," said his wife, "and there is no good to repeat. There! The machine is coming down. We will go and meet dearest Dodo."

The Prince considered this proposition on its merits.

"No: I will sit," he said. "I will eat a cake. And I will see what is a thimbleful. Show me a thimbleful. A pretty young lady could put that in her thimble, and I will put it now in my thimble inside me."

Fresh hedonistic plans outlined themselves.

"And when I have sat, I will have my dinner," he said. "And then I will play Bridge, and then I will go to bed, and then I will snore!"

Dodo had frankly confessed that she was a snob; otherwise her native honesty might have necessitated that confession when she found herself playing Bridge in partnership with Nadine against her princely guests. She knew well that she would never have consented to let the Prince stay with her, if he had not been what he was, nor would she have spent a couple of hours at the card-table when there were so many friends about. But she consoled herself with desultory conversation and when dummy with taking a turn or two in the next room where there was intermittent dancing going on. Just now, the Prince was dealing with extreme deliberation, and talking quite as deliberately.

"Also that was a very clever thing you said, Lady Chesterford, when you came in from your flying," he said. "I shall tell the Princess. Sophy, Lady Chesterford said to me what was very amusing. 'I flew to meet you,' she said, and that is very clever. She had been flying, and also to fly to meet someone means to go in a hurry. It was a pon."

"Yes, dearest, get on with your dealing. You have told me twice already."

"And now I tell you three times, and so you will remember. Always, when I play Bridge, Lady Dodo, I play with the Princess for my partner, for if I play against her, what she wins I lose and also what I win she loses, and so it is nothing at all. Ach! I have turned up a card unto myself, and it is an ace, and I will keep it. I will not deal again when it is so nearly done."

"But you must deal again," cried his partner. "It is the rule, Albert, you must keep the rule."

He laid down the few cards that remained to be dealt, and opened his hands over the table, so that she could not gather up those already distributed.

"But I shall not deal again," he said, "the deal is so near complete. And there is no rule, and my cigar is finished."

Dodo gave a little suppressed squeal of laughter.

"No, go on, sir," she said. "We don't mind."

He raised his hands.

"So there you are, Sophy!" he said. "You were wrong, and there is no rule. Do not touch the cards while I get my fresh cigar. They are very good: I will take one to bed."

He slowly got up.

"But finish your deal first," she said. "You keep us all waiting."

He slowly sat down.

"Ladies must have their own way," he said. "But men also, and now I shall have to get up once more for my cigar."

"Daddy, fetch the Prince a cigar," said Dodo.

He looked at her, considering this.

"But, no; I will choose my own," he said. "I will smell each, and I will take the smelliest."

During this hand an unfortunate incident occurred. The Princess, seeing an ace on the table, thought it came from an opponent, and trumped it.

"But what are you about?" he asked. "Also it was mine ace."

She gathered up the trick.

"My fault, dearest," she said. "Quite my fault. Now what shall I do?"

He laid down his hand.

"But you have played a trump when I had played the ace," he said.

"Dearest, I have said it was a mistake," said she.

"But it is to take five shillings from my pocket, that you should trump my ace. It is ridiculous that you should do that. If you do that, you shew you cannot play cards at all. It was my ace."

The rubber came to an end over this hand, and Dodo swiftly added up the score.

"Put it down, Nadine," she said. "We shall play to-morrow. We each of us owe eighty-two shillings."

The Prince adopted the more cumbrous system of adding up on his fingers, half-aloud, in German, but he agreed with the total.

"But I will be paid tonight," he said. "When I lose, I pay, when I am losed I am paid. And it should have been more. The Princess trumped my ace."

The entrance of a tray of refreshments luckily distracted his mind from this tragedy, and he rose.

"So I will eat," he said, "and then I will be paid eighty-two marks. I should be rich if every evening I won eighty-two marks. I should give the Princess more pin-money. But I will fly to eat, Lady Chesterford. That was your joke: that I shall tell Willie, but not about his music."

Dodo took the Princess up to her room, followed by her maid who carried a tray with some cold soup and strawberries on it.

"Such a pleasant evening, dear," she said. "Ah, there is some cold soup: so good, so nourishing. This year I think we shall stop in England till the review at Kiel, when we go with Willie. So glorious! The Cherman fleet so glorious, and the English fleet so glorious. What do you say, Marie? A little box? How did the little box come here? What does it say? Vane's patent soap-box."

Dodo looked at the little box.

"Oh, that's my father," she said. "Really, ma'am, I'm ashamed of him. His manufacture, you know. I expect he has put one in each of our rooms."

"But how kind! A present for me! Soap! So convenient. So screaming! I must thank him in the morning."

Then came a tap from the Prince's room next door, and he entered.

"Also, I have found a little box," he said. "Why is there a little iron box? I do not want a little iron box."

"Dearest, a present from Mr. Vane," said his wife. "So kind! So convenient for your soap."

"Ach! So! Then I will take my soap also away inside the box. I will have eighty-two marks and my soap in a box. That is good for one evening. Also, I wish it was a gold box."

418

Dodo went downstairs again, and found her father in a sort of stupor of satisfaction.

"A marvellous brain," he said. "I consider that the Prince has a marvellous brain. Such tenacity! Such firmness of grasp! Eh, when he gets hold of an idea, he isn't one of your fly-aways that let it go again. He nabs it."

His emotion gained on him, and he dropped into a broader pronunciation.

"And the Princess!" he said. "She speaking of Wullie, just like that. 'Wullie,' as I might say 'Dodo.' Now that gives a man to think. Wullie! And him his Majesty the Emperor!"

Dodo kissed him.

"Daddy, dear," she said, "I am glad you've had a nice evening. But you put us all out of the running, you know. Oh, and those soap-boxes, you wicked old man! But they're delighted with them. She is going to thank you to-morrow."

"God! An' there's condescension!" said he reverently.

3

Dodo had been obliged to go to church on Sunday morning by way of being in attendance on Princess Albert. She did not in the least mind going to church, in fact she habitually did so, and sang loudly in the choir, but she did not like going otherwise than of her own free-will, for she said that compulsion made a necessity of virtue. Church and a stroll round the hot-houses, where the Prince ate four peaches, accounted for most of the morning, but after lunch, when he retired to his room like a flushed boa-constrictor, and Jack had taken the Princess off in a motor to see the place where something happened either to Isaac Walton or Isaac Newton, Dodo felt she could begin to devote herself to some of the old friends, who had originally formed the nucleus of her party. For this purpose she pounced on the first one she came across, who happened to be Miss Grantham, and took her off to the shady and sequestered end of the terrace. Up to the present moment she had only been able to tell Grantie that she was changed; now she proceeded to enlarge on that accusation. Grantie had accepted (you might almost say she had courted) middle-age in a very decorous and becoming manner: her hair, fine as floss silk had gone perfectly white, thus softening her rather hard, handsome horse-like face, and she wore plain expensive clothes of sober colours with pearls and lace and dignity.

"You've changed, Grantie," said Dodo, "because you've gone on doing the same sort of thing for so long. Nothing has happened to you."

"Then I ought to have remained the same," said Grantie with composure. She put up a parasol as she spoke, as if in anticipation of some sort of out-pouring.

"That's your mistake, darling," said Dodo. "If you go on doing the same thing, and being the same person, you always deteriorate. I read in the paper the other day about a man whose skin became covered with a sort of moss, till he looked like a neglected tombstone. And going on in a groove has the same effect on the mind: if you don't keep stirring it up and giving it shocks at what you do, it vegetates. Look at that moss between the paving-stones! That's there because the gardeners haven't poked them and brushed them. The terrace has changed because it hasn't been sufficiently trodden on and kicked and scrubbed. It has been let alone. Do you see? Nothing has happened to you."

Miss Grantham certainly preserved the detached calm which had always distinguished her.

"No, it's true that I haven't been kicked and scrubbed," she said. "But all my relations have died. That's happened to me."

"No; that happened to them," said Dodo. "You want routing out. Why do you live in the country, for instance? I often think that doctors are so misunderstanding. If you feel unwell and consult a doctor, he usually tells you to leave London at once, and not spend another night there. But for most ailments it would be far more useful if he told you to leave the country at once. It's far more dangerous to get mossy than to get overdone. You can but break down if you get overdone, but if you get mossy you break up."

Dodo had a mistaken notion that she was putting Grantie on her defence. It amused Grantie to keep up that delusion for the present.

"I like a life of dignity and leisure," she said, "though no doubt there is a great deal in what you say. I like reading and thinking, I like going to bed at eleven and looking at my pigs. I like quiet and tranquillity——"

"But that's so deplorable," said Dodo.

"I suppose it is what you call being mossy. But I prefer it. I choose to have leisure. I choose to go to bed early and do nothing particular when I get up."

Dodo pointed an accusing finger at her.

"I've got it," she said. "You are like the poet who said that the world was left to darkness and to him. He liked bossing it in the darkness, and so do you. You train the village choir, Grantie, and it's no use denying it. You preside at mother's meetings, and you are local president of the Primrose League. You have a flower-show in what they call your grounds, just as if you were coffee, on August bank-holiday, and a school-feast. You have a Christmas-tree for the children, and send masses of holly to decorate the church. At Easter, arum lilies."

Miss Grantham began to show that she was not an abject criminal on her defence.

"And those are all very excellent things to do," she said. "I do not see that they are less useful than playing bridge all night, or standing quacking on a stair-case in a tiara, and calling it an evening party."

"Yes, we do quack," conceded Dodo.

"Or spending five hundred pounds on a ball——"

"My dear, that wouldn't do much in the way of a ball," began Dodo.

"Well, a thousand pounds then, if you wish to argue about irrelevancies. All the Christmas-trees and Easter decorations and school-feasts don't cost that——"

"Grantie dear, how marvellously cheap," said Dodo enthusiastically. "What a good manager you must be, and it all becomes more appalling every minute. You know that you don't boss it in the darkness because of the good you do, and the pleasure you give, but because it gives you the impression of being busy, and makes so little trouble and expense. Now if you ran races, things in sacks, at the school-feasts yourself, and pricked your own delicious fingers with the holly for the Christmas decorations, and watered your flowers yourself for the flower-show, there might be something in it. But you don't do anything of that kind: you only give away very cheap prizes at the school-feast, and make your gardeners cut the holly, and take the prizes yourself at the flower-show. You like bossing it, darling: that's what's the matter, and it's that which has changed you. You don't compete, except at the flower-show, and then it's your gardeners who compete for you. You ought to run races at the school-feast, if you want to be considered a serious person."

"I couldn't run," said Miss Grantham. "If I ran, I should die. That would make a tragic chord at the school-feast, instead of a cheerful note."

"It would do nothing of the sort," said Dodo. "The school-children would remember the particular school-feast when you died with wonderful excitement and pleasure. It would be stored for ever in their grateful memories. 'That was the year,' they would say, 'when Miss Grantham fell dead in the sack-race, and such a lovely funeral.' They wouldn't think it the least tragic, bless them."

To Miss Grantham's detached and philosophic mind this conclusion, when she reflected on it, seemed extremely sound. She decided to pursue that track no further, for it appeared to lead nowhere, and proceeded violently upwards in a sort of moral lift.

"And then I happen to like culture and knowledge," she said. "I just happen to, in the same way as you like princes. I know you won't agree about the possible advantage of educating yourself. Last night at dinner I heard you say that you had probably forgotten how to read, as you hadn't read anything for so long. That made me shudder. You seem to think that, because I live in the country, I vegetate. You call me mossy, and I am nothing of the kind. I read for three hours a day, wet or fine. I do wood-carving, I play the piano."

Dodo gave a long sigh.

"I know; it sounds lovely," she said. "So does suicide when you have to get up early in the morning. Sometimes Jack and I think we should like to live in a cottage by a river with a bee-hive and a general servant, and nine rows of beans like Mr. Yeats, and lead the simple life. But moral scruples preserve us from it, just as they preserve one from suicide. When I feel that I want to live in the country, I know it is time to take a tonic or go to Ascot. I don't believe for a moment that I was meant to be a 'primrose by the river's brim.' If you go in for being a primrose by the river's brim, you so soon become 'nothing more to him' or to anybody else. If Nature had intended me to be a vegetable, she would have made me more like a cabbage than I am."

Miss Grantham was hardly ever roused by personal criticism, partly because she hardly ever was submitted to it, and partly because it seemed to her to matter so singularly little what anyone else thought of her. But when Dodo began again, "You're a delicious cow," she interrupted firmly and decisively, dropped any semblance of defence and attacked.

"And now it's my turn," she said, "and don't interrupt me, Dodo, by any smart repartees, because they don't impress me in the least. I may be a cabbage—though as a matter of fact, I am not—but I would far sooner be a cabbage than a flea."

"A flea?" asked the bewildered Dodo.

"Yes, dear, I said 'flea.' All the people who live the sort of life which you have deliberately adopted as your own, are precisely like fleas. You hop about with dreadful springs, and take little bites of other people, and call that life. If you hear of some marvellous new invention, you ask the inventor to lunch and suck a little of his blood. Then at dinner you are told that everybody is talking about some new book, so you buy a copy next morning, cut the first fifty pages, leave it about in a prominent place, and ask the author to tea. Meanwhile you forget all about the inventor. Then a new portrait-painter appears, or a new conjuror at the music-halls or a new dancer, and off you hop again and have another bite. For some obscure reason you think that that is life, whereas it is only being a flea. I don't in the least mind your being a flea, you may be precisely what you choose. But what I do object to is your daring to disapprove of my way of life, about which you know nothing whatever. You called me narrow——"

"Never!" said Dodo.

"In effect, you called me narrow. Didn't you?" asked Grantie calmly. "Yes."

"Very well then. When you talk about narrowness, you seem unaware that there is no greater narrowness possible than to adopt that cocksure attitude. You think you are competent to judge modes of living about which you are quite ignorant. What do you know about me?"

Dodo surged out of her chair.

"Grantie dear, we don't understand each other one bit," she said, kissing her. "How sad it all is!"

Grantie remained unmoved and calm.

"I understand you perfectly," she said. "Though I am quite aware that you don't understand me."

Dodo suddenly ceased to attend, and held up a silencing finger.

"Listen!" she said.

From the open window of a bedroom just above their seat came a sound sonorous and rhythmical. Dodo had not meant to have the war carried into her own country, and she was rather glad of an interruption.

"Albert!" she said rapturously. "Albert snoring."

Any text would have done for Grantie's sermon that moment.

"Yes, I hear," she said. "We can all snore, but that particular snoring amuses you, in some odd way, because he's a prince. I don't love you any the less because you are a snob and a flea."

Dodo burst into a peal of laughter.

"Grantie, you're perfect!" she said. "Oh, how little did I think when I began calling you a vegetable, quite conversationally, that you would turn round and hustle me like this. And the worst of it is that you are right. You see, you arrange your ideas, you think what you mean to say, and then say it, whereas I say anything that comes into my head, and try to attach some idea to it afterwards if it's challenged. Usually it isn't, and we talk about something else, and everyone thinks 'What clever conversation!' But really you wrong me: I am something more than a snobbish flea."

"Yes; you're a parody," said Miss Grantham thoughtfully. "That is the deplorable thing about you. You have always made a farce out of your good qualities, and a tragedy out of your bad ones. What a waste! You need never have been either a farce or a tragedy, but just a decent, simple, commonplace woman like me."

Dodo knew perfectly well what Grantie meant by this considered indictment. It needed but the space of an astonished gasp, as this cold hose was sluiced on her, to understand it entirely, and recognise the basic truth of it. She knew to what Grantie alluded as her good points, namely her energy, her quickness, her vivacity, her kindliness. Of these, so said Grantie, she made a farce, used them to cause laughter, to rouse admiration, to make a rocket of herself. And there was no more difficulty in identifying the bad points, out of which tragedies had come. They were just the defects of her qualities, and could easily be grouped together under the general head of egotism.

Quite suddenly, then, there came a deepening in the import of the conversation which had begun so superficially. At first Dodo had used the lightness of touch, in discussing Grantie's mode of life, which, to her mind, befitted such subjects. But now she found herself gripped; something had caught her from below. For some reason—perhaps from having lived so long in the country—Grantie took matters like tastes and conduct and character quite seriously. Dodo did not mind that in the least; it was still she who was being talked about, and thus her egotism was fed. Even if it was being fed with 'thorns and briars of the wilderness,' it was still being attended to.

"Go on," she said. "Explain."

"It's hardly worth while," said Grantie, "because you know it already. But just think of your telling me with disapproval that I have changed! So much the better for me, though you think it is a matter for regret."

"Darling, I never said you weren't quite delightful as you are," said Dodo.

"I wasn't aware that there was any such complimentary *nuance* in your criticisms," said Grantie. "Anyhow there is none in mine. I find that you have not changed in the least: you are in essentials precisely the same as you always were, and I could weep over you. I talked to Edith last night, when you were taking off the Princess's shoes or something, and she quite agreed with me. She said that you were amazing in the way that you had retained your youth. But she thought that was lovely, and there I disagreed. I find it tragic. It's an awful thing, Dodo, to be youthful at your age, which is the same as mine. If you were worth anything, if you had ever got out of yourself, your life would have changed you. You say that there is a man covered with moss: well, there is a tortoise covered with its bony shell. You remain the same marvellous egotist that you were when you dazzled us all thirty years ago, and it is just because I have changed that I see through you now. You have thought about yourself for fifty-four long years. Aren't you tired of the subject yet?"

Dodo felt a keen sense of injustice in this.

"But you don't understand me," she said. "After all, I don't know how you could. You haven't got a husband and a son for whom you would do anything. Oh, and a daughter," she added hastily.

"How you enjoyed saying that!" observed Miss Grantham.

Dodo paid no attention to this very just remark, and went on as if nothing had been said.

"Dear Grantie, you only understand things on your own plane. You don't know what marriage and children mean. But I do; I've been married over and over again. Because you pat other people's children on the head, and give tea and shawls to their parents, you think you know something about devotion."

Miss Grantham looked at her watch.

"If Jack or you had to die in a quarter of an hour's time, that is to say at five minutes to four in horrible agony, which would you choose?" she asked.

"But that's impossible," said Dodo in some agitation. "You are putting ridiculous cases."

"They are ridiculous cases, because you know what your choice would be, and don't want to confess it," said Grantie. "I don't press for an answer, but it was your own fault that I asked the question since you talked nonsense about devotion which I can't understand. I merely inquired into its nature. That's all; it is finished."

"Grantie, I hate you," said Dodo. "Why don't you make the best of other people, as I always do?"

"Simply because they insist on making the worst of themselves, and it would be rude to disagree with them," said Grantie.

"You are a sour old maid," said Dodo with some heat.

Miss Grantham spoke to the terrace generally in a detached manner.

" 'Why don't you make the best of people as I always do?' " she quoted.

Dodo laughed.

"Oh yes, you scored," she said. "But to be serious a moment instead of pea-shooting each other. I allow you have hit me on the nose several times with devilish accuracy and hard, wet peas. What fun it used to be——"

"To be serious a moment——" said Grantie.

"That's another pea; don't do it. To be serious, as I said before, do you really suppose that you can alter your character? It always seems to me the one unchangeable thing. A thoroughly selfish woman can make herself behave unselfishly, just as a greedy person can starve himself, but they remain just as selfish and greedy as before. Oh, Grantie, I've got a dreadful nature, and the only thing to be done is to blow soap-bubbles all over it, so that it appears to be iridescent."

"You don't really believe that about yourself," said Grantie.

Dodo groaned.

"I know I don't," she said. "I know nothing about myself. When David thinks I am adorable, I quite agree with him, and when you tell me that I am a worm, I look wildly round for the thrush that is going to eat me. There's one on the lawn now; it may be that one. Shoo! you nasty bird!" she cried.

The thrush scudded off into the bushes at the sound of Dodo's shrill voice and clapped hands.

"So it isn't that one. What a relief!" said Dodo. "But what's to be done?"

"Knit!" said Miss Grantham firmly. "Sew! Get out of yourself! Play the piano!"

"But I should only think how beautifully I was playing it," said Dodo. "All you say is true, Grantie; that's the beastly thing about you, but it's all no use. Listen at that fortunate Cherman snoring! He isn't thinking about himself; he's not thinking about anything at all. I wish I was eighty. It's better to be in a bath-chair than in a cage. We are all in cages, at least I am, and you are a raven in a cage. You croak, and you peck me if I come near you. Iron bars do make a cage, whatever Lovelace thought about it, if the iron bars are your own temperament. I can't get out, and isn't it awful?"

Dodo gave a great sigh, and lit a cigarette.

"I shall forget all about it in two minutes," she said, "and that's the really hopeless thing about me. I feel deeply for a few seconds, and then I feel equally deeply about something perfectly different. Just now I long for something to happen which will break the bars or open my cage. And yet it is such a comfortable one. That's the matter with all of us, me with my egotism, and you with your school-feasts. We're all far too cosy and prosperous. 'See saw, Margery Daw!' We're all swinging in an apple-tree. The rope has got to break, and we must all go bump, if we hope for salvation. It must be something big, something dreadful. If Jack lost all his property, and went utterly bankrupt, that wouldn't help me. I should get an old wheezy barrel-organ and parade the streets and squares in London, singing in a cracked voice, and have a lovely time. Or I should get a situation at a tea-shop, or I should chaperon climbers, and it would all amuse me, and I shouldn't change one atom. Really I don't think anything would do me any good except the Day of Judgment. . . . Thank God, here's

Hughie; I am getting rather insane. Hughie, what have you been doing, and if so, are you happy, and if so, how dare you be happy? Why are you happy?"

Hughie considered these questions, and ticked the answers off on his fingers.

"I've been doing nothing," he said, "and I dare to be happy. I don't know why. But again, why shouldn't I be?"

"But why should you? What have you done to deserve it? Catechise him, Grantie, because it's Sunday afternoon, and make him confess that he's got a horrid nature, and ought to be miserable."

"Go ahead," said Hugh. "But it's no use trying to make me confess that I've got a horrid nature. I haven't. I've got rather a nice one."

"Then you are wrapped up in self-esteem," said Dodo, "and I'm better than you."

Hugh, seated on the terrace, looked up at Dodo with the mild, quiet surprise that he exhibited when his aeroplane engine miss-fired.

"Of course you are," he said. "So why not play croquet? Then I shall be better than you."

"But I want to know what makes you happy. Grantie's been stirring me up, and making me feel muddy. I've been telling her all the good reasons why I lead the life that suits me——"

Grantie gave a loud croak of dissent, like the raven to which Dodo had compared her.

"That bears not the most distant relation to truth," she said. "What you have been doing is to give all sorts of bad reasons why I shouldn't lead the life that suits me."

Dodo paid no attention to this.

"And she's been making me say that the Day of Judgment is the only thing that will do me any good. She has been ferreting me out, like a rabbit, and making me confused. It isn't the real me that she has bolted. When you ferret rabbits, you get rabbits that are fussed and frightened and in a hurry; they aren't normal rabbits. Grantie, you are a mixture between a raven and a ferret and a gadfly—a marvellous hybrid, as yet unknown to books on natural history. You have pink eyes, and a horny beak and a sting. I want Jack. Where is Jack? Oh, he's still out with that dear old Cherman governess. And listen—oh, it has stopped!"

Dodo looked up at the window from which the noises of repose had come, and at the moment a large suffused face looked down.

"Also, your garden-party awoke me," said its injured owner. "I was dreaming a pleasant dream, and then in my dream there came noise. I was in the restaurant at the Ritz, and it was dinner, and then people at the next table began talking and laughing, and I could no more attend to my dinner, and then I awoke, and it was all true except the Ritz and the dinner, for there were people talking and laughing, and so I awoke. And so it was a dream, and yet it was not a dream. Where is the Princess? She is not home yet? I will play croquet, and I will win and I will have my tea."

"Yes, do come down, sir," said Dodo. "It was me talking."

"Also, in English you should say 'I' not 'me,'" said this profound scholar.

"No, sir, you shouldn't," said Dodo. "You say 'I' when you're learning English, because that is correct, and when you've learned it you say 'me.'"

"So! Then me will come and play croquet. Ha! You see I have learned English so quickly. First will me put on my white pantaloons, and then I will play croquet. Auf wiedersehen."

Dodo looked across at Grantie.

"You shall play with him," she said in an encouraging whisper. "Devotion to others, darling! Duty! Change! Expansion of soul and development of character! All that we've been talking about which I haven't got."

Dodo strolled away with her son-in-law when she had seen Grantie firmly embarked on a game with the Prince, who played with even more deliberation than his opponents found so wearing when he played bridge, and with a thoroughly East Prussian thoroughness. He very soon made up his mind that he was a player of more resource than Grantie, and so arranged to have a stake of five marks on the game. This made it a peculiarly serious business, and one that entailed a great deal of stooping down behind the ball he was playing with, and accurately aligning his mallet in the direction of the object. Having done this he got up with creaks from his stiff white pantaloons, and clinging to the handle of his mallet, as to a life-buoy, while keeping it unmoved, bent down again to pick up his spectacles which had always fallen off. He answered, in fact, perfectly to Edith's definition of the German spirit as the unhurrying and relentless entity which spared no trouble in securing a certain advance towards its appointed end. As exemplified by Prince Albert the efficiency of this industrious labour had to be supplemented by a ruthless system of cheating. The moment he thought that Miss Grantham's eye was occupied in other directions, he rolled his ball by a stealthy movement of his foot into a more advantageous position for his next stroke, and made any little surreptitious adjustment that might tend to confound his adversary. Unfortunately it was a very short time before Miss Grantham awoke to these manoeuvres, and proceeded to take counter-offensive measures of a more than neutralising character. For instance, the moment he had aligned his mallet, and bent down for the second time to pick up his spectacles, she shifted the position of the ball at which he had taken his aim, and if possible, put the wire of a hoop between him and it, or if that was not feasible, merely kicked it a foot or two away, for she had observed that on rising again for the second time he paid no more attention to where the object ball was but devoted his mind to hitting in the direction in which he had laid his mallet. He hit his own ball extremely true. Grantie, so far from having any compunction about this, felt that she was merely doing her proper part; if these were the German rules, it was incumbent on her to observe them. . . . At other times, if she hoped to make a hoop herself, she merely trundled her ball into an easier position.

Slowly and calmly, like the light of morning, the fact of these manoeuvres made to match his own dawned on him, and he unblushingly proposed an abandonment of these tactics.

"Also, as it is," he said, "first I cheat, and then you cheat. I do not gain if we do so, so where is the use? Always there is a wire when I hit at your ball, and then I go bump, and I do not gain. So no longer will I move my ball, and no longer shall you. Shall that be a bargain, an agreement? There is no gain if we both do so. I did not know that in England you played so."

Dodo had returned by this time, with David holding on to her hand, and heard the ratification of this infamous bargain.

"Oh, Grantie, how I despise you," she said, "and how comfortable that makes me feel. You have lowered yourself, darling; you have come down from your pedestal."

The game had got to an exciting stage, and a loud hoarse voice interrupted.

"Also my ball skipped," cried the Prince. "It ran and rolled and then it did skip over the other ball. It is no game on such a carpet. It is madness to have marks on the game when my ball skips like that. It ran and it rolled and then it skipped. I play for nothing if my ball skips. If again my ball skips, I will pay no marks."

Edith had joined Dodo on the edge of the lawn.

"That's Berlin all over," she observed.

David lifted up a shrill treble.

"Mummie, I don't understand this game," he said very distinctly. "May I cheat when I play croquet? First he cheated and then she cheated: I watched them from the nursery. And what are marks?"

Dodo devoted her entire attention to David.

"They are slipper-marks," she said brilliantly. "You shall get them if ever I catch you cheating at croquet."

"But has he got——" began David.

"Quantities! Shut up, darling!"

This international event was protracted till dressing-time was imminent, and during the last half-hour of it the Prince was the prey of the most atrocious anxieties. If the game was abandoned, no decision would be reached, and he would not get his five marks, of which he, in the present state of affairs, felt that he was morally possessed. On the other hand, if they fought it out to the bitter stump, dinner must either be put off, which in itself made a tragedy of this pleasant day, or he would be late for dinner, which was almost as terrible. By way of saving time he debated these contingencies very slowly to his wife.

"If I stop I do not win," he said, "and if I do not stop, I may yet be beaten, and also it will be after dinner-time. I am puzzled. I do not know what I shall do. I do not win if I stop——"

"Dearest, you must stop talking," said she briskly, "and go to hit your ball. Dodo will put off dinner till half-past eight, but we cannot all starve because of your five marks."

"But it is not five marks alone," said he. "It is also glory. Ha! I have thought, and I will tell you what I shall do. I shall play till half-past eight and then if it is not finished, I will come to dinner in my white pantaloons, and I will not clean myself. So!"

"But you cannot dine in your white pantaloons," said she. "It would be too screaming!"

"But I will dine in my white pantaloons, whether they scream, or whether they do not scream. Often have I at Allenstein dined in my white pantaloons, and if I do not clean myself, I am still clean. So do not talk any more, Sophy, for I shall do as I please, and I shall please to dine in my white pantaloons if the game is not over. See! I strike! Ach! I did not stoop. I did not look. But I will not be hurried. . . . But look, I have hit another ball. That is good! My ball did not skip that time, and I will have five marks. Now you shall see what I do!"

The game came to an end while there was yet time for him to change his white pantaloons, even though there was considerable delay in convincing him that a half-crown, a florin and a sixpence were a true and just equivalent for five marks of the Fatherland. Victory, and the discovery that there was bisque soup for dinner put him into an amazingly good humour which blossomed into a really vivacious hilarity of a certain sort. Incidentally, some racial characteristics emerged.

"Also I am very happy to-night, Lady Dodo," he said. "Not ever have I felt so much hungry, and it is happy to be hungry when soon I shall not any longer be hungry. I will take again of the beef, and I will take also again of the long vegetable with the butter. It is good to be at dinner, and it is good to be in England. All Chermans like to be in England, for there is much to eat and there is much to study. I also study; I look and I observe and again I look and I study. We are great students and all good Chermans are students when they come to England."

Quite suddenly, so it seemed to Dodo, Princess Albert, seated next Jack on the middle of the other side of the table, caught something of what he was saying. In any case, she broke off in the middle of a sentence and leaned across to him.

"Dearest, you are keeping everybody waiting," she said. "Do not talk so much, but attend to your good dinner."

He nudged Dodo with his fat elbow.

"You see, I am a hen-peck," he said. "That is a good term. I am a hen-peck. Good! So I will myself peck the long sprouts with the butter."

He devoted himself to doing so for the next few minutes, and regretfully sucked his buttery fingers.

"I talked of study," he said, "and it is croquet I study, and I have five marks. Chermany is poor compared to rich England, and in Allenstein I play only for three marks when I play croquet. But we Chermans have industry, we have perseverance, also nothing distracts us, but we go on while others stop still. I am very content to be a poor Cherman in rich England. . . . No. . . . I will have no ice! If I am warm inside me, why should I make cold inside me? But soon I will have some port, and I am happy to be here. I could sing, so happy am I."

Once again the Princess must have been listening to him.

"Indeed, dearest, you shall not sing," she said.

He looked at her with a grave replete eye.

"But if I choose, I shall sing," he said, "and if I do not choose then I shall not sing."

Dodo felt that there was something moving below this ridiculous talk, which she could not quite grasp. Some sort of shifting shadow was there, like a fish below water. . . .

"Don't be a hen-peck, sir," she said. "Sing quietly to me."

He leaned a little sideways to her, beating the table softly with his hand. Edith, who was sitting on his other side, caught the rhythm of his beat.

"That's 'Deutschland über alles,' " she said, cheerfully.

He gave her a complicated wink.

"Also, you are wrong," he said. "It is 'Rule Britannia.' "

He leaned forward across the table.

"Sophy," he said. "This is a good joke; you will like this joke. For I thumped with my hand on the table, and this lady here said, 'Also, that is "Deutschland über alles." ' And I said to her, 'You are wrong,' I said. 'Also, it is "Rule Britannia." ' That is a good joke, and you shall tell that to Willie when you write to him. So! We are all pleased. Ach! The ladies are going. I will rise, and then I will sit down again."

Edith went straight to the piano in the next room, and without explanation, thumped out "Rule Britannia." She followed it up with the "Marseillaise."

4

Dodo had always firmly believed that boredom was by far the most fruitful cause of fatigue, and since she herself was hardly ever bored, she attributed to that the fact that she was practically indefatigable. Her immunity from boredom was not due to the fact that she, like the great majority of the women of her world, steadily and strenuously avoided anything that was likely to bore her: it was that she brought so intense and lively an interest to whatever she happened to be doing, that her occupation, of whatever kind it might be, became a mental refreshment. Last night, for instance, at dinner she had sat next Lord Cookham at a mournful and pompous banquet, an experience which was apt to prostrate the strongest with an acute attack of nervous depression, but the only effect it had on Dodo was to make her study with the most eager curiosity how it was possible that any one could be so profound a prig, and yet not burst or burn with a blue flame. He spoke in polished and rounded periods, always adapting his conversation to the inferior intellect of his audience, and it was impossible to hold discussion or argument with him, for if you disagreed with any of his *dicta,* he smiled with withering indulgence, and reminded you that he had devoted constant study to that particular point. Naturally if he had done that it was certain that he had come to the correct conclusion, and there was no more to be said except by him (which he proceeded to do). This table-conversation, moreover, could have been set up into type without any corrections, for he be-lieved, probably with perfect correctness, that everybody, except him-self, made occasional grammatical slips either in speaking or writing, and he winced if you used the expression "under these circumstances" instead of "in." He had never married, having been unable to find a wife of sufficiently fine intellectual calibre. But so far from irritating Dodo, this prodigious creature merely fascinated her, and when after dinner he took his place in the centre of the hearthrug, and recounted to the entire company the talk he had had with the Minister of Antiqui-ties in Athens, and the advice he had given him with regard to the preservation of the sculpture on the Parthenon, Dodo felt that she could have listened for ever in the ecstatic attempt to realise the full complacency of that miraculous mind. Thoroughly refreshed but slightly intoxicated by that intellectual treat she had gone to a party at the Foreign Office, followed by a ball, and was out again riding in the Park with David at eight. She came back a little before ten, and found her husband morosely breakfasting in the sitting-room, with his back to the window.

"Good morning, darling," she said. "It's the divinest day, and you ought to have come out instead of sleeping off your Cookhamitis. There was a blue haze over everything like the bloom on a plum, and a water-cart came down Park Lane just as we got out of the gate, so we followed it for half a mile going very slowly behind it, because it smelt so good. Jack, I am sure Cookham was like that when he was born; he could never have learned to be so marvellous. He probably told his nurse in Greek how to wash and dress him before he could talk. Now don't say that he couldn't speak Greek before he could talk, because my suggestion contains an essential truth in spite of its apparent impossibility. 'You must believe it because it's impossible,' as St. Augustine said."

Dodo poured herself out some tea.

"I got home at a quarter to four," she said, "and I was called at a quarter to eight, and I was out by eight and I shall have my bath after breakfast."

"What happened to your prayers?" asked Jack.

"Forgot them, you old darling. How delicious of you to ask! When I say them I shall pray that you will be less grumpy in the morning. What an unholy lot of letters there are for me! I like a lot of letters really; it shews there were a quantity of people thinking about me yesterday. When I don't get a lot, I think of the time when I shall be dead, and nobody will write to me any more. Or will they write dead letters? The dead letter office sounds as if it was for that. Oh, here's one from Lord Cookham in that dreadful neat handwriting which leaves no room for conjecture. Why couldn't he say what he had to say last night? Oh, it's something official, and he, being what he is, wouldn't talk officially at a private house. What beautiful correctness!"

Dodo turned over the page.

"Well, of all the pieces of impertinences!" she said. "Jack, listen! He is commanded to ask whether I will give a ball for the Maharajah of Bareilly——"

"That's not impertinent," said Jack.

"No, dear; don't interrupt. But he suggests that I should send the proposed list of my guests to him for purposes of revision and addition. Did you ever hear anything like that?"

Dodo read on, and gave a shrill scream.

"And that's not all!" she shouted. "He suggests that I should send him the choice of three dates about the middle of July and he will then inform me in due course which will be the most convenient. Is the man mad? There aren't three dates about the middle of July, and if there were I wouldn't send him them."

"What are you going to say?" asked Jack.

"I shall say that I happen to have no vacant dates about the middle of July, but that I am giving a ball on the sixteenth and that I shall be delighted to ask his Indian friend, who may come to dinner first if I can find room for him. About my list of guests I shall say that I should no more dream of sending it to him for revision and addition than I should send it to my scullery-maid, and that if my friends aren't good enough for a Maharajah, he may go and dance with his own. My guests to be revised by Lord Cookham! Additions to be made by him! Isn't he quite priceless?"

"Completely. Mind you don't ask him."

"Certainly I shan't. The soup gets cold when Cookham comes to dine. Also, as Prince Albert says, when he comes in at the door gaiety flies out of the window."

Jack took up the morning paper.

"The only news seems to be that he and the Princess have come up to town," he observed. "They are to stay with your Daddy a few days and then their address will be at the Ritz."

"Daddy will love that," said Dodo, recovering her geniality. "Jam for Daddy. They'll like it too, because it will save a few more days of hotel-bills. What a happy family!"

Jack turned back on to the middle page of the *Times*. He usually began rather further on where there were cricket matches and short paragraphs, in order to reawaken his interest in the affairs of the day.

"Hullo!" he said. "What a horrible thing!"

Dodo had not noticed that he had left the cricket-page.

"Has Nottinghamshire got out leg before?" she asked vaguely.

"No. But the Archduke Ferdinand and his wife have been murdered at Serajevo."

Dodo rapidly considered whether this made any difference to her, and decided that it did not matter as much as the letter she was reading.

"I don't think I ever heard of him," she said. "And where's Serajevo?"

"In Servia or one of those places," said Jack. "The Archduke was the heir to the Austrian throne."

Dodo put down her letter.

"Oh, poor man!" she said. "How horrid to be killed, if you were going to be an Emperor! What makes you frown, Jack? Did you know him?"

"No. But there is always trouble in those states. Some day the trouble will spread."

Dodo gathered up her letters.

"Trouble will now spread for Baron Cookham," she remarked. "I think I shall telephone to him. He hates being telephoned to like a common person."

"May I listen?" asked Jack.

"Do, darling, and suggest insults in a low voice."

Dodo sent a message that Lord Cookham was required in person at the degrading instrument, and having secured his presence talked in her best telephone-voice, slow and calm and clear-cut.

"Good morning," she said. "I have received your letter. Yes, isn't it a lovely day? I have been riding. No, not writing. Riding. Horse. About your letter. I am giving a ball on the sixteenth of July, and I shall be delighted to ask your friend. Of course I shan't give another ball for him, but if the sixteenth will do, there we are. And what a delicious joke of yours about my sending you a list of my guests! I think I shall ask for a list of the guests when I go to a dance. A lovely idea."

Dodo paused a moment, listening.

"I don't see the slightest difference," she said. "And I can't give you a choice of days, because I haven't got one to give you."

She paused again, and hastily put her hand over the receiver.

"Jack, he wants to come and talk to me about it," she whispered, her voice quivering with amusement. Then it resumed its firm telephone-tone.

"Yes, certainly," she cried. "I shall be in for the next half-hour. After that? Let me see; about the same time to-morrow morning. You'll come at once then? Au revoir."

Dodo replaced the instrument, and bubbled with laughter.

"Oh, my dear, what fun!" she said. "I adore studying him. I shall get a real glimpse into his mind this morning, and if he annoys me as he did in his letter about the list, he shall get a glimpse into mine. He will probably be very much astonished with what it contains."

It was not long before Lord Cookham arrived. He was pink and large and sleek, and could not possibly be mistaken for anybody else except some eminently respectable butler, in whose care the wine and the silver were perfectly safe. Dodo had not quite finished breakfast when he was announced, and proceeded with it.

"So good of you to come and see me at such short notice," she said. "Do smoke."

He waved away the cigarettes she offered him, and produced a gold case with a coronet on it.

"With your leave, Lady Chesterford," he said, "I will have one of my own."

"Do!" said Dodo cordially. "And light it with one of your own matches. Now about my dance."

He cleared his throat exactly as if he was about to make a speech.

"The suggestion that his Highness should come to a ball given by you," he said, "originated with myself. Such an entertainment could not fail to give pleasure to him, nor his presence fail to honour you. His visit to this country is to be regarded as that of a foreign monarch, and in the present unhappy state of unrest in India——"

"It will be nice for him to get away for a little quiet," suggested Dodo.

Lord Cookham bowed precisely as a butler bows when a guest presents him on Monday morning with a smaller token of gratitude than he had anticipated.

"In the present unhappy state of unrest in India," he resumed, "it is important that the most rigid etiquette should be observed towards his Highness, and that he should see, accompanied by every exhibition of magnificence, not only the might and power of England, but all that is most characteristic and splendid in the life of English subjects and citizens."

"I will wear what Jack calls the family fender," said Dodo. "Tiara, you know, so tall that you couldn't fall into the fire if you put it on the hearthrug."

Lord Cookham bowed again.

"Exactly," he said. "The fame of the Chesterford diamonds is world-wide, and you have supplied a wholly apposite illustration of what I am attempting to point out. But it is not only in material splendour, Lady Chesterford, that I desire to produce a magnificent impression on our honoured visitor; I want him to mix with all that is stateliest in birth, in intellect, in aristocracy of all kinds, of science, of art, of industrial pre-eminence, of politics, of public service. It was with this idea in my mind that your name occurred to me as being the most capable among all our London hostesses of bringing together such an assembly as will be perfectly characteristic of all that is most splendid in the social life of our nation."

These well-balanced and handsome expressions did not deceive Dodo for a moment; she rightly interpreted them as being an amiable doxology which should introduce the subject of the revision of her list of guests. She could not help interjecting a remark or two any more than a highly-charged syphon can help sizzling a little, but she was confident, now that Lord Cookham was well afloat, that her remarks would not hamper the majestic movement of his incredible eloquence.

"Daddy will do for industrial pre-eminence," she said, "though perhaps you would hardly call him stately."

Lord Cookham waved his smooth white hand in assent.

"I see already," he said, "that our list is not likely to cause us much trouble. Mr. Vane's name occurred to me at once, apart from his felicity in being your father, for he stands pre-eminent among our masters of industry as an example of one who has amassed a princely fortune by wholly admirable methods and is as princely in his public generosity as in the lavishness of his private hospitality. Your father, in fact, Lady Chesterford, is typical of the aristocracy of industry. Sprung from the very dregs—I should say from the very heart of democracy, he has risen to a position attained by few of those who have been the architects of their own fortunes. Among such you can be of inestimable assistance to me in making this gathering truly representative. You are in touch in a way that I cannot hope to be in spite of my earnest endeavours to make myself acquainted with our country's industrial pioneers, with the princes of manufacture, and while it shall be my task, in conjunction of course with you, to secure the presence of the most representative among our de Veres and Plantagenets, you will be invaluable in suggesting the names of those who by their industry, capital and powers of organisation, have in no less degree than our hereditary aristocracy, helped to establish on sure foundations the power of England. This ball of yours is to be like some great naval or military demonstration designed to set forth the wealth and the might of our country. In the present state of unrest in India from which as you so rightly observe, our guest is fortunate in securing a holiday, it must be his holiday-task, if I may adopt the phraseology of youth, to weigh and appreciate the power that claims his fidelity. We have no more loyal prince in India than he, and what he shall see on his visit here must confirm and strengthen that. Busy though I am this morning (indeed I am always busy) I was well aware that I could not spend a half-hour more profitably than in coming personally to see you. It would have been difficult to convey all this to you so unerringly on the telephone."

Dodo's mouth had long ago fallen wide open in sheer astonishment. She had shut it again for a moment in order to avoid laughing at the mention of Daddy as having sprung from the dregs of the people, but immediately afterwards it had fallen open again and so remained, as she drank in the superb periods. They soaked in quickly like water on a parched soil. He paused for only a moment.

"It is in this sense that I have alluded to the honour done to you," he resumed, "by my tentative selection of you as hostess in what I am sure will constitute the culminating impression on the Maharajah's mind. You will be for that evening the representative of England herself. Let us next consider the question of date, if, as I take it, you are at one with me on the topic of the list of your guests. Now though you, as hostess will have gathered together this amazing assembly, and will therefore be the queen of them all, the more dynastic represent-atives of England will, I have reason to hope, honour you with their presence in unique numbers. The date you propose, namely the six-teenth of July, may, I hope, be found suitable, but I should like to be in a position to submit other dates in case it is not. Shall we therefore temporarily fix on that night or one of the two following?"

This was getting down to business, and Dodo pulled herself together.

"We will fix on nothing of the sort," she said. "My ball is on the sixteenth. And, do you know, to speak quite frankly, I don't care two pins whether your Maharajah comes or not. In spite of my humble origin I have entertained scores of Maharajahs. Last year half a dozen of them were foisted on to me."

"I have given you some slight sketch of a unique occasion," he reminded her.

"I know you have. I enjoyed it enormously. But my ball is on the sixteenth; you don't seem to understand that yet. And if it doesn't suit anybody he needn't come."

Lord Cookham took a memorandum book from his pocket.

"I have of course been entrusted with all arrangements for his visit," he said, "and I see I have fixed nothing for the sixteenth."

"Very well, fix it now," said Dodo, "and let us go back to the question of the list of guests. There is no such question, let me tell you. I am asking my own guests. I shall be delighted to see the Maharajah (you must tell me something about him in a minute), and any other of those whom just now you called the dynastic representatives of En-gland. I love having kings and queens and princes at my house, because we all are such snobs, aren't we? But I believe that this notion of my submitting my list to you is your own idea. You weren't commanded to do anything of the sort, were you?"

He drew himself up slightly.

"My conduct in this as in all other such matters," he said, "has been dictated by my sense of the duties of my position."

"Same here," said Dodo. "I am the hostess and I shall do just as I please about my ball. Now I'm not going to have it stuffed up with scarecrows. A dozen fossilised Plantagenets spoil all the fun for yards round. They look down their noses and wonder who other people are. Of course there are plenty of Plantagenets who are ducks; they'll be here all right, but if the angel Gabriel said he wanted to make additions to my ball, I would pull out all his wing-feathers sooner than allow him. Worse than that would be the thought of allowing you or him or anybody to cut out the name of any friend of mine because he wasn't fit to meet a Maharajah. All my friends are perfectly fit to meet anybody. So, my dear, you may put that into your own cigarette and smoke it."

Probably Lord Cookham had never been so surprised, so wantonly outraged in his feelings since the unhappy day when he had been birched at Eton for telling lies, which subsequently proved to be true. Just as on that tragic occasion his youthful sense of his own integrity had rendered it impossible for him to conceive that the head-master should lift up his hand against his defencelessness, so now, even as Dodo's tongue dared to lash him with these stinging remarks, he could hardly believe that it was indeed he who was being treated in so condign a manner. And she had not finished yet apparently. . . .

On her side Dodo had (quite unexpectedly to herself) lost her temper. It was a thing extremely rare with her, but when she did lose it, she lost it with enthusiastic completeness. Up till a few minutes ago she had been vastly entertained by the glorious speeches of this master-prig, viewing him objectively and licking her lips at his gorgeousness. But then as swiftly as by the turning of a screw she viewed him subjectively and gazed no more at his gorgeousness but felt his impenetrable insolence. She proceeded:

"I appear to astonish you," she said, "and it is a very good thing for you to be astonished for once. You must remember that I am sprung, as you said from the dregs of the people, and when you go away and think over what I am telling you, you may console yourself by saying that a fishwife has been bawling at you. Now who the devil are you to order me about and invite my guests for me? Are you giving this ball, or am I? If you, ask your guests yourself, and don't ask me. Try to get together a wonderful and historic gathering for your Maharajah on the night of the sixteenth and see who comes to you to make history, and who comes to me. What you wanted to do was to patronise me, and make yourself Master of the Ceremonies, and allow me to have this old Indian for my guest as a great favour. Who is this Maharajah of Bareilly anyway, that for the sake of getting him into my house I should submit to your insufferable airs? Who is he?"

After the first awful shock was over, Lord Cookham conducted himself (even as he had done on that occasion at Eton) with the perfect calm that distinguished him. He appeared quite unconscious of the outrage committed on him, and answered Dodo's direct question in his usual manner.

"As a youth he was sent to Oxford," he said, "where I had the honour of being a contemporary of his. I had been asked, in fact, to put him in the way of knowing interesting people and directing his mind, by example rather than precept, towards serious study. I was asked, in fact, to look after him and influence him in the way one young man can influence another slightly his junior. After leaving Oxford he spent several years in England, and was quite well known, I believe, in certain sections of London Society. Personally I rather lost sight of him, for he went in for sport and, in fact, a rather more frivolous mode of life than suited me. Pray do not think I blame him in any way for that. He succeeded to his principality only a few weeks ago, on the death of his father——"

Dodo had stood up during her impassioned harangue, but now she sat down again. All her anger died out of her face, and her eyes grew wide with the dawning of a stupendous idea.

"It can't possibly be that you are talking about Jumbo?" she asked.

"That I believe was the nickname given him at one time," said Lord Cookham, "in allusion to the——"

Dodo put both her elbows on the table, and went off into peals of inexplicable laughter; she rocked backwards and forwards in her chair, and the tears streamed from her eyes. For a long time she was perfectly incapable of speech, for at every effort to control her mouth into the shape necessary for articulate utterance, it broke away again.

"Oh, oh, I must stop laughing!" she gasped. "Oh, it hurts. . . . My ribs ache; it's agony! What am I to do? But Jumbo! All this fuss about Jumbo! Jumbo was one of my oldest friends. How could I guess that he had become the Maha-ha-ha-rajah of Bareilly? Oh, Lord Cookham, I apologise for all I've said, and for all I've laughed. It's too silly for anything! But why didn't you say it was Jumbo at once, instead of being so pomp—no, I don't mean that. I don't know what I mean."

Dodo collected herself, wiped her eyes, drank a little tea, choked in the middle and eventually pulled herself together.

"Jumbo!" she said faintly. "Is it possible that you never knew that Jumbo used to be absolutely at my feet! I suppose that belonged to the time when he was frivolous, and you lost sight of him. My dear, he used to send me large pearls, which I was obliged to send back to him, and then he sent them again. What they cost in registered parcel post baffles conjecture. What's his address? I must write to him at once. He would think it too odd for words if I gave a dance and didn't ask him. I wonder he has not been to see me already. When did he get to London?"

"Last night only," said Lord Cookham. "He's staying at——"

At that moment the telephone bell rang.

"I believe in miracles," said Dodo rushing to it.

"Yes, who is it?" she said. "You're talking to Lady Chesterford."

There was a second's pause, and the miracle came off.

"Jumbo darling," she said. "How delicious of you to ring me up on your very first morning. I should have been furious if you hadn't. Oddly enough I've been talking about you for the last hour without knowing it, because you've been and gone and changed your name to Bareilly. What? Yes, of course, my dear. Come round in half-an-hour, and I'll take you out, and you shall write your name wherever you please, and then you'll come back and have lunch with me. What a swell you've become. Where's Bareilly? I don't believe you know. Shall I have to curtsey when I see you? This evening? No, dear, I can't dine with you this evening, because I'm engaged, and I never throw anybody over. Yes, afterwards if you like. Alhambra? Yes, take a box there, and I'll come on there as soon as ever I can. We'll make more plans when we meet. Oh, by the way, put down at once that you're dining with me on the sixteenth, and I've got a ball afterwards in honour of you. What?"

Dodo glanced at Lord Cookham.

"Yes, Lord Cookham has told me that he hasn't made any engagements for you that night," she said. "He'll put it down in his book, so there won't be any mistake. What?"

Dodo paused a moment, gave a little gasp, and spoke in a great hurry.

"Yes, Lord Cookham is here with me now," she said. "In this very room I mean, close by me. Do you want to speak to him? All right then. Now I shall rush and have my bath, and then I'll be ready for you. . . . Jumbo, don't be frivolous. I'm not alone. Hush!"

During this remarkable conversation Lord Cookham's long practise in dignity and self-posession had enabled him to appear quite unconscious that anything was going on. By the expression on his face he might have been sitting on the slopes of Hymettus, contemplating the distant view of the Acropolis, and hearing only the hum of the classical bees, so detached did he seem from anything that Dodo happened to be saying to the telephone. Being without the sense of humour, especially where he himself was concerned, and being also pleasantly encased in the armour of his own importance, it actually did not occur to him as possible that he was being spoken about from the other end of the telephone with anything but the deepest respect. Perhaps the instrument was not working well; that was why Dodo had said so very plainly that he was sitting in the room with her.

She put the receiver back on its hook, tried to be grave and once more broke down.

"I must send you away," she said, "because I'm beginning to laugh again, and I must have my bath. And it's all settled quite satisfactorily, isn't it? Oh, dear me, what a funny morning we are having."

Dodo made an heroic effort with herself and gave a loud croak as she swallowed the laughter that was beginning to make her mouth twitch again. Lord Cookham disregarded that, even as he had disregarded the telephone, but, though he would never have admitted either to himself or others that Dodo had failed in respect to him, some faint inkling that she had done so must have percolated into his inner consciousness, for when he spoke, he permitted himself to speak with irony, his deadliest and most terrific punishment for those who had been impertinent to him. When he addressed anyone with irony, he supposed that their souls popped and shrivelled up like leaves cast into a furnace.

"Good-bye, Lady Chesterford," he said. "Your instructions to me then are that His Highness will dine with you and go to your dance on the sixteenth. I will have the honour of conveying them to the proper quarter."

He did not look at her as he spoke, but addressed the air about a foot above her head. For a moment's silence, in which, no doubt, her soul shrivelled, his austere gaze remained there. When she answered him, her voice trembled so much, that he felt he had been almost unnecessarily severe.

"Yes, that's it," she said. "What a nice talk we've had. Delicious of you to have spared me half-an-hour."

She went out into the hall with him. Even as her footman opened the door for his exit, a motor drew up, and a huge and gorgeous figure stepped out. She saw Lord Cookham bow low, hat in hand, and next moment Jumbo caught sight of her, and bounded up the steps into her house.

"My dear, what fun!" she said. "How are you, Jumbo? You're ever so welcome, though I did tell you to come in half-an-hour and not three minutes. Oh, it's all been too killing! I'll tell you every word as soon as I'm ready. Go into my room, and wait. I'm ever so glad to see you."

Dodo was an admirable mimic. Jumbo, rolling about on the sofa almost fancied he was back at Oxford again being influenced by Lord Cookham.

5

Whenever Dodo was in London for a Sunday, as was the case on the day preceding her ball, she always gave up the hours until teatime, inclusive, to David's uninterrupted society. They breakfasted together at half-past nine, and immediately afterwards, usually before Jack had put in an appearance at all, set off on the top of a bus, if the weather made that delightful form of progress possible, to attend service in the dome of St. Paul's Cathedral. A mere sprinkle of rain did not matter, because then they crouched underneath an umbrella, and played at being early Christians in a small cave, while if the inclemency was too severe for any reasonable Christian to remain in a small cave, they dashed to the tube-station at Down Street, and after traversing an extremely circuitous route, like early Christians in an enormous rabbit-burrow, emerged at Post Office Station, where another dash took them into shelter. It was in fact only on the most tempestuous Sundays of all that they were reduced to the degradation of ordering the motor, and going there in dull dignity.

They did not always wait for the sermon; David had the option of going away or remaining, for Dodo considered that a tired boy listening or not listening to a sermon was likely to get a gloomier view of religious practices than if he had been allowed to go away when he had had enough and play early Christians in a cave again. But he had to decide whether they should remain or go away while the preacher was being conducted to the pulpit, and it was stipulated that if he decided to stop he must abide by his choice and not retire in the middle of the sermon, since it was not polite to interrupt people when they were talking to you.

To-day David had made a most unfortunate choice. The preacher was entertaining for a few minutes merely because he had a high fluty voice that echoed like a siren in the dome, but he said nothing of the smallest interest, and had no idea whatever when to stop. Between his sentences he made long pauses, and Dodo had got briskly to her feet during one of these, thinking that the discourse was now over. So she had to sit down again, and David, trying to swallow his desire to laugh, had hiccupped loudly, which made three people in the row immediately in front of them, turn round all together as if worked by one lever and look fixedly at them, which was embarrassing.

One of them happened to be Lord Cookham, and it seemed likely that Dodo would hiccup next. Then from a front chair close to the choir, Edith Arbuthnot got up, curtsied low in the direction of the altar before turning her back on it, and began walking towards them down the gangway.

"Why did she curtsey, mummy? Was Prince Albert there?" asked David in a whisper.

"Yes," said Dodo, not feeling capable of explaining it all just then.

One of Edith's boots creaked exactly an octave below the pitch of the preacher's fluty voice. This sounded ever louder and more cheerfully as she got nearer, and she stopped when she came opposite to them.

"Stop for the second service, Dodo," she said. "They're going to sing my mass. I can't. I'm playing golf at Richmond. Good-bye."

Her creaking boot sounded in gradual diminuendo as she tramped away down the nave.

"Mummy," began David in a piercing whisper. "If Mrs. Arbuthnot may go out in the middle——"

Dodo conjectured what was coming.

"Because you're not grown up," she said. "Hush, David."

It was impossible to listen to the flute-like preacher, for his words ran together like ink-marks on blotting-paper, and Dodo gave up all idea of trying to hear what he was saying. But she had not the slightest wish to follow Edith; to sit quiet in this huge church, dim and cool, charged with the centuries of praise and worship which had soaked into it was like coming out of the glare of some noisy noon-day, into the green shelter of trees and moisture. Dodo had already finished saying her prayers, but she tried to say to herself not very successfully, the twenty-third Psalm which seemed to her expressive of her feelings, and then abandoning that, gave herself over to vague meditation. Deep down in her (very effectively screened, it must be allowed, by her passion for the excitements and mundane interests of life) there existed this chamber of contemplation for her soul, a real edifice, quite solid and established. It was not in her nature to frequent it very much, and it stood vacant for remarkably long periods together, but just now she was ecstatically content, with David by her side, to sit there while the voice of the preacher hooted round the dome. There she recaptured the consciousness of the eternal, the secure, the permanent that under-lay the feverish motions of her days. They were like some boat tossing on the surface of the waves, yet all the time anchored to a rock that lay deep below all movement and agitation. Thus in such "season of calm weather" she rested in a state of inertia that was yet intense and vivid, and it was from just this power of conscious tranquillity that she drew so much of the indefatigable energy that never seemed to grow less with her advancing years. For her senses it was rest, for her soul it was wordless prayer and concentration.

"That's all," said David suddenly jumping to his feet.

Dodo came out of her place of rest with no more shock than that with which she awoke in the morning, and observed that the preacher had left the pulpit. Then Lord Cookham passed her with a fixed uncon-scious expression, which made Dodo think that he was cutting her until she remembered his avowed habit never to recognise even his nearest and dearest in church. On the way down the nave she was filled with consternation to find that her entire financial resources consisted of one shilling, sixpence of which was absolutely necessary to enable her and David to get home on the top of a bus, so what was to be done about the offertory-plate which she knew would be presented to her notice near the west door. She would hardly like to ask the verger for change. In these circumstances she thought she might venture to appeal to Lord Cookham, who was but a yard or two in front of her, and he, still without sign of recognition gave her a new crisp five-pound note. This also out of its very opulence rather than its exiguousness seemed to stand in need of change, but the idea of applying to him again with the confession that she did not want so much as that was clearly unthinkable. She noticed, however, with rapt appreciation that his own alms were not on this magnificent scale, for with silent secrecy, so that his left hand should not know what his right was doing, he slid a half-crown into the dish. It was fearfully and wonderfully like him to hand her the larger sum and reserve for himself the smaller. . . .

According to Sunday usage David had filled one of his pockets with maize to give the pigeons that bowed and strutted about the pavement outside the west door, and it was not till the early Christians had boarded their bus (there was no need to-day for any cave beyond that afforded by a parasol) that he could seek the solution of such theological difficulties as had occurred during the service. The first was as to why his spirit should long and faint for the converse of the Saints. Didn't "converse" mean opposite? In this case his spirit longed and fainted for wicked people. . . . Then there was the knotty point of "special grace preventing us." David could only suppose that it meant a very long grace, such as the bishop used when he stayed at Winston, which prevented you from sitting down to dinner. . . .

The "converse" of the early Christians drifted away to the more mundane question of what was to be done after lunch. Here Dodo had the privilege of suggesting though not of deciding, but her suggestion of the Zoological Gardens led to an immediate decision.

"And I shall see the blue-faced mandrill," said David, "which you said was so like Prince Albert. I shall stand in front of the cage and say 'Good-morning, Prince Albert.' "

Dodo had forgotten that she had made this odious comparison.

"You mustn't do anything of the sort, darling," she said. "The mandrill wouldn't be at all pleased. Monkeys hate being told they are like people, just as people hate being told they are like monkeys."

David considered this.

"It'll have to hate it then," he observed. "Does it cheat at croquet, too?"

"There's the Salvation Army," said Dodo, skilfully changing the subject. "And the lions in Trafalgar Square. We'll see the lions fed this afternoon."

"Yes. And we'll see the mandrill fed. Does the mandrill eat as much as——"

"No, not so much as the lions," said she.

"I wasn't going to say that. I was going to say 'does it eat as much as Prince——' Oh, mummy, look. There's Jumbo! Hi! Uncle Jumbo!"

Their bus was just moving on again after stopping opposite the Carlton Hotel, and there on the pavement, majestic and jewelled and turbanned was that potentate who had already won so honourable a place in David's heart that he had been promoted to the brevet-rank of an uncle. He looked up at his nephew's shrill salutation, saw him and Dodo, and with a celerity marvellous in one of his bulk, skipped off the pavement and bounced and bounded along the street after them, presenting so amazing an appearance that the conductor, instead of stopping the bus, stared open-mouthed at this Oriental apparition. After a few seconds the Maharajah giving up all thought of further hopeless pursuit stood in the middle of the road waving his arms like a great brown jewelled windmill, and blowing handfuls of kisses after them.

"Well run, Uncle Jumbo!" screamed David. "What a pity!"

A thin middle-aged lady, like a flat-fish (probably the person who tells the public who was in the Park looking lovely) sitting on the seat next to Dodo peered over the side of the bus, and turned to her with an air of haughty reproof.

"You should teach your little boy better manners," she said, "than to go shouting such names at the Maharajah of Bareilly."

"Yes, David," said Dodo with a glance that he completely understood. "Sit down at once, and don't be so rude, shouting names at people in the street. And was that really the Maharajah, ma'am?"

This very proper behaviour appeared to mollify the flat-fish.

"Dear me, yes," she said. "That's the Maharajah of Bareilly. And he's so good-natured, I'm sure he won't mind. He wears pearls valued at half a million sterling."

"Indeed!" said Dodo. "That would make you and me very good-natured too, wouldn't it?"

The flat-fish fingered a very brilliant cairngorm brooch, which she wore to great advantage at her throat, in case Dodo hadn't noticed it. (She had).

"So affable and pleasant too," said she. "Dear me, yes!"

"Oh, is he a friend of yours?" asked Dodo, thrillingly interested, with a side glance of approval at David, who was holding himself in, and biting his lips like a good boy.

"The dear Maharajah of Bareilly!" exclaimed the flat-fish, not quite committing herself. "Very full of engagements he is during his brief visits here. To-morrow he dines with the Marchioness of Chesterford, Lady Dodo, as her friends call her."

Dodo gave an awful jump as her name came out with such unexpectedness, but pretended to sneeze so promptly that the effect might easily have been confused with the cause.

"Where does she live?" she asked.

"At Chesterford House, to be sure, close to Hyde Park Corner. I will point it out to you if you go as far. Dear me, fancy not knowing Chesterford House and its beautiful ballroom, but I daresay it's very pleasant living in the country. It's a strange thing now, but for the moment when I came up on to the bus—though I seldom go by a bus—you reminded me of the Marchioness."

Dodo could not resist pursuing this marvellous conversation. David seemed safe, he was looking at the sky with blank frog-like eyes, and quivering slightly.

"Oh, how lovely for me!" she said, as the bus slowed down in Piccadilly Circus. "And do you know her too?"

They drew up a few yards down Piccadilly, and the conversation was interrupted by the exit down the gangway of dismounting passengers. During this pause the flat-fish was probably saved from direct perjury by the violent hooting of a motor immediately behind them. Looking round, Dodo saw Jumbo dismounting from his car, having evidently pursued them up Lower Regent Street. Her friend looked round too, and beamed with excitement.

"Here's the Maharajah again!" she exclaimed. "Now you be quiet, little boy, and we'll have a good look at him."

Dodo rapidly considered this dramatic situation. It seemed highly probable that Jumbo would board the bus, as soon as its outgoing passengers permitted him to do so. She decided on instant flight in order to spare the flat-fish unimaginable embarrassment.

"We've got to get down here," she said hurriedly, "and we must keep seeing Chesterford House for a treat some other day. Come along, David."

Jumbo's mission was to insist on Dodo and David coming back to lunch with him at the Carlton, where he expected Lord Cookham, but Dodo first of all hurried him away from the bus, over the top of which the face of the flat-fish appeared gaping and wide-eyed.

"Jumbo, dear, we must get round a corner quickly," she said, "or David will burst. There's a woman looking over the edge of it, who——"

David's pent-up emotion mastered him, and he staggered after them yelling and doubled up with laughter. There had never been so marvellous a Sunday morning, and the joy of it was renewed next day when a paragraph appeared in a certain journal with an admittedly large circulation.

"The omnibus is becoming quite a fashionable mode of conveyance for the aristocracy. I saw the Marchioness of Chesterford with her son, Lord Harchester, now grown quite a big boy, dismounting from one at Piccadilly Circus yesterday morning, where they stood chatting with the Maharajah of Bareilly who will be the guest of Lady Dodo (as her friends call her) at Chesterford House this evening."

At lunch Dodo vehemently defended her conduct on the bus.

"I could do nothing else," she said. "The other lady began. She rolled over us like a tidal wave, didn't she, David, and told me to stop your shouting at the Maharajah of Bareilly. I couldn't have explained that we really knew you, and that David actually does call you Uncle Jumbo, because she wouldn't have believed me. And what was I to do when she said that I had reminded her of myself? I couldn't have said that I was myself. She would never have believed that I wasn't somebody else. I almost thought I was somebody else, too."

Lord Cookham condescendingly unbent to this frivolous conversation.

"A humorous situation," he said, "and one that reminds me of a similar experience, though with a different ending, that once happened to me at Corinth, where I arrived one day after a tour in the Peloponnese. My courier had gone on ahead, but he was out on some errand when I found my way to the home of the Mayor—the Demarch, as they still call him—where quarters were prepared for me. He and his family, very worthy people, and a few of the leading local tradesmen were awaiting my arrival. And I arrived on foot, dishevelled, dusty and in my shirt-sleeves. For a moment they positively refused to believe that I was myself."

Dodo's face had assumed a rapt air.

"How did you convince them?" she asked.

He made a conclusive little gesture with his hand.

"I did nothing," he said. "I did not even put on my coat, but lit a cigarette, perfectly prepared to wait till the return of my courier. But somehow they saw their mistake, and were profuse in apologies, which I assured them were unnecessary."

"It's like clumps," said Dodo. "We've got to guess what it was that convinced them. I believe you gave them five pounds for a local charity, just as you gave me five pounds this morning. Or did they see the coronet on your cigarette case?"

The impenetrable man smiled indulgently.

"Scarcely," he said; "I imagine they just realised who I was."

"My dear, what a different ending, as you said, to my adventure on the bus! They all felt your birth and breeding. That was it. With me there was nothing of that kind to be felt. Wasn't it, that you meant?"

The bland superiority of his face suffered no diminution. He gave his butler-bow.

"I offer no explanation at all," he said. "I merely recounted an experience similar in some ways to yours."

"And in some ways so different," said Dodo. "How wonderful the perception of people at Corinth must be!"

Jumbo gave a loud quack of laughter like a wild goose, and entangled himself with asparagus. Lord Cookham noticed nothing of this, and proceeded.

"Talking of Greece, Lady Chesterford," he said, "I should like to remind you that the Queen of the Hellenes, to call her by her more official title, came up to London yesterday. I had the honour of waiting on her, and the fact of your ball to-morrow drifted into our talk."

Dodo licked her lips.

"Who is she?" she asked. "Is she the sort of person I should like my friends to meet?"

"The German Emperor's sister," said Lord Cookham.

"She shall come to dinner, too," said Dodo wildly. "There won't be room, so Jumbo and I will have high tea with David upstairs. I shall paint my face brown, and Jumbo shall paint his face white, and we'll be announced as the white elephant from the Zoo, and the Maharanee of Bareilly from India. Jumbo, dear, I'm going mad through too much success for one of low birth. I think we won't have a dance at all, but we'll mark out the floor of the ball-room into squares, and have a great game of chess with real kings and queens, and two black bishops from the Pan-Anglican Conference, and two white ones from the polar regions. Then Daddy was made a knight the other day, so we'll try to get three more knights, and we'll advertise for four respectable people called Castle. Then by hook or crook, probably crook, we'll entice in sixteen mere commoners to be the pawns. Lord Cookham, do you think we can get hold of sixteen commoners between us? I shall direct the game from the gallery, and I shall call out 'White Queen takes Black Bishop,' and then the Queen of Greece will run across and pick up the Bishop of the Sahara Desert, and put him in the nearest bath-room, where the taken pieces go. No, I think I shall be a pawn myself. I shall divorce Jack in the morning, and so I shall be a commoner again by the evening. And Edith shall sing the 'Watch by the Rhine,' to make the Queen of Greece comfortable. Then, we'll open all the windows and play draughts, and oh, Jumbo, may I go away? As long as Lord Cookham sits opposite me looking pained, I shall continue to talk this awful drivel. Let's all go to the Zoo, and see if the blue-faced mandrill reminds him of a certain royal personage or not. Oh, there are some delicious ices. I shan't go away just yet. Jumbo, what a good lunch you're giving us, and all because David howled at you from the top of a bus. Let me be calm, and see who is here."

The difficulty rather was to see who was not here, for that day the clattering restaurant overflowed with the crowds of those who live to see and be seen. Jumbo's party occupied an advantageous position in the centre of the room, and on all sides the tables teemed with the sort of person whose hours of leisure provide material for small paragraphs in the daily press, and many of them on their way out had a few words with our particular group. Prince Albert of Allenstein was there alone, "looking very greedy," as a veracious paragraphist might have remarked: here was a Cabinet Minister, Hugo Alford, lunching with a prima-donna, there an Australian tennis-champion with an eclipsed duchess, a French pugilist and a cosmopolitan actress of quite undoubtful reputation dressed in pearls and panther-skins. Then there was old Lady Alice Fane bedizened in bright auburn hair and strings of antique cameos, looking as if she had been given a Sunday off from her case in the British Museum, smoking cigarettes and leaving out her aspirates, and with her a peer, obviously from Jerusalem, the proprietor of a group of leading journals, a sprinkling of foreign diplomatists, and several members of the Russian ballet. Dodo, enjoying it all enormously, had kissings of the hand for some of these, notes scribbled on the backs of menu-cards for others, shrill remarks for nearer neighbours and an astounding sense of comradeship for all the ingredients of this distinguished *macédoine*. Only an hour ago she had been alone with David in the dim dome of worship, diving down to the secret chamber of her soul; now with equal sincerity and appreciation of the present moment she was a bubble on the froth of life thrilled with the mere sense of the crowd whose chatter drowned the blare of the band.

Never had the whirlpool of London life revolved more dizzily than in these days of July; never had the revolt against quiet and rational existence reached so murderous a pitch. Just now even the attraction of Saturday-till-Monday house-parties in the country had waned before the lure of London and the restaurant-life; at the most you would see thirty or forty people in your week-end at a country-house, so, if a breath of fresh air seemed desirable before Monday came round again, what was easier than to motor down to Thames-side after lunch

on Sunday, spend the afternoon in Boulter's lock, dine and get back
to town late that night, or, if some peculiar attraction beckoned, hurry
off again after an early breakfast on Monday morning? The twenty-
four hours of day and night must be squeezed of their last drop of
possibilities; they must be drunk to the dregs and the cup be filled
again. The round of hours passed like the last few minutes in some
casino before closing-time; there was such a little time left before London
was sheeted and silent, abandoned to care-takers and mournful cats.
In a few weeks now the squares would be littered with the first fallen
leaves, and the windows darkened. Till then leisure and sobriety of
living were the two prime enemies of existence.

"We're all mad," said Dodo breathlessly as this varied interchange
of greetings went on. "Why does it please everybody to see other
people like this, where you can't talk to them, and only scream a
word in greeting? Personally I love it, but I don't know why. Why
don't we have roast beef and Yorkshire pudding at home, and read a
book afterwards or talk to a friend instead of grinning at a hundred?
Oh, look, Jumbo! Vanessa hasn't got a stitch on except panther skins
and pearls and mottled stockings to match. How bad for David. David,
darling, eat your ice. Here she comes! Vanessa, dear, how perfectly
lovely you look, and I hear you're going to dance at Caithness House
on Tuesday. Of course I shall come. They didn't allow your great
Dane in the restaurant? What hopeless management, but perhaps you'll
find he has eaten the porter when you go out. Still, you know, if we
all brought great Danes, there might be rather a scrap. Hugo! I never
saw anything so *chic* as having a red despatch-box brought you by a
detective in plain clothes, in the middle of lunch. You frowned too
beautifully when you opened it, and are hurrying out now exactly
as if a European complication was imminent. I believe you've been
practising that all morning instead of going to church. Mind you keep
up your responsible air till the very last moment, and then you can
relax and go to sleep when you get back to the Foreign Office. Darling
Lady Alice, what delicious cameos! I believe you stole them; there
aren't any cameos like those outside the British Museum. Yes, of course
you're coming to me to-morrow night. I think I must have sent you
two invitations, and so they probably cancelled each other like nega-
tives. We shall finish up with eggs and bacon on Tuesday morning,
and I'm sure you'll look much fresher than any of us. Oh, there's
the Prime Minister talking to Hugo. They're doing it on purpose so
as to make us think that something terrific has happened. I like Prime
Ministers to be histrionic. He's taking something out of his pocket.
It's only a cigar; I hoped it would be an ultimatum. David, what a
day we're having!"

It was not till half-past three that Dodo remembered that the sea-lions were fed at four, and the land-lions half an hour later, and got up.

"We mustn't miss it," she said. "I've sworn an oath unto David—oh, that's profane. My dear, the keeper throws large dead fish into the air and the sea-lions catch them. Thank God, I'm not a sea-lion. I couldn't possibly eat raw fishes, heads and tails and bones and skins. And then there's the monkey-eating eagle, which I suppose they feed with monkeys. Once when I was looking at it with Hugo who is so like a small grey ape, the monkey-eating eagle brightened up like anything when it saw him. I took Hugo away, as the bars didn't seem very strong. Bless you, Jumbo, good-bye. Oh, may I take your motor just as far as Regent's Park and keep it for an hour? Then you can get a taxi and come and have tea with us at home, and reclaim it. And I haven't got any money; give me a sovereign, please, Lord Cookham, because the more you give me, the more chance there is of my remembering to repay you. How mean you were to give me five pounds at St. Paul's for the offertory, and then contribute half-a-crown yourself. I saw you. Look, there's Prince Albert coming; let's go away at once, David, before he sees us."

Dodo dodged behind a tall waiter, whom she used as cover to effect an unobserved exit, while the Prince made his ponderous way to the table where she had been.

"I saw here Lady Dodo," he said to Lord Cookham, "and also now I do not see her. And I wished to see her, for she has invited me to her dance, but not to her dinner. I would be more pleased to go to her dinner and not to her dance than to her dance and not her dinner. But now she is not here, and I cannot tell her so. But soon I will telephone to her."

His large red face assumed an expression of infinite cunning, and he closed one eye.

"I am here *en garçon,*" he said. "I have given the Princess the slip. She said 'I will go to church, and you will come with me to church,' and I said 'Also I will not go to church,' and while she was at church, I give her the slip. Ha!"

He lumbered out into the hall, and by way of amusing himself *en garçon* sat down close to the band, and fell fast asleep.

David's happy day terminated after tea, and when Jumbo went off in his recovered car about seven, Dodo found that she had still half an hour to spare before she need dress for dinner. With an impulse very unusual with her, she lay down on her sofa, and determined to have a nap rather than busy herself otherwise. But before she had done more than arrive at this conclusion, Jack came in.

"You and David had a good time?" he asked.

"Lovely! Church, bus, Carlton lunch, Zoo. Any news?"

Jack sat down on the edge of her sofa.

"I think there's going to be," he said. "Do you remember the murder of the Archduke Ferdinand at Serajevo?"

"Yes, vaguely."

"Well, Austria has sent an ultimatum to Servia about it," he said, "which Servia cannot possibly accept. Hugo told me. I met him this afternoon going back to the Foreign Office."

"With a red despatch-box which was brought to him at the Carlton," said Dodo. "How small the world is."

"Big enough. There's a meeting of the Cabinet to-morrow morning."

"Oh, then they'll have a nice long talk and settle it all," said Dodo optimistically.

6

On this Sunday evening, the day before her ball, Dodo had been engaged to dine at the German Embassy, but just as she was on her way upstairs to dress, a message had come, putting off the dinner owing to the Ambassador's sudden indisposition. Jack was dining elsewhere, so Dodo, not at all ill-pleased to have an evening at home, secured Edith Arbuthnot to keep her company. She had caught Edith on her return from her golf at Mid-Surrey, and she soon arrived in large boots with three golf-balls and a packet of peppermint bull's-eyes in her pocket, and an amazing appetite. As Dodo had not waited to hear her Mass at St. Paul's that morning, Edith consoled her after dinner by playing the greater part of it on the piano, singing solo passages in a rich hoarse voice that ranged from treble to baritone, with a bull's-eye tucked away in her cheek where it looked like some enormous abscess on a tooth. When no solo was going on she imitated the sounds of violin and bassoon and 'cello with great fidelity, and when it was over she arranged round her cigarettes, bull's-eyes and a mug of beer, put her feet up on a chair of Genoese brocade and lamented the frivolous complications of life. She took as her text the insane multiplicity of balls; since the beginning of June they had been like the stars on a clear night for multitude, and every evening from Monday till Friday three or four had bespangled the firmament. In spite of her general modernity, Edith was laudably Victorian in regard to her maternal duties, and considered it incumbent on her to chaperone her daughter wherever she went. As Madge was a firm, tireless girl, who got no more fatigued with revolving than does the earth, and as Edith wanted to marry her off wisely and well as soon as possible, she had of late seen as many dawns as the driver of a night-express.

"The whole thing is insane," she said. "We take a girl to balls every night in order that as many young men as possible may see her and give her lobster-salad and put their arms round her waist in the hopes that one of them may want to marry her and take her away from her mother."

"You leave out the dancing," interrupted Dodo. "Dancing takes place at balls."

"To a small extent, but the other is the real reason of them. Besides you can't call it dancing when everybody merely strolls backwards and forwards and yawns. It would be far more sensible to have a well-conducted marriage-market at the Albert Hall, under the supervision of a bishop and a countess of unimpeachable morals. The girls would sit in rows mending socks and making puddings, with tickets round their necks shewing what they asked and offered by way of marriage settlements, also their age and a medical certificate as to their general health and temper. Then the boys would go round and each would taste their puddings and see how they sewed and have a little conversation, and look at the ticket and find out if Miss Anna Maria was within his means. Those are the qualities that really make for happy marriages, pleasant talk and cooking and needlework. The market would be open from ten to one every day except perhaps Saturday. Instead of which," concluded Edith indignantly, "I have to sit up till dawn every night with a host of weary hags, who are all longing to take off their tiaras and their hair, and tumble into bed."

"Have a chaperone-strike instead," said Dodo. "You'll never get boys to go to the Albert Hall in the morning. Besides, no one ever got engaged in cold blood. But I really should recommend a chaperone-strike. It isn't as if chaperones were the smallest good; no girl who wants to flirt is the least incommoded by her chaperone, nor does the chaperone take her away till she feels inclined to go. Get up an influential committee, and arrange a procession to Hyde Park, with banners embroidered with 'We won't go to more than five balls a week' and 'Shorter night-shifts for mothers.' 'We will go home before morning.' I'll join that, for I do the work of half a dozen mothers who haven't so fine a sense of duty as you. Or why shouldn't fathers take their turn and chaperone boys instead? Girls don't want any chaperoning now-a-days, boys are much more defenceless. In a few years chaperones will be as extinct as—as Dodos."

Edith refreshed herself in various ways, finishing up with a crashing peppermint.

"I shall revolt next year," she said, "for I won't go through another season like this. Dodo, does it ever strike you that we're all mad this year? We're behaving as we behave when the ice is breaking up, and we will have one minute more skating. Thank goodness your ball to-morrow is the last, and there positively isn't another one the same night. There were to have been two so I thought I should have had to take Madge to three, but they have both been cancelled. I suppose it was found that everyone would stop all night at yours."

"I hope so," said Dodo greedily. "It's delicious to make other competitors scratch on your reputation."

Edith pointed an accusing finger at her.

"Now you've said competitors," she announced. "What's the competition? What's this insane will-o'-the-wisp that's being hunted?"

Dodo considered this direct and simple question.

"Oh, it's an art," she said. "It's a competition to see who can give most pleasure to the greatest number of people. That sounds as if it were something to do with a fine moral quality, but I don't claim that for it. It's partly a competition in success too, and Grantie, the sour old angel, would say that it is a competition in imbecile expenditure, and just for two minutes I should agree with her."

Dodo gave a great sigh, and shifted the subject of the conversation a little.

"And it concerns burning candles at both ends and in the middle," she said, "and seeing how many candles you can keep alight. It's squeezing things in, and don't you know what a joy that always is, even when it concerns nothing more than packing a bag and squeezing in something extra which your maid says won't go in anyhow, my lady?"

"My maid never says that," remarked Edith. "I'm a plain ma'am."

"The principle is the same, darling, however plain you are. Life in London is like that. We are all trying to squeeze something else into it, and to extract the last drop of what life has to give. You are just the same, with your bull's-eyes and your beer and your golfing-boots and your cigarettes. You're making the most of it, too. What will our luggage look like when it comes to be unpacked at the other end?"

"I don't care what mine looks like," said Edith. "I only do things because I think it's right for me to do them."

"My dear, how noble! But isn't it faintly possible that you may be mistaken?" asked Dodo. "You seem to think it right to cover that chair with large flakes of mud from your boots, but I'm not sure that it is. Oh, my dear, don't move your feet; I only took that as the first instance that occurred to me. Naturally, we don't deliberately do what we believe to be wrong, but then that's because we none of us ever stop to consider whether it is. When we want a thing we go and take it, and only wonder afterwards whether we should have done so."

"If you wonder afterwards whether you should have done anything," said Edith austerely, "it means that you shouldn't."

"Oh, I don't agree. It probably means that you are not certain that you wouldn't have enjoyed yourself more wanting it, than getting it. Nothing is really as nice when you have got it—I'm talking of small things, of course—as you thought it was going to be. Acquisition always brings a certain disillusionment, or if not quite that, you very soon get used to what you have got."

Again Edith pointed an accusing finger at her.

"That's the worst of you," she said. "You have a fatal facility. You have always got what you meant to get. You've never had to struggle. Probably that means that you have never had high enough aims. What will the world say about you in forty years?"

"Darling, it may say exactly what it pleases. If in forty years' time there is anybody left who remembers me at all, and he tells the truth, he will say that I enjoyed myself quite enormously. But why be posthumous? Have another peppermint and tell me about your golf."

Edith did not have any more peppermints, so she took a cigarette instead.

"I have a feeling that we are all going to be posthumous with regard to our present lives long before we are dead," she remarked. "We can't go on like this."

"I don't see the slightest reason for not doing so," said Dodo. "I remember we talked about it one night at Winston when you finished in my tea-gown."

"I know, and the feeling has been growing on me ever since. There have been a lot of straws lately shewing the set of the tide."

"Which is just what straws don't do," said Dodo. "Straws float on the surface, and move about with any tiny puff of air. Anyhow, what straws do you mean? Produce your straws."

She paused a moment.

"I wonder if I can produce some for you," she said. "As you know, I was to have dined with the Germans to-night and was put off. Is that a straw? Then, again, Jack told me something this evening about an Austrian ultimatum to Servia. Do those shew the tide you speak of?"

"You know it yourself," said Edith. "We're on the brink of the stupendous catastrophe, and we're quite unprepared, and we won't attend even now. We shall be swept off the face of the earth, and if

I could buy the British Empire to-day for five shillings I wouldn't pay it."

Dodo got up.

"Darling, I seem to feel that you lost your match at golf this afternoon," she said. "You are always severe and posthumous and pessimistic if that happens. Didn't you lose, now?"

"It happens that I did, but that's got nothing to do with it."

"You might just as well say that if you hit me hard in the face," said Dodo, "and I fell down, my falling down would have nothing to do with your hitting me."

"And you might just as well say that your dinner was put off this evening because the Ambassador really was ill," retorted Edith.

Dodo woke next morning to a pleasant sense of a multiplicity of affairs that demanded her attention. There was a busy noise of hammering in the garden outside her window, for though she was the happy possessor of one of the largest ballrooms in London, the list of acceptances to her ball that night had furnished so unusual a percentage of her invitations, that it had been necessary to put an immense marquee against the end of the ballroom fitted with a swinging floor to accommodate her guests. The big windows opening to the ground had been removed altogether, and there would be plenty of rhythmical noise for everybody. At the other end of the ballroom was a raised dais with seats for the mighty, which had to have a fresh length put on to it, so numerous had the mighty become. Then the tables for the dinner that preceded the ball must be re-arranged altogether, since Prince Albert, whom Dodo had not meant to ask to dine at all, had cadged so violently on the telephone through his equerry on Sunday afternoon for an invitation, that Dodo had felt obliged to ask him and his wife. But when flushed with this success he had begun to ask whether there would be bisque soup, as he had so well remembered it at Winston, Dodo had replied icily that he would get what was given him.

These arrangements had taken time, but she finished with them soon after eleven, and was on her way to her motor which had been waiting for the last half-hour when a note was brought her with an intimation that it was from Prince Albert.

"If he says a word more about bisque soup," thought Dodo, as she tore it open, "he shall have porridge."

But the contents of it were even more enraging. The Prince profoundly regretted, in the third person, that matters of great importance compelled him and the Princess to leave London that day, and that he would therefore be unable to honour himself by accepting her invitation.

"And he besieged me for an invitation only yesterday," she said to Jack, "and I've changed the whole table. Darling, tell them to alter everything back again to what it was. Beastly old fat thing! Really Germans have no manners. . . . Daddy has been encouraging him too much. If he rings up again say we're all dead."

Dodo instantly recovered herself as she drove down Piccadilly. The streets were teeming with happy, busy people, and she speedily felt herself the happiest and busiest of them all. She had to go to her dressmakers to see about some gowns for Goodwood, and others for Cowes; she had to go to lunch somewhere at one in order to be in time for a wedding at two, she had to give half an hour to an artist who was painting her portrait, and look in at a garden party. Somehow or other, apparently simultaneously, she was due at the rehearsal of a new Russian ballet, and she had definitely promised to attend a lecture in a remote part of Chelsea on the development of the sub-conscious self. Then she was playing bridge at a house in Berkeley Square—what a pity she could not listen to the lecture about the sub-conscious self while she was being dummy—and it was positively necessary to call at Carlton House Terrace and enquire after the German Ambassador. This latter errand had better be done at once, and then she could turn her mind to the task of simplifying the rest of the day.

There were entrancing distractions all round. She was caught in a block exactly opposite the Ritz Hotel, and cheek to jowl with her motor was that of the Prime Minister, and she told him he would be late for his Cabinet meeting. He got out of the block first by shewing an ivory ticket, and Dodo consoled herself for not being equally well-equipped by seeing a large flimsy portmanteau topple off a luggage trolley which was being loaded opposite the Ritz. It had a large crown painted on the end of it in scarlet, with an "A" below, and it needed but a moment's conjecture to feel sure that it belonged to Prince Albert. Whatever was the engagement that made him leave London so suddenly, it necessitated an immense amount of luggage, for the trolley was full of boxes with crowns and As to distinguish them. The fall had burst open the flimsy portmanteau, and shirts and socks and thick underwear were being picked off the roadway. . . . Dodo wondered as her motor moved on again if he was going to quarter himself on her father for the remainder of his stay in England.

A few minutes later she drew up at the door of the German Embassy, and sent her footman with her card to make enquiries. Even as he rang the bell, the door opened, and Prince Albert was shewn out by the Ambassador. The two shook hands, and the Prince came down the three steps, opposite which Dodo's motor was drawn up. It was open, there could have been no doubt about his seeing her, but it struck her that his intention was to walk away without appearing to notice her. That, of course, was quite impermissible.

"Bisque soup," she said by way of greeting. "And me scouring London for lobsters."

He gave the sort of start that a dramatic rhinoceros might be expected to give, if it intended to carry the impression that it was surprised.

"Ah, Lady Dodo," he said. "Is it indeed you? I am heartbroken at not coming to your house to-night. But the Princess has to go into the country; there was no getting out of it. So sad. Also, we shall make a long stay in the country; I do not know when we shall get back. I will take your humble compliments to the Princess, will I not? I will take also your regrets that you will not have the honour to receive her to-night. And your amiable Papa; I was to have lunched with him to-day, but now instead I go into the country. And also, I will step along. *Auf wiedersehen*, Lady Dodo."

Suddenly a perfect shower of fresh straws seemed to join those others which she and Edith had spoken about last night, and they all moved the same way. There was the note which she had received half an hour ago saying that the Prince could not accept the invitation he had so urgently asked for; there was the fact of those piles of luggage leaving the Ritz; there was his call this morning at the German Embassy, above all there was his silence as to where he was going and his obvious embarrassment at meeting her. The tide swept them all along together, and she felt she knew for certain what his destination was.

"Good-bye, sir," she said. "I hope you'll have a pleasant crossing."

He looked at her in some confusion.

"But what crossing do you mean?" he said. "There is no crossing except the road which now I cross. Ha! There is a good choke, Lady Dodo."

Dodo made her face quite blank.

"Is it indeed?" she said. "I should call it a bad fib."

She turned to her footman who was standing by the carriage door. "Well?" she said.

"His Excellency is quite well again this morning, my lady," he said. That too was rather straw-like.

"Drive on," she said.

Just as impulse rather than design governed the greater part of Dodo's conduct, so intuition rather than logic was responsible for her conclusions. She had not agreed last night with Edith's reasonings, but now with these glimpses of her own, she jumped to her deduction, and landed, so to speak, by Edith's side. As yet there was nothing definite except the unpublished news of an Austrian ultimatum to Servia, and the hurried meeting of the Cabinet this morning to warrant grounds for any real uneasiness as to the European situation generally, nor, as far as Dodo knew, anything definite or indefinite to connect Germany with that. But now with the fact that her dinner had been put off last night and the ambassador was quite well this morning, coupled with her own sudden intuition that the Allensteins were going back post-haste to Germany, she leaped to a conclusion that seemed firm to her landing. In a flash she simply found herself believing that Germany intended to provoke a European war. . . . And then characteristically enough, instead of dwelling for a moment on the menace of this hideous calamity or contemplating the huge unspeakable nightmare thus unveiled, she found herself exclusively and entrancedly interested in the situation as it at this moment was. She expected the entire diplomatic world, German and Austrian included, at her ball that night; already the telegraph wires between London and the European capitals must be tingling and twitching with the cypher messages that flew backwards and forwards over the Austrian ultimatum, and her eyes danced with anticipation of the swift silent current of drama that would be roaring under the conventional ice of the mutual salutations with which diplomatists would greet each other this evening at her house. Hands unseen were hewing at the foundations of empires, others were feverishly buttressing and strengthening them, and all the hours of to-night until dawn brought on another fateful day, those same hands, smooth and polite, would be crossing in the dance, and the voices that had been dictating all day the messages with which the balance of peace and war was weighted, would be glib with little compliments and airy with light laughter. She felt no doubt that Germans and Austrians alike would all be there, she felt also that the very strain of the situation would inspire them with a more elaborate cordiality than usual. She felt she would respect that; it would be like the well-bred courtesies that preceded a duel to the death between gentlemen. Prince Albert, it is true, in his anxiety to get back without delay to his fortressed fatherland had failed in the amenities, but surely Germany, the romantic, the chivalrous, the mother of music and science, would, now and henceforth, whatever the issue might be, prove herself worthy of her traditions.

Once more Dodo was caught in a block at the top of St. James's street, and she suddenly made up her mind to stop at the hotel and say goodbye to Princess Albert. Two motives contributed to this, the first being that though she and he alike had been very rude throwing her over with so needless an absence of ceremony and politeness, she had better not descend to their level; the second, which it must be confessed was far the stronger, being an overwhelming curiosity to know for certain whether she was right in her conjecture that they were going to get behind the Rhine as soon as possible.

Dodo found the Princess sitting in the hall exactly opposite the entrance, hatted, cloaked, umbrellaed and jewel-bagged, with a short-sighted but impatient eye on the revolving door, towards which, when-ever it moved, she directed a glance through her lorgnette. As Dodo came towards her, the Princess turned her head aside, as if, like her husband, seeking to avoid the meeting. But next moment, even while Dodo paused aghast at these intolerable manners, she changed her mind, and dropping her umbrella, came waddling towards her with both hands outstretched.

"Ah, dear Dodo," she said, "I was wondering, just now I was wonder-ing what you thought of me! I would have written to you, but Albert said 'No!' Positively he forbade me to write to you, he called on me as his wife not so to do. Instead he wrote himself, and such a letter too, for he shewed it me, all in the third person, after he had asked for bisque soup only yesterday! And I may not say good-bye to your good father or anyone; you will all think I do not know how to behave, but I know very well how to behave; it is Albert who is so boor. I am crying, look, I am crying, and I do not easily cry. We have said good-bye and thank you to nobody, we are going away like burglars on the tiptoe for fear of being heard, and it is all Albert's fault. In five minutes had our luggage to be packed, and there was Albert's new portmanteau which he was so proud of for its cheapness and made in Germany, bursting and covering Piccadilly with his pants, is it, that you call them? It was too screaming. I could have laughed at how he was served right. All Albert's pants and his new thick vests and his bed-socks being brought in by the porter and the valets and the waiters, covered with the dust from Piccadilly!"

"Yes, ma'am, I saw it myself," said Dodo, "when I was passing half an hour ago."

The Princess was momentarily diverted from the main situation on to this thrilling topic.

"Ach! Albert would turn purple with shame," she said, "if he knew you had seen his pants, and yet he is not at all ashamed of running away like a burglar. That is his Cherman delicacy. 'Your new bed-socks,' I said to him, 'and your winter vests and your pants you must have made of them another package. They will not go in your new portmanteau; there is not room for them, and it is weak. It has to go in the train, and again it has to go on the boat, and also again in the train.' It is not as if we but went to Winston—ah, that nice Winston!—but we go to Chermany. That is what I said, but Albert would not hear. 'By the two o'clock train we go,' he said, 'and my new vests and my socks and my pants go in my new Cherman portmanteau which was so cheap and strong.' But now they cannot go like that, and they will have to go in my water-proof sheet which was to keep me dry on the boat from the spray, for if I go in the cabin I am ill. It is all too terrible, and there was no need for us to go like this. We should have waited till to-morrow, and said good-bye. Or perhaps if we had gone to-morrow we should not go at all. What has Chermany to do with Servia, or what has England either? But no, we must go to-day just because there have been telegrams, and Cousin Willie says, 'Come back to Allenstein.' And here am I so rude seeming to all my friends. But one thing I tell you, dearest Dodo; we chiefly go, because Albert is in a Fonk. He is a Fonk!"

"But what is he frightened of?" asked Dodo. The Princess was letting so many cats out of the bag that she had ceased counting them.

"He is frightened of everything. He is frightened that he will be pelted in the London streets for being a Cherman prince, just as if anybody knew or cared who he was! He is frightened of being put in prison. He is frightened that the Cherman fleet will surround England and destroy her ships and starve her. He is frightened of being hungry and thirsty. He is a pig in a poke that squeals till it gets out."

This remarkable simile was hardly out of the Princess's mouth before she squealed on her own account.

"Ach, and here he is," she said. "Now he will scold me, and you shall see how I also scold him."

He came lumbering up the passage towards them with a red, furious face.

"And what did I tell you, Sophy?" he said. "Did I not tell you to sit and wait for me and speak to no one, and here are you holding the hand of Lady Dodo, to whom already I have said good-bye, and so now I do not see her. It is done, also it is finished, and it is time we went to the station. You are for ever talking, though I have said there shall be no more talking. What have you been saying?"

Princess Albert still held Dodo's hand.

"I have been saying that your new portmanteau burst, and I must take your vests and your socks and your pants in my water-proof sheet. Also I have been saying——"

"But your water-proof sheet, how will your water-proof sheet hold all that was in my portmanteau? It is impossible. Where is your water-proof sheet? Show it me."

"You will see it at Charing Cross. And if it is wet on the boat I will take out again your vests and your socks and your pants, and they may get wet instead of me."

"So! Then I tell you that if it is wet on the boat, you will go to your cabin, and if you are sick you will be sick. You shall not take my clothes from your water-proof sheet."

"We will see to that. Also, I have been saying good-bye to dearest Dodo, and I have been saying to her that it was not I who was so rude to her, but also that it was you, Albert. And I say now that I beg her pardon for your rudeness, but that I hope she will excuse you because you were in a fonk, and when you are in a fonk, you no longer know what you do, and in a fonk you will be till you are safe back in Germany. All that I say, dearest Albert, and if you are not good I will tell it to the mob at Charing Cross. I will say, 'This is the Prince of Allenstein, and he is a Prussian soldier, and therefore he is running away from England.' Do not provoke me, heart's dearest. You will now get them to send for a cab, and we will go because you are a fonk. There will be no special train for us, there will be no one of our cousins to see us off, there will be no red carpet, and it is all your fault. And as for dearest Dodo, I kiss her on both cheeks, and I thank her for her kindness, and I pray for a happier meeting than is also our parting."

That afternoon there began to be publicly felt the beginning of that tension which grew until the breaking-point came in the first days of August, and but for Dodo's shining example and precept, her ball that night might easily have resolved itself into a mere conference. Again and again at the beginning of the evening the floor was empty long after the band had struck up, while round the room groups of people collected and talked together on one subject. But Dodo seemed to be absolutely ubiquitous, and whenever she saw earnest conversationalists at work, she plunged into the middle of them, and broke them up like a dog charging a flock of sheep. To-morrow would do for talk, to-night it was her ball. Her special prey was any group which had as its centre an excited female fount of gossip who began her sentences with "They tell me. . . ." Whenever that fatal phrase caught Dodo's remarkably sharp ears, she instantly led the utterer of it away to be introduced to someone on the great red dais, managed to lose her in the crowd, and "went for" the next offender. The rumour that the Allensteins had left Charing Cross that afternoon for Germany was a dangerously interesting topic, and whenever Dodo came across it, she strenuously denied it, regardless of truth, and asserted that as a matter of fact they were going down again to-morrow to stay with her father at Vane Royal. Then perceiving him not far off, looking at the dais with the expression of Dante beholding the Beatific vision, she had dived into the crowd again, and told him that if he would assert beyond the possibility of contradiction that this was the case, she would presently introduce him to anyone on the red dais whom he might select. As he pondered on the embarrassment of such richness, she was off again to break up another dangerous focus of conversation.

An hour of wild activity was sufficient to set things really moving, and avert the danger of her ball becoming a mere meeting for the discussion of the European situation, and presently she found five minutes rest in the window of the music gallery from which she could survey both the ballroom and the marquee adjoining it. In all her thirty years' experience, as hostess or guest, she had never been present at a ball which seemed quite to touch the high-water mark here, and she felt that without Lord Cookham's assistance she had provided exactly the sort of evening that he had designed, in honour of Jumbo. It had happened like that; everybody was present in that riot of colour and rhythm that seethed about her, and at the moment the dais which stretched from side to side of the huge room was empty, for every one of its occupants was dancing, and she observed that even Lord Cookham (who had come in an official capacity) had deserted his place behind a row of chairs, and was majestically revolving with a princess, making little obeisances as he cannoned heavily into other exalted personages. The whole of the diplomatic corps was there, German and Austrian included, and there was the German ambassador, quite recovered from his curious indisposition, waltzing with the Italian ambassadress. The same spirit that had animated Dodo in breaking up serious conjectures and conversation seemed now to have spread broadcast; all were conspirators to make this ball, the last of the year, the most brilliant and memorable. From a utilitarian point of view there was no more to be said for it than for some gorgeously plumaged bird that strutted and spread its jewelled wings, and yet all the time it was a symbol, expressing not itself alone but what it stood for. The glory of great names, wide-world commerce, invincible navies, all the endorsements of Empire, lay behind it. It glittered and shone like some great diamond in an illumination which at any moment might be obscured by the menace of thundercloud, but, if this was the last ray that should shine on it before the darkness that even now lapped the edge of it enveloped it entirely, that gloom would but suck the light from it, and not soften nor crush its heart of adamant. . . .

From the moment that the ball got moving Dodo abandoned herself to enjoying it to the utmost, wanting, as was characteristic of her, to suck the last ounce of pleasure from it. She had that indispensable quality of a good hostess, namely, the power of making herself the most fervent of her guests, and never had she appreciated a ball so much. Not until the floor was growing empty and the morning light growing vivid between the chinks of closed curtains did she realise that it was over.

"Jumbo, dear," she said, "why can't we double as one does at bridge, and then somehow it would be eleven o'clock last night, and we should have it all over again? Are you really going? What a pity! Stop to breakfast—my dear, what pearls! I can't believe they're real—and don't let us go to bed at all. Yes, do you know, it's quite true—though I've been lying about it quite beautifully—the Allensteins left for Germany this afternoon, I mean yesterday afternoon. Oh, I don't want to begin again. . . . What will the next days bring, I wonder?"

She stood at the street door a moment, while he went out into that pregnant and toneless light that precedes sunrise, when all things look unreal. The pavement and road outside were pearly with dew, and the needless head-light of his motor as it purred its way up to the door gleamed with an unnatural redness. In the house the floor was quite empty now and the band silent, a crowd of men and women eager to get away besieged the cloakroom, and in ten minutes more Dodo found herself alone, but for the servants already beginning to restore the rooms to their ordinary state.

She felt suddenly tired, and going upstairs drew down the blinds over her open windows. She wanted to get to sleep at once, to shut out the dawning day and all that it might bring.

7

The morning papers were late that day, and when they arrived Dodo snatched at them and automatically turned to the *communiqué* from the French front. There was a list of names of villages which had been lost to the allies, but these were unfamiliar and meant nothing to her. Then she looked with a sudden sinking of the heart at the accompanying map which shewed by a black line the new position of the front, and that was intelligible enough. For the last fortnight it had been moving westwards and southwards with regular and incredible rapidity like the advance of some incoming tide over level sands. Occasionally for a little it has been held up, but the flood, frankly irresistible, always swept away that which had caused the momentary check. . . . In the next column was an account of German atrocities compiled from the stories of Belgian refugees.

Dodo had come back to London last night from Winston where she had been seeing to the conversion of the house into a Red Cross hospital, and just now she felt, like some intolerable ache, the sense of her own uselessness. All her life she had found it perfectly easy to do the things which she wanted to do, and she had supposed herself to be an efficient person. But now, when there was need for efficient people, what did her qualifications amount to? She could ride, as few women in England could ride, she was possessed of enormous physical and nervous energy, she was an inimitable hostess, could convert a dull party into a brilliant one by the sheer effortless outpouring of her own wit and infectious vivacity, but for all practical purposes from organisation down to knitting, she was as useless as a girl straight out of the nursery where everything had been done for her by assiduous attendants. She was even more useless than such a child, for the child at any rate had the adaptability and the power of learning appropriate to its age, whereas Dodo, as she had lately been ascertaining, had all her life been pouring her energy down certain definite and now useless channels. In consequence those channels had become well-worn; her energy flowed naturally with them, and seemed to refuse to be diverted, with any useful result, elsewhere. She could ride, she could play bridge, she could, as she despondently told herself, talk the hind leg off a donkey, she could entertain and be entertained till everyone else was dying to go to bed. And no one wanted her to do any of those things now; there was absolutely no demand for them. But when it came to knitting a stocking herself, or being personally responsible for a thing being done, instead of making a cook or a groom or a butler responsible for it, she had no notion how to set about it.

Very characteristically when David's nurse had announced her intention of being trained for hospital work, Dodo had warmly congratulated her determination, had given her an enormous tip, and had bundled her off to the station in a prodigious hurry, saying that she would look after David herself. But the things that a small boy required to have done for him filled her with dismay at her own incompetence, when she had to do them. If he got his feet wet, fresh socks had to be found for him; if his breeches were covered with short white hairs from his ride, these must be brushed off; buttons had to be replaced; there was no end to these ministrations. Dodo could not get on at all with the stocking she was knitting or the supervision of the storing of the furniture at Winston, while she had to produce a neat daily David, and incidentally failed to do so. She advertised for another nurse without delay, and David was exceedingly relieved at her arrival.

Dodo was, luckily, incapable of prolonged despair with regard to her own shortcomings, and by way of self-consolation her thoughts turned to the fact that before she left Winston she had contrived and

arranged a charming little flat in a wing of the house for herself and
David and Jack whenever he could find time to come there, for he
was in charge of a remount camp, knowing, as he certainly did, all
that was to be known about horses from A to Z. Dodo's mind harked
back for a moment to her own uselessness in envious contemplation
of the solid worth, in practical ways, of her husband's knowledge.
For herself, through all these frivolous years she had been content
with the fact of her consummate horsemanship: she had hands, she
had a seat, she had complete confidence (well-warranted) in her ability
to manage the trickiest and most vicious of four-legged things. There
her knowledge (or rather her instinct) stopped, whereas Jack, a mere
lubber on a horse compared with herself, was a perfect encyclopaedia
with regard to equine matters of which she was profoundly ignorant.
He could "size up" a horse by looking at it, in a way incomprehensible
to Dodo; he knew about sore backs and bran mashes and frogs and
sickle-hocks, and now all the lore which she had never troubled to
learn any more than she had troubled to decipher a doctor's prescription
and understand its ingredients, was precisely that which made Jack,
at this crisis when efficiency was needed, so immensely useful. . . .
However, after all, she had been useful too, for she had planned that
delicious little flat at Winston (necessary, since the house was to be
made into a hospital), which would give accommodation to them. Everything, of course, was quite simple; she had put in two bathrooms
with the usual paraphernalia of squirts and douches and sprays, and
had converted a peculiarly spacious pantry into a kitchen with a gas-
stove and white tiled walls. Naturally, since the house was no longer
habitable, this had to be done at once, and her energy had driven it
through in a very short space of time. The expense had been rather
staggering, especially in view of the cost of running a hospital, so
Dodo had sent the bill to her father with a lucid explanatory letter.

   The thought of this delicious little flat, which would be so economical
with its gas-stove for cooking, and its very simple central heating, in
case, as Jack gloomily prognosticated, there should be difficulties about
coal before the war was over, made Dodo brighten up a little, and
diverted her thoughts from the on-creeping barbarous tide in France,
and the sense of her own uselessness. After all somebody had to contrive, to invent, even though plumbers and upholsterers effected the
material conversion, and Daddy paid the bill; and she had come up
to town in order to superintend a similar change at Chesterford House.
That was to be turned into a hospital for officers, and Dodo was determined that everything should be very nice. The ballroom would be
a ward, so also would be the biggest of the three drawing-rooms,
but the dining-room had better be left just as it was, in anticipation

of the time when the invalids could come down to dinner again. She intended to keep a couple of rooms for herself, and one for her maid, since she could not be at Winston all the year round. . . . And then suddenly she perceived that behind all her charitable plans there was the reservation of complete comfort for herself. It cost her nothing, in the personal sense, to live in a wing at Winston and a cosy corner of the house in London. There was not an ounce of sacrifice about it all, and yet she had read with a certain complacency that very morning, that Lord and Lady Chesterford had set a noble example to the rest of the wealthy classes, in giving up not one only but both of their big houses. But now all her complacency fell down like a house of cards. Jack certainly had given up something, for his day was passed in real personal work. . . . He was on the staff with a nice red band on his cap, and tabs on his shoulders and spurs. And here, even in the moment that she was damning her own complacency, she was back in the old rut, thinking about signs and decorations instead of what they stood for. There was the black line of the tide creeping over France, and three columns of casualties in the morning's paper, and one of German atrocities. . . .

Dodo was expecting Edith to lunch, and since the *chef* had gone back to France to rejoin the colours, there was only a vague number of kitchen-maids, scullery-maids and still-room maids in the house to manage the kitchen, and even these were being rapidly depleted, as, with Dodo's cordial approval, they went to canteens and other public services. She had, in fact, warned Edith only to expect a picnic, and she thought it would be more picnicky if they didn't go to the dining-room at all, but had lunch on a table in her sitting-room. This did not, as a matter of fact, save much trouble, since the dining-room was ready, and a table had to be cleared in her sitting-room, but Dodo at the moment of giving the order was on the dramatic "stunt," and when Edith arrived there was a delicious little lunch in process of arrival also.

"Darling, how nice of you to come," said Dodo, "and you won't mind pigging it in here, will you? Yes, let's have lunch at once. The *chef's* gone, the butler's gone, and I shall have parlour-maids with white braces over their shoulders. My dear, I haven't seen a soul since I left Winston yesterday, and I haven't seen you since this thunderbolt burst. Do they burst, by the way? All that happened before the fourth of August seems centuries away now. I can only dimly remember what I used to be like. A European war! For ten years at least that has been a sort of unspeakable nightmare, which nobody ever really believed in, and here we are plunged up to the neck in it."

Edith seemed to have something in reserve.

"Go on," she said, helping herself to an admirable omelette. "I want to know how it affects you."

Dodo finished her omelette in a hurry, and drew a basket full of wool and knitting needles from under the table. Out of it she took a long sort of pipe made of worsted. She made a few rapid passes with her needles.

"I have been frightfully busy," she said. "If I'm not busy all the time I begin wondering if any power in heaven or earth can stop that relentless advance of the Germans. The French government are evacuating Paris, and then I ask myself what will happen next? What about the Channel ports? What about the Zeppelins that are going to shower bombs on us? And then by the grace of God I stop asking myself questions which I can't answer, and occupy myself in some way. I have been terrifically busy at Winston, clearing all the house out for the hospital we are having there, and just making a small habitable corner for David and Jack and me at the end of the east wing, do you remember, where the big wisteria is. Central heating, you know, because Jack says there will be no coal very soon, and my darling Daddy is going to pay the bill. Then I came up here, because this house is to be a hospital for officers——"

Dodo suddenly threw her hands wide with a gesture of despair.

"Oh, how useless one is!" she said. "I know quite well that my housekeeper could have done it all with the utmost calmness and efficiency in half the time it took me. When I was wildly exciting myself about blocking up a door in my room at Winston, so as not to have vegetable-smells coming up from the kitchen, and thinking how tremendously clever I was being, she waited till I had quite finished talking, and then said, 'But how will your ladyship get into your room?' And it's the same with this awful stocking."

Dodo exhibited her work.

"Look!" she said, "the leg is over two feet long already, and for three days past I have been trying to turn the heel, as the book says, but the heel won't turn. The stocking goes on in a straight line like a billiard cue. I can never do another one, so even if the heel was kind enough to turn now, I should have to advertise for a man at least seven feet high who had lost one leg. The advertisement would cost more than the stocking is worth, even if it ever got a foot to it. Failing the seven-foot one-legged man, all that this piece of worsted-tubing can possibly be used for, is to put outside some exposed water-pipe in case of a severe frost. Even then I should have to rip it up from top to bottom to get it round the pipe, or cut off the water-supply and take the pipe down and then fit the stocking on to it. Then again when David's nurse left, I said I would look after him.

But I didn't know how; the nervous force and the time and the cotton and the prickings of my finger that were required to sew on a button would have run a tailor's shop for a week. Oh, my dear, it's awful! Here is England wanting everything that a country can want, and here am I with hundreds of other women absolutely unable to do anything! We thought we were queens of the whole place, and we're the rottenest female-drones that ever existed. Then again I imagined I might be able to do what any second-rate housemaid does without the smallest difficulty, so when other people had taken up the carpet on the big stairs at Winston, I sent four or five servants to fetch me a broom, so that I could sweep the stairs. They were dusting and fiddling about in the way house-maids do, and they all grinned pleasantly and stopped their work to fetch me something to sweep the stairs with. I supposed they would bring me an ordinary broom, but they brought a pole with a wobbly iron ring at the end of it, to which was attached a sort of tow-wig. I didn't like to ask them how to manage it, so I began dabbing about with it. And at that very moment the grim matron leaned over the bannisters at the top of the stairs and called out, 'What are you doing there? You look as if you had never used a mop before!' I hadn't; that was the beastly part of it, and then she came down and apologised, and I apologised and she shewed me what to do, and I hit a housemaid in the eye and hurt my wrist, and dislocated all work on that staircase for twenty minutes. And then I tried to weigh out stores as they came in, and I didn't know how many pennies or something went to a pound Troy. And you may be surprised to hear that a hundred-weight is less than a quarter, or if it's more it isn't nearly so much more as you would think. I'm useless, and I always thought I was so damned clever. All I can do is play the fool, and who wants that now? All my life I have been telling other people to do things, without knowing how to do them myself. I can't boil a potato, I can't sew on a button, and yet I'm supposed to be a shining light in war-work. *'Marquez mes mots,'* as the Frenchman never said, they'll soon be giving wonderful orders and decorations to war-workers, and they'll make me a Grand Cross or a Garter or a Suspender or something, because I've made a delicious flat for myself in the corner of Winston, and sent the bill in to Daddy, and will be going round the wards at Winston and saying something futile to those poor darling boys who have done the work."

Dodo held up a large piece of hot-house peach on the end of her fork.

"Look at that, too," she said. "I'm an absolute disgrace. Fancy eating hot-house peaches in days like these!"

Edith had rather enjoyed certain parts of Dodo's vivacious summary of herself, but the most of it caused her to snort and sniff in violent disagreement. Once or twice she had attempted to talk too, but it was no use till Dodo had blown off the steam of her self-condemnation. Now, however, she took up her own parable.

"Wouldn't you think it very odd of me," she said in a loud voice, "if I began writing epic poems?"

"Yes, dear, very odd," said Dodo.

"It wouldn't be the least odder than you trying to sew on buttons or washing David. You are just as incapable of that as I am of the other. You only waste your time; you never learned how, so why on earth should you know how? We're all gone perfectly mad; we're all trying to do things that are absolutely unsuited to us. I really believe I'm the only sane woman left in England. Since the war began I have devoted myself entirely to my music, and I've written more in these last few weeks than I have during a whole year before. There have been no distractions, no absurd dances and dinners. I've been absolutely uninterrupted. Bertie has been taken on for the London Defence against Zeppelins. He has never seen a Zeppelin and knows as much about defences as I know about writing sonnets; and Madge pours out the most awful tea and coffee on the platform at Victoria. She never could pour anything out; if she was helping herself to a cup of tea she flooded the tray, and I should think that in a few days Victoria station will be entirely submerged. That will mean that troops will have to reach their trains in London by means of rafts."

"But one can't help doing something," said Dodo. "One can't go on being useless."

"You don't mend it by being worse than useless. That's why I devote myself to music. I can do that, and I can't do any of the things that everybody else is trying to do."

Edith paused a moment.

"There's another reason, too," she said. "I should go off my head if I wasn't busy about something. I wish there was such a thing as a clinical thermometer of unhappiness, and you would see how utterly miserable I am. You can't guess what being at war with Germany means to me. All that is best in the world to me comes from Germany; all music comes from there. And yet last night when I was playing a bit of Brahms, Bertie said, 'Oh, do stop that damned Hun tune!' Why, there's no such thing as a Hun tune! Music is simply music, and with a few exceptions the Huns, as he loves to call them, have made it all."

"He calls them Huns," said Dodo carefully, "because they've already proved themselves the most infamous barbarians. Did you see the fresh atrocities in the *Times* this morning?"

"I did, and I blushed for the wickedness of the people who invented them and the credulity of the people who believed them. They *can't* be true. I know the Germans, and they are incapable of that sort of thing. I bet you that every German paper is full of similar atrocities committed by the English."

"Then you'll have to blush for the wickedness and the credulity of the Germans too, darling!" remarked Dodo. "You *will* be red."

Edith laughed.

"Yes, I'm sorry I said that," she said. "But in any case what has Brahms got to do with it? How can any sane person develop racial hatred like that? Let's have a pogrom of Jews because of Judas Iscariot. To go back. I'm not sent into the world to empty slops, but to make symphonies. Very few people can make symphonies, and I'm one of them. Huns or no Huns, what have artists to do with war?"

"But, my dear, you can't help having to do with it," said Dodo. "You might as well say, 'What have artists to do with earthquakes?' But an earthquake will shake down an artist's house just as merrily as a commercial traveller's. You can't be English, and not have to do with war."

Edith was silent a moment, and suddenly her face began to tie itself into the most extraordinary knots.

"Give me some port or I shall cry," she said. "I won't cry; I never do cry and I'm not going to begin now."

The prescription seemed to be efficacious.

"Then there's my boy," she said. "Berts has left Cambridge and I suppose that before Christmas he'll be out in France. He's about as much fitted to be a soldier as you are to be a housemaid. Of all the instances of everybody wanting to do what they are totally incapable of, the worst is the notion that we can make an army. You can't make an army by giving boys bayonets. Germany *is* an army, for forty years she has been an army. Why compete? Germany will wipe up our army and the French army like a housemaid, which you want to be, wiping up a slop. Have you seen what the German advance has been doing this last week? Nothing in the world can save Paris, nothing in the world can save France. Out of mere humanitarian motives I want France to see that as quickly as possible. The war is over."

Dodo rose.

"Don't talk such damned nonsense, Edith," she said. "That port has gone to your head and given you *vin triste.* If anything was wanting to make me quite certain that we are going to win it, it is the fact that you say we are not. Do you remember when those beastly Allensteins were staying with me, and how he knocked out 'Deutschland über alles,' on the table with his fat fingers? The effect on you was that you played 'Rule Britannia' and 'God Save the King' as loud as you could on the piano next door. It was extremely rude of you, but it shewed a proper spirit. Why can't you do it now?"

"Because it's hopeless. Before Germany shewed her strength you could do that just as you can tweak a lion's tail when he is lying asleep behind bars at the Zoo. But now we're inside the cage. I don't say we are not formidable, but we don't make ourselves more formidable by sending all the best of our young men out to France to be shot down like rabbits. We were not prepared, and Germany was. Her war-machine has been running for years, smoothly and slowly, at quarter-steam. We've got to make a machine, and then we've got to learn how to run it. Then about the navy——"

Dodo assumed a puzzled expression.

"Somebody, I don't know who," she said, "told me that there was an English navy. Probably it was all lies like the German atrocities."

Edith threw her hands wide.

"Do you think I like feeling as I do?" she asked. "Do you think I do it for fun?"

"No, dear, for my amusement," said Dodo briskly. "But unfortunately it only makes me sick. Hullo, here's David."

David entered making an awful noise on a drum.

"Shut up, David," said his mother, "and tell Edith what you are going to do when you're eighteen."

"Kill the Huns," chanted David. "Mayn't I play my drum any more, mummy?"

"Yes, go and play it all over the house. And sing Tipperary all the time."

David made a shrill departure.

"Of course you can teach any child that!" said Edith.

"I know. That's so lovely. If I had fifty children I should teach it to them all. I wish I had. I should love seeing them all go out to France, and I should squirm as each of them went. I should like to dig up the graves of Bach and Brahms and Beethoven and Wagner and Goethe, and stamp on their remains. They have nothing to do with it all but they're Huns. I don't care whether it is logical or Christian or anything else, but that's the way to win the war. And you're largely responsible for that; I never saw red before you talked such nonsense about the war being over. If we haven't got an army we're going to have one, and I shall learn to drive a motor. If I could go to that window and be shot, provided one of those beastly Huns was shot too, I should give you one kiss, darling, to shew I forgave you, and go to the window dancing! I quite allow that if everybody was like you we should lose, but thank God we're not."

Dodo's face was crimson with pure patriotism.

"I'm not angry with you," she said, "I'm only telling you what you don't know, and what I do know, so don't resent it, because I haven't the slightest intention of quarrelling with you, and it takes two to make a quarrel. You know about trombones and C flat, and if you told me about C flat——"

Edith suddenly burst into a howl of laughter.

"Or C sharp," said Dodo, "or a harpsichord. Oh, don't laugh. What have I said?"

Edith recovered by degrees and wiped her eyes.

"In all my life I have never had so many offensive things said to me," she remarked. "I can't think why I don't mind."

"Oh, because you know I love you," said Dodo with conviction.

"I suppose so. But there's Berts going out to that hell——"

"Oh, but you said the war was over already," said Dodo. "Besides what would you think of him if he didn't go?"

"I should think it extremely sensible of him," began Edith in a great hurry.

"And after you had thought that?" suggested Dodo.

Edith considered this.

"I don't know what I should think next," she said. "What I'm going to do next is to get back to my scoring."

Edith's remarks about the absurdity of people attempting to do things for which they had no aptitude made a distinct impression on Dodo, and she totally abandoned the stocking of which she could not turn the heel, and made no further dislocation of work by trying to use a mop. But she found that if she really attended, she could count blankets and bed-jackets, and weigh out stores and superintend their distribution. Again, driving a motor was a thing that seemed within the limits of her ability, and by the time that Winston was in full running order as a hospital she was fairly competent as a driver. Awful incidents had accompanied her apprenticeship; she had twice stripped her gear, had run into a stone wall, luckily in a poor state of repair, and had three times butted at a gate-post. Her last accident, after a week really tedious from mere uneventfulness, had been when she had gone all alone, as a pleasant surprise, to the station to meet Jack, who was coming home for two days' leave. She had been both driving and talking at high speed, and so had not seen that she was close to a very sharp corner on the marshy common just outside the gates, and preferring the prudent course, as opposed to the sporting chance of getting round the corner without capsizing, had gone straight ahead, leaving the road altogether, until, remembering to apply her brakes, she stuck fast and oozily in the marsh.

"There!" she said with some pride. "If I had been reckless and imprudent I should have tried to get round that corner and had an upset. Didn't I show presence of mind, Jack?"

"Marvellous. And what are we to do now?"

Dodo looked round.

"We had better shout," she said. "And then somebody will come with a horse and pull us out backwards. It has happened before," she added candidly.

"But if nobody comes?" asked he.

"Somebody is sure to. It's unthinkable that we should remain here till we die of exposure and hunger, and the crows pick our whitening bones. The only other thing to do is that you should jump out and fetch somebody. I wouldn't advise you to, as you would sink up to your knees in the mud. But it's a lovely afternoon; let's sit here and talk till something happens. Haven't I learned to drive quickly?"

"Very quickly," said Jack. "We've covered the last three miles in four minutes."

"I didn't mean that sort of quickly," said Dodo, "though daresay I said it. Isn't it lucky it's fine, and that we've got plenty of time? I wanted a talk with you and somebody would be sure to interrupt at home. He would want sticking-plaster or chloroform or charades."

"Is that your department?" asked Jack.

"Yes, they call me Harrods. You never thought I should become Harrods. Oh, Jack, if you've got an ache in your mind, the cure is to work your body till that aches too. Then two aches make an affirmative."

"What?" said Jack.

"You see what I mean. And the odd thing is that though I'm entirely taken up with the war, I try not to think about the war at all, at least not in the way I used to before I became Harrods. One is too busy with the thing itself to think about it. In fact, I haven't looked at the papers for the last day or two. Has there been any news?"

"Not much. I've been busy too, and I really hardly know. But there's been nothing of importance."

"Jack, what's going to happen?" she asked.

"Oh, we're going to win, of course. God knows when. Perhaps after three years or so. But it's no good thinking about that."

Dodo gave a little groan.

"I know it isn't. If I realised that this was going on all that time, I think I should just get drunk every day. Let's talk about something else, and not realise it."

"When are you coming to see my camp?" asked he.

"I should think when the war is over and there isn't any camp. I don't see how I can get away before. How long has it been going now? Only three months, is it? And I can hardly remember what things were like before. How did one get through the day? We got up later, it is true, but then we went to bed later. Did we do nothing except amuse ourselves? I couldn't amuse myself now. And what did we talk about? I seem to remember sitting and talking for hours together, and not finding it the least tedious."

"I shall insist on your having a holiday soon," said Jack.

"Oh no, darling, you won't. I've had fifty-five years' holiday in my life and three months' work. That doesn't give much of a daily average, if you work it out; somewhere about five minutes a day, isn't it? I must have something better than that to shew before I have another holiday. . . . Jack, did you say that we must look forward to three years or more of this? Good Lord, how senseless it all is! What do you *prove* by setting millions of jolly boys to kill each other? Oh, I shouldn't have said that; I would have said, 'What do you prove by having our jolly boys killed by those damned Huns?' Yes, darling, I said damned, and I intended to. I told Edith that one day. The way to win a war is to be convinced that your enemy are fiends. 'Also,' as that fat Albert would say, 'we must therefore kill them.' But I wish I really meant it. There must be a lot of nice fellows among the Huns. They've had a bad education; that's what is the matter with them. Also, they have no sense of humour. Fancy writing a Hymn of Hate, and having it solemnly sung by every household! That odious Cousin Willie has approved of it, and it is being printed by the million. No sense of humour."

Dodo unconsciously hooted at her motor-horn, and looked wildly round.

"I didn't mean to do that," she said, "because I don't want to be rescued just yet. It's lovely sitting here and talking to you, Jack, without fear of being asked to sign something. What was I saying? Oh yes, humour! The Huns haven't got any humour, and the lack of that and of mirth will be their undoing. How wise Queen Elizabeth was when she said that God knew there was need for mirth in England now, just at the time when England was in direst peril. That is frightfully true to-day. We shall get through by taking it gaily. It's much best not to let oneself see the stupendous tragedy of it all. If I did that I would simply shrivel up or get drunk."

Dodo began a laugh that was near to a sob.

"I saw three boys this morning," she said, "all of whom had had a leg amputated. There were three legs to the lot of them. So they put their arms round each other's necks so as to form a solid body, and marched down the long walk shouting 'left, right, left, right.' Then they saw me, and disentangled their arms and grinned, and tried to salute, and so they all fell down with roars of laughter. My dear, did you ever hear of such darlings? That was the mirth that Queen Elizabeth said was so necessary. I wanted to kiss them all, Jack."

"I want to kiss you," he said.

"Then you shall, you dear, if you think it won't shock the magneto. I do miss you so horribly; you're the only link between the days before the war and the war. All other values are changed, except you and David. What a nice talk we have had, at least I've had the talk, so you must do your part and find it nice. Now let's hoot, until several strong cart-horses come to help us."

Dodo performed an amazing fantasy on the horn, while the early sunset of this November day began to flame in the west, which reminded her that there were charades this evening. A chance bicyclist was eventually induced to take a message to a farm about half a mile distant, and a small child came from the farm and took a message to his mother, who came out to see what was happening, and took a message to her husband, who did the same, and went back for a horse, which was found to be insufficient, so deeply were they stuck, and another horse had to be produced from another farm. After that they came out of the marsh like a cork being pulled out of a bottle, and Dodo was in time to be the German Emperor with a racing-cup upside down on her head for a helmet, an enormous moustache, and half a dozen sons. This scene represented the complete word, which was instantly guessed and hissed as being undoubtedly Potsdam.

8

There were not less than ten people in any of the compartments when the London train, which was so long that both ends of it projected outside the station, arrived at Winston, and so Dodo made herself extremely comfortable in the luggage van, feeling it perfectly blissful to be alone (though in a luggage van) and to be inaccessible to any intrusive call of duty for three whole hours. Indeed, she almost hoped that the train would be late, and that she would then get a longer interval of solitude than that. She had a luncheon-basket, and a pillow, and a fur-coat, and a book that promised to be amusing, and had very prudently thrown the morning paper, which she had not yet read, out of the window, for fear she should get interested in it and think about the war. If there was good news, she could wait for it till she got to London; if there was bad news she thought she could wait for ever. The friendly guard, rather shocked to see her preference for a luggage van, rather than a fraction of a seat in a crowded carriage, had drawn an iron grille across the entrance, so that she resembled a dangerous caged animal, and promised her an uninterrupted journey.

The book speedily proved itself a disappointment; it was clear that the war was going to creep into it before long, like the head of Charles I. into Mr. Dick's Memorial, and Dodo put it aside and looked out of the window instead. The blossoms of spring-time made snowy the orchards around the villages through which the train sped without pause or salute, while the names of insignificant stations flashed past. But the country-side was thick with reminiscence of hunting days for her, and with that curious pleasure in mere recognition which the sight of familiar places gives long after all emotion has withered from them, she identified a fence here, a brook there, or a long stretch of ploughed land, lawn-like to-day with the short spikes of the growing crops, all of which brought back to her mind some incidents of pleasant winter days, now incredibly remote. Then as the train drew up in deference to an opposing signal, she heard from a neighbouring coppice the first note of a cuckoo, and unbidden the words of the old song, still fresh and untarnishable by age, floated across her mind:

> Summer is i-cumen in,
> Lhoude sing cuccu:
> Groweth sed, and bloweth med,
> And springthe the woode nu,
> Sing cuccu.

"Oh, the old days!" thought Dodo to herself, feeling immensely old, as the train jerked and moved on again. Trains used not to jerk, surely, in the old days, and for that matter she used not to travel in a luggage van. Then she concentrated herself on the view again, for very shortly they would be passing the remount-camp where Jack was in charge. Of course she missed it; probably it was on the other side of the line, and she had been earnestly gazing out of the wrong window.

Well, it was very pleasant to renew the sense of travelling in a train at all. The rush past crowded platforms, the rise and fall of the telegraph-wires as the posts flicked by, the procession of green fields and blossoming orchards, the streams running full with the spring rains, the cuckoo, the fact of being on the way to London after four solid months of hospital life at Winston, the thought of the luncheon-basket with which she purposed soon to refresh herself had all the sweet savour of remote, ordinary normal life about them, and a semblance of pre-war existence, even when it would last but for a few hours, seemed extraordinarily delicious. Almost more pleasant was the smell of springtime that streamed in through the window, that indefinable fragrance of moisture and growth and greenness, and she drew in long inhalations of it, for of late the world had seemed to contain only three odours, namely those of iodoform, of cooking dinners and of Virginian cigarettes. For the last four months she had not spent a single night away from Winston, and even then she had only gone away, as she was doing now, to have a look at how things were going on in the officers' hospital at Chesterford House. Never in her life, as far as she could remember, had she spent anything approaching four months in the same place.

Dodo, who a few years before had literally no first-hand experience of what fatigue really meant, felt tired this morning, but she had got quite used to that to which she had been a stranger for so many years, and now it seemed as much a part of general consciousness to be always tired as it did in the old days to feel always fresh. But she had found that when you had arrived at a sufficient degree of fatigue, it got no worse, but remained steady and constant, and she now accepted it as permanent, and did not think about it. Both sight and sound were veiled with this chronic weariness, which took the keen edge off all sensation and she smelt and listened to the odours and sounds of springtime as if through cotton-wool, and looked at its radiance as if through smoked glass which cut off the brightness of sunray, and presented you with a sepia sketch instead of a coloured picture. Still it was very good to be quit of the smell of iodoform and the sight of bandages.

This busy life in her hospital had now for a year and a half cut her off from all the pursuits in which hitherto her life had been passed, so that even while she recognised a brook she had jumped or a fence she had fallen at, she realised how remote the doings of those days had become. They were severed from her not merely by these two winters of abstinence from hunting, but much more crucially by the chasm of the huge catastrophe which had wrecked and was still wrecking the world. Memory could accurately recall old incidents to her, but in her own consciousness she could not recall the atmosphere in which those days had been lived; at the most, they seemed to have been read about in some very vivid book, not to have been personally experienced by her. She realized that this was probably only a symptom of her general fatigue, a false claim as Christian Scientists would have told her, but its falsity was extremely plausible and convincing. The fatigue, however, and the symptoms arising from it were just those things which she was bound most sternly to suppress when she was at work. Her value, such as it was, in the day-long routine, lay, as she was well aware, in her being gay and ridiculous without apparent effort, giving a "frolic welcome" to her tasks, as if it was all the greatest fun in the world. She had, in fact, to pretend to be what she had always been. Deep down in her she hoped, she believed that the mainspring of her vitality was unimpaired, for now, as the train sped onwards, something within her hailed the springtime, like an awakened Brunnhilde, with ecstatic recognition. Only, it did not thrill her all through, as its custom used to be; there was this hard, fatigued crust on her senses. . . .

What she missed most, the thing that she did actively and continually long for was the society and companionship of her friends. Just as, all these weeks, she had done nothing but her work, so she had seen nobody except those professionally engaged with it. Her legion of friends were, with one exception, as busy over war-work as she was herself. Younger men, with terrible gaps already in their numbers, were fighting on one of the many battle-fronts, older men were engaged with office work or other missions for the more mature, and women and girls alike were nursing or typewriting, or washing dishes, or running canteens. They were too busy to see her, just as she was too busy to see them, and that was a very real deprivation to Dodo, for she had no less than genius for friendship. Many of these, however, were in London, and Dodo proposed to do something towards making up these arrears of human companionship during this next week. Her daughter Nadine Graves was dining with her to-night and going to the theatre; Edith (the sole exception among war-working friends) was entertaining her to-morrow with an evening at the opera; the next day there was a small dance somewhere, which would be full of boys from France and girls from hospitals. A social engagement or two a day, seemed to Dodo after these months of abstinence to be a positive orgy, and she ate her sandwiches with an awakening zest for life, and fell fast asleep.

The day was beginning to flame towards sunset when she got out at the London terminus, and at the sight of the crowds, brisk and busy and occupied with various affairs, this sense of stimulus was vastly increased. There was a little fog in the station with the smell of smoke and of grimy, beloved old London hanging there, and everyone seemed to have two legs and two arms and not to be bandaged and not to limp. No one had slings or crutches, and involuntarily there came into Dodo's mind the verse from the Bible about "the lame and the blind that are hated of David's soul." For one moment, as the intoxication of freedom and independence, of crowds and brisk movement mounted to her head, she felt a secret sympathy with that monarch's sentiments, which were so literally translated into actual conduct by Edith who still refused to have anything to do with war-work,

and occasionally wrote to Dodo saying how magnificently her new
symphony was progressing. But even while she sympathised with
David, she detested Edith's interpretation of him, though she realised
that she herself, not having a single drop of artistic ichor in her blood,
could not possibly understand the temperament that led Edith to remain
the one unpatriotic individual in all her circle. Edith similarly refused
to talk or hear about the war at all, because mention of it interrupted
that aloofness from disturbing thought that was necessary to give full
play to an artist's creative powers. Dodo would not, however, let a
divergence of sentiment even on so vital a topic interfere with her
friendship. Edith had a right to her own convictions, odious though
they might be, and to the ordering of her own life. Only, if your
own thoughts and actions were entirely concerned with the war, it
was difficult, so Dodo found, not to let some trace of that creep into
your conversation. However, when she met Edith to-morrow, she
would do her best.

Dodo had several businesses to attend to before she went home,
and when finally, rather behind time, she drove down Piccadilly on
her way to Chesterford House, the sun had long set, and such lighting
as, in view of hostile raids, was thought sufficient, illuminated the
streets. No blink of any kind shewed in the blank fronts of the houses,
but the road and pavement presented the most fascinating harmonies
in subdued and variegated tints. The glass of some street-lamps was
painted over with violet, of others with red; others were heavily blacked
on their top-surfaces but not obscured below, so that an octagonal
patch of pavement was vividly lit. Whether this delightful scheme
of colour helped to confuse possible raiders, Dodo did not consider;
she was quite content to enjoy the aesthetic effect, which did seem
very bewildering. The streets were still shining with the moisture of
some shower that had fallen earlier in the afternoon and they furnished
a dim rainbow of reflected colours while the whole paint-box of various
tints was held in solution by the serene light of the moon now near
to its full, and swinging clear above the trees in the Park. The thought
of a raid that night struck her as rather attractive, for she had not
yet been in one, and her re-awakened interest in life welcomed the
idea of any new experience.

She was just turning in at the big gates of Chesterford House when
it became likely that her wish was to be gratified. The hooting of
bicycle-horns and a sound of police-whistles began to pierce shrilly
through the bourdon rumble of wheeled traffic and this grew swiftly
louder. Instantaneously there came a change in the movements of foot-
passengers; those who were strolling leisurely along first stopped to
verify what they had heard, and then proceeded on their way at a

far livelier pace, many of them breaking into a run, and soon, tearing along the road, came half a dozen bicyclists hooting and whistling and shouting "Take cover."

Dodo had just got out of her motor and was absorbed in these new happenings, when Nadine in cloak and evening clothes came running in at the gate.

"Oh, mamma, is that you?" she said. "Isn't it lucky; I've just got here in time. Let us come in at once."

Dodo kissed her.

"Darling, I simply can't come in this minute," she said. "My legs refuse to take me. I want to see what happens so dreadfully. What do they do next? And how about our theatre? Would it be nice to be there for a raid? I don't much mind if we can't go, we'll have a cosy little evening together."

"Oh, I must go in," said Nadine. "It all gets on my nerves. I hate to sit in a corner, and shut my ears, and I get cold and my knees tremble. What do they do next, do you ask? They drop enormous bombs on us, and we let off all the guns in the world at them. It's all most unattractive. You must come in before the guns begin."

Dodo promised to do so, and as soon as Nadine had gone inside the house, went out of the big gates again into the street. Already the wheeled traffic in the road had mysteriously melted away, and almost entirely ceased, though the pavements were still full of hurrying foot-passengers, most of whom crossed the road a hundred yards further down towards the entrance of a tube-station which was already black with people. As they went they spoke jerkily and nervously to each other, as if vexed or irritated. But in ten minutes they had all vanished, leaving the street entirely empty, and it seemed as if some uncanny enchantment must have waved over the town a spell, which withered up its life, so that it was now a city of the dead. The pulse of traffic beat no longer down its arteries, not a light appeared in its windows, no trace of any animation remained in it. Not a whisper of wind stirred, the remote moon shone down on the emptiness, and Dodo, holding her breath to listen, found the stillness ringing in her ears.

Suddenly the silence was broken by some distant mutter, very faint and muffled, but sounding not like some little noise near at hand, but a great noise a long way off, for low as it was, it buffeted the air. Dodo felt that every nerve in her body was sending urgent messages of alarm to her brain, but with them there went along the same wires messages of tingling exhilaration. This was the real thing: this was war itself. In her hospital she had lived, till she had got used to it, with those whom that wild beast had torn and mangled, but the sound of guns, here in the secure centre of London, was different in kind from that; it was war, not the effects of war. She knew that the outer defences, away somewhere to the east, were already engaged with the enemy, whose machines, laden with bombs, were drawing closer every moment with the speed of swallows on the wing. Then that remote mutter ceased again, absolute silence succeeded, and Dodo, to her intense surprise, found that her hands were icy cold and that her knees were shaking. Quite clearly, though she had not known it, her brain was acting on those alarming messages that were pouring into it, but more vivid than these was her intense curiosity as to what was coming next, and her exhilaration in the excitement of it all.

Again the silence became intolerable, filling the air like some dense choking fog. One part of her would have given anything in the world to be safe back at Winston, or huddled in the cheerful recesses of the tube with those prudent crowds which had hurried by, but another part, and that the more potent, would not have accepted any bribe to miss a moment of this superb suspense. Then somewhere over the Green Park, but much nearer at hand, there came a flash as of distant lightning, silhouetting the trees against a faint violet background, a gun barked into the night, and a shell whimpered and squealed. Several times was that repeated, then some other gun barked more loudly and fiercely. At that Dodo's intense curiosity must have conveyed to her that for the moment it was quite satisfied, and before she fairly knew what she was doing, her feet had carried her scudding across the gravelled space in front of the house, and her fingers were fumbling with the latch-key at the door. She did not feel in the least afraid of German bombs or fragments of English shrapnel, but she was consciously and desperately afraid of silence and of noise and above all of solitude.

For the next hour there was no need to fear silence, so few moments of silence were there to be afraid of. Sometimes the firing died down to a distant mutter like that with which it had begun, and then without warning the Hyde Park guns from close at hand broke in with bouquets of furious explosions and screams of squealing things, making the windows rattle in their frames. Then, just as suddenly, they would cease, and more distant firing seemed but the echo of that tumult. Between the reports could be heard the drone of the engines of hostile aircraft; once for the space of half a minute the noise came loud and throbbing down the chimney, showing that the machine was directly overhead, and two or three times a detonation infinitely more sonorous than the sharp report of the guns gave the news that some bomb had been dropped. A clanging bell grew louder and died away again as a fire-engine dashed up the deserted street outside.

Dodo and Nadine sat together in the sitting-room that Dodo had reserved for herself when she gave up the rest of the house to be a hospital. The table for their early dinner before the theatre was half-laid, but since the raid began the arrangements had been left incomplete. Now that she was within walls and not alone any longer Dodo's fears had passed off altogether; she found herself merely restless and excited, incessantly going to the window and raising a corner of the blind to see what was visible. Outside the Park lay quiet under the serene wash of moonlight, but every now and then a tracer-shell lit a new and momentary constellation among the stars, and the rays of the searchlight swept across the sky like the revolving flails of some gigantic windmill. Nadine meantime sat in a remote corner of the room directly underneath an electric lamp, with a book on her lap on which she was quite unable to concentrate her attention, and her fingers ready to apply to her ears when the noise which she proposed to shut out had violently assailed them. Once she remonstrated with her mother for her excursions to the window.

"It's really rather dangerous," she said. "If a bomb was dropped in the road outside, the window would be blown in and the glass would cut you into small pieces of mince."

"Darling, how can you be so sensible as to think of that sort of thing in the middle of an air-raid?" asked Dodo. "Though it's all quite horrible and brutal, it is so amazingly interesting. I should like to go up on the roof in a bomb-proof hat. You must remember this is my first air-raid. Even the most unpleasant things are interesting the first time they happen. I remember so well my first visit to a dentist. And do air-raids make most people thirsty, I'm terribly thirsty."

Nadine shut up her book and laughed.

"You're a lovely person to be with," she said. "I don't mind it nearly as much as usual. Hark, don't you hear whistles?"

Dodo listened and beamed.

"Certainly," she said. "What does that mean? Is it another raid?"

"No, mamma, of course not," said Nadine. "What an awful idea! It's the signal 'all clear.' They've driven them out of London."

"That's a blessing, and also rather a disappointment," said Dodo. "Let's have dinner at once. I'll be dressed in five minutes, and then we can go to the theatre after all. Wasn't it exciting? Aren't I cramming a lot in?"

A weird melodrama thrilled Dodo that night, and the general thrill was renewed again next morning by a telephone message from Edith that a bomb had fallen in the road exactly in front of her house, completely wrecking two front rooms. She wanted to come round instantly to see Dodo over very important matters, and arrived a quarter of an hour late boiling with conversation and fury.

"Insured? Yes, we're insured," she shouted, "but what has insurance got to do with it? If I took up the poker, Dodo, and smashed your looking-glass, you would find no consolation in the fact that it was insured. It would be my infernal impertinence and brutality that would concern you. Those brutes deliberately bombed me, who have always . . . well, you know what my attitude towards Germany has been, and we'll leave it at that. There are twenty pages of my score of the new symphony which were on the table, absolutely torn to shreds. It's impossible to piece them together, and I can never re-write them."

"Oh, my dear, how dreadful!" said Dodo. "But why not write them again? Wasn't it Isaac Newton, who——"

"Isaac Newton, wasn't me," said Edith. "I daresay he might do it with a mere treatise, but there's a freshness about the first draft of music which can never be recaptured. Never! The wreckage: you must come at once to see the wreckage. It's incredible; there's a Chippendale suite simply in splinters. You might light a fire with the bigger pieces, and use the rest instead of matches. There are little wheels about the room which were a clock, there's half the ceiling down, and there's glass dust, literally dust over everything, exactly like the frosted foregrounds on Christmas cards. Inconceivably thorough! I always said the Germans were thorough."

"And where were you?" asked Dodo.

"In the cellar, of course, with the housemaid and cook singing. But the outrage of it, the wanton brutal destruction! Do those Huns——"

"You said 'Huns', " said Dodo gleefully.

"I know I did. Huns they are, brutes, barbarians! And do they think that they can win the war by smashing my clock? First there were the Belgian atrocities, then there was the massacre of peaceful travellers on neutral shipping without any warning being given, and now they must break my windows. That has brought it home to me. I believe every accusation of brutality and murder and loathsomeness that has ever been made against them. And that is why I came round to see you. I want to renounce all my previous convictions about them. I will never set foot on German soil again; the whole beastly race is poisoned for me. There's exactly the same callous brutality in pages of Wagner and Strauss, and I thought it was strength! I lay awake half of last night hating them. Of course I shall take up some war-work at once; best of all I should like to go into some munition factory and make with my very own hands high explosives to be dropped on Berlin. Why don't we prosecute the war with greater frightfulness, and, oh, Dodo, at the very beginning why didn't you convince me what brutes and barbarians they are!"

Edith walked rapidly about the room as she made this unreserved recantation, stamping with fury.

"My clock! My symphony! My front-door!" she exclaimed. "My front-door was blown right across the hall, and in its present position it's more like the back-door. If I hadn't been so furiously angry at the sight of the damage, I think I should have laughed at the thought that I once believed the Huns to be cultured and romantic people. I'm almost glad it happened, for it has brought enlightenment to me. That's my nature. I must act up to my convictions whatever they are and I don't care at what personal loss I learn the truth. Not one note more of music will I write till the English are strolling down the Unter den Linden. The Kaiser must be brought to justice; if he survives the war he must be treated like a common criminal. He must suffer for smashing up my rooms exactly as if he had been a hooligan in the street. He is a hooligan; that's precisely what he is, and once I was pleased at his coming to my concert. I talked to him as if he had been a civilised being, I curtsied to him. I wonder that the sinews of my knees didn't dry up and wither for shame. What a blind dupe I have been of that disgusting race! Never will I trust my judgment again about anybody. . . . Give me a box of matches and let me make a bomb."

Dodo was enchanted at this change of view in Edith. Though she had determined that nothing should interfere with her friendship, things had been rather difficult at times.

"How you can have tolerated me, I can't think," continued Edith. "And you showed marvellous tact, because if you talked about almost anything under the sun the war would creep in. Wonderful tact, Dodo; wonderful patience! I must begin to do something at once; I must set to work to learn something, and the only question is what shall it be. Luckily I learn things quicker than anybody I know, for I can concentrate in a way that hardly anyone else can. You never concentrate enough, you know. I have often told you that."

"Yes, darling, often and often," said Dodo. "How much more fortunate you are! What are you going to concentrate on?"

"I don't know. I must think. By the way, you are dining with me to-night, aren't you? That will be all right, if you don't mind there being no front-door; they left me my dining-room. But the road in front of the house is all torn up; you will have to walk ten yards. The Huns!"

Dodo, by way of a holiday, spent an extremely strenuous week. She took the convalescents out for drives in the morning, and to matinées in the afternoon, and got up a variety of entertainments for those who were in bed. Many of her friends were in town, busy also, but she sandwiched in, between these hospital duties, a prodigious quantity of social intercourse. Yet the spring, the sunshine, the aroma had for the present gone out of all that used to render life agreeable; it was an effort hardly worth making in these days when efforts were valuable, to wear even the semblance of a light heart when there was nothing more to be gained beyond the passing of a pleasant hour for herself. Fatigue of mind and soul lay within her like some cold lump that would not be dissolved and she had some sort of spiritual indigestion which made amusement taste queerly. Apart from the mere stimulus of human companionship, all this tearing about, this attempt to recapture a little of the pre-war *insouciance* was hardly worth the exertion. In the wards she could be amazing, but there she had a purpose: to play the fool with a purpose and see it fulfilling itself was an altogether different affair and was easy enough. What was difficult was to play the fool from mere ebullition of high spirits.

Edith came to the station to see Dodo off on her return to Winston. She had meant to stop another couple of days but already she was fidgeting to get to work again, and what clinched her decision to go back was that a medical inspector had given notice of his visit to her hospital to-morrow morning and it was unthinkable that she should not be there. She had secured a seat in the train, and the two strolled along the platform till it was due to start.

"It's a waste of time and energy," she said to Edith on this topic, "to make an effort to enjoy yourself. If you don't enjoy yourself naturally, you had better give it up, and try to make somebody else enjoy himself."

Edith was in rather a severe mood.

"Truly altruistic," she said. "Suck the orange dry, and then give the rind away."

"Not at all: squeeze the juice out of it, and give the juice away," said Dodo.

"Yes, as you don't want the juice yourself. That's precisely what I mean. But don't let us discuss abstract questions; I have bought a typewriter."

"A typewriter is a person," said Dodo. If Edith was going to be magisterial she would be, too.

"No; the person is a typist," said Edith. "I'm one, so I ought to know. In a week's time I shall be absolutely proficient."

"My dear, how clever of you," said Dodo, forgetting to be disagreeable. "What will you do then?"

"I shall make a round of hospitals and do all their correspondence for them for a week. I shall come to Winston."

"That'll be lovely," said Dodo. "But what about the munition factory?"

"They say I'm too old to stand the hours, and to stand the standing.

Old, indeed! Also you mayn't smoke, which is more important. One has to make the most of one's faculties, and if I couldn't smoke all day, I shouldn't be at my best. We've got to learn efficiency; we shall win when we all do our best."

They had come out of the dim arch of the station, and Dodo, helplessly giggling, sat down on a bench in the sunlight.

"That's so deliciously like you," she said. "You practically say that the war is won because you've bought a typewriter. It's the right spirit, too. I feel the Red Cross may be happy in its mind so long as I am at Winston. All the same the abstract question is interesting. I feel that the only way to laugh nowadays is to make other people laugh. And we've got to take short views, and get through the day's work, and get through to-morrow's work to-morrow. One is learning something, you know, through all this horror; I'm learning to be punctual and business-like, and not to want fifty people to look after me. We've been like babies all our lives, getting things done for us, instead of doing them ourselves. In the old days if I was going by train my maid had to come on first and take my seat, and watch by the carriage door till I arrived, and gave me my book and my rug, and the station-master had to touch his cap and hope I would be comfortable, and the footman had to shew my ticket."

An engine somewhere in the station whistled and puffed and a long train slid slowly by them and vanished into the tunnel just beyond.

"We were babies, we were drones," continued Dodo, "and we were ridiculously expensive. If a train didn't suit us, we took a special, if a new dress didn't come up to our hopes, we never saw it again. But now we wear a dress for years, and instead of taking specials we catch slow trains humbly, and travel in luggage vans. I don't think we shall ever go back to the old days, even if we had enough money left to do so."

She looked round, and a sudden misgiving dawned on her.

"Where's my train?" she said. "It ought to be standing there? What has happened?"

It was soon clear what had happened. . . . Half an hour later Dodo left in a special at staggering expense, in order to get down to Winston that night.

9

The morning paper had been brought in to Dodo with her letters, and she opened it quickly at the middle page. The German assault on Verdun was being pressed ever more fiercely; it seemed impossible that the town could hold out much longer. A second of the protecting forts had fallen, smashed and pulverised under the hail of devastating steel. . . .

Dodo read no more than the summary of the news. It was bad everywhere; there was not a single gleam of sun shining through that impenetrable black cloud that had risen out of Central Europe nearly two years ago, and still poured its torrents on to broken lands. On the Eastern front of Germany the Russian armies were being pushed back; the British garrison in Kut was completely surrounded, and even the sturdiest of optimists could do no more than affirm that the fall of that town would not have any real bearing on the war generally. They had said precisely the same when, a few months ago, Gallipoli had been evacuated, just as when in the first stupendous advance of the enemy across France and Flanders, they had slapped their silly legs, and shouted that the German lines of communication were lengthening daily and presently the Allies would snip them through, so that all the armies of the Hun would drop neatly off like a thistle-head when you sever its stalk with a stick. At this rate how many and how grave disasters were sufficient to have any bearing on the war? Perhaps the fall of Verdun would be a blessing in disguise. The disguise certainly seemed impenetrable, but the optimists would pierce it. . . .

Dodo pulled herself together, and remembered that she was an optimist too, though not quite of that order, and that it was not consistent with her creed to meditate upon irretrievable misfortunes, or indeed to meditate upon anything at all when there were a dozen private letters of her own to be opened at once, and probably some thirty or forty more connected with hospital work, waiting for her in the office. It certainly was not conducive to efficiency to think too much in these days, especially if nothing but depression was to be the result of thinking; and if all she could do was to see to the affairs of her hospital, it was surely better to do that than to speculate on present data about the result of the fall of Verdun.

A tap at her door, and David's voice demanding admittance reminded her that after she had attended to the immediate requirements of the hospital, she was to have a holiday to-day, as David was going to school for the first time to-morrow, and this day was dedicated to him. Thus there was another reason for liveliness; it would never do to cast shadows over David's festival.

"Yes, darling, come in," she said. "I'm still in bed like a lazy-bones."

"Oh, get up at once, mummie," said David. "It's my day. Shall I fill your bath?"

"Yes, do. While it's filling I shall open my letters."

"But not answer them," said David. "You can do that to-morrow after I have gone. Isn't it funny? I don't want to go to school a bit, but I should be rather disappointed if I wasn't going."

"I know, darling. I'm rather like that, too. I hate your going, but I'm sending you all the same."

"Anyhow, I shan't cry," announced David.

Dodo glanced through her letters while David was busy with her bath. There was one from Jack, announcing that he would be here for the Sunday, and that was good. There was one from Edith, and that made her laugh, for it informed her that she would arrive to-night bringing her typewriter with her. The speed at which she was getting efficient appeared to be quite miraculous, if her machine had not been away being repaired, she would have typed this letter instead of writing it. She had knocked it over yesterday, and the bell wouldn't ring at the end of a line. She was learning shorthand as well, and it would be good practice for her to take down Dodo's business letters from dictation, and type them for her afterwards. . . .

"Ready!" shouted David from the bathroom next door. "And I've put in a whole bottle of something for a treat."

From the thick steam that was pouring through the open door it seemed certain that David had treated her to a bottle of verbena salts.

"Darling, that is kind of you," said Dodo cordially. "Now you must go downstairs, and say we'll have breakfast in half an hour."

"Less," said David firmly.

"Well, twenty-five minutes. You can begin if I'm late."

The rule on these festivals, such as birthdays and last days of the holidays, was that David should, with his mother as companion, do exactly what he liked from morning till night within reason, Dodo being the final court of appeal as to whether anything was reasonable or not. She was allowed to be reasonable too (not having to run, for instance, if she really was tired) and so when he had gone downstairs, she emptied the bathwater out and began again, since it was really unreasonable to expect her to get into the fragrant soup which David had treated her to. But she was nearly up to time, and in the interval he had learned the exciting news that the keeper's wife had given birth to twins. This led to questions on the abstruse subject of genera-tion which appalled the parlour-maid. Dodo adhered to the gooseberry bush theory, and would not budge from her position.

An hour in her business-room after breakfast was sufficient to set in order the things that she must personally attend to, and she came out on to the lawn, where David had decreed that croquet should form the first diversion of the day. It was deliciously warm, for the spring which was bursting into young leaf and apple-blossom on the day that Dodo had gone up to town three weeks ago was now, in these last days of April, trembling on the verge of summer. A mild south-westerly wind drove scattered clouds, white and luminous, across the intense blue, and their shadows bowled swiftly along beneath them, islands of moving shade surrounded by the living sea of sunlight. Below the garden the beech-wood stood in full vesture of milky green, and the elms still only in leaf-bud, shed showers of minute sequin-like blossoms on the grass. The silver flush of daisies in the fields was beginning to be gilded with buttercups, the pink thorn-trees, after these weeks of mellow weather were decking themselves with bloom, and the early magnolias against the house were covered with full-orbed wax-like stars. Thrushes were singing in the bushes, the fragrance of growing things loaded the air, and David from sheer exuberance of youth and energy was hopping over the croquet-hoops till his mother was ready. Sight, smell and hearing were glutted with the sense of the everlasting youth of the re-awakening earth, and as she stepped out on to the terrace, Dodo recaptured in body and soul and spirit, for just one moment, the immortal glee of springtime. The next moment, she saw a few yards down the terrace, a bath-chair being slowly wheeled along. Two boys on crutches walked by it, its occupant had his whole face as far as his mouth, swathed in bandages. . . . And before she knew it, a whole gallery of pictures was flashed on to her mind. Hospital ships were moving out of port, and putting into port again, if they escaped the deadly menace of the seas; long trains with the mark of the Red Cross on them were rolling along the railways, and discharging their burdens of pain. Down the thousand miles of front the pitiless rain of shells was falling, Verdun tottered, in Kut . . .

Dodo pulled herself together, and overtook the bath-chair.

"Why, what a nice day you've ordered to come out on for the first time, Trowle," she said. "Drink in the sun and the wind: doesn't it feel good after that beastly old house? Ashley, if you go that pace already on your crutches, you'll be taken up for exceeding the speed-limit in a week's time. As for you, Richmond, you're a perfect fraud; nobody could possibly be as well as you look. Isn't it lovely for me? I've got a whole holiday, because my boy is going to school to-morrow and we're going to play games together from morning till night. He's waiting for me now. If any of you want to be useful—not otherwise— you might stroll down to the lodge across there, and tell them I shall come in to see the keeper's wife sometime to-day. She's had twins. I never did. Yes, David, I'm coming."

David had never forgotten that remarkable game of croquet he once witnessed when Prince Albert Hun, as he was now called, and Miss Grantham both cheated, and this morning as a reasonable diversion, he chose to impersonate him and cheat too. Naturally he announced this intention to his mother, who therefore impersonated Miss Grantham, as a defensive measure, and the game became extremely curious. David, of course, imitated the Albert Hun mode of play, but, having adjusted his ball with his foot so as to be precisely opposite his hoop, and having bent down in the correct attitude to observe his line, he found that Dodo had taken the hoop up, and so there was nothing to go through.

"Oh, I've finished being a Hun," he said, when he made this depressing discovery. "Let's play properly again. What made him so fat?"

"Eating," said Dodo. "You'll get fat, too, if you go on as you did at breakfast."

"But I was hungry. I could have eaten a croquet-ball. Should I have been sick?"

"Probably. Get on! Hit it!"

"All right. And why did Princess Hun always creak so when she bent down. Do you remember? Did she ever have twins like Mrs. Reeves? Can I have twins?"

"Yes, darling, I hope you'll have quantities some time," said Dodo.

"Can I have them to-day?" asked David. "Let's go to the kitchen-garden, and look among the gooseberry bushes."

"No, there's not time for you to have them to-day."

"Then I shall wait till I go to school. Ow! I've hit you," screamed David suddenly losing interest in other matters. "Now I shall send you away to the corner, and I shall go through a hoop, and I shall——"

David careering after the ball, tripped over a hoop which he had not observed, and fell down.

Thereafter came an expedition to the trout-stream, and since their efforts to throw a fly only resulted in the most amazing tangles and the hooking of tough bushes, it was necessary to suborn a gardener to supply them with worms, and to promise to say nothing about it, for fear Jack should have a fit. With this wriggling lure, so much more sensible if the object of their fishing was to entrap fish (which it undoubtedly was) David caught two trout and the corpse of an old boot which gave him a great deal of trouble before it could be landed, since, unlike trout, boots seemed to be absolutely indefatigable and could pull forever. Then David distinctly saw a kingfisher come out of a hole in the bank (naturally the other side of the stream) and had to take off his shoes and stockings and wade across, as there was a firm legend that the British Museum would give you a thousand pounds for an intact kingfisher's nest. He dropped a stocking into the water, and this was irrevocably lost, but on the other hand he found a thrush's nest, though no kingfisher's. But as he was totally indifferent as to whether he had two stockings or one or none, the fact of finding a thrush's nest contributed a gain on balance. After that, it was certainly time to have lunch, as was apparent when they got back to the house and found it close on half-past three. So they decided to miss out tea, or rather combine it with supper, and continue looking for birds' nests.

Dodo was the least envious of mankind, but she was inclined that day, when the sunset began to flame in the west and kindle the racing clouds, to be jealous of Joshua, and if she had thought that any peremptory commands to the sun and moon would have had the smallest effect on their appointed orbits, she would certainly have told them to remain precisely where they were until further notice. All day she had been playing truant; she had slipped her collar, and gone larking in the spring time. With none other except David, could she have done that; there was no one intimately dear to her who would not have shoo'd her back into the environment of the war. Jack even, the friend of her heart, must have asked about the hospital, and told her about the remount camp, and given her the latest War Office news about Verdun and Kut. But Dodo could lose herself in love with David, and all day he had never brought her up gasping to the surface again. The most tragic of his recollections concerned his going to school to-morrow, and knit up with that was the joy of new adventures, and the grandeur of leaving home quite alone with trousers and a ticket of his own. His world all day had been the real world to her, and it was with the sense of an intolerable burden to be shouldered again that she saw the evening begin to close in. Often had the complete childish unconsciousness of any terrific tragedy going on enabled her to slip the collar to get a drop of water from this boyish Lazarus, who alone was able to cross for her the "great gulf fixed," and now the giver of a little water was off to embark on other adventures. With an intuition wholly without bitterness Dodo knew that in a week's time she would be getting ecstatic letters from him on the joys of school and the excitement of friendship with other boys. She loved the thought of those letters coming to her; she would have been miserable if she had pictured David really missing her. She had no doubt that he would be glad beyond words to see her again, but in the interval there would be cricket to play, and friends to make, and cakes to share and stag beetles to keep. It was intensely right that a new life should absorb him, for that was the way in which young things grew to boyhood and manhood and learnt the part they were to play in the world. But as far as she herself went (leaving the consideration of the big affairs outside) she imaged herself as a raven croaking on a decayed bough. . . . Jack would come and croak too; Edith would croak; everybody except those delicious beings aged twelve or under, croaked, unless they were too busy to croak. But to David the war, that aching interminable business was just a pleasant excitement, like the kitchen chimney being on fire, or a water-pipe bursting. There were a quantity of agreeable soldiers in the house, who sometimes told him about shrapnel and heavy stuff and snipers, and to him the war was just that; an exciting set of stories connected with the smashing up of the Hun. He had a world of his own, of the things that truly and rightly concerned him. The most thrilling at the moment was the fact of going to school to-morrow, after that came the lost stocking and the other diversions of the day. Since morning he had wiled Dodo from herself, and as they sat down with great grandeur to a splendid combination of tea and supper, which included treacle pudding, the two trout and bananas, reasonably chosen by David for the last de-bauch, Dodo's jealousy of Joshua surged within her. In an hour from now, David would have gone to bed, and then she would go upstairs to say good-night to him, and come down again to welcome Edith and her typewriter and slide back into the old heartbreaking topics.

Dodo had made a glorious pretence of being greedy about treacle pudding, in order to show how much she appreciated David's house-keeping. Thus, when the hour for bed-time came, he got up, rather serious.

"Oh, Mummie," he said, "I shall never forget to-day, if I live to be twenty."

"My darling, have you enjoyed it? Have you enjoyed it just as much as you can enjoy anything?" said Dodo, feeling the shades of the prison-house closing round. "I have."

"To-morrow at this time," said David solemnly, "you'll be here and I shan't."

Dodo heard her heart-cords thrumming; joy was the loudest because the child she had brought into the world, flesh of her flesh and bone of her bone was a boy already, and with the flicking round of the swift years would soon be a man, and for the same reason there was regret and aching there because never again would she see one who was part of herself, her life, swelling into bud, and thereafter blossom-ing . . .

"Oh, David," she said, "your darling body will be there, and I shall be here, but that's nothing at all. There's love between us, isn't there, and what on earth can part that? You'll understand that some day. Hasn't to-day been delicious? Well, it was only delicious because you were you and I was I. Just think of that for a second! You wouldn't have cared about catching boots with Albert Hun."

He opened his eyes very wide.

"Why, I should have hated it!" he said. "It was the boot and you, Mummie, that made it lovely. Is that it?"

"It's it and all of it," said she. "Off you go. I shall come to say good-night before dinner."

David wrinkled up his nose.

"Dinner after treacle-pudding and bananas!" he shouted. "Who'll be fat?"

"I shall have to make a pretence to keep Mrs. Arbuthnot from feeling awkward," said Dodo.

"I see. *Now* you've promised to come to say good-night? It's a con— something."

"Tract," said Dodo.

Dodo kept her part of the contract. But there was never anyone so deliciously fast asleep as was David when she went to perform it. He lay with his cheek on his hand, and his hair all over his forehead, and his mouth a little open with breath coming long and evenly. His clothes lay out ready for packing in the morning, and the immortal warless day was over.

She went downstairs again, smiling to herself that David slept so well, back into the cage. The evening papers had been brought by Edith who was singing in the bathroom. Verdun still held out, and the news of the fall of the second defensive fort was unconfirmed. On the other hand, Trowle, the boy with the bandaged face, who had taken his first outing to-day, had a high temperature, and the matron had asked Dr. Ashe to come and see him. So there was David asleep and Edith singing, and Verdun untaken, and Trowle with a high temperature. Dodo felt that, on balance, she ought to have been very gay. But Trowle, one of a hundred patients, had a high temperature. She was worried at that in a way she wouldn't have been worried a year ago. If only they would stop maiming and gassing each other for a few days, or if only the hospital could be empty for a week!

By the middle of next morning, David had set off without tears according to promise. Trowle's temperature much abated, only indicated a slight chill, and Verdun still held out. Dodo had dictated a couple of letters to Edith, who with swoops and dashes of her pencil took them down on a block of quarto paper, and while Dodo opened the rest of her correspondence was transferring them on to her typewriter. She worked with a high staccato action, as if playing a red-hot piano. As she clicked her keys, she conversed loudly and confidently.

"Go on talking, Dodo," she said. "All I am doing is purely mechanical, and I can attend perfectly. There! when the bell rings like that, I know it is the end of a line, and I just switch the board across, and it clicks and makes a new empty line for itself. You should learn to typewrite; it is mere child's play. I shall never write a letter in my own hand again. We ought all to be able to use a typewriter; you can dash things off in no time. I think the work you have been doing here is glorious, but you ought to type. Let me see, you said something in this letter about aspirin. I've got 'aspirin' mixed up with the next word in my shorthand notes. Just refer back, and tell me what you said about aspirin."

Dodo turned up a letter which she thought was done with. "We want aspirin tabloids containing two grains," she said.

"That was it!" said Edith triumphantly. "You said 'grains,' and it looked like 'graceful' on my copy. Are you sure you didn't say 'graceful'? Now that's all right. I move the line back and erase 'graceful.' No, that stop only makes capitals instead of small letters. I'll correct it when the sheet is finished. Let me see; oh, yes, that curve there means 'as before.' It's all extraordinarily simple if you once concentrate upon it. The whole of this transcribing which looks like a conjuring trick—oh, I began writing 'conjuring trick'—is really like the explanation of a conjuring trick, which—did I type 'before,' or didn't I? Do go on talking. I work better when there is talking going on. I shan't answer, but the fact that there is some distraction makes me determined not to be distracted. Conscious effort, you know. . . ."

"Jack comes to-night," said Dodo, continuing the opening of her letters, "and we'll play quiet aged lawn-tennis to-morrow afternoon."

Edith paused with her hands in the air.

"Why quiet and aged?" she said, plunging them on to the keys again. The bell rang.

"Because the lights are low and I'm very old," said Dodo.

Edith forgot to move the machine, and began writing very quickly over the finished line.

"Nonsense!" she said. "You must be fierce and strong and young with all the lights on. I mustn't talk. Something's happened. But all that concerns us now is to be as efficient as we possibly can. We can't afford to make mistakes. We must——"

She pulled out the sheet she had been working on, and gazed at it blankly.

"Dear Sir," she repeated. " 'The Marchioness—' is it spelled like March or Marsh, Dodo? Oh, March; yes. I'll correct that. 'Aspirin in graceful conjuring trick,' that should be grains, and then four large Qs in a row. Oh, that was when I made a mistake with the erasing key. Very stupid of me. And what's happened to the last line? It's written over twice. Have you got any purple ink, Dodo? I always like correcting in the same coloured ink as the type; it looks neater. Well, if you have only got black that will have to do."

Edith shook the stylograph Dodo gave her to make it write, and a fountain of pure black ink poured on to the page.

"Blotting-paper," she said in a strangled voice.

Dodo began to laugh.

"Oh, Edith, you are a tonic," she said, "and I want it this morning. My dear, don't waste any more time over that, but tell me if you never feel in crumbs as I do. I think it's reaction from yesterday. I escaped. I played with David all day, and forgot about cripples and Kut and Verdun, and now I'm back in the cage again, and David's gone, and—and I'm a worm. If I followed my inclination, I should lie down on the floor and roar for the very disquietness of my heart, as the other David says."

"I shouldn't," said Edith loudly. "I want to dance and sing because I am helping to destroy those putrid Huns. Every letter I typewrite— I'll copy this one out again by the way, as no one in the world could read it—is another nail in their odious coffin. I don't care whether Verdun is lost or Kut or anything else. It's not my business. And it's not yours either, Dodo. You mustn't think; there's too much to do; there's no time for thinking. But what has happened to you is that you're overtired. I shall speak to Jack about it."

"My dear, you will do nothing of the kind," said Dodo. "It would be quite useless to begin with, for I should do exactly as I pleased, and it would only make Jack anxious."

Edith ran an arpeggio scale up her typewriter.

"When I feel tired or despondent," she said, "which isn't often, I read about German atrocities. Then I get on the boil from morning till night."

Dodo shook her head.

"No," she said. "Living surrounded by the wounded doesn't have that effect on me or anyone else. If you allow yourself to think, it simply makes you sick at heart. Two days ago a convoy of men who had been gassed came in, and instead of feeling on the boil, I simply ached. We are beginning to use gas too, and . . . my heart aches when I think of German boys being carried back into hospitals in the state ours are in. I suppose I ought to be pleased that they are being gassed too. But I'm not. And I began so well. I was simply consumed with fury, and thought that that was the way to wage war. So it is no doubt. But what do you prove by it? Was anything ever so senseless? The world has gone mad."

Edith fitted a new sheet into her machine.

"I know it has, and the best thing to do is to go mad too, until the world is sane again," she said. "You haven't had your house knocked to bits by a bomb. Now I'm going to begin the aspirin letter once again. I don't want to think and you had better not, either."

Dodo laughed.

"I know," she said. "And will the aspirin letter be ready for the post? It goes in a quarter of an hour."

"It will have to be," said Edith. "After that I insist on your coming out to play a few holes at golf before lunch. I shall work all afternoon. Give me a sheaf of letters to write, Dodo."

This time something quite unprecedented happened to Edith's machine, for six of the keys including the useful "e" would not act at all, and Dodo, already much behindhand with her morning's work, left her furiously tinkering with it. The aspirin letter was in consequence indefinitely delayed, and Dodo had to telegraph instead. Later in the day, the machine being still quite unuseable, Edith put it into its box and despatched it for repair to London, with a letter of blistering indignation. A day or two must elapse before it came back, and she devoted herself to shorthand, and gave a little series of concerts consisting of her own music to the astonished patients.

David wrote happily from school, Trowle's temperature went down, Verdun held out, and the convoy of gassed men did well. Under this stimulus, Dodo roused herself for the effort of not thinking. She did not even think how odd it was for her, to whom activity was so natural, to be obliged to make efforts. The days mounted into weeks and the weeks into months, and she ceased looking forward and looking back. It was enough to get through the day's work, and every day it was a little too much for her. So too was the effort to keep her mind absorbed in the actual work which lay to hand. That perhaps tired her more than the work itself.

10

Dodo was lying in bed, just aware that a strip of sunlight on the floor was getting broader. She was not precisely watching it, but, half-consciously she knew that it had once been a line of light and was now an oblong, the rest of her perceptions were concerned with the fact that it was extremely pleasant to have been commanded in a way that made argument impossible, to remain where she was, and not to get up or think of doing so until the doctor had visited her, for there was nothing so repugnant to her mind at the moment as the idea of doing anything. She believed that she had breakfasted in a drowsy manner, and believed (with perfect truth) that she had gone to sleep again afterwards, for now the sunlight made a broad patch on the floor. Collecting her reasoning faculties, and remembering that her room looked due south, she arrived at the brilliant conclusion that the morning must have progressed towards noon. That seemed something of a discovery, and having arrived at that conclusion she went to sleep again.

She dreamed—the dream being about as vivid as her waking consciousness—that she was a chicken, and was being put up to auction in the operating theatre. Two bidders were interested in her, but they could not buy her till she awoke. One of the bidders was Jack, who stood on the left of her bed, the other the hospital doctor, on the right, before whose advent she was not allowed to get up. Then her dream was whisked off her brain in the manner of a blanket being pulled from her bed, and becoming wide awake, she was aware that this disconcerting dream was, as the retailers of incredible stories say, "largely founded on fact," for there was Jack on one side of her bed and Doctor Ashe on the other. They did not look like bidders at an auction at all, nor, as her waking consciousness assured her, did they look at all anxious. Doctor Ashe seemed to have said "Fine sleeper," and Jack, as Dodo opened her eyes, remarked rather ironically, so she thought, "Good afternoon, darling."

This annoyed her.

"Why afternoon?" she asked. "Don't be silly."

Then looking at the patch of sunlight again, which seemed the only real link with the normal world, she saw it had got narrow, and was on the other side of her bed.

"Very well then, it's afternoon," she said. "Why shouldn't it be? I never said it wasn't."

"Of course you didn't," said Jack in an absurdly soothing manner. "And now you'll have a talk with Dr. Ashe."

Dr. Ashe was not in need of great explanations, for being the hospital doctor, he was already in possession of the main facts of the case. For the last month Dodo had been increasingly irritable, and increasingly forgetful. He had urged her many times to go away and have a complete rest; he had warned her of the possible consequences of neglecting this advice, but she had scouted the idea of being in need of anything except strenuous employment. Then, only yesterday afternoon, she had suddenly fainted, and recovering from that had simply collapsed. She now accounted to Dr. Ashe for these unusual proceedings with great lucidity.

"I forgot about dinner," she said, "and that came on the top of my being rather tired. I only wanted a good night's rest, like everybody else, and I've had that. I'm quite well again. Who is attending to the stores?"

Dr. Ashe slid his hand on to her wrist.

"Oh, the stores are all right," he said guilefully. "You've had Sister Alice under you for a couple of months, and you've made her wonderfully competent. But for your own peace of mind I want you to answer me one question."

"Go ahead," said Dodo. "I hope it's not crashingly difficult."

"Not a bit. Supposing I told you to get up at once and go back to your work, do you feel that you would be able to get through a couple of hours of it? On oath."

Dodo thought over this, trying to imagine herself active. It was difficult to imagine anything, for she seemed incapable of picturing herself otherwise than lying in bed. Even then everything was dream-like; Dr. Ashe did not seem like a real person, and Jack, dream-like also, had merely melted away. She was only conscious, with a sense of reality, of an enormous lassitude and languor unlike anything she had previously experienced. Even the burden of answering a perfectly simple question was heavy. Every limb seemed weighted with lead, but the bulk of the lead had been reserved for her brain. She had to make an effort in order to answer at all.

"I'm not sure," she said, "because I feel so odd. But I think that if you told me to stand up I should fall down. I can't be certain; that's only what I think. What's the matter with me?"

A dream-like voice answered her.

"You've got what you asked for," it said. "You wouldn't take a holiday when you could, and now you've got to. You're just broken down."

This sounded so alarming that Dodo had to make a joke.

"I'm not going to break up, am I?" she asked.

"Of course you're not. Not a chance of it."

"What's to happen to me then?" she asked.

"You're to spend two or three days in bed," said he. "After that we'll consider. Limit yourself to that for the present."

Something inside Dodo approved strongly of that.

"That sounds quite nice," she said. "I shall sleep, and then I shall sleep, and then I shall sleep."

That anticipation proved to be quite correct. Dodo was roused for her meals, resented her toilet, and for the next forty-eight hours was either fast asleep or at the least dozing in a vacancy of brain that she found extremely pleasurable. At the end of that time she entered with zest into future plans with the doctor and Jack.

"You may leave out a rest-cure," she said, "because if you want me to stop in bed for a month I won't. I should hate it so much that I would take care that it shouldn't do me any good."

"It would be the best thing for you," said the doctor.

"Then you must choose the second best. It would make me ill to
stop in bed for a month, and so I should have to recover all over
again afterwards. Oh Jack, you owl, for God's sake tell me what I
do want, because I don't know. I know lots of things I don't want. I
don't want you, darling, because you would look anxious, and don't
want David, because I couldn't amuse him, and I certainly don't want
a nurse to blow my nose and brush my teeth and wash me."

Dodo sat up in bed.

"I'm getting brilliant," she said. "I am beginning to know what I
want. I want to go somewhere where there isn't anybody or anything.
Isn't there some place where there is just the sea——"

"A voyage?" asked Jack.

"Certainly not; because of submarines and being unwell. I should
like the sea to be there, but there mustn't be any bathing-machines,
and I should like a great flat place without any hills. The sea and a
marsh, and nobody and nothing. Isn't there an empty place anywhere?"

Dr. Ashe listened to this, watching her, with a diagnostic mind.

"Let's hear more about it," he said. "You don't want to be bothered
with anybody or anything. Is that it?"

Dodo's right arm lying outside the bedclothes suddenly twitched.

"Who did that?" she said. "Why doesn't it keep still? I've got the
jumps, and I want to be quiet. Can't either of you understand?"

"And you want to go somewhere empty and quiet?" asked Jack.

"Yes, I've said so several times. And I don't want to talk any more."

They left her alone again after this, and presently when they returned, it appeared that Jack had once spent a couple of weeks one
November at a small Norfolk village near the sea. The object of the
expedition had been duck-shooting, but as far as duck went, it had
been disappointing, for they usually got up a mile or two away, and
flew out to sea in a straight line with the speed of an express train
and never came back any more. But apart from duck, the village of
Truscombe had promising features as regarded their present requirements, for Jack was not able to recollect any feature of the slightest
interest about it. It squatted on the edge of marshes, there was the
sea within a mile of it; he supposed there were some inhabitants, for
there was a small but extremely comfortable inn. Now in July there
would not even be any intending duck-shooters there; it promised
to be an apotheosis of nothing at all.

Dodo roused herself to take an interest in this, as the colourless
account of it proceeded, and even under cross-examination Jack could
not recollect anything that marred the tranquillity of the picture. Yes,
there was a post-office where you could get a daily paper if you wanted
one, but on the other hand if you did not want one, he hastened to

add, you needn't; there was also a windmill, the sails of which were always stationary. There were no duck, there was no pier, there was no band, the nearest station was four miles away; really, in fact, there wasn't anything.

The lust for nothingness gleamed in Dodo's eyes.

"It sounds delicious," she said. "When may I go to Truscombe, Dr. Ashe?"

"Have a couple more days in bed," said he, "and then you can go as soon as you like, if you will promise not to make any exertion for which you don't feel inclined——"

"But that's why I'm going," she interrupted. "Telegraph to the inn, Jack, and engage me a couple of rooms—oh, my dear, I feel in my bones that Truscombe is just what I want. They will meet me at the station with a very slow old cab, or better still with a dog-cart. It sounds just precisely right. Shall I call myself Mrs. Dodo of London? It's all too blessed and lovely."

Three evenings later accordingly, Dodo arrived at Holt. She found a dog-cart waiting for her, exactly as she had anticipated, and a whisper of north wind off the sea. Her driver, a serene and smiling octogenarian began by talking to her for a little, and his conversation reminded her of bubbles coming up through tranquil water, as he asked her how the war was getting on. They didn't hear much about the war down at Truscombe, but the crops were doing well, though the less said about apples the better. After this information he sank into a calm sleep, and so did the pony which walked in its sleep.

As the vanished sun began to set the north-west sky on fire, this deliberate equipage emerged from the wooded inlands into flat and ample spaces that smouldered beneath an enormous sky. Across the open the sea gleamed like an indigo wire laid down as in some coloured map along the edge of the land, and a spiced and vivid savour which set the pony sneezing, awoke him, and with a toss of his head he began of his own accord to trot. In time that unusual motion aroused his driver, and they jogged along at a livelier pace. The air seemed charged with the very elixir of life; it was like some noble atmospheric vintage that enlightened the eye and set the pulses beating full and steady. Presently they came to the village with the brick-facings of the flint-built houses glowing in the last of the sunset and the night-stocks redolent in their gardens. To the left stretched vast water-meadows intersected with dykes where loose-strife and willow-herb smouldered among the tall grasses, and tasselled reeds gave harbourage to moor-hens. Out of all the inhabitants of Truscombe but one representative seemed to be in the street, and he slowly trundled a barrow in front of him and let it be known that he had fresh mackerel for sale. Short spells of walking alternated with longer sittings on the handle of his barrow, but whether he sat or whether he walked no one bought his mackerel.

The Laighton Arms stood on a curve of the sole street through the village, and Dodo entered as into a land full of promise. An old setter, lying in the passage thumped her a welcome with his tail, as if she was already a familiar and friendly denizen, just returning from some outing. She dined alone at a plain good hospitable board, and presently strolled out again through the front door that stood permanently open into an empty street. It was night now, and the sky was set with drowsy stars that glowed rather than sparkled, and up the street there flowed, not in puffs and gusts, but with the current of a slow moving tide the salt sweetness of the marshes and the sea. Very soon her strolling steps had carried her past the last houses, and in the deep dusk she stood looking out over the empty levels. A big grass-grown bank built to keep out high tides from the meadows zig-zagged obscurely towards the sea, and there was nothing there but the emptiness of the land and the star-studded sky. She waited just to see the moon come up over the eastern horizon and its light confirmed the friendliness of the huge solitude. Then returning, she found a candle set ready for her, which was a clear invitation to go to bed, and looking out below her blind she saw in front a stretch of low land with pools of water reflecting the stars. Six geese, one behind the other, like a frieze, were crossing it very slowly in the direction of the saltwater creek that wound seawards.

For the next week Dodo pursued complete and intentional idleness with the same zeal which all her life had inspired her activities. She got up very late after long hours of smooth deep sleep, and taking a book and a packet of sandwiches in her satchel strolled out along the bank to the ridge of loose shingle that ran east and west along the edge of the sea. At high tide the waves broke against this, and since walking along it was an exercise of treadmill laboriousness she was content to encamp there in some sunny hollow and laze the morning away. Sometimes, for form's sake, she opened her book, read a paragraph or two, wondered what it was about, and then transferred her gaze to the sea. An hour or so passed swiftly in stupefied content, and then shifting her position she probably lay down on her back. Bye and bye hunger dictated the consumption of her sandwiches, and refreshed and revived she would begin a pencilled note to Jack. But after a few words she usually found that she had nothing to say, and watched the sea-gulls (she supposed they were sea-gulls) that patrolled the edge of the breaking waves for food, and dived like cast plummets into the water. Then on the retreat of the tide, the ebb

disclosed stretches of hard sand tattooed with pebbles, where walking
was easy, and she would wander away towards the point of tumbled
sand-dunes that lay westward. A coast-guard station stood there,
brought into touch with the world by means of the row of telegraph-
posts that ran, mile after mile, straight as an arrow, along this shingle-
bank, which defended from the sea the miles of marshes and sand
flats which lay on the landward side of it. Through the middle of
them broadening into a glittering estuary when the tide was high ran
the river that debouched into the sea beyond the point; at low tide
it was but a runnel of water threading its way through the enormous
flatness of shoal and mud-bank where flocks of sea-birds hovered.

This great stretch of solitude attracted Dodo more even than the
familiar emptiness of the sea. Once across the bank of shingle the
sea was out of sight, and it lay spread out, this strange untrodden
wildness, wearing an aspect of hospitable loneliness, and sun-steeped
quiet. Narrow channels and meandering dykes, full at high tide and
empty at the ebb, zig-zagged about the marsh which was clad in unfamiliar vegetation. There were tracts waist-high in some stiff heather-
like growth, and between them lawns of sea-lavender now breaking
out into full flower, and above high-water mark clumps of thrift and
sea-campion and horned poppy. Overhead the gulls slid and chided,
balancing themselves on stiff pinions against the wind, or, relaxing
that tense bow of flight were swept away out of sight across the flats.
For miles there was but one house set on a spit of stony land, and
even that seemed an outrage against the spell of solitariness till Dodo
discovered that it was undwelled in, and therefore innocuous.

For half a dozen days it was enough for her to sit on the edge of
the shingle or stroll through the sea-lavender of the marshes, hardly
recording the sounds and the sights that made up the spell, but merely
lying open to the dew of their silent enchantments. Then, as her vigour
began to ooze into her like these tides that imperceptibly filled the
channels in the marshes, she extended her radius and came at last to
the sand-dunes that were clumped together like a hammer-head on
the shaft of the shingle-ridge. There the telegraph-posts took a right-
angled turn towards the mouth of the estuary, where there were signs
of inhabited places, shanties nestling in hollows, stranded ships made
fast with chains, with the washing a-flutter on their decks. Votaries
of solitude, botanists and ornithologists she was told, spent summer
weeks here, but she never saw petticoat or trouser. Probably they
too avoided the presence of others and sought refuge in the sand-
dunes when her fell form appeared, just as she herself would undoubtedly have done at a glimpse of a human creature. Here then, while
physically she inhaled the vitality that tingled in marsh and sea-beach
and lonely places, she spent long solitary hours, dozing among the

dunes, following the arrow flight of terns, wondering at the plants that seemed to draw nourishment from the barrenness of sand, and yet all the time pushing her roots, like them, into some underlying fertility.

She was almost sorry when her mind, stained deep with these indelible days of unrelieved hard work in her hospital, began to show signs of its own colour again. Mental fatigue, too, had stricken her with a far severer stroke than had been laid on her body, and it was with something of a shock that she began to be interested in her surroundings instead of merely observing them. What started this first striving occurred during a walk she took along the upper ridges of the beach outside the sand-dunes. There had been shrill scoldings and screamings in the air above her from certain sharp-winged birds which clearly resented her intrusion, and, at this moment, she had suddenly to check her foot and step sideways in order to avoid treading on a clutch of four eggs with brown mottled markings that lay on the protective colouring of the shingle. A couple of yards further on was another potential nursery, and soon she found that the whole of this ridge was a populous nesting-place. It was natural to connect these aerial screamings from the hundreds of birds that hovered above her with the treasures at her feet, and her interest as opposed to her contemplation awoke. Someone had told her that a very high tide in June had washed away the eggs of hundreds of sea-birds, and here they were again industriously raising a second brood. . . . Had there been, instead of birds, hundreds of human mothers and fathers yelling at her to take care not to tread on their babies, she would have fled from adults and infants alike. But, though still shunning her own kind, she adored these shy wild things that gabbled at her, and wondered what they were.

On her way home she noticed a crop of transparent erect stalks growing thickly from a mudbank. It looked like some emerald-green minute asparagus. Then what was the shrubby stiff-stemmed thing that seemed to imitate a Mediterranean heath? And a pink-streaked convolvulus that, behaving as no known convolvulus had ever behaved, flowered out of the sand? Really if you wanted to avoid human beings, it might be as well to make acquaintance with these silent companions of solitude. So thinking to start with a known specimen, she picked a sprig of sea-lavender, and stepped into a remarkably deep bog-hole. Thereupon her leg, as far as her knee, wore a shining stocking of rich black mud, and it was necessary to cross the bank of shingle, wash it in the sea, and leave the shoe to dry. For the sake of symmetry she pulled off the other shoe and stocking, and paddled about, rinsing out the mud in the tepid water.

Dodo spread the mired stocking out to dry on the pebbles, just out of reach of the crisply-breaking ripples. Then she saw a most marvellous, translucent pebble, orange-red in colour, just being sucked into the backwash of a wave. Then a small crab, truculent and menacing, sidled towards her, and the next wave rolled it over with gaping pincers, and returned the cornelian to her feet. An interesting piece of drift-wood demanded investigation, and a little further on she found a starfish which she threw back into the sea. Then she remembered her stocking and turned back. There was no sign of that stocking, but the other one and her two shoes were just recoverable from the edge of the incoming tide. With them in her hand she paddled homewards along the "liquid rims" of the sea.

That evening Dodo sent an immense telegram to her housekeeper in London for a standard book on British birds and another on British plants. These were to be despatched to her immediately, with some field-glass highly recommended for the observation of small distant objects. That done she spent a studious evening in planning out a scheme of study. She would take out with her in the morning the books on birds and flowers, and make a *cache* for them in the shrubby thing of which she would soon know the name. Then for two hours she would collect plants in the marsh, and, returning with her spoils, identify them in her book. After lunch she would take the book on birds to some commanding spot and bowl out the gulls with her field-glass and her authorities. There must be a note-book and a quantity of well-sharpened pencils. Two note-books, in fact, one for birds and one for botany.

Imperceptibly and instinctively after the start had been made Dodo began to run in the strenuous race again. She bought a bathing-dress and a morning paper at the post-office and some bull's-eyes, and there arrived for her an admirable field-glass of German manufacture, with a copy of Bleichroder's "Birds of Great Britain" in six volumes and Kuhlmann's "English Botany" in eight. She was rather shocked at this exhibition of Hun industry, but speedily got over it, and drove down to the sea with these treasures and the key of a bathing-hut which she proposed to convert into a library. With the help of Bleichroder's "Birds," and Zeiss's field-glass she was almost certain that she saw a golden eagle and a hoopoe (those rare visitors to Norfolk), of which she made an entry with a query in the ornithological note-book. Then she bathed and then she had lunch, and then, after smoking four cigarettes, she went to sleep in the shadow of the library and had an uneasy dream about Berlin. After that she botanised: the heathery-looking shrub proved to be "shrubby sea-blite," and she duly noted its name in the botany note-book. Then there was orache and thrift, and sea-campion and stinking Archangel (this was thrilling) to be noted

down, and then, returning to the birds, she put down tern, and great
black-backed gull, and ringed plover and sparrow (probably Tree).
Subsequently she crossed out the golden eagle and the hoopoe, for it
was hardly possible that her first glance through her Zeiss should have
revealed a couple of such distinguished visitors. Of course, it was possible that she had seen them, since the possible could be stretched to
any degree of elasticity, but it was better to be cautious and wait for
further appearances before astounding the entire world of ornithologists.

Dodo took a volume of Bleichroder's "Birds" back to her hotel that
night, leaving the rest of the library in the bathing-hut. It contained
admirable pictures, but what really struck her most about those pictures
was the vivid resemblance between the birds which they portrayed
and human beings. The Shoveller, especially with the addition (lightly
pencilled and then erased) of spectacles looked precisely like Dr. Ashe,
while Richardson's Skua without any addition at all recalled Edith
with extraordinary vividness. She wondered who Richardson was; if
he had sent in his card just then, she would have been entranced to
have a talk to him about his Skua. She wondered also how they were
all getting on at Winston that evening; she wondered if Jack had got
back from France, if David was asleep, if Edith was composing an
unrivalled symphony, if Lord Ardingly was meditating on the duties
of the upper classes towards the lower. . . . And then she became
aware that the human race was beginning to interest her again. Up
till now she had, at the most, been concerned with star-fish and terns
and shrubby sea-blite, things that touched her mind impersonally. Now
she began to picture herself shewing these pleasant creatures to a person
of some sort; she imagined herself directing David's field-glasses towards Richardson's Skua. When he had seen it, they would restore
Bleichroder's monumental work to the shelf in the sea-library and
go to bathe.

Suddenly the thought of the three weeks more which she had promised to spend here became intolerable, if she had to stay here alone.
The hotel was quite empty, save for herself and her maid, and why
should not her beloved David come straight here for a week when
his term was over? A telegram in the morning would settle that, and
if Jack was home from France, he could easily run over for next Sunday.
She would continue this rest-cure just as before; in fact, if somebody
didn't come down she would get bored with it to-morrow or the next
day, and undo all the good that it had brought her. Sea-blite and
skuas had helped her enormously, but their efficacy would begin to
wane if now she could not shew them to somebody. She had shewn
a piece of sea-blite to her maid, and told her how very local it was,

but Miss Henderson had replied in an acid voice, "It looks to me quite like a common weed, my lady. . . ."

Somewhere down the street a gramophone was jigging out a lively tune, and Dodo stole forth, making a pretext to herself that she wanted to observe the stars of which there was a great number to-night, but she knew that she longed to be near human movement again. A rhythmical thump accompanied the gramophone's shrillness, and she wondered if there might happen to be a little dancing going on. She soon localised the sound; there was a room facing the street with curtains discreetly drawn, so as to conform with the lighting order, but the thump of feet went gaily on inside. She forgot about the stars; they belonged to that steadfast imperishable thing called Nature that could be appealed to when you were tired. A dance to the wheezings of a gramophone, with the handsome girls of the village and the boys back on leave from France had become far more enthralling than Bleichroder's "Birds" lying open on her table in the inn, or the wheeling heavens above her. There she lingered, rather like the Ancient Mariner without a wedding-guest to whom she might soliloquise.

Jack arrived on Saturday night, and next morning Dodo seemed to feel that what she called a "picnic-service" on the beach would be rather a treat instead of going to church. Accordingly they took out a Bible and Prayer Book, and Dodo, whose bent was not strictly ecclesiastical, read a quantity of chapters out of Ecclesiastes for a first lesson and for a second lesson the chapter out of Corinthians which the Church had mistakenly appointed for Quinquagesima. Then she read the twenty-third Psalm, and rapidly turned over the next leaves.

"There's at least one more," she said, "and I can't find it. It's about the House of Defence and the satisfaction of a long life."

"Try the ninety-first," said Jack.

"Darling, how clever of you. I never had a head for numbers. After that we'll talk; I'm beginning to want to talk dreadfully."

Dodo read her psalms quite beautifully, and lay back on the warm shingle.

"Oh, Jack, I feel so clean and washed," she said. "These weeks which I've had quite alone have been like a lovely cold bath on a hot day, or, if you like, a lovely hot bath after a cold day. I'm beginning to see what they have done for me, besides resting me. I think people and things are meant to cure each other."

"How?" asked Jack.

"Well, take my case. I was absolutely Fed Up with people, human beings, when I came here. You see, ill human beings are concentrated human beings. All the material side of them is exaggerated; you only think of them as bones to be mended and flesh to be healed. My soul got so sick of them, and when I came here I wanted never to see anybody again. Nor did I want to think any more; that I suppose was mere fatigue. The whole caboodle—living, I mean—wasn't worth the bother it gave one. Are you following, darling, or are you only thinking about those pebbles which you are piling so beautifully on the top of each other?"

"Not on the top of *each* other," remarked Jack. "Otherwise——"

"Oh, don't be grammatical. On the top of *each* other."

"I'm following," said Jack.

"Very well. So I took the lid off my brain, let the stuffy air escape, and let in the wind and the sea. Now don't say 'water on the brain,' because it isn't true. It just lay open, and then after a time the sea-gulls and—and I've forgotten the name of the blighted thing, and that reminds me that it's sea-blite—the sea-gulls and the sea-blite got in; I think the gulls nested in the blite. So I got interested in them, but still I didn't want to see a single soul, not even you and David. But I sent for enormous books on birds and botany, and you'll find them in my bathing-hut with the bill: unpaid. Those jolly insolent things, going where they chose and growing where they chose healed me of people-sickness. They didn't care, bless them, if a convoy of wounded came in, or if nobody loved me. One of them squawked, and the other pricked my large ankles."

Dodo sat up.

"Yes, what made me want to see you and David again," she said, "was a course of sea-blite and Richardson's skuas. That's what I mean by people and things healing each other. I think I shall go back to Winston to-morrow."

"If I thought you meant that," said he, "I should tell you that you would do nothing of the sort."

Dodo looked wildly round.

"Oh, don't tell me that!" she said, "or out of pure self-willed vitality I should do it."

"Very well; you will go back to Winston to-morrow," said Jack.

"That's sweet of you; now I shan't. I think if Sister Ellen came and asked me if the seven-tailed bandages had arrived, I should gibber in her face. She hasn't got a face, by the way, she has only two profiles. How funnily people are made! She's got two profiles and no face, and David has got a duck of a face and no profile: just the end of his nose comes out of a round, plump cheek. I wish I was eleven years old again. I wish I was a cat with nine lives, or is it tails? Seven lives, isn't it? Or is seven rather too many? How many lives do you want, Jack? Choose!"

Jack threw down his beautiful tower of stones.

"Oh, this one will do," he said. "This and the next. If I must choose, I choose whatever happens. I might spoil everything by choosing."

"But if you could have your life over again, wouldn't you choose that many things should be different?" she asked.

"I don't think so. If things had been different, they wouldn't be as they are at this moment. You and me."

Dodo laid her hand on his.

"My dear, are you content?" she asked.

His eyes answered her.

11

It was within ten days of the completion of the fourth year of the war, and since the spring every morning had brought an extra turn of the screw, tightening a little more and again a little more the tension of the final and most desperate campaign of all. Late in March there had opened the last series of the furious German offensives, any one of which, it seemed, might have battered its way through to Paris or the Channel ports. Day by day territory captured by the enemy in their first irresistible invasion of French soil, and won back yard by yard in three and a half years of warfare, had been passing behind the German lines again. Once more the Germans advancing in that grim dance of death as in some appalling quadrille had taken Peronne, had taken Bailleul, had swarmed up over Kemmel Hill, had recaptured Soissons, had broken across the Marne. All that could be said was that neither materially nor psychically had the tension quite reached breaking-point. No irremediable breach in the lines had been made, and there was still enough spirit left in the nation to shout over the glorious adventure of Zeebrugge. Finally the counter-offensive of the Allies had begun, and to-day Jack brought to Winston, where the hospital was crammed to overflowing, the news that the Germans had been forced to retreat over the Marne again.

Dodo had entirely refused to learn any sort of lesson from her breakdown, and for the last two years had taken no further holiday beyond an occasional day off when David was at home from school, or a flying expedition to the hospital in London. But instead of being "served out" for her obstinacy, she had remained a glorious testimony of the health-giving properties of continuous over-work, and had shewn not the faintest signs of another collapse. Jack, the matron, the doctor, had all done their best to induce her to be more sensible without the slightest success, and to-day she was lucidly explaining to her husband how wrong they had all been and why.

"The only thing that really can tire one is thinking," she said, "and since I came back from Truscombe two years ago, I haven't thought for two minutes. My mind has been like a 'painted ship upon a painted ocean,' and very badly painted too. That's why I'm the life and soul of the party; I have become like one of the cheerful beasts that perish and I have thought as little about the war as about astronomy. It didn't occur to any of you that it wasn't the acting of silly charades or the ordering of aspirin or the giving out of bandages and books that made me collapse: it was letting my mind dwell on the reason for which I was doing it. But if you will only become a machine, as I have, and go on doing things without thinking why, they are as effortless as breathing. I shall never get out of the groove now, you know: I shall go on counting blankets and going to bed at eleven, and getting up at seven, till the end of my life. My dear, what did we all do before the war? The only effort I ever make is trying to remember that, and I never succeed. I think we talked, just talked. Precisely what I'm doing now, by the way. But I used to be an agreeable rattle, such clever chatter, God forgive me!"

Jack began to laugh.

"Go on; rattle!" he said.

"I couldn't. If you rattle you have to say anything that comes into your head, and try to think what it means afterwards. It was the old style of conversation which I invented when I was young. Nowadays I mean something first and say it afterwards. At least I do sometimes. When the war is over I shall become a Delphic oracle."

"Do! How will you set about it?" he asked.

"I shall advertise in the Personal Column of the *Times,* for some retired oracle who will give me lessons. Besides, when once you get the reputation of being an oracle you have only got to say nothing at all, and everyone says how extraordinarily wise you are. Rich silences. Such nonsense!"

"I thought you were going to stop in your groove and give out blankets and aspirin," said Jack. "I was looking forward to a remarkable old age."

Dodo looked round her on the quiet familiar scene. She had strolled out across the park to meet her husband, and they had sent the motor on with his luggage and had sauntered home through the woods. At the edge of them, when they had come within sight of the house, stately and sunny below them, with the Red Cross flag drooping on its staff, they had sat down in the shade before facing the heat of the open ground now yellowed and parched by three months of strong heat. Even in the middle of summer the beeches were already tinged with gold; now and then a leaf dropped from its withered stem, and came spinning down through the windless air.

"Oh, don't let us be remarkable whatever we are," said she. "Let us go gently Darby-and-Joaning it down the hill, Jack, and watch David skipping about. He got swished the other day at Eton—oh, I promised not to tell you!"

"Go on, then," said Jack.

"Well, I've done it now. He made a book on the Derby, or whatever did duty for the Derby last month, and won thirty shillings, so he considered it well worth it. He bought me a delicious little mother-of-pearl box out of his winnings, which came to bits at once. Then, when he was caught, he had to return his winnings, so the poor darling was out of pocket!"

"So you sent him a tip," remarked Jack.

"Naturally; that's all by the way. But it really does worry me to wonder what we shall all do when the war is over. Personally I shall be extremely cross and bored; I know I shall, and yet it will be very odd of me. Considering that there is nothing that I have really wanted for the last four years, except the end of the war, it seems rather strange that I should miss it, the great brutal, bloody monster. I would give literally anything in the world except you and David and a few trifles of that sort, if it would stop this minute, and if it did I—I should yawn. And the thought of beginning other things again would make me feel lazy. But I daresay I shall be dead long before that. Gracious me, Jack, what was my life before the war? If you had to write my biography, you could only say that I rattled. I suppose that has been my profession, while yours has been to listen to me without ever really wanting to divorce me. But I never talked in my sleep; there's that to be said for me. You do: last time you were here you woke me by calling out, 'Sickle-hocked: take it away.' "

"The further the better," said Jack.

Dodo wrinkled up her eyes as she looked out over the hot, bright noon.

"All the same I had a very good mare once that was sickle-hocked," she said. "I called her 'Influenza,' so that I shouldn't get it and she had rather long eyes like Nadine. Oh, Jack, I quite forgot to tell you. I had a joyous telegram from Nadine to say that Hughie had crashed out in France, and had broken his arm. She was pleased."

"But why?" asked he.

"Darling, you are dull. He's safely tucked up in hospital and with any luck he will be transferred to town. Isn't it lovely for her? He won't be able to fly again for months."

Dodo gave an awful groan.

"Oh, I'm thinking about the war," she said. "What are we coming to? Here are Nadine and I simply delighted because Hughie's broken his arm. That's singular, you know, if you come to think of it. We hope it will take a long time to mend, so that he won't be able to fly again yet."

"Perhaps he won't be wanted to," said Jack.

"Why?"

Jack lit a cigarette, and with the flaring match burned a withered beech-leaf that had fallen on the turf without replying.

"I don't want to say too much," he began at length.

"Darling, you're not saying anything at all at present," said she.

"I know. Perhaps it's best not to. Besides, you don't want to hear about the war."

Dodo waved her hands wildly.

"But get on," she said. "You speak as if there's something good to be heard. What do you mean? As if I wouldn't give my—my shell-like ears to hear something good. My dear, the number of times I've chucked the paper away because the headlines only said, 'New German offensive. Slight loss of ground near Parlez-vous.' Go on, Jack, or I shall burst."

"Well, do you know anything about the position on the west front?" asked he.

"Nothing whatever. I only know it's a beastly front."

Jack took his stick and drew a long line with two bulges in it on the short turf.

"That lower bulge is the Marne," he said, "and the upper one is round about Amiens."

"Where one has coffee on the way to Paris," said Dodo breathlessly.

"Yes. They battered away at the Marne bulge, and have now had to go back. Then they battered alternately at the Amiens bulge, and it isn't bulging any worse. There was no earthly reason why the Huns shouldn't have walked straight through to Abbeville, which is there, last week. They meant to give us a knock-out in one place or the other. But—how shall I explain it?"

"Anyhow," said Dodo.

Jack clenched his fist and drew back his arm.

"Well, I'm the Hun," he said, "and it's a boxing match. Your chin there, darling, is quite defenceless, and I can knock you out, if I have enough weight behind me to give you a good punch. But I haven't; it looks as if I was exhausted. I can just advance my arm like that, but I can't hit. You're rather done, too, but you can just grin at me, and wait till you get stronger. But I shan't get stronger; I'm fought out."

Dodo put up her hands to her forehead.

"But ever since March we've been thrust back and back," she said.

"Yes. And now we're going to begin."

Dodo made a wild gesticulation in the air.

"I won't think about it," she said. "You must remember the idea of the Russian steam-roller, and the Queen Elizabeth steaming up the Dardanelles. Oh, Jack! It's a trick! They're going to break through in Kamkatka or somewhere and I won't think about that either. We've got to go pounding along, and not attend to what is happening. I want a map, though. Do be an angel, and get me an enormous map with plenty of flags and pins and I'll hang it up in the dining-room. One may as well be ready, and you have to order things long before you want them. Jack, if you were obliged to bet when the war would be over, obliged I mean, because I should cut your throat if you refused, when would you say? Name the day, darling!"

"Can't," said he.

"Don't be so ridiculous. Name the year then. Or the century."

"Nineteen hundred and eighteen," said he.

"Pish!"

"Very well, pish," said Jack.

Suddenly Dodo's mouth began to tremble.

"Jack, you're not playing the fool, are you?" she said. "Do you mean that?"

"I do. There's a man called Foch. And there are a million Americans now in France. An Australian boy the other day told me that they are rather rough fighters."

"Bless them!" said Dodo.

"By all means. Now don't build too much on it. It's only what some people think."

"I won't think about it. But I want a map. Gracious, it means a lot to want a map again. I got an atlas August four years ago and coloured Togoland red."

Dodo sniffed the air.

"I really believe I can smell greens cooking for dinner," she said. "And I certainly can see a lot of those boys in blue suits, moving about on the lawn like ants. That's all I must think about. But do you know what I'm stopping myself from thinking about? Don't laugh when I tell you. David's thirteen, you know, and in four years from now——"

For quite a long time Jack didn't laugh. . . .

Dodo got what she described as a life-size map of France, and an immense quantity of pins to which were attached cardboard flags of the warring nations. The map was put up at one end of the men's dining-room practically covering the wall, and morning by morning, standing on a stepladder, she gleefully recorded the advance of the Allies, and the retreat of the Huns, in accordance with the information conveyed by the daily *communiqué*.

"Amiens!" she said. "We must take out all those German flags and put English ones in instead. We shall be able to get coffee again there on the way to Paris, unless the Huns have poisoned all the supplies in the refreshment room, which is more than probable, and put booby-traps in the buns, so that they explode in your mouth. Look! A German flag has fallen out of Bapaume all of its own accord; that's a good omen, it's hardly worth while putting it back. Isn't it a blessing we've got more French flags? Now we can make Soissons a pin-cushion of them. But it's a long way to Berlin yet. I believe you'll have to join up, David, before we get there. Why not make a betting-book about the date we get to Berlin? Oh, there's a place called Burchem; what an extraordinary coincidence. Give me some more American pins."

Through August the advance continued, sweeping on during September back through Peronne, and through the Drocourt-Quéant line, until late in the month the Hindenburg line was broken, and Dodo pulled out the most stubborn of all the rows of German pins.

" 'All according to plan,' as the German *communiqué* tells us," she said. "What a good thing their plans coincide so exactly with ours! They didn't want to hold the Hindenburg line any longer. They had got tired of being so long in one place and thought they would like a change, and by the greatest good luck we agreed that a change would be nice for them. That's all that's happened: they had been abroad for four years, and it was high time to think of getting home. What liars! My dear, what liars. Presently they will get tired of being in Cambrai, and so, according to plan, they will leave that. I should love to be the German Emperor for precisely five minutes to see what he feels like. Then I would be myself again, and gloat. Wanted on the telephone, am I? Nobody must touch those pins. I must put every one of them in myself. To-morrow I will be unselfish and let somebody else do it, but not to-day. Just according to plan!"

October came and flung a flaming torch among the beeches, and the thick dews brought out the smell of autumn and dead leaves in the woods and meadows. Once for two days a gale from the south-west roared through the grey rainy sky, strewing the lawn with the wreck of the woodland, but when that was past the weather became crystal clear again, with days of warm windless sun, and evenings that grew chilly and mornings when the hoar-frost lay white on the grass. Cambrai was regained and the British armies marched back into Le Cateau of evil memory, and the French flag flew once more over Laon. The tide of victory swept too along the Channel, and before the end of the month the waters of freedom washed the whole Belgian coast clean of the dust of its defilement. And not along the French front alone was heard the crash of the ruinous fortress of the Huns, nor there alone leaped the flames that rose ever higher round the crumbling walls of their monstrous Valhalla, shining brighter as the dusk deepened to night in the halls of their War God. For to the east Damascus had fallen; nearer at hand Bulgaria lay like a cracked and rotten nut, black and shattered; the Italian armies recrossed the Piave and on the last day of the month the Allied Fleet steamed through the Dardanelles past silent guns and deserted bastions to receive the surrender of the Turks. For four years of war the grim tower of Central Europe had stood firm: now as its outlying forts surrendered it shook to its foundations, the fissures widened in its tottering walls, and the dusk gathered.

It tottered, and with a crash a wall fell in, for in the first days of November, Austria surrendered, and at Kiel the German sailors mutinied. Two days later full powers were given by the Versailles Conference to Marshal Foch (of whom Dodo had now heard) to treat with the German envoys who came to sue for an armistice. And next day Sedan fell to the Americans.

"Sedan was rather a favourite town with the Huns till just now," said Dodo, as she dropped the German pin on the floor and made an American porcupine of the place. "Now they won't like it quite so much, and I'm sure I don't wonder. What did the cocks say in Sedan when they woke up the hens in Sedan this morning? Nobody can guess, so I'll tell you. They said, 'Yankee-doodle-doo. Amen.' Give me some more American pins! Yankee——"

She gave a loud squeal.

"I've put an American pin into my finger instead of into Sedan," she said. "I want a disinfectant and a sterilised bandage, and some more pins. Look, I've shed my blood on the French front. Give me a wound stripe and a Sedan chair, and let me try to be sensible. It won't be any good, but we may as well try."

Dodo had arranged a week ago to run up to London on November the ninth, because David was coming up from Eton on leave that day to see a dentist, and because Monday had been notified to her as a day of inspection for the hospital at Chesterford House: it must therefore be distinctly understood that the fall of Sedan and the powers granted to Marshal Foch had nothing to do with the date of this expedition. The visit to the London hospital had to be made, and if David was coming up on the ninth, it was indicated, with the force of a providential leading, that she should amalgamate these two events into one visit. Saturday afternoon, when the dentist was numbered with past pains, should be given to David; Sunday would be Sunday, and she would get back to Winston on Monday night. David would see his dentist in the morning, and Dodo accordingly left the house early, before the paper had come in, so that she would be ready for him by lunch time in London. That day the German envoys were to be received by Marshal Foch, who would hand them—so it was understood—the terms on which Germany would be granted an armistice. It was believed also that if the terms were accepted, the armistice would come into force on the morning of the eleventh. The terms, whatever they were, had been agreed upon by the Versailles Conference earlier in the week. . . .

David appeared soon after Dodo had reached Chesterford House.

"Oh, it was too exciting," he said. "I had gas, mummie, wasn't it grand? They put a cage over my mouth, and I began to get buzzy in my head, and then before I got really buzzy I was all bloody instead and the beastly thing was gone. It was like a conjuring trick, and the Emperor has given up, and I am so hungry. Look where it came out."

"Darling, what's happened to the Emperor?" she asked.

"Resigned, whatever they call it. Look at the hole."

David opened his mouth to the widest.

"I never saw such a big hole," said Dodo. "But where did you hear about the Emperor?"

"On a news-board. May we have lunch? And what shall we do all this afternoon? I needn't go back till the six o'clock from Paddington. Has it stopped bleeding?"

The terms of the armistice were accepted, and at eleven o'clock on Monday morning the roar of cannon and moan of shells, which for more than four years had boomed and wailed without intermission over Europe, were still. The news of that, and the silence of it, came with a reverberation as stunning as had been the first shock of war; even as England breathed one long sigh of relief to know that her honour had demanded war, so now, silent for a moment, she sighed as she put back in its scabbard the sword that her honour had drawn. Then she proceeded to celebrate the event.

Dodo was not so foolish as to struggle against the invincible, and with greater wisdom sent a long telegram to Winston announcing that she was unavoidably detained in London that night. That was quite true, for the necessity of being here, in the hub of all things, was inexorable. To see the streets and the crowds to-night, to hear the shouting, to be one with the biggest mass of people that could be found, was as imperative as breathing. Nadine rang her up on the telephone and asked her to dine and look at the crowds, and she said she was dining with Edith. Edith rang her up and suggested looking at the crowds, and she said she was dining with Nadine. Jack, who had come up that day, proposed a window at the Marlborough Club, for there was certain to be a demonstration opposite, and she said she was dining with Edith and Nadine. A further enquiry came from a place where the biggest crowds were expected, as to whether she was up in town, and she said she was at Winston, and almost curtsied to the telephone. Having told so many lies, nothing else mattered, and after eating a poached egg she went quite mad, put on a mackintosh and an old large hat and sneaked off from the house into the streets, forgetting to take a latch-key, but remembering to take a quantity of small change. She wanted only to be in the crowd and of the crowd and not to be shut up in the window of a club, decorously watching its passage, but to be merged in it, to get shoulder to shoulder with it, to look into its heart.

Hyde Park Corner was in flood; from the gate of her house to St. George's on one side and to the top of Constitution Hill on the other, pavements and roadway seethed with the glad huddle of humanity. Here and there was a motor or an omnibus quite unable to move forward through the crowd, being used as a vantage point for those who wanted to see more. There was a taxi just opposite her gate; half a dozen folk were sitting on the roof of it, two more were by the driver, and were in charge of the horn. . . . During the day an attempt had been made to scrape the obscuring paint off the street lamps, and something of the old warm glow of London diffused itself over the long-darkened ways. Everywhere were vendors of festive apparatus, and Dodo instantly bought balls of coloured paper ribands which shot out in an agreeable curve when you projected them, and whistles, and a small lead phial which she incautiously uncorked, and which instantly discharged a spray of odious scent into her face.

"Born from the dregs of the people," she thought exultantly to herself. . . .

There were two strong tides at the corner, one setting towards Constitution Hill, the other flowing along Piccadilly. Dodo meant to go along Piccadilly, but she got into the other tide, and after a vain attempt to extricate herself, was swept along by it. It was running so strongly that it was surely going towards some place of importance, and then she suddenly remembered that at the bottom of the hill lay Buckingham Palace. That would do excellently; and as she got near it, above the chatter and songs of the crowd there rose a long, continuous roar of shouting voices. Quite helpless in this great movement, she was cast

forth upon the steps of the Victoria monument, and there in front
of her was a row of lighted windows with a balcony, and the silhouette
of heads and shoulders against the light. The shouting had collected
itself into singing now, a certain rhythm directed it, and a kind of
fugual chorus was in progress, some singing one line of the National
Anthem, and some another, and stopping every now and then to cheer.
"Frustrate their knavish tricks," shouted Dodo at the top of her voice,
and then being very hoarse she blew piercingly on her whistle.

The tide swept her off again into the comparative gloom and quiet
of the Mall, but the roar of the streets and their illumination increased
as the crowd flowed up between St. James's Palace and Marlborough
House. She got into the stream which flowed along the south side of
Pall Mall, noticed Jack at the window of his club, and tried to attract
his attention with as much success as if she had attempted to signal
to the man in the moon. She passed Edith, who, jammed in the crowd
along the north side, was passing in the reverse direction; and they
screamed pleasantly at each other, but were powerless to approach,
and away she went up Regent Street into the central Babel of all London
in Piccadilly Circus. Here like a leaf in some resistless eddy of bright
eyes and shouting mouths she was trundled helplessly up the Quadrant,
till at length, spent and breathless, she was cast out again, jetsam from
that wonderful tide, into a backwater in Vigo Street, where voluntary
movement was once more possible. What the time was she had no
idea; she scarcely knew even who she herself was except in so far
that she was just one drop of hot victorious English blood that flowed
through the heart of London.

She made her way through the deserted streets of Mayfair into Park
Lane, and finding she had left her latch-key at home, rang for a long
time before she could get the door opened to her. When she succeeded
it was still necessary to establish her identity. . . .

Dodo found that it was already half-past two. Outside the streets
were beginning to grow empty, and the crowd surfeited with rejoicing,
was moving homewards. And then, all at once, a wave of reaction,
as irresistible as the wave of exultation had been, swept over her.
The war was done, and the victory was gained, and along the thousand
miles of battle fronts no gun that night boomed into the stillness, no
shell screamed along its death-bearing way. Since the news had arrived
no thought but that had visited her. She had burned in the glorious
fire of sheer exultant thanksgiving. Now, as she undressed, her thoughts
turned from the past and the present towards the future. There would
be no more convoys of wounded arriving at Winston; there would
be no more pinning up the record of the advancing Allied Armies.
In a few weeks or at the utmost in a few months the wards would

be empty, and the work which had occupied her to the exclusion of all that had made her life before would be finished. The smell of iodoform and Virginian tobacco would fade from the house; there would be no beds along the drawing-room walls, and no temperature charts hanging above the beds. There would be no more anxiety about the men who lay there, no repression of the rowdy, no encouragement of the despondent, no soothing of pain, no joy in recovery, no watching of the wounded creeping back into vigour again, no despair at seeing others lose their hold on life. Now that the four years of war, intense and absorbing with all their heart-breaks and exultations, were over, they seemed to have passed like the short darkness of a summer night, and here was day dawning again. What would fill the empty hours of it? . . .

The reaction passed, though the question remained unsolved, and once more Dodo recollected the stupendous event that had sent the millions of London shouting along the streets. And then her eyes, bright with excitement, grew dim with a storm of sudden tears.

12

Dodo went back to Winston on the morning after her night out, and had a second celebration of the armistice there. A gardener remembered that there was a quantity of fireworks, procured in pre-war days for some garden-fête, slumbering in a tool-house, and she arranged that there would be an exhibition of these on the lawn, under the direction of a convalescent patient who had embraced a pyrotechnical career before he became a gunner.

As an exhibition of smoke and smell these fireworks which had become damp and devitalised were probably unrivalled in the history of the art. Faint sparks of flame appeared from time to time through the dense and pungent clouds that enveloped the operator: Roman candles played cup and ball on a minute scale with faintly luminous objects; Catherine-wheels incapable of revolution spat and spluttered; rockets climbed wearily upwards for some ten feet and then expired with gentle sighs, and Bengal fires smouldered like tobacco. Very soon nothing whatever could be seen of the display through the volumes of smoke which completely shrouded the lawn, and all that could be heard was the convulsive coughing of the asphyxiated gunner, who emerged with streaming eyes and said if being gassed was anything like that he would sooner be wounded ten times over. He was sorry that he had been absolutely unable to stop there any longer, but before rescuing himself had lit a remaining half-dozen of rockets, and a fuse attached to a square box called a "mine" of which he knew nothing whatever, and hoped less. He had hardly explained this when the mine went off with an explosion that caused all the windows to rattle, and a couple of rockets shot up to a prodigious height and burst in showers of resplendent stars. Half an hour later, a policeman groped his way up to the hospital through the fumes, and having ascertained that there had been fireworks, felt himself obliged to report the occurrence to a local tribunal, and Dora fined Dodo fifty pounds. Altogether it was a joyful though an expensive evening.

It had been arranged by the military authorities that the private hospitals should first be evacuated now that the stream of wounded no longer poured into England from across the Channel, and gradually as the patients at Winston were discharged, the wards began to empty. Dodo resorted to all possible means to keep her hospital full. She besieged the War Office with such importunity that, had she been a widow, she must surely have had her request granted her; she threatened, flattered, and complained about the management of the Red Cross, she even considered the possibility of suborning an engine-driver of a Red Cross train going to York or some northern depôt, to bring his waggons to a standstill at the station for Winston, and then go on strike. Thus the wounded must be conveyed somewhere, and as the train could not proceed, it would be necessary to bring them to Winston, and had strikes then been as popular as they soon became, this brilliant plan might possibly have succeeded. As it was, she saw her beloved establishment growing emptier and emptier every week; there were no more operations to be performed, so the surgeon went back to his practice in Harley Street; all but one of the staff of nurses departed to get married or take up the normal threads of life again, stretchers stood in disconsolate heaps in the passages, bedding and bedsteads, drugget, tables and bath-chairs were put into lots for sale, the big ward was closed, and the beflagged pins so gleefully stuck into the map of France fell out one by one on to the floor, and were swept up by the housemaid. Soon there were but half a dozen men left in the whole place and these, like the little nigger-boys, vanished one by one. The gramophones grew mute, the smell of Virginian tobacco grew faint, nobody banged doors any more or played "There's a Little Grey Home in the West" on the cracked piano, hour by hour with one finger and a wrong note coming after a pause always in precisely the same place. Finally one man alone remained, who had missed his train and had to stop till the next morning. He tried that evening with very small success to teach Dodo a game of cards called "Snick," and she with even less success tried to entertain him with agreeable conversation. Under this enchantment he grew ever more morose, and when she could think of nothing more to say, a long silence fell, which was broken by his remarking, "Gawd, this place gives a man the hump!". . . With that heartfelt ejaculation he shuffled up to bed, and was gone next morning before Dodo came down. The hospital fizzled out, like an oil-less lamp; it ceased to flame, the wick smouldered a little and then expired.

Dodo had, rather mistakenly, arranged to remain here for a couple of days after everyone had gone, in order to taste the sweets of leisure in a place where she had been so absorbingly occupied, for she hoped that this would draw the fullest flavour out of the sense of having nothing to do. From habit she awoke early, and tried to cajole herself into imagining how delicious it was to stop in bed, instead of getting up and going down to her business-room. It was a dark, chilly morning, and she heard the sleet tattoo on her window-panes; how cold the business-room would be, and how warm she was below her quilt. Instead of arising and shivering, she would doze again, and tell her maid to light a fire in her bedroom before she got up. Then, instead of dozing, she made lazy plans for the day; after breakfast she would read the paper, and then, not stirring from the fireside, would go on with that extremely amusing French book which made Jack say "Pish!" and throw it into the waste-paper basket, from which Dodo had rescued it. After lunch, fine or not, she would go for a ride, and stop out just as long as she chose, instead of hurrying back to duties that no longer existed, and she would have tea in her bathroom, and lie there hotly soaking, and she would go to sleep before dinner, and have a quail and some caviare and a hothouse peach and half a bottle of champagne and then she would finish her book, go to bed early and go on reading when she got there. There was nobody except herself to please, and nothing to do except exactly that which she chose to do. To-morrow morning Jack arrived, and the day after they would go up to town together. Chesterford House had also been evacuated a week ago and by this it should have resumed its usual appointments.

Dodo (though with slight internal misgivings) was so anxious to begin enjoying herself by doing nothing at all that she rang for her maid and got up. It was a perfect day for thinking how comfortable it was by the fire, for outside the wind screamed and scolded, and the sleet had turned to snow. She was rather glad to find that there was nothing of the smallest interest in the paper, for that made it more imperative to throw it away, put her feet on the fender and smoke one cigarette after another. "Too heavenly," she thought to herself. "I could sit and toast myself for days and days. I haven't got to give out bandages, nobody is going to have an operation, I haven't got any letters to write, and if I had I shouldn't write them. How wise I was to stop here and be lazy. The luxury of it!"

The house was perfectly quiet; how often she had longed for an hour's quiet during these last years, for the gramophone to be mute, and the piano to be silent, for the cessation of steps and whistling everlastingly passing down the corridor outside her door! Now she had got it, and she tried hard to appreciate it. No one could possibly come to interrupt her, no one wanted her, she had leisure to amuse herself and taste the joys of a complete holiday. So she made up the fire and got her French book which she need not begin reading till she felt disposed. But she opened it, skimmed a page or two, and thought that Jack was really rather prudish. She would have argued with him about it if he had been here. Then the clock on her mantelpiece struck the hour, which she was surprised to find was only eleven, when she had imagined it was twelve. All the better; there was an extra hour of doing nothing.

The snow had ceased, and a patch of pale sunlight brightening the floor brought her to the window. There had been no heavy fall, but it still lay smooth and white on the broad gravel path and the lawn, for no footsteps that morning had trodden it. Just about a year ago there had been a similar fall, and by the middle of the morning the path had been swept clear, and the lawn had supplied sufficient material for the erection of a snow figure, which had been begun as a man, but had been transformed into a lady since skirts were more solid and easier of execution than legs. But she was not a satisfactory lady, and so she was snow-balled into even a more complete shapelessness. . . . Below the window this morning the warmth of the sun on the house had already melted the thin covering on the flower-beds, and snowdrops and aconites made a brave heralding of spring. But there was no object now in going out and picking them and making them into bedside posies. Dodo did not in the least want any snowdrops for herself; they seemed to her a depressed, frightened kind of flower that wished it had not blossomed at all. Then suddenly with an immense feeling of relief it occurred to her that she had not tidied up the business-room; there were all sorts of files and bills and papers, connected with the work of these last four years, to be arranged and put away, and delighted at having found something to do she spent a strenuous day, not stirring out of doors and sitting up into the small hours of next morning. That day there was the auction in the house of hospital furniture, and Dodo from pure sentimentality bought a gramophone, an iron bedstead with bedding complete, a bath-chair and five packets of temperature charts.

"Darling, they'll be so useful," she explained to Jack, who arrived in the afternoon. "We're growing old, you see, and either you or I, probably you, will be crippled with arthritis before many years are over, and then think how convenient to have a beautiful bath-chair all ready, without having to order it and wait for it to come. Very likely there would be a railway strike at the time, and then you wouldn't get it for weeks and weeks, and would have to remain planted on the terrace, if you could get as far, instead of having the most delicious pushes—I suppose you call it going for a push, don't you?—all over the woods. And the cheapness of it! Why, a new one would cost double what I paid for it, and it's quite as good as new, if not better."

"I see. That was very thoughtful of you," said he. "But why all those temperature charts? There appear to be five packets of twenty."

Dodo felt perfectly able to account for the temperature charts.

"My dear, supposing the influenza came again this spring as it did last year," she said. "It often attacks an entire household. Suppose we've got a party here, suppose there are twenty people in the house; that will mean at least fifteen valets and maids as well and that makes thirty-five. Then there are all our own servants. Bang comes the 'flu, and without a moment's delay everybody's temperature chart is hanging up above his bed. Now I come to think of it, I wish I had bought more. Two such visitations will use them all up. It was penny-wise, pound-foolish not to have taken the opportunity of getting them cheap."

"You certainly should have bought more," said Jack. "These will be used up in no time. I didn't know you kept charts for people who had influenza, but——"

"But you know now. Don't apologise," said she. "Oh, my dear, I'm so glad to see you. I thought I should like being alone here with nothing whatever to do, but it was hellish. And that beautiful iron bed. Wasn't it a good thing I bought that?"

"I'm sure it was," said he. "Tell me why!"

Dodo raised her eyebrows in commiserating surprise.

"How often has it happened that somebody has proposed himself and I've had to telegraph, 'So sorry but not another bed in the house'? Now that will never happen again, for there it is!"

"There usually was another bed in the house," remarked Jack.

"Then with this that will make two," said Dodo brilliantly. "We can always have two more people. As for the gramophone—let me see, why did I buy the gramophone? A gramophone is much the most odious thing in the world for its size, worse than flees or parsnips. I think I bought it because I hated it so. Shall I turn it on? Jack, I think I shall put it in the drawing-room where it used to play all day, and turn it on and then come back here, and you'll guess what it was

like when it went on from dewy morn to dewier eve. Frankly, I bought
it to remind me of the hospital. My dear, how I miss it! Without it
this house gives me the hump, as Wilcox said."

"Who is Wilcox?"

"The last man who was here. He missed his train, and I tried to
amuse him all evening with that result. The war's over, by the way,
I have to say that to myself, for fear I should howl at the sight of
this emptiness. What are we going to do with ourselves in London
all March?"

Jack licked his lips.

"I'm going to sit down," he said. "I've stood up for four years strolling
about in mud. I'm going to sleep in my nice chair, and play bridge
when I awake. I'm going to matinées at theatres——"

"When you wake, or in order to sleep?" asked she.

"Both. I'm going to get up later and later every morning until there
isn't any morning, and go to bed earlier and earlier until there isn't
any evening. I'm cross and tired and flat. I never want to see a horse
again."

Dodo looked at him in consternation.

"Oh, but that will never do," she said. "You've got to wind me
up, darling, and stimulate me incessantly until I perk up again and
hold myself upright. At present I feel precisely like one of those extremely frail-headed snowdrops—I always despised snowdrops—and
wish I had remained comfortably underneath the ground, and hadn't
come up at all. We shall never get on if you mean to be a snowdrop
too! Jack, you can't be a snowdrop: I never saw anyone so unlike a
snowdrop. You really mustn't attempt to imitate anything that you
resemble so little. I might as well try to be a penny-in-the-slot
machine!"

Jack had taken a cigarette and held it unlit as he looked about.

"Do try," he said. "I happen to be in want of a box of matches."

"I daresay you do," said Dodo, "but I'm not in want of snowdrops.
You must think of me, Jack."

He took a coal out of the hearth with the tongs, lit his cigarette
and singed his moustache.

"My job is over too, as well as yours, Dodo," he said, "and I'm
damned if I want to have another job of any sort. I believe the railway-
men are going to strike next week——"

"My dear, we must get up to town before that happens," said she.

"I don't see why. What's the use of going anywhere, or doing anything? I'm quite in sympathy with people who strike. Why shouldn't
I sit down if I choose and do nothing? I have worked hard; now I
shall strike."

Dodo gave him a quick, sidelong glance.

"Are you tired, Jack?" she asked. "Fed up?"

"No, not the least tired, thanks, but I'm the most fed-up object you ever saw. I shall strike."

Dodo tried a humourous line.

"Get up a trades-union of landowners," she said. "Say you won't perform the duties of landowner any longer. My dear, you could hold on with your strike for ever, because you are rich. Other strikes come to an end, because the funds come to an end, or because the Government makes a compromise. But you needn't compromise with anybody, and as long as you live within your income, you will never starve. I shall join you, I think. What fun if all the peeresses went on strike, and didn't give any more balls or get into divorce courts, or do anything that they have been accustomed to do."

"Very amusing," said Jack drily.

"Then you ought to laugh," said Dodo.

"I daresay. But why should I do anything I ought to do?"

Dodo suddenly became aware that she had got somebody else to think about besides herself. Up till to-day she had been completely engrossed in the fact that, with the passing of the hospital, she had got nothing to do, and, for the present, did not feel inclined to take the trouble to bestir herself for her own amusement. But now it struck her that other people (and here was one) might be feeling precisely as she felt herself. She had supposed that some day somebody or something would come along and begin to interest her again, and then no doubt she would rouse herself. She had thought that Jack would be the most likely person to do that; he would propose a month's yachting, or a few weeks in London, and be very watchful of her, and by all means in his power try to amuse her. She knew quite well that the faculty of living with zest had not left her, for long before her first twenty-four hours of complete laziness were over, she had pined for employment, and hailed the fact of an untidy business-room as a legitimate outlet for energy. But now she found herself cast for a very different part; she had imagined that Jack would help her on to her feet again, and it seemed that she had to help him. For all these years he had found in her his emotional stimulus without any effort on her part. He had never failed to respond to her touch, nor she, to do her justice, to answer his need. But at this moment, though the symptoms were so infinitesimal, namely the failing to be amused at the most trivial nonsense, she diagnosed a failure of response. . . . And at that, she felt as if she had been suddenly awakened by some noise in the night, that startled her into complete consciousness, and meant danger; as if there were burglars moving about the house. All her wits were about her at once, but she moved stealthily, so that they should not guess that anyone had heard or was stirring.

"My dear, you've hit it," she said in a congratulatory voice. "Why should we do anything we ought to do? Don't let us. Oh, Jack, you're old and I'm old. For a couple of years now I have suspected that our day was done. We've had the hell of a good time, you know, and we've had the hell of a bad time. Let's have no more hells, or heavens either for that matter. Probably you thought that I should want to go skylarking about again; indeed, I've said as much, and told you that you had to stimulate me, and get me going again. But oh, I wish I could convey to you how I hated the idea of that. I thought you would come back with your work over, and all your energy bursting to be employed again, and that you would insist on my ringing the curtain up, and beginning all the old antics over again. I would have done it too, in order to please you and keep you busy and amused. But what a relief to know you don't want that!"

Dodo suddenly became afraid that she was putting too much energy into her renunciation of energy, and gave a long, tired sigh.

"Think of Edith," she said. "How awful to have that consuming fire of energy. The moment the war was over she threw her typewriter out of the window and narrowly missed her scullery-maid in the area. She had locked up her piano, you know, for the period of the war, and of course she had lost the key, and so she broke it open with a poker, and sat down on the middle of the keys in order to hear it talk again. She has gone straight back to her old life, and oh, the relief of knowing that you don't want me to. I couldn't possibly have done it without you to whip me on, and thank God, you dropped your whip. Jack, I thought you would expect me to begin again, and would be disappointed if I didn't. So, like a good wife, I resigned myself to be spurred and whipped, just telling you that you would have to do that. But the joy of knowing that you want to be tranquil, too! Don't let us go up to town to-morrow, or next week, or until we feel inclined."

Dodo ran over what she had said in her mind, and thought it covered the ground. She had fully explained why she had told Jack that he mustn't be a snowdrop, and all that sort of thing. She was convinced of her wisdom when he put up his feet on a chair, and showed no sign of questioning her sincerity.

"We've all changed," he said. "We don't want any more excitements. At least you and I don't. Edith's a volcano, and till now, I always thought you were."

Dodo made a very good pretence at a yawn, and stifled it.

"I remember talking to Edith just before the war," she said. "I told her that a cataclysm was wanted to change my nature. I said that if you lost every penny you had, and that I had to play a hurdy-gurdy down Piccadilly, I should still keep the whole of my enjoyment and vitality, and so I should. Well, the cataclysm has come, and though it has ended in victory, it has done its work as far as I am concerned. I've played my part, and I've made my bow, and shall retire gracefully. I don't want to begin again. I'm old, I'm tired, and my only reason for wishing to appear young and fresh was that you would expect me to. You are an angel."

Dodo's tongue, it may be stated, was not blistered by the enunciation of these amazing assertions. She was not in the least an habitual liar, but sometimes it became necessary to wander remarkably far from the truth for the good of another, and when she engaged in these wanderings, she called the process not lying, but diplomacy. She had made up her mind instantly that it would never do for Jack to resign himself to inaction for the rest of his life and with extraordinary quickness had guessed that the best way of starting him again was not to push or shove him into unwelcome activities, but cordially to agree with him, and profess the same desire for a reposeful existence herself. She regarded it as quite certain that he would not acquiesce long in her abandoning the activities of life, but would surely exert himself to stimulate her interests again. For himself he was an admirable loafer, and had just that spice of obstinacy about him which might make him persist in a lazy existence, if she tried to shake him out of it, he would be first astonished and soon anxious if she did the same thing, and would exert himself to stimulate her, finding it disconcerting and even alarming if she sank into the tranquil apathy which just now she had asserted was so suitable to her age and inclinations. This Machiavellian plan then, far from being a roundabout and oblique procedure, seemed, on reflection, to be the most direct route to her goal. Left to himself he might loaf almost indefinitely, but a precisely similar course on her part, would certainly make him rouse himself in order to spur her flagging faculties. And all the time, it was she who was spurring him.

She proceeded to clothe this skeleton of diplomacy with flesh.

"I always used to wonder how this particular moment would come to me," she said, "and though I always used to say I would welcome it, I was secretly rather terrified of it. I thought it would be rather a ghastly sort of wrench, but instead of being a wrench it has been the most heavenly relaxation. I had a warning you see, and I had a taste of it, when I collapsed and went off alone to Truscombe; and how delicious it is, darling, that your resignation, so to speak, has coincided with mine. I thought perhaps that you would preserve your

energy longer than I, and that I should have to follow, faint but pursuing, or that you would fail first, and would have to drag along after
me. But the way it has happened makes it all absolutely divine. I
might have guessed it perhaps. We've utterly grown into one, Jack;
I've known that so many years, dear, and this is only one more instance
out of a thousand. Just the same thing happened to Mr. and Mrs.
Browning——"

"Who?" asked Jack.

"Brownings—poets," said Dodo, "all those books. After all, they
were Mr. and Mrs., though it sounds rather odd when one says so.
Don't you remember that delicious poem where they sat by the fire
and she read a book with a spirit-small hand propping her forehead—
though I never understood what a spirit-small hand meant—and
thought he was reading another, and all the time he was looking at
her?"

Dodo suddenly thought she was going a little too far. It was not
quite fair to introduce into her diplomacy quite such serious topics
and besides, there was a little too much *vox humana* about it. She poked
the fire briskly.

" 'By the fireside'; that was the name of it," she said, "and here
we are. We must advertise, I think, in the personal columns of the
Times, and say that Lord and Lady Chesterford have decided to do
nothing more this side of the grave, and no letters will be forwarded.
They inform their large circle of friends that they are quite well, but
don't want to be bothered. Why, Jack, it's half-past seven. How time
flies when one thinks about old days."

Throughout March they stopped down at Winston, and the subtlety
of Dodo's diplomacy soon began to fructify. She saw from the tail
of her eye that Jack was watching her, that something bordering on
anxiety began to resuscitate him, as he tried to rouse her. Once or
twice, in the warm days of opening April, he coaxed her down to
the stream with him (for fishing was a quiet pursuit not at variance
with the reposeful life) to see if she would not feel the lure of running
water, or be kindled in these brightening fires of spring-time. If fish
were rising well, she noted with a bubble of inward amusement that
he would forget her altogether for a time, but then though hitherto
he had always discouraged or even refused her companionship when
he was fishing, he would come to her and induce her to attempt to
cast over some feeding fish in the water above. So, to please him,
she would take the rod from him and instantly get hung up in a tree.
But oftener when he proposed that she should come out with him,
she would prefer to stay quiet in some sheltered nook on the terrace,
and tell him that she was ever so happy alone. Once or twice again

he succeeded in getting her to come out for a gentle ride, solicitous
on their return to know that it had not overtired her, eager for her
to confess that she really had enjoyed it. And then Dodo would say,
"Darling, you are so good to me," and perhaps consent to play a game
of picquet. He did not disquiet himself over the thought that she was
ill, for she looked the picture of health, ate well, slept well, and truthfully told him that she had not the smallest pain or discomfort of
any kind. Often she was quite talkative, and rattled along in the old
style, but then in midflight she would droop into silence again. Only
once had he a moment of real alarm, when he found her reading the
poems of Longfellow. . . .

Then one day to his great joy, she began to reanimate herself a
little. A new play had come out in London, and some paper gave a
column-long account of it, which Jack read aloud.

"Really it sounds interesting," she said. "I wonder——" and she
broke off.

"Why shouldn't we run up to town and see it?" said he. "There
are several things I ought to attend to. Let's go up to-morrow morning."

"Yes, if you like," she said. "I won't promise to go to the play,
Jack, but—yes I'll come. You might telephone for seats now, mightn't
you?"

Certainly the play interested her, and they discussed it as they drove
home. One of the characters reminded Dodo of Edith, and she said
she had not seen her for ages. On which Jack, very guilefully, telephoned to Edith to drop in for lunch next day, and arranged to go
out himself, so that Dodo might have a distinct and different stimulus.
Unfortunately Dodo, hearing that Jack would be out, scampered round
about lunch-time to see Edith, and drink in a little froth of the world
before returning to the nunnery of empty Winston, and thus they
both found nobody there. She and Jack had intended to go back to
the country that afternoon, but Dodo let herself be persuaded to go
to the Russian ballet, which she particularly wanted to see. Jack took
a box for her, and in the intervals several friends came up to see them.
He enjoyed the ballet enormously himself, and longed to go again
the next night. This was not lost on Dodo, and she became more
diplomatic than ever.

"Stop up another night, Jack," she said, "and go there again. I shall
be quite, quite happy at Winston alone. Let's see; they are doing 'Petroushka' to-morrow; I hear it is admirable."

"I shouldn't dream of stopping in town without you," said he, "or
of letting you be alone at that—at Winston. You won't stop up here
another day?"

Dodo was getting a little muddled; she wanted to see "Petroushka"

enormously, and had to pretend it was rather an effort; at the same
time she had to remember that Jack wanted to see it, though he pretended that he wanted her to see it. He thought that she thought.
. . . She gave it up; they both wanted to see "Petroushka" for their
own sakes, and pretended it was for the sake of each other.

"Yes, dear, I don't think it would overtire me," she said. "But let's
go to the stalls to-morrow. I think you will see it better from straight
in front."

"I quite agree," said Jack cordially.

About three weeks later Dodo came in to lunch half an hour late
and in an enormous hurry. She had asked Edith to come at 1.30 punctually, so that they could start for the Mid-Surrey links at two, to play
a three-ball match, and be back at five for a rubber before dinner
which would have to be at seven, since the play to which they were
going began at eight. She was giving a small dance that night, but
she could get back by eleven from the play. They were going down
to Winston early next morning (revisiting it after nearly a month's
absence), so that Jack could get a day's fishing before the Saturday-
till-Monday party arrived.

"I don't want any lunch," said Dodo. "I'm ready now, and I shall
eat bread and cheese as we drive down to Richmond. Things taste
so delicious in a motor. Jack, darling, fill your pockets with cheese
and cigarettes, and give me a kiss, because it's David's birthday."

"We were talking about you," he remarked.

"Tell me what you said. All of it," said Dodo.

"We agreed you had never been in such excellent spirits."

"Never. What else?"

"We agreed that I was rather a good nurse," said he.

Dodo gave a little squeak of laughter, which she instantly suppressed.

"Of course you are," she said.

"And I was saying," said Edith, "that the war hadn't made the slightest change in any of us."

"Darling, you're wrong there," said Dodo. "It has made the most
immense difference. For instance—nowadays—we're all as poor as rats,
though we trot along still. Nowadays——"

A tall parlour-maid came in.

"The car's at the door, my lady," she said.

"Put the golf clubs in," said Dodo.

"Tell me some of the enormous differences," asked Edith.

Dodo waited till the door was closed.

"Well, we all have parlour-maids," she said.

"That's an enormous difference."

She paused a moment.

"Ah, that reminds me," she said. "Jack, I interviewed a butler this morning, who I think will do. He wants about a thousand a year. . . ."

Edith shouted with laughter.

"Poor as rats," she said, "and parlour-maids! Any other differences, Dodo?"

"I wonder," she said.